KRISTA & BECCA RITCHIE

ADDICTED SERIES
Addicted to You
Ricochet
Addicted for Now
Kiss the Sky
Hothouse Flower
Thrive
Addicted After All
Fuel the Fire
Long Way Down
Some Kind of Perfect

LIKE US SERIES
Damaged Like Us
Lovers Like Us
Alphas Like Us
Tangled Like Us
Sinful Like Us
Headstrong Like Us
Charming Like Us
Wild Like Us
Fearless Like Us
Infamous Like Us
Misfits Like Us
Unlucky Like Us
Nobody Like Us

BURN BRIGHT

KRISTA & BECCA RITCHIE

Bloom *books*

Copyright © 2025 by Krista and Becca Ritchie
Cover and internal design © 2025 by Sourcebooks
Cover design by Krista & Becca Ritchie and Nicole Lecht/Sourcebooks
Cover images © Studio 2am/Creative Market, Davide Bassu/Creative Market, Samran wonglakorn/Shutterstock, MicrovOne/Getty Images, 2shoes4blues/Shutterstock

Sourcebooks, Bloom Books, and the colophon are registered trademarks of Sourcebooks.

All rights reserved. No part of this book may be reproduced in any form or by any electronic or mechanical means including information storage and retrieval systems—except in the case of brief quotations embodied in critical articles or reviews—without permission in writing from its publisher, Sourcebooks.

No part of this book may be used or reproduced in any manner for the purpose of training artificial intelligence technologies or systems.

The characters and events portrayed in this book are fictitious or are used fictitiously. Any similarity to real persons, living or dead, is purely coincidental and not intended by the author.

All brand names and product names used in this book are trademarks, registered trademarks, or trade names of their respective holders. Sourcebooks is not associated with any product or vendor in this book.

Published by Bloom Books, an imprint of Sourcebooks
1935 Brookdale RD, Naperville, IL 60563-2773
(630) 961-3900
sourcebooks.com

Cataloging-in-Publication data is on file with the Library of Congress.

Printed and bound in the United States of America.
LSC 10 9 8 7 6 5 4 3 2 1

CHARACTER LIST

THE COBALTS
Connor Cobalt & Rose Calloway

First Born:
Jane Eleanor (26)

Second Born:
Charlie Keating (23)

Third Born:
Beckett Joyce (23)

Fourth Born:
Eliot Alice (22)

Fifth Born:
Tom Carraway (21)

Sixth Born:
Ben Pirrip (19)

Seventh Born:
Audrey Virginia (16)

For anyone who has ever felt like they don't quite belong.
You belong here.

PARTY WITH KAPPA PHI DELTA BEFORE FALL SEMESTER BEGINS!

Say goodbye to summer and ring in the greatest year of our lives at KPD House on Frat Row.

Doors open @ 10 p.m.

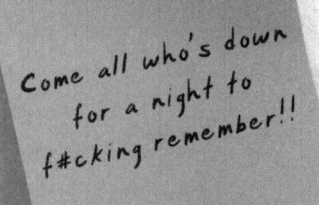

Come all who's down for a night to f#cking remember!!

ONE

HARRIET FISHER

I take my beer and my scowl to the wall. Me and the wall—great friends. My only current friend.

This party feels like an amalgamation of hipsters, jocks, beauty queens, and outcasts. A total *Breakfast Club* scenario. But instead of five people sharing detention there are a hundred-plus sharing a frat house.

My white crop top and red-and-black checkered, very low-rise pants—which I love in all their early 2000s punk glory—shouldn't cause me to stand out that much. I'm positive I saw a guy wearing a spiked collar five minutes ago.

I take a stiff sip of beer.

Alone.

Avoiding direct eye contact with others.

Maybe I thought things would be different at Manhattan Valley University.

New city, new college, new outcomes. But I might be part of the problem when it comes to making friends. I don't know how to be warm and inviting. I can blame it on my scowl and permanent

Resting Bitch Face, but the truth is I could try harder to be softer. More approachable. Yet, the thought of being someone that people actively *want* to approach makes me scowl even harder. Is it weird? To want friends but also *not* want them?

Sure, the idea of friends sounds amazing. People to hang out with, laugh with, go to the movies and venture to the mall with. But friends also come with drama—like what if they judge me? Hate me? What if I do something wrong to mess it all up? Or worse, what if they're amazing friends, and they start wanting more from me? So I'd have to start sharing about my life and get into my past, and all that sounds so incredibly taxing that I'd like to just fling myself into a dilapidated cabin in the South Pole where no one can find me.

Friends…sometimes the fantasy seems better than the reality.

And it's not just girls that I struggle to connect with in that way. I've never had a friendship with a guy. I've never wanted to be adopted as one of the *bros*. I can't wrap my head around what a guy's girl even looks like. It sounds like phony fucking baloney.

I'm not even really attempting to make a friend tonight. Literally, my goals are on the floor. I just want to have a better-than-average time at this party.

When I go to the backyard for some fresh air, a thought slams at me.

I shouldn't have come here.

Maybe I should've stayed inside and melted into the plaster. Kappa guys play beer pong on the grass while couples giggle-fight during a game of chicken in the pool, and I'm *just* trying to reach a corner of the fence.

"She's so tiny," a six-foot-something asshole with a humongous smile says. He wears an MVU Row Team shirt, and he elbows his preppy friend in the side. "Like a little Polly Pocket." They snort together.

I try to walk around the jock for the second time.

He side-steps *again*. "Whoa, Polly, how tall are you?" He tries to pat my head, and I jerk backward.

"Leave me alone." I raise my voice which contains rasp and grit.

But their glassy eyes say they're four beers in and I'm as threatening as a Chihuahua. "Come on, you're supposed to be *fun-sized*." He downs a big gulp. "Be *fun*."

His friend laughs, then leans into the jock to mutter, "Those are definitely party-sized, though." Their heavy-lidded eyes drop to my chest.

Yeah, I have larger than average boobs. I've been told this super uninteresting fact since the tenth grade. Guys like to act as if it's surprising to me. Like I don't realize my tits are, I don't know, *attached* to my fucking body.

I can see them.

I know they're big.

And I wish I didn't finish off my beer in the house. I'd throw it at his face. Cup and all. Instead, I flip them off with two middle fingers. "How's this for fun?"

They snicker, like I'm playing around. Like this is just a game and I should lighten up. It's a party, right? We're at a frat house on campus. People aren't taking anything seriously here.

I'm the buzzkill.

But maybe I don't want to be the five-foot-one party favor.

"Seriously," I growl. "Just let me through." I try to slip past the jock. He blocks me.

I glare. "*Dude*."

"*Polly*."

What the fuck?!

"Oooh, you made her mad, Cameron," he says off my scowl.

"Does she bite?" Cameron laughs, then tries to pat my blond hair again.

I swat his hand away. "Don't touch me."

"Aww, she's a snapping turtle." Cameron passes his beer to his preppy friend. "You know what turtles need?"

My pulse races. I try to back away, to return inside, but I barely even rotate before Cameron hoists me around the waist. I kick out as he tosses me over his shoulder and shouts, "Water!"

"Let me down!" I yell, banging a fist against his back. I squirm and try to pull away as he carries me to the pool. No, no, *no*. Panic envelops me alongside raw anger, and I fight against his rower strength.

"You've gotta go in the water, turtle!" He grunts as I writhe against his hold. He pins me harder on his shoulder. "I'm saving you!"

"Water! Water! Water!" People chant around the pool.

"No, no!" I shriek so loudly, so furiously, my throat sears. As he prepares to launch me into the pool, I scream bloody murder. "LET ME DOWN!" Fear guts me. "LETMEDOWN!" I can't see beyond the hot glassy film in my eyes.

I just hear a strong, commanding voice. "HEY! Let go of her! What the hell are you doing?!!"

I feel the tug around my waist from behind. Someone is ripping me out of Cameron's rower arms. Someone is setting me gently on my feet. Someone is letting go of me.

As soon as I spin around to see who, I'm thunderstruck at the sight of him. I stumble back a step, breath caught deeper in my lungs. I have to crane my neck just to meet his carved jawline.

Fury flexes his cut muscles, his athletic body. He's sky-scraping tall. Taller than most students here. His wavy brown hair peeks beneath a faded blue baseball cap. No one wears a ballcap as attractively as he does—with this rugged sexiness that shouldn't exist in New York. It should look so out of place, but he doesn't.

He just fits.

He seems to always fit among people. And there is something so devastating about his blue eyes, about the way he looks at you. Like you're his whole...entire...world when I know it's not true.

His world is massive and illustrious.

I'm small and dull inside it.

My eyes drop to his chest. He's in an old Penn Hockey shirt, even though we're not at the Ivy League anymore. And didn't he quit hockey?

"Is that Ben Cobalt?" I hear the whispers.

"Holy shit, that's a Cobalt."

"Ben!" someone calls out in familiarity.

"Hey, there you are, Ben," Cameron says brightly like they're buddies. "You should stick around us, man. The party's right here."

Ben is ignoring them and staring right at me. He's sweeping me for signs of damage. "You want out of here?" he asks me.

Yes.

I still can't slow my pulse. I can barely form a single word. A lump swells in my esophagus. I sense Cameron coming up behind me. I flinch, and Ben reaches out and shoves him backward.

"Get *the fuck* away from her," Ben warns with visceral heat.

I don't wait around. I bolt on instinct and race back inside the frat house. My heartbeat pounds in my ears.

"Harriet!" Ben calls after me, and I feel him desert the party and his surplus of friends. He sprints after me. I've never had anyone come check on me for anything good.

I'm not thinking. I rush up the flight of wide stairs littered with beer bottles and ping-pong balls. I land on the second floor and quickly find a bathroom. Once I'm inside, I slam the door shut.

Breathing heavy, I keep my palms glued to the wood.

"Hey," Ben says from right outside the door. It's unlocked, but he doesn't come in. I feel a weight against the door, and I imagine his palms are on the other side. That he's pressing against it too.

I let out a slow breath, starting to ease. "Hey," I say, trying to make sense of the weird flip of my stomach and the even stranger tug at my lips. Am I...am I smiling?

I shake my head to myself. *What the hell, Harriet?*

I blink back the jumbled emotion. I never thought my messed-up life would collide with a Cobalt.

Really, *this* Cobalt.

There are five brothers and two sisters and a mom and dad any kid would dream of having—a tight-knit family who go to battle for each other. And they're rich.

Blue-blooded, high society Philadelphians who might as well be

New Yorkers with how often they're in this city. They have McMansions, private jets, yachts, and trust funds, all the things that come with owning the world's most popular soda corporation.

But they are so much more than the typical billionaire.

They have bodyguards.

They have millions of followers on their socials.

There are Reddit forums and fandom pages on Fanaticon dedicated to them. Fans follow their every move and theorize what they're doing at every minute of every day.

Their names are as commonplace as the most recognizable actors and pop stars of our generation. Yet, they're not in movies and they're not known for charting the Billboard Hot 100. Their fame has an origin so deep-seated in the fabric of American society that most have forgotten *how* they became noteworthy in the first place.

They should've just been like every other billionaire who owns Fortune 500 companies. Like the faces behind Pepsi and Coca-Cola. They should be *irrelevant*. But that's about the last thing you can say about a Cobalt.

None are irrelevant.

All of them matter as pillars of elegance and intelligence and power. That is the mythos of the Cobalt Empire.

People talk about them like they're spawns of Zeus—godly, some full of hubris, but so unbelievably *mighty*. Like if you run into one, your whole world will spin on its axis. You'll be *changed*.

No one talks about what happens when you try to enter their orbit (under good pretenses) and you're rejected. That it feels like getting spit out of a whale's mouth. The lions roared in your face and then turned their backs. The animal kingdom dubbed you less than.

But the Cobalt who tossed me aside—he's not the one at this party. Of the few times we've crossed paths, Ben has never scorned me. We both went to Penn and transferred to MVU this semester—for different reasons, I'm sure—but if anyone can understand what this move feels like it's him.

So it's natural to grab the knob. And I let him in.

I'm eye-level with his sternum. He's six-*five*. The top of my head barely reaches his shoulders. Being this close to his chest quickens my heartbeat. I back up and sink against the wooden cupboards, sliding to the scuffed tile.

Ben shuts the door. I can feel him assessing my state, which is mostly pissed.

I pick at the gray fuzzy bath rug next to me. "Your friend is an asshole," I say.

"Cameron Dunphy?" He joins me, sitting against the wooden cupboard that's covered in Kappa Phi Delta decals and beer stickers like Budweiser, Koning Lite, Coors. "He's not really my friend."

"You know his last name," I say like it's proof enough.

Ben smiles first with his eyes. Even shadowed with the curved brim of his hat, those baby blue orbs carry his emotion so clearly before his lips tic upward. "I know a lot of peoples' last names. Including yours, Fisher."

Flush tries to reach my cheeks.

Especially as he adds, "But you are my friend."

Right. I wonder how many times he's used this line on girls.

I glance over at him. "And we have a lengthy text thread to prove it."

Ben pulls out his phone at this. The last encounter I had with him, we exchanged numbers, but we never texted, never called, never did anything other than exist in each other's cellphones. I considered sending him a casual message about a cool grunge band I like, but I figured he has a thousand randoms spamming him with memes and invites, and he didn't need one more.

To sum it up, I would be absolutely *delusional* to consider a Cobalt a real friend off a five-minute interaction at Penn.

His thumbs fly over the screen.

My phone suddenly buzzes on a clip at my hip, resembling an old school pager. I see his text.

> **BEN**
> I like what you did with your hair.

I let my buttery-blond bangs grow out a little this summer, and they touch my eyelashes as I stare at his message. I remove my phone from my hip and text back.

> **HARRIET**
> Thanks, Friend.

He's fast.

> **BEN**
> I knew we'd get there again.

He's slipping me coy glances, and I chew on the inside of my cheek to keep this strange feeling at bay.

> **HARRIET**
> Were we ever here before?

I anticipate his response more than I should. I watch his fingers dance across his phone with precision. There is no hitting the delete button. He's not overcomplicating his response. He just presses *send*.
I look.

> **BEN**
> Yeah. We have been here before. This isn't the first time you've called me Friend.

> **HARRIET**
> That's right. It was your birthday.

> **BEN** 🌿
> Happy you could remember.

His side glance at me steals my breath, and I have to look at the tiny hole patched in my checkered pants.

It was March. His birthday. That was our last encounter. He ran into me in a science lab at Penn. This isn't the first time Ben has been in the right spot, the right time, and helped me.

I don't respond, and my phone vibrates in my palm.

> **BEN** 🌿
> Unless you're trying to forget?

"Sorry to bring it up," he says out loud. "I know it wasn't a great day for you."

I shrug. "It happened, it passed. I'm not letting it fester or anything." I wrap my arms around my legs, bringing them closer to my chest. "You know, I saw online that you were transferring here," I say, resting my temple against the cupboard.

He does the same, looking at me. "Tabloids?"

"Yep. Sorry to say you weren't a headline, just a footnote."

"That's preferrable," he breathes. "The siblings and cousins who are headlines have it harder. My fame is easy in comparison."

I nod. "How long have you even been on campus?"

He checks the time on his blue-plated Omega watch. It's one of the only evident signs of his wealth right now. "Two hours. This is actually my first time at MVU."

I frown. "But you toured the campus and met Cameron Dunfuckface weeks ago, right?"

Ben laughs, the corner of his mouth pulling higher. It sends a flutter throughout my entire nervous system. I don't know what it's like to be overcharged. I probably exist on 30% battery life. I'm not chipper. I'm not fucking bubbly, that's for sure. If I'm a dying battery, then I'm also a flat beverage, but who cares?

I'm not trying to be Miss Energizer Bunny.

I tear my gaze off his. *Get it together.*

Some of his brothers can be described as lethally charming, and he could fall into this quadrant of the Venn diagram too.

"I never took a tour," Ben admits as his smile softens on me. "I just met Cameron and half the row team an hour ago."

Of course he did.

Ben isn't a loner. He's not a loser.

He's a social fucking *butterfly*. Who could make friends with the sun, the moon, and a trashcan. Within an hour or less.

And he's out of his mind. "You're seriously unhinged," I say. "You transferred to this college without ever stepping foot here when you were going to an Ivy."

"You transferred too."

"I bought a brochure. I took a three-hour tour. I made an Excel spreadsheet listing the financial expenses of this move—not that you'd need to do that."

"I did Google search MVU," he smiles, almost teasingly.

"Oh, he Google-searched." I mime pompoms to cheer him on, my lips somewhat rising with his. "That has to at least dock you a point or two with the studious fam, Cobalt boy."

"Probably five points. Don't tell my mom. She'd have a heart attack knowing my research consisted of typing in *Manhattan Valley* in a web browser and not a one-on-one with Dean Ferreira."

"Like I would ever come face-to-face with *the* Rose Calloway Cobalt," I say without thinking. His mom is a certified bomb-ass-bitch, and I would idolize her feminine ferocity if I didn't prefer hero-worshipping the dead. The dead can't disappoint you as much as the living.

"You never know," Ben says like life has taken stranger turns. It causes the air to tense and for the focus to draw to us. To how we've run into each other *again*. How we're on a collision course. Our eyes clash in the sudden quiet, fighting to stay glued for longer than a couple seconds.

"How'd you hear about this party anyway?" I ask.

"Through a friend of a friend who knows Leif Westergaard. He's president of the frat."

"Already three-degrees from the Kappa prez," I tease.

He laughs, then checks the time again. "I'll probably head back to Philly in a couple hours."

My stomach sinks, but then twists in more confusion. "You aren't staying in New York?"

"Classes don't start till next week. I'm not moving here before then." He asks fast, "What about you? How long have you been here?"

"A few days. I have to take a week-long orientation for the Honors Program."

"Overachiever," he calls me out.

I make a heart with my hands and crack it apart. "You want half?"

He glances down at my hands, then up to my eyes. "You always break your heart for your friends?"

He would be my only friend.

If this were real.

"It's imaginary, Ben," I murmur. "Tomorrow, you'll act like I never existed until our next strange encounter. Is that not what this is?" I motion between him and me.

"No." He shakes his head, scans the bathroom, then rests a forearm on his bent knee. "No, it's not, Harriet." His voice is nearly a whisper, and he lays his gaze even gentler on me. "We don't have to be strangers."

I'm lost for words.

So he adds, "I want to be your friend."

Did Cameron Dun-fuckface drop me on the pavement outside? Did I hit my head? "Okay."

"Okay," Ben repeats, then narrows his gaze. "I get the sense you still don't believe me."

"I'm trying, Friend."

He smiles a little, which is coaxing mine out. Wow, he is *really* good at this...

I should probably take notes on how to make friends, but what he possesses feels like a gift. A trait inherited, not one learned.

"Thanks for the backup tonight," I say too quietly. I'm unsure if he hears until I see the ire flashing through his eyes.

"Parties like this can be such a fucking wreck." He gazes at the wall, his jaw muscle ticking. "I'm sorry that happened to you. Someone should've stopped it before me."

"At least you did something at the cost of social suicide."

"I'm a Cobalt. That cost is low." He exhales a long, tired breath. "We've been here before." *Here* as in helping me.

He already said that over text.

I hold my knees, seeing him stare unblinkingly at a stain in the ugly brown paint. "Yeah, but it'll be me helping you out next," I promise. "Right place, right time, I'll be there. And when I make commitments, I don't usually break them."

You can count on me, I think about adding, but how much weight does this cliché phrase even hold when you barely know someone and they barely know you?

Ben cradles my gaze for a steady beat, and just as he inhales like he's about to tell me something, a knock pounds the door.

"Ben, you in there?!"

"Man, of course he's in there. His bodyguard is standing right out here."

"Ben, come do a shot with us!"

I rise to my feet first. "You've been summoned, Cobalt boy."

He takes a taxingly long time to pick himself off the floor. He stares at the door, then down at me. I forgot about our height difference while we were on the ground. He is *towering*. I try not to imagine being scooped up in his arms.

I try not to imagine being held by him. I felt it for point-two-seconds tonight, and I'm worried I'll want more when *everyone* already wants so much more out of him. How much can a person like him even really give to someone like me?

"I'll probably head out," I tell him. "I've got some stuff I need to get to." Like sleep. Me and my pillow—also friends.

Does he look dejected? Or is that wishful thinking—that *maybe* he wanted to hang out with me for longer?

"Ben!" his friend calls.

"I'll find you in the kitchen, Reece!" he shouts back while only looking at me, his gaze rooting me here. It's one of the hottest sensations that slips into my body, the feeling of being *kept* and *grasped* with a single intrusive, caring stare.

Their footsteps pad away.

I intake a short breath and tuck a strand of blond hair behind my ear. "Catch you later?" I hear my doubt.

A part of me does believe this friendship is an illusion. It's not that I've been met with total misfortune in my life—I'm at a *dream* college, for fuck's sake—but it's still hard to accept beautiful spots inside my reality that I didn't work for. Having good things fall into my lap...that rarely happens.

Ben likely hears my cynicism too.

Is that why he lingers? Does he wish I believed in him more? My stomach backflips, and I realize how much I want to believe this won't end here between us.

He glances at his phone. I wonder if he'll text me or if there'll be a new wave of tumbleweeds, and then he says so suddenly, so abruptly, "I need a job."

I'm thrown off.

I nod slowly, seeing he's messing with me. "Right. I also need a job, but for real. I used to give drumming lessons in Philly to this snarky little prep school kid, and I'm not sure a gig will be as easy to find in New York."

"I'm for real," Ben says fast, eyeing the door, then me. As if this is a secret.

I shift my weight in confusion. "But you're...*rich*."

"I'm broke."

My jaw is on the floor. "Whaa...how? Is that even possible? Don't you have a trust fund?"

"Our trust funds aren't limitless. I'll explain later." He's running out of time with me. "But if you find anything worth applying for jobwise, let me know. Maybe we can work together."

Work *together*...?

He wants to work with me now? Maybe *he's* hit his head. Because no one, and I mean, *no one* has acted thrilled to spend more than an hour with me. Unless I'm on my knees.

But Ben isn't asking for a blow job.

He's asking for *friendship*. The one thing I've never really given out.

"Maybe, yeah," I say in one trapped breath. I think I would want to work alongside Ben Cobalt. Who wouldn't?

One question is plaguing me as he goes to the door, adding distance between us, and I call out, "Who knows?"

"Who knows I'm broke?"

"Yeah. Who'd you tell?"

"Just you."

My brows catapult, and my lips part but only breath comes out. Just me?

Just me?

JUST ME????

It's not computing fast enough. It's not computing *at all*.

He grips the doorknob but faces me. "No one in my family knows, and I need to keep it that way."

What the...?

This isn't just a secret big enough to implode his life. It's massive enough to spill to tabloids for cash. It could help pay for my housing.

I could turn on Ben in a heartbeat. It'd be so easy to pocket the ammo and payday. There's nearly nothing stopping me from destroying him.

"You're unhinged," I say again. "You barely even know me, but you know enough that I could ruin you out of revenge—I hate your brother and he hates me—or out of desperation. Because you know that I could use the money."

"Yeah...I'm hoping you keep it a secret."

"Hope?" My stomach churns hearing that word out loud, and I come closer to him. "That's what you're banking this on?"

"I'm banking on you." He stares down at me from beneath his ballcap. "I'm banking on *you*, Harriet." His deep voice is a caress. It's terrifying how much I want to feel it all over my body. "I might not know you that well yet, but I think your heart is good."

"You think," I repeat like he's lost it. "You're out of your mind." I lace my hands on my head before they fall to my neck, my pulse on an ascent. I grip my shoulders like I pulled a muscle. The one class I almost failed was P.E. in ninth grade.

As a non-endurance runner, fuck the mile death run.

But I don't hate this weird out-of-breath feeling with Ben. It's one born from anticipation, from the things that slam through walls and soar. I've experienced so much of life alone that to share this moment with another is heady, dizzying, *maddening*.

And I realize...I'm losing it too.

Ben looks me over. "Tell me not to believe in the good in you. Tell me I should be scared." Our eyes can't unfasten.

"You should have some fear for your life. Where's the self-preservation, Friend?"

"Courage doesn't exist without fear. We all have to confront things that scare us at some point."

So this does scare him.

The idea that I could betray him.

I can't imagine screwing over a person who's helped me not once but *twice*. This secret isn't a grenade that could blow me up. It feels more like his heart. Like he was the one who cracked the organ in half. He was the one who gave it away.

"You might've chosen the wrong person." Better to warn him now. "I've never been a safety net for anyone. My parachute probably has holes in it."

He twists the doorknob. "Guess we'll be on a fast descent together, Fisher." He gives me a salute from the brim of his hat. "See you around, *Friend*."

My heart can't slow. "See you, Friend."

TWO

BEN COBALT

one week later

What is it like to have four older brothers? What's it like to have two sisters? What's it like to be the son of a feminist icon and a legendary billion-dollar man? What's it like to be a part of the Cobalt Empire?

Everyone wants to know the truth.

Very few ever will.

Entrance into my family is like finding a golden ticket in a Wonka Bar, only then to be battle-tested in a Colosseum. Death is more likely than victory.

Despite feeling like I'm the black sheep among lions, there's so much I love about my unshakeable family. I love that it's not easy to gain access to all of us when there are people in the world with cruel intentions. I know they exist—even if Charlie will claim I'm so *naïve* to the atrocities of others.

I see it.

I see it overwhelmingly. I see that trust is too valuable a commodity.

Still, I give my trust more freely than many of my siblings, but in a way, I think we all know which pieces to hold back from strangers. And I think we all know which pieces will always belong to each other.

It's far from misery to be bred from the kind of love that pulls you to your feet when you've crashed hard. And this past year, I've fucking *crashed*. This low was worse than being body-slammed into ice. Worse than any hit I've ever taken in a hockey rink.

It's why I left Philly.

But I didn't want to leave Audrey this soon. I dragged my feet for so long because of my little sister. Even now, I don't know if this is where I should be, if this is just another mistake I'm making, but my college records have already been transferred to Manhattan Valley University.

My first class is tomorrow.

I just have to see where this choice takes me. Even if it wasn't part of the plan.

Clutching my phone to my ear, I grip a handrail with my other hand. The subway car rattles along the tracks, and I hear my older brother's smooth, calming tone.

"What time are you getting in?" Beckett asks. "I'll pick you up."

"You mean your driver will pick me up," I whisper while I'm in public. Girls in business casual blouses and skirts read on tablets, and I can't be sure if they're close enough to overhear or if they even recognize who I am. Or if they even *care* that I'm a Cobalt.

How the public perceives me—I don't pay much attention to. But some in my family are extremely private. Beckett being the *most* private, I don't want to be the one to air any aspect of his personal life to fans, press, the media—so I try to be mindful.

"I'll be with my driver," Beckett says. "I'm taking tonight's performance off—"

"Don't."

"Ben—"

"Don't miss ballet for me." I dip my head down, the rim of my old baseball cap shielding my eyes. "I'll get there when I get there."

Beckett exhales a long breath. The truth is, I'm only moving to New York because *he* asked me to. If it were any other brother, I would've just suffered alone under the weight of my mistakes. But Beckett Joyce—I've loved him for as long as I can remember.

I'm number six out of seven.

He's number three. And when it felt like every older brother poked and poked and *poked*, he was the one who just held and hugged. Hell, sometimes I loved him more than I loved our father, who we all revere and admire in our own way.

But there were times I wished Beckett were my dad.

Then he married ballet, and he left home at sixteen to be with the love of his life. *Dance*. He was trained in a prestigious conservatory, then accepted to the New York Ballet Company. It's the best in America. He's a principal dancer, and people who've never seen him perform might think he got handed it because of his last name.

But once you see him on stage, the truth is palpable.

He landed the coveted title on pure talent. He is grace and beauty, and according to ballet critics, his technique is unmatched.

I can't take him away from that—not for something as temporary as me crashing at his apartment for…for hopefully not that long.

I'm not just living with Beckett. All four of my older brothers share a four-bedroom apartment in Hell's Kitchen. I was *twelve* the last time we all lived under one roof, and I can't see how it won't cave in if I'm there for more than a few weeks.

So yeah, this has to be temporary.

I'm not trying to make their lives harder. It's bad enough they feel the need to scoop me up like I flew too close to the sun and melted my wings.

I hear muffled voices in the background of the call, and Beckett quickly says, "I have to go. We'll talk later, okay?"

"Yeah," I get in right before he hangs up, and I just really wish he weren't the busiest of my brothers. Catching quality time with him is like ensnaring a bird.

The subway car rolls to a stop.

I sense a person hovering near my back. I barely glance over my shoulder to catch the brown eyes of my bodyguard.

Olive skin from his Italian-Croatian heritage, shaggy walnut-brown hair styled meticulously, khakis and a linen shirt. He blends in like an average thirtysomething living in the trendy parts of Brooklyn.

Chris Novak has been assigned to my detail since I was ten. He's been unfortunate enough to be around for my two growth spurts. Shot up to six-foot in middle school and then wrecked my back with stretch marks in ninth grade when I climbed to six-foot-five. That was a real pissy year for me, and Novak heard most of my complaining.

"Next stop," I tell him.

He gives me a short nod. His gaze has left mine and roams the cramped subway car. I know I don't make his life easier. Could've hailed a cab. Could've done a lot of things differently. But even if I wasn't penny-pinching right now, I'd still be trying to leave the world better than when I entered it. My carbon footprint matters to me, and I don't give a shit what people think of me for it.

I check my texts.

As the subway car halts again, Novak follows me off the platform while I scroll and move. Usually, he'll slip in front of me to clear a path, but people rush out and we both naturally walk with the flow.

My messages have blown up in the past three hours.

SANTIAGO A.P. ENGLISH LIT (DALTON ACADEMY)

> You're moving to New York? Dude!

RITA CARRAWAYS SHOW

> Heard you moved to NYC. Let's grab drinks

> **PRESCOTT KAPPA PHI DELTA (MVU)**
> Hey, Ben. Don't forget to rush Kappa Phi.

I sift through another five sent from different people I've met over the years, and I smile when I come across a thread from thirty minutes ago. I click it and reread.

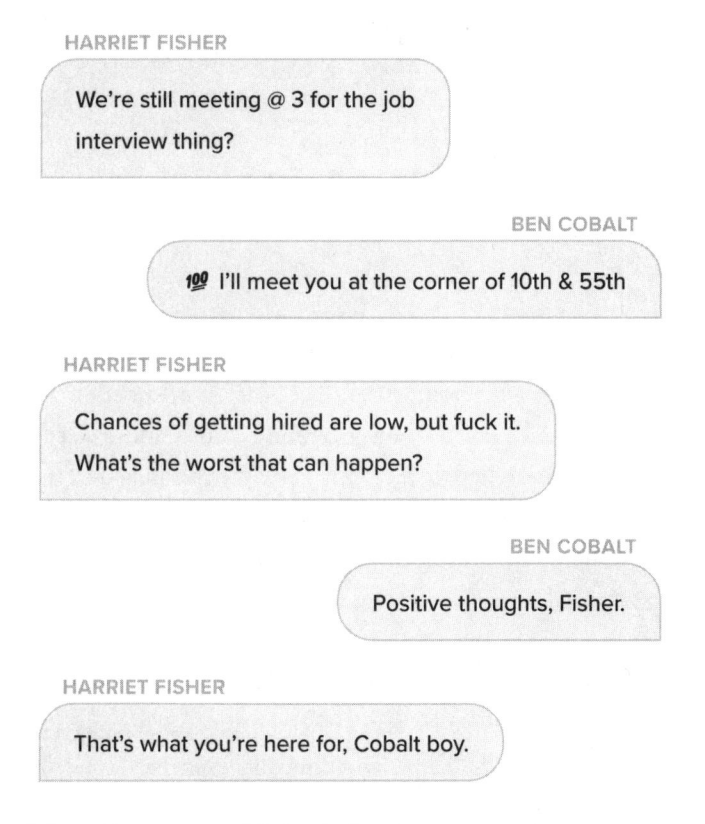

> **HARRIET FISHER**
> We're still meeting @ 3 for the job interview thing?

> **BEN COBALT**
> 💯 I'll meet you at the corner of 10th & 55th

> **HARRIET FISHER**
> Chances of getting hired are low, but fuck it. What's the worst that can happen?

> **BEN COBALT**
> Positive thoughts, Fisher.

> **HARRIET FISHER**
> That's what you're here for, Cobalt boy.

My smile grows, and I check the time on my phone.

It's 10 a.m., and I have a canvas duffel bag strapped across my chest with my essentials. I wish I could fast-forward to three and just meet up with her now, but I can't delay this move-in any longer.

It's time to be with my brothers.

The thought is both comfort and tension. A paradox. And funny enough, my family loves those.

THREE

BEN COBALT

This isn't some cheap apartment complex. It's high-end and ritzy with a bellhop, entrance security, a member's only club lounge, an infinity pool, steam room and sauna, and other luxury amenities. I've been here before, but never for this long of a stay.

The elevator dings, and I walk out onto the 21st floor. Yeah, I wouldn't call this inviting. Ominous, maybe. The hallway has an eerie elegance with deep red walls, dim lighting, and gold fixtures. It's like I'm stepping foot in The Shining. A potential bloodbath could occur.

And I know exactly which brother it'll be with.

Blowing out a large breath, I shake out my arms, my muscles burning in hot bands before anything has even happened. I stare down the gold-plated 2166 apartment number on the dark wooden door. I'm not lacking in confidence.

That's engrained too deep within me.

I think it makes these situations easier. The ones that feel like I'm about to hurdle the Empire State Building. I dig out a key to their place from my dark jeans.

Their place—yeah, it hasn't sunk in that it's about to be mine too.

When I'm inside, I quickly see I'm alone.

I'm just met with a spacious, overly clean marble kitchen. Most appliances stored away except for a dual coffee and espresso machine. It smells like lemon Lysol and fabric softener. The floors are immaculate, and I have a feeling they had a service do a deep-clean.

I wonder if it's something that happens weekly.

The apartment is an open floorplan, and stepping farther inside, I pass barstools tucked against the spotless kitchen island. Industrial lighting hangs in the vaulted ceiling of the living room, and a camel-leather couch faces two dark-blue lounge chairs that can rotate 360-degrees.

There is no TV.

Just a Van Gogh on one wall and a marble fireplace on the other with built-in dark wooden bookshelves.

I can't take in all the vases, knickknacks, artifacts, various leather-bound books displayed fast enough. From a kantharos (a type of Grecian cup) to a glass figurine of two bodies intertwined to a carved wooden pipe to an old flute to Shakespeare's entire works in thick black binding.

Most, I'm positive, belong to Charlie from his travels. Jet-setting around the world could be his occupation if he posted *anything* about it on social media, but most of the time, we don't even know where the hell he goes.

No family photos on the shelves. It's not that my brothers aren't sentimental, but more personal items are contained to their bedrooms since they've held parties here before and things have "mysteriously" gone missing and then "mysteriously" been up for bid on eBay.

I toss my duffel on the couch and stride closer to the humongous windows overlooking the city. It's late morning, and the sun refracts against the glass high-rises. But with the tinted window, the natural light is dulled.

A concrete jungle.

I don't love New York.

I've never loved it. As a kid, I'd cry and beg my mom to take me home because I didn't want to hear the gurgle of exhaust or the honk of pissed-off drivers. I wanted to listen to the rustle of leaves as the wind swept through oaks. Even in Central Park, the city *loomed*.

Now I'm living inside it.

My nose flares as I consider the possible outcomes of being here. Honestly, some don't feel great. Some feel fucking terrible.

"And so he arrives." The dry, slightly bored tone could only belong to one brother.

Fuck.

I was hoping to run into Eliot first.

Tensing, I reluctantly turn to see Charlie leaning a shoulder on the arched entryway of a short hall. Which I remember leads to his bedroom and Beckett's. His ankles are crossed, and his hands are loosely threaded over his white button-down, the shirt partially untucked from his khaki slacks.

His golden-brown hair is unkempt. He looks like he gives zero fucks because he does give *zero* fucks. About almost everything.

Charlie Keating—he's number two.

I've hated him for as long as I can remember, but not before he started hating me.

"Welcome home, little brother," Charlie says with the enthusiasm of a defective confetti popper. "Though, by the looks of it, you don't want to make this one yours."

"What do you mean?" I know what he means.

I just don't love that Charlie acts like he's in my head when he has no real clue what goes on inside of me. But to be fair, he's *unbearably* intelligent and can read a room as well as he can people.

"You only brought one bag." He sounds irritated and gestures a stiff hand to the duffel. "Unless you're planning to bring the rest later."

I'm not. He knows I'm not.

I say nothing.

Charlie rolls his eyes. "This is going to be fun." He stands off the doorway and comes closer. He favors his right leg, and when he catches me staring at his slight limp, I cut my gaze to the window.

Guilt festers in my chest. It's a knot I can't loosen because I caused his injury.

I thumb an elastic cloth bracelet that says *don't worry, be capy* with an embroidered Capybara. Winona Meadows, my cousin, gave it to me years ago, and thinking about my obliterated friendship with her just tightens the knot.

I snap the elastic against my wrist.

"Get over it," Charlie says harshly while slouching back onto one of the blue chairs.

I clench my jaw.

The truth about Charlie? He has *no* real empathy for anyone outside of his twin. His unconditional love for Beckett is the best thing about him.

It's the only thing I relate to, but it's never been enough.

Now he's acting like it's so fucking easy to dispose of emotions. As if he understands them at all. If it were up to him, he'd carve out every single one from my body and grind them into dust.

He wants me to feel *nothing*. I'm the most sensitive Cobalt, in his eyes. The one without armor. The one with the most vulnerabilities. The one with the most fatal flaws.

To him, I'm just weak.

The runt of the pack.

The one who should've died early on. I was not meant to last, and maybe I only have because of our parents. Because we have a lioness for a mother who would snatch any struggling cub by the neck and keep them with the pride.

No matter the cost.

"*Ben.*"

I shoot my lowered gaze up to Charlie's. He's bowed forward in his chair, staring me down with a look I don't recognize.

"Just leave me alone," I say in a tensed breath. I take off my baseball cap, rake my fingers through my wavy hair, then toss the hat on the top of my duffel.

Charlie is blatantly annoyed. "It was a car accident from three years ago."

"Yeah and I was the one driving!" I shout as my eyes burn with heat. "I'm sorry I care about the impact it had on everyone in the car, including *you*." I sneer out the last word.

Charlie groans and slings his head backward. "Get the fuck over it."

I grit down on my teeth and stare unblinkingly at the window. What was I thinking? There's no way we'll last a few weeks together. At this rate, we might not even make it twenty-four hours. I fit my ballcap back on and snatch the strap to my duffel.

"Is that Ben I hear?!" a masculine voice calls out, mirth seeped in every syllable. Truthfully, mirth has been seeped in every *bone* of his body since birth.

I want to smile but it's lost beneath the heat of Charlie's heartless stare.

Eliot emerges from his side of the apartment, and his burgeoning, sly grin could light the room on fire.

In a perilous way.

I've always run toward a certain kind of danger, but maybe not the hedonistic kind Eliot supplies.

He's wearing gray sweats that ride low on his sculpted waist. It looks like I might've woken him up. He has the brawn of an NHL player, more built than even I am, but he's never been into sports. He just lifts.

"I'll be back later," I tell Eliot, about to make the trek to the door. Maybe I can meet up with Harriet early to grab lunch.

"Later?" Eliot's leisurely stroll morphs into an urgent sprint. He vaults over the couch to reach me faster and presses a hand to my chest. "You just got here, dear brother." He levels a look at Charlie, then smiles back at me. "I'll take that. Merci beaucoup." He takes my duffel before I can protest and slings the strap on his broad shoulder.

I guess I'm staying.

Until three.

I turn my baseball cap backward right as Eliot squeezes me in a suffocating bear-hug. I swear one time he cracked my rib. I was nine, and I said nothing because I never wanted him to be afraid to hug me. I never wanted him to stop.

He's number four.

Eliot Alice—he's pleasure and delight unencumbered, I've always believed. He's almost the same height as me. *Almost.* He's six-four like our dad. Really, out of everyone, he looks the most like our father. With perfectly wavy brown hair, a strong jawline fit for modeling, and deep captivating blue eyes.

As we pull back now, I don't even need to look down to meet those deep blues.

"You're going to love it here, Ben." He has a monster grin. "The things we're going to get up to."

"I have college," I remind him.

"After hours." He points at me. "You're mine."

I'm picturing Dionysus scales of debauchery, but the truth is, I don't know what Eliot does in New York. I've never been old enough to spend a day in the life with any of them here, and I can't lie—it *is* enticing. To be closer to them.

To be loved by them.

But I don't ever want to hurt them with my shit.

He scans the living area for more luggage. "Where's Theodore?" My cockatiel that him and Tom gifted me a while back. I love that bird, and I even convinced the administration at Penn to let me keep him in my dorm. I know my brothers would've had even less issues with him here.

"I left him with Audrey. I didn't want her to feel alone now that I'm gone."

"I like this. We move to New York; we give you the bird. You move to New York; you give her the bird. You know what we call that? *Symmetry.* Perfect circles." He glances around again, then pats the duffel. "This is it?"

I feel Charlie's mocking head-tilt behind me. I look. *Yeah.* There it is. He also has his feet kicked up on the glass coffee table, his fingers to his temple. "Is that it, Ben?" Charlie says like an annoying older brother.

"Hecklers," Eliot banters. "Ignore them, Ben. I always do."

"You love getting heckled," Charlie says plainly. "Any avenue for attention, you'll take."

He gasps. "Did the heckler just call me an attention whore?" His grin spreads.

"Point made."

Eliot leans into me and feigns a whisper. "He's obsessed with me."

"It is painfully the other way around," Charlie says.

"Ben can be the judge of that." Eliot adjusts the strap on his shoulder and gives me a short once-over, as if gauging whether I'm about to bolt. "Seeing as how you'll be living with us now. Front row seat to the chaos." His smile is genuine. It draws mine out. "Welcome to the bachelor pad." He raises and lowers his brows. "Where sins are made and prayers are kept."

It's a true bachelor pad in the fact that all my brothers are single and in their twenties.

As am I...except for being nineteen. I don't feel my age, though. The past few years, I feel like I've aged about ten more.

"I'll show you to your room, young prince," Eliot says, turning on his heels like we're in a play. For him, life is one beautiful stage.

I start to smile, but it wanes fast at a realization. "My room?"

He walks backward, eyes on mine. "You think we'd let you sleep on the floor?"

I was hoping.

A rock wedges in my ribs, and I follow Eliot to his side of the apartment, just as Charlie calls out to me, "Does Beckett know you're already here?"

"No." I stop in place. "I told him not to worry about picking me up."

Charlie curses under his breath, drops his feet to the ground, and immediately calls our brother. Phone to his ear. "He's already here… okay. Il est énervé contre moi." *He's angry with me.* Long pause. "Je ne peux pas être tenu responsable de lui." *I can't be held responsible for him.* "Oui, oui. À plus tard." *Yes, yes. See you soon.* He hangs up.

"Beckett has a performance tonight," I tell Charlie.

"He's taking tonight off for you."

I wince. "I told him not to."

"Well, congratulations. You're one of the few people he would sacrifice an evening performance for."

Fuck. I grimace and expel heat from my lungs with a big exhale. "Is that supposed to make me feel better?"

"I don't care what it makes you feel," Charlie says. "It's just the truth."

"Brutal, brother," Eliot says with less levity.

"I warned all of you that I wasn't going to be soft on him."

Irritation scrapes down my neck, and like word vomit, I sling back, "I wasn't expecting you to be Maximoff." Our older cousin who has an off-again, on-again friendship with Charlie. I think they're currently *on*, but there is one undying truth: where Maximoff is purely good, Charlie is purely evil. Day and night. Hero, villain.

For some reason, I got stuck with the villain brother.

Charlie is equally as irritated as I am now that I brought up Moffy. "Sorry he's not here to coddle you like you're twelve."

"Only you would think *coddling* is equivalent to being *kind*."

"I'm unkind. Moffy is the best. Moffy is the greatest," Charlie says in a mocking, disinterested tone. "Don't you get sick of smelling his shit? Or do you really, truly believe it doesn't stink?" He cocks his head at me. "You're going to be in a world of hurt when you realize he's not perfect."

I never thought he was. But at the very least, Maximoff Hale has never made me want to punch my fist through a fucking wall.

This time, I ignore Charlie. "Where are we going?" I ask Eliot.

"This way." He guides me down the short hall and opens a door. "After you." He extends his arm, and I stride inside...his bedroom.

The whole space is engulfed by an ornate four-poster bed with a thick burgundy canopy and even darker bedding. Squished in the corner is a reading nook, and beneath heavy curtains lies a desk that houses piles upon piles of manuscripts and treasured copies of Poe. It's familiar and as gothic as his childhood bedroom. The walls are even the same blood-red.

He drops my duffel. "It'll take me about ten minutes to strip the bed and put on a fresh set of sheets, and I'll have all this cleared out." He gestures to manuscripts—what I assume are plays. He used to be in a prestigious theatre troupe in Hell's Kitchen, but that job fell apart late last year.

He grabs a cardboard box from the floor. I come forward to stop him. "I don't want your room," I tell him.

"Is it the paint? Tom said it might scare you. You can always paint it blue." He wears an endearing smile. "For the Empire."

I laugh, the sound light in my chest. "Yeah, for the Empire. Because I fit in so well." I'm not bitter about being the odd one out. *This* is just a fact to me.

"None of us are the same, brother," Eliot reminds me. "That's what makes us gods among men."

"I thought it was just being born from *the* Rose Calloway and Connor Cobalt."

"The mother and father of gods," he hollers like he's in a stadium announcing their entrance.

I smile, but it's harder to hold these days. "I'm not displacing you, man. I can't."

"We don't mind. Tom and I willingly shared a room ninth through tenth grade."

"You're not in high school anymore."

"Ah, but to some, I have Peter Pan syndrome. So in certain eyes, I will never grow up." He opens his hand with this reasoning. "So what say you?"

"I say *I can't*."

He tosses the empty box aside, then clutches my face with two strong hands. "You can."

"I can't."

Eliot squints. "You can." He nods to himself like it'll process within me.

"I can't."

"I don't think I like this game."

"Probably because it's not a game."

"Vrai, vrai, vrai." *True, true, true.*

Then the door flings open. "Dude, I can't *fucking* believe him…" Tom trails off as he looks up from his phone and sees me. "Oh, you're here."

Eliot punches Tom in the arm.

"Oh you're here!" Tom changes his tone with fake excitement.

I rub the side of my neck. "Don't worry, it won't be for long," I mention.

"What? No, *no*." Tom raises his hands with the phone. "Sorry, Ben. Like I am *super* fucking happy you're living with us. Trust. *Please*. But I'm just dealing with the biggest pain in my ass."

Eliot leans on a bedpost and muses, "Is he a pain in the ass because you want him there?"

"I'm not talking about Phoenix, and *no*—no, dude, I don't want to sleep with Phoenix either." Tom groans all the way to the bed and plops face-down into the rumpled comforter.

He's number five.

Tom Carraway—he's eleven-months younger than Eliot, and they've been thick-as-thieves since they were kids. Eliot was right when he said none of us are the same. They might be alike in how they play with fire, but Eliot is usually the one who goes up in flames.

It feels like I should be closer to Tom since I'm sixth-born and he's fifth, but he spent his whole life at Eliot's side.

I can understand why.

Eliot knows how to make people feel extraordinary. So many

times, he's made me feel like I'm everything. Number one brother. Best person on the planet. A star in an undying constellation. Then there are times where I feel like he's forgotten I even exist. The shadow he leaves in his wake is unbearable. Everyone wants to be in his light.

I pick up my duffel while I ask Tom, "Who's bothering you?"

He rolls onto his back, forearm over his eyes. He looks the most like Charlie. With the same golden-brown hair, but Tom's is shaggier and often hangs in his eyes. He has on Vans and a The All-American Rejects band tee. Nothing that Charlie would wear.

"No, today is not about Alfie Bugsby," Tom says, naming the problem. He rises up like he's a zombie awakening from the dead. "It's about you. I'm completely focused on you, dude."

Honestly, I don't want him to be. My brothers have lives outside of the mess I'm fucking dropping on them by even being here, and I don't want them to change their worlds for me *at all.*

"Alfie Bugsby," I repeat. "Isn't that your new drummer? The one that your label put in your band?"

"That's the one." Tom physically winces at his phone. "He's seriously trying to rewrite three of my songs. After he already changed the tempo to our EP *live.* Fucking *live*, Ben. On stage at Tangerine. He screwed the entire show. At this rate, we'll never release our first album."

"Let's not doom The Carraways," Eliot says.

"My band *is* doomed. The second I didn't choose Phoenix as my drummer because I was worried he was too hot and he'd distract me—it was doomed." Tom gives me a distraught look. "You don't listen to them, do you? The band that Phoenix plays drums in?"

"Nothing Personal?" I ask.

"He knows the name of the band," Tom says to Eliot.

"He knows the name," Eliot echoes like this isn't good.

I almost laugh. "You vent about them at every Wednesday Night Dinner," I remind Tom.

"Never by name."

"Their rock single is also all over the radio."

"When did you start listening to the radio?" he interrogates, like this has to be some elaborate ploy to cause him distress.

I lift my shoulders. "I listen to a lot of things, including your music. Which I love." This barely edges him away from a cliff. The Carraways' EP is cycled in my repeat plays all the time. It's just more emo-punk like My Chemical Romance and not as mainstream as Nothing Personal.

"Radio is banned," Eliot announces. "No one's allowed to turn it on until the band that shall not be named breaks up."

Tom nods repeatedly like this is a great idea. Albeit dramatic, but *great*. It's nuts. My family is certifiably *nuts*. I smile a little more. Until he says to me, "You don't have their songs saved in your playlists, right?"

Uh, yeah.

I do.

I like all kinds of rock music, and Spotify has recommended their songs to me about a billion times. I've known Tom has a feud with the band, but I didn't think he'd ever see my playlists or grill me on it.

I could lie.

I have the ability *to* lie and do it pretty well. Evidence: I've lied to my therapist before, and he never noticed. Though I'm definitely not the best liar out of my siblings. Being cunning and skilled enough to deceive receives applause among Cobalts. It's a positive attribute.

But I don't love lying, especially to them.

Which is why skirting around the truth of my empty bank account is going to be impossibly *fucking* hard.

I thumb at my cheek where I have a beauty mark. "So I might've saved a couple of their songs—"

Tom groans before I even finish and flops backward on the bed. "Fuuuuck me, dude."

"So incestuous of you," Eliot banters.

"Shut up," Tom moans into his palms. "Ben Pirrip, you're giving them listens, numbers, *hits*."

Eliot tilts his head to me. "Don't listen to the enemy's music. Solidarity, baby brother."

"I'll delete it." I pull out my phone and easily remove all traces of Nothing Personal. I'm just reminded of how much Tom and Eliot eat, breathe, and shit *loyalty*. It runs through all our veins to certain degrees, and theirs is to the extreme.

I tense when I shove my phone back in my pocket.

Tom has very bad history with Harriet Fisher. If he knew I'm meeting up with her for a job interview…yeah, this isn't going to end well. But no one gets anywhere being careful.

So I can delete a song I like for Tom. But I can't delete a person. Which means I suck at the whole loyalty thing.

Probably because I can't be pressured to do anything I don't want to do. I have a titanium-strong backbone.

Which does make me a Cobalt.

I'm just not a very good one.

"House meeting!" Charlie calls from the living room. "Beckett is home!"

Tom springs off the bed and pushes his hair out of his eyes.

Eliot follows.

I'm the last one out—but I'm trapped for a beat by the humongous, ornately framed painting on the wall.

My eyes grow wide at the dark oils illustrating the sack and annihilation of an ancient Roman city. A storm brews in the background as warriors kill and seize prisoners. A woman in white is being yanked backward by an aggressor. Marble pillars are crumbling. A bridge is broken. People drown in the water. Buildings and boats are on fire.

It's *The Destruction of the Empire* by Thomas Cole.

The fourth of five paintings in his *The Course of Empire* series. Our parents gave us each a replica of a particular one. They depict the rise and fall of a civilization. This one—the one given to Tom and Eliot—has always disturbed me.

It's an empire at war.

"BEN!" they all call.

I tear myself away. "Yeah, I'm coming!" Duffel on my shoulder, I go to my brothers.

FOUR

BEN COBALT

"I'll sleep on the couch," I tell Beckett directly even though I'm facing all four older brothers. I'm the only one even sitting on the couch right now. He's in the matching blue chair beside Charlie.

"It's not a pull-out," Beckett says with a mountain of confusion knitting his features—features that can only be described as *angelic*.

It's weird that he shares that in common with Charlie when A.) Charlie is a demon and B.) they're fraternal twins. They don't look that alike, really. Beckett has much darker brown hair, and he's a couple inches shorter at six-one. They do have the same penetrating yellow-green eyes and lean builds.

But Beckett is *ripped*.

His body could probably be studied in art and humanities courses.

He shrugs off his leather jacket, and I notice the floral tattoos crawling up his arm. He has the reputation of being "the bad boy of ballet" at his company, which I've never completely understood how it could be true. Not until the past few years.

"The couch is long enough to fit me," I tell him. "I can just throw some blankets on it."

"You'd rather take the *couch* than a king-sized bed?" Beckett is very confused. He slips a look to Charlie like *how much did I miss?* They share short glances. Talking through their eyes.

They do that a lot.

"Maybe Eliot's room has a funk that we're nose-blind to," Tom says, straddling a kitchen chair backward. He dragged it over here.

"Bronwyn would've said something," Eliot replies, the only one standing. His bare foot is on the glass coffee table which has to be bothering Beckett because it sure as hell would bother our mom. "She was here two nights ago."

"Bronwyn?" I ask, the girl totally unfamiliar, and I'm fairly good with names.

He presses his tongue against the inside of his cheek and jerks the air. Miming a blow job.

He fucked her. Probably a casual hookup. Eliot isn't quiet about how he sleeps around.

"You'll change the sheets?" Beckett asks Eliot.

"I already told Ben I would."

"It's not about that," I jump in. "Okay, I just think the couch is better." I'm doing a piss-poor job at reasoning with them.

In their minds, my request is absurd.

I make no sense.

The logical thing is to sleep on a bed.

"There's no privacy out here," Beckett reminds me.

I shrug. "I don't care."

I don't plan to be here for long.

I'll be out of your hair soon.

Don't worry.

"We could get a pull-out," Tom suggests, opening and closing a Zippo lighter. The *click, click* fills the tense silence.

Charlie stares at me like he's mid-excavation from five feet away. Digging through my insides.

I'm burning up.

Eliot rests his forearm on his bent knee, bowing toward me as he asks, "Is there something wrong with my room, Ben?"

I smash my ballcap in my hands. "Can we not act like we're on the set of Clue and you're Mr. Green?"

"We can because I'd only play Colonel Mustard."

I open my mouth to respond, but I end up laughing. The lively sound dies too fast, and I lean farther back and try to look anywhere but at the brothers I sincerely love, which leaves me glancing at Charlie. I blink a few times, then say, "Nothing is wrong with your room, Eliot."

He nods once. "I detect no lies."

"When has he ever lied?" Charlie says like it's just another shortcoming.

"Because you know me so well," I snap at him.

"Because you're so complicated."

"Because you're the *only one* who can be," I retort.

Charlie laughs dryly, his annoyance contorting his face, and he shoots to his feet like he's done with me. I don't know why that hurts. It's what I want, isn't it?

For him to stop digging into me.

"Charlie," Beckett pleads, then looks to me. "We just want you to be comfortable here, Ben."

I watch Charlie lower back down.

Tension never leaves my body. "I could sleep on the floor and I'd be fine. I can make up the couch every night, and I'll put the blankets up every morning. You won't even notice I'm here."

Beckett scrunches his face in a physical manifestation of the phrase, *what the fuck.* "That's not the point of you living with us."

I scrape a rough hand through my hair. My eyes sear as one of the worst nights of my life tries to tunnel back into me. Anger amasses in my chest that I can't throw off.

Then fear.

Because I left Audrey.

I left Audrey.

Maybe I shouldn't have left her this soon. I could've stayed in Philly until she graduated from prep school. She's only sixteen.

"Pip," Beckett says so softly, so gently. He's one of the few people who call me *Pip*. Our older sister is the only one who calls me Pippy.

I swallow a boulder to tell him, "This isn't permanent."

Charlie arches his brows. "Somewhere else you have to be?"

Anywhere but here with you.

On-campus housing would've been my first choice. Second would be an apartment *not* with Charlie. Both cost money that I don't have right now, and I'd rather cut out my tongue than advertise I'm broke to him.

"What do you care?" I sling back. "You don't even want me here."

Beckett slips him a look I can't read.

Charlie sweeps the length of me. "What I want doesn't matter. You need to be here."

"I need to be here," I echo and nod a few times. "Je vais bien. Vraiment." *I'm fine. Really.*

"Tu ne vas pas bien," Beckett says so smoothly. *You're not.*

I love hearing him speak French the most, not just because his cadence is beautiful—but because his silky voice is practically a morphine drip. It reminds me of our dad, how he can calm me with a few words. I hang on to that and not how my muscles are on fire like I need to escape my entire body. I rub at my brow and scrub a hand down the side of my face. "Je vais bien," I repeat. "Je vais bien."

I hate how they're staring at me.

Like I'm a malfunctioning nuclear reactor. And my brothers are confident enough to house one. They are prepared to be blown into smithereens because they know they can't be injured.

Cobalts are invincible, haven't you heard?

All but me, apparently.

Beckett comes over and sits next to me. His arm slides over my back with such familiarity. He holds my shoulders, and I breathe out deeper at his consoling touch. I'm four, five, seven—and he's wrapping his arm around me while I'm crying over something seemingly dumb.

A bird fell out of a nest in our backyard and wheezed painfully on the grass.

Tom and Eliot lit a rosemary bush on fire.

A girl scraped her knees at Disneyland and her dad was being an ass to her. I didn't understand why.

Beckett was there when we were kids. Before he left for his dream. I'm nineteen, and he's here again. Right beside me.

This feels like my dream—like I am *dreaming*. Because it can't last. I have to wake up.

"You need to be in the city with us," Beckett says quietly to me, drawing my gaze to his. "New York is where you get to *live*, and I mean truly live. This is your time to be selfish, follow your ambitions, fuck the night away, let it all go—and we'll be with you. You aren't alone here, Pip."

I nod a few times, trying to cool the simmer in my blood.

"Have you talked to Dad?" Tom wonders. "About what happened that night?"

That night.

I can barely see what I did. Rage tore through me. I think I blacked out for half of it. I smashed a Porsche in with a bat. Then I knocked out the guy who owned it. I assaulted him on his front lawn, and I think I would've killed him if I wasn't pulled off.

So have I talked to our dad? Who relates almost 100% with Charlie? Who would never rage like an unhinged ape? Yeah, no. "I'm not looking for Dad to psychoanalyze me," I mutter quietly.

"Then Mom?"

I shake my head. "Not really." She's already told me she would've skewered that guy with her high heel. *She* is a proponent of revenge. But it didn't make me feel much better.

My brothers wanted me to come to New York almost immediately after I lost control. After they heard I did all of this alone. I don't think anyone expected it.

"Something's going on with you," Jane had said. "Pippy? Just talk to us. We're all here."

She's number one.

Jane Eleanor—the best of us. And for once, no one would disagree.

I try to breathe.

I relax more when they concede to the couch idea. Beckett says they'll get a pull-out. I offer to pay. I'll put it on my credit card.

They get weird when I bring up the cost. It's August, and less than three months ago our trust funds were replenished with a jaw-dropping amount. We should all be beyond flush.

All trust funds are different, depending on who sets them up. Ours isn't free money raining down from cobalt-blue skies.

I don't have access to the billions my family is worth either. My inherited and gifted stock from my family's companies is unattainable until a specific date. *Years* from now.

I don't make dividends. I can't sell stock for cash. It's all inherited wealth locked behind pearly gates that only means something when someone Googles my net worth. I'm only nineteen. I'm not hurting enough that I'd need to cash out pots of gold at the end of a rainbow.

My trust fund, though—that is more accessible.

Our parents planned all our trust funds the same in an effort for us to learn fiscal responsibility. A hard lesson for kids born of billions. On May 15th of every year—starting at whatever age (within reason)—we could draw a lump sum from our trust. A portion had to be used for education, but the rest, we could do whatever we wanted with it.

Spend, splurge, invest. Doesn't matter.

It's up to us, and if we fuck it all away, then we suffer the consequences of those actions. They won't bail us out or offer us more money.

We have to wait for the next May 15th.

The sum we receive every year—it's far, *far* beyond the median annual income. Enough to start a new business, enough to secure our futures, and there are no rules. My parents have given us the opportunity to sink or swim, and currently, I'm an anchor at the bottom of the Atlantic.

My savings account is a whopping *zero*.

My checking account is *zero*.

I'll have to wait almost a whole year for that number to grow. All I really have are some credit cards, and I'm not too eager to use them when I can't afford to pay them off anytime soon.

I tune in as Eliot says to me, "You can use our bathroom." He's referring to his bathroom with Tom, even though I had no intention of using Beckett's. I'm not really messy, but Beckett has a particular way in which he keeps his things. Product labels facing outward, bath towels symmetrical and aligned on the rod, Q-tips lying flat in a container. And those are just the ones I know about.

"Or I can just use the powder bath," I suggest.

"There's no shower," Tom says, which derails us into banter about sponge-bathing and maybe I'm the one with a stink. I don't fucking stink. Eliot sniffs under my armpits. Confirms I smell like cedar and pine.

Then they talk about demoing the powder bath. Making it bigger.

"HOA won't allow it," Charlie says. "I've already tried."

"We *own* the apartment," Tom complains. "They can't just tell us *no*."

"They can actually."

"We could buy the apartment complex," Eliot considers. "What do you say, let's each chip in?"

"What do you think it'd go for?" Beckett asks Charlie, as if this is a plausible option.

Blood tries to drain out of my face. For once, I don't like that we're rich *rich*.

"With financing, a hundred mil, easily," Charlie says.

"Twenty million apiece," Eliot nods. "Cough it up, boys."

"Fuck no," Tom gapes.

"*Brother.*"

"Do you know what else I could buy with that? For what—a bathroom?"

I keep my mouth shut.

Beckett tells Charlie, "We could just buy a bigger condo in the same complex."

"Bigger with a worse view."

I rub at my face. Uprooting them is the last thing I wanted to happen.

Eliot motions to the floor. "Let's have Luna and Xander go in on it. They're living in the apartment complex too." Our obscenely wealthy cousins are three levels below us on the 18th floor. Our moms are the Calloway sisters, and our Grandfather Calloway (may he rest in peace) was the one who created Fizzle, one of the most popular sodas in the world. It's where the majority of our fortune comes from. Though, our families all have a shit ton of companies beyond the soda dynasty.

I rub my face harder at the mention of the Hales.

Luna Hale.

Xander Hale.

The two of them moved in during the summer. They're also going to MVU this semester, and Xander will be a freshman. Luna is *best friends* with Tom and Eliot, so I always figured I'd see her here, but I've been hoping Xander and I don't cross paths anywhere.

An arctic freeze exists every time we share the same air as we've gotten older. It's like being naked in the Tundra and I can't melt the snow.

"I'll call Luna," Tom says, about to pose the idea.

I'm on my feet. "No one needs to fork over twenty million."

"Could be fourteen million," Eliot points to Tom's phone. "We just need two more takers."

"I'll use your bathroom," I announce. "Like right now." I show them that I am happy with this outcome. I even smile on my route there. "Thanks for sharing!"

"Always!" Eliot calls out. As he lowers his voice to our brothers, I just barely hear him say, "I think he's going to be fine."

My chest tightens, and I shut the door.

The spacious bathroom has a *massive* glass shower. Black tile, black grout, and a humongous rainfall showerhead with LED lighting. Eliot already told me to download the app so I can shower in any hue of choice. I imagine he chooses the hues of hell. Bathing in red.

None of their hair products or razors are out on the counter. The stone sink is squeaky clean, and I smell sandalwood from incense. My brothers keep a tidy bathroom. Definitely not tidier than Beckett, but this is a habit from having very put-together parents who didn't always let housekeepers clean our shit for us.

They were probably afraid of raising spoiled, nepo brats, and in a life surrounded by private jets, yachts, magazine covers, unimaginable wealth—they had to humble us somewhere.

Eliot and Tom were also consistently grounded in their youth, and our mom preferred to dole out chores as punishment. They'd joke about being well-acquainted with the Scrub Daddy.

I take a seat on the toilet lid.

My leg jostles while I scroll through the forty new text messages I received in the last half hour from various people. My eyes slow on several.

> **MOM**
>
> Did your move go well, gremlin? If ANY of your brothers gave you grief, I will personally smite them with receding hairlines.

A warm smile inches up my face, and we text back and forth for a second.

> **BEN COBALT**
> I'm not sure you have the power to cause hair loss.

> **MOM**
> I'm your mother. My powers are limitless.

> **BEN COBALT**
> They can probably be put to better use than on me.

> **MOM**
> I disagree. The greatest force of my power will always be reserved for my children. And that includes you.

"I know," I whisper to the phone. She's so scared I don't feel included since I'm the least "intellectual" of our very academic, creative-minded brood. I'm the athlete who dislikes Shakespeare and has never read Austen and don't get me started on Faulkner. It's migraine-inducing.

All the things the great and mighty Rose and Connor love, I just don't click with.

But my parents have never treated me like I'm inadequate for not reaching the *perfect* Cobalt standard. They've valued our uniqueness and have even fostered it. I've never felt pressure to achieve more or be more than I am. At least not from them.

I scroll to another message.

> **DAD**
> While you're in New York, would you want to see Frederick?

His life-long therapist? He hasn't even let *Charlie* see Dr. Frederick Cothrell. From what I've gathered, our dad is afraid Charlie would mind-fuck Frederick into giving details about his own sessions. We're all in therapy, by the way. To either vent or make sense of our strange place in this world or for unknown personal reasons that we don't openly share. The latter, being *me*.

All seven of us have gone at various points. Some more than others. As far as I'm aware, Tom and Charlie go the most.

With maybe me at third place.

I reread the text about twenty times, my leg bouncing again.

I trust my dad.

But I also trust that his concern for me has reached Mount Everest elevations. I trust that my parents would do *anything* to ensure my safety and well-being. Even if it means secretly prying without my knowledge.

Is it still an invasion of privacy if the intent is pure?

Yeah, probably.

But it's more difficult not to love how deeply they care about me. I'd never choose their apathy. Which just makes me think of Charlie. I can't even *imagine* him as a father. I fucking *fear* for that child.

And Frederick—would he break doctor-patient confidentiality and tell my parents about our sessions? I want to say *no*. My dad has only ever said Frederick is unbiased and reasonable. But I do know that my dad is smart enough to also mind-fuck Frederick, so no…I don't want to see his therapist.

At times, being in my family feels like one ginormous game of chess.

Thing is, I also hate chess.

I lose nearly every time. But that's not why I play the least of everyone. I'd just rather be stretching my legs than stretching my mind.

BEN COBALT

> I prefer to continue seeing Dr. Wheeler.
> He said he'd take video calls.

I wait a second after I send the text, my hand clamped over my mouth, and I hope my dad doesn't suspect anything amiss. Like, maybe, Dr. Wheeler isn't good for me. Like, maybe, it's because I haven't been treating therapy like I should be. With *honesty*.

It takes him a few seconds to reply.

> **DAD**
> If you reconsider, just let me know.
> I'm always here for you.

Yeah.

I know that too.

When I drop my hand off my mouth, I thumb through more messages and come up to the old thread with Harriet. I stop on her name.

Harriet Fisher.

She shouldn't stick out to me, but our one run-in at Penn has played on a loop in my head for so long. I'd been hightailing it to an Intro to Biology class and chugging a blue Ziff sports drink. I had my gym bag on my shoulder since hockey practice was right after. It should've been a typical, ordinary day at college.

Nothing special.

Nothing monumental.

Average.

I peered into a science lab as I strode past, but I caught a glimpse of a girl staking a glare at an older professor. It jerked me backward. Because they were alone.

The lab was nearly empty with untouched beakers and vials and clean black desks.

It felt...wrong.

Doors down the hall began to slam. Footsteps faded away. Class was about to start. The building went hushed, and I was going to be late.

I cared about my grades. Failing Bio meant the coach would

never let me touch the ice. But my relationship with hockey was... *is* complicated.

I didn't head to class. I heard the steam off her words. I saw him encroaching her space with similar aggravated heat. They were disagreeing. Not civil enough to be about a poor exam or grading dispute. It was personal.

I entered the lab on instinct. The professor hadn't seen me yet. Not until he grabbed her elbow, and I shot forward, yelling at him, scaring him off too easily.

When he was gone, she breathed so hard, I wondered if she was on the verge of a panic attack. I was about to ask if she needed some water, but her scowl narrowed her dark ocean-blue eyes into furious waves. I didn't move, and it felt like even a single sound would cause her to lash out.

But I wasn't going to flee.

I wasn't even afraid of her.

If anything, her silent hostility drew me closer.

She was short enough that I could feel the muscles strain in my neck as I looked down. Five-foot, five-one, maybe? She righted her slipping bookbag—a blink-182 patch sewn in the canvas fabric, plus a laughing skull and a coffin that said *are you dead yet tho?*

Strands of her flowy blond hair caressed her soft, delicate face. It was the only thing soft about this girl. Her plaid pants were ripped at the knee, her maroon leather jacket swallowed her tiny frame, and her combat boots were laced to the ankles. I recognized her instantly. She was my cousin Luna's lab partner from the semester before.

As she sucked in a breath to speak, I was ready for her to tell me to fuck off. But she said, "Thanks."

I've wondered if that was the moment. Was that when she got in my head? Was that when I couldn't excise her from my thoughts? I hadn't expected her to thank me. I wasn't even looking for a *thanks*.

I frowned and glanced back at the door where the professor ran out of the lab. "What was that?"

"Professor Turner. He teaches Molecular Biology of Life. Luna and I took him last semester."

I gestured my sports drink at her. "No, I meant *what* was that. Why was he grabbing your arm like that?"

She blew out a breath so hard it rustled her blond bangs. "He's a fuckwad, that's why."

I pressed on because I couldn't let it go. Not after what I'd just seen. "Why is he a fuckwad? What'd he do?"

"What are you Scooby Doo?" She frowned deeper, her scowl darkening. Maybe she was used to people just leaving her pissed-off face alone. Turning their backs. Walking away.

"I don't know. Is this a mystery that needs to be solved, Harriet Fisher?"

She flinched, probably surprised I remembered her name. Then she lifted her chin higher to meet my gaze. "No mystery here, sorry to break your heart. Turner just got the wrong impression after we made an agreement." *An agreement?* She crossed her arms. "And you do realize your brother Tom hates me?"

It always came back to Tom.

She added, "Pretty sure you'll be disinvited to the next Cobalt soiree."

"That's actually impossible," I told her. "I could piss off every sibling, and they'd still invite me and try to hold some elaborate family intervention."

She nodded slowly. "Ruthless love." She said it, not with distaste or jealousy, but how someone would appraise a foreign treasure. Unsure of the true value of something they've never held before. "But from where I'm standing, Cobalts don't like strangers or interlopers."

"I can be friends with who I want."

"Since when are we friends?" Harriet asked.

We went on a tangent about the definition of friendship, similar to the one I had with her at the frat party. I told her that she was officially my only friend. She believed me about as much as she did at the Kappa Phi Delta house, but I wasn't really lying. Right then, I would've deleted every contact in my phone to prove it.

I didn't know her, but I knew I didn't want to lose her.

She finally returned to the "agreement" she made with the professor. "Look, it's not a big deal, dude. I gave Turner a blow job in exchange for a favor, and now he wants more than one blowie, so I'm fending off an ugly hammerhead shark."

I couldn't stop looking at her. My brain worked a mile a minute over what that meant.

She raised her brows at me. "Say something, Friend."

"What favor is worth blowing a hammerhead shark?" I glared back at the door, wishing I could've laid my fucking hands on him. Wishing his face met the *fucking* floor. Ire bubbled in my blood, and my hand twitched at my side, dying to curl into a fist.

He was her *professor*. He was a *teacher*. And he took advantage of a *student*. Of *her*.

Harriet let it spill that the favor had been for Luna, who'd missed labs. Their professor apparently refused to let Luna finish the course off-campus, even though it'd been national news that my cousin was in the hospital after an assault.

Harriet bartered with Professor Turner to give my cousin take-home work, so that Luna could pass the course.

"Can you not tell Luna? Please?" Harriet pleaded. "She didn't ask me to make the deal. I did this on my own accord because I felt bad she had to miss labs."

Of all the favors…she didn't even blow him for herself. It'd been for a girl that I'm sure Harriet just considered a college lab partner and not even a friend.

And she thinks *I'm* unhinged.

"Again, not a big deal." She made sure to say. "It meant nothing, and I've given blow jobs for less. It's not like I got naked for the guy."

We went back-and-forth on whether he should be reported, but I left it in her court and gave her my number in case she was ever in trouble again. She told me she was transferring to MVU in the fall. Pre-med, which I didn't peg her for. She was a mystery to me, and I thought I needed to be okay with never uncovering the answers or the stormy depths to Harriet Fisher. Having her phone number was enough.

So I let her go. I watched her walk down the hall. "See you around, Fisher."

"See you, Birthday Boy."

I rocked back. My heart stopped for a beat. Just dumbfounded. Not a single friend, not even one of the twenty that I ran into that morning on campus, wished me a happy birthday. Family, sure, but my friends...they either didn't realize or they forgot. I didn't make my birthday a big deal. I didn't mention it. I didn't seek out attention from it.

She walked backward, moving more slowly away from me. "I didn't stalk you exactly. I was doing my homework on Tom a while back. For the drum audition. Your page was pretty small." She squeezed her fingers together. "Where's all the accolades?"

I smiled, one that spilled warmth into my body. "Siblings took them all."

She mimed tears with her fists, her lips rising. The smile surprised her, and she startled into a frown. I thought it was cute. She gave me a stiffer wave before she disappeared completely.

We didn't stay in contact.

Despite really, *really* wanting to, I never texted her. My move to New York was never part of the plan at the time. I didn't think I'd follow her to MVU, and a friendship with Harriet didn't feel genuine if it was miles away. But then I did move to New York, and...the frat party happened.

Twice now, my presence averted some sort of catastrophe in her life. Twice, I was able to get some bastard's hands off her. That doesn't always happen. Being at the right place, right time. Especially with me. I don't really believe in destiny or fate, but I do believe there's something about Harriet that makes me feel like I won't fuck everything up.

All I really want is to be able to hold on to that feeling for a second longer.

FIVE

BEN COBALT

I'm applying for a job. It's not a great thing to tell my brothers on my way out the door. I already picture Beckett's classic "what the fuck" face, and Tom's double-blink like he can change the channel on me—to one that makes more sense.

So I just tell them I'm meeting with a friend. They know I have many. They also know my friendships are about as deep as a Neapolitan pizza.

"Don't wait up for me!" I call out as I open the door.

"Wasn't planning to," Charlie deadpans.

"Duuude," Tom groans like Charlie is beating a dead horse—that horse being *me*.

It's easy to tell myself, *don't let Charlie get under your skin.* Harder to accomplish when he lives in my bloodstream. I escape into the hall and breathe out the smoke-cloud of aggravation in my chest, then I text my bodyguard to just meet me on the lobby level.

Waiting for the elevator, I punch the button a couple times, and my phone buzzes in my jeans' pocket. I slip the cell out, my pulse skyrocketing. Is it her?

My heart jumps seeing the "H," then the "a" but then plummets at the rest of the name. Haddock (Coach MVU). I stare at the screen, processing this brutal anticlimax. Disappointment has sufficiently smothered a brief millisecond of exhilaration. That's what I get for getting excited over a fucking *phone call*.

I answer it as the elevator opens on the twenty-first floor. "Hi, Coach." I slip inside and hit the lobby button, vaguely listening to his pitch about trying out for the team. It's his third attempt to recruit me.

Hockey. First time I remember really thinking, *I could do this forever. I never want to leave the ice*, I'd been seven. I wasn't on an indoor rink. It'd been a freezing Christmas, and the lake had iced over at my family's vacation home in the Smoky Mountains. Orange sun crested over the spruce-lined peaks, and I held a stick and flew toward the net. I wasn't alone. Ryke Meadows and Maximoff Hale, my uncle and my cousin, were there, playing with me, and as I sucked the frigid air in my lungs, I just felt alive.

I played nearly every day that year. If I couldn't get on the ice, I'd put on rollerblades and shoot pucks into a goal in the Meadows' cul-de-sac. Then I played on a team, helped a group of boys win a dinky little trophy, but their elation was *everything* to me. I fed off the high of their happiness.

So I kept going. I played for my prep school throughout my adolescence. Then at sixteen, I played junior hockey to improve for college. When I was young, hockey had been a constant source of love. I could rely on it, depend on it.

The last few years, things started shifting in my head. It's been a steady decline, the slow decaying of what I once enjoyed. My college experience with the sport didn't help.

I warmed the bench more than my blades touched the ice. I was consistently told I wasn't good enough and that "not everything can get handed to you"—even if I thought I was at least the fourth-best on the team.

Coach Haddock, who I'm on the phone with now, likely found little footage of me playing back at Penn. He also admitted to contacting my old coach for a recommendation. Which, I gathered, my old coach told Haddock that I suck and not to waste his time on a "prick of a kid" like me.

Why would Haddock even want me on his team badly enough to call again? MVU is a D1 college. A good percentage of players end up being drafted for the NHL. He's a *dream* coach who could have his pick of a potential hockey prodigy.

I'm not that wonderkid, and MVU's hockey team isn't hurting for a win. They consistently advance to the playoffs in their division. So in the back of my head, I'm considering how he could just want fanfare.

The Cobalt to ride the bench and sell-out tickets.

Except, he's only ever discussed my potential. He's only ever been *nice*. So I have this desire to please him. I can't shake it.

"If you're worried about the publicity, we can do a private tryout," he even tells me, further eliminating the notion he's interested in my family's notoriety. "It'll just be me and Coach Zamora."

That's not the issue. "Can I think about it some more?" I ask, mostly to avoid hurting him with an axe to whatever idea he's constructed in his mind. My mom would shake her head at me with the subtlest of smiles. "Let them down gently" is not a phrase in her guide to dealing with…anyone.

Both my parents are business-oriented—my mom in fashion; my dad in anything with a high profit margin. Cobalt Inc., our birthright, owns subsidiary companies that sell magnets, paints, ethically-sourced diamonds, video games, and more sectors than I can name. Though in another life, I wonder if they would've worked in academics and argued over old British literature and texts written in Middle English.

"Of course you can." Haddock's tone goes upbeat, which makes me feel good but also makes my stomach roil. Because…I'm not playing hockey. I can't play anymore. "Season doesn't start until late September. We've got plenty of time, Ben."

I get tripped up on how he says *we* as if I'm part of the team already. My old coach went out of his way to exclude me when I was actually *on* the team. I was the shining celebrity star he was trying to ground every day.

I couldn't even blame him. Cobalts are born in the sky. Feeling for the earth has always been a struggle, but it's where I've loved to be, rolling around in the dirt and mud. Literally. My mom used to hose me off after a long day playing outside before she'd let me in the house.

I smile to myself at the memory as the elevator descends, and I listen to Coach Haddock make a final plea. "You'll love the facilities. They redid the rink a couple years ago. If you haven't seen it yet, I'll give you a tour anytime. Or I can get some of the guys to show you around. Get you introduced to the team."

The elevator suddenly jerks to a stop at the eighteenth floor. Not even close to the lobby yet. I keep the phone rooted to my ear while the doors slide open to reveal a long-limbed guy who slouches on the opposing wall, waiting for *this* elevator.

Red bulky headphones cover his ears, and a black hood is drawn over his head, shadowing striking features that could cause doubletakes and four-car pileups. Elevator doors are now fully open. It lets out a *ding*. He straightens off the wall, then stops when he sees me.

He has sharp cheekbones and amber eyes like melted caramel, but they're far from sweet when he looks at me.

"Hey, I need to call you back," I tell Haddock fast, and I only hang up when Coach says, "I'll be here." Then I grab the side of the elevator as the doors try to shut.

I wait for him to come inside.

He settles back against the wall. "I'll take the next one."

I'm about to ask if he's sure, but he's already staring at everything but me. The line of his jaw could cut glass as he clenches down. I let go and the elevator doors shut on him. My muscles cramp.

Yeah.

I take it personally.

Because that's my cousin.

Xander Hale.

HARRIET IS WAITING FOR ME ON A CONGESTED CORNER, dodging the shoulders and elbows of power-walking New Yorkers. When she finally spots me, her chest collapses in a relieved exhale. It brightens something inside me, knowing my presence brings *relief.*

A smile crawls across my face. "Harriet Fisher," I say as I reach her short height.

"Cobalt boy." She adjusts her backpack strap. I'm only carrying a water bottle. The blue aluminum is decaled with different environmental and wildlife stickers.

"I don't even get a *Ben?*" I tease.

"Maybe later." She looks me up and down. I'm just wearing a white '70s-style ringer tee with the words *Give a Hoot, Don't Pollute!* and an owl. She's stuck on my biceps, the fabric tight around my carved muscles. "Nice suit and tie."

"Same to you." She has on low-rise, acid-wash jeans and a mesh camo top that barely covers her ribcage. Not changing her punk-rock style for this interview. I respect the *come as you are* approach. "I like the belly button ring."

She prickles, shoulders raised as if preparing to combat the punchline.

I give her a softer look, then block her from being sideswiped by a leather bag as a man rushes past us. "I was serious," I tell her. "I like it." I point to the bejeweled piercing hooked through her tiny belly button.

Her shoulders lower. "Thanks." She jerks her head toward the sidewalk ahead of us. "Let's go bomb this interview."

I tsk. "No faith, Fisher."

"Well, my odds have now increased with you here. I have faith in that," she says while we walk side by side, not too far from my brothers' apartment in Hell's Kitchen. "But I might be the one bringing us down."

Yeah, I can't see how that'd be true. Unless she breaks a martini glass trying to make a cosmo. But the bar manager might not even test our mixology skills.

We aren't applying to work at a high-end restaurant with collar-and-tie uniforms, fifty-dollar cocktails, and linen tablecloths. The End of the World is a dive bar, as far as we've been told by her friend. It has no social media, no website, and a lone 5-star on Yelp. No pictures.

"It might not even exist," Harriet tells me.

"It might be a crack den."

She gives me a hard side-glance. "I love how you said that with so much apprehension."

My lips rise. "No point in freaking out. We're not even there yet."

Harriet nods, then expels a long breath, and when we come up to the bar, I hold my hand out to the full name scrawled in spray paint styled font on the dark window outside. **WHERE YOU WANT TO BE AT THE END OF THE WORLD.**

"It's real," I tell her.

"A miracle," she says dryly. "You used to those?"

I grin. "Yeah, every time I ace a science exam."

She lets out a snorty laugh, then goes ahead of me to push inside. That's when I see the back of her hair. White residue trickles down blond strands in a slimy river.

"Harriet." I catch her backpack, tugging her backward.

"Don't tell me you have cold feet." She spins toward me, then scrunches her face at my winced expression. "What's wrong?"

I just come out with it. "A bird shit in your hair."

Her eyes pop. "Wh…no way, *no.*" Her voice pitches abnormally high, then her eyes ping to pedestrians who stroll past and couldn't care less about us. We're not in Times Square where I'd draw attention from tourists like I'm a superhero street performer doing the worm on cement. We step closer to the brick siding outside the bar. "How bad is it?" She's asking while I pop open my water bottle. Her hands hover around her head. "You know how many diseases pigeon shit has?"

"Don't touch it."

"You don't touch it," she shoots back. "Just cut if off, Ben."

"I'm not cutting your hair because of bird shit." I grab my tee at the back of my neck and pull it over my head. Then I wet the fabric with water. "Turn around."

She's frozen and wide-eyed on my bare chest. She's slowly, *slowly* processing my shirtless state while we're out in public. I catch her staring at my abs for a beat too long.

I almost laugh. "Petit oiseau." I whirl my finger in the air. "Tourne-toi." *Litle bird, turn around.*

"Just when I forgot you're both brains and brawn."

"More brawn than brains," I correct her. "Everyone in my family can speak fluent French." I can tell my confidence in handling this situation is easing her panic. Enough that she rotates, her back facing me. Still, she's a rigid punk-rock statue, and I have a feeling she's never taken a trust fall in her life.

She's taking one now. I recognize how she's trusting me to clean her hair when she could've shoved me off and ran into the bar's bathroom.

Her head barely reaches the height of my shoulders, and using my damp T-shirt as a rag, I comb it through the blond strand, cleaning off the white slimy residue. "If it makes you feel any better, I've been shit on by birds a lot worse than this."

She shifts her head a little, trying to look at me, but stops herself. "What kinds?"

"Mostly cockatiels."

"*Pet* birds? Ones you feed yourself and probably aren't carrying a petri dish of bacterial infections?" Her voice spikes weirdly again. "We should just cut it."

"I'm getting it all out," I assure. "I promise. I've done this before." I need a better hold on Harriet, so I say, "I'm going to touch you."

"You are touching me."

"Yeah, a little more than this, Friend."

She goes quiet. She's clutching her backpack strap like it's the safety holster in a fighter jet, prepared to fly away from me. I wait for her to say *no*. Instead, she says gruffly, "You don't need to warn me."

I smile at her hot tone. "Your body kind of says otherwise." But taking her cue, I just go ahead and clutch her shoulder with my left hand, working on her hair with my right.

She tries to relax. "What are you—a master of reading body language?"

"More like novice level."

"You've got to be the least cocky Cobalt."

"Just honest." I try to get out a nasty chunk stuck between two strands, and for a better grip, I slip my fingers from her shoulder up to the soft nape of her neck and into her silky hair. I'm holding the side of her head, and I try not to concentrate on the warmth of her against my palm. Or how she careens back toward my chest, closing in on me. Her breath deepens like she's on the ascent of a rollercoaster, and I have the sudden urge to pull her into my body and wrap my arms around her in a vise.

It looks like she could use a hug. A million questions swarm me at once. Like whether she's ever been held. Does she even like being hugged?

"Is it out?" she asks, her voice husky.

My cock twitches in my jeans. *Fuck.* "Yeah, almost." For her sake, I finish pretty fast, but I have to drench more of her hair with water. The back of her head is wet when I'm done. So I take off my baseball cap and fit it on her head. It's huge on her, so I tighten the back strap, pulling the fabric through a metal clasp.

Good enough. "There you go. Bird shit free."

Harriet spins around, the brim of my hat totally concealing her eyes from me. I push it up and see her murderous scowl.

I laugh. "I really hope this is the absolute *worst* thing that's ever happened to you."

"Far from it," she notes, a smile fighting its way through her beautiful features.

I tilt my head in thought, hoping she is just joking with me. "What's worse than being shit on before our big interview?"

She shrugs, her smile disappearing, and I almost regret asking. Then she nods to me, "You're really going in there without a shirt?" She watches me stuff my dirty tee in my back pocket.

I shrug back at her. "Why not?" At this, I enter the bar, and Harriet follows with more intrigue. She never takes off my hat.

SIX

BEN COBALT

I have no experience in bartending. Neither does Harriet, and even though we're not twenty-one yet and can't legally drink, it's legal for us to serve alcohol in New York.

Gavin, the bar manager, is a copper-haired, thirtysomething around Novak's age. He has a body as thin as a pencil and a mustache-goatee combo like he should be hosting a poetry slam and not taking wooden chairs off the scuffed tables before the bar opens at six.

"Ben Cobalt, you really showed up," Gavin says with a lopsided, silly grin like he just struck gold.

"In the bare flesh," I joke and motion to my chest. "Bird shit on me. You wouldn't believe it, man."

He laughs. "You're kidding?"

"Deadass. Though if it helps me get the job, then maybe I should thank the little bird." I peer down at Harriet.

She scrunches her nose at me, but her cheeks pinch like she's a teeny-tiny fraction of a second from a smile. It morphs into a full-blown scowl when Gavin appraises her head to toe.

Fire roars in my chest as he lingers too long on her tits.

"This is Harriet Fisher," I cut in, drawing his attention back to me. "We're applying together."

He nods. "And who's that?" He juts a thumb toward the stoic guy posted at the door.

"Chris Novak. He's my bodyguard. He won't get in the way, but he'll be around if I'm here."

"Personal security detail. That's fucking badass, man." He slaps a hand to the bar, going around the counter to pluck off a pint glass from the shelf. "So this is the End of the World." He motions around the space. "It's small but a stubborn old bitch. Been here for decades, but I've been running things for the owner for the past eight years. Terry is retired and just kicks back in his brownstone. He'll pop in for a whiskey sour from time to time, but he lets us do whatever, whenever."

I can see why this place has survived since the '80s. Ripped up magazines cover the plastered walls in a hodgepodge of ads and torn articles like we're in a teenager's bedroom during grunge days of Nirvana and Stone Temple Pilots. It has warmth and charm with several weathered vinyl booths, bumper-sticker vandalized tables, and a projector screen over a brick wall playing *Breakfast at Tiffany's*.

Gavin catches me staring as an orange cat paws at a sleeping Audrey Hepburn who wears an iconic turquoise eye-mask. My stomach tightens seeing my little sister's namesake.

"Movies play every day of the week," he explains. "It's the only requirement Terry has. And they all need to have one thing in common."

"What's that?" Harriet asks.

"All the films are set in New York."

I let out a laugh. Of course I choose to apply for a job in New York that's going to torment me *with* New York.

Gavin pours himself a beer, then takes a frothy sip. "Let's get started."

It's a majorly short interview. Except for the part where Gavin spends five minutes talking about how his girlfriend is obsessed with the ballet and has seen my brother Beckett dance about two-hundred times. "He's her hall pass," he says casually like he didn't just mention how he'd let his girlfriend fuck my brother.

Harriet's face contorts like she swallowed curdled milk. I half-expect her to tell him this is a shit interview. More surprised when she doesn't. She's not impatiently rocking on her feet or sighing out in frustration. She's quietly assessing Gavin, which is pulling her face between a cringe and a scowl.

I'm not a psychiatrist, but it seems like she's biting her tongue. Maybe Harriet is more used to suppressing whatever tumbles around her head.

I'm more used to being around unfiltered people. And by *people*, I mean my family.

Gavin doesn't ask for our experience behind the bar. Just has us make a whiskey sour in case Terry ever stops by. Harriet precisely measures out the bourbon. I confidently wing it.

With not enough shame (where did it go? Pretty sure it never existed), I copy off her. I think she's pissed at first but then she rolls her eyes and shows me exactly what goes into the drink. Because I have no fucking idea.

"You make these a lot?" I ask her while Gavin sets out the last chairs and leaves us alone behind the bar.

"Once or twice." Harriet dips down to be eye-level with her lemon juice in the measuring cup. Being *very* exact.

"You hate the taste?" I wonder.

She stiffens a little as she straightens up. "I never tried it. I didn't make it for myself."

For who then?

I probably shouldn't pry, but as I skim her, several theories crash too aggressively into me. I let one out. "Ex-boyfriend?"

"Yes and no." She pours her lemon juice into a cocktail shaker. "Mom's ex-boyfriend." Her cheeks redden with hot flush. I wonder if she's burning up all over.

Okay. It's a sensitive topic. *Tread lightly.* "You've one-upped me because I've never made this in my life."

"You don't say?" Her brows lift into her bangs. "I couldn't tell at all."

I'm smiling while I guess how much lemon juice she used. I dump what I think is a healthy amount into my shaker.

"It's three-fourths ounce," she tells me, her voice pitching like I'm about to cut my hand when there are no knives near us, no threat of harm.

I stop and watch her intake a big breath to calm down. I'm not panicked at all. This isn't a life-or-death situation, but I wonder why she feels like it's one. "That looked like three-fourths," I say. "Don't you think?"

"No," she says seriously. "It looked like a half a cup. Which is *four* ounces."

Fuck. I grab the bottle of bourbon, adding a touch more *without* measuring.

"You're diabolical," she says, watching closely. "Keep going. Keep going." I take her advice. When I add enough liquor to combat the citrus that might still leave Gavin with permanently puckered cheeks, I set the alcohol aside.

She finds the simple syrup under the bar counter. "So you've never made one of these, but have you had one before?"

"No, I'm not much of a drinker." I'd typically leave it there, but as our eyes catch, her ocean-blues are rough swells on me. And I find myself diving deeper. "Occasionally, I'll have a beer, but the first time I got drunk, I felt too out of control around people I hardly knew. I ended up trying to fight the effects like I was in a duel with vodka."

"Who won?" she wonders.

I scratch the back of my head at the memory. I was fifteen at a teammate's house party. His parents weren't home. "The vodka, probably."

She nods slowly when I don't elaborate, like she understands it might be a bad moment I'm not willing to share, but as she looks away, I just want her back.

"I could feel myself about to pass out at my friend's party," I explain, drawing her gaze to mine again. "So I locked myself in his parents' wine cellar and called my older sister to come pick me up."

Harriet processes this. "You were afraid someone would mess with you while you were out of it? I thought you trusted easily." She's short of saying, *you trusted me*.

"Not everyone," I nearly whisper.

She nods more strongly, then slides the simple syrup to me. "You need to triple what I did, and if you're going to cheat, then maybe you should cheat *well*, Cobalt boy, and measure it out this time."

"Cheat," I almost laugh. Not at all bruised over being called out. "You know that's a fighting word in my family?"

"Then you must fight a lot with them."

She's not wrong. "If I were smarter, I'd tell you I'm not cheating, I'm just flexing my observational skills."

"You mean if you were cockier."

I meant *smarter*, but maybe she's right. Maybe it's not my lack of wits but my lack of arrogance that separates me from my siblings. I've never had anyone give me a new perspective into my life like this, but I've also never been this forthcoming with a friend either.

We focus on finishing our whiskey sours as the bar manager returns to us. When Gavin taste-tests, it's clear mine is still brutally heavy on the lemon. He triple-blinks and is knocked backward. "Whoa, lay off the citrus next time," he advises.

There'll be a next time?

He simply nods when he tries Harriet's, but I know it has to be perfect. Before he can give a final verdict, Harriet gets a call.

"Sorry." She's about to mute the ring.

"Go ahead and take it," Gavin urges, and Harriet hesitates before accepting his permission. She slips into a booth by the window, a good distance away.

I come around the bar beside Gavin, and he leans an arm on the scratched wood, bowing toward me. "So listen," he says under his breath.

He didn't want her to hear this. Anger begins gathering in my lungs. I push it down. "Yeah?"

He eyes Harriet for too long. Her phone is propped to her ear, her finger plugging the other to block out the movie, and I see wrinkles creasing her eyes in a heavy frown before she turns away from us.

It pulls my lips downward.

"You're great," Gavin says to me, snapping my attention back to him. "Terry is going to love a Cobalt in the bar on the weekends, but I can't give your friend a job."

"Why not?" I ask and sidestep to obstruct his view of her. It's deeply fucking irritating how he keeps staring at her like she's a problem. "She's the reason we got interviews. Her friend who worked here referred us."

Gavin makes a face. "You mean Ashton? She blew him and spent the night on his couch. I don't think they're friends, man."

I force myself not to glance back at Harriet in confusion, in a tsunami of concern, in muddled emotions that I can't make sense of right now. Muscles burn in my neck, and my aggravation toward Gavin intensifies as I come to terms with what he's saying. "Regardless, Harriet is *better* at making cocktails than me. If there's only one position available—it should go to her." I'm not containing the raw heat in my voice.

He hears I'm pissed.

I am a page-turn away from growling out, *Hire her.*

"That's not it." Gavin holds out his hands in defense. "She's..." He attempts to glance past my shoulder to get another glimpse of her. I block his eyesight, forcing his gaze on mine. "She's unapproachable. This entire time, she's looked *pissed* to even be here. Hell, she's looked angry at *me.* Like she might rip out my jugular."

Maybe she should.

Fuck, *I* might rip out his jugular at the end of this.

"She can't be the only pissed-off looking bartender in New York," I retort.

Gavin opens his palms like, *you might be right.* "Look, I'm not denying that, but ninety-nine percent of our patrons aren't going to stop by the bar if she's behind it. Some might even start fights with her."

Dammit. I scrape a forceful hand through my hair. I want to prove Harriet wrong—that this interview wasn't a waste of time or a flop or that she's the issue, and there's no way I'm going to accept a job without her. I'm not abandoning Harriet. I'd rather not take the job at all.

I straighten up, no longer slouched while I face Gavin. He doesn't realize it yet, but I almost always get what I want.

"That's too bad," I tell him, glancing at the door like I'm seconds from leaving. "Because the two of us are a package deal. If you don't hire her, then you don't have me."

Gavin groans, "Ben. I'm telling you, she *won't* last out here. I'm doing her a favor."

I speak hotter under my breath. "You haven't even given her a chance."

He threads his arms and stares at his feet. This is where he's supposed to say, *I'll give her* one *chance.* It doesn't leave his mouth.

I clench my jaw. "You want a Cobalt here on the weekends, then you're going to hire us both. Put us on the same shift if you have to." It's what I want anyway.

He grinds his teeth, then assesses me as if weighing the benefit of my presence behind the bar. I can see the gears cranking in his head like he's trying to find a loophole.

"This doesn't work if you put her in the back," I add swiftly. "She needs the tips, so you'll let her bartend with me."

Gavin expels a heavy, resigned sigh, unfolding his arms just to rub his goatee. "And I thought you were the nice one."

"Huh?" I frown.

"You know, out of the 'Cobalt Empire'." He uses finger quotes. "I heard the youngest boy was supposed to be the nicest, but you're out here trying to bargain like you're Connor Cobalt making a business deal."

My blood goes cold for a second. He doesn't get it. I'm really not like my dad. *I'm not.* I'm just trying to be a good friend. That's all.

"Do we have a deal then?" I ask, casually ignoring his comment.

"Yeah, deal." He extends a hand to shake on it. After which, my bodyguard approaches the bar, and I check my phone for texts, only reading the important one.

ELIOT COBALT

> Our little sister is going to guilt-trip you into moving back home. Don't let her. Stay strong, brother.

"We'll need to discuss security on nights Ben is working," Novak says to the bar manager, and I slip away to let him do his thing.

Harriet's head is face down on the booth, my baseball cap on the graffitied table, and she slowly bangs her forehead onto the worn wood.

"Whoa, Fisher." I slide in on the other side, a heartbeat away from catching her head before she pounds it into the wood again. "Is this a new drumming method?" I tease with a smile.

She groans as she looks up at me. A red welt already forms on her forehead, and my smile vanishes when I see it. "It's a patented method," she says sadly. "Don't go trying to recreate it. I'll sue."

"Yeah, lucky for you, I don't have any musical talent like my brother." She, on the other hand, is pretty fucking spectacular at drums. Or so I've heard. I've never actually seen her play. I nod to the cell on the table. "Who was that?"

"Manhattan Valley's admission's office. Apparently my transfer credit for Logic & Critical Thinking doesn't code as a humanities class, so it won't count toward the twelve credit hours of humanities and arts we need to graduate."

We need. Yeah, I need those twelve hours too since the humanities and arts is a core requirement, regardless of a major.

"And that's a big enough issue to go all Meg White on your forehead?"

She narrows her eyes at me. "You know who Meg White is?"

"Drummer for *The White Stripes*." I give her a look while I swig my water, then swallow. "What kind of music do you think I listen to?"

"I don't know." She shrugs. "Instrumental with emphasis on the violins."

I laugh hard.

She chews on her lip as a smile forms. "Someone in your family has to be into Chopin and Tchaikovsky."

I tilt my head, thinking. "That'd probably be Beckett since he has to listen to it all day, but he'll go off on how he hates the music to Cinderella. You don't want to get him started on that rant."

Harriet leans back in the booth. "You act like I'm going to meet your brothers." She shies a little from my gaze, digging in her bookbag and unearthing a…Jolly Rancher. I watch her slowly unwind the plastic ends. Bright glittery beaded bracelets jingle on her wrists. The kind you'd string together yourself or buy with a quarter in an old vending machine. Blocked letters. Smiley faces. Hearts.

I've seen her wear similar chokers with beads spelling out words like *bitch* and *whatever*.

"You might," I say. "You've already met one."

Her face pinches into a grimace at the mention of Tom.

Shit. "Sorry, I didn't mean to bring him up—" I cut myself off as my phone vibrates from a video call. "Hold on a sec," I tell Harriet. On instinct, I answer my phone, and my little sister emerges. I flinch in surprise at the black veil and puffy black sleeves of her Victorian dress.

Audrey typically wears *pink*.

"Did someone die?" I ask her.

"Philly is in mourning, as am I." She plops on the chaise at the foot of her four-poster bed. "I already told Eliot and Tom that I'm to wear all black until they relinquish you to me." She flings her veil off her fair face. Tendrils of her carrot-orange hair caress her soft cheeks.

She's number seven.

Audrey Virginia—the youngest of us all, and arguably the most dramatic. (Eliot won't relinquish that title without a fight.) She became my closest sibling as our brothers left our childhood home one by one, but I've vowed to always protect her since we were little kids.

Leaving is festering a wound inside me that won't exactly heal.

"I'm out in public, by the way," I warn Audrey. "I'm with my friend Harriet."

Harriet, thankfully, hasn't put the cherry-red Jolly Rancher in her mouth because I think she would've choked on it. Her big doe-eyes bug in surprise.

"Hi, Harriet," Audrey says morosely. "Tell Ben to come home."

Harriet sweeps me. "Go home, Friend." She says it rather unconvincingly.

I smile at her, then draw my gaze back to my phone as Audrey lets out a breathy whine. "*Ben*. It's so very unfair. They're all together in New York. They didn't need to take you too."

"They haven't kidnapped me, Audrey. Hey, look at this." I flip the camera and crane over toward *Breakfast at Tiffany's* on the projector screen just as Audrey Hepburn sits in a cab while rain splashes the windows. "Isn't that cool? It's like you're here with me."

"She looks as forlorn as I feel." Audrey Hepburn is seconds away from crying, and as I frame the camera back on my face, I realize my sister Audrey is too.

"Audrey—"

"I hate being the youngest," she cries into a hiccup like she's trying to suppress the waterworks. She wipes them fast, but it's gutting me seeing them stream more silently down her cheeks. "The house is too quiet without you."

You'll be okay without me. She has to be.

"I'll be back for a Wednesday Night Dinner," I promise. I wasn't planning on skipping those, even if the idea of facing our parents twists my stomach. It's better to stay the course and act like nothing is wrong. If I skip a bunch of Wednesdays, it'll sound the alarms. *Ben isn't okay! What's going on with Ben?!*

Don't need that.

I typically always go to these dinners for Audrey, so that can't change yet.

Keeping anything from our parents takes mental gymnastics none of us can land for too long. They're certified geniuses with high IQs, and they consume knowledge like it's the foundation of the food pyramid.

They know how to pull truths out of us—or they already see the answers before we've confessed. I've wondered if my parents already know I'm broke, but they don't have access to my bank accounts. They believe in our autonomy and independence, and they wouldn't invade our privacy in that way.

"I hope so," Audrey says with a breathy sigh. "Theodore!" She calls out for the cockatiel, then sighs heavier. "He never listens to me."

"He loves you."

"No, I think he misses you most of all."

A weight sinks in my lungs. "You'll take care of him," I assure her.

"Of course I will." She lifts her chin. "I am the world's best bird-sitter."

"He's yours now," I remind her. "It's more than just bird-sitting."

She looks away, trying to control the sudden brimming tears. "I'm sorry."

"Don't be sorry for crying."

"I'm not trying to make this harder on you—well, actually I am," she says, and I laugh while she continues, "I just really miss you, Ben. And it's been *days*."

"A day," I correct.

Her chin trembles. "I will be okay." She blows her nose in a monogrammed handkerchief. "Because I'm a Cobalt, and we are built to withstand everything."

I give her a few big nods, that statement not sitting as confidently inside me as it is within her. After we say our goodbyes in French, we hang up, and I shove my phone in my pocket.

Harriet has questions in her eyes. She shifts the Jolly Rancher slowly in her mouth with her tongue, then says, "Wishing you never transferred to MVU?"

It's not what I thought she'd ask. "Going back to Philly didn't even cross my mind," I say honestly. "So I'd say no." Then I nod to her, "What's going on with the forehead, Friend?" It's still red as fuck, and I didn't forget where our conversation ended.

She bites down on the hard candy and rotates her bracelet on her wrist. "I busted my ass in that class, and now I have to retake it." Her eyes tighten, more upset. "Which could set me back for applying to med school if I can't stack certain courses together or if some aren't offered in the right semesters. It's just another roadblock, and I'm tired of those."

Pre-med. I can't imagine how intense and arduous the path to becoming a doctor is. I haven't even declared my major yet. I'm not striving for a specific career. It's not like I've been great at anything other than hockey.

"You don't want to pack it all up and become a drummer?"

"Like that's any easier," she mutters, pulling a bracelet off her wrist, just to put it on the other.

I scrape my hand across the back of my neck, then bow toward her. "Maybe there's a bright side to this."

She looks interested. "I'm listening."

"I have the same core requirements for humanities," I tell her. "Why don't we take the same class?"

"Take…the same class?" she repeats like I'm speaking French.

"Yeah," I nod. "If the course you need is filled, I'll go to the dean and get us in it. They'll usually pull strings for Cobalts."

Her face draws into a confused wince. "What the hell do you get out of it?"

"I don't have to suffer through a humanities course alone. I like taking classes with friends." I tip my head in thought. "And I get to help you."

Her brows rise. "I'm your charity case?"

I seesaw my hand. "I get off on making people feel good. So in that instance, maybe, but maybe not because I feel like it's more for me in a way, less for you."

She fights against an emerging smile. "You're weirdly honest."

"You don't hate it," I state.

"I don't," she agrees, sitting forward. Closer to me. Our knuckles nearly brush. She goes quiet. Deep in thought while sucking on the Jolly Rancher.

I feel on the verge of being rejected. "Unless," I say, "you don't like having friends in your classes, which I get if you think I'd be a distraction. But I'm a decent classmate. I won't bug the shit out of you. Though, I do make an average study partner. My flashcards are always pretty fucking basic."

She blinks for a second before she says, "You realize you don't have to ask, right? You could just wait and see if I can get in it myself, then figure out which humanities course I'm taking and…enroll in the same class."

I smile. "I don't much like stalking."

"Is it stalking or using your resources?"

"Just trying not to give you a jump scare when you see me in your class, Fisher."

She glances at my ballcap on the table, then at me. "What if I choose a class that you'll absolutely hate?"

"I don't really care what it is," I admit. "Just pick whatever you need to get into med school on time."

"Yeah, okay—"

"You two," Gavin cuts her off, and the rise of my pulse suddenly flat lines at his presence. "You both start this Saturday. I'm sending you your onboarding paperwork by email."

"Wait…" Harriet frowns. "Both of us?" She casts a skeptical glance from me to the manager. "I got the job?"

Gavin, thankfully, doesn't stare me down when he says, "Yeah, you'll work the same shift together. It'll be easier to train you at the same time." He pauses. "And Harriet."

I slip him a warning glare. *Don't be an ass to her.*

"Yeah?" She's bracing herself for a wrecking ball swing.

"You can smile once in a while, you know." He says it like a jab and not like friendly advice.

Still, Harriet nods, "Yeah, I'll work on it."

Once he's gone, I tell her, "You don't have to smile if you don't want to. He probably won't even be around when we're bartending."

She grabs her backpack strap. "It's not the first time I've heard it." She snatches my ballcap, then holds it out to me. "Here you go, Friend."

"Keep it." I like seeing her wear it.

Harriet sucks in, not releasing the breath. "Uh, I can't." She slides out of the booth, then shoves the hat in my chest when I stand up. "It's yours. See you later?" She's bolting toward the exit, but she slows and spins around, just to wait for my response.

"I'll call you," I tell her.

I swear she smiles as she walks out the door.

SEVEN

HARRIET FISHER

I cannot stop thinking about *him*.

The entire subway ride after leaving the End of the World, I replay our conversations, which were easy and natural and not at all taxing. I'm buzzing like I drank three Lightning Bolt! energy drinks back-to-back.

I dazedly touch the damp tendril of my hair. I remember his strong hand sliding up against my neck and cradling the side of my head. I remember the skip of my pulse, the urge to lean my weight into his bare chest, the comfort and growing euphoria of being around him.

A bird shit on me, and he made me feel like nothing was ruined. Not my hair, not the day, not the moment, not *me*. I was okay.

He made me feel okay.

He let me wear his hat. It's seriously nothing I should freak out over, but my heart floats higher in my body as I rerun how he fit it on my head, how he tightened it for me. I'm weirdly breathless all over again.

Harriet. I want to groan out my name into the pits of my palms, but I stay quiet and still as the passenger car rattles on the tracks. I feel fucking ridiculous for being giddy over something so *basic*, but if this is what friendship brings…then I think I could get behind it.

Friendship.

I stare at my empty hands. I could be holding Ben Cobalt's worn ballcap right now, and I know it seems dumb that I gave it back. Who'd ever reject an article of clothing worn by a Cobalt boy? But I don't regret it. Because I can't imagine never seeing him wear it again.

So yeah, I didn't accept the hat. I'm sure a good percentage of girls would thank me profusely.

I take the subway north to the Upper West Side where MVU's campus resides. My housing isn't directly on campus, but it's only ten blocks away. If I don't want to walk to class, I can bike.

I just have to get a bike. And learn to ride it.

Another task for another day.

I mentally file it away, which is too easy considering Ben is occupying about 80% of my brain right now.

Once I'm on foot and in the old apartment complex, I take the elevator to the fourth floor, and I think about him *again*.

I want to tear him out of my head, but then I don't. Because I like this weird, feather-light feeling swimming through me every time I remember and recall and replay. Memories aren't always worth revisiting in my experience. Most of the time they bring an uncomfortable swelter that feels like I'm being cooked alive.

Not these, though.

These ones, I think I really like.

"Why don't we take the same class?"

My lips twitch, aching to rise higher. Having a friend in a class is like gaining an instant advantage. We can share notes. We can study together. We can discuss lectures and help each other with assignments. The only time I ever have this perk is during classes that assign lab partners.

Humanities don't have labs. I'd normally never have this advantage. I'd have to slog away alone.

Yet, Ben offered it to me like it was nothing.

And why—why couldn't my initial thought be one of elation and utter happiness? Instead, I kept thinking, *he's going to get sick of me.*

We're working the same shifts. We're bound to spend more and more time with each other.

And now we'll be in a class together.

I've been told that my mere presence drains people like a battery sucking vortex. And that was from my own mom. I'm not trying to ruin this friendship before it leaves the starting line, but I just worry that Too Much Harriet will likely wear down even the mightiest of extroverts.

I haven't determined where on the extrovert scale my new roommate Eden Marks lands. She has a dramatic chin-length bob suited for the streets of Paris. Nearly black hair, pale-white skin, and a freckleless, clear complexion like she hibernates during the summertime. A denim overall dress, frilly white top, and Mary Janes remind me we are on two different scales of the style spectrum.

She's going into her fourth year and majoring in accounting, which means we won't have any classes together. It's better this way. No risk of having Too Much Harriet here.

When I'm barely two steps through the door, Eden asks me to take off my shoes. "I'm sorry, it's like a personal thing."

"It's fine," I say, not caring at all. While I unlace my boots, I try to work my jaw out of its normal resting place. *Smile*, I hear my mom in my head, as well as her next words, *but not like that.* I return my jaw to its OG position.

Eden is busy bustling around, clearing stray dishes off the butcher-block countertop and starting a pot of coffee in the cramped kitchen. Which is home to the world's skinniest stove and fridge. No microwave, no dishwasher.

The tiny, but cute, one-bedroom apartment is under 500-square feet. I haven't really contributed to any of the furniture here. Not that there's room for much. A lumpy lime-green sofa faces a small TV on a wooden media console, and an orange armchair sits beneath the only window. I get the sense that Eden likes to thrift anything from the '70s. Her brown-and-orange-rimmed dishware even looks authentic.

My mom would rent this place fully furnished as is. She'd add Fleetwood Mac vinyls on the walls. Her obsession with the band led to my middle name being *Stevie.* After Stevie Nicks.

I probably adopted a love of music from her, but not her love of the '70s. The décor isn't really my taste, but I'm so far from picky where my housing is concerned right now. Eden could have a thing for stuffed rabbits or toenails in jars, and I would deal with it.

What's noticeably not from the '70s: the black-and-white photographs framed on the brick walls. Eden's family photos, I've deduced, from the beachy posed pics where she's gathered with her mom, dad, and four siblings near a sand dune.

Several others are of a gorgeous couple suntanning on a dock. The girl snuggled against the guy is clearly Eden. "That's my boyfriend," she claimed him proudly, and he's smoking hot so I can see why. Apparently, the photos were taken on their summer vacay at Lake Champlain.

I'm shocked she didn't ask him to move in, considering he's made the family wall *and* his abs are displayed for all to see. She briefly mentioned it was "too soon" for that commitment since they'd only been together for four months. I guess it's easier to trash a photo if things go bad. Not as easy to kick someone out of your place.

As I slowly untie my laces, I stare dazedly at her family photos, and my stomach clenches with bits of envy. I'd almost rather she had an addiction to taxidermy, but it's good—this is fine. She loves her family, and I don't even know her, so I'm not going to wish her a deadbeat dad and a shitty mom.

Dishes clink as Eden sets a daisy-embellished plate in the cupboard. "I'm actually so glad you answered me on the Valley Boards," she says. "For a second, I thought I wouldn't have any takers this semester."

Valley Boards are ways for MVU students to connect with each other. Locating study partners, announcing new intramural sports, and even posting for roommates. I'd been quick to contact Eden as soon as my transfer to MVU was accepted.

Her ad was simple: `Pull-out couch, shared bathroom, and parking spot all yours for just $700 a month!` (Ten blocks from campus.)

The parking spot was the real get for me. My car has been my lifeline since I was sixteen, and trying to decide what to do with it when I moved here had been the biggest thorn in my side.

It's also startlingly cheaper than the price of on-campus dorms. That luxury would cost an arm, leg, kidney, and possibly the spleen of my firstborn.

The coffee machine rumbles to life. "So you're pre-med?" Her eyes narrow disbelievingly, and they sink down to my combat boots as I pry each one off. "I don't know any doctors who wear Doc Martens, no offense."

I'm a little surprised she thinks my TJ Maxx boots are actual Doc Martens. "I know of a doctor who's covered in tattoos and piercings," I say. "Believe me, the boots won't make a difference." Though I won't be wearing them to my med school interview. I didn't put in much effort for this bartending job today because I didn't think the manager would care.

Physicians *will* care if I show up in a crop top and jeans. That's even *if* I get an interview. There's about a thousand hundred moves I need to make before I can reach that hurdle.

Eden eyes me for another solid beat. "Med school is *really* difficult. Besides accounting, pre-med is the hardest path at MVU. You have to be a brainiac."

I nod slowly and place my shoes on a checkered mat beneath a coat hook. "I know it's hard."

She smiles stiffly. "Just making sure. It's easier changing majors as a sophomore than it is as a senior." She checks on the pot of coffee. "Where'd you say you transferred from? NYU?"

I never actually told her my previous school—and now saying it will make me look like an overachieving dick. There were so many times growing up that I'd get the side-eye for setting a curve on tests, for winning academic awards, for being "the teacher's pet" in sixth grade. Just because I cared about my grades. Took them seriously. I *enjoyed* school.

Big shock, right? So there's always this sudden urge to shrink back when people ask me about myself. To downplay. Just so I can avoid the narrowed looks.

But Eden is my roommate, and I shouldn't hide basic shit from her. So what if she thinks I'm an overachieving dick? So fucking what.

"Penn," I say tightly.

She pours coffee into a vintage diner mug. "Penn State is a good school, but MVU is way harder."

I wince. "Actually, it was the University of Pennsylvania."

She grimaces at the slip-up. We're both basically in full grimaces at this awkward miscommunication, and I am completely the one to blame.

"Oh…" she breathes out.

"Yeah," I say into a long nod.

"That's an Ivy League," she says like she's having a light bulb moment. "It must have been so rigorous. Is that why you're transferring?"

I don't mention my straight As at Penn. I do tell her the truth. "They don't have an Honors House like MVU does."

Eden's brows jump. "You're applying for the Honors House?"

"Yeaaaah," I say slowly. "Is that okay? If I get in, I might only be here for a few months." I've had my sights on the Honors House from the very first moment I transferred here. It's a prestigious academic society on campus that provides free on-campus housing to undergrads.

Basically the equivalent of a co-ed sorority/fraternity.

Only downside, it's extremely exclusive. It might be easier discovering a new planet in the Milky Way than be accepted, but joining the Honors House is number one on my master plan to becoming a doctor. I need a place to live that won't put a meteor-sized crater into my bank account, and it'll be a highlight on my med school applications.

Eden nods. "That's totally cool." She looks me over. "So you're like *really* smart then?"

No, I'm delusional. The sarcasm in my head doesn't help the scowl on my face, I'm sure.

I refrain from rolling my eyes, and I'm definitely not telling her I skipped the fifth grade. "I'm all right," I say, downplaying it unfortunately.

She motions to the living room. We can see the lumpy lime-green sofa directly from the kitchen. "How has the pull-out been? I know the mattress is kind of…springy. If you'd rather just sleep on the cushions, I won't judge."

"It's been comfortable," I say with a nod.

She snorts into a laugh. "You don't have to lie."

"No, seriously," I shrug. "It's been comfortable."

"Okay." Eden squints like I'm weird for thinking a pull-out is even marginally comfy.

I try not to wince at myself. I sort of wish we didn't run into each other today. She's been a ghost roommate this first week after a ton of missed connections. Our interactions have been *very* infrequent.

I sling my backpack onto the couch. Potted plants sit on the windowsill, and I have a view of the back of another brick building. The sun is beginning to set, and I smile a little, staring out at New York. Even the worst view of the city, my life feels on a better track now.

I have a job. I have a place I can call home for the time being. The lighting is warm and comforting in the apartment. All in all, it's cozy. Quaint.

"If you need more storage space, I cleared out the coat closet this morning," Eden says into a sip of coffee while she texts. "It's all yours."

"Thanks." I try to smile a bit bigger, not that she's looking at me.

She's focused on her phone.

I glance over at two white doors. One leads to her bedroom, the other to a tiny bathroom that we share. It's better than taking showers at the gym, which I'd been doing back at Penn.

Relief burrows into me. I have a bed (a couch) and a bathroom and even a closet for my clothes. I don't have to live out of my duffel bag anymore. I don't want to soak it in too much. Don't want to over-celebrate in case it all vanishes in an instant.

Anyway, I can't get complacent. This isn't my finish line. It's a steppingstone in the direction I want to go.

"I know it's not much," Eden says.

"It's great," I say, genuinely.

She smiles. "So where are you from originally?" she asks, then her cell rings in her hand. "Sorry, I should get this. It's Austin." Her boyfriend.

She splinters off to her bedroom, shutting the door behind her.

I've been hesitating to bring too much of my stuff into her place, but now that I have the closet, I decide to go grab more of my belongings. Leaving the apartment, I venture into the parking garage and visit Harold—my Honda Civic that's been my prized possession since I bought it off my old boss at Wendy's when I was sixteen.

"Harold," I greet and pat his silver trunk. Pillows, blankets, and my backpack crowd the backseat. Opening the driver's door, I snatch my phone charger from the middle console and remove an old empty Taco Bell bag from the footwell on the passenger side. From the trunk, I retrieve a small duffel and check the contents.

Clothes. Bra. Underwear. Three gallon-sized plastic baggies containing shampoo and conditioner, toothpaste and a toothbrush, and then my small vibrator in a third.

I sigh. Sleeping in the middle of a living room will be wreaking havoc on any self-love time. I'm not about to be kicked out of the apartment because Eden walked in on me fingering myself. No, thank you. Dry spell, here I come.

Yay.

Not that I have good material in my spank bank these days anyway.

Ben's chiseled jawline suddenly flashes in my head. The way his fluffy brown hair blew in the wind after he gave me his hat. How his smile crawled up his face when he looked down at me.

I imagine his hands on me again, and flush bathes my cheeks. He's melted some stone-cold part of me, and I could definitely create some toe-curling sexual fantasies in my head. Especially when I picture his six-foot-five stature lifting me in his arms. I wonder how big his cock would feel just rubbing against my pussy.

"Oh my God," I groan to myself. "You're just friends with him." I zip up my duffel. "Just friends, Harriet."

Last time I checked, friends don't fuck each other. They certainly don't masturbate to images of each other, right? That sounds really hot, though.

I slow my movements, my breathing getting shallow with arousal as I picture his sculpted body up against my smaller frame. As I picture him wrapping his arms so tight around me. I've *never* enjoyed being hugged, but why am I obsessed with the idea of him practically suffocating me?

I imagine his hand descending between my legs. My clit throbs for touch, and I try to snap out of it, slinging my duffel's strap on my shoulder.

Friends can be attracted to each other, I think, and under certain circumstances, maybe they can entertain those attractions too. But those circumstances haven't risen for us, and I'm not going to actively create one.

My phone buzzes on my hip clip, and I nearly jump out of my skin like God, Himself, has been eavesdropping inside my carnal mind.

Not that I'm a very religious person, but Mass was one of the few things I remember going to with my dad when I was little.

Shutting the trunk with one hand, I answer the call with my other.

"Harry, are you on the moon? Jupiter? I know you're smart

enough to get into NASA and board a rocket ship to Mars, but I still expect you to keep your location services *on*. How else will I know if you're sitting in a crater or floating through open spa—*shit,* Fava get out of that plant, you little toad."

Hearing my Aunt Helena's voice sends a lightness through me like I'm stepping on a fluffy cloud. She's the only person I'll let call me Harry. And even though I haven't seen her in person since I was eleven, I can picture Fava (one out of her three hairless cats) digging into a potted fern. My aunt has the biggest green thumb. Plants crowd her small two-hundred-and-fifty-foot studio apartment in San Francisco along with Fava, Pinto, and Lima.

The Three Beans look like wrinkly little dicks, but in the cutest way.

I put the call on speaker so I can click into my cell's settings. "Location services might have turned off on the last update." Sure enough, it's off. I swipe it back on. "Fixed."

After a long moment, Aunt Helena gasps. "New York? No, that can't be right. Angelica said you'd be in Baltimore. She's never wrong."

Angelica is her close friend and a psychic.

"Maybe her crystal ball is dusty."

"Darling, she reads cards. Why are you in New York?"

"School. I transferred—"

"Goddammit," she curses. Not at me. Pretty sure I hear a loud groaning in the background. "These pipes are going to bust any day now. I swear it." She's living in a rent-controlled apartment. The same one she moved in to when she was eighteen. She has said more than once that her landlord will have to kick down the door and drag her decomposing body out of it. I just hope the Three Beans don't eat her first—at least, I've heard that cats will start chowing down on their dead owners.

"Sorry," she apologizes. "You transferred schools? That's great. Or I assume that's great. You don't make those kinds of moves without thinking fifteen steps ahead." She gasps. "Unless, is there…a…*boy* involved?" She asks like she's tiptoeing around the subject.

My cheeks heat and another flash of Ben Cobalt's panty-dropping smile graces my brain. Oh *God*. Sorry, God. Shit. Fuck. I pinch the bridge of my nose.

"There's not a boy—"

"I feel like you might be lying," she cuts me off swiftly. "Maybe we should put Angelica on a three-way call—"

I interrupt her before she has a chance to speed dial her psychic friend. "All right, it's boy-adjacent."

Aunt Helena sucks in a breath. "What in the hell does that mean? Like…is he…part amphibian?"

I almost laugh. "He's not a merman, Aunt Helena."

"I suppose it'd be more likely he's part robot," she says, all too seriously. "I heard they're starting to put microchips in people's *brains*, Harry. When you're a fancy-pants doctor, please side with the humans and not the AI."

"Always Team Human," I tell her.

"So boy-adjacent. My theories have ended. What does that mean?"

"I transferred for school," I explain, "but there's this guy who kind of also transferred? Our worlds are…revolving, I guess." I take a beat before I add, "We're friends." I say it confidently, believing it more, and I smile to myself.

There's a long pause on the other end.

My smile falls. "Aunt Helena?"

"I'm not crying." She's sniffling. I roll my eyes, but I can't help but laugh a little. "It's just…you have a *friend*. You haven't had a friend since the fourth grade."

Thank you for that reminder.

"It probably won't last," I mutter. "No need to go through the waterworks."

"Manifest, Harry. *Man-i-fest*. It'll last if you want it to."

I'm not sure that's true. Every time I've tried to manifest something, the universe doesn't grant it to me in a package and bow. I have to work. And work. And *work* for what I want.

Though I really, *really* want to be Ben's friend. Maybe I can't manifest it to last, but I can try my hardest not to fuck it up.

"Do you still have Hope's number blocked?" my aunt asks, changing the subject so abruptly that I have mild whiplash.

"Yeah." My skin goes cold hearing her name.

Hope.

My mother.

Her little sister by about fifteen years.

"Good," Aunt Helena says. "She tried to reach out to me. I thought she might have found a way to contact you too."

The thought of having to speak to my mom again actually gives me acid reflux. "Radio silence," I mutter, and I could ask my aunt what the circumstances of the call were, but I don't want to know. Ignorance is bliss when it comes to my mom.

"Dammit, not you too, Pinto!" Aunt Helena yells at one of the Beans. "I have to go before they destroy the Monstera. Love you, Harry."

"Love you too."

We hang up, and I stare at the phone for a solid minute, just trying to be grateful to have her in my life. Someone who cares. Someone who calls me when they don't know where I am. And maybe we don't talk enough. Maybe our once-a-month phone call isn't a normal check-in for most, but for me—it's everything.

It's all I really have.

EIGHT

HARRIET FISHER

"Why do you look like you're going to throw up?" Ben asks me as we settle in our seats. I'm sitting stiffly, and I do feel like I might hurl at any second. It's not the chair's fault. These things are wide, cushiony, and comfortable. Gold birds are stitched into burgundy fabric. The mascot and colors of MVU.

The bird isn't an eagle or hawk, but a thrasher. I try to train my eyes on the **SOAR, THRASHERS, SOAR!** banner above the projector screen so I don't fixate on the podium at the ground level. No one is standing behind it at least. Class hasn't officially started.

It's one I picked out of necessity. There were slots available, so Ben didn't need to butter up the dean to get us in. Probably due to the sheer size of the class.

I crane my neck left and right. Ben and I are sitting next to each other in a middle row of an enormous lecture hall. One that could easily fit two hundred students.

Why do you look like you're going to throw up? Ben's question rolls around in my head.

"Because we're taking *classical mythology*," I whisper-hiss like the room has ears. But we're practically alone. Ben's bodyguard quietly took a seat right behind us. Only two other students are here, and they've chosen chairs way down in the first row, much closer to the professor's podium.

Maybe that's where I should be. Closest to the person who will be doling out the grades.

Or maybe not.

Last thing I need to do is projectile vomit on the professor. I'm just glad we're here early. Twenty minutes early to be exact. But I could be here twenty-four hours early, and I'd still be nauseous.

Ben wears concern like he's seconds away from snagging the trashcan by the door and holding it under my chin. He leans an arm on the back of the auditorium-style chair, facing me fully, and I try not to get flustered by his all-encompassing attention on me. I can't remember the last time someone gave me so much of their energy, their interest.

"Why are you whispering?" he asks.

"I don't know," I say, my voice rising to a normal level. "I'm nervous, okay? I've avoided taking most of my humanities requirements. Biology, I get. Chemistry, no problem. Calculus, a breeze. But if you ask me to write an essay…I get…I get hives." I slump down. It's not an exaggeration. I broke out *in* hives my first semester at Penn when I had to take English 102. I barreled through with determination, sleepless nights of rewrites, and Benadryl.

To distract myself, I try to concentrate on how Ben's burgundy MVU sweatshirt blends into the chair and how he pushed the sleeves up to his elbows. Veins spindle down his strong arms, and those beautiful, masculine forearms should bring me out of my panicked state.

But really, it's his baby blue eyes caressing me that help the most.

His brows are fully raised. "Hives?" He skims my body like he's checking for a breakout.

"Yes, Benjamin. *Hives*."

"It's just Ben."

That takes me aback a second. I sit up a little. "Wait, your parents named you *Ben*. Just Ben? Not Bennet? Not Benedict? Not Benvolio?"

He chokes out a bright laugh. "*Jesus*. Benvolio?" He's looking at me with far too much intrigue for someone who clearly didn't read his Wikipedia page thoroughly enough.

"Your parents love Shakespeare," I remind him, which I quickly realize is a silly thing to do. Of course he knows his parents better than someone who's picked up rudimentary facts online. I'm hot (and not in a good way) thinking about it. "Benvolio was a good guess," I say fast, but I can't help the defensive bite in my voice.

Ben doesn't seem to care about it. His smile reaches his glittering eyes. "That's the first time *anyone* has offered that guess, so you get all the creative points."

I make a face.

He frowns. "What?"

"Creative?" I say the word like it has necrotizing fasciitis. It's about as foreign in my life as flesh-eating bacteria. "No one's ever called me creative. My third-grade teacher once told me my imagination was about as vast as a puddle."

He leans forward, and I lose sight of his face but I'm making an educated guess that he's full of pity.

Shit. Why do I even open my mouth? "I'm not saying this for you to pity me—"

"I'm not pitying you," he interrupts swiftly, leaning back now, and I see the look in his blue eyes. Oh...he is *pissed*.

His expression flames. "What kind of shitty third-grade teacher says that to a kid?" It's as if he wants to storm out of the lecture hall, hunt down my elementary teacher, and have some tough words with them. I am not used to whatever *this* is. Protection? Defense? An armed firing squad? I don't hate it. I'm just not sure I deserve it.

"In defense of Ms. Larsen, I had been correcting her on her geometry lessons. She wasn't good with quadrilaterals. I was kind of a dick in grade school. I also only used the yellow crayon, which annoyed her greatly."

Ben shakes his head. "I don't care how much of an asshole you were at eight. You were still a kid."

"I guess," I say into a shrug. I unzip my backpack and take out a red pencil pouch. He casually steals one of my blue ballpoint pens as soon as it's on my desk. Is this what friends do? Share pens?

It feels comfortable like we've been this way for a hundred years. Maybe that's why I'm not shriveling in my seat with him knowing more about my childhood. Normally, I'd find ways to avoid talking about it. It's embarrassing how much of a know-it-all I was when I was young, but I don't feel judged by him.

Ben's still reeling. I can see it in his eyes like a thousand wheels revolving in his head. I take it he's not someone who can brush something aside so easily. He slips the pen behind his ear, his baseball cap on backward. He leans against my shoulder to get closer, and his voice lowers as more students file into the lecture hall. "Did you tell your parents about your teacher?"

"A little," I say. "I told them she didn't like me, and I mentioned the whole 'puddle' thing."

His shoulders slacken in relief. "So what'd they do?"

"Do?" I slow as I flip open my college-ruled notebook.

"Yeah," Ben nods. "My mom would have stormed the school and told your teacher that imagination comes in different shades and sizes and if it's yellow then it's yellow and to not knock you down… in so many words."

"She sounds amazing," I say, trying not to be wistful. I don't *need* a mom like that. I've been fine without a legion to go to bat for me.

"She is," Ben says fondly, but his concern has now tripled on me because I haven't exactly answered his question. "They didn't do anything?"

"They had a lot going on," I say softly. "I was told to be nicer to Ms. Larsen."

He shakes his head once more, his anger manifesting through the veins in his arms down to the clench of his knuckles. He blows out a frustrated breath. "You know my brother—"

"Depends which one," I cut in.

He tilts his head to me. "The smart one."

"Aren't you all smart?" I banter, and we share emerging smiles. Our eyes drift up and down—from our gazes to our lips. Acknowledging that we're causing each other to smile introduces a new heat among the feather-light sensations.

Attraction is a wild beast that wants to stampede over me. I've never felt it this powerfully—and definitely not in the most ordinary of moments. This isn't a date, okay. I'm in a *classroom*.

About to endure the worst class on my schedule (a necessary evil).

"The smartest brother," he clarifies in a husky voice. He clears out the noise, and I can't even mentally categorize how hot that was because I focus on his words. "He was a lot like you. Talked back to teachers and stuff when he was little…or so I was told."

"*Or so you were told*," I repeat. "Perks of you being the youngest brother. Getting all that information second-hand. Like a little thrift shop of memories."

"And she said you weren't creative." He takes his pen and bops me on the nose.

I scowl instantly. Why did I not hate that?

He smiles. "Anyway, Charlie was a dick—as you put it—to his teachers. My dad was in parent-teacher conferences all the time, and then he told Charlie something had to change. That he wasn't being challenged, and he needed to skip some grades."

He has an above-average father. Not that I ever questioned it.

Don't want them. Don't crave them. I've gone this long without dreaming of another set of parents replacing my own. My dad, he's not all bad. I don't want to shade the man in a dark light. My parents are just different than the iconic Rose Calloway and Connor Cobalt.

Mention of Charlie reminds me of last night. Ben talked to me on the phone. "Just because." I've never had someone call me out of the blue to simply chat.

He asked me what I was doing. I'd been listening to Paramore while painting my toenails deep red and reading some of my O-Chem textbook. I'd just rented it from the on-campus bookstore.

"What are you doing, Cobalt boy?" I replied after describing my uneventful night. "Bathing in the tears of your enemies?"

He laughed. Just remembering his vibrant laugh sends an electric current down my body. "I'm sure Eliot showers with the tears of his foes every night." After a pause, he ended up saying, "I survived the move-in."

"Were you afraid you weren't going to?" I asked, capping the polish.

"There was a chance. I'm pretty sure Charlie has wanted to make my heart bleed since birth. I guess it's a good thing I gave you half." His voice was teasing, and I could feel my lips inching upward. The smile didn't take hold though.

"So the rumors are true then?" I wondered with a frown. "You and Charlie don't get along?"

I don't live under a rock. I've heard that Charlie clashes with Ben. Tabloids haven't caught them verbally laying into each other the way they've captured fights between Charlie Cobalt and Maximoff Hale, Ben's older cousin, so I figured *maybe* it's all fake to line the pockets of a phony friend who dished to the media.

"Those are unfortunately true, yeah," Ben confirmed on the phone.

It panged my heart then, and hearing him describe Charlie pangs my heart now.

I hold his gaze in the lecture hall. "Charlie needed to skip some grades," I repeat what he just said. "The brother you have beef with?" I ask under my breath so no one can hear.

Ben nods. "The one and only Charlie Keating Cobalt."

Shit. "Sucks to say, Cobalt boy, but I now have more in common with your nemesis than you." My chest tightens at the words, and I don't know why.

"What do you mean?" he frowns.

"I skipped fifth grade," I tell him. "Guidance counselor realized the same thing your dad realized about Charlie. Told me I needed to hike it over to sixth and stop being an asshole to the educators who were just trying to do their jobs."

He slips the pen back behind his ear, but I can't read the expression on his face anymore. "Good. I'm glad someone was looking out for you." He says it in a way that definitely targets my parents—and the sad thing is, I can't really defend them. Other than admitting they were busy. Distracted. A nasty divorce will do that.

We go quieter as the room fills up with more and more bodies. A white girl and her friend with dark brown skin strategically pick seats right in front of Ben's chair. They pretend to take selfies with each other, but it's clear he's caught in the frame. He turns the ballcap around, dips it low over his eyes, and slumps down.

Seeing him use it as a shield from attention, I'm even happier I returned it.

Students pull out laptops and tablets for notetaking, and I check the time on my phone. We still have ten minutes to go. Nausea returns. Science courses are far easier, in my eyes. They have specific answers. True or false. Multiple choice.

Essays are too subjective, and based on experience, the teacher weighs them more favorably to whoever they like. It's a popularity contest, and when it comes to those, I'm a big loser.

Ben pulls out a tablet from his bookbag, and I give him a look. "Why'd you need a pen?" I ask him, staring at my cheap ballpoint he placed on his desk. I stole it from the waiting room of an ED.

"So I could do this." He picks it up and then twirls it between his fingers like he's mastered the finger baton.

It's moments like these that I remember…he is a jock. A popular, hot *jock*. And I'm stupid enough to find his pen baton routine charming.

Something gnaws at me, and I have to ask. "So why *just* Ben?" I wonder. "Why not something Shakespeare related?"

"Because," Ben says, slipping the pen back behind his ear. "My parents love Shakespeare, but they love my Uncle Loren more. They let him name me."

Oh, that's sweet…but also diabolical. If I had a kid, I wouldn't trust a single soul to name them for me.

It's also strange hearing him say *Uncle Loren*, when I know full well that he's referring to *the* Loren Hale, the husband to *the* Lily Calloway.

Lily is his mom's younger sister. Basically because of the three Calloway sisters, there are three famous families.

The Cobalts.

The Meadows.

The Hales.

Fans choose allegiances to different families like they're sports teams or Hogwarts houses.

The Cobalts are the intellects, the ones to revere for their aptitude and prowess. They're the gods among royalty.

The Meadows are the adventurers, the ones who climb mountains and race down highways on motorcycles. They're more likely to be caught camping at a national park than fine-dining at a Michelin-star restaurant.

The Hales are the pop culture geeks, the ones who love superheroes enough to own a comic book publishing company and a comic-themed coffee shop. Plus, they're behind a mega corporation that makes baby products. *Hale Co.* It's generational wealth.

Ben has it too.

And beyond the surface-level stuff, Lily Calloway is notorious for being a recovering sex addict, and her husband is a recovering alcoholic. They go in depth about their lives on an Emmy award-winning docuseries that's been running off and on for decades. I've never tuned in, but I do know most of Ben's family have made appearances on the show. Because of the Hales' relatability and candidness about their struggles with addiction, they're the most popular in the media, maybe even the most beloved, but also the most criticized.

I never showed my love to a family online by posting memes or putting "adopted Cobalt daughter" in my bio. But I did wonder what life would be like if the Hales opened their door and let me live with them. They'd be the ones most likely to bring me into their fold since they're known for taking in misfits and broken toys.

The Cobalts are the *opposite*. They're renowned for slamming the gilded gates on anyone who doesn't bleed Cobalt blue.

There are far less Hales than there are Cobalts too, so it seemed more reasonable in my imagination to be a Hale. There was room for me in a family of six, but it's not like I wanted to ditch my parents for the Hales. I was just picturing myself in the lineup.

It'd be Maximoff, Luna, Xander, *Harriet*, and then Kinney. A complete and utter fantasy.

If I were shrewder, maybe I would've tried to be Luna's best friend at Penn and not just her lab partner. I had an *in*, but it felt gross to use that relationship to gain entry into a family. That's *her* family.

Not mine.

It was always supposed to be just a fantasy. One that made me feel better when only-child syndrome struck harder.

I look to Ben beside me. I do really like this reality where I'm friends with a Cobalt (specifically, *this* Cobalt). It feels just as unbelievable in a way, but I want to embrace it fully and not construct more defensive walls.

"Why'd your uncle name you Ben?" I ask him in a frown, trying to figure out a connection. Are there Marvel superheroes named Ben? I don't read comics, but I've seen enough of the movies and remember an Uncle Ben from Spider-Man.

He angles his body more toward me, no longer facing forward in the direction of the girl's unsubtle selfies. "My uncle is big into Star Wars," he explains. "I'm named after Obi-Wan Kenobi, who went by the name 'Ben' when he was in hiding on Tatooine. Personally, I think there was a missed opportunity to name me Anakin. That would've been badass."

I roll my eyes. He's such a guy. "Be glad he didn't go with Jabba the Hutt."

Ben laughs. "I'd like to think my mom would have vetoed that one." His voice is almost drowned out by a sudden hum of loud whispering. The volume escalates across the entire room, and both Ben and I swing our heads for the source.

It takes less than a second to spot the disruption.

Even with red headphones around his neck, a black hoodie drawn up over his head, it's impossible to not recognize Xander Hale. When he shrugs off the hoodie like he's suddenly overheated from the thick fabric, the audible feminine gasps and squeals reverberate and echo in the auditorium. *Especially* as his T-shirt sticks to the hoodie and rises a little too high on his chest, revealing his carved abs before he quickly tugs the black tee down.

A girl is close to hyperventilating. I hope her friend tells her to take some deeper breaths or she actually might pass out.

It's not a total overreaction either.

The allure of Xander Hale is real. He has tousled brown hair, a sharp jawline, and a slender build with defined muscles in his biceps—notably different than years ago when girls in my high school used to call him Jack Skellington chic. But it's his arresting, amber-colored eyes that completely disarm onlookers. I'm not sure I'm immune. I weirdly feel almost oxygen-deprived by his beauty.

Everyone who's arrived early has rotated in their chairs to watch him, film him on their phones, entrench his image in their memories.

I don't think anything of it until I realize he's frozen on a stair ten rows below us. He peers over his shoulder and speaks under his breath to the tattooed guy behind him. *His bodyguard.* Paul Donnelly.

Last semester, I ran into Xander and Donnelly on occasion when Xander was visiting his sister Luna at Penn. I don't know what feels more unreal—the few months I was circling the Hales in Philly or the present situation in New York where I'm friends with Ben Cobalt.

On the stairs, Xander continues whispering to his bodyguard.

Donnelly wears a white MVU Thrashers tee, probably to blend in. His inked arms, pierced ears, and casual-cool demeanor should make him stand out more than Xander, but it's clear the Hale is the one being ogled of the two.

I'm sure it's partly because Xander is a known recluse. He's rarely spotted out, despite his level of popularity online.

Admittedly, I'm not the best at reading body language, but there must be a reason he hasn't moved off the stairs. Is he inwardly freaking out? I mean—*I* personally would be flipping the fuck out if that many people were staring at me.

I turn quickly to Ben, expecting him to be waving Xander over because, you know, they're *cousins*. But Ben is just silently watching Xander like the rest of the students. Confusion throttles me. "Are you going to wave him over?" I ask.

Ben looks from me to Xander, then back to me. "Do you want me to?"

That's not the reply I was anticipating. "He probably doesn't know where to sit. Right?" I ask, not even sure myself. There are girls literally on the edge of their seats, hoping he'll choose the empty chair beside them. The two girls in front of us have abandoned taking "selfies" and have aimed their cells more blatantly in Xander's direction. Not hiding the fact that they're filming him.

Ben opens his mouth to reply to me.

"Xander!" That voice originates from the other side of the auditorium. A petite brunette waves a hand and bounces up in her seat. "Come sit over here!"

Xander pretends not to hear and continues up the stairs. The girl goes beet-red and shields her face with a textbook. Ugh, I feel the rejection secondhand, and my stomach cramps.

Ben takes a deeper breath the closer his cousin comes to our row, but Xander hasn't exactly spotted us as the lecture hall begins to crowd. "I just think he'd prefer to sit in the back," Ben whispers to me.

"You think?" I frown. "If a ton of strangers were bombarding me, I think I'd like to sit with my cousin. You know, a friendly face." I shrug.

"I'm not a friendly face, Fisher," he says tightly.

Wait. "You have beef with Xander too?" I whisper back, shocked. *This* is not advertised, to my knowledge. Granted, I'm not diving into the depths of Fanaticon. People on those forums dissect every breath these families have taken, so maybe there are theories or videos about discord between Xander and Ben.

"Beef isn't the word I would use," he whispers hurriedly because Xander is getting closer. "I don't have anything against him. But he hates me."

He hates me. I have to repeat the words in my head because they don't fully make sense to me. Who could hate Ben? He's one of the kindest people I've ever met—and okay, maybe I don't know him completely yet, but *hate* feels too brutal of a word.

It just baffles me more, and I watch his cousin continue ascending the flight of stairs. The lecture hall has gone extraordinarily quiet now like everyone is caging breath, wondering where he'll choose to sit.

Xander climbs three more stairs, then his eyes flit to his right, and they land directly…on…me.

NINE

HARRIET FISHER

With Xander's gaze firmly on me, recognition shoots through his expression, and then immediate relief pours over his emotive eyes. Flashes of all the parties I've been to hit me.

Parties where I was alone beside a wall.

Parties where I wished I knew a single person to at least fill the awkward tension in my bones.

I relate to the feeling I see wash through him. I just never thought *I'd* be the friendly face in the crowd. We barely know each other. We're acquaintances through his sister—who I don't even talk to anymore now that we're no longer lab partners.

He takes a step toward me, entering our row.

One foot in, he stops. His gaze passes over my shoulder to see Ben. The color drains from Xander's face.

"Hey," Ben acknowledges in a friendly up-nod. "We saved you a seat." He motions to the open one beside me.

Xander looks from Ben to me and back to Ben. "It's all right." His voice is a low husk. "I'd rather sit in the back." He backsteps out of the row and hightails it up the rest of the stairs.

My stomach twists and twists. It feels like I rejected Xander now, and I hate how he's on an island alone when he was so clearly searching for a life raft. Did he think there wasn't room for him on the inner tube? That Ben occupied the lone spot?

My neck aches as I strain to watch Xander reach the back row and slump into an open chair, Donnelly claiming the one to his left.

All of Xander's muscles tense when he notices a bold blond powerwalking to make her claim on the vacant seat to his right.

I could cut her off.

I have a major brain-freeze on the words: *help Xander*. My body reacts as I spring to my feet, snatch my backpack, and climb the stairs.

Being casual enough, I make it to the seat quickly and sink into the chair beside Xander. I feel the blond screech to a halt, then choose a random place several rows away.

Xander releases a breath. His entire body slackens. "Thanks," he whispers with such depth that I should feel great about my choice.

I nod back, my stomach not unwinding from a vicious pretzel shape.

As I face forward, I realize what I just did.

I abandoned Ben.

My heart drops out of my body and rolls away from me. Fuck, fuck, *fuck*. See, this is why friendships are too complicated. This is why I might not be built to maintain them.

What's worse is knowing I left Ben for his cousin that apparently hates him. Ughhh. I want to bring my legs to my chest and hide in my kneecaps.

"Are you all right?" Xander murmurs.

I shrug and swallow the ball in my throat.

Xander searches his backpack. "I'd give you some water, but…I don't think I have any in here."

"I'll survive," I whisper, finally able to speak. "Will you?"

"Age old question." He presses the back of his head to the wall while looking down at me. "This is the only course I don't have with my best friend."

"Who's that?"

"Easton Mulligan."

"Never heard of him."

"Not famous. We grew up in the same neighborhood." Xander unwraps the headphones from around his neck. "Knowing someone beforehand just makes situations like this infinitely easier."

I had the same thought earlier today.

I don't point out the obvious though. How he should know *Ben* the best. "What about the bodyguard backup?"

Donnelly acknowledges me with a *rock on* hand gesture.

I give him a stiff wave as a friendly *hello*.

"I wouldn't have gone to college without Donnelly," Xander admits, then lets out a weak laugh. "Which, I know, probably seems stupid."

I meet his eyes. "Why would that be stupid?"

"Maybe because I can't exist without backup."

"Dude, did you hear the audible intake of *oxygen* when you appeared? I'm shocked you didn't get mauled. No one should knock you for wanting to be safe."

He must hear the ball still partially stuck in my throat. Or maybe I look sickly. "You sure you're all right, Harriet?"

I find a Jolly Rancher in my backpack, hoping it'll make my stomach feel better. "This class isn't really my jam," I admit in a whisper, trying to get over the Ben thing. *Let it go, Harriet.* It's not like I can rewind time or return to him. I just need to believe I did the right thing, but I can't stop staring at the back of Ben's head several rows below me.

Is he upset? Devastated? Am I overstating my importance in his life? What if he doesn't even give a shit? What if he's hardly batting an eye? And why does that hurt more?

"Classical Mythology?" Xander asks.

"Yep." I pop the green candy in my mouth, then point to myself. "Science nerd."

Xander points to his chest. "History nerd. I could help you out."

Plenty of people have more than one friend, but I'm not sure a friendship with Ben and one with Xander can co-exist. I swish the candy from one side of my cheek to the other as I contemplate accepting the offer.

Then the professor walks in. Our attention veers forward as the lecture hall falls hushed.

He looks like he might have lived among the likes of Athena and Achilles. He's *that* old. Professor Wellington's hair is white and fluffy like a cluster of clouds, and he hobbles to the podium so slowly we're all holding our breath like we're each on red alert to call 9-1-1 in case of a fall.

He passes the podium and shakily hands a stack of papers to a student in the first row. "Welcome to Classical Mythology," he says in a soft, buttery voice. I need to strain my ears to catch everything even though he's speaking into a microphone. Okay, sitting in the front row was the move.

As students begin passing the papers and the stack reaches Ben, I see him take one, then he stands to hand over the stack to a guy in the neighboring aisle. Once Ben has delivered the goods, I expect him to return to his seat.

Instead, he climbs the stairs with his backpack over his shoulder. Beneath the brim of his hat, he's smiling at me.

My pulse skips, and confusion melts into blissful relief when I realize he's headed straight for me. He claims the vacant seat at my side.

"You forgot this, Fisher." He places my pen pouch on my desk.

"My hero," I tease. "You going back to the middle row with the cool kids?" *Please say no.*

He folds out the retractable desk and sets his water bottle on it. "Nah, I think I'll stick with the cooler backrow kids."

Xander slouches more, his cheekbones sharpening as if he's clenching his jaw.

Ben can see. "That okay with you, man?"

"Yeah, do whatever you want." He stares unblinkingly at the blank projector screen.

When the papers come to our row, Xander slips one off the top and passes me the stack. My pretzeled stomach plummets when I see the handwritten scrawl. The professor handwrote the syllabus and scanned it. Does he not own a computer? My confidence swirls down a drainpipe when I skim the course curriculum.

Four exams.

Two essays.

And a group fucking presentation.

My ears ring from the hysteria pulsing inside of me.

"The tests will be given orally," Professor Wellington says. "I will read aloud the questions and you will write your answer on a sheet of paper."

Murmurs echo in the room, and I let out a soft, "What the fuck."

Ben skims my body in a slow onceover. "Are the hives starting?"

"I might be contracting something worse." I pull at the collar of my shirt, feeling suffocated suddenly.

He hands me his water bottle, and I side-eye him like, *are you sure?*

A smile crawls over his face. "Cooties don't exist."

"Herpes does."

"I don't have herpes," he assures while I take a grateful swig of water. Xander catches my eyes while I cap the bottle, and I tense, thinking back to him wishing he had water to offer me.

"Thank God for Cobalts, right?" Xander says quietly, with a hint of bitterness. "We'd never survive without them." It sounds like a personal shot at Ben, but guilt instantly twists Xander's face for even saying it. He mutters a soft, "Fuck."

Ben heard. "Thank *Cobalts* for Cobalts, actually." He says it pretty jokingly.

"Thanks for the correction, man. I forgot you're gods among us mortal humans." The sarcasm drips from Xander. He smears a hand down his face, then eyes the exit.

"We're ceasing fire." I reread the syllabus, panicking on too many accounts. "I really don't need to take any stray bullets."

Xander lets out a laugh. "My aim is terrible, so your worry is valid." He glues the back of his skull to the wall again, staring straight ahead with reddening eyes.

Ben looks down to me, then back up to his cousin. He seems worried about him. I try to concentrate on the potential presentation that we'll need to deliver to over a hundred students and not how I'm sitting between two insanely hot guys, notably a Hale and a Cobalt, and a potential feud I didn't even know existed until ten minutes ago.

"Hey, on the positive," Ben whispers to me, "if the professor doesn't own a computer, which seems likely, you can probably just get all your information from Wikipedia for the essays."

I raise my brows. "You're already plotting to cheat?"

Xander also makes a face like Ben has morphed into an unknown creature. I am getting the sense Ben has never advertised his duplicitous academic habits.

"Whatever helps the hives, Friend," Ben says.

"Cheating will probably cause stomach ulcers."

"We can't have that. Tell your stomach to stay out of it."

I almost smile. "My stomach is a nosy bitch."

I half-expect him to drop his head and speak to my belly button ring, but he seems highly aware Xander is beside me.

We both go quiet when the professor instructs everyone to settle down. The next half hour goes by painstakingly slow as Wellington draws out explaining the topics for the semester.

When class ends, Xander is a rocket. He says a quick, "Bye, Harriet," then exits before most students are even on their feet.

Ben watches Xander go while we gather up our things. By the tension in his face, I can tell that interaction bothered him. He's half-focused on returning my pen to me but mostly peering at the door that Xander disappears through.

Leaving the auditorium, we head down the black-and-white checkered marble hallway. The arched ceilings and intricate beam work remind me how some rich architect built MVU back in the day to resemble European cathedrals. Nearly every building has stained glass windows and gargoyle turrets.

We step foot outside together, and the sun beats on the grassy quad where students sprawl out with their textbooks and friends. New York high-rises jut in the background, reminding me we're actually *in* the city, but I'm digging the secluded collegiate feel of MVU's campus.

"Sorry back there," I say fast, needing to get this off my chest. "I didn't mean to bail on you for Xander. I just—"

"You saw a guy who needed an assist, and you came in with the save. Nothing to be sorry about." He skims me up and down. "You'll be a great doctor someday, petit oiseau."

It lifts the weight off my body and goes further by filling my heart. It's a total head-rush. His confidence really is a thing of beauty. "I know you're calling me *little bird*, but the correct nickname based on what happened would be *little bird shit*."

"Merde de petit oiseau?" He laughs, then says a much longer phrase in French.

I'm completely stumped, but my cheeks are on fire. "Is this going to be a Google translate situation?" I ask him.

His grin is infectious. "I said there's nothing shitty about you." His translation dives deeper into me.

I chew the inside of my cheek, feeling my smile reaching uncharted levels.

"Where are you off to next?" Ben asks after gulping some water.

I pull up my schedule on my phone. "I'm meeting with my honors advisor," I say, "over on...north campus."

"We are on north campus," he says into a smile.

"Lucky me, then." I hike the strap up to my falling backpack. "Where are you headed?"

He holds up his phone for me to see. Twenty-two missed texts. He must have kept it on silent because I never heard it go off in class. "My brothers," he explains. "They're relentless."

"What do they want?" I ask.

"The usual. For me to hang out with them. I think Beckett must have put them up to it. They're worried I'll hate New York."

"So now they're on a group mission to make sure you love it?"

"More like to make sure I won't move out in under two weeks. They want me to stick around."

I frown. "Are you in threat of leaving?"

He nods, which plummets my stomach. "I can't live with them all year. Charlie and I might kill each other."

Okay, so he plans to stay in New York. He just needs to find new sleeping accommodations, which must be hard with his financial situation. I'm still not sure *why* he's broke, even after he explained the stipulations behind his trust fund to me.

Maybe it's an embarrassing story. Like he got duped or hustled out of a large fortune. It makes sense why he wouldn't want to tell his family.

I figure when he's ready, he'll open up. It's not like he's taking an axe to my past. He's been swinging gently. So I do too.

"Are you looking for an apartment?" I ask him.

"Not yet. First, I need to convince my brothers I'll be fine on my own. It means hanging out with them a lot more than I would."

I have so many questions. Why don't his brothers think he's fine? And why wouldn't he want to spend time with them? Charlie, I get, but he doesn't have any vitriol for the other three.

I want to ask but I'm running late.

Ben sees me check the time. "I'll let you know how it goes with my brothers." He eyes me. "Let me know how your honors advisor thing pans out too?"

My chest inflates with oxygen so suddenly that I feel like I could float into the sky. "Yeah, sure," I say, trying to sound casual. Cool.

I tell my brain, *Relax. A hot guy asked you to update him on your day and he'll update you on his. He didn't profess his love and ask you to bear his children. We're good.*

We're good.

TEN

BEN COBALT

My first week in New York, sleep has been tough, and it's not because of the pull-out. I haven't slept well this entire year. My phone is blowing up beside me. Silent messages light the screen on fire, and typically, I'd reply to my friends as something positive to do.

Smile emoji. Laugh-cry emoji. Send.

Now I just toss the phone onto the mattress and rest my elbows on my bent knees, the white sheet stretching with the movement.

It used to be enough, knowing I was a good influence in the lives of others, but I'm plagued with the reality that I could be hurting the people I love most. My family. My sisters. My brothers. It feels fucking...irrational. Because I haven't done anything wrong. I'm not setting bombs in the living room. But I can't rid the thought at night when my mind spins.

Being here sends a quiet panic under my skin, but I must be a living contradiction. Because seven days in and I still feel myself longing to stay. To be more than a voyeur.

I've seen how Beckett is always the first to wake. Before the sun bleeds the sky in orange, he's showered and opening the fridge for a hearty, high-protein breakfast. Turkey sausage, avocado, four sunny side up eggs, a slice of sourdough. Fuel for his rigorous ballet schedule.

He'll make me an almond butter, banana smoothie before I even ask. We've eaten every breakfast together since I moved in, and there's been no pressure to dig into the night I went postal.

Beckett is just interested about my life in this moment. He's been like that ever since he left for New York at sixteen. He plays catch-up better than the rest of us because he's done it for so long, and there's such genuine intrigue in his need to know. It's as if my words paint a picture of all the moments he's missing, and for a brief second, he can see it play like a film.

The fact that he wants to watch the movie of my life makes me love him even more, but I just wish it were a riveting one. Yesterday, I talked mostly about hockey. How I was considering trying out for Manhattan Valley's team.

"Do you want to play?" he asked, his fork hovering over his eggs.

I thought about it for a second. "I want to be great at something. This is the only thing I've ever excelled at, Beck, and I'm not even that good at it."

He made a face. "You *are* good."

"I'll never be *that* good."

"In comparison to what?" he asked in confusion. "You're not as good as the other guys on the team? Or you're not good enough for the NHL?"

"Both, probably."

"Are you sure?" He frowned, disbelieving. "You're *really* good, Pip. We've all seen you play."

"You're family. You would see me as the best. It's natural bias."

His brows didn't uncinch. It felt like he disagreed, but he let it go to ask point-blank, "Do you like hockey?"

"Do I like it?"

"Yeah," he nodded. "Like it's all you think about. All you dream about. You would lose sleep for it. You would wake up in pain and still get on the ice because you're more afraid of the day where it all comes to an end."

I stared at him for a long beat. "Is that what ballet is for you?"

"It's everything," Beckett said from his soul. "And hockey…?"

"Isn't that," I breathed. "I just like being better-than-slightly-average at something."

I didn't tell Beckett about my ultimate plan.

The one I've been constructing for a while now. No one would want me to go through with it, but it's already been set in motion. The biggest derailment has been New York. I was never supposed to be here.

One new step: I need to drop out of MVU before the semester ends. Well before January. So there's really no point in joining the team if I can't stay through the season. I just want Coach Haddock to feel like his effort to recruit me wasn't in vain. Maybe trying out can give him that.

But I hate this new step more than I ever did. Because of Harriet. Because I've already started getting attached to going to class with her. Because I'd rather be with this resilient as fuck girl than anywhere without her, really.

At breakfast, I changed the subject off hockey and asked Beckett, "Do you usually eat alone? Before I moved in, I mean." No one had joined us this past week.

He glanced toward the hallway to Eliot's and Tom's rooms. "On occasion Eliot will wake early enough before he works out." His yellow-green eyes darted to me, then to his avocado. "And most of the time, Charlie would already be up, but not always." He added fast, "He's rarely in New York all seven days of the week. That's not because of you."

I've borne witness to that too.

Charlie has been MIA for entire days. I never catch him leaving the apartment, but suddenly, his suitcase will be propped against the door. His passport on the kitchen island. He'll have returned from someplace outside the country.

"Where'd you go?" I asked on Saturday. It was past three a.m.

He stared me dead in the eyes. "I'm not the one who just got home." He'd heard me come inside the apartment. I'd just returned from my first shift at the End of the World with Harriet.

"I've been out," I said.

Charlie studied me for too long.

So I added, "At a bar. And you?"

"Montreal." He walked to his room and shut the door. Leaving it at that.

It was honestly a bigger answer than the usual Charlie brush off.

This past week, if Beckett occupies my mornings, then Eliot tries to seize my nights.

"Come to a play with me, Ben."

"You'll love Duke's on 10th, Ben. Best fries of your life."

"Have you seen *Chicago* yet? I have an extra ticket that has your name on it, Ben. What say you, brother?"

I said *no*.

I said *I have to study*. Which, I kind of did. Over the phone with Harriet, we talked about downloading *The Odyssey* on audio for our mythology course.

I said *I'm meeting up with friends*. Also, met up with Harriet at work.

It hurt each time I declined Eliot, but he's the brother who'd take several stabs to the heart and keep walking toward you and the blade. He would die before giving up on any of us.

Being the resident of the living room, I've caught glimpses of Eliot and his nights without me in them. He'll bump inside at two a.m. with a giggling girl at his waist. He'll playfully shield her eyes with his hands—just so she can't see me on the pull-out when they go to his bedroom. He'll even give me a wink.

When she leaves a few hours later, I'm usually in a half-sleep, and I hear him wish her goodbye at the door. It's nearly a nightly occurrence, but not with the same girl. Never more than twice.

Beckett was more discreet the Friday night he brought a girl home. He thought I was sleeping. His quiet footfalls wouldn't give him away, but her awed voice did. "Whoa, this is your place?" She gasped. "Is that your brother?"

I couldn't make out his whispered reply. He carted her toward his bedroom. I never heard her leave, but it's not like she evaporated. Knowing Beckett, he likely insisted she be quieter on her exit.

When I asked about her at breakfast, he said, "She was just a girl I met at Pink Noir." It was a club where all the dancers frequented after performances. Beckett invited me to go out with him that night to meet his friends in the ballet company, but I bailed on him too.

That one still fists my lungs painfully. Even if Beckett hasn't acted like I'm the worst brother alive, it's pretty clear that I am.

"Will you see her again?" I asked him.

"No," he said definitively. "Relationships are work, and I have too much going on *at* work with *Leo*." The uncommon bite to Beckett's voice was reserved for his rival at NYBC. "The company is casting him as Albrecht in the first cast of *Giselle* in a couple weeks."

Giselle is Beckett's favorite ballet to dance in, and as a principal, he's been given the lead spot before. But he competes with Leo Valavanis for the top-billed male roles in every production. Most have double casts, and I know that Beckett being relegated to the lead role in the second cast is like being kicked to the JV team.

I was about to offer him some words of affirmation. My siblings and I know that the New York Ballet Company loves pitting Leo and Beckett against each other to drum up drama, which has increased ticket sales before. It's not a reflection of our brother's talent.

But he added, "There is no room in my life for the complications of love. Sex is simple." He cut his eggs with a fork and knife. "L'amour romantique est une maladie." *Romantic love is a disease.*

I wondered if that's what's happening to me.

Have I been unwell since I met Harriet? The times I'm with her, where I'm even *thinking* of her, the panic subsides. The restlessness inside me goes so still. The crawling beneath my skin begins to freeze.

Every breath I take is deeper. Every smile is bigger.

If romance is a disease, then I want to be stricken with whatever malady she's plagued me with. I feel myself chasing after it like a drug.

It's why I'm on my bed now and staring at my phone. Debating whether to text her at an obscenely late hour like a junkie needing a hit.

Don't suffocate her. You'll scare her off.

Harriet seems to startle easily, and if I come on too strong at the start, I might chase her away. Most people I talk to absorb into my sphere like they plan to make a home there.

Harriet, though, she's more guarded. Balanced on her tiptoes, prepared to sprint and save herself.

I wonder if someone hurt her.

That kills me.

The urge to talk to her intensifies, but baby steps, maybe.

I drag myself off the pull-out. Unable to sleep, I near the built-in shelves. Only wearing dark-blue boxer-briefs, the cold air from the AC chills my warmed skin. I notice French novels like *Les Misérables* by Victor Hugo. More French writers: Proust, Voltaire, Émile Zola.

They aren't unfamiliar to me. Neither is the language. We all learned French from our parents, who were taught at a young age in school. They fostered our knowledge through carrying conversations at home and our travels to Europe. It feels like I've always known French, the same way my siblings have.

Another book draws my attention. Tugging it out, I thumb through a hardcover titled *Grandes Esperanzas* by Charles Dickens.

I can speak Spanish better than I can read it—thanks to all the time I spent with the Meadows. My Uncle Ryke is fluent from learning in school as a kid too, and he helped teach some of us, including his daughters (Sullivan and Winona) and Maximoff Hale and me.

I'm really close to my Uncle Ryke and Aunt Daisy. Hell, I spent more time at the Meadows Cottage than the Cobalt Estate some months as a kid. They were right down the street, but they had the most acres of woods, the most secret hideouts, the most creeks to wade through.

I haven't hung out there since I left for college. Since I distanced myself from Winona. Losing a friendship with my cousin was painful, but losing time I loved spending with my aunt and uncle hurts more somehow.

I stare at the book in my hands. This Spanish edition of *Great Expectations* has to belong to Charlie. He's a polyglot like our dad and knows more languages than I can count. Spanish is on that list.

As the yellowed pages brush my fingers, my thumb catches one, and I see *Pip. From Pirrip.*

My middle name.

My pulse skips. I shut the book. Put it back between other classics. Then I pick up the kantharos by one of the two swooping handles. The black Grecian cup has intricate artwork of a girl cradling a fruit...maybe a pomegranate?

I can't see much else in the dark. So I turn to grab my phone to use the light. As I tap on the flashlight app, I lose grip of the cup. It slips and drops.

And shatters on the hardwood.

Fuck.

Wide-eyed, unbreathing, I stare at the shards of pottery at my bare feet. It must've made a decently loud noise because I hear the pitter-patter of footsteps like I woke someone.

Please be Beckett.

Please be Beckett.

I squat down to pick up the pieces. Just as a shirtless Charlie emerges. He wears gray cotton pants and a blank expression.

He comes closer, then roots a hand to the blue revolving chair. Using it as a brace, maybe. I don't fucking know.

I do know that I just broke a prized memento of his. It was *displayed*. It had to have meant something to him.

He sees the mess. "Planned on drinking wine?" His voice is void of emotion. Unreadable.

"What?" I breathe out my first breath.

He rolls his eyes. "It *was* a kantharos. It's meant for drinking wine."

I know what a kantharos is. I'm full of random facts that'd make me a decent Jeopardy competitor. A lot I learned during Wednesday Night Dinners. Some have been permanently etched in my brain. Some I've completely forgotten out of disinterest.

I still can't get a solid read on Charlie. "I broke your cup," I say as I gather the scattered fragments. "Sorry. It just fell out of my hands..." I shouldn't touch anything of his. I shouldn't be here. If I just called Harriet, I wouldn't have picked it up. I wouldn't have broken it. This wouldn't have happened.

"It's a cup, not an organ," he says like I'm overreacting.

Does he really not care? "Where'd you get it?"

"Sifnos."

I frown. "Where's that?"

"Greece."

I'm not shocked it's authentic. I wish it was a knockoff from Crate & Barrel that I could order online. "So I can just fly over there and get another one, right? This exact cup?" I know I can't. My entire stomach is lodged in my throat. I feel like throwing up.

"You don't have to get me anything. *I* can get one like it." Charlie pries himself from the chair, nearing me. As he takes a knee, he strains his bad leg and winces a little.

"Don't," I tell him. "I can clean this up myself. It's my fault."

He cocks his head, his brows pinching. "Why are you acting like the world is caving in?"

"I broke an irreplaceable artifact you found halfway across the fucking world," I say in one taut breath.

"I. Don't. Care. About. *It*. So why the fuck do you?" He's glaring.

I glare back. "Just let me clean this up." I have to make it right, and what if he cuts himself on the pottery? I've injured him *enough*.

Charlie rakes a frustrated hand through his golden-brown hair. He tosses the same hand at me. "Go back to bed."

"I can't—"

"*Stop*," he sneers at me. "The self-flagellation routine is tired. You're not the cause of my pain. You can't hurt me. Not by breaking a stupid cup. Not by living five feet from me." He sweeps me. "Do you understand?"

All I understand is the crater-sized rock in my throat. "No," I choke out.

Charlie stares so deeply into me; it almost overwhelms me to sudden, scalding tears as he says, "You feel everything. I feel *nothing*."

It pushes me like a shove against my chest.

"Go to sleep," he says numbly.

At this, I hand him the pottery. He collects the last of the shards, and I walk to the bathroom. Unable to be present while he sweeps up the remaining bits and pieces.

I tuck myself on the floor beside the toilet. And I cry. I don't even know why the fuck I'm crying, other than it's releasing this knot in my body that so badly wants to untangle.

Charlie must've called Beckett.

He comes in and takes a seat on the floor across from me. His hair is disheveled like he abruptly woke up. His black drawstring pants hang low on his waist, his tattoos visible along his carved bicep. The light in the bathroom causes him to squint a little as his eyes adjust.

"You need the sleep," I rasp out. "Don't worry about me. I'm fine." I'm screwing everything up. I rub roughly at my wet face.

"I'd rather be here," he whispers, his voice so soothing in comparison to Charlie's. He wears remorse. "Whatever Charlie said to you—"

"It's not that." And this wouldn't be the first time Beckett has tried to apologize on his twin's behalf. *I broke his Grecian cup.* He doesn't care. *So why do I?* I don't know.

I don't know.

Am I the only Cobalt who doesn't know enough? Am I the only one who would think, *I don't fucking know?*

I press the heel of my palm harder against my eye, trying not to groan out my gnarled emotions. I manage to get out, "I'll get over it." I hope.

He rests his forearms on his knees. "You should talk to Dad."

I shake my head so hard, a muscle screams in my neck to stop. *He wouldn't understand.* I'm being unreasonable. "I'm okay," I promise. "I'm okay, really, man. This is just...me being me, you know?"

Sensitive.

Fragile.

Irrational.

Ben.

I use the side of my fist to dry the last of my face.

Beckett slides over to me, wedging himself on my other side. He wraps an arm around my shoulders. "I love you, Pip. You being exactly who you are, I love you." He squeezes me a little fiercer than usual. "N'en doutez jamais."

Never doubt that.

It burns my eyes. "I love you too, Beck." I breathe in, breathe out. Deeper. Until I can swallow the rock back down. "N'en doutez jamais." *Never doubt that.*

"Je n'ai jamais pu," he murmurs. *I never could.*

I don't want to leave. In this single second, I want to exist quietly beside my brother, in the safety of this bathroom. I want to freeze time and know that everything is okay. Everything will be okay forever.

I'm okay.

ELEVEN

BEN COBALT

The next morning, hot water drips off my eyelashes. Steam fogs the bathroom in a cloudy haze. LED lights glow in a neon-blue color from the showerhead, bathing the entire stall in a calming cocoon.

I rest my palm on the black tile as water pelts my skull and the back of my neck. Expensive shampoos and body washes line two shelves. If I had to unearth a guess, the Dior shower gel is Eliot's.

He likes name-brand things, but Tom doesn't cheap out on any skincare products. So who the fuck knows? I never grew up sharing a bathroom with my brothers. Not until now.

Our childhood home is affectionately called the Cobalt Estate, but you can't find horse stables, multiple pool houses, or private tennis courts on the property. There aren't even million-dollar sunset views.

Don't get me wrong—our parents' house is a mansion.

The marble entryway with the dramatic staircase and crystal chandelier is fit for a Disney castle, but it's not twenty-thousand square feet to get lost in. It's not even a fraction of what my family's money could buy.

Our parents purchased a home in a gated neighborhood where households with mid-seven-figure incomes live. They picked it because it's where my mom's sisters wanted to be, and she wanted to be close to them and for us to grow up alongside our cousins.

So we did.

The Hales and Meadows lived just down the street from us in a rich little suburb of Philadelphia.

Some of our cousins became our best friends, and in my case, they *were* my best friends. Past tense. At one point, I would've said Xander was one of them too.

I try to push him so far out of my head, along with the cold chill he gives me every Tuesday and Thursday in Classical Mythology with Harriet wedged between us in the back row. The arctic blast from Xander hasn't stopped me from sitting beside her.

It's weirdly easier to focus on my brothers and being here. Each of us had our own space and privacy at the Cobalt Estate, and my brothers chucked that out of the window when they moved to New York. Now they're in a 4 bed/2 bath apartment that would be luxurious to most in the city, but it's honestly a shoebox compared to where we grew up.

When I was a little kid, I used to avoid bath time like the plague, mostly because I just liked the smell of dirt, of the muddy earth. As I got older, I'd race through my showers in under a minute flat. Soap all the important parts, rinse, and hop out. I thought maybe if I used less water, I could tip the scales in favor of the planet.

Then one day during my usual sprint through my shower routine, I just...stayed there. Frozen underneath the rainfall of water, I let it drip down my skin and pool into the drain. The warmth was an embrace I didn't want to abandon. Couldn't abandon. Despite the screaming in my head to *leave. Jump out, you wasteful bastard.*

I stayed there for twenty minutes. It had been the longest shower of my life.

That was three months ago.

And today, I find myself stuck in the shower again, the water a comfort I can't shake. Only instead of berating myself, I start thinking about a short, beautiful blond with angry eyes. I don't carve her image out of my head. I'm almost afraid of what'll fill its place once she's gone.

Nothing that'd feel as good. Nothing that'd stir emotion or my blood. Nothing I'd really want.

I picture her now.

Fully clothed in the shower with me, Harriet is underneath the waterfall with her chin tilted up to meet my eyes. Wet blond strands stick to her soft cheeks. Her cute pierced ears peek out of her soaked hair. Her arms are crossed at her ribs in a guarded, defensive posture, but as she clings to my confidence, she lets them fall to her sides. She trusts me, like I trust her.

I slowly drag my gaze down her body where the white cotton of her top suctions to her tits. Her shirt is drenched. Her nipples are perked buds against the fabric, but I look back at her face as her pink lips part, an aroused breath escaping. I feel myself harden.

"Fuck," I grunt out as my cock throbs. I want to run my hands down her hips—to see how her body reacts to me. I want this girl to shake in unknown fucking pleasure. I want her to crumble to the shower tile in ecstasy so that I'll have to pick her up to keep her against me.

I want inside Harriet.

Her mind, her heart, her pussy. Deep...deeper. Like how she's rooted herself in my head. I want to fuck her until she can't see straight and the only word she can mutter is *Ben*.

I stroke my rock-hard length with my right hand, balling my left into a fist against the tiled wall. My breath goes labored, and a groan tries to scratch against my throat. Has she ever been eaten out before?

I imagine dropping to my knees, then shimmying her soaked panties to her ankles. They're black. Lace, maybe.

She's gripping my shoulder, uncertain of what's about to happen. I'll make her see stars.

"Don't mind me!" Eliot's muffled voice startles me out of the hot visual, and I instantly drop my hand off my dick.

What. The. Fu—the bathroom door bursts open.

I rub a fist to the fogged glass just to confirm, yes, my older brother has barged in here.

Eliot shields his eyes with a hand in a mock display of modesty while he ventures to the vanity. "Goddamn, brother, you take long showers. I thought you were in conservation mode?"

"Is it a mode if it's his default?" Tom's voice precedes his appearance in the bathroom.

Unlike Eliot who's only in navy-blue boxer-briefs, Tom is fully dressed, wearing a black muscle shirt and ripped acid-wash jeans. He immediately bends down to the cupboard below the sink. I don't know whether to be annoyed, pissed off, or dumbfounded.

"Good point," Eliot replies to Tom.

"What the fuck?" I speak to both of them. "Hello? I'm showering."

"Well, if that's all you're doing, I'm not rushing out," Tom proclaims. "My hair is all fucked up, dude. I have a photoshoot in a couple hours. These are *dire* circumstances."

A groan of frustration rumbles in my chest. I pinch the water out of my eyes. "I locked the door," I tell them. What—do they have a key or something?

"We forgot to mention the lock doesn't work anymore." Eliot speaks to himself in the mirror. "Broke during a party last month."

"Four months ago," Tom corrects him.

Eliot whistles. "Time is a bastard."

I wonder if Beckett told them about finding me crying in here last night, but they're not hovering like I'm about to self-combust. Then again, Eliot *is* a professional stage actor, so he could probably hide his concern if he wanted.

Tom, maybe not. But he doesn't seem ready to chuck a fire blanket and first-aid kit at me. It eases my apprehension.

Hard-on officially soft, I shut off the water and the LED lights fade out. "Can you at least toss me a towel?" My brothers clearly have zero boundaries with each other, and I don't know whether to be envious or aggravated. Eliot and Tom were practically raised as twins since Eliot had to retake kindergarten, which landed him in Tom's grade for the rest of school.

Whereas the actual twins, Charlie and Beckett, didn't go to school together really. Charlie skipped third and fourth grade, so he ended up in the same year as our older sister Jane, while Beckett chose to be homeschooled after ballet took over his life.

Eliot throws the plush black bath towel into the shower, and I catch it before it lands on the wet tile. Swiftly, I wrap and knot it at my waist. When I step out of the shower, the steam follows me. Tom's busy digging in the cupboard for something, while Eliot squirts a glob of toothpaste on a toothbrush.

Eliot eyes me, a wicked grin playing at his lips. "Did we interrupt something?"

Tom, head-half-hidden below the sink, says, "He was definitely jacking off."

I groan. "This cannot be real life."

"We can pretend this is all a dream if you want," Eliot says, mumbling through his toothbrush. He waves a hand like he's putting a spell on me. "We were never here."

Tom chuckles.

Yeah, they're both amusing, but I'm not in the mood to laugh. Pressure compounds on my chest that I can't throw off. I'm fine, really. And they need to believe it too.

Beads roll down my temples. Using the heel of my palm, I wipe water off my jaw, but my damp hair tracks more droplets down my neck, so I take the towel off my waist to dry my head. Not caring about being naked in front of them. I'm not shy. Undressing in locker rooms pretty much cured me of that.

I just care that I was *jerking off* when they came in here.

"Can you just not do it again?" I ask.

"Only if you tell us who you were rubbing one out to." Eliot spits into the sink, and I'd think he were joking if I didn't know him. But I know him—too well. *Quid pro quo* might as well be tattooed on his ass. Right alongside *lex talionis*. An eye for an eye.

I evade, "I didn't say I was—"

"Dude, you take thirty-second showers." Tom interjects as he comes out of the cabinet with an armful of hair products. "If you weren't masturbating, what were you doing?"

Fuck my life. "You want to know, then you'd have to tell me the last person you jacked off to." This'll get them to back off...I think.

Eliot opens his hands. "That's only fair. Mine was a hate-jerking."

I make a face. "What does that even mean?"

"It means I was jacking off to my enemy's sister as a fuck you."

Do I even want to ask who that is? Anyone who marginally slights our family, Eliot has written off and the list is long.

Tom acts busy reading a product label.

"And you?" I wonder.

"Hmm?"

Eliot shoves his arm. "Share."

Tom shoots him a wide-eyed look. So...he doesn't want to share with me? Great, he's giving me an out too. I say, "We don't have to tell each other anything—"

"It's not that I don't want to. It's that, uh, it's secret-ish." Tom cinches one eye closed. "From Beckett."

My brows jump. "You're keeping a secret from Beckett? Why?"

Eliot's lips drop in disappointment at Tom. "Brother, no."

"I can't fucking help it, Eliot. He's *hot*. Like extremely fucking hot, and he winked at me."

"That was one time, and it might've been an eye twitch," Eliot refutes, then clues me in, "it's Leo Valavanis."

My frown heavies. "Beckett seriously *hates* him." I've never heard Beckett curse someone out like he does Leo. Honestly, I'm not even sure Tom's hostility toward Harriet is equivalent.

Eliot nods. "It's one thing to hate-jerk to get back at an enemy. Another thing to fuck your brother's mortal foe."

Tom groans, "I'm not actually going to hook up with Leo. I know it's probably not possible."

"Impossible," Eliot amends.

"Impossible," Tom agrees, then stares me down. "Your turn."

I'm really going to have to admit this. Telling them I was just standing in the shower wasting water will send off a million alarm signals. Eliot is already laser-focused on me, waiting for the answer.

I want to say the truth, but how the hell do I do that? There's a war within me to even say her name. Tom's not a fan of hers after she auditioned to be his drummer, and it'd only draw tension between us. I'm trying, *trying*, not to cause any further friction.

I run the towel against the back of my neck. "She's a girl from college."

Eliot rinses his mouth. "Do we know her?"

"You might." I act like it's unimportant, trying to throw them off the scent.

"Seems like we do," Tom says, appearing satisfied with my answer. He's half-reading the label to a hair product, then tossing the bottle back in a bin.

I reknot the towel around my waist. "I have a meeting with my advisor." I wind past both their bodies to reach the exit, but Eliot quickly puts a hand on the door before I grab the knob.

"Why the caginess?" His brows furrow. "We're brothers, *brother*." He leans more of his weight on the door, impeding me from leaving. "Which reminds me, I'm creating a group calendar. We're all going to share our schedules with each other. I'll send you the link."

I frown. "Charlie too?"

"He's been informed."

I laugh. "There's no way in hell he's going to participate."

"We're working on him," Tom says, dumping the bottles and sprays on the sink counter.

Eliot chimes in, "And I, for one, would love to see where Charlie fucks off to every day."

This can't be about Charlie, or else they would've concocted this group calendar thing prior to me living here.

"I'm mostly just on campus," I tell them. "It's boring."

"We're not asking to be entertained, Ben Pirrip," Tom says. "We just want to know where everyone is. We're not nobodies. Luna was assaulted last year." Mention of our cousin, *their* best friend, tenses the bathroom.

It wasn't a random assault. It was targeted. She's famous, and her attackers wanted a quick payout and sold the story to the media. Our parents have harped on us to "always have your bodyguard present" this year. It's why Novak is basically superglued to my shadow now.

"We should be keeping tabs on each other," Tom adds. "It's safer that way."

I let out a deep exhale. "Yeah, okay," I agree. I'm mostly trying to conceal my bartending job. I can just omit that from the calendar.

Eliot still has a palm planted on the door. He studies me, but if Charlie feels like the king, queen, rook, and bishop on a chess board, then Eliot is only the knight. He's far less threatening to me.

He straightens up so we're almost the same height. "You know, we'd be much closer, you and I, without so much mystery between us."

"Maybe I don't want to be any closer to you," I say without thinking. It's not the truth, but it's also not a total lie.

Tom lets out a breath. "Damn."

Guilt fists my insides. I try not to feel bad. Eliot and Tom aren't Charlie. They don't actively hate me. And the last thing I want is to become an asshole like Charlie.

"Harriet," I blurt out like a busted dam. "That's the girl." I jerk my head toward the shower.

Tom suddenly freezes. "I beg your pardon. *Who?*"

"Harriet," I repeat.

"I know a Harriet." He stares at me like *please don't say it's her*, but I don't want to hide her like a dirty dark secret. Like something to be ashamed of.

"Yeah, same Harriet."

Tom pushes his golden-brown hair out of his face with a hot hand. "Dude, she's trouble. You do not need to add her to your spank bank. Okay? She needs to stay far, *far* away from any indecent thoughts."

What? I give him a strange look. "*You're* telling me to stay away from trouble? You're jerking off to Beckett's ballet rival, and you literally got the word *troublemaker* tattooed to your bicep three weeks ago." I point to the cursive letters inked on his arm—very visible since he's wearing a muscle shirt.

"Ignore my tattoos," he says in a slight panic. "Ignore what I do, but don't ignore what I'm saying."

He's saying to stay away from the one girl who's made me feel happy to be in New York. "I can't. We're friends."

His jaw unhinges. "*Friends?*" He whips around to Eliot for confirmation. "Did I hear that right?"

Eliot's staring at me. "Parfaitement." *Perfectly*.

"I don't understand your issue with her," I tell Tom. "So she tried out for your band when she was seventeen. You were the one who rejected *her* just because she was under eighteen. If anything, she should be pissed off at you and not the other way around."

"Pissed off at me?" Tom touches his chest in disbelief. "Yes, I rejected her, but she's the one who emailed me when she turned eighteen and asked if she could be in the band. I told her *no*, and what does she do? Let it go? Move along with her life? No, she fucking *emailed* our bassist this long rant about how I was going to sink The Carraways. Pissed off at ME?" He's pacing. His hands on his hips. "Dude. She. Is. Batshit."

I wave a hand to Tom but look at Eliot. "He's getting this worked up over an email?"

"Are you fucking kidding me?" Tom almost lunges, but Eliot grabs a fistful of his shirt, dragging him backward.

Tom spins out of his hold and rests his hands on his head again, trying to cool off.

"It's his band, Ben," Eliot reminds me. "It might as well be a third appendage."

His band. Tom first formed The Carraways when he was fourteen with Warner, the bassist, during their time in prep school. The three-person punk-rock band has cycled out drummers over the years, but Warner has never abandoned Tom in the seven whole years the band has been together. I'm guessing if Harriet's email struck a nerve, then there might've been strife between Warner and Tom before she even hit send.

"Sorry," I say to Tom with more sympathy. "Honestly...I don't know what it's like to love something enough to grow a third arm for it." I shift my weight, gripping the towel at my waist. "I wish I did."

Tom settles down for a second, letting his hands fall to his sides. He's frowning. "You love hockey?"

He's unsure. I have a feeling all my siblings have been questioning my love for the sport lately. Leaving Penn, quitting the hockey team—it didn't gut me. Quitting something you love should feel devastating.

"Not like you love music," I say to Tom, similarly to what I told Beckett. Then I stare at Eliot, silently telling him to back off the door.

He doesn't move. "There's a party. Friday night at one of our favorite clubs. Come out with us, little brother."

"No thanks," I say, on automatic.

"Beckett will be there," Tom jumps in.

"No," I say again. The last place I need to be is an overcrowded club on a Friday night with my brothers. Too many things can go wrong.

Tom and Eliot share a wordless look before Eliot says, "Bring Harriet then."

"*Eliot,*" Tom snaps angrily like this is betrayal.

Eliot is only staring at me now, his eyes pleading.

I glance between them. "Tom won't want me to—"

"But he'll allow it," Eliot cuts me off. "Right, Tom? For our little brother."

"Right," Tom says like he just swallowed battery acid. "But you also could bring literally *anyone* else. Like someone Charlie hates. I'm sure that list is longer than a CVS receipt."

"Or you can bring Harriet," Eliot offers again.

Tom shifts just as I catch the contortion of his face. He's having an internal meltdown. I'm half-surprised he doesn't press his forehead to the counter and groan.

Eliot clutches my shoulders, prying my attention off Tom. "Bring her," he says strongly. They really want me to go out with them this badly.

I'm caving beneath the temptation. Beneath the idea of spending more time with Harriet outside of college, outside of work. Beneath the desire of being with my brothers. It feels like it'll be better if she's there.

It all entices me.

"I'll think about it."

TWELVE

HARRIET FISHER

"I can't," I say, my stomach dropping as soon as I reject Ben's invite. Friday night out with Ben Cobalt sounds like an image right off most girls' dream boards, but if I had a board, two pictures would engulf all the rest.

Get into the Honors House.

Become a doctor.

Being body-to-body in a sweaty, sticky club in Hell's Kitchen shouldn't even sound that appealing, but as soon as I imagine Ben and his hands on me, tucking me to his build so no one bumps into me, I crave it a billion times more than a solo night with old episodes of CSI while modeling carboxylic acids with my molecular model kit for O-Chem.

Ben leans against the windowsill of my apartment as rain beats against the pane. His buff arms are crossed with casualness. Barely any tension in his body, despite the big fat rejection I just cast upon him.

Did I mention he came to my apartment tonight to ask me *in* person? Luckily, I made up the couch before he arrived. The knitted blankets are folded and tucked in the closet with my pillow.

I'm sitting cross-legged on the lumpy lime-green sofa, a flimsy paper plate with my sandwich balancing on my thigh. My stomach grumbles. I had to skip lunch because of an interview at a genetics research lab on campus. A necessary sacrifice even if my stomach does not agree.

"You always eat sandwiches for dinner?" Ben wonders.

"It's a top three supper staple." I pick up the white bread cut in a diagonal. "I'm not exactly a Michelin-star chef."

"Same." His lips start to rise. "What kind of sandwich is it?"

"Tuna salad." I've learned a lot more about Ben, including his refusal to consume any animal products. I take a large bite and speak as I chew. "Does this hurt your vegan soul?"

He has a slanted smile. "I'll survive."

"Shucks," I deadpan.

"Trying to kill every Cobalt off one by one?" he teases.

"I gotta take my shot considering your brother aimed first." My next bite is bigger. I quickly realize I'm more ravenous than ladylike. Whatever. It's not like I'm courting Ben Cobalt or trying to woo him with feminine wiles. We're just friends. Licking my thumb, I continue, "And I know I sound bitter and butthurt over the auditions, but I was the *best* drummer there. I was watching everyone go up on stage and perform for the band, and I was the best. I know my worth, and Tom—"

"He messed up," Ben says in agreement. He might as well have thrown a brick at my face. The surprise is all the same.

"You've never seen me play."

He raises his shoulders up and down in an easygoing shrug. "I don't have to. Tom admitted you were the best one who tried out, but you were just too young." He eyes the half-eaten sandwich. "Don't kill me off yet, okay?"

"I doubt I could." I lift my sandwich to my mouth. "Cobalts never die."

His smile is fond for a second. "I like that one."

"I'll take the praise, but I'm not the originator."

"I know," he laughs. "I've heard it before. My family has many mottos."

It reminds me. "How'd the whole pride of lions come about?" I wonder, since Cobalts are associated with the animal. The color blue is obvious. *Cobalt blue,* duh. But lions, less so. "Is it a king of the jungle thing?"

"Maybe partly."

"You don't know for sure?"

"No, most things like that about the Cobalt Empire feel like myths. Legends. Told too many times from person to person over decades, and they've created a life of their own. We embrace them because why the hell not? Some, I'm sure, my parents even started. Some were definitely started by us. Whatever the case, it's always just bonded us closer as a family." He tips his head in a thought. "Though, among my siblings, I'd say I'm more black sheep than lion."

"Hmm," I chew slowly, then swallow. "Same."

"Black sheep of your family?"

"Yep. It seems we're the same breed, Friend."

"Knew I sensed a connection, Fisher." His smile edges across his mouth.

Do not blush at your tuna fish, Harriet. Too fucking late.

Ben lifts a ceramic pot off the windowsill. He inspects the sad little plant and the drooping heart-shaped leaves. "The actual drum audition isn't why my brother has a problem with you, is it?" His eyes flit back to me.

The tuna fish sinks to the bottom of my stomach. "He told you I emailed the bassist," I guess.

He nods like it's nothing, which feels a lot like another brick to the face.

Another realization strikes. "You knew, and you still asked me to go to this party with you?" I question like he's delusional. "I was a vindictive brat who tried to get Tom kicked out of his own band."

"Vindictive brats could literally describe most people in my family, and I still love them." Is he saying he loves me too—*no*. Absolutely fucking not. *Don't be ridiculous, Harriet.* Ben isn't even flustered like he slipped up and confessed deep feelings for me. He just touches the heart-shaped leaf. "This hoya needs more water."

My head is spinning. He's a plant expert too?

"It's not mine. But I'll let Eden know."

With the hoya in hand, he passes the couch, just to reach the nearby kitchen. He turns on the sink and waters the plant for Eden. His baby blue eyes drift around the apartment. "I see the sticks." He nods toward the drumsticks on the coffee table. "But where's your drum kit?"

Huh?

I'm still mentally attached to the fact that he knows about my bratty email. I wash down the lump in my throat with a gulp of lemonade, then say, "I don't own one…I've never actually owned one."

Ben shuts off the faucet. "Then how'd you learn to play?"

"A music store in Pittsburgh." I watch him return the pot to the windowsill, his eyes on mine as he crosses the living room again. "It was down the street from where I grew up. I used to go in there every day after school and just bang on the drums. The manager could've kicked me out—because a ten-year-old *clearly* isn't going to buy shit—but she started teaching me to play instead."

Ben looks deeper into me with this powerful comfort that makes sharing easy. Almost too easy. It's like he sees, understands, and will protect. I stop asking myself if he's this way with everyone.

I just start believing it's only for me.

"What was her name?" he asks.

I fight a tiny smile as he sinks beside me on the couch. "Sunny…I can't remember her last name. I don't think she ever mentioned it. For all I know, Sunny might've been a nickname too." I chew the inside of my cheek. "She was in her late twenties, and she played in a local band that'd do small gigs around Pittsburgh. I *begged* my mom to take me to one of Sunny's shows, but she always said no."

He gives me a baffled look while he picks up a drumstick. "Your mom said no to that, but she let you hang out at a music store alone?"

I laugh at my tuna sandwich. "Yeah, she had her moments of being super strict, then times where she totally forgot about me. It was like she had selective amnesia and when she suddenly remembered she was a mom, she wanted to triple-down." After another sip of lemonade, I put the glass on the coffee table. "It probably had to do with the divorce and wanting to prove to my dad that she was a better mom than he was a father."

"Was your dad as strict?"

"Not really…but I only ever spent a few summers with him."

Ben captures my gaze with a softness. "Divorced parents?"

"Yeah, I was only five when they split. He left Pittsburgh without really fighting to have more time with me. Then he remarried and had two more kids pretty quickly after that."

A whole new family.

I only briefly mention my stepsiblings Siggy and Chance. "I have a closer relationship with the pharmacist down the street than I have with them," I explain. "And I've seen the lady at Valley Drugs a whopping single time just to pick up my birth control pills. But we've said *hi* to each other at least."

I just so casually dropped being on birth control, but it's not an indication that I'm sexually active. There are a handful of other reasons to take birth control. To help with cramps or PCOS, relieve endometriosis symptoms, prevention for ovarian cysts, clearing up acne. The list is long, really.

What's weird is that I want him to ask me about my reason. *Why, Harriet?* I force myself not to groan. My reason is *basic*.

It's to avoid pregnancy.

Why do I want him to know this?

Maybe I just like this feeling. Of being so comfortable with someone that these intimate questions aren't off the table, but they're freely given and taken with no judgment and no reservation.

Ben twirls the drumstick between his fingers. I feel him studying my reaction. *Ask me about it. Ask me. Ask me. Don't stop asking me things. Please.*

"Do you still talk to Sunny?" Ben wonders.

It's not the question I wanted, but I like this one all the same.

I shake my head once. "I went to the store one day, and she wasn't there. I didn't have her number, but the new manager said she moved to Sedona. Out west." I frown. "I was fifteen, and I didn't think she owed me an explanation. People move to new cities all the time. People don't always stick around." I think about my dad. "But it did suck…knowing she was gone and she wasn't coming back." I swallow the lump forming in my throat. "And I realized that maybe she meant more to me than I meant to her."

His lips downturn. "Why do you say that?"

I shrug. "Because if she thought about me, maybe she would've left a note. I would've liked a note, at least."

He stops spinning the drumstick between his fingers. His brows crinkle as he considers something. "I'm not saying Sunny didn't care about you, but I don't get why she wouldn't have called your parents. Or tried to figure out why you were always there."

"She knew I liked playing the drums and that I didn't have a kit at home."

"Did she even know if you had a home?"

My frown deepens, then I shake my head again. "She never asked much about my life."

Ben shoots a fleeting glare to the ceiling, before he tells me, "I would've asked."

It wells up in me. *He would've asked.* My heart thumps as I feel closer to this guy in ways I've *never* felt close to another person. And we still barely know each other. "Thing is, Cobalt boy," I whisper, "I was glad she never asked. It made it easier to keep going back at the time. Maybe she knew that."

"Yeah, I hope she did." He holds my gaze. "I'm sorry she left."

Me too. "Shitty things happen every day. It's not like we can control them."

He stares off for a beat, then taps the stick to the top of my head. It should annoy me, but my lips twitch into a partial smile. "So you don't have a drum kit," he says, "but you love playing the drums enough that you auditioned at seventeen."

"It wasn't that long ago. I'm only eighteen."

"I know," he states with a playful smile. "I can do math. Not better than Jane, though." He mentions his older sister, but before I can ask about her, he says, "You still love playing?"

"Yeah. I'll always love playing."

He lets this sink in. "What do you love about it?"

I've never been asked this before, so it takes me a moment to find the words. "I love the physicality of it…how it almost feels like dancing without exposing yourself in a crowd. I love the…raw energy. The *aggression*. Everything I kept inside could come out and it was socially acceptable. Destroying my bedroom would not only get me severely grounded but probably piss off my mom's boyfriend enough that he'd—" I cut myself off abruptly, my heart jumping to my esophagus.

Ben's jaw muscle tics, then he slides his arm against the back of the cushion near my shoulders. Somehow, it relaxes me—his reaction to come closer and not spring farther away like I've suddenly contracted an STD…or scurvy.

"He'd be a dick," I finish vaguely. "She mostly dated dicks until she met Kenneth, her current husband. But she could be a dick too, so…match made, right?"

Ben doesn't press. He just nods.

He's sweet.

I'm not as nice.

I can't ignore the gnawing in my stomach any longer. I deathgrip my paper plate. "I need you to know that I don't regret the email to Tom." My heart pounds hard in my chest. I didn't expect to say this out loud to anyone, but keeping it to myself feels more like a crime than the crime itself. "And if I had to go back in time, I'd make the same choice ten times out of ten. Because…because…" My pulse hammers in my ears.

Ben grabs on to the other side of the paper plate, and the movement unleashes my ironclad grip on it. When our eyes meet, he just nods as if to tell me, *it's okay.*

"I was angry," I confess. "So damn angry. I'd been living out of my car and that gig felt like a safety net. A lifeline. And Tom just so casually ripped it away. I wanted him to hurt as much as I hurt—and I know that's wrong because it's Tom's band. It wasn't owed to me. But ten times out of ten, yeah, I'd do it again." I take a deeper breath, a weight bearing heavy on my chest. "So I'd understand if you don't want to be friends with me."

Ben is quiet for a long second, but I don't see judgment in his eyes. "What if I told you, I still want to be your friend?"

"I'd say you're certifiable."

He smiles. "That's not even an insult to me."

It makes my lips upturn too. We're quiet as he passes me the paper plate, and I finish off the tuna sandwich. He doesn't seem to mind that I'm eating fish around him. Not that I'd be able to accommodate. I don't have much else on the pantry shelf besides tuna and bread and some boxes of rotini.

Ben spins the drumstick again and looks me over. "If you're worried about running into Tom at the club tonight, I can make sure he doesn't cause any trouble."

"I'm not worried about Tom or trouble." I stand to toss the plate in the trash. "I just don't have time to go to a party tonight. I'm pre-med. Getting into medical school isn't as easy as handing over a report card with straight As. I need to stand out among other applicants, and that requires a boatload of extra shit."

"Like what?" Ben asks.

"I don't want to bore you."

"If I were bored, I'd have already left, Fisher. What's on your to-do list?"

I hold up my hand, fingers splayed, and I start by counting off my thumb. "One. I need an undergrad research position, which I secured this morning with Dr. Venison's research lab."

His brows rise. "Dr. Venison?"

"Don't worry, it has nothing to do with Bambi."

"I'm relieved because I was definitely thinking you were dissecting poor Bambi's mom." He waves me forward with the drumstick. "Continue."

I avoid telling him I will be dissecting mice. I'm not sure Vegan Ben will approve, and not getting his approval suddenly feels about as spectacular as swallowing nitric acid.

"Two." I list off my next finger. "Volunteer at the hospital. I applied this morning, and there will likely be an interview process later. Three: Join a club. Four: Get a shadowing position."

Shadowing is the holy grail of a perfect resume, and it's also incredibly difficult to find a doctor willing to let some undergrad shadow them. Most of the time students whose parents are doctors or who have connections in the hospital get these shadowing positions. It's a "who you know" atmosphere that doesn't benefit me…yet.

"Five: Be accepted into the Honors House by the end of the semester. That involves submitting an application, going to their events, completing their rigorous exam, and hopefully getting brownie points with the current members, who have all sorts of connections into the medical field. And six—"

"Jesus, there's a six?" Ben's grimacing.

"The MCAT," I say, using my other hand to count. "I'm currently a sophomore, and I'll be taking the test spring of my junior year. That means I have a little over a year to study, so I have to start now." I drop my arms completely, and I feel horrible for a second. I didn't scare him away by being an asshole to his brother, but I surely have scared him away now that he knows what little free time I have.

He stands up like he's ready to leave. "Okay," he says, grabbing his blue bookbag from the floor. My heart might as well be at my feet. Why...why did I have to go and ruin this *one* good thing? *He needed to know my reality,* I remind myself.

He slips the bookbag strap over his shoulder and gives me a long expectant look. "You coming?"

I frown. "What?"

"Number three. Join a club. You didn't say you've done it yet, so let's go join a club." He pauses before he adds, "Preferably not chess, though. Is that all right?"

I don't ask why. My heart has risen from my feet and nestled back inside my chest. I feel high as I grab my backpack from the closet and follow him out the door.

DESPITE LIVING IN THE TWENTY-FIRST CENTURY AND THE internet being a true essential, clubs are advertised on a bulletin in the student center. So Ben and I are back on campus in a little study room with glass walls and a conference table. Colorful fliers with meeting locations and times are push-pinned into a corkboard.

His bodyguard waits silently at the door, but barely anyone roams the halls. It's a Friday night during the second week of college. Most students are probably having dorm parties or occupied with rush.

"Badminton Club?" Ben points to a bright yellow flyer.

"Sadly, I have never picked up a racquet of any kind." I see him eyeing the Ultimate Frisbee Club. "In fact...let's just steer clear of sports altogether. I don't remember the last time I did a push up."

He laughs. "You'd probably fit in better with my family than I do."

"I *highly* doubt that. I lived out of my car, remember?"

"Are we going to talk about that?" he asks me, tilting his head. "You were only seventeen." I bet he's wondering where my parents were at that point.

"Sixteen, actually," I say under my breath. "I called my Honda my home at sixteen." I add more loudly, "And there's nothing to talk about since I'm no longer living out of my car."

"Hmm...okay." He nods a couple times. "I'll drop it for now."

It's harder to tear my eyes off his baby blues. I'm trying not to be totally enamored with Ben, but he knows just how much to pry and let go at the right times. I like that about him. I don't think I have that skill.

Social butterflies are an interesting species. I could learn from him, but more so, I just really love being around him.

I force myself to focus, trying to search the bulletin board. But my head is somewhere else entirely. "So tell me about your brothers. If I'm going to see them tonight, I guess I should know more about them from a better source than Wikipedia."

His smile expands to new degrees.

I shield my eyes. "*Whoa*, it's like looking into the sun. You realize your teeth are perfect? Did you even go through an awkward puberty phase? Did you have braces? Pimples? An ugly wart on your toe—"

"Do you want to know more about me or my brothers?" he asks.

You. "Both."

"To clarify, this does mean you're coming to the party tonight?"

I jab a thumb toward the board. "You are helping me knock off an item on my list. It's only proper to pay it back, Friend."

Plus, it sounds fun to finally attend a party with someone and not just show up alone. Ben makes me feel like my goals won't crash and burn if I give into this one temptation. Maybe it'll even be worth it in the end.

"Something about my brothers..." Ben thinks hard as he peruses the corkboard. His gaze falls off the flyers and settles on me with a sudden intensity. "They called me to New York. Well, Beckett did first, technically. I had zero plans to move here, but they were insistent after what happened right before the summer."

The room suddenly feels smaller as if his words aren't meant for a space this large. I had no clue he's only here because his brothers begged him to come. I don't know what it's like to have family that actively *wants* me around them. But I'm stuck on his foreboding last words. *What happened right before the summer.* A nagging feeling tugs at my insides. I get the sense he wants me to ask, and I can't help the pull to want to know. It's not so I can jot down Ben's secrets in a diary or slip them to the tabloids for cash. It's just so I can understand him more.

My voice is almost a whisper as I ask, "What happened before the summer?"

THIRTEEN

BEN COBALT

"I'm not a good person," I warn Harriet. "Even when I try to be…" I take off my baseball cap, just to scrape a hand through my hair. Then I gesture to her with the hat. "You should probably sit for this."

Her brows furrow in a cuter scowl. "Afraid I'll faint?"

"You're the doctor-to-be, you tell me."

"I'm fine on my feet." She threads her arms over her chest. "You're not going to scare me away either."

"Yeah?" I sweep her up and down, how staunch and fixed she is. Harriet is a determined girl, but I didn't think her determination would revolve around me. "I was a little worried about that."

"I'm not going anywhere, Ben."

It catches me off guard, hearing her call me *Ben* and not Cobalt boy or Friend. She's craning her neck past comfort to even look at me, so I rest my ass against the edge of the conference table. At a lower height.

I thumb the Capybara bracelet around my wrist. "I've lied to my therapist for a long time—I have a therapist, by the way. Dr. Wheeler." Guess I should start there. "I've never gone to therapy to make myself feel better. First, it was so my parents wouldn't worry about me. Then it was to get prescribed Adderall."

She frowns. "Adderall?"

"I made him think that I needed it."

"So you're abusing the drug to…stay awake?"

"No, I didn't even take it. I gave it to this one asshole in prep school who wanted it. We made a deal. I supply him Adderall and then he'd stop harassing my best friend. And he did stop for a while. Then I graduated and…I figured he had no reason to keep picking on Winona. He was messing with her to get a reaction out of me, and I was no longer *there*."

"Winona Meadows?" She names my cousin, my ex-best friend, who is insanely private. It's ironic that Winona loves photography. Nearly every lock screen on my phone are pictures she's taken of forests, rivers, mountains, the sky. Yet, she can't stand when her face shows up in magazines. The tabloids all usually say the same thing:

Winona Meadows is just like her supermodel mom! Another bombshell sex symbol in the making!

It doesn't matter that her "supermodel" mom—my Aunt Daisy—has publicly stated she didn't have a great experience modeling.

We all deal with being the children of larger-than-life, globally-recognized parents, but because Winona looks so similar to her mom, it's harder in a different way.

It'll get worse for her when she turns eighteen in March. When she's no longer a minor and the media can print whatever the hell they want about her body. And I've seen her cling to her youth like it's the end of a lifeline.

I'm older than her, and she's always sort of chased after me. When I climbed a tree, she'd try and *try* to reach the branch I scaled.

I had to grab her hand and pull her higher.

That's how it's always felt between us. If I hiked through waist-deep mud in a creek, she'd be chin-deep, so I'd put her on my back.

She'd make these silly animal noises as a kid. Elephant, goat, koala, hyena. I thought they were hilarious. We laughed so much our voices would go hoarse.

We got older and older, and I didn't want to tug her into college life too early. I didn't want to ruin the last *good* she'd been experiencing. So I added physical and emotional distance between us.

I tell this all to Harriet—because I don't know how to describe what happened that night without describing Winona. It's about her.

And it should probably weigh on me sharing private details about a private girl, but I'm so *tangled* in this mess about Winona that it's more painful keeping it inside.

Who is Harriet even going to tell? I trust she won't run to a tabloid. I trust she won't narc to a stranger. I trust she'll protect this knowledge because it'd hurt another girl if she didn't.

I put my worn ballcap on the table behind me. "When I left for college, it's not like I was leaving Winona all alone. She has three other best friends. They're the four youngest girls in my family." I pause to see if she knows.

Recognition glints in her eyes. "Your sister is one?"

"Yeah, we kind of refer to them as the girl squad since they're all around the same age. It's Audrey Cobalt, Winona Meadows, Kinney Hale, and Vada Abbey."

"Vada…? I think I've heard of her, but hate to break it to you, I didn't do my homework on this one."

I smile a little. "How very un-Harriet of you."

"You mean un-Cobalt?"

"Ah, you're not a Cobalt yet. I haven't proposed, Friend."

Her cheeks go bright red. *Did I go too far?* I skim her features more, but she says, "Okay, you're fucking with me."

"Just a little bit." My smile widens, and honestly, I can't believe I'm even smiling while in the midst of describing this agonized past. A smile toys at her lips too. "I wouldn't fuck with you that hard, Harriet."

She drops her backpack to her feet. "Think I can't take it?"

"You probably could. I just prefer teasing lightly…gently."

Harriet studies me like I've been studying her. As our eyes brush and caress, blood drives south in my body. I wonder if she's picturing me in bed—because now I'm picturing her beneath the sheets in my arms.

I clutch the desk on either side of me. Pressing my fingers harder into the wood to keep my cock from throbbing. "So Vada?" I have to clear the arousal out of my throat.

"Who is she?" Harriet asks while shrugging off her oversized leather jacket. She must be hot. I glance at her belly button piercing. Red plaid pants ride low on her hips, and her white crop top is tight against her chest, her tits big for her small frame.

Yeah, my blood is still surging downward. I want to hook my finger in the very thin strap of her panties that just *barely* peek out. Mostly to see if she'd like my hands there.

I shake the thought away. *You need to get this out.* "Vada is related to the Meadows and Hales through my uncles. Not blood-related to me or any Cobalt."

"But you grew up together?"

"Yeah," I nod. "She went on a lot of the same family trips. She races bikes. BMX. Her and Winona are in the same grade, so they're really close. So when I went to Penn, I thought Winona would be okay, but Vada was…" I roll my eyes at myself, pissed off *at* myself. "Vada was bugging me *a lot* this year about Winona. Trying to get me to mend the friendship, and I just didn't want anything to do with it. For some reason I thought…" My eyes burn as I stare unblinkingly at a dark water stain on the carpet. "I thought when Vada said the asshole was being a dick to Winona again in school, she was trying to emotionally manipulate me to fix things with her. Tug on my heartstrings, you know?"

Harriet hops up on the table, sitting beside me. "Is Vada like that?"

I let out a laugh. "*No.* That's the stupid thing. She's *not*, but Winona kept saying everything was fine. She's never lied to me like that before, but I get why she didn't tell me the truth. I'd put this giant wall between us, and for the first time, I'd stopped helping her over it." My nose goes runny as emotion builds, and I wipe it with the side of my fist. "So I was a callous dick to Vada. She didn't understand why I was icing her out, why I was cold-shouldering Winona, and the whole time, I thought everything was fixed. Fine. Done."

A vicious knot cramps inside my chest, and I can't let it unravel. I've never really figured out how, not when I remember what happened next.

"Vada convinced Winona to finally tell me what was going on," I say in a tight breath. "Winona came to me *bawling* while describing how she thought she was drugged. *In school.* He put something in her water bottle, and she almost passed out in the bathroom."

Harriet goes still. "Did he…?"

I shake my head hard. "She called Vada in enough time." I look up at the ceiling. "Her bodyguard wasn't in the building. The administration at Dalton Academy was terrible and barely listened to our parents complain about the harassment. Even when I was there. This asshole's grandfather practically paid for the east wing of the prep school. He was old money, and some teachers thought we needed to get thicker skin because we were the 'famous' kids. Like we were exaggerating what was going on."

I pause to swallow the rock that, honestly, won't go down. So I uncap my water bottle, take a hefty swig, and I offer some to Harriet.

Before she takes a sip, she says, "I don't see how you're the bad guy in all of this."

"I lost it," I choke out. "That night, when Winona told me what he did, all I thought about was hurting him like he'd hurt her. So I went to his house with a bat. Smashed his Porsche. Smashed him. He wasn't moving, Harriet. I almost…I almost killed him. I think I would've, but Donnelly—"

"Donnelly?"

"Yeah, Xander's bodyguard. He was the one on my security detail that night. He got me off him before I did any permanent damage." I run my tongue over my molars. "I'd say he saved me, but funny thing is, I didn't want to be saved." I blink a few times, my eyes on fire. "I scared my family. It's one thing to enact revenge *together*. Another thing to do it alone. They think I've been suffering *alone*." I glance over at her now. "Maybe they're right. But there were just too many variables if I involved them. Too many things could go wrong."

She caps the water bottle slowly, then passes it back to me with a deepening frown. "You really think that?"

"Yeah," I nod assuredly. "I do." I stare at her laced combat boots. "After Winona told her parents what happened, she decided that she wanted to go to an all-girls school for her senior year. *Boarding school.* She's not too far from here in Upstate New York. Vada went with her. It's another reason my sister has been so upset this year. I left Philly. Two of her closest friends left Philly. She only has Kinney Hale now."

"Why'd your sister stay behind?" Harriet asks.

"She won't admit it, but Audrey is pretty attached to our mom and dad. She's only sixteen. I don't think she was ready to live without them yet."

"I can't blame her." Harriet unwraps a Jolly Rancher, and it reminds me that she was sixteen and living in a Honda. Even without all the facts, it's hard not to feel anger toward her mom and dad for deserting their teenage daughter. I try to let it go as she tells me, "If I had your parents, I'd probably never leave them behind, no offense."

"None taken." I smile down at her. "Leaving anyone you love behind is the hardest thing in the world, but if you ask my Uncle Ryke, he'd say the hardest things are usually the right things."

She swishes the candy in her mouth. "Does Meadows wisdom even apply to a Cobalt?"

I hope it does. "Seems universal to me." I hop off the desk, then clasp her hand and tug her onto her feet. She stays at my side as I approach the bulletin, and I tear off a neon-orange flyer from its pushpin and flash it to her. "What about this one?"

"Board Game Club?"

"No push-ups required."

Her teeny-tiny smile returns, then she reads the fine print. "It looks like they're gathering to play Catan next. That's a strategy board game, right? I've never played before."

"Yeah. It's not too hard. Beckett loves it, so I've played a handful of times."

"Better than chess?" she teases since I said Chess Club was off-limits.

I almost laugh. "I can handle Catan for you, Fisher. Don't worry about me."

"I'll try not to, Friend." Her budding smile is now drawing mine even higher. Yeah, we're making each other smile. My chest feels lighter, and it takes me a second to realize something.

We've never let go of our hands.

FOURTEEN

BEN COBALT

No fucking way.

I reread the address on my phone ten times before it starts sinking in. Eliot didn't give me directions to a party. Sure, I thought The Labyrinth Library was an odd name for a nightclub, but I figured he found some Edgar Allan Poe themed hangout spot.

It'd be on brand for my Poe-loving brother.

Cabs honk in the distance. The night sky is a cloudy haze, and rain has quit pouring. I'm staring at a typical brownstone with a tiny brass plaque for a sign that feels less like an underground club and more like I'm being duped.

My brothers have to be inside. Seeing as how all four of their bodyguards are congregated on the wet cement steps. They stop shooting the shit as soon as I appear with Harriet and Novak. My bodyguard gives them a friendly wave from the sidewalk and joins them outside the entrance. I'm guessing the venue is secure. Maybe even private if they're not going in with us.

Harriet scrolls on her phone after I tell her I never looked up The Labyrinth Library on the internet. I just plugged it into Maps with an abundance of trust. I didn't think Eliot would go so far as to prank me. Not when he wants me to live in New York.

"Okay, I found it on Yelp." Harriet squints as she reads. "Four point seven stars. Oh..."

"Oh? Oh, what?" I try to read over her head. "Did he send us to a porn shop or something?"

"Better. It's an escape room."

What the fuck.

"Eliot," I groan out from my chest.

"Eliot?" She pushes her frizzing bangs out of her hostile eyes. "What'd he trick you on purpose?"

"Probably, yeah."

Her gaze darkens. "I was joking."

"He's a master of chaos. Will enact elaborate plots to repair broken friendships in the family." I grimace at the brownstone. "The amount of times he's tried to stick me and Xander together is obnoxious and impressive. But it's never worked. It will *never* work." I see pretty quickly that Donnelly isn't among the bodyguards on the concrete steps, so Xander can't be here.

It's not about the Hales.

This is about my immediate family. About my brothers and me. I comb a hand through my hair, my hat tucked in my back pocket. Agitation amasses. "No, you know what, I'd have preferred shopping for dildos and anal plugs over this."

She slides me a wide-eyed look. "Seriously?"

"Seriously. Having to do an escape room with my brothers sounds nightmare-fueled."

She tosses her phone in her black-studded messenger bag. Chains are strung across the zippered pockets. We'd taken a pit stop at her apartment where she left her backpack, thinking we were going to a *club*. Now she's telling me, "We don't have to go if you don't want to. Pretty sure I saw a sex shop two blocks away."

I almost laugh but I can't tell if she's joking, not even as her stormy ocean blues meet mine. I can't really tell what *she* wants to do.

I'd honestly go anywhere with Harriet. It's her company I'm seeking above everything else, and I wonder if she'd rather bail now that plans have changed.

Meeting my brothers all at once isn't a miniscule thing either. They're a powerful force, and it'd be nerve-wracking for anyone to walk into a Cat 5 hurricane. Even a girl who has weapons for eyes.

Cars fly past us. City lights flicker in the misty night, but I'm only staring at her.

"Fisher," I say in a calmer breath.

"Friend." Her lips inch up in one of those pinched smiles.

"What are your thoughts on escape rooms?" I ask her.

She hugs her leather jacket to her frame as a gust of wind comes through. "Never been to one." Her eyes linger on the door. "I've seen videos though, and they look like giant logic puzzles. Could be fun, I guess."

"You choose," I say. "Sex shop, escape room, or an actual club we find on Yelp."

"And if I choose a sex shop?" she says like I'm nuts. But every time I give Harriet more of my trust, I'm stepping on a high wire. It's an adrenaline rush. A euphoric hit.

"Then we go pick out some fun toys." I plaster on a smile that she immediately scowls at.

Her brows almost touch together as she thinks harder. "You know what, *no*. I'm not going to be the reason you bail on your brothers. One hates me already. I don't need all four to be on the Anti-Harriet train. You choose."

I hadn't thought about that, but she is right. My brothers might blame her if I dip out on them this time, and then they might not include her in any other invites. That sounds shittier than evading this whole trap.

"Escape room it is."

FIFTEEN

BEN COBALT

We enter the dusty, dimly lit brownstone. The heavy door *thunks* as I shut it behind us. Harriet sneezes into her elbow.

"Bless you," I say.

"Thank—" She sneezes again. I keep a protective hand on her shoulder, unsure of what we're actively walking into. Other than a musty, dingy-looking library.

Weathered texts line floor-to-ceiling, dark oak bookshelves. Globes and old artifacts pile on towering stacks of hardbacks. If someone told me we entered a movie set for an 1800s antique bookshop, I'd believe them.

I touch the top of her head, rounding her body. "Stay behind me, yeah?"

She doesn't protest. "Scared I might sneeze up a dust storm?"

"More like I'm afraid bats will come flying at us."

"Bats?" Her light brown brows vault into her uneven bangs. "I do *not* want to have to take the rabies vaccine. I don't care if they're not as painful as they used to be, it's a *series* of shots, Ben."

I slip her a smile. "You're scared of needles?" It'd be ironic since she's pre-med, but it's not that outlandish to me. So many times, I feel like I'm too many conflicting things at once.

"It's just my pain tolerance…it's not that high." Red flush creeps up her neck, like this is an embarrassing trait. I wonder if her parents told her to "suck it up" a lot.

"That's why I'm taking one for the team. Stay behind me, petit oiseau."

Harriet tucks herself closer to my back, and I reach behind me and hold her hand. Her grip is much tighter than it'd been earlier tonight in the study room.

We go farther into the disorganized foyer. No one is seated at the ornate wooden podium. I tap a brass bell. It dings. Harriet looks left and right, up and down, and as her fear subsides, I spot her intrigue.

"Okay, this is cool," she whispers like we're in a real library.

No one responds to the bell. So we follow muffled voices down a winding footpath. It's not a hall exactly. Stacks of leather-bound hardbacks on the floor create partitions and leave a twisting, curving space that guides us forward.

The sheer number of books reminds me of a shop in Italy called Libreria Acqua Alta. One hot summer day during a family vacation in Venice, my eldest brother did his typical routine of wandering off.

Charlie was fifteen at the time, and a fleet of bodyguards fanned out to try to locate him in the maze of Venetian streets. I was eleven and hanging around my dad when he had the idea to check Libreria Acqua Alta. We found Charlie inside with one of the bookstore's tabby cats circling his legs. He'd been flipping through *La Divina Commedia* by Dante Alighieri like nothing was out of the ordinary.

Instead of lecturing Charlie, our dad talked to him about Dante and the Inferno.

It pissed me off. Charlie gets special treatment because he's *Charlie*. Because he's a genius stuck inside a world that will never understand him.

I don't pretend to understand what torments Charlie. I just hate how the same grace isn't offered to me.

You feel everything. I feel nothing.

His gutting, mind-fucking words from the apartment ring in my ears as we walk toward the muffled voices and come into a vintage parlor. On instinct, I want to leave. I'd rather play Frogger in city traffic than be in breathing distance from Charlie.

I look down at Harriet. At how her scowl intensifies to "fuck you" levels. At how she keeps her determined gaze forward. At how she's here for me.

And then I want to stay.

We step into the parlor. Black lacquer walls, ornate gold-framed portraits of revolutionaries on horseback, red velvet Chesterfield sofas, and an oil painted ceiling of gods in fluffy clouds immerse us in a regal space reminiscent of sitting rooms in Versailles.

Flames flicker in a roaring fireplace, and I feel the heat in the confined space as we arrive.

All four of my brothers go silent and turn their heads. They resemble a still frame. A photograph out of an issue in Vogue, and I'm not sure what's more magnanimous. Them or the gods illustrated above us.

Beckett brings a lit cigarette to his lips, his lithe movements too compelling. It's impossible to look away. He has on a black leather jacket and dark jeans, and for as calm as Beckett is, his yellow-green eyes can puncture with unmitigated intensity. He's assessing Harriet—since he's only ever heard of her. I bring her up a lot during our breakfasts together. He takes a long drag, then passes the cigarette to Charlie.

Eliot grips a high shelf on a bookcase. He chose a khaki trench coat for the occasion, unsurprisingly on theme. The polished buttons and tailored fit seem expensive enough that I'm positive it's designer. Tom is sitting on top of a club chair, his Sharpie-doodled Vans on the cushion. He's in ripped jeans and a black muscle shirt.

Charlie looks the most editorial. Standing near the fireplace in black slacks and an oversized black cardigan with a deep V-neck, clearly not wearing a shirt underneath, he pinches the cigarette and fixates on *me*.

Harriet releases a tensed breath. She stiffens, then tears her hand out of mine. It's very clear they notice.

I'm not hurt. She's crossing her arms as a defensive measure. If I thought she couldn't handle them, I wouldn't have invited her here.

Charlie casually leans an arm against the wall and cuts an annoyed look between Harriet and me. "Nice of you to show up." He sucks on the cigarette while checking his watch. "Twenty minutes late." He blows smoke in my direction.

I narrow my eyes and waft the air. "I didn't know this was time sensitive. I thought we were going to a club."

Beckett swings an accusatory look at Eliot. "You lied to him?"

"I didn't think he'd show if he knew it was an escape room," Eliot confesses without a hint of remorse. And he's not wrong.

I would have rejected him. Again.

Charlie returns the cigarette to Beckett. "There's this thing called Google." He lifts his brows at me. "But of course you didn't look it up."

I glower. "Yeah, because I didn't think my own brother would lie to me."

Beckett slices a powerful, warning look to Charlie like *shut up*. Whatever Charlie was going to say next remains a mystery because he thankfully goes quiet.

Placing a hand on Harriet's shoulder, I introduce her. "This is Harriet Fisher. She's my friend at MVU."

"We know who she is," Tom says, the spite in his voice clear. Beckett lets out an exasperated sigh, and I wonder if he had a pep talk with the rest of our brothers to *be nice*.

I warn Tom, "Don't be a dick to her."

"It's fine, Ben." Harriet stares Tom down like she's the headlights and he's the deer caught in her way. "I know who you are too."

Tom flips open a silver Zippo lighter. "Let's hear it, Harry. Who am I?"

"Okay, *Tommy*. Lead singer of The Carraways. Horrible taste in music." She'll have to strike harder to land a blow in my unyielding family. I don't love that Tom is egging her on, but at least she's not backing down.

"*I* have horrible taste in music?" Tom makes a face. "Says a girl who's trying to be an Avril Lavigne knockoff. Where'd you get those pants? Hot Topic."

She glares. "At least my vocals didn't sound like shit in my most recent live performance."

Tom stews. "At least I have live performances."

"Probably not for long."

That strikes a nerve. Tom chokes on a coarse noise. "*You* begged *me* to be in *my* band."

"And I might've improved it, but you'll never know."

Tom spreads his arms. "A mystery I don't care to solve."

"Glad we're here to solve one you're interested in," she slings back.

Eliot has moved closer to Tom, as if to aid him in battle. Charlie and Beckett are exchanging indecipherable looks from across the parlor.

I never leave Harriet's side.

Frustrated, Tom spins to Eliot for backup. "Dude?"

"'Though she be but little she is fierce'," Eliot quotes. I almost laugh, which slices through the tension.

Tom groans. "You did not just whip out the Shakespeare for her."

Charlie rolls his eyes. "You act like he reserves it for special people. He's a walking lexicon of sixteenth century plays."

Eliot takes a dramatic bow, then steals the Zippo from Tom. The lighter actually belongs to Eliot, and he clicks it shut with one swooping motion. "Shall we begin, brothers and Harriet?"

"Please," Beckett says smoothly, blowing more smoke away from us.

Eliot wags his brows playfully at Harriet while he approaches me. Her scowl deepens, and he laughs while he hands me a sheet of paper with game instructions. He's a natural flirt, but I'm not even marginally threatened by my brother.

For one, I'm confident if we were competing for a girl's attention, I'd win in the end if I wanted the W. But mostly, Eliot would never hit on a girl I brought over. The depth of that betrayal would eviscerate him inside-out. So in a lot of ways, I will always and forever trust my brothers, even when they deceive me. The intent is always pure.

Mine is too.

I take the instructions, having trouble concentrating on the typed font when some tension still swarms the parlor.

From what I can tell, Eliot seems to like Harriet. Charlie has zero opinion of her so far, and Beckett watches my reaction more than hers. I didn't expect to be most worried about my favorite brother, but if he continues being this overly observant of me, I might have problems.

Fuck.

Yeah…I'm hiding a lot from them. Like being broke. Like *why* I have money issues in the first place.

I don't need Beckett digging too hard tonight. Before I figure out how to shrug off the attention, a man—wearing what I can only guess is a Sherlock Holmes costume—pops into the room.

"Welcome to The Labyrinth Library. The exit door is about to be locked, and it will remain locked until you find the key. No phones are allowed once the game begins." He holds out a basket for us to deposit our phones.

I'm about to chuck mine in there.

"Wait," Beckett says while putting his phone to his ear. He's calling his bodyguard to come collect our cellphones for us, not trusting this game master guy to hold on to them.

No phones. Stuck in a room with my brothers. Only one way out.

Sounds like the start to a very big disaster.

I'M GOING TO KILL HIM. MURDER SEEMS A REASONABLE solution after I learn that Eliot chose an escape room *without* a time limit. Meaning, it doesn't end in an hour if we don't get the key. We're fucking stuck here.

Ten minutes in—and I've never been more goal-oriented in my life.

After a quick sweep of the parlor, we discover three different padlocks in the room. The first on a drawer of an antique desk, the second attached to a tin box, and the third locking a cupboard of an apothecary cabinet. It's clear we need to find three keys to open the padlocks. Hopefully that'll lead us to the final clue for a way to exit the escape room.

Charlie has plopped down on the couch to read *Far from the Madding Crowd*—as if this isn't a team activity. Tom thinks the color of the books matter and is meticulously rearranging hardbacks on a bowed, wobbly shelf. Eliot and Beckett hover over an ink-blotched map spread on the antique desk, while Harriet and I comb through the apothecary cabinet for clues.

"That went really horrible, sorry," Harriet whispers fast, her gaze darting to the bookcase where Tom balances on a chair to reach the highest shelf.

"I think it actually went well." I give her a slanted smile.

She crunches down on a hard candy. "You're full of shit."

"No, really." I rifle through the glass vials in the apothecary cabinet, not sure what I'm looking for. "You stood up for yourself and you didn't piss off any of my other brothers. Honestly, it couldn't have gone any better."

She expels a deeper breath.

I eye her. "That was weighing on you?"

"Noooo," she draws out with thick sarcasm. "I *totally* came in here expecting to start a fight with Tom." She makes a lackluster hoorah motion. "I even brought ammunition. Bombs. Knives. Brass knuckles."

"Okay, Killer," I say into a laugh.

Her lips quirk in an almost-smile. It's hard to look away. Hell, it's hard not to pull her away somewhere more private so I can try to eke that smile out more. I don't get a chance to imagine it further because Eliot sidles near and hangs an arm over my shoulder.

"How are we doing?" he asks.

"Terrible," I say seriously since we're no closer to finding a key than we were fifteen minutes ago.

"Terribly amazing," Eliot rephrases. "We're Cobalts, brother. We can solve anything." He gives my broad shoulders a motivating squeeze, then picks up a leather-bound book. He acts like its yellowed pages carry the answer for point-two seconds before chucking it disinterestedly over his shoulder.

It thumps to the ruby red rug. Beckett trains his eyes on the discarded book, then the crooked shelves where Tom repositions texts, then the several papers scattered over the antique desk. With tension in his hand, he lights another cigarette and leaves the mess to sit on the sofa beside Charlie.

I watch Charlie rise while reading, and without looking, he scoops up the fallen book and slides it on one of Tom's shelves. "Your theory about the color isn't going to amount to anything," Charlie says. "Move on to—"

"Don't tell me," Tom whisper-hisses. "Dude, you promised you wouldn't help until an hour in. What gives?"

"You're taking too long," Charlie sneers. "*Hurry.*"

Tom doesn't see me staring, and Eliot has uncorked a cabernet. He drinks from the bottle of wine while making leisure laps around the parlor.

Yeah, only Harriet seems intent on figuring out how to open the padlock. She's filling vials with a glittery pink liquid from a carafe, then balances them on a brass scale.

"We *just* got here," Tom tells Charlie, not quietly enough. "You can't solve this in under five minutes flat like last time. A—it's no fun, and B—this is literally the *only* night we've gotten him to come out with us."

Guilt returns like a sledgehammer.

Charlie is glaring at Tom like he's the problem now.

"Chill, dude," Tom retorts. "We're all doing things we don't want to do tonight. You think I love being locked in a room with her?"

Harriet isn't listening. She's now pouring liquid out of a bulbous glass vial.

My pulse beats harder in my ears.

"Your issues with her can be resolved in a handful of different ways," Charlie says, "but you choose to harbor animosity because you don't enjoy life without *conflict*. You and Eliot thrive on strife."

"You are the main supplier," Tom quips with an impish grin, never letting Charlie dig under his skin. "You hear that, Eliot Alice? Charlie's got us clocked. We thrive on strife."

"Trouble is empty without us," Eliot decrees, then swigs wine and flips another book onto the floor.

Charlie looks thoroughly annoyed. Which causes Tom to grin even wider. "Don't start a war you can't win, Charlie Keating."

"There is no winner in a war against brothers," Charlie says plainly, and briefly, so very briefly, his eyes reach mine. It knocks me back a step, and I shift around, not sure what I feel other than this amalgamation of guilt, hurt, longing, and fear.

"Truer words," Eliot golf claps against the wine bottle.

I move out of Harriet's way so I don't impede her pursuit of a new vial. My chest is tight, especially as Beckett shuts his eyes. Charlie sees him, then tells Tom, "Let me solve this—"

"Charlie, I'm fine," Beckett cuts in, massaging his temple with the cigarette between two fingers. He opens his eyes on him. "We don't need to rush out of here."

"Isn't that the point?" I interject, feeling their attention redirect on me. I glance from each of my brothers. "We should want to *escape*."

"We just want to spend some quality time with you, Ben Pirrip," Tom says.

I open my mouth to say there are better ways, but are there? They've orchestrated this for me. To be with me. Because I keep shoving them away at every turn. So many people would beg for one brother who'd go through this amount of effort to be with them—and I have four.

Yeah, even Charlie. Though, he likely got dragged here by Beckett.

I meet Harriet's eyes while she corks a vial. *Ruthless love*, she once said about my family. She's never known love this deep, and I hate that I can't even let myself enjoy this time with them.

I can't relax.

Relax. Enjoy this. "Yeah, that's what we're doing," I tell them. "I'm here."

Eliot raises his bottle by the neck. "A cause for celebration." After a large swig, he hands me the wine. I take a swig too, the rich liquid going down smooth, and I offer some to Harriet.

She surprisingly sips from the bottle, then licks the red residue off her lips. *I want to kiss her.* The blip of a thought skips my pulse.

Looking away, I laugh when Eliot jumps on a towering stack of books and nearly busts his ass, but he manages to catch his balance.

Tom cackles too. Then laughter streams from Beckett, and the lively noise fills my lungs in ways I love. For a second, I even think Charlie might have a shadow of a smile.

"Gods and mortal lady," Eliot announces, "I hereby sanction tonight as a secret family affair. What happens within these four walls on this foggy night is to be protected and never misused. By Cobalt decree, we all promise one another. Say aye if spoken true."

"Aye," Beckett smiles.

"Aye." Tom pumps a fist in the air.

"Yes," Charlie agrees.

I nod, more tensed as all my brothers focus on me. "Aye."

They look to Harriet. She shifts her weight, her eyes darting up to me. "Aye, I guess?" She hands me the wine bottle, then asks in a whisper, "Are we playing the escape game or…?"

"I think they're just trying to bond with me," I murmur back. They're trying to reach me. I'm floating in the night, drifting farther and farther away into darkness, and they're reeling me back in.

Part of me aches for them to succeed. The other part is terrified if they ever do.

I down a bigger swig. My muscles try to constrict.

Eliot hops off the book tower, then flips open the Zippo, a flame in hand. He's been spending most of his time auditioning for new plays in the city. "I tried to do the jobless wandering routine like Charlie, but it's beneath me," he told me last night after he said he might be cast in *The Mousetrap*, an Agatha Christie murder mystery. So I'm not surprised he's treating this outing together like a rehearsal.

Harriet tentatively picks up another vial. "Why does he look like he's one step away from sacrificing a virgin?"

"Because he's Eliot," I say as if that explains everything. Honestly, I'm smiling so wide now that my face starts hurting.

Eliot spins on Harriet. "Is there a virgin in this room to be sacrificed, mortal lady?" He must've heard her.

She's scowling. "You tell me."

"Gladly."

SIXTEEN

BEN COBALT

Eliot raises and lowers his brows with a gleam in his eyes. Surprise freezes Harriet for a beat. Maybe she thought they'd be more tight-lipped about their lives, but she basically just took an oath to not spill anything outside of this room. Eliot gestures an arm out to Beckett on the sofa. "Virgin?"

"You're many years too late," Beckett says, cigarette burning between his fingers. He brings it to his lips.

"Charlie?" Eliot flicks his Zippo closed, then back open. "How virginal are you, brother?"

"Not at all." He's still irritated. I hear it in his voice, and he's scrutinizing the map on the antique desk from afar.

"Care to elaborate?" Eliot prods. "The people want to know."

"*You* want to know," Charlie rephrases, "and you will never."

"Challenge accepted, dear brother," Eliot grins, and at this, Charlie bends toward Beckett to whisper in his ear. He whispers back, ignoring Eliot, who's telling Harriet, "If sex were a competition, I'm fairly certain I'd claim the victory." He motions toward Tom. "Virgin?"

"Nope." Tom flips through a book while standing on the chair. "Our only virginal hope is our baby brother and his girlfriend."

"We're not dating," Harriet clarifies first. "*Friends.*" She emphasizes, pointing between us.

I nod once in agreement, but it's hard not to study her reactions. Would she want more? My cock twitches at the thought. *Fuck.*

I take a hearty swig to drown the arousal. Afterward, Eliot plucks the wine bottle from my grip and asks, "You're friends who fuck? Or non-fucking friends?"

"The latter," I say while flush bathes Harriet's cheeks. I'm very used to the constant prying, so it's not really fazing me. But just so she knows, I tell her, "You don't have to share if you've slept with anyone before."

"Thanks." Harriet moves the candy in her mouth while she assesses this situation. "But it's not a big bad secret." She places the half-filled vial on the scale as she tells Eliot, "Not a virgin."

"What a revelation," Charlie says dryly while checking the time on his irreplaceable Philippe Dufour watch.

Eliot smiles deviously at me. "And Ben? You lose it yet?" He knows this answer. Just like he knew none of us are virgins.

"Several years ago. Thanks for the condoms, by the way." I asked Eliot if he had any the night of Homecoming. I'd thought there'd be a chance I'd go all the way with Courtney, but I didn't have time to run to a drugstore and buy them.

"I have plenty more wherever the night may bring you." His eyes ping from me to Harriet and back to me with a Cheshire grin. Seconds from playing the part of Cupid.

Fucking Eliot. No one in their right mind would give him a bow and arrow and let him be a matchmaker. He can't even fix my decayed friendship with Xander. He doesn't repair. He destroys.

"No thanks, dude," Harriet says, biting on her candy. "I already have condoms. I don't need anything of yours." She studies the apothecary cabinet again, leaving an intrigued Eliot in her wake.

He tips his head to me. "Does she always look like she's about to rip off a cock?"

"Pretty much."

He laughs and pats me on the back, "I'd say protect your balls, but maybe you like the challenge."

"I don't think it's that," I whisper, even knowing Harriet feels like a flighty, rabid bat that might bite if caught. She *is* a challenge, but that's not what interests me the most about her. I like how she might feel the safest with me—that I'm a place of solace for her when she's never had a good place to land.

I want to wrap my arms around her. Protect her. Give her security and the kind of love she's lacked her entire life. I feel it gnawing at me like a hunger I won't be able to feed. Because of my plan.

I'm leaving.

Still, I can't stop fixating on how much I like her. On how when I return to her side at the cabinet, she hands me a vial and orders me around like I'm her lab partner. How she's trusting me to pour the liquid when she should know I'm a hundred times more focused on her. On how she blows out a disgruntled breath from her lips and squats to jerk open a cabinet drawer. On her furrowed brows that pinch harder with concentration.

She catches me smiling at her, and blush coats her cheeks again. I want to say, *yeah, I'm checking you out right now when I shouldn't be.*

I shouldn't fucking do this with her.

But I. Can't. Stop.

I love how she's overpowering this edged panic inside me. I'm not fixating on the possible worst outcomes of tonight. Or any dangers present. For once, I let myself have fun with my brothers.

All of us but Charlie have returned to the quest at hand, and fifteen minutes through, Harriet has balanced the correct weight on the brass scale. Fake lightning flashes through the room, along with the sounds of thunder. Then the fireplace extinguishes, and a metal cigar box drops onto the faux logs.

I blow a loud two-finger whistle, then clap for Harriet. "That was all you, Fisher."

Beckett and Eliot applaud her with rising grins of pride. Tom's hearty yet reluctant claps—like the sheer effort is pulling teeth—make me laugh.

"It was nothing," Harriet says, shying from my gaze while she treks over to the logs.

It takes me aback. No one but Harriet has solved a single part of this escape room yet. "That was not nothing."

She shrugs, minimizing what was an achievement she should be stuffing in all our faces.

Beckett slips me a furtive look. "Auto-dérisoire." *Self-deprecating.*

Eliot adds, "Doux." *Meek.*

I don't believe she's either of these things, but I'd love for her to celebrate her intelligence. It's worth the applause. Defending Harriet is an instinct, and I shoot back to my brothers, "Elle peut être sans prétention." *She can be unpretentious.*

Beckett raises his hands, saying he's not attacking. "Ce n'est pas un mal à moins que quelqu'un ne la fasse se sentir petite." *It's not bad unless someone made her feel small.*

Eliot narrows his gaze. "Cette personne devra mourir." *That person must die.*

Dramatic as fuck and on brand for my family, yeah, and my flexed muscles are agreeing with the sentiment. I head over to Harriet as she pops open the metal cigar box and retrieves the first key. After unlocking the cupboard of the apothecary cabinet, she finds a slip of paper to a three-part riddle.

with pointed fangs I sit and wait

This is going to take a while, and I catch myself smiling. Excited about it. Beckett and I work on the map together.

"This is pointing to the sconces on the wall," Beckett draws his finger over the inky line. "We probably need to reposition the lights."

Tom leaps off the chair to rotate the lights toward the ceiling, which illuminates a code for the antique desk.

Beckett and I share a grin as we roll the numbers into the steel padlock. It clicks, and we find a key to the third drawer. Inside, we discover the second piece to the riddle. Eliot tries to read the creased paper in my hand, but his brows scrunch in a way I've seen a thousand times growing up.

"Here." I hand it to him, thinking maybe he just needs a closer look and extra time to process the written scrawl. On occasion that's all it takes, or maybe he fakes it really well, making me believe he can comprehend it when he still can't. This time, though, he passes the paper back.

"Read it to me."

"'*With piercing force I crunch out fate,*'" I tell Eliot, and I hope he knows I think he's one of the most impressive people in our family. More so than Charlie. He has such a severe case of dyslexia, but it never stopped him from having a passion for literature or pursuing a career in the arts. He could've so easily been the jock of the Cobalt Empire, outperforming me in hockey, but he never did what came easy. He did what he loved. Above all else.

I should tell him before I go.

The sudden thought overturns my stomach. Reminding me this is finite. My time with them isn't forever.

All that's left is the key to the tin box for the last section of the riddle. It stumps us for the next ten minutes. Like Charlie said, Tom's theory about the color of the hardbacks comes to a dead end.

Harriet and I are on the floor flipping through books for a clue. Tom has dumped the drawers and broken half the vials. Glass litters the rug and hardwood. Eliot wrenches the paintings off the wall, tearing the canvas out of its frame. He checks for hidden messages but finds nothing.

It looks like a violent storm swept through the room. There is shit *everywhere*. The mess isn't bothering me, but I notice how

Beckett is back on the sofa. He smokes while rereading the one-sentence riddles on both slips of paper. I'm betting he's trying to block out the demolition around him.

Charlie seems more in tune with Beckett. He slams his book closed, then catches me staring at him.

My joints solidify to concrete. Charlie has a way of making me feel like a lightning bug trapped in a glass jar. I'm about to avert my attention when he suddenly asks me, "Why her?"

Harriet freezes.

I tighten my gaze on him. "What do you mean?"

"Why *bring* her?" he clarifies with aggravation. Being stuck in this room is making him more of an asshole. He rakes a hand through his golden-brown hair, tugging at the strands, especially when Tom shatters *another* vial. Beckett snuffs out his cigarette on a marble ashtray.

Charlie stands.

"I'm fine," Beckett says smoothly. "*Charlie. S'il te plaît.*" *Please.*

"He's fine," Eliot pipes in.

Charlie changes direction to Tom, and I hope his glare remains there. "Stop breaking shit. You're so far off, it's embarrassing."

"I'm not trying to amaze you, Charlie Keating." Tom frisbees a top hat to Eliot, who catches it and flips it on his head. Then Eliot opens a black umbrella indoors, not superstitious at all. He takes after our dad in that way, but Tom is cringing like he now eternally cursed himself. "Dude, no."

"*Ben,*" Charlie recaptures my attention, unfortunately. "Why her?"

Harriet busies herself with the stack of books, but tension cinches the air.

"She's my friend," I defend.

He sets his ass against the armrest. "I've seen your phone contacts. You have a million numbers, but why haven't we met any of your so-called friends besides her?"

"Dealing drugs, baby brother?" Eliot quips, but there is concern behind the joke. Because he's not sure if it's untrue.

They don't know about the Adderall. Just that I beat the shit out of Tate Townsend for what he did to Winona. Yeah, the asshole has a name. I just don't like remembering it.

"You've met my teammates from prep school—"

"That's not the same as this," Charlie cuts me off. "You know this is different. Why her?"

"What's with the inquisition?"

"There is none," Beckett says softly. "That's not what tonight is about." I believe him, but I also believe they want to dig deeper into what's going on with me and they're afraid I'll bolt if they come at me with every weapon in their arsenal.

They wouldn't be wrong.

I ease a lot, but Charlie is subzero frost. His cold sights turn on Harriet, and I worry enough that I tell Eliot, "One time, I did deal drugs." It causes everyone to look at me. "I gave a guy Adderall."

They go quiet. Motionless. I only hear the crunch of glass under Tom's sneakers as he shifts his weight.

"To whom?" Eliot asks.

"Tate Townsend. I made a deal to stop him from messing with Winona. It obviously didn't stick."

"Shit," Beckett curses with a deep frown, likely realizing why my rage was a level twelve that night.

Charlie cocks his head. "How'd you get the Adderall in the first place?" I hate how he's always asking the hardest questions.

"Another friend." It's not a total lie. I am *friendly* with my therapist.

"You conveniently have many of those," he says as if I'm so transparent.

"Maybe if you had a friend you'd understand," I counter, the guilt balling up as soon as I launch a mini grenade.

Charlie arches his brows, unaffected. "You're right, I have none. My definition of friendship differs from yours, and under my definition, I have a feeling you'd have only...*one*." He snaps his finger and points at Harriet, then gives her a sardonic wave with the same hand.

She's stiff as a board on her knees, unsure of what to do.

I rise to my feet and block her from his direct line of sight. Charlie lets out a dry laugh. "You think I'm going to hurt your little girlfriend? All you're doing is showing me you have another vulnerability. Add that on to the never-ending list of ways to make you cry."

"Because I'm so easy to attack."

"Yeah, you are," Charlie states plainly. "You are so susceptible to manipulation that you got conned into giving some prick Adderall, and he *still* drugged your former best friend—"

I shoot forward as rage blisters inside me, but Eliot is fast and captures my shoulders, tugging me away from Charlie who didn't even flinch. Does Charlie want me to punch him? Is that it? Is he seeking a fist to the fucking face?

"Can we not?" Tom asks him.

I'm zeroed in on Charlie, and if he wants to feel something, then I know exactly where to strike. "The world thinks you're so much like *Dad*, but you are a sick, *malignant* version of him."

His Adam's apple bobs, but his face carries no emotion. No response. "I guess that makes you the most pathetic version then."

"No," Beckett nearly groans, and I jerk in Eliot's hold, trying to launch forward to *hit* my oldest brother. The urge bangs through me like a pinball made of corrosive metal.

Charlie weaves his arms casually over his chest. Then he leans over to peer past my body, eyeing Harriet. "Does this turn you on?" He's referring to my anger.

"Fuck off," I growl out.

"I'd say *get thicker skin and maybe I will*, but I don't enjoy lacerating fragile things. I prefer ripping into people who can take it." He's calling me weak.

"People who can take it," I repeat hotly. "Like Moffy?" They've been in so many fistfights. Yet, I've never been able to land a blow against Charlie. I could've injured him out of aggravation and pent-up fury so many times, but someone is always there to separate us. I can't tell if it's methodical. If he provokes me during moments where he knows it won't end in physical violence.

Because when Moffy and Charlie go at it, blood is spilled. And it's not as if Charlie is more scared of my fists—because our cousin is stronger than me...I guess in every way that matters to Charlie.

His jaw muscle tics. "You love Moffy so much then where is he now?" He makes a mocking show of canvassing the parlor with a cutting gaze. "Maximoff Hale, are you around? Your least favorite cousin wishes you were here."

Least favorite. I try not to let it sting.

"Moffy loves you," Beckett tells me with certainty. "Charlie, that's enough."

"It's not even a morsel of what I could do."

Harriet shoves past me. "What the fuck is wrong with you?"

Charlie only stares at me. "Let her fight for you. Maybe you'll survive this harsh fucking world if you do."

I blink a few times, my eyes searing raw. "I'm not defenseless on my own, *Charlie*. You think I don't know when I'm being played?"

"If you do know and you willingly walk into a trap, then you're not just naïve—you're a *fool*."

They can't know I'm broke.

Ever.

My muscles cramp.

"Lay off him, Boy Genius." Harriet glowers.

Charlie barely acknowledges her. "You're not clever."

"And I don't believe you're that smart," she retorts. "You're just a bitter fucking *asshole*."

He's about to respond when a shrill noise *blares* through the parlor. *WEE-WOO! WEE-WOO!!*

It's a siren. *Fuck.* My hands fly to my ears, the sound louder than a fire alarm. We're all on our feet. My first thought is *Harriet.* She digs the heels of her palms into her ears and jerks her head to the door, signaling me to go. I rush over to it and turn the knob. Locked.

Shit—we're still locked in here. I rake a hot hand through my hair. Beckett comes beside me, checks the exit too. His mouth is moving, but I can't hear the words. When he repeats it again, I read his lips, *Where is the noise coming from?*

I shake my head, scanning the ceiling. Unsure. It's not an alarm attached to the wall either. No lights are strobing.

Eliot is talking but I can't hear.

Same with Tom.

Harriet grabs the two slips of paper off the floor. The riddles. If we can solve this, then maybe we can shut off this ear-splitting noise.

"IS THIS PART OF THE ESCAPE ROOM?!" Tom screams at the top of his lungs.

Eliot tries to respond but his words are drowned out.

"I CAN'T HEAR YOU!" Tom yells.

Charlie goes to Harriet, which has me striding protectively toward her. He rolls his eyes at me, then glances point-two seconds at the slips of paper like I do.

> *with pointed fangs I sit and wait*

> *with piercing force I crunch out fate*

We're missing the last piece of the riddle. The tin box—we need to figure out how to open it.

WEE-WOO! WEE-WOO!!!!! Fuck, *shit*. I grimace as sharp pain stabs my ear. Is it getting louder?

"YOU OKAY?!" I shout at Harriet.

Her face is one giant wince. She's abandoned the papers just to cover her ears again. I encase my palms over her hands to help muffle the sound.

Her brows knit together in confusion. I read her lips. *What about you?* She jerks her hands, trying to pull mine off her.

I don't let her. "I'M OKAY!" I yell, trying to ignore the piercing noise. All I care about is her. All I care about are my brothers. I don't care what happens to me. I haven't for a long time…maybe…maybe for my entire life.

She settles down, letting me help her.

Tom and Eliot have resorted to banging their fists on the door. Tom is screaming against the wood. "LET US OUT, YOU FUCKERS!! YOU'RE GOING TO BLOW OUT MY FUCKING EARDRUMS!!"

Even though Tom is a musician, I'm ninety-nine percent sure he wears earplugs on stage, so he's not used to this violent sound either.

"TOM, STOP!" I yell at him. "JUST COVER YOUR EARS!"

He doesn't hear me. He's screaming at the door.

Eliot slams his foot against the wood, trying to physically break it. Beckett has the tin box and tries to crack the lock with a paperclip.

Harriet kicks my shin, stealing my attention. I bend down to her height, and she murmurs into the pit of my ear, "Snake, bat, vampire." The riddle. She's trying to decipher the riddle.

I uncover our hands from her left ear and cup my palm around my lips. Whispering back, "Were there any books about animals on the shelf?" I shield her ear again while our gazes veer to the bookcase. A key could be inside the pages.

Just as we set our sights on the bookcase, Charlie yanks open drawer after drawer in the desk until he takes out a stapler. He pops it open, and where there should be a row of metal staples, there's a slender skeleton key.

He found it.

"THANK FUCKING CHARLIE!" Tom screams in glee, shaking Charlie's shoulders, practically jumping on his back. Our eldest brother ignores him as he fits the skeleton key in the door. It easily swings open.

The answer was a stapler. I would've never guessed that, but I'm just glad the alarm suddenly stops.

My ears ring like I've just vacated the front row of a heavy metal concert. I drop my hands off Harriet. Her breathing seems shallow, her neck splotchy with flush, and I recognize we've been touching each other a lot more tonight than usual.

"You okay?" I ask again, having trouble even hearing my own voice.

"I'm not the one who just withstood ear-splitting decibels." She bounces up to her tiptoes, trying to peer into my ears but not getting anywhere close.

A smile toys at my lips. "Trying to give me a check-up, Dr. Fisher?"

"Just making sure you can still hear me, Friend."

My smile softens on her while she falls flat on her feet. "I can still hear you." My voice is almost a whisper. Her guards drop, her eyes clinging to mine, and I think about pulling her into my chest. Until she diverts her gaze and gives Charlie a once-over.

Her brows furrow in frustration. "I can't believe he cracked that without the third clue." The one from the tin box, she means. We never even opened it.

Charlie isn't gloating, but Harriet's scowl has reformed. She even crosses her arms.

"Wish you figured it out first?" I ask.

"A little bit...okay, yeah. It was an easy riddle." She cringes at herself. "I was thinking about it too literally."

"I'd still give you a solid A," I tell her. "And not just because I think you're cute."

Her brows spring, and her lips part. A groan rumbles in my chest. She's fucking adorable, and the thought quadruples when her grouchy disposition returns. "I'd give myself a B minus, and I'd give you an A *only* because I think you're hot."

I laugh hard. "My good looks are really pulling through for me."

"You are very blessed, Cobalt boy."

It's too difficult not to put my hands on her now. I slide my fingers through her bangs, just to see her beautiful stormy eyes fastened on mine. A smile teases her pursed lips. I just slide my hand farther through her choppy blond hair, then hold the back of her head and bring her into my chest.

I wrap my arms around her small frame in a hug. I don't even care if she reciprocates, but my mouth curves upward as her arms coil around my waist.

Sherlock Holmes rounds the corner. "Congratulations on escaping The Labyrinth Library! Apologies for the alarm. It's supposed to trigger when the door is opened by force, but it activated unexpectedly. And there was no way to disable it without opening the door, which would have broken immersion. But you all figured it out in the nick of time!" His smile is forced, and I see a hint of worry behind his eyes.

He knows who we are.

My family has a hundred different lawyers on retainer, and he's probably crossing his fingers we're going to walk out of here without trouble. But I doubt any of my brothers will put up a stink about an alarm when they're usually the ones setting them off.

I only let go of Harriet when Beckett's bodyguard appears with the basket of phones. I hand hers back to her, then I collect mine and see fifteen missed calls from my little sister.

Blood drains out of my head.

"Fuck," I mutter, my pulse accelerating. This many incessant calls from Audrey means something is wrong. Four or five and maybe it wouldn't be anything dire, but fifteen? If she were in *serious* trouble, she'd call all our brothers, especially Charlie and Eliot.

My brothers check their phones, but no one seems distraught or panicked. Eliot even listens to his missed texts and grins.

I keep my phone in my fist, then spin to Harriet as she goes to grab her messenger bag. "Hey, can you give me ten minutes? I need to call my sister back."

"Yeah, sure."

I head out to use the bathroom for privacy, but when I step through the doorway, I hear Beckett say, "What's wrong, Tom?"

My stomach nosedives. Rotating back, I see Tom clutching at his throat. "I fucked up," he croaks. "Beck—" His voice *cracks*. Panic lances his widening eyes. He's the lead singer in his band.

Fuck.

Fuckfuckfuck. Wind is knocked out of my chest, and it takes everything to reach the bathroom in one choked breath.

The door swings shut behind me.

I don't call my sister right away.

I brace my hands on either side of the sink. What the fuck...what the fuck? A raging anxious heat swarms me. Sweat quickly builds up on my forehead, and I yank at the collar of my shirt. Suffocating— am I suffocating? Why is it so fucking hard to breathe? I intake an unsteady one and splash water on my face.

Groaning out, I try to calm down, but I can't...I can't because all I'm thinking about is how Tom likely just *damaged* his vocal cords. I shouldn't have come here. I shouldn't be here. This wouldn't have happened if I stayed at the apartment. Folding my arms on the rim of the sink, I press my forehead to them, feeling ill.

It's so dumb.

I'm being fucking dumb. This isn't my fault. *This isn't my fault.* But I caused this. Being here caused this. There are consequences to everything.

Hot tears burn the creases of my eyes. "Stop," I grit at myself. "*Stop.*"

Now I'm on my knees, and I'm puking in the porcelain bowl. I white-knuckle the top of the toilet, my insides on fire. All of me is trying to turn inside-out. I try to think of Harriet.

I didn't hurt her.

I haven't hurt her at least.

Harriet.

With a few deep breaths, I begin to slowly...so very slowly... calm down. I spit, then wipe my mouth with the back of my hand and hang my head. Breathing. I'm just trying to breathe.

SEVENTEEN

HARRIET FISHER

Beckett and Eliot are consoling a seriously freaked-out Tom in the small foyer of the brownstone. I followed them out of the parlor when Ben left for the bathroom, and I hang back while Tom paces left and right. His elbow knocks into a tower of books.

He whirls around, trying to catch a few of them. "Shitfuck." The hoarseness of his voice widens his gaze. Panicking, he laces his hands on the top of his head.

"Don't talk," Beckett advises.

"I'll call your laryngologist," Eliot says, taking Tom's phone and searching through his contacts.

"It's past midnight," Tom squeaks out, tears cresting his eyes. "He's probably asleep. OhmyGod." His scratchy voice is a whisper now.

"*Don't talk*," Beckett emphasizes.

Tom runs his fingers through his hair multiple times and begins pacing again. I know he's my nemesis and I should be inwardly jumping for joy seeing him rattled, but I kind of feel…bad. If someone broke both my thumbs and left me incapable of becoming a surgeon, I'd be devastated. No part of me wants to celebrate a dream being potentially ripped away. Even if it is *Tom's* dream.

"I hope it's nothing permanent." I regret uttering the words as soon as they're out of my mouth. The three of them look at me like I hexed Tom. Did I not sound genuine enough? Am I scowling? Oh, God, did I sound sarcastic? "I mean it," I say quickly, adjusting my messenger bag strap on my shoulder. "I'm not trying to be a bitch. I mean, I can be a bitch, but it's not one of those times." My face is burning up. I might just self-combust.

Tom just nods rapidly like he's trying to convince himself this isn't permanent too. He's pinching his eyes. And Beckett—he's doing this thing where he's boring his gaze into me. It's so intense that I take a step backward. The one fanfic I stumbled upon (when I was in my paranormal fanfic era) about the Cobalts being mind-readers pops into my brain. But that's just silly. Powers don't exist. Still…

"I'm…find Ben," I say inarticulately before darting off. *What the fuck, Harriet?* I take deep breaths to slow my spiked pulse. I glare and mutter, "Get it together. You are a savage. You are a bomb-ass bitch. No one and nothing can intimidate you." Except Beckett?

Does he not like me? Is he just being overprotective of his brothers? Does he think I'm going to hurt them?

I'd never intentionally hurt Ben. After seeing how Charlie chisels *deep* into him and doesn't let up, the urge to join Ben Cobalt's defense squad has escalated to extreme heights. But first impressions aren't my strong suit, so I don't know why I thought this would be any different with his brothers. I'm not ditching Ben, though. They'll all just have to deal with me.

I weave along the makeshift pathway, trying to find the bathroom. Only to immediately get lost.

Retracing my steps, I slow to a stop at the vintage parlor where we were all trapped. Charlie is still in there. He's lying on the velvet red couch, smoking a cigarette while gazing up at the oil mural on the ceiling.

The room is trashed.

Shards of glass speckle the dark floorboards and crimson rug. Bent picture frames hang sadly on the walls while the paintings are torn out. Books are scattered everywhere, and then there's Charlie—just lying among the wreckage, just watching the streaks of white paint as if the clouds are real. I'd wonder if he's high if I couldn't see his eyes. They aren't bloodshot. Pupils aren't dilated.

I can't tell if he's remorseful or indifferent to what just occurred between him and his youngest brother. Maybe it's not on his mind at all. Maybe he's just admiring the art.

It twists my stomach, and the need to protect Ben keeps compounding. So I check over my shoulder—no one behind me—and I slip inside the parlor, shutting the door.

I press my back to the wood.

"'Apothéose d'Hercule'," Charlie says, not looking at me. "Painted by François Lemoyne around 1736. Hercules is ascending to Mount Olympus while everyone celebrates him. Gods. Goddesses. Zeus, Hera, Athena." He takes a drag, letting his arm hang off the couch cushion. "This is a replica. The real painting is on the ceiling in the Salon d'Hercule."

I grind my teeth, afraid I'll snap at him if I speak.

Charlie sits up. "Which is in the Palace of Versailles," he says, like he sees I don't know. "France." He taps ash on the floor.

"I know where Versailles is," I say with heat.

His gaze narrows at me, and his yellow-green eyes fill with their own judgments. "Considering you can't find the exit, I had my doubts." He wags a finger toward the door. "Back that way."

I don't move.

Charlie sizes me up while snuffing out his cigarette on an ashtray. He has no visible tattoos, and the only piercing I see is a small gold hoop in the rook of his ear. "I'm not giving you a crash-course in Classical Mythology so you can get an A with my brother."

"You know we're taking Classical Mythology?"

"My brothers and I share a calendar now." His bitter voice is abrasive to my tender ears. "Ben has also mentioned you're taking the course together. You might think I'm only an asshole, but I'm not fucking obtuse. I do listen."

"I'm not here to ask you to tutor us." I'm not sure how he jumped to that conclusion.

"What do you want from me, Harriet?" Charlie asks point-blank. If there is a bush to beat around, he seems to prefer taking a chainsaw to its branches.

I drop my messenger bag on the ground. My heart thumps and descends like a sinking weight in my body. "I need you to back off Ben."

"Afraid I'll hurt his little feelings?" Charlie leans back on the sofa. "Poor *Ben*. Can't handle the heat when he steps into the fire."

I glower. "That's easy to say when you are the fire."

"She has teeth." Charlie stares straight into me as I approach. "Bite harder, Harriet. I barely felt that one."

I don't take that stupid bait. I have my own goal, and it's not to enter a verbal showdown with Charlie Keating Cobalt. "I'll make a deal with you," I tell him, my voice as gruff and scathing as I feel in this moment. Power surges through me, and it's not foreign. I've felt this before. I am in control. I have control. Even over someone like Charlie.

He rises to his feet, stalking toward me while I head for him, but before I can reach Charlie, he turns for the unlit fireplace. Confusion pummels me, almost giving me pause. I can't stop now.

So I follow him.

He stares at the logs for a second, then spins around while I meet him there. He has many inches on my height, and it forces me to crane my neck upward.

Charlie tilts his chin down to meet my eyes. "I'm not someone you want to make a deal with, Girl Genius."

Ben. He's all I can think about. How he's been there for me before he ever really knew me. How he deserves the same effort in return. He deserves to be cared for with the same ferocity, and I know I've never had a friend to love and one that loved me back. I know I've never had anyone except my Aunt Helena give a shit about me, but Ben does.

And I give a shit about him.

I *care*.

"I know what it's like to live with people who put you on edge, and Ben doesn't deserve that from his *own brother*. Leave him alone, dude. No more snide comments. No more incitement. Just walk the fuck away if you feel the need to be a dick, *Boy Genius*."

Charlie isn't blinking. "You can think whatever you want about me."

My unamused laugh sounds breathy. I can't believe half the twelfth grade at my high school was obsessed with Charlie Cobalt. He's the enigma. The one no one really has an accurate perception of, but the one they could place all their wild fantasies upon.

Would they even like him knowing he treats his little brother like absolute dirt? The answer is probably *yes*, and that breaks my heart for Ben.

"What's even your problem with him?" I ask.

Charlie leans an elbow on the mantel, his fingers to his jaw before he lets them fall. "If you haven't figured it out yet, Ben and I have *very* differing opinions on the world. I'm apathetic about humanity. He's idealistic to the point of *annoyance*. It fucking grates on me in ways you will never understand. Because nine times out of ten, the ruthless and self-serving always win, and he thinks he has a shot when he will be used and abused by them. You think I'm the fire? I'm more certain he will drown before he ever burns."

"Then help him," I shoot back.

"I can't change the core of who he is, even if I wanted to."

I wouldn't want Ben to change, I realize. He's the furthest thing from selfish. He so often thinks of others before saving himself. Hell, he just risked permanent hearing loss so I wouldn't.

Where's the self-preservation, Friend? I once asked him.

I'm not cowering away from Charlie. "Then the least you can do is back off Ben. Make his life easier. Take the deal." I shrug off my oversized leather jacket, then toss it on the red velvet couch behind me.

Charlie looks me over. "And what do I get out of being a perfect angel to my little brother?"

I slip a black scrunchie off my wrist, and I feel him attentively watching as I tie my hair back into a pony. "I'll blow you." These three words flow off my tongue like wine. Nauseatingly sweet. A bottle I've chugged too many times to be sick from now.

Strangely, though, my stomach begins to churn.

Charlie tips his head at me, his gaze more intrusive as he studies my features. "And what makes you think I want you to suck my cock, Harriet?"

My pulse suddenly races, but I take a shallow breath to stay in control. "It'll be worth it." I regain some confidence. "I've never had a complaint before. You'll probably want another one by the end of it." *Guys usually do.*

Charlie is considering. I see the gears shifting rapidly in his head. I see his eyes drop over me. Then he nods his chin toward the floor in a silent instruction to get on my knees.

Help Ben. I lower, the cold hardwood digging into my kneecaps—along with something sharper. Fuck, *fuck.* The glass. I forgot about all the broken vials, but I don't stand. I just let the pain flare as little jagged fragments rip through my pants. It's okay.

It's okay. I concentrate more on the searing of my skin than the sickness in my stomach. I'd rather feel pain than this jumbled, nauseous sensation. I've done this so fucking much, so I don't know why tonight feels any different.

Be a good friend. My heart is a thunderous drumbeat in my ears, timed to my sudden panic.

Be someone he deserves. I look up at Charlie, and his yellow-green eyes, the hue of a snake, are void of emotion.

Soft tendrils of his golden-brown hair swoop over his forehead, and he just stares at me. Waiting. Watching. Seeing what I'll do.

Unzip his pants, I try to command myself. I lick my dried lips. My pulse tries to run away from me. His eye contact is a magnetized intensity, and I can't break it. I'm under the power of it, which scares me. And still, I reach for his zipper. As soon as my hand is midair—he drops to his knees in front of me.

He doesn't touch me, but the impact of that movement knocks the wind out of my lungs. What the fuck is he doing? He makes no pained reaction as he kneels on glass too. Closer to eyelevel now, his gaze searches mine, excavating me like he's unearthing every time I put myself in this position. Like he knows.

Like he *sees*.

I feel violently, uncontrollably exposed. After a long minute of just staring at one another, he finally speaks.

"We are crooked things in this world." His voice is a soft, brutal blow. "Bent, gnarled, twisted things." It sounds like a line from a poem I don't know.

Tears well up in my eyes. "I don't know what that means."

"It means get off your knees."

"It does not." I swipe angrily at a traitorous tear.

His jaw twitches. "You might be friends with Ben, but he clearly has feelings for you. And you just tried to blow his brother. I don't hate him enough to let you. I've never hated him." His words sink heavy weights inside my stomach, drifting down to the pits of my belly. He doesn't even blink when he adds, "You're very fucked up."

Breath catches inside my lungs. Air is thin.

Charlie says, "We're all fucked up in our own ways. I just can't tell whether you'll be the worst thing that ever happened to my brother or the best."

"I—"

"What the fuck is going on?" Beckett's smooth voice triggers an alarm in my body, but I am unnaturally frozen when I see him hovering in the doorway. I didn't even hear him open the freaking door. He's glancing between me and Charlie with so many corrosive questions in his narrowing eyes.

Both Charlie and I are on our knees, which doesn't look great. Not that it's any worse than what I had planned. *What I had planned.* Oh God. Oh fuck.

I jolt to my feet. My vision blurs with more hot tears. I embarrassed myself for what? For *nothing*. It all meant nothing.

This was all for nothing.

I ruined…everything.

I run. Swiping my black messenger bag off the floor, I push past Beckett in the doorway and slip out of his grasp as he tries to catch me. "Harriet," he calls out, then I hear him ask, "Charlie, what the fuck did you do?"

I'm a mess navigating the pathway of tipsy-turvy books. I trip over a stack, and I pull my messenger bag closer to my body. Righting myself, I stumble toward the front door where Eliot and Tom linger inside.

I reach for my leather jacket—just so I can cover my reddened, tear-streaked face from them—but my fingers only catch the fabric of my crop top. Nooo, fuck. I left my jacket in the parlor. There's no chance I'm backtracking to retrieve it.

"Are you crying?" Eliot asks with darkening eyes. His head whips toward the pathway I just barreled through. "What happened?" He's about to rush into the danger that he thinks I met and escaped.

I say nothing. I sprint past Eliot and Tom like my feet have caught fire.

Ben is going to know. Charlie is going to tell him. Bile rises and sears my throat as I push out the front door into the warm, muggy night. Rain drizzles on the stone steps. On the stoop, I do my best to inhale a single breath.

I tried to blow his brother.

I'm very fucked up.

I would have done it had Charlie not dropped to his knees.

I would have done it.

I would have.

My heart beats so forcefully, and it takes me a moment to realize the five men casually standing on the sidewalk are the Cobalt brothers' bodyguards. They're all turning toward me like I'm a wet, stray cat that just scampered from the building.

Avoiding eye contact, I jog down the steps, and my boots hit the sidewalk.

"Harriet!" Eliot calls after me.

"I'm fine!" I yell into the night air at him. At security. At anyone who cares so they won't follow me. They don't need to chase me down. I'm fine. *Fine.*

I tried to blow Ben's older brother—when, really, I think I'm falling for Ben. But I'm fine.

I. Am. *Fine.*

Footsteps thunder behind me, and I pick up my own pace. I'm not slow. I run away from this moment. From my shame. From this life.

I'm going to be one of those girls that they all laugh about years to come. Remember Harriet? Yeah, that crazy chick who tried to blow Charlie in a deal to help Ben. Wild times.

Everything hurts.

"STOP! HARRIET!" Tom's blown-out voice almost causes me to trip. *Tom* of all people? I risk a glance over my shoulder. He's the one running after me at a break-neck speed.

I don't understand why. I don't want to stop and find out.

I just want to leave. I want to disappear. I want to have never met Ben Pirrip Cobalt and his four brothers.

EIGHTEEN

BEN COBALT

My little sister can't catch her breath as she cries into the phone. I've been in the bathroom at The Labyrinth Library for only a few minutes—a couple of those were dedicated to me disposing my stomach contents in the toilet.

I'm not that close to figuring out the cause of her distress. Mostly, I'm trying not to jump to the worst-case scenario since this could be about literally anything. A failed grade. A fashion emergency. A shitty day at Dalton—especially now that Winona and Vada aren't there. Maybe she's regretting not going to boarding school with them.

What's strange: Audrey didn't immediately put me on a video call. Normally, she'd ask to see my face to ensure Eliot and Tom aren't impersonating me as a prank.

"Audrey, breathe," I instruct, my frown deepening. "Just take a breath."

She inhales between sobs.

"What's wrong? What happened?" I ask.

She mumbles incoherently as her cries intensify. I press a hand against the porcelain sink and try to concentrate and piece apart her words. The smell of lavender overwhelms my senses. The dim lighting gives off a yellow-gold glow so it's not too harsh on my eyes, but my throat is sandpaper as I swallow. And my ears still ring from the siren.

It's hard to focus. Especially when all I can picture is Tom rubbing a panicked hand at his windpipe. I should have asked about emergency exits. Guilt craters a wound in my gut, and I'm just trying not to puke again.

"Theo…" Audrey's voice shoves me out of my head. In between her cries, I hear, "Theodore."

I go eerily still at the mention of my pet cockatiel—or rather *her* pet. I gave him to her. "Put me on video, Audrey."

"I ca-can't." She hiccups. "I don't want you to see him like this."

I scrub a hand down my face. "What's wrong with him?" My ribs constrict around my lungs. *This can't be happening. Why is this happening?*

"H-he's just a little slow to move." She intakes a sharp breath.

"*Theodore.* Theodore, come on. *Please.*"

"Is he in his cage?"

She's quiet.

"Audrey?"

"He's lying on the bottom. Possibly, he's just sleeping." Her voice fractures and goes high-pitched. "He could be sleeping."

My heart rate keeps accelerating. Sweat suctions my shirt to my chest. It's doing everything to suck in oxygen and speak clearly. "Where's Mom and Dad?"

She doesn't answer. In the next short pause, I picture her silent tears streaming down her fair cheeks as she nudges the lifeless, gray-feathered bird. He has an energetic personality, which I attribute to being raised first by Eliot and Tom. He *loves* hopping around. Tossing his little head to the beat of music.

I don't want to imagine him motionless.

The corners of my eyes go wet, and two involuntary tears drip into the perspiration of my skin.

"Did I kill him, Ben?" She's no longer sobbing or hiccupping and that concerns me even more. "I-I gave him water. I fed him. He ate sliced apple out of my hand. We were learning how to play a fun ring toss game together. We were *bonding*."

I lift my shirt and wipe my entire face with the damp fabric. Maybe he ate an apple seed. Which is highly poisonous.

"H-he *must* be sleeping. He must be."

"He might be," I console, exhaling a few times. "Go get Mom or Dad, or I'll hang up and call them myself."

I hear the thud of her footsteps, and while I wait, I stare at my reddening eyes in the gold-framed mirror.

I made another mistake. Giving Audrey my bird. I thought it'd be a *good* thing for her to have a reminder of me when I'm gone. Something she could hang on to. The average lifespan of a cockatiel is fifteen to twenty-five years, some living to thirty, so why would I be worried he'd pass away anytime soon? Let alone *two* weeks after I gave him to her.

I shake my head slowly to myself.

Life isn't full of loops and repeats. It's not cyclical. Audrey wasn't meant to have Theodore because Eliot and Tom had once gifted him to me. Isn't this proof enough of that? Fate *doesn't* exist.

Life is a swerving, unpredictable line of falling dominos. There are reactions to every action. Consequences.

Some brutal. Some eviscerating.

I'm just hanging on to the slimmest chance that he might be alive. Maybe his breaths are weak. Maybe he's ill.

"Audrey? What's wrong, mon petit?" I hear my dad's calming voice.

They both grow more muffled. I wonder if Audrey is cupping the phone to protect me from the news.

Seconds later, I hear, "Ben?"

"Mom?" I ask. "What's going on?"

"Hold on, I'm putting you on video call."

In the background, Audrey wails, "Wait! Please don't show him!"

"I'm just talking to him," she assures.

Emerging on the video, my mom pushes glossy brown hair off her shoulder. Her collarbones are strict, lips pursed, and eyes flamed. Her black silk robe contrasts the glittering strand of diamonds at her neck. She is the antithesis of soft, maternal warmth. She is cold, sharp battlement. And I've rarely, in all my life, wanted or needed for anything else, not from her.

Her hugs might be steel, but they've always been loving.

It's a comfort when she appears. I take a breath. "Is he okay?" I ask.

"We don't know." Her tone is icy. My mom frames the screen so I can only see her face. Likewise, she only sees mine. Based on her iron-willed expression—like she's ready to murder my sorrow, so even sadness can't hurt me—I know he's dead.

I know he's gone.

I internally nod to myself, trying to accept this without buckling. *Trying.* It's easier to just focus on my little sister. I want her to be okay.

In the background, I hear my dad tell Audrey, "He's not breathing."

"Give him CPR," she insists.

"Rigor mortis is setting in, Audrey. He's been dead for too long."

"There must be something we can do," she cries.

"Outside of pretending he's alive, there is nothing."

"*Richard,*" Mom glares over at him.

"Rose," Dad replies with less heat, a smile almost inside his voice. "It's the cycle of life. They know the dead can't be resurrected. And this isn't the first pet that's passed."

My mom accidentally rotates the phone, and I see Audrey on the floor of her room. Her head buried in her black satin pajamas. My dad is on the chaise at the foot of her four-poster bed, and he rubs her back in soothing circles.

"He had so many more years, though," Audrey sobs. "This is my fault."

"It's not your fault," I tell her. "I don't blame you." I really don't. I only blame myself. This is on me. She shouldn't have had to take care of him, and I should've accounted for this possibility. It was always there.

"We can take him to the vet tomorrow morning," my mom says to me, her face filling the screen again. "We'll get an autopsy to learn the cause of death."

"No," I say fast. "No, I don't want that." I'm most likely in the minority of my family, not wishing for knowledge. Answers. But I believe there's more peace in not knowing. Especially for Audrey. If he really died from an apple seed she accidentally fed him, it'd wreck her.

"We'll bury him," Mom assures me. "It'll be a *proper* burial too. A ceremony under your favorite oak tree. May his feathery little ass rest in bird heaven."

"*Mother*," Audrey cries. "It's been mere minutes. Can we not joke?"

"I was being serious," she says sharply, but I sense her studying my reaction, wondering if she upset me.

I'm fine. My chest hurts and my throat is scorched, but I'm fine.

"Ben?" Dad asks.

"I'm fine," I mention out loud.

"You'll come back for the burial?" he asks off-screen.

My mom's eyes ping over to him, then back to me. "You're coming." It's a demand, but she won't force me there if I can't make it.

"Yeah, I'll try." My voice goes soft. "Just make sure Audrey's okay. I don't want her to take this too hard."

Her lips flatline, and bottomless pools of concern fill her eyes. She struts out of the bedroom, taking the phone on her march to a home office downstairs. For privacy, probably. Once she's sitting pin straight at a mahogany desk, she says, "We're all more concerned about your feelings. Audrey cares about the bird, but she cares about you more."

I nod a couple times, my jaw locking.

"*Ben*." The aggressive way she says my name—the way her fierce yellow-green eyes drill into me—I wonder if she's worried about something else.

"What?" I ask.

She blinks and shakes her head like she's shooing a thought away. "I just...it's not like you to not even cry over Theodore. He was yours for years."

"I did cry before you got on the phone." Barely. Definitely not typical, and I think she can tell it couldn't have been a lot. So I add, "You rarely cry over anything."

"You're not an ice-cold bitch. You're my sweet-natured, fearless son—"

"I'm just in shock," I say fast. "Believe me, the waterworks are going to come during the burial." *I haven't changed, Mom.*

She pushes more hair off her shoulder. "You've been happy out there with your brothers?" she asks. "Because if you need me or your dad, you can come home."

"No, I want to stay. It hasn't been terrible in New York. I eat breakfast with Beckett every morning, and I'm out with all of them now. We're at an escape room together."

Her lips twitch in a smile. "What's the damage?"

I laugh. "Eliot and Tom definitely incurred a bill, let's just say that."

She makes a throaty noise of disapproval. "Ugh, I swear they are unrestrained little shits."

"Eliot thinks he's the big shit, actually."

"His ego is rivaling your father's by the day."

"By the hour," I banter with a smile, which brings hers out too.

"And Charlie...?" She hesitates to ask. "How are you handling living with him?"

I called him a sick, malignant version of Dad and he called me a pathetic one, so I'd say we're doing *great*. Exactly what any parent would want for their two sons. Sign us up for a three-legged sack race together and we'd most definitely face-plant off the starting line.

It's hard to muster a cheery lie, but there is a silent understanding between me and all my siblings that we don't tattle to our parents.

We're not five years old. They don't need to know Charlie's an absolute demon—and truthfully, I don't want them to know. A part of me truly believes they'd brush away his comments. Make an excuse for him. They haven't yet, but that's because I haven't given them the chance.

"It's been okay with Charlie," I tell her. "They all just met a friend of mine tonight."

"From hockey?"

"No, I haven't tried out for the team yet, but she goes to MVU."

Her eyes narrow in suspicion. "She?"

I smile wider. "Yeah, my friend is a girl—"

"Ben." Beckett pounds a fist at the bathroom door.

"I have to go," I tell her quickly, hoping she can't hear the urgency in Beckett's tone. "They must be ready to leave."

"I love you, sweet gremlin."

"Love you too, Mom." I hang up just as Beckett knocks again. When I open the door, the distress on his face crushes me.

"Harri—" He doesn't finish saying her name before I'm wrenched into the hallway by my own concern.

"Where is she?" I thought leaving her with my brothers would be fine. Beckett snatches the back of my T-shirt, stopping me short, and I twist out of his grip.

We're face-to-face when he holds up his hands to try and calm me. "Just take a breath, Pip."

I said the same thing to Audrey.

But I'm not crying.

I'm not sobbing.

No one has died—right?

"What the fuck happened, Beck?" I ask. "Where's Harriet?"

He keeps a hand raised as if he's anticipating I'll react poorly. Her leather jacket is draped on his forearm. Everything dials up my concern to new, unstable heights. "She ran off—"

That's all I hear before I'm sprinting to the front door. I push it open and meet the New York night with angered footfalls. Bodyguards stand on the wet sidewalk with the rest of my brothers as light rain mists the air. I'm lasered in on just one person.

The guy smoking a cigarette next to a lamp post.
The guy rolling his eyes as soon as he sees me approach.
The guy who I know had something to do with this.
"Charlie!" I scream. "What the fuck did you do?!"
He flicks his cigarette to the pavement and casually scuffs it with his polished shoe. I'm ten feet from him when Eliot and Tom sidestep in front of me, and all I want to do is bulldoze. Rage rips through my body, and I am ready to unleash. But Eliot's hands fly to my chest, and he's the only brother who's strong enough to physically restrain me.

"Stop." Eliot's urgency elevates my pulse. I shove him, and he grasps the side of my neck, pinning me closer to his chest.

"*Eliot.*"

"You can come to blows with Charlie later. There's no time."

"Harriet ran away," Tom rasps out in a faint whisper. "She was sobbing. I couldn't catch up to her. She's little but she's fucking fast." He grumbles the words *speed demon*.

My fury fractures into a new focus. "I need to find her." I pull away from Eliot and turn in the direction of the nearest subway station.

"Ben Pirrip!" Tom strains his voice, which stops me in place.

My eyes burn. "Don't hurt yourself for me." *Please.*

Tom just points to one of the two identical Range Rovers parked at the curb. Security vehicles. Some of my brothers use their bodyguards as private chauffeurs. Riding in their car isn't the better option for multiple reasons—the main one being it's *slower*.

"If we hit traffic, I'm fucked," I tell them.

"You might get mobbed on the subway," Eliot explains. "If someone recognizes—"

"No one recognizes me, man," I interrupt. I'm not my brothers. I won't get spotted that easily.

"Yeah, but they might recognize me," Tom rasps.

"And me," Eliot adds. "We're coming with you, whether you like it or not."

Jesus. Fuck. *Fine.*

My head spins, but I'm on autopilot. I hop into the Range Rover, and when Tom follows me, he flips the seat to crawl into the third row. Then Eliot locks it back upright. He slips next to me in the second row. Barely a heartbeat later, Beckett climbs into the car and sits on my other side.

As the passenger door jerks open, I blink a couple times to make sure I'm seeing correctly.

Charlie is suddenly sitting in the front seat without a single glance backward. As if it's reasonable for him to be in this car with me.

It feels so seamless. Like there was never any question. My four brothers were always going with me to find Harriet. My nerves haven't calmed. I don't think they will until I see her.

Who's driving? The mystery is solved quickly as Charlie's bodyguard gets behind the wheel.

Oscar Oliveira is a thirty-four-year-old seasoned pro, a Yale graduate, an ex-professional boxer, and one of my family's favorites in security. Seriously, I think my dad would rather saw off an arm than fire Oscar. He's the only bodyguard that's been able to last on Charlie's detail. All the others quit or were canned.

Oscar has a loose grip on the wheel, the sleeves of his white button-down rolled to his strong forearms. He's Brazilian-American with golden-brown skin and dark curly hair, and I'm sure this is just another hectic Cobalt night. He's unfazed.

He gazes through the rearview, meeting my eyes. "Where are we headed, Ben?"

I tell him Harriet's address from memory, then I crane my neck behind me and peer past Tom. Seeing the second Range Rover through the back windshield. Our other bodyguards pile into the vehicle and peel out onto the street as Oscar relays the destination through their radios.

They end up following us though. Once we're on the road, everyone is so fucking quiet, my ears start ringing again.

I'm about to speak, but Tom shifts forward to croak out, "See, this is why you don't open umbrellas indoor, Eliot Alice. Bad shit follows. I'm probably going to lose my voice *forever*."

Nausea churns.

Beckett gives him a look. "You're going to lose your voice because you keep talking."

"No, let's blame the umbrella," Charlie says, sarcasm thick. "Because that's definitely what made him scream like a banshee for five minutes straight."

"You were timing me?" Tom rasps. "He was timing me?" he asks Eliot.

"Brother, I love you," Eliot says, "but shut up. For your own sake."

Tom slides back in his seat with a heavy sigh, and I crack my stiff neck, my nerves tensing every inch of muscle. "Is anyone going to tell me what happened?" I ask. "I wasn't in the bathroom that long."

"I don't know, dude," Tom whispers, his voice getting softer. "She ran out of the building *crying*. That's all I saw."

"Likewise," Eliot says. "They weren't tears of joy either."

My stomach knots, and while I talk, I send her a text, asking where she is. "What was she running away from?"

Beckett takes a deep, readying breath. "She was in the parlor with Charlie before she ran out. He won't tell me what happened." He glares at the back of Charlie's headrest, and I wonder if this has been a point of contention.

I lean forward, prepared to stick my head between the driver and passenger seat to strangle my eldest brother. "So you did do something," I accuse as both Eliot and Beckett pull me back against the seat.

Of my brothers, I'm the most hot-tempered, and that's very blatant tonight. Hockey used to help—I blew off a lot of steam on the ice. I just let all the tension go.

That outlet is gone, and my fuse has been cut shorter.

"I did nothing." Charlie rotates in his seat to face us. "And like I told Beckett, I'm not in the mood to recount the events of tonight. She's your so-called friend. If she wants to tell you, she can. Otherwise, I guess we'll never know what happened in the Library."

"I bet it was Professor Plum with a candlestick," Eliot quips. "That purple bastard." His attempt at eradicating the animosity falls flat with me. Charlie cracks a smile though, and it ramps up my festering anger even more.

I'm hanging on to something he said. *So-called* friend. Charlie doesn't mince words. He says exactly what he means.

"She's my friend," I tell him. "There's nothing *so-called* about it, Charlie."

"Whatever you say." He flips on the radio. Soft pop fills the car, and I can't stop thinking about how Charlie didn't even tell *Beckett* what went down. Why? Who the hell is he protecting? I'd say himself, but Charlie has never cared about being painted as a villain.

He's never given a shit what people think about him.

I rest my forearms on my thighs, feeling winded. I'm not sure interrogating Charlie will get me anywhere. I just need to find her.

Beckett has a hand on my back. It's calming, and I take a few deeper breaths. *I'll find her*, I assure myself.

I'll find her. Because I'm not stopping until I do.

No one talks the rest of the way. Mostly so Tom quits interjecting. We help save his voice for him, and when Oscar pulls up next to the apartment building, I'm already unclipping my seatbelt before he even brakes.

"All of you stay here," I tell them as Eliot unbuckles too.

He reluctantly nods. "As you wish."

Beckett locks eyes with me. "Let us know if you find her."

"Yeah, I will." The car rolls to a dead-stop, and as I grab the handle, Oscar says, "Wait for your bodyguard. The other vehicle is stuck at a red light."

I don't have time to wait. Shaking my head, I open the door.

"Ben!" Oscar yells, and I just barely hear him mutter, "Novak is going to love this," before I launch myself toward the brick apartment complex. It's about a third the size of the luxury high-rise I'm living at. Chunky AC units stick out from windows, and the fire escape looks rusted.

Less than a minute later, I'm inside the echoey building and waiting for an elevator. I'm so focused that it takes me a second to realize Charlie has strolled up next to me. Oscar lingers behind, speaking hushed in a mic at his collar.

I frown at my brother. "I told you to stay in the car."

"And I didn't. Whoops." His sarcasm surprisingly doesn't grate on me. I have a feeling he jumped out of the car so Oscar could follow. So I could have security by proxy of being around him. Still, he's being eyed by a young white woman who grabs mail from a brass 92 box. I figure she's trying to place where she knows Charlie from.

He notices her, then holds out his hand to me. "Give me your hat."

I pull my baseball cap out of my back pocket and unfold it into his hand.

Putting it on, he dips the brim down over his eyes. It's not a great disguise, but not the worst either. I study him. How he angles his body but strangely braces more weight on his right leg—the one he's had surgery on. And are his knees wet?

Since he wears black pants, I can't tell exactly, but glass had been scattered all over the parlor, so... "Are you bleeding?"

"It's nothing." His cold gaze is cemented on the elevator.

Oscar sends Charlie a seriously concerned look. I wonder if he's already spoken to my brother about the issue. Because Oscar remains quiet, then faces forward again. They have a closer relationship than I have with Novak, and it's not strange to think Oscar might know things about my brother that I don't, considering he's with him nearly all day, every day.

We don't say anything else. Not even when we reach Harriet's apartment.

I knock on the door, my pulse on a fiery ascent.

Maybe it's good Charlie is here. If he did something, he can apologize. He can make it right...not that he's ever been good at *either* of those things.

No one answers. Shit, she has to be here. I don't know where else I would search otherwise. I run a hand through my hair and knock again. The door swings open to reveal a tall girl in a polka dot pajama set. Her dark bangs are pinned back with silver clips, and her eyes go as round as her mouth.

"Oh my fucking *God.*" She's staring right at my brother, and it's almost laughable how bad my baseball cap hid him.

He forces a tight smile.

She gasps like he dropped on one knee.

"You're Eden, right?" I cut in. "Harriet's roommate."

Her jaw drops even farther when she swings her gaze to me. "You know my name?"

"Is Harriet home?" I ask as Eden opens the front door wider for us. I step inside, but my brother stays back like he's some immortal vampire who hasn't been invited in yet.

"She's not here," Eden says, quickly pulling out the clips from her hair. She brushes her bangs down with her fingers.

"Can I check her room just in case?" I ask.

Eden frowns. "She sleeps on the couch." She points to the lumpy lime-green sofa in the middle of the living room. "She's renting the pull-out."

My stomach nosedives. I'm sleeping on a couch too, so I don't know why Harriet crashing every night on one is driving more worry into me. I also don't know why I assumed that she shared a room with her roommate. Like a dorm. Bunk beds...I never actually went into the bedroom, I realize.

"Do you know where she could be?" I ask.

Charlie's leaning a hip in the doorway, listening to everything. Probably analyzing all the ways in which I don't know Harriet that well. But he'd be wrong. So I didn't know she was sleeping on a fucking couch? She doesn't know I'm sleeping on one too. It doesn't mean anything.

"Noooo," Eden draws out the word, her eyes pinging from me to Charlie like she's etching this in her memory. "To be honest, I don't talk much with Harriet. We kind of keep to ourselves. How do you know her anyway?"

"College," I say vaguely, then I remember something. Harriet lived out of her car. If she needed to go somewhere more private than a shared living room, I bet it'd be there.

I turn back to Eden as the lightbulb moment surges hope through me. "Does your apartment come with a parking spot?"

NINETEEN

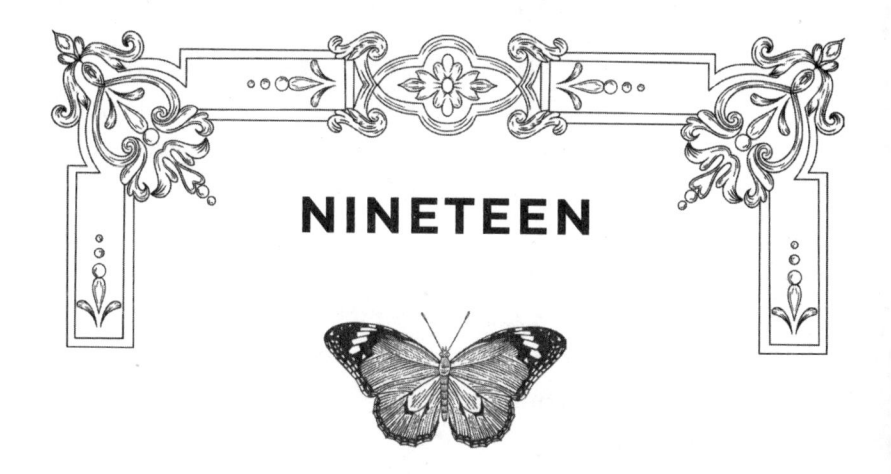

BEN COBALT

Oscar parks in an open space three cars down from the Honda, and my brothers thankfully stay in the Range Rover as I hop out. My pulse is climbing as I close in on Harriet's car, and the smell of urine in the parking garage doesn't fucking help.

I'm at the bumper and peering through the rear windshield and—*shit*. I don't see anyone sitting in the driver or passenger seats.

Slipping between the silver Honda and a blue Dodge Charger, I squint through the tinted window into the backseat. My shoulders fall in relief when I see her. Eyes closed, chunky headphones on, and a pillow under her head while she lies longways. A fuzzy hot-pink Hello Kitty blanket partially covers her slender frame.

I rap my knuckles against the window. Her eyes instantly pop open in alert. It takes two seconds for recognition to sink in, then her brows draw together in deep confusion. Did she not think I'd check in on her?

She doesn't make a move to the door.

I point down to the handle, trying to signal for her to unlock it.

She blinks four times as if she's shaking off a heavy thought. Leaning forward, she flips the lock for me.

I slide into the backseat and shut the door behind me. I rest my shoulders against the window. Facing her. A fir tree air freshener dangles off the rearview mirror, giving off a festive pine fragrance to the car. Harriet pulls her headphones to her neck and hugs her pillow to her chest. She scoots back to lean against the opposite door. First, I'm stuck on how bloodshot her blue eyes are. The puffiness of her eyelids makes it hard for her to open them fully.

I just want to take her hurt away. I'm not thinking about how I could be the cause. Because if I descend too deep into that, I might never come out of the abyss.

"I didn't think you'd be into Hello Kitty," I say with a peeking smile, but this time, it doesn't draw hers out.

Her lips pull into a massive frown, and her voice is barely a whisper. "I'm more into a ninety-percent-off clearance sale at Walmart."

I nod, my ribs compressing as her gaze drops to her legs. She tucks them closer to her body. I'm scrunched up back here, but I don't invade her space. I skim her car, then see a first-aid kit in the footwell, along with band-aid wrappers, a plastic grocery bag with bloodied paper towels, and the plaid pants she'd been wearing tonight. Her pants—the kneecaps appear stained with blood too.

Right now, the blanket hides her legs, her knees, her waist, but I'm putting some pieces together. *Did she get down on her knees for him?*

As my throat swells and my eyes feel scrubbed raw, all I care about is her. I hate, with everything in me, that she's hurt right now. Not just emotionally, but fucking physically...

"Harriet," I breathe.

"What are you doing here, Ben?" she chokes out. Her confusion is confusing the fuck out of me. I feel as if this should be obvious.

"I'm here to check on you," I say. "When my friend runs away crying, I'm not going to just go home and bake a frozen pizza like nothing happened."

She shakes her head, her bangs falling in her eyes. She pushes them away with a quick hand. "I don't understand," she says, then her lips part in shock. "He didn't tell you?" Her nose flares.

My stomach coils in a vicious knot. "Charlie did something. That's all I know."

Her frown deepens, but her jaw hasn't closed. "He told you that?"

"No, I..." My voice trails off as her face shatters. Her fingers curl tighter to the pillow, and I can tell she's fighting off tears. The realization that I might be wrong slams into me like a thousand gallons of water after a dam break. My throat is sandpaper as I add, "Beckett said he saw you and Charlie in the parlor, and that's when you ran away crying." I want to bring up the first-aid kit, the blood, her pants, but her chin begins quivering. "Harriet?"

"You should leave, Ben," she tells me, her voice surprisingly monotoned compared to the fracture of her face.

I can't leave things like this. I can't leave her like *this*. It's all impaling me. "I'm not sure I can. The Hello Kitty clearance blanket looks pretty comfy."

She chokes out a hoarse noise, her eyes daggered on me. "You can't be serious right now." I'm smiling a little, and her lips twitch up just a bit until her face contorts in a near-cry. "Stop, Ben."

"Yeah, I'm not sure I like you using my name when you're upset. Go back to Friend, *Friend*."

She chucks the pillow at me, her smile battling its way against her sorrow, and I just want it to stay. I just want her to be unscathed, unharmed...happy.

I catch the bed pillow.

Then she crosses her arms and sits up higher against her door, scowling at me.

I prop the pillow against my back. Getting comfortable. She sees and rolls her eyes into a headshake. "You're going to want to go," she says, her voice so unsteady. "After tonight, you're not going to want to be friends with me. So we can say our goodbyes now." She bows forward, just to hold out a hand for me to shake. "It was nice knowing you, Cobalt boy."

It feels like she's closing our last couple weeks together, packing them away, shipping them off into the past to be long forgotten memories. I'm not ready for that…I'm not willing to shut this chapter in this painful way.

I can't accept it. Not for her. Not for me.

I don't even look at her hand. I don't give it my attention. My gaze remains on her eyes in an unwavering beat. "This isn't how we end, Friend."

"How can you be so sure?" Her eyes start to well, but her words never lose their bite. "You rubbed a crystal ball? Cobalts can see the future now too?"

"It is because I'm a Cobalt," I tell her, "but we can't see the future—we just know how to carve out the ones we want. And you're in mine for longer than this, Harriet. This isn't how we end."

She swipes the heel of her palm beneath her eye before the tear can fall. "I don't want it to end here." Her chin trembles violently. "But I fucked up, Friend." Her whole face twists in the precipice of a guttural sob, and I can't sit still. Rocking forward, I cup her soft, warm cheeks with two strong hands, her body heaving in a good release at the touch, and she grips onto my forearms.

I can't decipher whether she'll shove me or bring me closer, but I whisper, "Let me hold you."

Her breath hitches, and her reddened eyes fill again. "I tried to make a deal with your brother," she gets out faster. "You won't want to hold me after I almost blew him."

"Yeah, I do," I say, not surprised at all by her confession. Without falter, I pull Harriet on my lap, her legs splaying across the seat while I curve my arms around her back. Her hands fist my shirt, but she's giving me her weight, wanting this closeness like I do.

The Hello Kitty blanket has slid down to her calves. She's only wearing cotton black panties with red font spelling *Monday* above her pussy. It's Friday. Her knees—they're bandaged. It did cross my mind she might've knelt on glass. Thing is, I don't understand why Charlie would've too.

"What was the other end of the deal?" I ask her.

Her eyes go dark. "Does it matter?" Her fists loosen, letting go of my shirt, and her palms lie flat on my chest—which I don't like as much. Next step will be Harriet pushing herself off me. "I got on my knees for your brother. The brother you just fought with." Her voice rises in distress. "I'm *disgusting*, Ben."

"Please don't ever say that again," I say sternly, my hand slipping into her hair. "And yeah, it *does* matter. Because the girl I know gave a blow job to a 'hammerhead shark' to help a lab partner. So I wouldn't put it past her to give a blow job to the fucking devil just to help a friend."

She doesn't pull away. "Knowing won't change anything."

"I still want to know."

She takes a breath. "I told him to stop harassing you. That was the deal."

My mind whirls for a solid second. "He didn't take it," I say, assuming the better of Charlie here, because I want to believe he wouldn't do that to her. I don't know if I could ever forgive him if he took that deal, if he took advantage of Harriet…it'd obliterate my relationship with him, one that's already hanging on a frayed thread.

"I thought he did. I got on my knees. I almost unzipped his pants, and then he just…backed out of it."

I glance at the window. "His knees are bleeding, I think."

Harriet chews the corner of her lip, trying not to cry. "He dropped to his knees too…and he said that he didn't hate you enough to do it. That he didn't hate you at all."

Charlie doesn't hate me?

It's harder to believe in this when he's only ever disregarded my feelings. But he did protect our relationship from imploding tonight. He has to care a little bit about me, right? Or maybe he knew Beckett would be irate with him, and he's protecting that relationship instead.

While I'm processing, her arms extend, her chest lifts farther away from mine. She's pushing off me.

I hold her thigh. "Harriet—"

"You don't get it." She presses her palm to her sternum, as if she wants to feel each breath she takes. "I would've done it, Ben. I would have gone through with it—you need to know that." I never desert her gaze. Not even as she asks, "So you see now, why we can't be friends?"

"No, this is exactly why we're friends. Because I understand why you did it."

She shakes her head over and over and over. "No, Ben. You can't. *We* can't. Do you honestly think I can be around you after this? Every time I look at you, all I'll think about is the deal and how fucked up I am. How I always, *always* think sex is the answer to problems. A currency. It's a loop I can't escape, not even around you."

I figured this might be an issue for her, but hearing her admit it has turned the theory into reality. It only makes me want to stay. I pinch my watering eyes, then say with confidence, "You don't need to replay it on repeat when you see me. I'm not judging you—"

"Your brothers—"

"Would probably pat you on the fucking back, Harriet. They would see what I see."

She's very still. "What do you see?"

"You go to the ends of the earth to help people you barely even know. Imagine what you'd do for someone you loved."

She looks away, out the back windshield, and then bursts into sudden tears as this reaches a vulnerable place that I think surprises her. I hold Harriet while she collapses into my chest. Lifting the blanket back up her legs, I feel her body shuddering against me.

"You haven't fucked up," I whisper, stroking her hair before wrapping my arms so tight around her small frame. She buries into me, and I rock her a little, resting my chin on her head. "This doesn't end here, petit oiseau."

Feeling her calm is calming me too. I'm not hurting her. I haven't hurt her. After a couple minutes, her tears stop and her breaths slow. She looks up at me while I stare down at her.

"You're not alone, you know," I tell her. "I'm far from perfect. We all do things we wish we could take back."

"You offer blow jobs in exchange for things too?" Her deadpan voice makes me smile.

I'm happy to hear her joke again. "I wish. Seems like a very effective trade."

"It was, until tonight."

Damn. The urge to protect her throttles me to the core. I want to ask if she was safe. I want to ask if any of the guys hurt her. I want to hurt them, if they did. She's been doing this for…fuck-knows how long. "Can I ask when it started?"

She turns her head, her cheek against my bicep that curves around her. "Years ago, I guess." It takes her a couple minutes to gather the next words. "One of my mom's ex-boyfriends, arguably the worst one, used to be strict and…angry over dumb shit. I came home too late without texting. I forgot to take out the trash before school. She microwaved the lasagna for too long. He'd throw TV remotes, lamps, chairs at me…at her, and she always made excuses." I see Harriet's cringe forming. "She'd claim I hated him because I was *jealous*. She'd get pissed at *me* when he stared at my body, but that was par for the course with Hope. It was always *my* fault if her boyfriends looked at me like they…" Her voice tapers out.

I tuck her closer while she expels a long, heavy breath. Then she says, "One day, I guess I realized I could use his gross fantasies against him. I told him I'd blow him if he'd leave my mom and never see us again. He'd be gone for good." She inhales. "And it worked. Mostly because he thought I might've recorded him. He'd be in jail, so…he chose life without bars and without us."

I stare up at the car's ceiling. My head heavies. "How old were you?"

"Fifteen."

I cut my glare to the window, feeling the weight and pain of that. "Fuck him," I let out. "He deserves to be in prison."

"I didn't actually record him." She sits up a little more. "It wasn't my first blow job so don't think that perv messed me up or anything. I was in control. It was *my* idea, and he's not in the back of my head doing damage." She clings to my gaze, seeing I'm not looking at her like she's broken. "How can you still want to be around me...?"

"You don't give yourself enough credit, Fisher," I whisper. "We all have different starting lines, and yours was much farther back than mine. Yet, you got yourself so fucking far without any help. When you had more reasons to fall, you kept getting back up. You kept going. You don't think that's admirable?"

She shrugs. "No one's every really admired me, so I don't know."

"It's a fucking shame I'm your first. It feels like the whole world should admire you."

Harriet gives me a *come on* glower. Like I'm blowing smoke up her ass.

I smile into a laugh. "You want my eyes? I'd take them out and give them to you. Just so you can see exactly how I see you. You're driven, compassionate, sharp, beautiful—in so many ways. You're everything I'd want to be around."

Her tears well. "That's not how that organ works, Cobalt boy. So don't go plucking your eyeballs out for me."

My smile stretches, and I can't stop staring at her. Watching her smile reemerge just hushes all the noise in my body. It's like walking barefoot through dewy grass. Feeling the stickiness of morning air. Smelling the wet earth and budding magnolias. "You're the one person who..." I trail off, not knowing how to describe this out loud.

"Who what?"

"Who I feel like...I won't harm."

She's a little puzzled, and I can't blame her. I'm sure it's fucking ridiculous. But I feel this quiet sense of ease with Harriet. Somewhere in my brain, I'm so certain that I'm a positive force in her life. My presence caused the hammerhead shark to swim away. She wasn't thrown in the pool at the frat party. She's no longer upset in the back of her car.

She's slowly smiling at me, at the way I'm looking at her. She's something good in my life I don't want to lose. I'm afraid to lose, but I have to…I shake the stabbing thought away.

Then my phone buzzes in my ass pocket against the seat, disrupting the peaceful silence.

"You getting that?" Harriet asks, about to slide off me, but I hold her still and dig out my phone to check the caller ID.

"It's Beckett. They all probably want to know if you're okay." I motion my head to the window. "They're parked a few cars over."

Her brows spring. "They're here?"

"Yeah." I try not to laugh at her surprise. "We're typically a 'come one, come all' kind of family."

Her lips are parted while she's staring out the window, maybe contemplating if they're in view.

Tension stiffens her body, and I ask, "You want to rip off the Band-Aid? Confront them now?"

"Now?"

"Right now. I'd just suggest putting on some pants before we go out there." I slip her a teasing smile. "Breathe, Fisher."

She inhales through her nose, then says, "Why the hell not, right? Better now than later." She's digging around, then unearths black sweatpants. "Let's see how many of your brothers have jumped on the Anti-Harriet train."

TWENTY

HARRIET FISHER

The Cobalt brothers—they are so fucking intimidating when they're all together. It took me half a second to psych myself up to air this out myself and decide to "rip off the Band-Aid" as Ben put it. Now that they've all piled out of their Range Rover and I'm facing them in this echoey, empty parking deck with Ben thankfully at my side—I feel their confidence stampeding mine like a pride of lions versus a panicky hare.

God, I'm calling myself panicky.

I'm standing completely still. I'm not on the verge of running. My eyeballs feel swollen, and if I never shed a tear again, I think I'd kiss the piss-stained concrete. Which says *a lot*.

And look, there's not much to lose. Ben has made it so clear he still wants to be friends, and that matters more than anything that happens next.

So before they can utter a word, I bite out, "I offered Charlie a deal. I'd blow him so he'd back off Ben. He didn't take it, and the deal is completely off. Rescinded." I'm pretty sure my entire face is one massive glare.

Tom's brows have sprung off his forehead.

Eliot is grinning.

Beckett is only looking at Charlie.

And Charlie is leaning against the shut car door, staring directly at me like I'm made of cellophane.

"Let it be known"—Eliot speaks first, which doesn't seem to surprise any of his brothers—"Charlie cannot be swayed by blow jobs."

Is Charlie smiling?

"And you." Eliot points a finger at me, then claps. The applause is overly loud in the parking deck, like twenty hands coming together and not two. "Very inspired ploy to protect our little brother."

"Therapy can't come soon enough," Tom mutters in a breathy whisper, then gives me a lackluster thumbs-up. Which is way better than the middle finger I was expecting.

"You're okay?" Beckett asks *me*.

I try not to startle in shock. I nod once, my cheeks roasting at the attention. "Yeah, fine." A warm, unfamiliar feeling washes over me that I instantly wish would stay. I cross my arms, shifting my weight with uncertainty.

"Ben?" Beckett asks.

"All good," Ben tells him, then glances down at me with a rising smile.

Tension slowly ekes out of my body as I realize they're not brandishing pitchforks. It's the exact opposite. Do they really not see me as an enemy? Or in the very least, too unhinged to be friends with their brother?

No one gets another word out—not when we hear a car rumbling closer. Everyone turns as a sleek black Audi with red stripes slows to a stop at the butt of the Range Rover. I gauge their complete lack of apprehension right before the driver's door opens.

Stepping out, black boots touch the ground, and I look up to see black slacks, black belt, and tucked-in black V-neck on a fit, masculine body. So many tattoos scatter his white skin, all the way up his neck. He swings out a trauma bag. Blows a bubblegum bubble, pops it in his mouth. Then lifts sunglasses up to his ash-brown hair—

which I've seen dyed white, black, even blue before (but never in person, always online and in tabloids).

If "effortlessly cool" were a person, it'd be this guy.

"Famous ones," he says to the Cobalts, his voice sounding naturally rough and deep while he stays chill. "Pop the trunk." He's already snapping on medical gloves. "Whoever's bleeding goes first."

I find myself locked in on him. On how he's triaging Charlie and Tom. On his assured demeanor. He's not a paramedic. He's a Yale medical school graduate. He went through residency at Philadelphia General Hospital, according to my Wiki search on him.

He's a doctor.

Seeing one in the wild isn't like spotting a rare albino moose, okay, but this little seed of envy-adoration grows being so close to someone who's *made it*. Who knows their shit. Who's done the arduous leg work, came out with the M.D., practices medicine, and his patients trust him to help them. It's clear the Cobalt boys called him at two a.m. to come to the rescue. Now he's at a random NYC parking deck acting like this is just any regular Friday night.

"That's Farrow," Ben whispers to me, probably seeing me ogle the fuck out of him while Charlie hops up on the opened trunk. I sincerely hope Ben doesn't think I have the hots for their family's on-call concierge doctor.

I'm like ninety-nine percent positive that's his job title because I've researched the position out of curiosity.

We're all congregated at the rear of the Range Rover. Charlie's bodyguard has even joined us, but I keep my distance from everyone.

Only Ben hangs beside me, and I whisper back, "Farrow Redford Keene, I've heard of him."

"*Hale*," Ben corrects with a small smile. "He's married to my cousin Maximoff." There's a sweet reverence in the way Ben mentions his oldest cousin, and seeing as how he brought up Maximoff in the escape room, I'm sensing a lot of love there.

It's cool knowing his issues with Xander haven't tarnished his relationship with the other Hales. If Ben somehow hated Farrow, I would feel like shit for being *this* laser-focused on him. I don't even tell Ben that I only know of Farrow because of his highly-publicized relationship with Maximoff. Otherwise, I doubt their family's concierge doctor would be all over the internet.

Farrow crouches down and rolls up Charlie's pant leg slowly, then faster (but carefully) once he sees shards of glass still lodged in his kneecap.

I bet he'll need stitches. His cuts seem deeper than mine—like he anchored his weight on the glass. I'd feel guilty, but I didn't ask him to drop to his knees. He could've just told me to stand up.

Red rivers of blood track down Charlie's legs.

Tom sucks in a wince.

Eliot grimaces. "Oof. Don't pass out, Tom." He clutches his brother's shoulder when Tom begins gagging. The bloodied wounds are fully displayed.

"That's worse than what you described, Charlie," Beckett says quietly to his brother.

"It's barely even bleeding," Charlie tells him.

"Eh, try again, Cobalt." Farrow inspects the depth and size of the visible gashes. "This is not barely." He asks him a few questions about how he feels. Like, "Dizzy? Nauseous?" After Charlie answers, Farrow cleans the wounds, then gathers a needle and vial of…lidocaine? I squint but can't read the label from here. He explains to Charlie, "I'm going to give you local anesthesia—"

"Skip it," Charlie interjects. Is he nuts? I would've gladly numbed my cuts before bandaging them.

Farrow frowns. "It's just lidocaine." I was right about that, *fuck yes.*

"I don't need it."

"Man, you have about *five* pieces of glass I'm going to extract. Then I'm going to suture at least two cuts. One might need *four* stitches. You'll want the lido."

"Charlie," Beckett murmurs.

"Fine," Charlie says. "Just hurry, I'm sure Tom is panicking about never being able to sing Bohemian Rhapsody again."

"Not funny," Tom croaks.

Farrow side-eyes him. "Don't talk until after I check you out."

Banter escalates between Ben's brothers, but my attention has been usurped as Farrow administers a lidocaine shot in each knee. He asks Charlie if he can feel anything when he presses near the wound. When it's numb, he moves on.

I watch him use forceps to pluck glass from Charlie's skin. He's in a squatting position, but he's so still. Quick. Meticulous. His hands never tremble.

When he brings out a suture kit, I stop myself from moving closer. *Don't be that fucking nosy, Harriet.* I'm lucky to have permission to watch this at all.

Once Charlie's wounds are stitched, cleaned, and bandaged, Farrow removes his dirtied gloves and puts on a fresh pair. Then asks Tom's brothers, "How'd he strain his voice?"

"Stupidity," Charlie answers.

Tom flips him off with two hands.

"He was yelling over a siren," Ben tells Farrow.

"A siren?" His pierced brows rise while he chews gum.

"An escape game gone poorly," Beckett clarifies.

Farrow spins around to Tom. He has a couple inches on him, so maybe he'll do this examination standing. I'd need to make my patient sit down. "I'm going to touch your neck and check out your throat. You okay with that?"

Tom is a little red in the face. He's also jittery, shifting his weight around and nodding. "Do it," he rasps in a whisper.

Farrow presses his fingers around Tom's neck. "Everyone be quiet for a second except for Tom." He's asking him to speak, and I wonder if he's listening for rattling. Then Farrow has a little handheld light. "Stick your tongue out and say *ahh*."

Tom does as instructed. "Ahhhh." His voice sounds wheezy.

Farrow shines the light down his throat, then assesses. I can't decipher the severity of the prognosis from his face, but he doesn't take long to tell Tom, "You likely just have vocal strain, but I can't rule out vocal bruising without a laryngoscopy."

"Are you doing a laryngoscopy here?" I say, my excitement getting the better of me. Fuck, *fuck*. Everyone is staring at me. I death-grip to the fact that Ben is smiling.

"Harriet Fisher?" Farrow guesses. "Luna's lab partner?" His memory recall must be insane because I've never interacted with him, and I highly doubt any Hale has mentioned me more than once.

"Former lab partner," I nod.

"Farrow," he introduces himself, and I'm shocked he doesn't say Dr. Hale. He must offer his first name to all strangers, because there is no fucking way I've leveled-up to one of the inner-circles of these families. I have to still be somewhere on the outskirts.

To me and Tom, Farrow says, "I need to do the laryngoscopy in the office. It's sterile and all the equipment is there."

"That's back in Philly," Beckett reminds Tom.

Farrow runs down Tom's options, which include having Farrow's uncle, also a physician, bring the equipment up to New York. It dawns on me that Farrow isn't the sole concierge doctor these families must hire.

Tom can also go to a hospital in the city if he wants this resolved like immediately.

"What happens if there's a bruise?" Eliot asks.

"No permanent damage. A superficial bruise will heal quickly by itself, but if there's a hemorrhagic polyp…a blood blister, it will require surgery, but the voice will typically return to its original capability even with surgery. So whichever way you flip it, your odds look great, Tom. Don't stress. Just try not to talk at all. If you have to, you can whisper. Drink lots of fluids, use a nebulizer and humidifier, and don't smoke. If it's only vocal strain, your voice should heal in a few days."

Tom decides on the option where he'll have Farrow do the laryngoscopy tonight in Philly. No shot at me seeing it then. I try not to be bummed. Eliot offers to go with his brother, that they'll just crash at their parents' house, which is in the Philly area.

Must be nice to have an open-door policy with their mom and dad. Welcome back home whenever.

Farrow pries off his gloves. "Anyone else need looked at?"

That's when Ben peers down at me. My heart flip-flops strangely, especially when I realize all four of his brothers are staring at me too.

"Yeah, Harriet does," Ben says. "She knelt on glass."

I'm frozen. "No...no, I..." My brows are furry little caterpillars of confusion. Farrow is already approaching. "Dude, I don't pay for concierge treatment. I'm not a 'famous one'." I use air quotes to quote him.

"If you're hurt, I'm going to treat you. I don't give a flying shit about the pay." He crouches down again, unzipping his trauma bag. "I've never been into medicine for the money."

Me neither. I heard residents don't make much anyway, I want to say. *Is that true?* I keep it inside and just roll up my sweatpants while he snaps on a new pair of gloves. "I already cleaned and sealed the cuts. They weren't as deep as Charlie's. I bandaged them too."

"You sealed them?" Farrow asks, peeling off my bandage. "With...?"

"Superglue." Why the fuck is my heart beating out of my chest? I'm so freaking nervous as he inspects the several cuts I sealed along my kneecaps.

"Keep an eye out for infection."

I nod stiffly, my pulse still out of whack as I watch him adhere clean bandages to each of my knees. Then he rises so very high above me and peels off his gloves. "Nice work," he says with so much light in his brown eyes. It's a smile before his lips stretch. Then he's packing up to go. Nice work?

Nice work.

Nice work.

Nice fucking work?!?!

I think I black out in joy.

And I only come to focus when Ben quietly teases, "You think he knows you're pre-med?"

I'm hopefully not blushing. "No way. A baby could do what I did."

"What babies are you trusting with superglue?" He's near a laugh, and my insides do an odd floaty maneuver.

"Baby geniuses like your brother."

"Like you," Ben smiles.

I start to shake my head but stop myself short, especially as Charlie comes closer with Beckett. Tom and Eliot are gathering their things out of the Range Rover, but they hear Charlie say loudly, "What have you learned, children?"

"Tom can't speak for days," Beckett says.

Eliot calls out, "Life is nothing but a maze." What...is happening?

"Umbrellas can be set ablaze," Tom whispers and slams the car door.

"Harriet deserves all the praise," Ben smiles down at me.

I wait for an explanation, but they give none. Their little word rhyming thing just ends, and I look around at each of them. "You all are really fucking weird."

Ben laughs, "You have no idea."

My lips nearly twitch into a tiny smile. As everyone starts climbing into vehicles, I'm hooked on him for a moment.

After my mistake, I expected tonight to be absolutely *gutting*. Then he found me. He held me in my car, stroked my hair, rocked me—and I thought I'd hate it. But I never wanted those intimate moments with him to end.

I've never had anyone try to make me feel better when I've been down in the dumps. Not as deeply as he just did. I've had to crawl out of the overflowing, suffocating dumpster myself.

And to have someone care enough to even open the dumpster, let alone crawl into it just to pull me out, overwhelms me. It's like

I'm stepping onto a beach my toes have never touched as the sun rises and bathes my skin. It's warmth. Tonight has been so warm when I expected it to be bone-chilling cold.

I try not to fear wanting more. Because it's terrifying to long for a feeling that another person provides when all I've ever done is rely on myself. What happens if it stops? Now that I've experienced this warmth, will life feel ten billion times colder without it?

I wonder if I've crossed the "no turning back" sign. If this is the moment a Cobalt has forever changed me.

TWENTY-ONE

BEN COBALT

Tom and Eliot aren't the only ones who return to Philly this weekend. When my brothers hear my bird died, everything changes, and by Sunday, we all end up at the Cobalt Estate.

My childhood home brings an aching nostalgia I've been trying to avoid. The humongous oak tree deep in the backyard beyond the stone patio and heated pool had been one of my favorite spots as a kid. I spent more hours lost in the thick gnarled branches than I did in the extravagant home library.

Honestly, most of my siblings find these backyard funerals silly, but it's not odd for them to attend.

Growing up, I had a goldfish that Eliot tried to feed to Jane's black cat, Lady Macbeth. Instead of flushing the fish when it died, Mom orchestrated this elaborate funeral procession that none of them really took seriously. Tom wielded a plunger like a bandmaster's baton, and Eliot snuck a flask of whiskey. Which got him in so much trouble.

Even when he said, "It's ceremonial whiskey. What's a funeral without a toast to the dead, Dad?"

He was fourteen.

Later, when Pip-Squeak passed, it crushed me. I grew up with the cockatiel, but my mom got him when he was relatively old, so I knew he wouldn't live long enough to be with me in college. I loved that she chose the unloved bird who really needed a home.

Though for her, I think she liked the idea of Pip-Squeak being a temporary thing and not a thirty-year commitment. She's not an animal person, but somehow, our pets always warm up to her cold nature.

I remember Pip-Squeak's backyard funeral like it was yesterday. The utter fucking chaos.

My siblings made this elaborate, giant paper mâché cockatiel sculpture. To which Jane, Charlie, and Beckett rigged on a zip-line from tree to tree. During the ceremony, as the five-foot cockatiel took flight, Tom and Eliot threw firecrackers at it.

The paper mâché went up in flames. And so did the branches to my favorite oak tree.

Jane's white cat, Ophelia, escaped her arms and scaled the tree trunk. Some of us were wearing wings, and without thinking, I ran after the cat.

Beckett ran after me.

Right as I captured Ophelia, Beckett pulled me down—but his wings caught fire.

I'd never seen Charlie sprint that fast in my life. He pried the burning wings off Beckett in seconds. Even before I could. Mom stomped on them with her heel. Dad drew us all back and called the fire station.

The tree and Ophelia survived.

It's hard not to think about old pet funerals when I'm at one. Typically, I was the only one who cared enough to cry. Most of the pets we buried were mine.

They did this for me, and no matter how silly or dumb or senseless they thought these funerals were or however chaotic they became, I loved every second of them—because they all showed up.

They always showed up for me.

Even now as adults, they're here.

One through seven. We've all gathered around a fresh mound of dirt. White cotton-candy clouds float in the bluest August sky, and we're barely into the funeral and I can confidently say this one is by far the strangest.

Because everyone is on their best behavior.

Charlie has yet to desecrate the grave by flicking a cigarette. Hell, he's not even smoking. No one's made a wisecrack about the afterlife or Big Bird. Most everyone has actually dressed in funeral blacks like this is a serious event.

Beside me, Audrey straightens her wide-brimmed black hat, the veil matching her Victorian dress with puffed sleeves and a bell skirt. She must be sweating in this heat.

Mom chose a staple black dress. Not that uncommon. She's always in black. At her side, Dad ditched his white button-down for a black one. He'd normally show in a navy-blue suit, but will you look at that? He's also in *all black*.

I can't stare at him for long. His deep blue eyes touch mine, and a nervous sweat pricks the back of my neck.

My burgundy MVU shirt sticks to my skin, and I flip my baseball cap backward. All my brothers wear black too, and for Charlie—*Charlie* to conform to a dress code is just bizarre.

I realize quickly my brothers are wearing the men's suits our mom designed. This year, as a bonding thing with her, we helped our mom create suits after our styles. She named each one after us—the Charlie, the Beckett, the Eliot, the Tom, the Ben—and half the net profits are supposed to go to us since we all modeled the Calloway Couture men's collection on a runway and in ads.

The fashion line debuted this spring, and we'll see our first paycheck in January. But it won't help me much by then.

Anyway, I highly doubt *the Ben* sold well—it's the most basic black suit, unlike Eliot's Romeo-inspired tailcoat and undershirt, and Tom's punk-rock jacket with zippered arms and a chain along his belt loop and pocket. Fans have clamored to buy *the Charlie* purely because it's from Charlie. His material is black velvet, and he has no shirt underneath the jacket. Or maybe they'll buy *the Beckett* since, in my opinion, it's the best—a slim-fitting black suit and black undershirt with silver stitching around the cuffs. Sleek and cool.

I wait for someone to speak.

A weird, respectful silence takes place for—uh, *five* minutes and counting? Yeah, one minute is usually pushing it.

Not *this*.

I look to my older sister.

Jane. With her wavy brown hair and splash of freckles on her cheeks and sly smiles—she's a bubbly combination of our mom and dad. The ultimate big sister who will drop everything for us with one SOS text.

For this Cobalt affair, she has on a black tulle skirt and zebra-print top. She's *matching*. What the hell?

Her outfits never match to the point where she's been on *Celebrity Crush's* Worst Dressed list for forever. Which should rattle our fashion designer mom's world, but our mom wants us to be *us*. Terrible style and all, Charlie would quip.

Jane catches me staring. She flashes a beaming smile at me, then mimes the tip of a top hat. She would be the first to try to cheer me up. Right before Beckett.

"Oh Pippy," she'd say when we were younger. "Don't cry. I'm here. I'll make everything better, and as your big sister, I will wish upon every star for it to be true."

Jane was the one I went to for advice, so when she first left for Princeton, it'd been devastating. We talked on the phone, and I tried to convince myself that it was the same. But it wasn't really. I think that's the toughest part of being among the youngest. My older siblings were able to spend their entire adolescence with all or most of us.

Audrey and I—we had a finite amount of time where the house was full. For three years, it was just us and our parents here in Philly while my brothers were in New York and Jane lived with Moffy. Three whole years that they'll never understand.

I try to smile back at Jane, but it's a little difficult considering my brain is spinning. Why are they all acting normal?

Did I miss the memo? One definitely got sent around. I'm afraid it said: *Take Theodore's funeral seriously for Ben. Act like church mice.*

Jane peers up at her six-foot-seven stoic husband. He's the only person taller than me here. Brown hair curls behind his ears. His strong, clenched jaw is unshaven and makes him appear overly stern and brooding all the time.

Thatcher Moretti is a Marine vet, identical twin, full-time bodyguard to Jane, and the only person who's breeched the Cobalt walls. It took a literal *Marine* to enter my family. I'm not so sure it will happen as easily again, and it wasn't really easy for him. For months, we all tested him with a series of elaborate Truth or Dares. Prying into his personal life. Seeing how far he'd go for Jane.

He's bouncing their unusually fussy nine-month-old in his arms. Maeve Rose Moretti. My niece is the only one crying. And it's a literal conundrum how *no one* is commenting on the baby bawling at a funeral.

Mom has her fingers to her temple in a slight cringe, hating infant cries, but it's obvious she absolutely adores Maeve because she's not banishing the baby out of the circle.

"Shh, shh," Thatcher coos, rubbing Baby Maeve's back.

Jane waves a very old stuffed animal. "Look, Mr. Lion! You *love* Mr. Lion."

Tom cringes at the ratty toy. "Ew," he whispers, trying to save his voice. Thankfully no vocal bruising. It was just strained, Farrow diagnosed.

"I bleached Mr. Lion," Jane says. "He's good as new."

Tom opens his mouth to respond, but Eliot kicks Tom's shins. He shuts up.

Jane's blue eyes flit to me, then she also goes quiet.

They're being really obvious now.

"Shall we begin, Mother?" Audrey asks.

"Yes, that silence was long enough."

Agreed.

Our mom hands out white roses from a bouquet to each of us. I swear she tries to smile *warmly* at me, and her face makes a robotic twitch.

What the fuck is happening?

When she returns to our dad, I hear him whisper, "You're overdoing it, darling."

She smacks his side. "He's watching us."

Our dad makes direct eye contact with me, and I give him a short, confused headshake. His features are impossible to read.

So I just try to concentrate on Theodore. He's why we're all here. I think.

Audrey has on black silk gloves. Reaching down, she takes my hand, and my chest swells with more emotion as I feel my sister trying to comfort me over seeking comfort for herself.

"Theodore," she says. "You were beloved. And I would like to read a poem in your honor." She takes a deep breath before reciting it by memory. "'Do not stand...By my grave, and weep. I am not there, I do not sleep—I am the thousand winds that blow, I am the diamond that glints in snow. I am the sunlight on ripened grain, I am the gentle autumn rain.'"

I recognize the poem. "Immortality" by Clare Harner. Tom has recited it a handful of times at Wednesday Night Dinners.

I've never heard Audrey deliver it, and in her whimsical, breathless voice, it twists the raw parts of me.

"'As you awake with morning's hush, I am the swift, up-flinging rush. Of quiet birds in circling flight. I am the day transcending night. Do not stand...By my grave, and cry—I am not there.'" She exhales deeply. "'I did not die.'"

I blink, expecting tears. Waterworks. Something.

Emotions feel coiled inside my chest. Tightly balled rather than unspooled threads. "That was beautiful, Audrey," I breathe. "Thanks." I wrap an arm around her shoulders and cup the back of her skull below her hat, trying to let her know I don't need the comfort. *I'm okay.*

"Theodore." Mom tosses her white rose onto the grave. "What can I say about you? You were a beloved winged creature that didn't abide by nightly quiet hours. You once yanked my diamond necklace right off my throat when I *graciously* changed your water. And your favorite word to mimic was *Satan*, to which I blame Eliot and Tom as your teachers."

Eliot mutters, "Terrific student."

"The best," Tom whispers.

They set their roses on the dirt.

Mom continues, "But you would also say, *bird*, and I found that endearing in its self-awareness. All in all, you weren't bad." She intakes a sharp breath. "I guess…I will miss you." She eyes me and adds, "Very much."

I smile now. That sounds like her, and it's about as good of an admission of my mom liking Theodore as I'll ever get. Dad squats down and puts the white rose on the dirt. "Memoria De valens vivat tamque vestri."

I can't translate the Latin, but I think it has something do with *memorial…memory?*

Audrey nods like she understands it, and I have no doubt Jane and my brothers know the translation too. But it's one of those many times in my family that I'm not really in the mood to ask for it.

Charlie says nothing, just places the rose with the others.

"You'll be missed," Beckett whispers, crouching to rest his rose on the earth.

"Forever loved and cherished," Jane says in her breezy tone. Another rose tossed.

Thatcher adds his flower to the stack, then helps Baby Maeve with hers. Jane is seriously smitten.

I'm up last, and my knees sink into the dirt. I press a hand to where I buried the shoebox. "We had a good run," I murmur. "I'm sorry." It was my fault. *I'm sorry.* "Thank you." I nod a couple times, then stand back up.

No one says a fucking thing.

It is hilariously quiet.

"Any other words?" I ask them.

Mumbles of *no, non, nope.*

I nod repeatedly, letting this sink in. "No one's going to mention why Eliot and Tom named him Theodore?"

A wicked grin spreads over Eliot's face.

Mom skewers him with a glare. "Your tongue will be in a jar on our bookshelf *fermenting.*"

He puts a hand to his heart. "My own mother would make me mute."

"A gift to the universe."

"A gift to your bookshelf."

Mom raises her hand. "We are at a funeral. This is a *serious* matter."

Eliot stops grinning. It just vanishes from his face completely. He concedes way too early. I look around, expecting someone else to chime in.

"Charlie?" I ask.

He shrugs, appearing bored.

I frown at the earth, then the sky, squinting. It hits me suddenly. Maybe they feel like they've hurt me in the past by not being more respectful. And so they're trying now. "I hope you all know I love you as you are," I say so quietly, but in the harsh silence, they can all hear. "I might be nothing like any of you and you may've never loved my pets the way I did—but I've loved you for caring enough to be here. I've loved the chaos."

My life would've been less full without it.

"Don't change," I whisper, even knowing in time everything changes, nothing is ever stagnant. The earth shifts beneath us even if we can't feel it. Trees will grow. Eventually someone might cut them down for lumber, then hopefully plant a new one its place. "Please."

"Can we...?" Audrey glances not that furtively at our oldest siblings. "Should we...speak?"

"So there was a plan?" I ask them.

Audrey bursts out, "Mother said we should employ the kindergarten rule that none of us can seem to follow. *If you have nothing nice to say, say nothing at all.* That also, she said, includes anything remotely egregious or bitchy or vulgar."

"Audrey Virginia, tattling on Mom," Tom whispers.

Her cheeks roast. "I-I did not."

"She did not," Jane backs her up. "She was just being...thorough." She nods confidently to Audrey, who nods just as resolutely back. Mom has a rare heartfelt smile that appears mostly for my sisters.

"Thoroughly annoying," Charlie mutters.

Audrey gasps. I have no clue why she looks for his praise. She wants Charlie to tell her she's the best sister, the best listener, the best secret-keeper, the best *everything*. When, in reality, he spends most of his time teasing the shit out of her.

Our dad has a burgeoning, powerful grin on our mom. "Were you not the first to break your own kindergarten rule?"

"Your memory is going," she retorts. "It's about time."

"A time you will mourn."

She purses her lips but doesn't deny. His arm slides along her lower back, and before they catch me watching again, I tell everyone, "Say whatever you need to say."

Eliot steps forward, clearing his throat as he announces, "To the greatest named bird in the history of the avian species—"

"Let's be real here," Mom interjects, "to get a rise out of your father you named this poor little fragile animal after a dull, uninteresting person. Specifically his boarding school fling of *one month*."

"Dad's reaction could have been better," Tom whispers.

"There's still ample time," Eliot tells our father. "An eye twitch of anger? A prickle of irritation?"

Dad is grinning into a laugh. "I can't be irritated at something that will never bother me, but you're welcome to keep trying. As always, the effort is amusing."

"Don't encourage them," Mom says. "They *cursed* a defenseless tiny beaked creature."

Jane stifles a laugh.

It makes me smile.

"Curses don't exist, darling," Dad says.

"Oh please, you're cursed with an ego that could choke out Godzilla."

We all laugh.

"Gifted," he corrects.

"Did you gift it to yourself too?"

"That is the definition of ego, Rose."

She raises her hand at his face. "And that is enough."

His grin never dims on her.

"Mom and Dad are going to make out," Tom whispers into a cough.

"*Tom*," we all say together. He literally can't help himself, and I end up laughing—swiftly, their laughter follows mine. Soul-filling, vibrantly loud noise cascades through the trees around us. It feels good until it doesn't.

I still feel like I can't live with my brothers long-term. Tom nearly losing his voice because of me—it's just a reminder I can't be around them. Even if I want to be, even if I love *this*. My plan has to move forward.

Everyone but me and Audrey go inside for the breakfast Chef Michael whipped up. He's been my family's private chef for years and he'd make mouth-watering blueberry vegan pancakes every Sunday for me.

Ignoring my growling stomach, I spend extra time with my sister while I'm here.

She spreads out a quilt that Beckett sewed for her years ago. "His love language is gift giving," Audrey says, seeing me staring at the quilt, then she smiles at the baseball cap on my head.

My favorite worn-out blue ballcap was a gift from Beckett. It'd been his when he was a kid. "He does it well," I say.

"Too well. I'm envious." She plops onto the quilt while I lie on the earth, staring up at the clouds. She's quick to tell me, "Everyone just worries about you, you know."

Turning onto my side, I prop on my elbow to face her. "No one needs to walk on eggshells around me. I'm doing fine."

"But you're still not speaking to Winona. She was your best friend."

"She's one of your best friends."

"We can both have the same best friend, like we had for years. It was a pleasant time, wasn't it, Ben?" She slips off her gloves, waiting for my response.

"Yeah," I nod. *It was.* I have no complaints about my childhood and adolescence. Even the saddest days couldn't wash away the love. I felt rich because of my enormous family, including the Hales and Meadows. Not because of the trips around the world, the trust fund, the luxury cars, the mansions. Even now, my pockets might be empty, but I'm going to feel the most broke when I never come back home.

I know this.

I push past the ache in my chest. It's hard not to think of Harriet when I do. I thought about inviting her to this backyard funeral, but I'd rather introduce her to my parents one-on-one and not among all my siblings. It'd overwhelm most anyone, and after what happened on Friday night, she might need a breather from the chaos.

Plus...it might not be a good idea to do yet. I shouldn't draw closer to her unless I explain more of my situation. So yeah, I need to do that first.

I focus on my sister. "How's school going?" She updates me over text every day. "Did you finally convince drama club to let you in?" Her and Kinney have been getting more involved in extracurriculars to take their mind off not having Winona and Vada around.

"No, I fear it's a lost cause. I found out that Mandy Dean hates me because Eliot wouldn't give her older sister a third date when he was at Dalton. And Father might not believe in curses, but Eliot most assuredly cursed me. So now you can't rest easy living with a curser." She lifts her veil, so I can see her face more clearly. Hurt creases her eyes.

I didn't choose Eliot over you, I want to tell her.

But I did.

"No one's giving you crap though? No guys are messing with you or Kinney?"

Audrey sighs. "You don't have to ask me that every time we talk." She slowly folds her gloves. "I'd tell you if someone were harassing me."

"Like you told me about Winona?"

"It wasn't my place, and I didn't even know the extent. Not like Vada did." She removes her hat completely now. Her carrot-orange hair blows in the soft wind. "And anyway, *no one* is going to try anything with Kinney or me. Not after you sent Tate to the hospital. I think that scared everyone at school."

Even though Tate drugged my cousin, I should have still been charged with assault. I realize how lucky...privileged I am to have parents with the best lawyers in town. The threat of litigation alone was enough for Tate's family to quietly settle.

"That's an unintended benefit, I guess." I pick a weed out of the grass. "Have you been regretting not going to boarding school?"

"Not even for a second." She speaks so quietly, as if it's a secret. "I feel guilty, almost, for not wishing I were with them. But I didn't just stay in Philly to be close to our parents."

"Jane and Thatcher?" I guess since they're here too.

"Not just them either."

I frown. "Okay, I'm confused."

"You and our brothers." She explains further, "You do realize the commute from Philly to see you in New York is only two hours? From boarding school it'd take over three hours to reach Hell's Kitchen. Even longer to come back here. It's forever away, really, and I don't want to be forever away from all of you. And one day, I'll be in New York City, too. We'll be together again. You can count on it."

I won't be there, Audrey.

This conversation is more painful than I thought it'd be. "New York would be better with you in it." I try to smile at her.

"All of us. We're the best together."

"Or the worst."

"Impossible." Her blue eyes narrow on me, studying my face. "It's so strange. You still haven't cried."

"You told me not to," I say lightly. "Remember? The poem?"

She rolls her eyes, but a soft smile touches her lips. "Yes, but—it's just...it's frankly *weird*. Tom even said if you didn't cry this morning, it'd be sus."

Hearing her say "sus" makes me laugh hard. I fall back into the grass.

"What?" She smiles at my laughter.

"When you quote Tom, it's just the best." She speaks like she's stuck in a Brontë novel, and Tom uses slang like a typical twenty-one-year-old.

"You are *sus*," she jabs my arm with a finger, her smile flickering in and out.

I sit up. "Everything's fine, really, Audrey." I take off my ballcap. Running my fingers through my hair.

She searches my eyes, trying to uncover a lie, but finds none. Unfurling a black laced fan, she wafts her glistening face. "I overheard Mother and Father talking."

"What about?"

"They said you're working at some bar in New York. As a bartender."

I suppress a groan in my chest. *Fuck*. Fuck. I rub at my eyes. "Really?" Only one person could've leaked that information to my parents. One person I've trusted for years.

My bodyguard. *Chris Novak.*

I clench my jaw. The betrayal sinks heavy, even though I have no idea why he'd tell them. Was it a security reason? Did he feel like they needed to know? He's kept way worse shit a secret, but then again, maybe his loyalty is askew after I went full Rambo mode.

She frowns. "Is that not true? They said you were bartending so you could be closer to a girl. They didn't name or describe her, but I assumed it was Harriet."

After the video chat where Audrey met Harriet, I've mentioned her to my sister. Once. Twice…a lot of times. I like talking about her.

"Yeah, it is Harriet," I nod.

She perks. "Can I have her number? Which bar?"

"When you meet her in person, you can ask for her number. It's not mine to give." I scratch the back of my head. "And if I tell you the bar, you *cannot* tell our brothers. Seriously, I don't need Tom and Eliot to come crash my place of work and get me and Harriet fired."

"I promise. I won't."

I shouldn't tell her. "Even if they press you—"

"I will not crack." She puts her hands together. "Please, *please* give me a chance. I know I haven't been great at keeping secrets before, but I just need the opportunity to succeed and—"

"Okay, okay." I trust her, but this is a big risk. "We're bartending at a placed called Where You Want to Be at the End of the World. It's where *Breakfast at Tiffany's* was playing when we talked on the phone."

Her eyes brighten. "Can I visit you there?"

"You have to be eighteen to get in."

Her shoulders slump. "Being the youngest Cobalt is truly abhorrent."

I smile. "I know. You're almost there though."

"I'm sixteen. Eighteen is a *lifetime* away." She falls back onto the quilt dramatically, and really, fuck Mandy Dean for not letting her into drama club.

"When are cheer tryouts?" I ask.

"Next week," she says to the sky. "If I don't make varsity, bury me right here."

"You're going to make it." She was on the JV cheer squad last year, and she's good enough to be on varsity. We talk more about my classes and how MVU is about the same difficulty as Penn. She updates me on the fact that *zero* boys in her class are cute.

She's had plenty of crushes, but never on guys at school. Great for me, since I never had to deal with my little sister potentially dating one of my friends when we were at Dalton together. Too many of my hockey teammates wanted to hook up with her. It was very fucking annoying.

"Boys are so immature," she laments. "And soft. I just want a *man*." She speaks loud enough that Charlie can hear while trekking over to us. "Is it really too much to ask to be manhandled?"

She worries me when she says shit like that. "Depends on which guy you're asking, seeing as how you're still *sixteen*." I throw a dugout weed on the grass.

"La tragédie." She shuts her fan. "The man of my dreams is out there. And he'll sweep me off my feet so very *roughly*."

Charlie stops at the quilt. "Look, it's the worst conversation I've heard all day."

She lifts her chin. "Don't make fun of my romance."

"I'm not. I'm making fun of your imagination."

Her jaw drops, and I glare at Charlie, but he's not paying attention to our sister. He nods slightly to me. "Dad wants to talk to you."

"Later, I will—"

"Before breakfast, he said."

Fuck. I pick myself off the grass. "Is this you warning me?"

"No, I just wanted the fresh air." His dry tone and irritation are apparent. "He'll find you if you don't find him first."

So he is giving me a heads up. "Thanks," I tell my brother, a weird feeling rolling around my stomach. Is Charlie being nice?

Hiking back to the mansion, I run into my dad in his pursuit of me. And sure enough, he says, "Can we talk before we eat?"

I don't love the seriousness in his eyes. Avoidance is futile. This is going to happen.

TWENTY-TWO

BEN COBALT

I expect my dad to lead me to his office, the den, or the library, but we never go inside. Once we reach the patio, he chooses the wicker-cushioned couch. I loved swinging on the hammock by the pool as a kid, but this couch was consistently one of my favorite spots. Because of the iron pergola. Vines of purple wisteria crawl up the four posts and hang down the iron slats overhead.

I'd stare up at the bees for hours and whistle at the birds.

I wonder if that's why he chooses this place, the outdoors. Or am I reading too much into this?

Yeah, fucking doubtful.

My dad's IQ surpasses most. Even my mom—who is viciously smart. He ranks high on every scale. Deduction. Memory. Ambition. His brain is an encyclopedia of random information, and he can speak even more languages than Charlie.

Not a day goes by that I don't think how astronomically different I am from this man. We're not different sides of the same coin. He's an archaic Roman provincial coin and I'm a standard American penny.

"Let's hear it." I sink down on the cushioned chair across from him. "You're so worried about me. I didn't cry for Theodore. Something must be wrong, and I need to ditch Dr. Wheeler and see your therapist in New York."

He arches a brow, leaning back casually. His ankle is propped on his knee, arm extended over the top of the couch. Everywhere Connor Cobalt goes, he has an aura as if he owns the earth, the air, the water—all of life's necessities, and it's easy to believe it's true. And I don't understand how I was born from him.

I'm confident, but not even remotely in that way.

He's nonconfrontational and calm as he says, "You've already told me you don't want to see Frederick. I'm not going to press you further."

"Then what?" Baseball cap in my hands, I curl the brim in a tightening fist.

"When you were three, Tom stepped on a caterpillar and you cried," he tells me. "The next week, you stepped on an ant, and you were inconsolable for days. Even when I explained that an average garden ant would live around a year, when I gave you the rundown of their life cycle, it didn't change your despair. When you were seven, you made sure no one squashed the spider in Jane's room. Instead, you captured it in a cup and released it outside—"

I let out an annoyed breath, cutting him off. "Yeah, I don't like needlessly killing things. It's not a revelation. I shouldn't be the only person who wants to protect the fucking—" I stop myself, trying not to drop a thousand *fucks* around my parents—"the planet and the things inside of it."

"It's not a revelation, Ben," he says. "It's who you are. The depth of your compassion has never waned over the years."

Compassion. It's not something my dad actually values. It's like a genius telling you you're good at finger painting. So I'm not deluding myself into thinking this is some grand gesture to tell me he's proud of me. I don't need that.

He has a son who's his replica in mind. *Charlie.*

He has a son who's his replica in body. *Eliot.*

He has a son who's his replica in ambition. *Tom*.

He has a son who has surpassed him in raw talent. *Beckett*.

And then he has me.

I'm not a disappointment in his eyes. I know that. But I'm nothing special either.

I don't have a reply for him, and I choose to let the silence eat the air.

He takes a moment before he speaks again. His fingers slide through his wavy brown hair, then fall to his knee. "We haven't talked about that night, Ben," he tells me, his concern slipping over me.

There it is.

It always comes back to me attacking Tate. He knows the full rundown about the drugs and Winona. I confessed about the Adderall last night to my dad since I let the cat out of the bag to my brothers, and he was *extremely* concerned—specifically about how I obtained the Adderall in the first place. It's now another reason he wants me to change therapists so badly.

"Yeah, we did talk," I reply. "I told you why I did it."

"And I'm supposed to believe you've become Niccolò Machiavelli overnight?" he asks me. "When have you ever believed the ends justify the means?"

"Beliefs change," I tell him. "Shouldn't *you* out of everyone understand that? I've read about how you didn't believe in the concept of love before Mom about a billion times in the press. And you've *talked* about it to *us*." He's been very open and honest, and when he tells us that he loves us—a man who loves few and sparingly—I believe him.

Because even among our differences, I've felt my dad's love. We wouldn't be having this conversation if he didn't love me even a little bit.

"That didn't happen overnight, Ben. I didn't meet your mom and magically fall in love. I thought I was *incapable* of certain emotions. Believing I could love—that was *work*. That was therapy and investment in myself."

I say nothing. I'm not sure what to say, to be honest. A current of panic and agitation move through my bloodstream, and I'm having trouble even sitting still. *He can't find out I'm broke.* My knee tries to jostle.

I want to lean back, then forward.

It's taking everything in me to remain rigid.

His expensive sole drops off his knee and lands on the stone. He cups his hands, and his soul-burrowing gaze never leaves mine.

He might be this godly Zeus-like figure, but right now, I'm not intimidated by him. At the end of the day, he's my dad.

He continues, "You hurt someone, and the Ben that I know wouldn't care if the other guy deserved it or not, it'd affect him. It'd crush him."

It is crushing me, but not in the way he thinks. I'm not crying like Tate is that dead caterpillar. I'm not devastated. I don't even regret it.

But I am terrified of retribution. Of the universe course-correcting pain that I caused. It feels inevitable that my family will get hurt. How can I even explain that to *him*? He won't understand.

"Do I look crushed?" I ask.

"No, and that's what scares me," he says. "You're hiding your feelings, burying them, or avoiding them—"

"And this is your expert opinion, seeing as how you're a master of emotions since you have a total of five of them." I immediately regret my words for how callous they are, but I shove that guilt so far down.

He slowly blinks, but he's not looking at me like I'm a stranger he doesn't know. He stares at me with deep, unbridled worry. If I was determined to cast his concern into the ether today, I'm doing a fucking awful job at it.

"I'm not a therapist, you're right," he says. "But I think you should see someone other than Dr. Wheeler. I don't think he's a good fit for you."

The truth is, I don't believe any therapist would be good for me. If my brilliant dad doesn't understand me, then how the fuck would a professional? I already know I'm being irrational—they don't need to tell me that.

I fit my ballcap on and rise to my feet. "He's my choice. You're going to have to live with it."

He follows me to my feet. "Something has to change." He holds out a hand for me to wait because I'm facing the house. "I know you're hurting—"

"Something did change," I combat. "I moved to fucking New York." My voice rises with my frustration. "Is that not enough?!"

"Ben—"

"You want to reminisce?" I ask him, my chest rising and falling with heavy, uncontrolled breaths. "You remember when I was really little? Remember how Mom said she was going to cut out your lungs in your sleep and you told her she can have them—but it'd be a mistake because she'd miss breathing your air? I *wept* in my fucking bed that night for hours thinking my parents were going to murder each other. I called Uncle Ryke so distraught I could barely form words. I was *seven*." Tears try to burn my eyes. "It took me too many years to even understand what my brothers and sisters understood from day one—the exaggerations, the banter, the wit—I am not like all of you. I don't think like you."

"You can always talk to Ryke. Just because Winona—"

"Dad, I can't do this." My pulse is out of control. A knot is contracting painfully in my ribs. I am crawling out of my skin, and I wish Harriet were here. I wish I could divert whatever's rattling me for a second. I want the panic to just fade. "I just need you and everyone else to just *stop*." Please.

Let me go.

We both aren't blinking.

"Tu nous repousses," he says in a gentle whisper. *You're pushing us away.* "Pourquoi?" *Why?*

I shake my head, about to lie and say I'm not.

I have been distancing myself from everyone, and their biggest triumph in bringing me closer has been me moving in with my brothers. Even that, though, I am one foot out the door.

"Tu n'es pas obligé," he whispers. *You don't have to.* "Nous pouvons t'aider." *We can help you.* He reaches out, and partly to pacify him, partly because I crave my dad's embrace more than even conceivable—I let him draw me into his chest. I grip his shoulder like I'm hanging on to a jagged cliffside, not wanting to let go. Scared to fall. Scared to meet what's below.

But for their sake, I feel like I eventually have to. *Courage.* I've never lacked the courage to race after the dangerous, terrifying thing. Especially when I know it'll save someone else.

He hugs me, his hand rising to the back of my skull. The same way that I comforted Audrey at the funeral. I notice it, a subtle similarity between me and him, and my heart skips.

Breathing out the tension in my body, I just hold on to my dad for a long moment. When we pull back, he cups my jaw and nods to me. "It doesn't matter which direction your mind takes you, you're still a Cobalt. You're still my son."

It almost breaks me.

And for the first time this morning, I cry.

TWENTY-THREE

HARRIET FISHER

It's a slow, rainy Sunday night at the End of the World when Ben tells me his pet cockatiel died. The 2002 version of *Spider-Man* plays on the oversized projector screen with Tobey Maguire web slinging his way through New York, and Ben rubs a wet rag over the sticky bar counter. He says he's not crushed by Theodore's death, and he doesn't know why. When his childhood bird, Pip-Squeak, passed away, he struggled to leave his bed for seven days straight.

I wish I had the right words to say.

Death isn't something I'm all too familiar with. I never had a pet growing up. Never had a relationship with my grandparents. Never had a friend or loved one who passed away unexpectedly… or expectedly. I've been lucky. But I'm also planning to become a doctor, and death will likely be a large factor in my life.

"Maybe you're in shock," I tell him as I slice limes for the dwindling container in the mini fridge under the bar.

"Maybe I'm just checked out," he replies in a defeated tone. "When I gave Theodore to Audrey, I'd already said goodbye."

I think about my mom. In my head, I've said goodbye to her. I don't think I'd be devastated if she passed away. "I can understand that. Some goodbyes feel more final than others."

He eyes me curiously, but we don't expand on the topic because a rush of drenched college students stumbles into the empty bar. They shrug off sopping rain jackets. "Cool, Spider-Man is on tonight," one says.

The next Sunday *When Harry Met Sally…* plays to the delight of many patrons. I enjoy the cycle of New York centric films. *West Side Story, Annie, Paris is Burning,* and *Big.*

Bartending on the weekend rapidly becomes a highlight of my week. Then soon, it tops as my favorite activity. I can admit it's because of Ben. Getting to spend time with him outside of class still makes me weirdly giddy, and as we've grown closer, I feel myself anticipating it. Counting down to Saturdays and Sundays to work alongside him.

In three weeks, he's perfected the art of a good beer pour, and his whiskey sour has even outclassed mine. Whenever I fear I've accidentally ticked off a customer, he slides in with a charming smile and all the right words.

He smooths over my bumps. My hard edges. But never makes me feel as if I need to apologize for the gristle and the bite. It's *easier* being myself when he's around. Attaching myself to this feeling means attaching myself to him, right?

At times, it scares me to want Ben around this much, but fuck, isn't this what life is about? To find and surround yourself with people that make living feel *less* difficult.

The End of the World goes from a sleepy dive bar to a hot spot for twentysomethings once news around Manhattan Valley's campus gets out that *the* Ben Cobalt periodically works here.

Ben says it's a miracle his brothers still don't know since he told his little sister the truth, and especially because his parents learned from his bodyguard. Without even realizing it's a secret, Rose and Connor have kept it for him.

I wish I had that relationship with my mom.

If I did still talk to her, she probably would've typed and printed out my deepest secrets and taped them to every lamppost in the city. She has a way of always being right. Of making sure I'm wrong. Of letting me know I will never *ever* be better than her.

Aunt Helena says it's because Hope hates my dad so much that she can't see past the half of my DNA that belongs to him. Punching me down is her way of socking it to him, I guess.

Luckily, my busy college schedule casts out most thoughts about her.

August bleeds away in a fever dream of homework assignments, undergrad research, volunteering at the hospital, first exams of the semester, and bartending. Ben comes over to my apartment too many nights to count. He helps make flashcards for my anatomy class, quizzes me on the circulatory system, and reads my essay for my application into the Honors House. I listen to him vent about whaling and learn way more about microplastics than I ever have in my life. He doesn't urge me to change my ways, but with knowledge comes great responsibility (semi-thanks goes to Spider-Man), and I decide it's better to switch my plastic Tupperware for a glass one I find at a thrift store.

He introduces me to jackfruit, which blows my mind. It has the same texture as shredded meat and a tasty, mild flavor. I start swapping it for tuna in my sandwiches after he explains overfishing and bycatches. All I can think about are the little sea turtles and seabirds being scooped up in fishing nets and thrown away like trash.

I can honestly listen to Ben talk for hours. And I do. Surprisingly, I find myself talking just as much.

Even more surprisingly, he hasn't tired of me.

I could stand in the middle of Time Square and scream those words into throngs of tourists. It's revolutionary. And even with my jam-packed schedule, I still yearn for nightly phone calls with him as if this is the new episode in the addictive TV show called My Life.

Tonight, I chew on the end of a Twizzler, earbuds in, and scroll through a shared notes app where we plugged in our class schedules—our attempt to find an available window to meet for a bite to eat together on campus.

HARRIET SCHEDULE
Monday, Wednesday, Friday
11:30am – 12:20pm: Latin III

Wednesday
8am – 11:10am: Organic Chemistry I Lab
1:50pm – 5:00pm: Anatomy & Physiology Lab

Tuesday, Thursday
9:35am – 10:50am: Classical Mythology
12:45am – 2:00pm: Organic Chemistry I
2:20pm – 3:35pm: Anatomy & Physiology

BPC SCHEDULE
Tuesday, Thursday
9:35am – 10:50am: Classical Mythology
12:45pm – 2pm: Marine Biology
2:20pm – 3:35pm: World Civilizations
3:55pm – 5:10pm: Beginner Volleyball

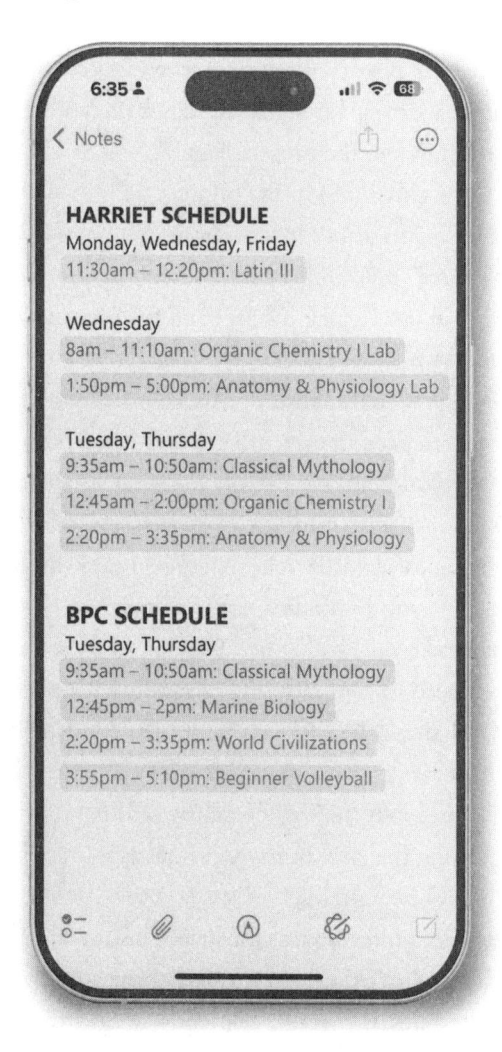

I smile reading it. I knew he picked the Tuesday, Thursday strategy of stacking all his classes on those two days. I would've done the same, but Latin was only offered on the Monday, Wednesday, Friday schedule, and trying to fit three-hour labs on Tuesday or Thursday was near impossible.

"I should've joined you in Beginner Volleyball," I say, my voice picking up in the mic of my earbuds. My phone is face-up on the coffee table. Ben's picture on the screen.

He took the pic at work when he realized I didn't have his photo in my contacts. Wearing his signature baseball cap, he holds up a peace sign and smirks in the camera. Can't lie—he's hot.

I have a hot jock's photo in my phone.

I have *Ben Cobalt's* photo in my phone.

All things that make me slump down in the lumpy couch cushion like I'm about to kick my feet and fucking *giggle*.

What are these feelings, Harriet?

I'm not in high school anymore. This feels like something I should have already experienced in eleventh grade. Missed that, apparently.

But is there really an age cut-off to being infatuated? Oh my God, am I *infatuated* with him?

"No, you would've hated volleyball," Ben says through my earbuds. "Hannah Payne broke her nose yesterday after some Kappa Phi douchebag spiked the ball at her. Whole court was full of blood."

I've gotten used to him referring to random people by their full names. Some of them, he's friends with. The kind of friends who invite him to parties or who sit beside him in class to share notes. Others, he just met, but the way he talks, you'd never know.

"Really putting the *pain* in Payne," I deadpan.

He laughs. "Clever girl."

I almost choke on my Twizzler. My face burns, and I'm thankful he can't see the flush. *Get it together, Harriet, he didn't call you a sexy vixen.* I disagree with my brain. Somehow what he said was even better. New turn-on unlocked.

Not that I should be turned on by my friend. And after he found out I almost gave head to his brother, I think that's where I'll firmly remain. Even if there was a small, microscopic chance we could be something more, I blew it up in one explosive chemical reaction called The Charlie Cobalt Blow Job Combustion.

I return to the topic at hand before I destroy this even more. "I'm just dreading having to take the P.E. requirement—which should really be banned in college. Running the death mile every week in high school was bad enough." I blow out a stressed breath. "It would've been easier doing it with you."

"Then you'll do it with me. I'll sign up for whatever P.E. course you want next semester."

I chew on the candy slowly. "That's a repeat of a credit you don't need."

"Ah, you don't know that, Fisher," he says. "I'm still Undeclared, remember? I could go into Kinesiology and then I'd be right on track."

"Or I could be unintentionally tanking you," I mutter and narrow my eyes at his schedule. "Wait, how are you getting from Marine Biology to World Civilizations in twenty minutes? Those are on opposite sides of the campus."

"I have long legs."

I gape, the Twizzler falling out of my mouth. "You're *running*?"

"I think we should direct this energy toward the fact that your science lab only gives you one credit hour, but it takes up three hours of your time. That feels way fucking wrong."

I'm about to agree with him when the door lock jangles. "Hold on," I tell Ben and sit up to make sure it's just my roommate.

The door bangs open with a fit of giggles, and I relax when I see Eden kick off her heels. Behind her, a tall Black guy with a strikingly chiseled jawline slips into the apartment and fingers the strap to her tank top. She swats his hand away when she sees me staring. "Oh, Harriet."

Austin gives me a friendly wave and takes a gentlemanly sidestep away from his girlfriend. "Hey, Harriet. How's pre-med stuff?"

"It's going well so far," I say into a nod.

Eden rocks on her feet. "I thought you were volunteering at the Urology department tonight."

"Nephrology," I correct her. "And that's on Monday nights." It's not an adrenaline-fueled position. I mostly just restock gloves and emesis bags in patient rooms and then wait in the nurses' station for any other basic tasks an undergrad can fulfill. At least the nurses are nice enough to make small talk with me when they could so easily just pretend I'm wallpaper.

Eden winces and whispers something into Austin's ear. His gaze slides down the length of her in a slow, propositioning onceover that makes me look away. *Good for Eden.* At least one of us is getting dicked down in this apartment.

"So Harriet." Eden walks to the front of the couch while Austin disappears into her bedroom. "I have a teensy, tiny favor to ask."

I'm already grabbing my backpack off the ground. "I can give you the apartment for the night."

"Really?" Her brows hike in surprise. Maybe she thought I'd put up a stink or something.

I tuck my Twizzlers under my armpit and sling my backpack over my shoulder. "Yeah, no problem."

"You are the best. *Thank you.*" She almost goes in for a hug but stops about a foot short and then slides her hands down her skirt to cover the slip up. *Shit.* It must be my face. I'm scowling, or else why would she abandon a hug midway through committing?

An awkwardness flits between us. "I'll just...go."

She nods. "Thanks again."

I want to tell her to have fun, but maybe that's too forward for our roommate relationship. So I just grab my bed pillow out of the closet and leave.

"You're not sleeping at your apartment?" Ben's voice causes me to jump.

"Fuck," I curse, totally forgetting he's still on the phone with me through my earbuds. "You scared the shit out of me."

"Sorry," he says. "Where are you headed?"

"Harold," I say the name of my Honda.

"You're going to sleep in your car?"

"I did it for two years. One more night won't kill me."

"Just come here," he says. "Stay with me for the night." His words are so casually cool that you would never think Ben Cobalt just invited me to spend the fucking night! I'm freaking out, and my feet decide now is the time to lose momentum.

I stop in the hallway, my boots frozen beside a stain on the ugliest purple carpet I've ever seen. "In case you've forgotten, Friend, you sleep on a couch."

"It's a pull-out. I can take the floor."

"No, see, car trumps floor."

"Then we can share the pull-out. It's big enough for two people."

I grumble a noise of disbelief, but my cheeks are likely fire-engine red. I am set ablaze at this idea.

"My legs fit on it, Fisher. What does that tell you?"

"That you're curling up in the fetal position at night." I chew on my lip, feeling the start of a smile.

He laughs. "Jesus. What do I need to do to convince you? Do you want me to video call while I pull out a tape measure?"

My lips tug into a bigger smile. My heart pounds so deeply. "That's unnecessary—" He's video calling me.

When I click into it, his face fills the frame. Tendrils of his hair swoop over his forehead, and his blue eyes are so captivating that I wonder how many girls he's charmed into bed. Ten? Twenty? Is our body count even similar? Friends probably shouldn't actively want this information. Maybe that makes me an overly curious friend. I can live with that.

"Harriet Fisher," he says, all too seriously. "Please spend the night at my place." Spending the night with him, even as friends, does beat sleeping in a car ten times out of ten. Resisting is futile, but I do have questions.

"Are your brothers okay with it?" I ask.

I haven't seen any of them since that night at the escape game a month ago. In truth, I have been full-on avoiding. They're intense and truly the first people to intimidate me who don't have an M.D. after their name. But I know being friends with Ben means I will run into his brothers sooner or later.

"If they weren't okay with it, they'd be the biggest hypocrites on the planet." Oh, his brothers bring home hookups.

That is…information I never thought I'd have. He flips the camera to a long camel-leather couch that honestly looks like it might've been picked out of a designer showroom.

It must be made of eco-friendly leather. Ben has told me there are a bunch of different kinds made from things like mushrooms, teak leaves, and even cacti.

So I can't see Ben sleeping on cow hides, especially after he asked if my jacket was authentic leather. I almost laughed. It is 100% pleather. No way could I afford the real deal, not that I had a big desire to anyway.

I asked him if any of his family is as environmentally conscious. He said his brother Beckett won't wear real leather, but it's mostly just out of respect for him.

I'm still staring at the couch. Where Ben sleeps. And…where his brothers live. That is a *shared* living room.

"But are your brothers having friendly sleepovers or *friendly* sleepovers." I emphasize the second 'friendly' with a raise of my brows.

Ben is grinning. "Probably the latter."

"So won't your brothers think we're having *friendly* sleepovers too?"

"I will make sure they know it's the normal kind of friendly."

I bite the corner of my lip. "Okay."

His face lights up. "Okay, see you in fifteen."

We hang up and my feet start working again. But it's only when I make it to the street that I realize what's happening. I'm about to spend the night at the Cobalt brothers' apartment.

Holy shit.

I'm about to spend the night with Ben.

TWENTY-FOUR

HARRIET FISHER

This isn't just the fanciest apartment building I've stepped foot in—this is the nicest *place* period. Besides the gold fixtures, the pristinely clean marble floors upon entering the lobby, the lavender smell like I've been bath-bombed by Lush—the exclusiveness is nothing I've encountered before.

The bell hop, entrance security, and some manager lady named Susanne all ask me *multiple times* who I'm here to see. They scan my ID in a machine. They flag down *more* security like I'm lying. They start making me believe Cobalt Stalker is printed on my forehead.

Ben did offer to meet me in the lobby. I told him, "I have feet, Cobalt boy. I don't need an escort. Just tell me your apartment number."

Mistake made.

This is just a giant reminder that having Ben at my side isn't a knock on my capabilities. He just makes tough moments less fucking tiresome. By the end of this exchange, I have verified my name ten times.

Yes, I am Harriet Stevie Fisher.

The Harriet that Ben Cobalt said would be arriving.

And the staff gives me a lukewarm apology. "People your age are usually the ones trying to sneak into the building to see the Cobalts. We've had over twenty attempts this summer since the Hales moved in. We can't be too careful. Have a nice night, ma'am." ID returned to me, I am now headed up the elevator, just glad there wasn't a full-body search.

Clearly the average twentysomething isn't renting an apartment here. Before I step on the 21st floor, the elevator lets out a polite ding.

Wow, even the elevator is prissy.

I'm out of my element, but it never stops me from trudging ahead. Shifting the weight of my backpack on my shoulder, I march down the hallway. Deep red walls. Warm lighting. I dig it. I could live here—*not* that he's asking me to move in, okay. *Take a thousand hikes backward, Harriet.*

I'm not obsessed with Ben Cobalt. I just like the building's moody décor. Yep…I smack my lips, then I stop at door 2166.

I knock.

Fast-building anticipation rouses my nerves. I wait, smoothing my lips together, glancing left and right. Is there a doorbell?

Nope.

I rap my fist harder. He's not standing you up. *This isn't a practical joke.* He's your friend. You're fine. I hush the dusty insecurities that crawl out from under an ugly old sofa in my brain. He's probably just taking a shit or watering a plant or…

A door opens from down the hall, and I twist my head to see a gorgeous girl slipping on silver high heels while tucking a glittery clutch under her armpit. She's bouncing in an attempt to cram her foot in the shoe.

Shit, she sees me watching—or scowling.

Confusion pinches her brown brows. *Stop staring, Harriet.* After the pseudo-FBI interrogation downstairs due to being young, I expected to run into middle-aged Wall Street brokers. Not someone who looks around my age.

"Hey," she calls out, more curious. I am the guest. She's a tenant... maybe? She could be visiting someone too.

"Hi," I say, more gruffly.

Heels on, the girl tugs down the short silver cocktail dress that molds her slender, athletic frame and complements her golden-brown skin. Fuck, she's walking this way. She never takes her eyes off me, not even as I knock again.

She's quickly undoing her double French braids. Shaking out the dark brown curls, she slows and sees which apartment I'm trying to enter.

2166.

She laughs hard. "Oh trust me, whoever you are. You don't want to go in there. The whole apartment has a stench of smug male ego. It's foul." The door swings open on her last word.

I flinch but don't move as...ugh fuck, it's not Ben. I'm greeted by one of his older brothers.

Beckett is only in a white terry cloth *towel*. He has one hand on the door frame, another on the knot of the towel at his waist. Water drips down his jawline, his hair wet, but it's his body—not even the tattoos on his bicep—that literally tries to magnetize my eyeballs.

Every inch of his abs is defined. Every lean muscle is carved like he's chiseled from marble.

Even the girl behind me teeters in her heels like his presence steals oxygen. Righting herself, she wiggles her toes in her heel, then bends over to adjust the ankle strap. "And there's the worst offender."

Huh?

Off my limited experience with the Cobalt boys, I wouldn't have picked Beckett as the most arrogant. The most intense, definitely. Like right now. His yellow-green eyes are latched on her.

"And there's the resident squatter," Beckett says smoothly. "Or do you prefer the brat down the hall?" There is slight annoyance in the angles of his face. I'm guessing he does not like her.

She straightens up. "I prefer Joana Oliveira...from her." She points to me. "From you—you can keep my name out of your mouth."

"Then stop coming around to bother me, or I might start to think you enjoy being in my mouth."

She begins to look at me, maybe to shut him out, but he's compelling her attention too much. I get it. Cobalts seem to be proficient at catching and reeling. His hook is already in her.

"She's a little young for you, don't you think?" Joana asks him.

I stiffen, wishing I was actual wallpaper. There is an awkward beat, and I know I appear younger than my actual age, but *come on*.

Beckett frowns a little, then asks me, "How old are you?"

"Eighteen."

"Right on the cutoff," Joana raises her brows at him.

He glares. "She's *Ben's* friend," he says, no coarseness in his silky tone. "And what are you still doing here?"

Annoying him, apparently. "Checking on the mattress on your back. The one you always lug around. Worn out and springy. Just concerned about the girls you're breaking in on that old thing."

"You still carrying one?" His voice is so sensual. "Or did you finally realize you'd prefer to be pounded from behind. By me."

Holy fuck.

I should not be standing between them right now.

She staggers on her heels again. "No."

"No?" His gaze drips down her body.

"Hmmmm-no. In your dreams, Cobalt." She nods to me. "Later, Ben's friend."

"Harriet Fisher," I introduce.

She smiles at me, then walks backward toward the elevator and says, "My big brother is Charlie's full-time bodyguard. Oscar Oliveira. And I've been *staying*, not squatting, at Oscar's apartment."

"Paid for by security," Beckett tells me. "She's squatting."

Her smile spreads. "A girl's gotta use her connections."

I watch her go. She's pretty badass.

Beckett stares at her all the way until she disappears into the elevator. Opening the door wider, he lets me inside the apartment. I see him subtly adjusting his junk over the towel, as if he's trying to subdue a hard-on, and when he catches me staring, my face ignites. He looks completely unaffected. Not angry, not remotely ashamed. Totally unbothered. It's masculine big dick energy. He simply says, "Ben's on the phone. He should be out soon." He has a relaxed stride as he goes farther into the kitchen.

Beckett Cobalt is a mood.

He swipes a half-opened box of Lucky Charms off the marble counter just as Ben enters from a hallway.

"Hey, sorry," Ben tells me, pocketing his phone in gray sweats. The action guides my eyes down toward his crotch. Lingering there because those pants reveal a fact I did not know. Ben is hung.

Oh my God, Harriet. I didn't come here to torture my pent-up self. I came here for a place to crash—as in *sleep*.

He's also shirtless. Staring at his cut biceps should be safer territory, but I just remember being held by him in the sanctuary of my car. The force of his caring embrace, and I ache to be wound up in Ben's stronghold again.

Ben has a peeking smile, as if he can tell I'm attracted, but thankfully, he rolls over it to explain, "I was talking to MVU's hockey coach. I'm trying out on Monday."

I nod. "Glad you got off the seesaw, Friend." I knew he'd been debating on trying out. I told him he can always reject the offer if he makes the team. And if they say *no*, then the choice is made for him anyway.

"Did you leave this out for her?" Beckett asks Ben, lifting the cereal. "Because I'm going to put it away if not."

"No. Tom probably forgot to put it up." Ben nods to me. "You hungry, Fisher?"

Beckett rattles the box of cereal.

"I'm good. I ate a ton of Twizzlers earlier." I watch Beckett place the cereal in a very organized kitchen cabinet.

I ease at this normalcy and look around.

I've seen flashes of the apartment over video call. Being here is wildly different. I don't know why I pictured Animal House with dirty hampers of laundry and empty beer bottles. This place is spotless and smells even better than the lobby.

So Joana was wrong. There is no foul stench. Just a really attractive musk-and-pine scent wafting off Ben. Especially as he nears.

My heart jumps as he slides my backpack off my shoulder. I ignore the goose bumps forming on my arms to say, "You live in a well-guarded castle. I'm surprised they didn't strip me to see if I'm wearing *Cobalt4Ever* panties."

"Did they pat you down?" Concern darkens his baby blues.

"No," I say. "I'm just messing with you. It wasn't that bad." But his worry about my well-being is a flutter-kick in my lungs. It's weird how much I like it.

Ben is staring at Beckett, and his older brother comes around the kitchen island to tell him, "Have your bodyguard escort your friends up here next time." He puts a calming hand on Ben's shoulder, then says on his way out, "If Eliot throws a condom at you, tell him I said—" He speaks in French.

Ben laughs from his chest, then replies in the same language. His luminous smile descends on me. It somehow makes me feel included and not on the outskirts, despite knowing zero percent of what they said.

A thought passes over me in an engulfing wave. Is this what it's like to feel loved? Or is this just run-of-the-mill infatuation? How would I even know the difference?

Once Beckett is gone, Ben loops me in. "He said to tell Eliot that he doesn't need to be the condom Santa, gifting protection, when he fucks too much to spare one."

I almost smile, but I'm too stuck on how much Ben trusts me. He's giving me so much info about his brothers—when maybe Beckett spoke in French to keep Eliot's sex life a secret from me.

My heart keeps swelling. I follow Ben as he brings my backpack to the pull-out. Couch cushions are already stacked near the floor-length windows. The glittering, mesmeric city-view nearly siphons oxygen from my lungs.

At nighttime, everything sparkles.

Wow.

He sets my backpack on the unfurled mattress. "My brothers know we're not together," he says, "and that you got booted from your apartment and just needed a place to crash."

I nod a couple times, trying not to frown at how easily he said, "We're not together." Of course we're not. It's a fact I haven't tried to overturn. Neither has he.

I glance around. "Has he been pelting condoms at all your friends?"

"You're the only one I've ever brought to their place." Ben re-enters the kitchen, not making a big deal about me being the first, but I notice how he didn't call this apartment *his* place.

This is still a temporary living situation for him. He hasn't earned enough tips to pack up and find better housing in the area yet.

Ben spins around to tell me, "I'm sorry about downstairs."

"It's fine," I assure, trailing after him while he nears the fridge. "Really, I should've just let you come meet me. Lesson learned. Having a Cobalt sidekick isn't the *worst* thing in the world, especially if that Cobalt is you."

His smile stretches to sexier levels. "I'd say *wise choice*, Fisher, but you'd be choosing the last picked Cobalt."

"Well, you know what they say"—I lean on the sink—"saving the best for last."

I watch his expression go gentle on me, yet our gazes crash together like we're the turbulent sea. I chew on the corner of my lip, my pulse thumping.

He scrapes his fingers through his wavy hair, then clears arousal out of his throat. God, that might be my favorite noise on earth, which is so dumb. There are a billion other noises that should be better—like the sound of the snare and bass when I drum to "She" by Green Day.

"Security has just been tighter than usual." Ben rests his shoulders on the fridge, not turning away from me but not bridging the distance either. "I'm not as famous as Xander or Charlie. But our parents still worry about all of us getting kidnapped and extorted for money."

"Oh to be that famous," Tom suddenly appears in the kitchen. Ben and I quickly tear our gazes off each other.

Tension ramps up more. I rotate to the sink, combatting the impulse to stick my flaming face beneath the faucet. It's good Tom is here—not that Ben and I were about to do anything normal friends wouldn't do.

Tom plops on the barstool, only wearing black drawstring pants. A tattoo of a black skull with red devil horns is inked over his heart.

Must be new-ish.

I definitely would've noticed that tattoo on YouTube. He'll sometimes peel off his T-shirts during high-octane performances. I'm almost positive he has millions of views online for his arresting stage presence alone. Prickly feelings toward him aside, the dude is talented.

He has the "it" factor. Which is why I'm salty he didn't think I was worthy enough for the drumming position. Maybe I did want Tom's approval, okay. It would've been nice to be validated.

Now, if he gave it—I'd grind it into the garbage disposal.

Tom grabs a clementine out of the fruit basket. What he said, with a wishful longing, registers with me all of a sudden. "Wait, *you're* not that famous?" I ask in disbelief.

I'll never admit it out loud, but The Carraways were in my top three most listened-to bands last year. I almost uninstalled the music app on my phone when I saw it, but it's hard to deny I love the EP they put out.

Emo punk-rock has been in my soul since I discovered Green Day, which spiraled me into Simple Plan, Panic at the Disco, My Chemical Romance, and The Carraways. But I've loved The Carraways the most because they're my generation. And sure, it was a sucker punch in the gut when I didn't make the band—but I didn't stop listening to their music.

I still watch YouTube videos of their live performances just to see if they're singing a new song at a show. Then I'll stream it on repeat until they drop the single.

"Get Lost" is my constant go-to "fuck my life" song that I belt in my car when I'm feeling like the world is out to get me. So I'm just a little dumbfounded how Tom thinks he's not famous. In my eyes, he's *incredibly* famous.

Tom squints at me in his own confusion. "Do *you* think I'm famous?"

"You have three million views on your music video for Get Lost," I tell him. "And before you say something about me watching it, remember that I was trying out for your band. I had to do my research, Thomas."

"Obviously not well enough, *Harry*, because A. My name is *just* Tom—"

"I know."

"—and B. Three million views is nothing. I might be known to people who like the genre, but the random Joe down the block doesn't know shit about The Carraways. I'm basically a nobody."

"He wants mainstream popularity," Ben explains as he kicks the fridge closed with his foot. He brings out two cans of Fizz Life and offers me one.

I take the soda, still baffled. "Then why don't you play pop?"

"Because I don't like pop music." Tom peels the orange with his thumb. "If I have to be a trendsetter and set the trends back to emo-punk, then that's what I'm going to do."

I remember Ben mentioning that Tom's ambition is high, and I'm now realizing how high. Maybe this is why he keeps losing drummers. His goals are fucking lofty.

"You could just use your 'Cobalt' name to get popularity." I pop the tab to the soda, and it lets out a bubbly fizzle. It's an honest suggestion, but I worry it comes off a little sarcastic.

"Wow, why didn't I think of that before?" Tom tosses a slice of orange in his mouth and slides off the stool. "Don't let her near my records, Ben Pirrip. I wouldn't put it past Harry to practice her drumming skills on them."

"Not even on my death bed, *Tommy*." I flip him off.

He gives me a middle finger in return and leaves for his bedroom. Just when I thought we were having a civil conversation. I whirl around to Ben, who's taking a large swig of his Fizz Life.

"Did I sound sarcastic?" I ask.

He shakes his head and sets the can on the counter. "No. He agrees with you. He'd use his last name to get popular, but it doesn't really work like that. The people who follow our family online don't necessarily love the kind of music he plays. His genre is niche."

So he either has to sell out and make different music or continue playing for his loyal but small following. I'm guessing if Tom wants more popularity, it must be for something other than money. It can't only be for fame though…right?

Who would *want* to be famous? Xander Hale looks like the definition of soul-crushed every time I see him in Classical Mythology. Random strangers film him, yell his name, try to seize his attention. It's exhausting to just observe from the sidelines. I can't even imagine *being* Xander.

I don't think Tom wants that—but then what does he want?

And why do I even care? It's Tom fucking Cobalt. My nemesis. Ben's watching me intently, his lips lifting the more I scowl.

"Tom wants fame?" I end up asking.

"He wants people to listen to his music. A *lot* of people. Naturally fame would come with that, yeah." He opens a bag of sea salt popcorn that must be vegan-friendly, then looks me over. "What do you think about being famous? Would you be okay with it?"

I'm not sure why he's asking. It's not like I'm in jeopardy of being some noteworthy superstar. My life will be common. I'll be a surgeon at a hospital in the city, hopefully New York. The most exciting thing about me will be my friendship with him, but it's not as if Ben Cobalt's friends even have a drop of fame.

He has too many friends for that.

"Honestly," I say, "I'm not a fan of fame after what I've seen Xander go through."

Ben winces. "Yeah but...that's different. Xander is different..." His voice trails off, and I know I struck a tense chord. Xander's not a good name to toss around Ben.

It's been a month, and the most they say is "hey" and "hi" and the occasional "what's up"—which never has an actual verbal reply. Just a head nod.

Sometimes I feel like an invisible wall sitting between them. Only, they both can see me but can't see each other.

I don't want to make this night awkward before it's begun, so I ask quickly, "Are you tired or do you want to stay up?"

His lips slowly stretch into a grin that is too attractive for words. Literally. Words fly so far out of my head the dictionary might as well be planted on the moon.

"I'm not tired at all, Fisher." His voice is like a cool wind traveling over my skin, creating goosebumps of anticipation.

It is not a sexual suggestion, Harriet. But damn, my body wishes it were one. This dry spell is seriously messing with my head, and we still have the entire night to go.

TWENTY-FIVE

HARRIET FISHER

We end up on the pull-out sofa together. Side by side. Not before I changed in the bathroom. I'm wearing a baggy Evanescence band tee over my black *Thursday* panties. Unfortunately, I forgot to pack my pajama shorts. I usually just sleep in an oversized T-shirt, so it didn't cross my mind.

Until I had to walk back into the living room. Fabric barely covering my thighs.

Ben just smiled.

Which, really, felt more intimate than it should. He makes no attempt to act like I'm an ugly duckling. It's very clear he finds me at least a teeny bit hot, and I also haven't exactly pretended he's a grotesque swamp monster.

He is fucking *gorgeous*.

I try to stare at the laptop balancing on his thigh and not up at his eyes. I'm still thunderstruck that the Cobalts don't have a television in here. I thought that was a basic living room requirement.

Ben has bent one knee, his arm resting on top, lounging comfortably above the sheets and navy-blue quilt. My brain has circled back to the fact that this is where we'll both also be sleeping. *Together.* I try not to get into too much of a thought loop or my cheeks will be cherry-tomato red.

He scrolls through a streaming service when he says, "He lives three floors below me, you know."

I frown. "Who?"

"Xander." Oh, his mind must not have left his cousin.

"I didn't know he lived in this building until the entrance security mentioned the Hales." I crunch on a kernel of popcorn. He gave me the bag earlier. "Do you…talk to him?" I realize how silly that question sounds when I say it.

His brows hike. "I think he'd rather eat staples." He takes a handful of popcorn when I hold out the bag. "But I mention it in case you want to say hi to him or whatever. I know you're friends."

Not like I'm friends with you. Those words sit on the tip of my tongue, but I can't seem to release them through my swelling throat. He shoves the popcorn in his mouth, chewing slowly while swiping through movies.

Setting the popcorn bag aside, I sit up a little against the mound of fluffy pillows and hug my legs to my chest. My T-shirt rides up. I'm not full-on flashing Ben, but that's not even worrying me right now.

I glance over at him. "Does sitting in class together count as friends?" I wonder. "It's not like I have his number."

"You're definitely friends, Fisher."

I don't know why that makes my stomach roll worse. I should be happy that he thinks Xander and I are friends, but in a way, it feels a little like betrayal. No?

His eyes are on the laptop screen as he adds, "I would understand if you wanted to be more than friends with him. Most girls would kill for the chance." His gaze flashes over to me. "He's Xander Hale."

This is not where I thought the night was going. Ben giving me permission to date his cousin. I'm so much farther in the friend zone with Ben than I even thought. Does he not feel even a smidge of attraction toward me? Has it been one-sided this whole time?

That…doesn't make sense.

His muscles are flexed. He's letting out tighter breaths through his nose.

My cheeks are hot. "I'm not really interested in Xander like that." And there's a good chance Xander wouldn't like me if he really knew me. Not all people would be as cool as Ben hearing about my past blow job deals. Or even proposing to blow their brother.

His shoulders loosen as he leans back into the pillows beside me. "Then he'll be a good friend to you." He runs his fingers through his hair before holding on to the top of the laptop. Like he's bracing for something. He checks behind his shoulder. Coast is clear. Then his voice becomes a whisper. "I'm leaving the city in November, so you'll at least have him to hang with."

A deep scowl seizes my face. "You're leaving New York in November?" I roll those acidic words on my tongue. *That's two months away.* "You just talked about taking a P.E. class with me next semester."

He goes pale. "I shouldn't have offered that. Sorry." He places the popcorn bag over on the side table, so nothing is between us, then scrapes another hand through his hair. "When I'm around you or talking to you, I sometimes forget that I'm not planning on staying." His voice is tight—like a knot is in his throat.

I feel it in mine.

My breath cages, and I try my best to stifle the sudden, swelling pain that permeates through me. "Where are you going?"

Ben's voice stays hushed. "The wilderness. Somewhere remote."

"Going to live off the grid, nature boy?"

"Something like that."

My stomach twists. "I was joking."

He tries to smile, but it looks pained. "I'm not though." My future friendship with Ben takes a serious nosedive. I could never live off the grid, and how would I even visit him? I can't imagine hiking through dense foliage. Mosquitoes alone terrify me. Would there even be cell reception? I hate the idea of losing our phone calls. Of never being able to talk to him again. I think that's the worst part.

He glances warily at the hallways that lead to the bedrooms. "My brothers don't know."

"I won't tell them." Another secret to keep. Being quiet, I speak under my breath. "Does being broke have to do with this remote wilderness plan?"

"Yeah, in a way." Before I ask, he says, "You won't be able to call. You could write though."

I swallow hard. "Will you write back?"

He nods.

"Why are you going?" I ask. But the question I really want answered is: *Is there any way I can convince you to stay?* I can't manage it. It feels like too much of an ask from me.

"It's something I just really need to do. I planned to go a while back, before moving to New York, but my brothers—they're persistent." Maybe he misses nature, and he has some sort of soul-deep calling to be in the woods.

I don't know what else to say to him. Tension pulls all my muscles taut, and I'm glad he put the popcorn away because I've completely lost my appetite. But I can't loosen my grip off my legs. Hugging them to my chest gives me protection from feeling utterly fucking exposed.

My eyes burn as I focus on the laptop screen, unable to even glance at Ben.

He was never really mine, so I don't understand why I feel so shattered at the idea of losing him.

"Harriet…" His voice is a soft, broken whisper. "I didn't mean to upset you."

"I'm not upset," I lie. "I'm just processing. It's not like I expected us to be best friends forever and graffiti *Ben and Harriet BFF* on a toilet stall. That would be silly. We're just hanging out for a few months, sharing a class, working together. It's not that deep." I partly say the words out loud to make sure my subconscious is getting this memo. The other part is to see Ben's reaction.

His lips flatline, but he nods tensely. "But to be clear," he tells me.

"I've never invited a friend to spend the night with me. I'm usually over at their house, so it might not be that deep but it's not my norm."

It might not be that deep.

But it's not his norm.

I'm a vessel for conflicted emotions. His words are a paradox gifted with a bow. Maybe I shouldn't have said "it's not that deep" to begin with. The lie hurts. This has been the deepest friendship I've ever had, and we've only been hanging out for a month and a half. I just didn't expect him to agree with me—but I'm an idiot because I rolled those dice.

I don't know how to do this. Friendships. Relationships that last longer than a full moon. I'm saying the wrong things in some wasted effort to protect my heart.

At least he told you, Harriet.

At least he didn't just leave out of the blue.

"What's your favorite movie?" he asks.

My eyes sear as I restrain more emotion. "*Sugar & Spice*. I don't think you'll like it though."

He frowns. "Why not?"

"It's about a group of cheerleaders who plan to rob a bank when one of them gets pregnant. It's a chick flick."

"I have a little sister, remember? I'm well-acquainted with chick flicks. Let's do it." He's clicking on his laptop and pulling up the film. He keeps glancing at me. Not that I've made eye contact. I am successfully avoiding that. But I can feel the heat of his concern bearing on me in three-second increments.

He nudges my shoulder with his. "Harriet," he breathes. "Can you look at me at least?"

I bite the inside of my lip before turning my head and catching the depth of his baby blues.

"I'm sorry," he murmurs. "I should've told you sooner that I didn't plan on staying in New York. If you don't want to hang out anymore—"

"No," I wince. The idea of cutting him out of my life *right now* is too abrupt. I'm eviscerated just thinking about it. "I want to hang out. We have the rest of September and all of October, right?"

He nods strongly. "Yeah."

"Okay, then we have two months, and I will try my best not to be the world's grumpiest person during that span of time."

He laughs. "I'll take what I can get. You want to be grumpy, that's not going to bother me." He pauses a beat before he adds, "I just can't stand it when you're sad."

Then don't leave. I still can't manage the words. "I'm trying not to be."

He wraps an arm over my shoulders, pulling me closer to his side, and I instinctively unfurl from my roly-poly position, my body subconsciously craving his embrace, his comfort. I rest my cheek on his bicep, and his arm falls to my waist. He's holding me against his sturdy, athletic frame, and I start to will myself to forget about his impending departure from the city. From my life.

The movie plays, and we sink down a little together. I'm lying into him like he's a pillow, and his hand makes small soothing circles on my arm. I've never half-watched *Sugar & Spice*. I'm usually engrossed by the campiness and dark humor, but tonight my mind wanders so easily.

His fingers slip under my black sleeve and brush my skin in a casual way, but the skin-to-skin contact has my brain buzzing.

I glance up at him every so often, and he'll glance down. An emotional undercurrent tethers me and him together when maybe it should've torn us further apart. I seek out his comfort in the same way he seems to be seeking out my presence.

My breathing shallows. I imagine what it'd be like to be underneath Ben. Cocooned and protected by his strong build. I imagine him pushing inside me. Closer than we've ever been.

I want it even more than I did.

As the movie plays, I don't stop myself from visualizing Ben leaning in to kiss the nape of my neck, his erection digging into me. Why would I stop? He's leaving. There's no friendship to protect anymore. I can have as many illicit thoughts as I want.

But I don't have to picture his hand skating down my elbow to my wrist. I feel it.

My arm lies against his warm chest. I've never cuddled anyone like this, but I want to keep curling up against Ben. Our eyes meet again. Oxygen has thinned. I shiver a little when his hand drops to my thigh. *Keep going*, I think. *Don't end it.*

He's thumbing the soft skin that peeks beneath the hem of my T-shirt.

I hear his breathing deepening. He cups my ass—then the front door opens while the pregnant cheerleaders storm the supermarket on screen.

Ben tugs down my T-shirt quickly. I unhook my leg from his waist and fall onto my back. It's already past midnight, and we crane our heads to see Eliot twirling a chestnut-haired girl into the apartment. Her green velvet dress flows gracefully as she spins.

They laugh together. When she whirls to a halt, her focus lands on Ben with a gasp. "Is that—?" she starts, but Eliot slips a hand over her eyes.

"Nothing to see here." Eliot gives Ben and me a smirk and wink. "The bedroom is this way, milady." He guides her to his room, and it takes all my energy not to call him back.

Because I understand now.

Why Eliot and the rest of them have been trying to spend time with Ben. Why they've been "bonding" and why they begged him to move to New York. Ben thinks his brothers don't know he plans to leave, and maybe they don't know he's ready to pack his bags for the wilderness.

But they suspect something.

Why else would they be trying so hard to get him to love New York?

And I'm not deluding myself. *I* will never be the reason Ben stays in the city. The only shot will be if his brothers can convince him. I want that. More than anything I want the Cobalt brothers to succeed.

"Sorry about that," Ben apologizes and rewinds some of the movie.

"I'm guessing that's not a girlfriend."

"New night. New girl," he confirms, his gaze dropping down to me for a long, sweltering beat. He's not restarting the movie.

His hand slides through his hair, and I'm reminded how classically attractive he is. He might as well be the jock in any teen movie. The heartthrob in a rom-com. The boy next door that the girl has always pined for but never had.

He has a natural charm that lessens my nerves, whispers words of comfort and ease, and tonight, more than any night, I feel emboldened.

Turning toward him, I just come out and ask, "How many girls have you slept with?"

His lips edge into a powerful grin the same time his eyes go big in surprise. "That's unexpected."

"You're leaving in two months. There's no reason to be shy or wait around for the hard-hitting questions." It's not like I'll ever be able to talk to him while he's foraging in the woods. And maybe something *good* can come out of knowing he's not sticking around. I don't have to worry about pushing him away or being too nosy or not doing the right things.

"You really want to do hard-hitting questions tonight?" His eyes dance over mine.

I nod. "Yeah, I want that." I want to know all about him. Everything. And I know it'll be more painful when he vanishes from my life, but at least I got to say I knew him…and he knew me.

He shuts the laptop and sets it on the end table. When he twists to face me, he says, "Twelve. You?"

I can't stop my eyes from bugging.

He reads me. "That surprises you?"

"Yeah, but not why you might think. Our numbers are the same. Mine's twelve too."

"Not including head," he clarifies.

Flush burns my neck. "I didn't include it. Did you?"

"No." He's not balking or wincing or grimacing. He's nodding, thinking it over. "A lot of mine were just casual hookups at parties. Only a few were girls I dated briefly in high school."

"Did you enjoy it?" I wonder, doing my best not to visualize him hot and heavy with someone else.

"The sex? Yeah," he smiles. "But honestly, I never really had a meaningful connection with anyone I've slept with. I don't think I let anyone get to know me enough to feel that." He holds his bent knee. "It was very surface level. Tip of the iceberg."

Feeling way more forward, I ask him, "What do you call this?" I motion between us.

"Not that," he murmurs, as though what we share is a fragile thing he's cradling. "We're below the iceberg. In the water."

"The hypothermic water?"

His smile rises. "I'll keep you warm, Fisher."

I bite my lip, feeling the start of my smile. "I think I'll let you, Friend."

His gaze clasps mine so tightly. "I've never been this open with someone who's not family."

It stirs so much emotion inside me, but I plow through it to ask, "Are you scared of the thirteenth girl? The thirteenth lay? It being the unluckiest number and all."

Ben laughs. "Yeah, I don't believe in that. Now, Tom, might freak out if he ever hits thirteen."

"You don't think he already has?"

"No." His brows scrunch. "Tom doesn't really sleep around. He used to talk about this one Russian-American guy he'd hook up with consistently. I think his name was like RJ or something, but I'm not even sure they're a thing anymore. He hasn't really brought anyone home that I've seen." He knocks his knee into mine. "You scared of the thirteenth guy?"

I shake my head. "I'd be freaked out all the time if I was scared of the number thirteen." I explain, "I was born on the thirteenth. *October* thirteenth, so I guess you'll be here for my birthday, Cobalt boy."

His smile grows. It almost beckons mine to surface again. "Looks like thirteen is lucky for us then."

I knock my knee back into his. "Don't jinx it."

"But I thought you weren't superstitious," he teases.

"Not unless you give me a reason to be."

"Fair." His eyes skim me in a slow-burning caress. "How was your first time? Did you like it?"

"Physically, it hurt," I say into a shrug. "A senior I had a crush on invited me over to his house, and we hooked up on the floor in his basement because he was nervous about getting cum on the couch. He let me spend the night afterward, and I slept on the comfiest La-Z-Boy chair, so I thought he was sweet." I adjust my back on the pillows, and my foot slides against Ben's calf. He leans closer to me while we talk, and the air thickens for a hot second. "What about your first time?"

"It was typical. I was fifteen, and we went back to her place after Homecoming. Her parents were out of town, and we had sex in her bedroom. *On* her bed." He flashes me a smile that heats my core, and my lips threaten to match his. "I wasn't invited to spend the night though. She was nervous about her parents coming home early and finding me in her room."

"Did you date?" I wonder.

"Short stint, just casually in high school for four months. She broke up with me when I refused to bring her to a Wednesday Night Dinner."

He's told me about those. Though, I'd heard of them before. I mean, it's a proper noun with its own Wiki page. *Wednesday Night Dinner.* All caps.

They're the most exclusive and elusive nights that his family spends together, and it's one of the greatest Cobalt Empire mysteries. Ben explained how he can't even describe them to me. To elaborate on what happens during those nights is the ultimate familial betrayal. I would never assume I'd be allowed to attend, not even if we were dating.

"What happened to La-Z-Boy?" he asks me. "You two become a couple?"

I lean more of my weight into Ben, his arm already around me. "Well, not really. He ignored me in school."

Ben's eyes darken. "Asshole."

My heart flutters at his protectiveness. But I quickly say, "No, it wasn't like that. I preferred that he ignored me. That way, I was able to concentrate on my schoolwork. He never badmouthed me or spread rumors to his friends. He just...invited me over occasionally to have sex and let me sleep in his basement. It was nice, actually. I was sixteen, so...I didn't have anywhere else to spend the night. Other than my car." I shrug tensely, but his arm is more secure around me. He's holding me closer.

It feels better than he realizes.

Ben lets out a deep exhale. Concern has ensnared his face. I can tell what he's thinking. I know I've skirted this topic so many times, and I know he's patiently waited for more details. So I'm not surprised when he says, "If we're doing this hard-hitting thing, then I'm going to ask some personal questions, Fisher."

"I know."

"Why were you homeless?"

My throat swells. "She kicked me out." I explain how my mom was on her fourth or fifth boyfriend at the time, and she hadn't always hated me. Maybe resented me for being smart like my dad. Maybe resented me for caring about school and grades. But no hate. Not at least until I hit puberty.

"It was a flick of a switch," I tell him. "As soon as I had boobs and men started to notice me—she despised me. I didn't want their attention. It was fucking gross to have her old nasty boyfriends stare at me. I just had to pretend not to notice. She'd end up cutting things off with them, then turning it around on me, telling me *I* was the problem. I was wearing slutty outfits to turn them on. I was flirting with them, which was all news to me."

My esophagus is dry and raw, and my voice sounds scratchier as I keep going. "I could deny it every day. I wanted *nothing* to do with those dudes, but in her head, I was the source of all conflict. Then she met Wilson, and he was less of a dickhead and more of a moron. But a sweet moron. Someone who brought her roses on Valentine's and saved their anniversary on his calendar. I tried my best to stay in my room. To avoid. To be invisible. But with Hope, it was impossible. Wilson was just being nice when he bought me a new pair of drumsticks for my sixteenth birthday. She threw them in the garbage, spit-screamed in my face and told me to pack my bags and get out."

I stare off at the quilt. It's been almost three years, and I can still hear Hope's voice ravaging my brain.

"I have had *enough* of you," she seethed. "You ruin *everything*. You don't know how not to. Get out of here. *Go,* Harriet. Call your dad and let him deal with you."

I did call my dad. I hear his voice too.

"Harriet? I can't talk. I just got paged for an emergency thoracotomy."

"She kicked me out," I told him.

There was a pause before he said, "Call your Aunt Helena. I'm sure she'll let you stay with her. I have to go." He hung up.

I never asked my Aunt Helena if I could live with her. She'd never leave her little rental in San Francisco, and I wanted to finish school in Pittsburgh. So I just made it work with my Honda and my resolve.

Ben lifts my chin, and my eyes reach his again. His compassion burrows into my body and warms me just like he promised he'd do. "Hypothermia really is impossible with you," I mutter.

He's not smiling. "I really hate your parents. What your mom did to you—it makes me viscerally angry. You shouldn't have had to go through that."

"Don't hate my dad," I whisper. "He didn't know I lived out of my car. He assumed I went to stay with my Aunt Helena."

Our legs have tangled, we're so close now. He tucks a strand of hair behind my ear. The movement so simple yet pulses my heart in unsteady beats. His voice goes hushed too. "Why didn't you just ask if you could stay with him?"

"Because I was scared of the answer. There's a chance he could have said *no*. He made a whole new life for himself after he divorced my mom. One that didn't include me. His new wife, his son and daughter—they're everything to him. I always just got the occasional call on my birthday, but that ended when I turned eleven. And for all I know, he could've hated me because I have fifty percent of my mom's DNA." I raise my chin, looking directly at Ben. "But I have a plan. I'm going to become a trauma surgeon just like him—and *then* he'll realize that I'm more Grant Fisher than Hope Danes. Maybe he'll even let me shadow him and invite me on vacations with my half-siblings."

I don't say the unspoken words.

Maybe I'll be a part of a family.

I swallow the biggest lump, and Ben's thumb moves in soft circles against my knuckles. Until he's holding my hand. Lacing our fingers.

"That's why you want to be a doctor," he realizes.

"It was the first initial reason. Then I fell in love with medicine, so I have more reasons now." I unlace our hands, just to pull off my beaded bracelets. "What about you and hockey?"

"Me and hockey?" He's watching me slip the bracelets onto his wrist.

"Yeah. If it's taken this long to even try out, then...do you even like playing?"

Ben scratches the back of his head, then slumps a little against the pillow mound. I follow suit. Our heads turn to each other as he says, "I think I hate it."

My brows catapult, not expecting that. "Hate is a strong word, Friend."

He reaches over, grabs his blue water bottle, takes a hearty swig, then offers it to me. I take small sips, listening.

"The aggressive part of hockey, I never disliked. There've been times where I think I need it. Until the last three years…I guess I just started hating the brutality," he breathes out. "I'd try to skate around the body slams, but I was a target during every game I played. And if I didn't want to keep getting concussions, then I needed to defend myself." He rubs at the little beauty mark on his cheek. "I've knocked out teeth on four different guys, Harriet. I've laid even more out on the ice. I hate causing *physical* harm to people, and I know it seems ridiculous after what I did to Tate…but there's enough suffering in the world, I just don't want to contribute to it." His eyes redden as he stares at the bracelets. "It fucking tears me up every time I do."

"Then why even try out?"

"I love the feeling of being on the ice. Of flying toward the net. Like nothing can catch me. I imagine maybe it's what birds feel like in the air." He scrapes his tongue over his molars in thought. "And I love helping my team win. I love feeling like I *excel* at something like Cobalts are known to do. But the past few years, the hate has drowned the love. Now I think I'm just trying out for Coach Haddock. He's a good guy, and I don't want to let him down too hard."

Ben has a really big heart. I can see why his brothers might fear someone hurting him. I feel more protective of his heart too. Especially since it feels like he keeps giving it to me.

"I'm glad you're trying out," I tell him. "You'll get that last time to feel like a bird. Be all Nelly Furtado on the ice."

He laughs hard. His face is one beautiful smile. "You aren't worried I might fly away?"

It hurts a little, even knowing he's teasing. "Oh no, I am very worried." I try to joke back. It comes off more serious than I intended.

"Don't be," he says softly. "Everything's going to turn out okay, Friend."

"What if you get third-degree sunburn? Or a splinter that causes a bacterial infection? You could accidentally chop off your hand—"

"That's not going to happen," he laughs.

"Have you ever swung an axe before?"

"Yeah."

"And chopped wood?"

"*Yes*," he says like it's not hard and common practice. Now I'm picturing outdoorsy Ben. Which has to be one of his natural states of mind, considering he loves the earth. Being stuck in the city isn't where he's meant to be.

All birds need to be set free, I realize, and maybe convincing him to stay would be like trapping a wild creature.

I tuck myself more to his side. Trying to be okay with his plan.

He cups the side of my head and scrunches my hair a few times. It's so effortlessly comforting. I'm drawn to him. To his energy and affection, and there's a sudden urge to want more. To be consumed by Ben Cobalt.

I look up at him.

He looks down. The electrical charge between us pumps my blood. It's paddles to my heart. On impulse, I slide my leg over his waist and roll onto his lap.

My palms meet the back of his warm neck, and his large hands fall to the soft divots of my hips.

Ben drinks in my bare thighs around him, and I run my fingers over the ridges of his abs. I can feel his dick hardening against me as his gaze fixes back on mine.

"Harriet," he breathes out a knotted breath of arousal. "We can't do this."

"Because we're friends? Or because we're in the living room?"

"Neither." He rolls me off him so easily—as if I weigh nothing. My head sinks into the soft pillow. He sits up and watches me scowl at him. He smiles when he says, "Glare at me all you want, but it's not happening."

"Give me a good reason because you already rejected two."

"You're my guest," he says, grabbing a pillow to put over his semi-hard cock—because it's distracting me. He's fucking huge. "I don't want sex in return for you spending the night here."

Oh…

My face is on fire. "That's not why I crawled on top of you."

"It might not be your intent, but you obviously have a history with sex being transactional. Am I wrong?"

No, he's not. Our body counts might be considered high for our ages, but my number rose to twelve because I did get more than sex out of it. Most of my one-night stands came with a place to lie down for the night. A bathroom to freshen up in the morning.

"This…" I choke up a little. "This isn't like all those other times though." He's searching my eyes as vigorously as I search his.

I'm not all mettle and guts because I struggle to say what's in my head.

This isn't the same, Ben.
I have feelings for you.
I like you.
Half my heart might be in your hands too.

Instead, I breathe out, "I don't want this to be transactional. I just haven't had an orgasm in months. Not since I moved in with Eden. And I just thought, maybe we could…"

"We can't," he reaffirms. "But *I* can."

My lips part in shock. "*You* can…what?" I'm imagining too many scandalous things, and I comb his gaze again for answers.

He roots a palm on the mattress beside my arm, leaning more over me. His voice comes out in a soft, husky whisper. "I can give you an orgasm, Friend."

Holy fucking shit. Did I manifest this? I've never believed in the whole "ask and you shall receive" mantra, but I might be a new convert. Aunt Helena will be thrilled.

"That sounds nice," I rasp because I'm not sure what else to say other than *yes, please*. But I'm not ordering an orgasm off a menu here. This is Ben fucking Cobalt. This is my best friend. The closest I've ever been to a person.

I instantly dig into the bed, aching for his touch. He studies me, how I'm clenching the quilt, how my knees squirm, how my body rises and falls with hitched breaths.

He clasps my cheek, which nearly does me in. "You're okay with this even if I'm leaving?" he asks, concern planted in each word.

"Yeah," I whisper. "You're not leaving tonight, Cobalt boy." This might make his departure in two months even harder, but it's just an orgasm. It's just fooling around. It doesn't have to be intense and emotionally complicated. I'm more eager to experience these moments with Ben than never feel them at all.

"Now what?" I ask and skim him, how his legs tangle into mine, how his muscles flex in hot bands, how his gaze consumes and cradles me.

He scoops me up in his arms, just to throw the quilt and sheets farther down the mattress, then he brings them over our heads. I cage a moan in my throat. My legs instinctively break apart around him, and I wrap my arms against his neck. My pulse beats faster, thumps harder.

Ben lays me flat on the mattress, then hovers over me. "We're going to be very fucking quiet," he breathes, his lips ghosting over mine. The threat of a touch, a kiss, intensifies every single nerve-ending in my body.

This is happening.

I want to memorize each tantalizing second. I glance down at our pelvises, not at all lined up because I'm so much shorter than him. That'd be an issue if his dick were slipping inside me, but he made it clear he's not going that far tonight. I imagine the problem would be resolved by me being on top.

My imagination becomes irrelevant as soon as he lowers more of his weight on me. The quilt tents over his back and cocoons us in darkness and warmth. A heady, drugged feeling dizzies me.

"I want to make you feel good," he whispers into my ear.

Those words might as well be a long-forgotten ancient language. I've never heard them before. Never dreamed of their existence. I bite the inside of my cheek to stop my heavy breathing.

We're in his living room.

If one of his brothers comes out here, this won't look innocent *at all*. A massive blanket lump screams indecent activity.

All I can hope is that we're quiet enough to not attract attention. Maybe we'll also be able to hear any incoming footsteps. We'll have time to break away and pretend we're just sleeping. My acting skills aren't up to par, so I'm really banking on being super silent here.

Ben isn't making it easy.

Not as he skates a molten palm from my knee up to my thigh. Anticipation causes me to shudder just as much as his physical touch. His hands, *on me*. My hands, *on him*.

Our eyes catch every other second, escalating this new feeling I can't make sense of yet.

My shallow inhales and exhales sound like fog horns in the silence. I find myself confining oxygen in my lungs to be quieter, not releasing breaths. *Do not pass out before you have an orgasm, Harriet.* The thought makes me intake small lungfuls of air.

Ben hooks a thumb in my black *Thursday* panties and drags them down my thighs, my legs, my ankles—off me entirely. I quake against him as his knuckles brush against my skin, and I let my hands drop to his broad shoulders. Hanging on.

I don't see where he discarded my panties, but his hand returns to the soft flesh of my thigh. Our eyes lock again, and it steals all my thoughts.

My mouth opens. I can't shut it. My esophagus tries to tighten closed. Why is he looking at me like that? Am I looking at him the same way too? It's the depth. Like he's reaching into me, even though we're not two pieces of metal welded together.

We're two separate entities. Aren't we?

He stretches my legs open even wider, and an ache spirals through me. *Don't make a sound. Don't even breathe.* Then his fingers slip against my wet heat. My body nearly spasms at the sensitivity. The blanket slips off our heads. *Fuck.*

I side-eye the darkened living room, nervous about his brothers appearing.

He turns my chin, so I look back at him. When Ben becomes my sole focus, the anxieties fade, and I sink into how he's lighting my body on fire, how my lungs feel fuller and simultaneously oxygen deprived.

He rubs my clit in slow strokes, and I grind against his hand on impulse. His muscles contract, and our eyes slam together again. Holy. *Fuck.*

I almost cry out.

He immediately covers my mouth with a strong palm.

He grunts out a sexy, hoarse breath into a deeper, "*Harriet.... fuck.*" His forehead lowers toward mine, and I reach down and grab his wrist, feeling how he's between my legs. *This is really happening.*

His lips brush against my ear. "Wet…you…" His words stick to his throat like they're coated in thick honey. My head is spinning. Dizzying. Me.

Then he slips his finger inside my pussy. *Oh my God.* The fullness curls my toes, even more when he begins pumping. He starts toying with my clit at the same time, and I think, *this is where I'll lose it.* But it's not what's setting me off the most.

It's his eyes.

This exhuming look that I'm more positive we're sharing. He's mining my heart, and I'm chiseling out his. Uncontrollable sentiments surge in me, overwhelming every part of my mind.

I instinctually arch my hips into the movement of his hand—the pull-out couch lets out a sudden sharp squeak. *Oh fuck, fuck.*

We both freeze like we've been caught under a giant searchlight. Our heavy, half-captured breaths are the only thing I hear in the quiet. Ben listens and scans the living room. When he glances back at me, his self-assurance tries to ease my panic.

Still, we silently wait a minute for footsteps. I strain my ears. Each second aches with his finger motionless inside me. It's the longest, hottest minute of my life.

My muscles pulse around his finger in want, and his brows arch at me. He can feel that. *He can FEEL that?!* I'm beet-red. Hot all over. I just want more. Deeper. But we're determined to not fuck this up, to not end this in a horrible way. I won't be able to construct a halfway decent lie if Charlie or Beckett come out here. I'll have to confess to his older brothers that Ben's finger is inside me.

And then I'll have to go pick out a headstone for my grave.

Risks are high. Hooking up in the Cobalt brothers' living room. I never thought I'd do it, okay, but there are no signs of regret or remorse. I'm all-in on this dangerous path with Ben.

The minute subsides in slow slipping seconds, then he fits another finger in me. *Fuckfuckfuck.* "Fuck," I rasp out loud, hopefully soft enough. I writhe beneath him, not even sure how many times I've cursed into the air.

I look down beneath the sheets. To his hand cupped against my pussy. When my eyes meet his, we exchange intimate awareness that he has two fingers inside me now.

His lips skim my ear. "G-spot." He's not asking. He's telling me. One single word has cranked up my arousal to smoldering degrees.

I try to whisper back, but all I think is, *no one has ever found...* Oh, what the...*fuck*. I shake against him. Full-body vibrations. His smile is even sexier with his pleasure. And I feel like he's getting off on this just as much as me.

Ben skillfully pumps his fingers in an expert tempo, mimicking thrusts. It feels like sex. Like I'm being fucked, except I don't know if I'd call it that. A fucking. Because as he clasps my face with one hand and pulses inside me with the other, our eyes haven't broken apart.

Our aching breaths become in sync again.

Our bodies cake with sweat.

My gaze burns, and I watch his eyes redden as we're pulled under a powerful riptide together. He's nodding to me, as if to tell me it's okay. That I can give into this feeling with him. Water wells in my eyes, spilling into the creases. *What the fuck, Harriet?*

I've never experienced *this*. What is...*this?*

He's choked on a gruff, deep noise, and I claw at his arms, hoping he never stops. Hoping this never has a true end.

I lose myself to the friction, the scorching affection, *Ben*.

A high-pitched moan tears through me—he catches the sound with his hand quickly. But we don't even pause like before. I don't think either of us can.

He smothers my whimpers against his large palm. His nose flares as he grits down to detain his own sounds. They release like masculine, grunting breaths. I think he wants to tell me something a couple times, but all he gets out are one or two indistinguishable words. It's as if communicating has slipped away from us under these heightened feelings.

I come so suddenly.

My whole body arches up into his chest as the orgasm ripples through me. His palm tightens over my lips to shelter as many noises as he can. Tendons strain in his neck as he controls himself from coming. To be honest, I wouldn't even be able to hear footsteps. Not over the ringing pulse in my ears.

It takes seemingly minutes to gather oxygen in my lungs. He peels his hand off my mouth, then slips his fingers out of me.

I'm propped on my elbows, unable to fully catch my breath.

He's on his knees, the blanket falling a little bit. I watch him palm his hard length over his sweats, but he's scrutinizing me, maybe to make sure I'm okay.

I'm scared. Because... "What...what was that?" I almost *croak* out, then wipe the residual wet streaks from the corners of my eyes.

His Adam's apple bobs, and he shakes his head.

"Is this how intense it always is with you?" I whisper. "Do I need a defibrillator on standby?"

He cracks a smile that fades too fast. "It's not usually…that's a first for me, Fisher." He seems afraid too. This was just supposed to be a quickie. A friend helping a friend out. He was doing me a solid. Granting me a long-lost orgasm. Instead, he served a side dish of emotional turmoil, and I must be a masochist because I don't think I want to send it back.

TWENTY-SIX

BEN COBALT

Yeah, I'm out of my fucking mind. Because my feelings for Harriet are so raw, I couldn't even *speak* while I had my fingers inside her. I choked out words against her ear. She only let out these cute little raspy *fucks*. Her scowl melted into this overcome expression I'll engrain in my head for *all fucking time*. All her guards, all her defenses dropped into this fragile surprise.

The emotion stunned her as much as it obliterated me. It took everything not to take her all the way. My throbbing cock strains against my sweatpants now, and my breath sounds more ragged because I'm terrified to love her and leave her.

I've never been in love in my life, and of course this is happening to me now. Maybe it's been slowly, imperceptibly happening for longer than this moment. Love probably isn't a flip of a switch. It's not a malady contracted overnight. Beckett would say I've been diseased, and didn't I ask to be?

Didn't I want to roll around in this feeling with her?

Yeah.

I'm already going to leave five siblings who I love more than planet Earth.

What's one more love lost?

I pinch my eyes that try to well. "Sorry," I breathe.

She shakes her head now. "It's a lot…I get it." She's never felt this before either, but I can't change the expiration date…it needs to stay. For my family. She glances around, making sure no one is creeping, before she whispers, "Thanks for the orgasm, Cobalt boy."

I try to smile but end up just nodding to her. I want to hold Harriet, to remind her that I'm here. Right now.

Bending closer, I lift her in my arms and bring her higher up the pull-out. I place her head on a pillow.

Harriet eases into the mattress, and this tranquil, teeny-tiny smile tics up her lips. It's a new one that I drink in and treasure.

I'm grateful that none of my brothers needed a glass of water or a midnight snack. Tonight, with her, was worth the risk, and I wouldn't take it back.

Under the sheets, we lie on our sides, and I curl my arms around her small frame, drawing her back into my chest. She burrows against me and clutches my forearm. Everything about us is so natural, I'd almost think we've been together for years.

I wish we had been.

She yawns, exhaustion tugging her. I stroke sweaty blond hair out of her face, behind her ear, and I rest my chin on her head. Feeling her body slacken against me is untensing my muscles.

I just need to stop revisiting her full-body convulsion when she climaxed. If that's how she reacts with my fingers, I wonder what it'd be like if I—*Jesus. Not tonight, Ben.*

Maybe not ever.

I blink away that thought.

Soon, she's completely knocked out.

Seeing Harriet so quickly and so easily fall asleep in my arms catapults me to cloud nine. My chest rises as my lungs inflate, and a smile edges across my mouth. I'm in some kind of paradise, just existing with her in this second. Where worries can't find me. Where fears don't flourish. Where panic doesn't thrive.

I want to live here.

I want to stop time again.

I want to freeze this peaceful moment with this one girl.

Very softly, I breathe, "Bonne nuit, petit oiseau."

Being this close to her body heat while pent-up has set me on fire, and I gently pull away, bringing the quilt higher up her shoulders before sliding out of it.

My feet touch the ground. I stand and inhale a few deep breaths through my nose, glancing back at Harriet. Forceful emotions barrel into me.

How do I leave her in two months? *I have to leave her.*

Warring sentiments. I'm at odds with myself, but this clash is nothing new. My mind has been a battle zone for the past three years with no winner.

I walk away from the pull-out. The microwave clock glows in the dark kitchen. Flicking on the sink faucet, I wash my hands hurriedly, trying not to waste water. I hear the soft creak of a door down the hall that leads to Tom's and Eliot's rooms.

Seconds later, Eliot emerges in nothing but deep-red boxer-briefs. His bare feet pad quietly along the floorboards.

I shut off the faucet with my elbow. Even in the dark, I can see the gleam of sweat along Eliot's toned muscles.

Running two hands through his damp hair, he slicks back the wavy strands, then flashes me a wry smile that personifies *debauchery*. "Greetings and salutations." He meanders to the coffee pot like it's eight in the morning and not *two*.

My forehead creases. "Coffee?" I ask in a whisper.

"The night is young." He wags his brows.

I smile from his infectious energy.

Eliot comes to my side to fill the reservoir with sink water. "I'm only on round two. You?"

He's talking about sex. I know he is. Oversharing is commonplace with Eliot, and I'd like it more if I didn't feel like it was a tactic for me to spill my guts too.

I lean on the counter. "I didn't need to know that, man."

"Knowledge is power, little brother." He tilts his head to me, then toward the couch where Harriet sleeps. "Do you know what you're doing with that one?"

His question is a slingshot to my brain. I don't fully understand what he's asking. If he were inquiring about whether I hooked up with her, he would just come out and ask if we fucked.

"Doing?" I lower my voice.

"Yes, doing." He returns the filled reservoir to the machine and grabs a bag of Colombian coffee from the cabinet. His gaze drops to the beaded bracelets on my wrist. The ones that belong to Harriet.

My head whirls. I grip the marble counter. "She's my friend."

Eliot slides me a darker grin as he shakes out a generous amount of grounds into the paper filter. "So you've said."

I'm not in the mood to argue with him, especially not when I just made Harriet come. It's one thing to defend myself from a baseless accusation, but now…I don't know what to call this. We *are* still friends. But I definitely don't give orgasms to all my friends. I definitely don't imagine sliding my cock in my friends. I'm definitely not this emotionally invested in my friends.

I've definitely never fallen for *any* friend.

Fuck.

I scrub a tensed hand down my hard jaw. I should just call it a night and return to the couch, but something roots me in the kitchen. Maybe it's Eliot's calmness. He's rarely ever this subdued. It relaxes me in a way that usually only Beckett can.

Once he starts the coffee machine, he rotates to face me fully while it brews. "There's a reason I tend to keep my flings short-lived."

"Yeah," I nod. "You get bored." Once he's figured someone out, the interest wanes and Eliot moves on.

"True." His grin softens. "But that's not all. I'm not in the occupation of breaking hearts, and the longer you keep them around, the more attached they inevitably are. Not just to you."

Now I want to argue with him. Tell him he's full of himself. He's wrong. But the words glue to the back of my throat. Sometimes I forget that the whole "Cobalts are gods" saying isn't much of a joke. Not to some people. It has nothing to do with our wealth, our fame, or our limitlessness.

It's the love.

The loyalty.

The unfailing, undying, unblistered power of family. It's how there's light in each of my siblings so bright that it's not a question of whether they can illuminate the night sky. They just do. Being around them is like finding a way out of darkness, a way home.

"The gates to our family rarely open," Eliot warns. "You bring them closer and closer, they start seeing what's inside and believe they'll have it one day. It'll break them knowing they can't."

"Could the gates open for her?" I ask him.

My family's fierce devotion—it's everything she's never had growing up, and I want her to experience love that never leaves you cold. To not just look up and see a constellation, but to be among those eternal stars.

He casts a glance toward the couch, the coffee machine gurgling softly behind him, then looks me over. "Oh, to be nineteen again."

"What does that have to do with it?"

He picks up a mug, tossing it in his palm. "Girls will come and go out of your life, little brother."

His words stab me. "She's different," I say, my voice hostile. "She's not coming or going. She's here, and *she's staying*." I say this from my absolute core. I want her to stay. I want them to be there for her. I need them to let her through those gates without trouble, and it's asking a lot.

I know it is.

He lets out a weighted breath, and his gaze no longer pins to the pull-out. He's staring at me. *Through* me. He processes for a long moment, squinting in the dark. All I can hope is he can see how much I care for her. How much she means to me.

Then he breathes out, "Well, shit."

"What?" I frown.

"I'll have to put her on my *fuck with her and die* list."

I start to smile. It's very much what I want. "Tu promets?" *You promise?*

"De tout mon être." *With my whole soul.* He comes closer and curves an arm around my head, bringing our foreheads together before messing my hair and letting go.

I smile even wider. Promises from Eliot carry the most weight in my family. He'd choose death over breaking one he made to us.

He's grinning off my happiness. "It's not too long of a list, just so you know. One cannot go to battle for every soul."

I nod strongly. "Thanks, Eliot," I tell him with depth.

He nods back, holding my gaze for another beat, as if seeing there is something deeper at play. But the coffee machine beeps. He spins around and pours himself a cup, then raises the mug to me. "Off for round three."

TWENTY-SEVEN

BEN COBALT

My mind keeps whirling back to that night. The couch. The "friendly" sleepover. After I cooled off and climbed back into bed, I thought about turning away from her. Letting a pillow separate our bodies. But I couldn't resist shifting closer.

Harriet naturally reached for me when I brought my arm over her. She curled up into my biceps that I tucked around her frame. She let me hold her while we slept, and it's those innocent hours underneath the blankets that I've replayed over and over just as much as the volatile quakes of her climax.

She left in the morning before my brothers even woke.

It's been three days. Three fucking days and my brain has made about a million revolutions around her. She returned to her pull-out couch. I stayed on mine.

It's better this way, I remind myself. She has a history of using sex transactionally, and I don't want to risk her sliding into that loop with me. Separation is good.

My brain hasn't picked up that message yet, but we'll get there.

I comb some wet strands of hair out of my face. The showers

at MVU's gym have shit water pressure, but that's about my only complaint today at tryouts. A true shock to my system considering I had a laundry list of complaints on my old team.

Former captain called me a "nepo baby" after every game—which sidenote: not an insult when it's a fact—but he always made sure to sling it like a slight. The coach made me do more suicide drills on the ice than I care to admit.

Usually alone.

Usually after practice.

He'd have the assistant coach stay behind to blow the whistle. And fuck if I don't hate that shrill sound in a near empty rink with no teammates around me. It ruined any peace I felt while skating.

So this morning, I fully expected some extra laps or an underhanded dig from at least one of the guys on the MVU team. But the left wing gave me a slap on the shoulder like I already belonged. The goalie invited me out for a beer. (I don't think he knows I'm nineteen.) The center complimented my pivots. It felt like the fucking Twilight Zone. I half-expected Eliot to pop out of the stands and tell me they were all actors he hired.

Turns out, it was real.

Coach Haddock even shook my hand at the end of practice, and it startled me for a long moment. With hockey, I had forgotten what it feels like to be treated like a functioning human being and not a sack of shit.

Only problem…I can't like the team here.

I can't start to love hockey again.

I won't be in New York for the full season. Trying out was always more for Coach Haddock than myself, and he seemed grateful that every phone call and encouragement at least got me out on the ice tonight.

As I kick the apartment door shut, all I can think about is calling Harriet. She's the first person I want to talk to about tryouts, but it's Monday night and she keeps her phone off while she's volunteering at the hospital. So I make my way farther into the quiet apartment, but I don't fool myself into believing it's empty.

Most of my brothers have participated in the shared calendar, so I know that Beckett is dancing in *Giselle* tonight, Tom's band practice finished hours ago, and now that Eliot landed the role of Christopher Wren in *The Mousetrap*, he spends post-rehearsals in his room running lines.

Charlie hasn't updated his portion of the calendar so he could be drowning in the Pacific Ocean, for all I know. I toss my gym bag and hockey stick on the couch, and my phone pings in my pocket. My stomach knots as soon as I see the text.

DR. WHEELER

> Ben. Are you around for your session? It was supposed to start 10 minutes ago.

Shit. Fuck. I completely forgot. I scrape my hand through my hair and glance around the apartment. I've been pretty strategic in doing my tele-therapy sessions on campus in a quiet study room. Last thing I want is for one of my brothers to overhear.

I could bail on Dr. Wheeler tonight, but if word gets back to my parents that I'm skipping sessions, it'll give my dad more reason to encourage me to find a new therapist. And that's a drum I don't want to beat again.

Fuck it. I'll just take the call here. Not in the bathroom—the lock hasn't been fixed, and I'm not making that mistake a second time. I slip into the coat closet, shut the door, and take my puffer jacket off the hook to bunch up at the gap between the floor and the door. I'm not sure how soundproofed it is in here, but that'll have to do.

Sinking onto the hardwood, I'm wedged between the wall and an umbrella. I shift a heavy bag off to the side, and I unzip it to see a bowling ball. What the fuck? I don't even know which one of my brothers bowls.

Zipping it back up with one hand, I send a quick text with my other.

> **BEN COBALT**
> Available now. Not for video chat though. Can you call?

Less than ten seconds later, my phone rings, and I answer it.

"Ben." Dr. Wheeler's voice is friendly and casual. "Is everything all right? You're usually not late to a session."

I rest my head back against the wall. "Sorry, I had hockey tryouts. I forgot to reschedule."

Dr. Wheeler blows out a breath of surprise. "Hockey tryouts? You mentioned you didn't want to play…"

"Yeah, about that." I rest an arm on my bent knee, my limbs cramped in the closet. "I decided to give it a go. Coach Haddock has been nice…really nice."

"You seem surprised."

My brows furrow. "He told me I was faster than most players he's ever seen at MVU. That I'm even good enough to make it to the NHL, like third-round draft pick good enough. So I'm just wondering if he's blowing smoke up my ass."

"Why would you think that?"

I laugh and run another hand through my hair. Memories torpedo through me in a crushing onslaught. "My old coach said the opposite. Said I would never amount to that. It's just confusing. Who to believe." I grind my jaw and try to roll out the tensed muscles in my shoulders.

A short stretch of silence bleeds over the phone before he replies. "Of what you've told me about your old coach and your interactions with him, there is a chance he was singling you out because he thought you had an ego. So it's possible he never told you that you were good because he thought you already knew you were."

I try to process this as he adds, "He could've been bringing you down to humble you."

I squint in contemplation. "To humble me?" Because of my last name. As if being a Cobalt somehow brands me with an overinflated, oxygen-sucking ego.

"It's a theory," Dr. Wheeler says. "Because there's no real reason your new coach would lie to you."

"If he wants me on the team this badly, he could just be telling me what I want to hear so I'll join."

"Why would he want you on the team if he didn't think you were good?"

I circle around to the idea he's using me for ticket sales, but he's still shown no interest in publicity. Just shown interest in me...in my abilities on the ice.

Dr. Wheeler fills the silence. "If he thinks you're good enough, then you're good enough, Ben. It's okay to believe that."

My jaw aches. Muscles won't relax. I'm not sure I'll get there. Not tonight. Not talking to Dr. Wheeler. All I really want to do is hear Harriet's voice.

"Yeah, okay," I say hurriedly. "Anything else?"

Dr. Wheeler laughs. "I think I'm supposed to be asking you that."

"All good in the neighborhood," I tell him. "Classes great. Friends great. Brothers great. Sisters great. Nothing new to speak of."

"Next semester, are you still planning to major in Ecology?"

"Yep," I say, keeping up the lie I fed him last month.

"Good, good. It's great to have goals." Dr. Wheeler chats a little longer, and I give him some perfunctory answers before we end the call.

I'm about to stand and shake out my limbs when the closet door swings open. Fuck. *Fuuuck.*

Of course, it has to be Charlie on the other side.

His hair sticks up in five different directions. With his white button-down wrinkled and untucked in a pair of black slacks, he could have just finished fucking someone or had a meeting with a Fortune 500 company. When it comes to Charlie, you never know.

He leans a hand on the door, appraising me slowly. "What the fuck?" he asks in a causal, unbothered tone.

"What the fuck, *what*?" I shoot back, my adrenaline suddenly surging even though he hasn't really come at me.

He rolls his eyes. "You really need me to spell this out?"

I rise to my feet. "No, I don't." I'm waiting for him to move away because he's blocking my exit.

He grips harder onto the door. "Why are you in the coat closet?"

"You're the smart one," I snap. "You tell me."

He blinks. "Not a mind reader, but I see how you can get those two confused."

"Fuck you," I say with less heat. "I don't have a bedroom; in case you've forgotten."

"So shoving yourself into a four-by-four space makes total sense," he says. "Got it." He opens the door wider and lets me pass him. I'm halfway to the couch when he adds, "If you need privacy for a phone call, to jerk off, or just to get away from Eliot and Tom, you can always use my room or Beckett's. One of us is usually not home."

That stops me cold in the middle of the floor. I almost think I misheard him. I'm about to ask if he's for real when I glance over and see him pop something in his mouth. He catches me staring and his brows rise like *what the fuck are you looking at?*

Adderall? Ecstasy? Fucking Zoloft? I don't know. It could just as likely be an Allegra to combat seasonal allergies, but there's not a chance in hell I'm going to ask.

"I'll be sure to use your room to jerk off in," I tell him.

Charlie flips me off, then rotates his hand to check his watch on the same wrist. "Not that I care, but shouldn't you be at some board game thing?"

Fuuuuck.

I check the calendar on my phone. Board Game Club starts in twenty minutes. How did I even forget that? How did Charlie remember? I grab my jacket on the back of the couch, and as I hurry out the door, I hear a faint, "You're welcome."

TWENTY-EIGHT

BEN COBALT

She's not here.

Harriet should have finished volunteering for the night about ten minutes ago, and the hospital isn't too far from campus. I've shot her a couple texts, but I don't expect a reply if her phone is still off.

Still, I'm stressed. It's past nine p.m., and if she doesn't respond, I might head to the hospital.

Would that be too much? I know she's independent, and I don't want to seem suffocating. *Fuck.* Why is this so difficult? I usually know *exactly* what to do with friends. But she's not a typical friend. She's...more.

Maybe I could just send Novak.

"Hey, Ben." Quentin Tupu rounds to my table of *one*. I'm oddly alone in a back corner, an arched stained-glass window beside me. Four other circular tables have five to six people packed around them. The board game, Catan, sits unopened two feet from me.

Quentin is the club president, Samoan, and incredibly friendly. To the point where my ass is partially in this seat and not in a jog to find

Harriet because I'd hate to offend him or ruin his attendee numbers. And yeah, I've only had two interactions with him. The last club meeting and tonight.

He places a casual hand on the Catan box. "Looks like you're missing some players. You can join Table Three."

"I'm waiting for someone actually."

Quentin's gaze veers past my shoulder toward the door. "Ah, right on time then."

My relief floods me only to wash out to shore as soon as I rotate around. *Fuck.* I know Xander plays super intense strategy games like Warhammer 40k, LARPs on the weekends, and watches every fantasy show on TV. He's even currently wearing a *Game of Thrones* House Stark T-shirt, and yet, I didn't expect him to be here.

Geeky shit might be his thing, but clubs never were.

What's not shocking? He's here with Easton Mulligan. His best friend. He looks like he hasn't seen the sun in five hundred years and will suck your blood if you get too close. He's quietly threatening. Exactly what Xander would need in a friend, since he's harassed at least once a day by paparazzi or obsessive fans.

I would've thought I'd be that friend for him. Battling off unwanted attention. I would've never predicted the turn of these tables when we were kids. That his protective best friend would be the one glaring at me.

Easton isn't fond of me...to put it lightly.

I can't tell if he sees me right now. He has on sunglasses *indoors*.

His styled chocolate brown hair is shorter on the sides, a little longer on top, and he's tall, lanky, and pale white with a confident, unperturbed stride. What's funny is he could so seamlessly fit in with my family.

He wears his wealth.

Expensive, fashionable style. Tailored suit pants, crisp button-down, black leather jacket, and dark Prada sunglasses. He's a Burberry ad come alive.

He might look like a Cobalt, but he lived with the Hales for several months before graduating prep school. They took him in, even though his family's home was only a street over in our gated neighborhood.

I should know him better than I do.

But I purposefully avoided Easton at family functions, at school when we'd attended Dalton together, and I wish I could avoid him now in college. It's one thing to confront Xander's cold shoulder, another to be stared down for an hour like I've put shaving cream on his pillow.

Xander scopes out the room, and when he catches my eyes, his whole chest sinks like a deflated balloon. He whirls around to leave.

Easton grabs onto his shoulder, then whispers in his ear for a long beat. With several words, he must convince my cousin to stay. I watch Xander nod a couple times and face my way again.

I imagine Easton said, *Don't let Ben ruin this for us. We're already here. Let's play the game.*

I lean farther back in my chair as Quentin waves them over, unaware of the arctic frost he's summoning toward me.

"Hey, guys, I'm Quentin, the club president. You can take a seat at this table." He points to where I'm sitting. Xander looks everywhere but at me.

I might as well have evaporated into the air.

Quentin isn't registering the tension, but his gaze does flit to the tall, tattooed bodyguard lingering in Xander's shadow. "So that makes four," he continues.

Donnelly readjusts the mic at the collar of his acid wash The Cure band tee. "Nah, I'll be sitting this one out."

Quentin nods. "Three is still enough players for a game." He smiles excitedly like it was a stroke of fate that Xander and Easton walked right in.

More like shitty happenstance.

Or maybe I did something that caused this. My mind tries to

reel for a split-second, but Xander's presence is kicking me out of my head.

He's hovering near the chair across from mine. I'm almost positive he's about to ask Quentin if he can join a different game.

Then Easton sinks down in a chair, hands stuffed in his leather jacket. "Sorry we missed the first meeting," he apologizes to Quentin. The cadence of his voice is flat and smooth. "We were in between this and LARPing Club, which meets on the same night. But we found out they only do post-apocalyptic."

"It's not really our thing," Xander adds, rubbing a hand against the back of his tensed neck. He's still standing. Still diverting his gaze from mine.

Quentin is beaming at him. Star-struck.

He must've recognized Xander the moment he walked in, but he isn't mentioning it. I like that for my cousin. Instead, Quentin tells them he'll bring over an attendance sheet and questionnaire to get a sense of their experience level for strategy games.

I already know these two will beat my ass at Catan—but if Harriet doesn't text me in…I check my watch. Five minutes. I'm not going to stay long anyway.

Quentin leaves, and I watch Donnelly follow him, probably to have him sign a non-disclosure agreement. Xander and NDAs are one of the dynamic duos in the family. It's moments like these that I appreciate not having obsessive, all-consuming fame. Novak is chilling by the doors, in eyesight but not glued to my heels.

I pop open my water bottle. "Why don't you like post-apocalyptic LARPing?" I ask Xander as he finally sits.

He gives me a pointed look. "We don't have to do this."

Jesus. "It was an honest question, man."

Easton has a casual arm on the back of Xander's chair. "Pretending to survive a nuclear war and fight zombies isn't fun. I'd much rather be drinking mead in a tavern with my Elvish brethren." He makes geeky shit sound cool.

Xander's lips quirk into a smile.

Yeah, they're meant to be best friends. Maybe more than I ever was supposed to be, and I like that even more for my cousin. Xander would've lost me eventually, and Easton will stick around for him.

Speaking of friends. Where the fuck is mine? I glance at my phone *again*.

Easton hooks his sunglasses to his collar. "Everything okay?" I'm about to mention how Harriet is supposed to be here, but he adds, "Or is that another cousin you're ignoring?"

I frown. "Xander is right here. I'm not ignoring—"

"I'm not talking about Xander. I mean Winona. *Vada*." Easton went to Dalton with the girl squad, and I knew he became friends with them through Xander, but I was at Penn during this time. Graduated. Gone.

I deflect. "Vada Abbey isn't technically my cousin, man. We're not blood related."

"I'm aware." He's irritated by this. Why? I can't process quickly enough. He's already saying, "If you told anyone—Winona, Vada, me, Xander—that you'd been giving Adderall to Tate so he'd lay off the girls, then we could've done something when you left." He tips his head to Xander, including him.

Xander's jaw sharpens. He's also pissed that I didn't loop him in on what was happening right under his nose.

I didn't want to put that pressure on Xander. He was home-schooled most of his life. He didn't need to deal with the awful parts of prep school. The social piranhas who'd feed on you if you let them. The douchebags who'd say they'd fuck your sister just to get a volatile reaction. I wanted Xander to enjoy his time there.

I wanted to bubble-wrap him.

And I felt like I had it under control.

"I'm sorry," I apologize from a deep place within me, but I can't take it back. I can't reverse what happened.

"I'm sorry too," Easton says with heat. "Because if I knew, I wouldn't have had to find Winona almost passed out in a fucking bathroom."

A brutal chill ices my body. I've already thanked Easton for being there when she got drugged, but that's not enough. I'm the cause.

People I love keep getting hurt because of me. It's fucking inevitable at this point. Taking a hot swig of water, I swallow. "What's your major?" I ask. "Hating me?"

"That'd mean I spend fifteen hours a week thinking about you, which I don't."

Point taken. "Debate then."

"Business. Unfortunately, I have parents that don't let me do whatever I want when they're paying for my college." Shots fired, but I don't feel the bullet go through.

My frown deepens. "I thought you cut that leash when you moved in with the Hales?"

"No," he says flatly. "I only moved in with Xander under the guise that it was a 'learning experience' for a potential internship with Hale Co."

His parents just shipped him out to live with the wealthiest family on the block? It seems cold. I nod to him, then check my incoming texts. None from Harriet.

"Can we play the game?" Xander asks, unboxing Catan. "It's the only reason I'm still here."

I miss her. I'm worried about her. I need to see her.

"Ben is going to bail," Easton says, reading me as I glance at the door. It's like having one of my brothers at the table, and right now, that's not helping abate my panic.

"You don't know me, man," I say, trying not to get worked up. I'm white-knuckling my water bottle.

Xander is more uncomfortable. He's slowly pulling out decks of cards.

"I know this is your MO. You ditch people. You cut them dead. I've heard enough from Vada."

"I'm sorry, are you Vada?" I sling back. "She can say this shit to me herself."

"Can she? How many texts have you responded to?"

None.

I dig my back into the chair. He's right, I want to bail on this moment. On this club. On them. The truth isn't just hard to hear, it's setting me on fire. I'm burning up, and I can't find the extinguisher. *Stay?* I need to stay, but how can I when staying just hurts everyone around me.

Either way, I inflict some kind of pain. There is no victory inside my head.

I think I need Harriet.

Xander pieces together the weird hexagon-shaped game board. His amber eyes briefly rise to mine. The past is haunting. Because I did ditch him too. I cut him dead. At fourteen, every invite I had to a house party or a soccer game, I used to bring Xander with me.

We were friends.

He just wanted to fit in, and my "buddies" wanted to use *the* Xander Hale for clout. They would try to get him to take shots and film him. His dad is a recovering alcoholic, so yeah, Xander being caught with vodka underage is headline-worthy news.

Xander took the shot. His first taste of liquor, and I was there. It was my fault. I put him in that position, and I didn't get him out fast enough.

I did make the guys delete the footage. The peer pressure kept escalating. I've never been afraid to say *no*, to be a dissenter among a crowd, but Xander just...he did not want to stand out. His whole life, that's all he's ever done.

And I should've ditched the toxic social circle and kept him.

I just stopped inviting Xander around instead. To save him from those situations.

Being friends with guys I didn't care for—that was pretty normal. At times I tried to find reasons to like them, to make it easier, but mostly,

I was just keeping an eye on people I distrusted. It was a misguided attempt to protect my family while we were all at school together.

Maintaining superficial relationships with insufferable pricks—I'd say it's a skill, but all it did was make me feel like shit.

Charlie and our father could probably do what I couldn't. They have the stomach for it. Or maybe they have the right kind of impenetrable heart.

Hell, in Charlie's case, he might not even have a heart to penetrate.

I look at Xander now, and I do miss the simplicity of what we had when we were younger. I miss sharing a bunk room at the lake house and tossing a foam ball up in the air while Xander talked about *The Silmarillion* from Tolkien for hours. Even the days he'd be sad and quiet, we'd listen to the rain beat against the windowpanes together and draw on an old Etch A Sketch. Passing it back and forth to add more gray lines to the picture.

A dick and nuts would end up somewhere. We thought it was hilarious.

Making him smile, just once, was the highlight of my whole summer. I loved him.

I'll always love Xander.

A phone pings, and my heart jumps, thinking it's Harriet. Only, it's not my phone. Easton shoots up while reading the text. "Fuck, I have to go."

"What?" Xander is about to rise out of his chair.

Easton puts a hand on his shoulder, telling him to stay. "My dad is here."

"On campus?"

"Seems that way." Fear—no, literal *terror*—has widened his eyes. He's no longer unperturbed.

"You want us to go with you, man?" I ask him.

Xander is worried, halfway out of his seat again. "Easton—"

"He just wants a tour of the business building. It's better if I go alone." He's in a hurry, and Xander is partially standing as Easton sprints out into the hall.

"*Fuck,*" Xander curses, conflicted. He ends up lowering back down.

"His dad wants a tour at"—I check my Omega watch—"nine-thirty p.m. on a Monday?"

"I think it's a power trip thing. His dad is so strict, he's literally picked every single one of his classes for the semester. He'd probably have a conniption if he knew Easton was coming from a 'useless' board game club and not chess."

Easton was a chess *champion* at Dalton. I always wondered who'd win if he ever played Charlie. Very few people can beat my brother.

Xander starts packing up the game.

"We aren't playing?" I sound dejected because I strangely am. Minutes ago, I was ready to run. Somewhere, deep down, I want to play this game with him, and that desire surges so suddenly, so fucking powerfully, to the surface.

I want to be here.

"We can't with only two players."

"Counting me out already, House Stark?" Harriet appears, biting on a Jolly Rancher and taking Easton's abandoned chair. She's in khakis and a white button-down, her outfit for volunteering at the hospital, and my smile has fucking exploded.

Xander has a similar one. "Hey, I didn't know you were coming."

"Gotta pad the resume with extracurriculars." She scrapes her chair closer to the table.

"Fashionably late, Fisher," I tease.

She sucks on the hard candy, but her lips try to perk. "You need new eyes, Cobalt boy. *This* isn't fashion." She plucks at her button-down. "It's necessity."

"I'm pretty sure you could make a heavy-duty trash bag look cute."

Xander deals out some cards, more tensed.

Harriet notices him and talks more to the cards she's stacking in her hand. "Maybe you should keep those eyes. They're clearly painting me in the best light."

"You know how to play?" Xander asks her.

"Nope. You want to teach me, Paul Atreides?" The first time

Xander and Harriet met, he was dressed as Paul Atreides from the *Dune* movies...or books. I have no idea what he was going for. I've neither watched nor read them.

Hurt flares in my chest seeing Harriet give him attention. It shouldn't. Three days ago, I literally told her I'd be fine if she got with Xander—and saying those words out loud felt like shoving pushpins in my mouth. Witnessing this possibility now is like swallowing them.

"It's not too hard." Xander tosses her the dice.

She catches with a slight smile.

Jealousy hammers against my ribcage. They're not even really flirting, and breathing already becomes painful. Fucking fantastic. I down a large swig of water.

"You'll get the hang of it fast," Xander sits back down.

"I love the vote of confidence." She rests her elbows on the table. "Lay it on me."

He describes the rules, then the goal of being the first to build the largest army or road, or the first to create the most settlements and cities. Soon, we're all playing together. Rolling dice. Trading our resource cards—a critical component of the game.

"Either of you want to give me all your brick for a couple sheep?" Harriet asks us.

"All my brick?" Xander's brows jump. "For *two* sheep?"

She nearly laughs. "It's called shooting your shot."

He laughs back. "Savage."

My stomach knots. Cards. Focus on the cards.

Harriet pumps her bicep. Barely any muscle. I smile over at her, and I'm not sure she notices me until she says, "What about you, Friend?" Her ocean blue eyes dart to mine. I swear flush creeps up her neck. "Give me all you've got for a couple Bo Peeps?"

My entire hand is brick. "You run a hard bargain." I lean toward her. "But okay."

"Okay?"

"I'll take the deal."

"What?" Xander scrunches his face at me, especially as I pass over all my cards. "Whoa, whoa, whoa." He spreads out his hands. "Pause the game." He shoots a harsh look at me, reminding me of his dad, my Uncle Loren, who can kill with one glare. Xander can be soft one second and lethal the next. "You're going to be left with *nothing*, Ben."

"She's giving me two sheep."

"To do what with? Sheep are practically worthless."

"Hey, they're cute," Harriet defends with not much fight.

"Cute but worthless unless you have brick, wood, and wheat." He turns to me. "Which is going to be hard to get when you have nothing."

I stare at little brick pieces on the colorful board. "I don't think I have much of a chance here, anyway."

Xander scoots his chair closer to me. "You care if I help him?" he asks Harriet, and I'm not sure who's more surprised—me or her.

"You are family. I would only expect as much." She chews on a smile. "Make sure he doesn't pawn off his T-shirt too."

"Jesus, if Ben strips, we have worse problems."

I laugh and nod to Harriet. "You wouldn't want this shirt?" It's a white ringer tee that says *love the planet* in blue lettering.

"If you want to include it with the brick, I won't complain."

Xander cuts me another look like, *please don't show your abs in here*. It will draw attention to our table, and since he's allergic to the spotlight, I'm not trying to make my cousin go into anaphylactic shock. I just show him my cards, letting him help me.

Xander inspects them. "Ben will give you *one* brick for two sheep."

"Cheapo."

"We can't let you make the longest road and end the game in two seconds, and he needs the brick to do literally anything."

"Fine. I won't leave him destitute. Here you go, Cobalt boy." She slides over two sheep. "The Hale to the rescue."

I wonder if she knows the impact those words have on Xander. If she can see him intake a deeper breath. He tries to play it off by concentrating on my hand and his. My smile widens, and we end up joking, laughing, trading cards, trying to thwart each other from building new settlements.

Xander helps me win.

I'm used to my brothers being out for blood during *Candy Land*. Don't even talk about Monopoly. Eliot will buy up every property you need. Taking the W isn't why my chest rises, my lungs fill, though. It's feeling the ice melt between us for the first time in years.

I shouldn't gamble with today. I should leave this one good thing exactly where it is. I could ride this feeling into the morning. The euphoria of knowing something has gone epically right.

Then Xander invites us back to his apartment to hang out and discuss our group presentation for Classical Mythology. Yeah, we're presenting together and not by choice. Our professor chose groups depending on seat arrangements, and we were all sitting side by side by side.

I'm torn on being around him for longer.

The desire to hang out with Xander overrides the fear. Maybe because Harriet is with me. So I take the risk.

TWENTY-NINE

BEN COBALT

Xander's apartment is similarly laid out to my brothers' place three floors above, except Xander's is a two-bedroom he shares with Easton and resembles more of a casual crash pad. Gray sectional, ginormous television, gaming system, and state-of-the-art surround sound.

He moved in this summer, but this is my first time stepping foot here.

My effort to rebuild anything with Xander hasn't been great. Tonight, I realize how much I want to leave things better than they were with him. I feel like I finally have a chance to.

He's opening the fridge. "You two want a beer?"

"Sure, what do you have?" Harriet asks, slinging her backpack on the sectional. She slides into the corner cushions.

"Koning, Miller, Yuengling."

"I'll take a Yuengling."

He pulls out two glass bottles, then asks, "Ben?"

"I'm good with my water." I sit on one side of Harriet and watch Xander pop the caps. I wonder how often he drinks.

His jaw muscle tics when he notices me staring. He's giving me a brutal look. "Don't judge me, man."

"I didn't say a word," I defend.

"You have that look." He takes a seat on the other cushion beside Harriet and hands her a beer. "Okay, I'm not an alcoholic just because my dad is one—and yeah, it is hereditary, but I have *zero* signs of addiction. So cheers." He lifts the beer, then takes a bitter swig. His brows pinch afterward. Guilt for being an asshole causes him to slump back into the couch.

My muscles flex, and I sit more on the edge of the cushion. Well, this is blowing up really fucking fast.

Harriet glances cautiously between us. "So...should we talk about Ovid's *Metamorphoses* or the fifty-ton elephant in the room?"

"Have you read it yet?" I ask Xander, choosing the easy subject matter—our presentation topic.

"I read one of the translations four years ago." It's a Roman epic poem originally in Latin. "You?"

I shake my head. "I know most of the poems. Ovid gets mentioned so much, he might as well be a tenth member of my family." I flip the cap of my water bottle. "Of what I remember, it's mostly about the gods being immoral and how they inadvertently inflict pain upon others." I glance at Harriet.

She sinks back. "Don't look at me. I haven't even gotten the book yet." She sips her beer.

Xander picks at the label on his glass bottle. "Yeah, but I don't think we should focus the presentation on that aspect. Ovid isn't like Homer where there's a clear epic hero. There's no Achilles or Odysseus, no courageous battletested warriors to root for. Instead, he shows us that we're all flawed. Gods and mortals alike."

I frown. "So there aren't any heroes?"

"No, there is," Xander says. "I think at the foundation of every poem, the hero is love."

"Love?"

"Yeah, and change. It's literally called *Metamorphoses*. I think there's a quote too." He squints at the ceiling in thought. "'What we have been, or now are, we shall not be tomorrow.'" He nods. "Something like that." He shrugs. "I just think it's a more interesting concept."

"I'm down," Harriet says.

Love and Change as heroes? I don't know what I feel. My brain speeds beyond me. "Yeah, sure."

"Or, I mean, if you want to go in a different direction after you read it, I'm open to anything. I *really* don't want to be the one to say more than a couple words when we present. It'll be a miracle if my voice doesn't shake."

"I've got you covered. I can memorize whatever." Public speaking has never been hard for me.

He eases, then nods in thanks.

Harriet frowns at her beer. "The presentation is one of the last big grades for the course."

"Yeah...?" I don't follow where she's going.

"Professor Wellington hasn't set a date yet, but it'll probably be toward the end of the semester. Like November or December." *When I'm gone,* she doesn't add.

I sit up a little stiffer. "Maybe it'll be October."

"Yeah, maybe."

Xander isn't catching onto the problem. Easton calling me out for ditching people comes crashing back.

To bail or not to bail? I hate that sticking around feels more fatal somehow, but I can't even picture leaving Xander or Harriet alone in front of two hundred students. She might break out in hives, and I could so easily carry the weight of the presentation for them.

I'll be there.

I'll make it. I have to make it. I can make it.

Another swig, more water washes down my throat. Cooling me off, and then an awkward silence passes between us.

"I think the elephant is back," Harriet says casually. "You have a name for him?"

I rest my forearms on my knees, more hunched, and I glance over at Xander. He takes a sharper swig of beer.

"I guess not." Harriet widens her eyes.

"You want to tell her?" I ask him.

"Why not?" Xander turns to her. "Ben, here, thinks I'm a porcelain doll. One crack away from shattering."

"That's not—"

"It is true," Xander retorts. "Look, we can blame the total annihilation of our friendship on your shitty friends, on you feeling like I couldn't stand up for myself, whatever, but when we were kids, you *never* treated me like I was this fragile, broken thing. You don't even get how much I fucking loved you for that." His nose flares. He's avoiding Harriet and rises to his feet.

I stand up too.

He stops in place.

Pain envelops me, just seeing his and knowing I'm the origin. "I just wanted to protect you," I tell him.

"I am not one step away from self-destruction." He points at himself with the beer bottle. When he sees me glancing at the alcohol, he lets out a dying laugh. "Jesus Christ."

"Xander—"

"You look at me, Ben, like I'm *still* that thirteen-year-old that you found…" His voice tapers out. He's unblinking.

I'm unblinking.

It hurts to breathe as we both see the memory in front of us. Christmas at the lake house. The night of his thirteenth birthday. One or two a.m. I needed to piss, and I slipped off the top bunk, not realizing Xander wasn't on the bottom.

I went into our bathroom. Flicked on the lights. I saw blood, him, the bathtub, and a razor in his fingers. He was cutting the top of his thighs.

I was only thirteen too, and I got the blade out of his hand, watched him slump down into the tub in anguish I wished I could take away, and he just kept crying and pleading, "Don't tell anyone. Don't. *Please*, Ben."

When Xander was around eleven, twelve his depression had taken an all-time low. It wasn't a secret to our families that he wasn't doing well.

I helped him out of the tub. "We can just sit for a sec. I'll get bandages." I got him to calm down, and we sat on the floor while I peeled off Band-Aids and he stuck them on his cuts.

He was blinking through streaming tears. "You can go. I'm making your night worse, maybe your life…I don't know."

"It's not worse." I caught his drifting gaze. "Honestly, I'd rather sit on this bathroom floor with you for a billion years than not have you in this world at all." His chin quaked, and I added, "I bet it'd get pretty crammed in here because all our families would feel the same too."

Xander nodded a bunch.

I nodded back and asked, "You think Eliot would stand on the sink?"

He choked out a weak laugh. "And recite some weird soliloquy." Then he wiped his runny nose. It took him a while to speak again, but he whispered out, "Thanks, Ben."

I didn't tell anyone what happened. In a way, I thought he'd trust me more. I thought we'd grow closer. I thought if he hit another low, I'd be someone he'd go to, but he's right that I started treating him like he was always in harm's reach.

Gone were the simple times of penis Etch A Sketch drawings. Things got real. I did not want to lose my cousin to anything.

I'm still naturally searching for the bubble-wrap when he's around.

Harriet casts tense glances between us. "Ben found you where…?"

I'm floored when Xander admits, "Cutting. I was cutting myself in the bathroom." He's only looking at me.

"Oh," she murmurs.

I take a breath. "Maybe I should've told someone what happened."

His brows scrunch in confusion. "Why?"

I lift my stiff shoulders. "Because after that I felt responsible—like if *anything* bad happened to you, it'd be because of me. Because I didn't tell your parents. I didn't even tell Moffy...and you know how badly I wanted to run to him that night?" I shift my weight. "You have one of the best brothers in the world. Back then, I would've given a left kidney to switch him with Charlie."

"Back then? Not now?"

"I don't know what's happening, but Charlie hasn't been that horrible." I don't mention how he gave me a heads up about the Board Game Club tonight, and how he told Harriet he doesn't hate me. The latter still feels unreal.

Xander loosely fists the neck of the beer. "You know if you ran to Moffy, there is no chance he would've kept it a secret. He would've told our parents."

"Yeah, he would've done the right thing." I hear my voice rising. "Everyone would've, except for me."

"You were thirteen too," Xander defends me. "If anything happened to me, it would've never been your fault. If anything does now, it won't be either." He motions to my water bottle. "Is there holy water in there? Because you're absolved. Spritz it on yourself or whatever."

It won't be my fault.

I let that ping around my brain, but it's not helping me relax. Something feels wrong with me. I don't know...I lift my gaze to his. "If it means anything, I don't really see you as breakable as much as everything is breaking around me." The door begins to creak open. Easton is here. "I should go."

"Wait," Xander calls out.

"See you in class." I nod to him with a smile. "I am glad we did this."

He nods uncertainly.

And I salute Harriet. "Fisher." My chest is tight. I'm leaving her with Xander. Don't do it. Don't do it.

I want her at my side.

I want her in my arms.

I want her to be mine.

Instead, I'm veering toward the door like a tornadic wind, and Easton blows out of the way. Glaring, he says, "It's not a French exit. It's the *Ben* exit."

I shoot a glare back.

When I'm in the hall, I head to the elevators. Each step away from her hurts. The sound of a shutting door jolts my body, and I look backward.

Harriet is running to catch me.

My lungs expand. I hang on to her appearance, not even caring if she's a mirage and I'm imagining shit now. I'll take this fantasy. But full disclosure, she's real.

She slows at my side, digging in her black backpack. Our eyes meet a few tender times. Then I say, "You looking for a cross to excise the demon within me, Fisher?"

"You're a Cobalt. The only demon within you is hubris, and sorry to say, you seem to lack it the most of your immortal fam."

"So you say," I smile more and more.

It pulls a tiny one out of her too.

Harriet does make me feel so much fucking better, and I can't explain it at all. I've stopped trying to figure it out.

"Damn," she mutters, a plastic baggie of hard candies in her hand. Her shoulders drop in defeat when we reach the elevator. "How are these not vegan?" She's reading the ingredients label.

She wanted to give me candy? I smile down at her.

She looks up at me. "What?"

"Nothing," I whisper, then I drape my arm over her shoulders. Harriet leans a little into me. I feel her skin go warm, and I scrunch her hair with my hand. *I think I'm falling in love with you. I wish we could be together. I'm sorry.*

Thank you.

It all rolls over me like a tidal wave.

THIRTY

HARRIET FISHER

"What birthday presents did you get them?" Tom asks me. He's leaning his arms on a sticky bar, waiting for a bartender to notice him. It might be a decade before that happens. This club is *packed*. The bouncers stopped letting people in about fifteen minutes ago.

Tom and I are wedged up by the bar side by side like we don't hate each other, when *he* was the one throwing popcorn at me in our boxed seat at the ballet tonight. Okay, I might have been throwing popcorn back, but I wasn't going to surrender with kernels stuck in my hair. And now my head spins at his words. *Birthday presents.* Did I lose this memo in the mail? Surely, Ben would have told me if I needed to get Charlie and Beckett gifts.

It's September 19th.

Girls in high school were *obsessed* with this random ass day all because *the* Ryke Meadows was born on it, and then twenty-eight years later—his nephews, Charlie Cobalt and Beckett Cobalt, came into the world on the same exact day.

I've never marked it on my calendar. I honestly forgot all about it until Ben invited me to the ballet for Beckett's "birthday" performance. He's invited me to see *Giselle* before, but I've opted out in favor of studying. Tonight should've been another easy pass since I have a Latin exam tomorrow.

But my heart won over my head, and I blurted out, "I'll be there."

Little did I know that "there" also included an afterparty at Pink Noir.

I'm digging the cool '80s *Blade Runner* slash Disco Barbie vibe of this club. Hot pink strobe lights stroke sweaty bodies in the dance pit, and the light refracts colorfully against revolving disco balls. Film noir posters hang on the black walls, and racks of liquor bottles at the bar are backlit with a pink neon glow.

Apparently, most ballet dancers from NYBC frequent this club after their performances to blow off steam. So while I should be memorizing Latin adverbs, I'm crossing my fingers and toes that the bartender doesn't ask for my I.D.

I'm also really wishing Ben were next to me right now to clear up this "birthday present" confusion. But he left five minutes ago to use the restroom, and I'm almost positive he's not making it back through the crowds anytime soon.

That leaves me with *Tom*.

He's waving a hand for the bartender, who's busy helping a group of girls at the other end of the bar. He lets out a heavy sigh and rotates back to me. "If you got them both a book, I'm going to warn you now, that's just so generic of you."

My face heats. *He's serious?* "Was I supposed to get them something?"

Tom's brows lift. "Harry? You didn't get my brothers *anything?*"

"They're turning twenty-four," I say in defense. "Not five." As soon as I utter the words I feel like an asshole because I don't really mean it. I'd gladly accept a birthday gift at the ripe age of fifty. I just don't know how else to deflect the brewing guilt bubbling in my stomach. I was the only "friend" invited to sit in the Cobalt brothers' boxed seat at the ballet with them. So maybe I should've bought

Charlie and Beckett something just to be nice...even if they're mind-bogglingly wealthy.

Rich people still like presents. Right?

Tom narrows his eyes at me as he studies my expression. "Are you—actually—wrecked by this?" His face twists. "And here I thought you were made of iron. Relax, relax. Don't cry—"

I'm scowling. "I'm not crying, *Tommy*."

He holds up his hands in surrender. "I was fucking with you."

"Clearly," I shoot back. "So what did *you* get them?"

"Nothing." He tries flagging down the bartender again. "No one gives them gifts. Pretty sure Charlie would chuck it into the dumpster. In front of your face." He laughs at the visual.

On the other side of me, an old stocky man lets out a frustrated curse before he grumbles under his breath and abandons the bar. His presence is quickly replaced by a younger, taller, more athletic, more picturesque-looking guy in a gray sweatshirt and jeans. He pushes back the wet strands of his dark dirty-blond hair. Perspiration isn't beaded up on his olive skin, so he's not sweaty from dancing. More like, he just showered. He has a soap scent and "just shaved" smoothness to his strong jawline.

I wonder if he's one of the dancers from *Giselle*. Seems likely, but I wasn't exactly memorizing their faces during the performance tonight.

He glances to his left *over* my head and makes direct eye contact with Tom. I watch him assess Tom in a quick sweep—up, down. "*You're* having trouble getting a drink? Fucking hell. This is going to be a nightmare." He puts two elbows on the counter and leans half his body over. "Marjorie!" he shouts at one of the brunette bartenders. "Marj!"

"In a minute!" She shoos him like she's swatting a fly.

He lets out an annoyed breath, then peers back at Tom. "What do you want to drink?"

Tom's brows spike. He points at himself where a silver skull necklace hangs against his black muscle tee. "Me?"

"No, the bodyguard behind you." He jerks a thumb to the towering guy that's standing directly behind Tom. "Because I'm sure he's allowed to drink on the job."

I am thoroughly lost now. "How do you know he's a bodyguard?"

This maybe-dancer looks *down* at me as if the mouse on the floor just decided to squeak. "Who are you?"

"Harriet," I snap into a scowl. "Who are you?"

Tom's eyes bug so wide at me like I'm making a fool of myself. I don't understand. Does this guy piss gold or something? He seems to be a grade A asshole from my point of view.

"She's new," Tom says swiftly. "Tonight was her first time watching an NYBC ballet."

"What a shame." The maybe-dancer gives me a tense smile. "Your first would've been better tomorrow night when I'm the lead." He outstretches a hand for me to shake. "Leo Valavanis."

I hold in a breath. This is…messy. Tonight, Beckett danced the lead male role, and I recognize the clear shot taken at Ben's older brother. The literal Birthday Boy tonight. No way am I touching Leo, not even with the tip of my pinky.

Five seconds pass, and he drops his hand like he never offered it to begin with. He turns his attention back to Tom in a casual, cool way. "Drink?"

"Yeah, uh, sure." Tom bops his head to the beat of the music, but he's clearly into whatever charming asshole vibes Leo is projecting. "Vodka and Fizz."

"I'll take a Modelo," I tell Leo, shooting my shot. Hey, there's a ten percent chance *I'm* going to be the one to get a bartender over here.

Leo doesn't let on if he heard me, but he pulls himself halfway over the bar again. "Marjorie!" he yells. "I'm grabbing the Grey Goose!"

"No, you are not, LV!" The brunette whirls toward us in a rush, then swats his back off the bar. "What do you want?"

"Two vodka and Cokes. And a Shirley Temple for the shortie." He points at me in the middle of him and Tom. My face flames.

"He means a Modelo," I correct.

Marjorie scans me in a quick sweep, then offers a pitying smile. "Sorry, hun. That won't fly with me." *Great, so why am I standing here?* She starts pouring the Grey Goose when I feel a body walk up behind me. At first I think it might be Ben, until I glance up to see Beckett's chiseled, angelic jawline and hardened expression. I've found it's scarier when someone like Beckett—who's considered the calmest of the Cobalt Empire—goes nuclear. And right now, he is *pissed*.

"What the fuck are you doing?" Beckett snaps at Leo.

Oh, I really don't want to be in the middle of this. But it appears I'm stuck between Tom and Leo with Beckett *right* behind me. No way out.

Leo leans a casual elbow on the bar. "What's it look like I'm doing?"

"He's fine, Beckett," Tom interjects. "Harmless, even."

Leo throws a hand toward Tom. "See that—I am *harmlessly* buying your little brother a drink." The smile crawling across his face is just for Beckett. A big FU.

Beckett glowers. "You're going to walk away."

"And why would I do that?" Leo asks into a laugh. "You don't own this bar, Cobalt."

"It's my birthday," Beckett reminds him, and I think that Leo might just laugh even harder. But something passes between their eyes. Understanding? I can't read body language as well as Ben, but it's clear these two have bucketloads of history.

Leo smiles. "Sure," he says, then tips his head to the side. "See you around, Tom."

Tom up-nods but concentrates mostly on the drinks being poured.

Leo lingers like he's considering recapturing Tom's attention, but Beckett angles himself at Leo in a show of dominance and masculine posturing. Then he says one firm, "No."

I'm guessing this dissuades Leo since he just looks down at me. "Shortie." He leaves at that dumb insult, and I pin my glare to his fucking back. Ugh.

"I hate that guy," I say.

Beckett's not even listening to me, he's fixed on his little brother. "Don't entertain him, Tom."

"He was going to buy me a drink. Why would I turn down a free drink, dude?"

"Because you can buy your own drinks," Beckett says smoothly. I must be getting to know them better—since I can see his subtle aggravation.

Tom groans and side-eyes the general direction Leo walked off to. "I can't help it, Beckett Joyce—I was just a bystander. *He* was flirting with *me*. Right, Harry?" He twists to me for confirmation.

But Beckett doesn't give me a chance to reply. "He's using you to piss me off," he tells Tom. "Letting him inside of you will be the worst decision of your life. Just stay away from him."

Marjorie pushes the three drinks toward us, her eyes darting warily between Beckett and Tom like she doesn't mean to interrupt.

"What is this, Marj?" Beckett asks her.

"Two vodka Cokes and a Shirley Temple." She's summoned to the other side of the bar and rushes away.

Beckett gives Tom one of his supremely famous *what the fuck* faces. "Coke?" Ah, this must have to do with the fact that their family owns Fizzle, the competing soda company.

"Dude, I did not order this." Tom takes the Shirley Temple. "I'm going to go find the other birthday boy." He sidesteps away from the bar, and Beckett lets out a deep exhale before turning to me. I'm still not used to being in Beckett's presence. It's easier when another Cobalt boy is around. But if it's just him—I find myself sweating. Especially now that I'm keeping a giant secret from him.

Ben is planning to move to the remote wilderness in November.

I ache to tell him. Maybe Beckett would be able to convince Ben to stay, but if I utter the truth—I'd blow up my friendship...or whatever I have with Ben in a single instant.

I'm fucked up.

Not a great person.

Selfish.

Because I can't manage to speak the truth. I just say, "Happy birthday." And scamper away as quickly as Tom did. Pushing through the crowds, I find Ben stuck in a cluster of people. Surrounded by a wall of bodies. I think about shoving toward him, fighting through the small gaps of people.

But I don't have to. He towers over everyone and looks around, his gaze planting on mine in milliseconds.

He smiles and weaves his way toward me.

When he's in front of me, I imagine the world's most epic reunion (not that we've been away from each other for long), but there is some sort of fairy tale in being swept up in each other's arms and spun around on a dance floor in a public display of affection. It's a silly thought. Even though we've hooked up once, we're still just friends.

It is what it is…he gave me an orgasm to help me out during a dry spell, not to build a foundation to some long-lasting relationship. But if he asked to fool around again, even with the threat of emotions slipping through the cracks, I'd say yes. I'd say *hell* yes. Because the hot mental image of his fingers disappearing inside me has been cycling through my head on repeat since it happened six days ago.

It's not really a question whether he's been thinking about that night. I can see the way he slowly undresses me, as if he's recalling his hands on my bare skin. It gives me free rein to check him out too.

He's in more formal attire for the ballet. Black slacks fit his ass and muscled thighs too well, and I could thank the club's heat index for making Ben roll up the sleeves of his royal-blue button-down. I wonder if he can tell how obsessed I am with his strong forearms. With the veins spindling down to his large, masculine hands.

He definitely can, Harriet. Neither of us tuck our attraction away. Nope, it is very fucking present.

He stops inches away, his eyes flitting from my lips back up to my gaze in a quick, sexy beat. It skips my pulse.

"Fisher," he greets with a wide grin. "How have you survived without me?"

"Well, I was denied a Modelo. Called *Shortie*. And your brothers had a heated exchange in spitting distance of me, so I would say, I am thoroughly alive."

Ben frowns. "Who called you Shortie?" His gaze narrows to hot pinpoints at the crowds, and I bite my lip, feeling my perpetual scowl morph into a smile.

"This Leo Valavanis jerk," I say more upbeat because I am fucking *giddy* right now at Ben wanting to defend my honor. *Calm yourself, Harriet.*

Recognition hits Ben. "That's Beckett's rival in the company."

"Makes more sense. He was definitely taking jabs at him."

"Which of my brothers were going at it?"

"Tom and Beckett."

"Because of Leo?"

"Yep."

He nods strongly like that checks out. He peeks at his phone into a deeper frown.

"What's wrong?" I ask.

"I'm just seeing if Guy Abernathy is stopping by. Beckett let me invite him to the afterparty."

I go cold. "Guy Abernathy?" My jaw drops. "As in the *president* of the Honors House?"

"The one you've been insta-stalking all semester, yeah that one," Ben slides me a teasing smile.

My cheeks are hot. "You invited him?" I'm about to ask how he got his number, but this is *Ben*. I wouldn't be shocked if he had Patroclus on speed dial and every other Trojan War hero.

"Yeah, you said networking was a big deal to get in."

So he invited him to Beckett and Charlie's birthday outing at Pink Noir? The thoughtfulness nearly dampens the anxious anticipation surging through me. "And he said yes?" I ask, my pulse racing.

"He said yes," Ben tells me. "But the bouncers cut off the line, so I'm just trying to make sure he'll be let in if he shows late."

Yes...yes. That's a good idea. I try to waft my shirt, but the fabric of my crop top is too tight. Pit stains are likely. Thankfully it's white. My phone buzzes at my hip. I unclip it, and all my nervous, excited energy plummets in a pit of despair.

"Fucking...*no*," I growl.

Ben leans closer, placing a hand on the small of my back. He's leading us to a darker, more secluded corner of the club near a metal trashcan. His towering concern should calm me, but this night is seriously taking a turn. "What's wrong?" he asks.

"The grad student who's mentoring me with my research project just texted. And I need to go into the lab."

He frowns. "Now? It's midnight."

I don't know how to explain this without divulging the truth. I speak so quickly, I half-hope he can't piece apart some of it. "I can't access the clean room as an undergrad, so I rely on the grad student to pull the pregnant mice for me. She was supposed to pull one this afternoon, but she got busy and just did it now. I need the embryos to be exactly seventeen days in gestation. So I have to dissect tonight."

His eyes go big. "*Dissect? As in...?*"

My heart hurts. "I'm killing the mouse, Friend."

"The pregnant mouse," he says without blinking.

"...yeah."

I can't read his expression. I'm not sure I want to. He says nothing else, and I think this might be too much for him to process.

Air is brittle in my lungs, but I manage to say, "I...I have to go. But I think I might be able to come back." It's not just for Guy Abernathy. I don't want to bail on Ben or this night or his brothers, but mostly just Ben.

He nods slowly. "We'll be here late-late. Four, maybe."

I let out a breath. "Okay, I might be able to make it back." I crane my neck to hold his gaze. "If you want me to come back, that is?" My chest tightens, dreading his response. I hate that I've hurt him, and by the pained look in his eyes, I know I have.

He nods even slower. "Yeah. I want you to come back, Friend."

I repeat those words over and over in my head as he walks me out, hails me a cab, and makes sure I leave safely.

THIRTY-ONE

BEN COBALT

After Harriet texts that she's on campus, I think I'll relax, but tension still flexes every tendon in my body. I'm back inside Pink Noir, and Eliot and Tom have already pulled me onto the dance floor.

I have to pretend for thirty minutes that I'm not dying inside. The club feels too small. Bodies packed too tight. I can spot the NYBC dancers on the floor, not just because I recognize their faces.

The beat of the music seems to flow through their limbs, their veins, with soul-bearing rhythm in each lithe movement. Leo rolls his neck like the melody is a drug he's high on. Beckett lifts a girl in his arms and twirls. She sways her hands upward like she's skimming the surface of a lake and not the air. A couple dancers drift off to the side complaining about being sore and exhausted from their performance earlier tonight.

I try to let the remixed songs absorb my thoughts like the most powerful sponge, but I just keep thinking, *Harriet dissects mice*. And now she's gone. I'm not sure which one feels worse. There is a definite void she's left behind.

She dissects mice? I wish it were a question and not an absolute fact. I'm so conflicted that my stomach is caving in on itself. I might hurl.

"Ben! Brother!" Eliot cups my jaw, then the back of my skull with love. "No pouting allowed!"

"No pouting, Ben Pirrip!" Tom hollers in agreement. "It's our brothers' motherfucking birthday!" Half the dance floor cheers with them.

I want to smile and join the fevered elation. Not that long ago, I would've been bellowing with joy. Tonight has been entirely worry-free, stress-free, panic-free. I never stopped grinning during the ballet. Of the countless times I've seen my brother dance, this was hands-down my favorite watching him on stage.

His favorite ballet. On his birthday. Then I looked next to me and saw Harriet entranced with the way Beckett glided and took each turn with perfect precision. His sky-high, effortless jumps made the whole theatre audibly gasp, including her. After his variation, a booming roar of applause erupted. We were all on our feet.

I haven't even feared the terrible outcomes to being around them. I just existed in the moment with my brothers and with her.

We left the ballet and wandered down the sidewalk toward the club, singing "Happy Birthday" to Charlie and Beckett, with all of Beckett's friends. I picked popcorn kernels out of Harriet's blond hair, and she tried not to trip while she walked in front of me. I thought about scooping her up in my arms, thought about kissing her under the sparkling city lights, thought about all the ways in which I never wanted this to end.

Eliot led the way into Pink Noir, all of us cutting the velvet ropes and the long, weaving line out the entrance.

It's been a flood-my-lungs, stay-out-forever, soar-to-the-stars kind of night.

Now it's crashing to the concrete.

In the middle of a pop ballad, I feel my phone vibrate in my palm—I've been keeping it there in case Harriet or Guy texts. Before I even look at the screen, I'm wishing it's from her.

My stomach plummets.

> **GUY ABERNATHY (HONORS HOUSE PRESIDENT)**
> I got held up. Really want to make it, but it looks like I'll need to take a raincheck.

Could this night tank even harder? I skate a frustrated hand through my damp, sweaty hair before I stuff my cell in my pocket. Fuck tonight. Truly. I try to slip away from my brothers, but Eliot seizes my shoulder and leans into my ear. "Where are you off to?"

"To find Beckett!" I yell over the music as it changes to a bass-heavy song.

Eliot fists a handful of my shirt and pulls me away from the amps to a quieter side of the club. I let him drag me there. I'm not sure I have a lot of fight in me tonight. He wipes dripping sweat off his temples with the side of his fist. "Did you have an argument with Harriet?"

My muscles cramp. "What?"

"You were fine before she left." Eliot kicks a crumpled beer can out of my vicinity, like its mere two-inch radius to my feet might hurt me.

I wonder how crushed I look. "And I'm still fine," I lie and pat his shoulder. "The music is just loud. I want to be outside. I'm going to go find Beckett and say goodbye."

"Souviens-toi." *Remember.* Eliot grips my shoulders with two hands. "Tu n'es jamais seul." *You are never alone.*

I'm okay.

I'm okay, I want to tell him, but I struggle to lie twice in a row. I hate doing it just once. "Je dois y aller," I choke out. *I have to go.*

He drops his hands off me. "I saw Beckett head toward the bathroom. Tom and I will be out front waiting for you."

"You don't have to leave too."

"The party is played out anyway." He wears a wry smile, in part to lighten my mood. Last thing I want is to ruin his night, but arguing with him is futile. So I just let out a *thanks* and try to hang on to the relief of having my brothers around. It's been more in reach tonight than it has been the past three years.

But I feel it being drowned by this stupid fucking feeling. The severe need to pull away begins to escalate.

I pat his shoulder again, then slide past him, but I can practically feel his worried eyes follow me as I curve my way around the dancers. When I take a sharp turn down the dimly lit hall that leads to the bathrooms, my feet skate to a sudden stop.

I've found Beckett near the bathroom door, but he's not alone. He's standing two short inches apart from Leo Valavanis, and they're both talking in hurried, enraged words that I can't decipher—but that's not what has my shoes glued to the sticky floor.

Their bodies curve *inward* not outward. Beckett has a hand bracing the wall above Leo's head. I'm decent at reading body language, and these aren't two people about to throw punches, even if their voices carry ire.

But it doesn't make sense—Beckett is straight…I think?

I don't know his sexual history, but I can't imagine a world where he'd have hooked up with guys and not told Tom. All my life, all I've ever known is that Tom likes guys. It had never been a big deal or a question. And I was there that Christmas when Maximoff, our cousin, came out as bisexual to the family. I was there when my ten-year-old brother broke down crying. I think that might've been one of the happiest days in Tom's life.

We're all out here just striving for empathy. Connection. A common bond between the people we love. I know I've gone to bed *begging* for it. It's hard to wrap my head around Beckett withholding that from Tom.

So yeah, this doesn't make any fucking sense.

Personally, I don't need it to make sense. I just need air.

I reroute out of the hallway without disturbing Beckett and Leo. My bodyguard follows. Novak's presence feels more like a weighted blanket than a shadow, and I'm keenly aware of his concern as soon as I head for the back exit doors and not the front. He doesn't say anything as I push them open—grateful no alarm goes off—and meet the night air.

The doors swing shut behind Novak, and I don't even have time to think or process. On this empty sidewalk, there's a girl sitting on the dirty cement in a sparkly pink halter dress. Her back leans up against the wall, and her face is an ashen gray. She looks incredibly fucking unwell. "Heyhey!" I rush to her, dropping to my knees. "What's wrong?"

Soft brown curls frame her round cheeks. Pieces stick to her clammy forehead. She's staring beyond me. "I can't see…I'm going to faint—" The whites of her eyes come into view as her eyeballs roll back.

Shitfuck. Her head slumps, and I catch her cheek in my palm before her skull can collide with the cement. She's fully passed out on the ground. Looking up at Novak, I shout, "Get help!" He tries the double doors, but they locked behind us. So he sprints around the corner, speaking hurriedly into his radio.

I press my fingers to her damp neck, her pulse a steady thump. Then I find her cell phone beside her, and I turn it in front of her face. The security interface recognizes her features and unlocks. Her last call was to a *Nikolai Rurik Kotova Jr.*

I don't know who the fuck that is—but I'm about to dial him when a voice of panic pitches into the air.

"There she is!"

I look up to see the girl that Beckett had lifted on the dance floor earlier. Tight red mini dress, pin-straight bleach-blond hair, long ballerina legs—she's one of the NYBC dancers. Beth Anne Blanchard. I met her tonight when Beckett introduced me to more of his friends.

She races over with Leo and Beckett at her heels. She squats down to her unresponsive friend while I'm beside her. "Roxy. Roxy. Roxanne." She snaps her fingers in the brunette's face, then glances quickly to me. "When did she pass out?"

"Five seconds ago." I'm still cradling her head.

Beth Anne lets out a breath of relief, and Leo wets a bandana with his water bottle and hands it to her. I'm guessing Leo shares friends with Beckett in the company since he's out here. I watch as Beth Anne lightly dabs the damp bandana to Roxanne's forehead. Whatever's happening seems to be familiar for all three of them because they wait for another few seconds before Roxanne's eyes flutter open.

"Oh my God," she moans, warmth returning to her features. Her skin is a light golden-brown hue, and her face pinches in more embarrassment than anything. "This didn't just happen. Whywhy-why?" she mutters quickly to herself.

"Welcome back to the living, Roxy," Leo says. "You picked a disgusting place to pass out."

"Just take it easy," Beckett advises her and shoots Leo a look.

"Yeah, don't sit up right away, babe," Beth Anne adds.

She moans again, more mortified, and sits up straight. Seeing me squatting beside her. "Uh, hi? You're…Ben Cobalt." She's losing color again. Her horrified hazel eyes soar to Beckett above us. "I fainted on your brother?"

"Not *on me*," I say lightly. "I just caught you."

"Yeah, okay, that's great." She face-palms herself. "Ifaintedon-BenCobalt."

I look up at Beckett for clarity, and he introduces, "This is Roxanne Ruiz. Ballerina."

"Hi," she squeaks out. "And I already said that…" She shuts her eyes like she'd prefer to disappear.

"I would've introduced you earlier," Beckett tells me, "but she had to run out to meet with her family."

Beth Anne presses a hand to her collarbones. "You scared the shit out of me when I couldn't find you."

Roxanne blows out a long breath, still not fully a hundred percent yet. "I walked out here to take a call, and I was burning up. It's colder outside, so the temperature change got to me." It is a brisk night, but she's still shy about it.

"Rox, it's fine," Beth Anne assures. "We're all just glad you're okay."

"I'm scared if I stand, I might get light-headed," she mumbles into her water bottle. Her cheeks are on fire.

"Blood pressure thing?" I ask Beckett and back up.

He nods. "Vasovagal." Then he easily lifts Roxanne in a cradle, his arm under her legs and another behind her back. So routine that I wonder how many times he's done this.

Beckett has a whole world in ballet I've never delved this deeply into. The desire to be an integral part of his life is overwhelming. It slams into me and lifts the carriage of my body. I love feeling closer to Beckett. I would've given *anything* to tag along on his adventures in New York when I was a kid.

I'm here now.

I want to murder the ugly monster that says I shouldn't exist in breathing distance of him. There hasn't been a moment where I haven't wished it dead. I wish it never arrived. I wish it never crawled out beneath my bed. I wish it never stood in the corner of my room and grew.

I hope it's shrinking. Until it's so small, I can squash it beneath my foot. But it's terrifying because when have I ever willingly exterminated something? Is this thing alive in me?

Beckett's yellow-green eyes zero in on me. Confusion draws on his face. "What were you doing out here?"

"Saving the day," Beth Anne answers for me. "Roxy might've had a full-blown concussion if your brother *wasn't* here."

I nod slowly, but I don't speak. Beckett is staring *through* me like my intentions are visible etchings in my agonized heart. I was leaving without saying goodbye. And he knows that's out of character for me.

"Let's call a cab and get her home," Leo says, "because I, for one, Roxy socks, do not want a run-in with your Russian family after you fainted."

I don't hear the response. I'm the forceful gust being propelled away by my own need.

"Ben!" Beckett calls out. "Can you wait a minute for me?" I take too long to respond, and he shouts—literally *shouts* in a way that Beckett almost never does, "S'il te plaît, attends une minute!" *Please wait a minute.*

His friends go wide-eyed and still. They've likely never heard him raise his voice. It's a well-regarded fact among the public that Beckett is like idle water while the rest of us are the tempest—the turbulent, torrid storm.

All the ballet dancers are staring at me.

I nod tensely, solidified to the sidewalk. "Désolé." *Sorry.*

"Ne t'excuse pas," he says much quieter. Softer. *Don't apologize.* He takes a tight breath before he disappears around the corner with everyone. For the first time in a long while—I'm alone.

Truly alone on this sidewalk.

Beckett knew he'd be risking that by leaving me. I hear Eliot in my head, "Tu n'es jamais seul." *You are never alone.*

No bodyguard. No people. The air is much cooler out here than in the crowded club. I close my eyes for a second, trying to hear the birds. But the sound of exhaust, of a faint ambulance siren, and squealing clubgoers around the corner murders the chance.

When I snap my eyes open, I hear footsteps behind me. Novak readjusts the radio on his waistband. Before our eyes crash together, I look away and listen to an impulse.

I stride down the sidewalk and head toward the nearest station. I've always liked Novak, but knowing he probably ratted out my bartending job to my parents is fucking *unnerving.*

Maybe that's why I have this itch to run.

I'm five blocks away from Pink Noir when a black SUV rolls up beside the curb at the same pace as me. My pulse accelerates as the car keeps in time with my stride. Fuck—am I about to be kidnapped? Mugged? Assaulted?

THIRTY-TWO

BEN COBALT

Fear slams at me.

I shouldn't have left my brothers—the thought is hacksawed as the rear passenger-side door whips open. While the car is still fucking moving. Sure, it's going like a mile per hour, but for a split-second, my muscles flex in preparation to fight.

When I see Charlie in the car, glaring at me, I'm so caught off guard that I almost run into a lamppost.

Novak catches my arm and yanks me to the side so I don't make a head-on collision with metal and gain a massive goose egg.

"Get in," Charlie says more calmly than his eyes let on.

"Did Beckett send you?" I stop at the curb.

Charlie tilts his head. "Of course he sent me. *Get the fuck in.*" When I don't move, he lets out an exasperated sigh. "It's my birthday, Ben."

Swiping the birthday card should not have this much power, but our mom treats birthdays like they're coronations. Our day to reign. Even if some of us don't care much about them. Honestly, if Charlie weren't a twin, I think he'd Houdini himself on his birthday so no one could celebrate him.

Novak is silent, but I sense his utter relief when I step toward the SUV. My bodyguard rounds to the front passenger-side door, and I climb into the backseat beside my older brother. Oscar Oliveira mans the wheel, and I avoid making eye contact with Charlie's bodyguard through the rearview.

Really, I just want this night to end.

I'm splintered open from feelings I can't wrestle with properly. I still haven't texted Harriet not to return to the club when she's done at the lab. Because I worry if I tell her I've left she'll think it's because I'm angry at her.

Charlie lowers his window. "I don't want to ask." Cigarette between his lips, he lights it, then actually blows smoke outside and not in my face. "But this is my birthday present to Beckett, so I'm going to ask..." He raises his brows at me. "What's wrong, Ben?"

The question sounds like he couldn't care less for the answer.

"Consider your birthday present given," I tell him with heat. "You asked me."

He rolls his eyes. "I need an answer."

I turn my gaze to the blurring city lights. "I'm not talking to you about this."

"Eliot and Tom seem to think it has something to do with Harriet. They say she left, and your mood turned to shit, so what happened?"

I don't reply.

He lets out an irritated exhale. "Let me guess. She offered to suck another guy's dick—"

"Fuck off." I shoot him a glare.

"He's alive," Charlie golf claps with the cigarette pinched between his fingers.

"Do not *fucking* talk about her like that." Anger lances my voice. Novak is casting glances back at us. He might need to physically restrain me from strangling my brother in the next minute.

Charlie takes a drag from his cigarette, then taps the ash casually out the window. "Then explain why you looked like you just saw roadkill?"

"I thought I was about to get kidnapped off the street!" I shout.

"I had no fucking idea it was you."

"This is a security vehicle," he says like I'm a moron.

"We aren't the only people who own Range Rovers!"

He pinches his eyes like my lack of forethought is a bullet to his brain. We're both grating on each other. "Before you stupidly thought you were going to be kidnapped, you were upset." He drops his hand from his face. "So let's not do this pointless runaround tonight. I'm not in the mood to chase you."

"When are you ever in the mood?"

"Good point," he deadpans. "You've made one in a blue moon. Now explain what the fuck went wrong." He hangs his wrist out of the windowsill.

I exhale a rough breath, trying to cool down. "You of all people aren't going to understand."

Charlie takes the longest drag, then slowly blows smoke outside. When he slings his head back, he says, "Try me."

I release another coarse breath. Why not? What do I have to lose? My nerve? I'm already on edge. So I tell him, "Right before Harriet had to leave, I learned her research involves animal work."

Charlie doesn't laugh. He doesn't roll his eyes. He just asks, "What are we talking about? Rats, mice, guinea pigs, rabbits?"

"Mice."

He looks me over. "And you hate her now?"

My face fractures. "*No.* I don't hate her." *I could never hate Harriet.* "But I don't approve of what she's doing. It's just as unethical to experiment on animals as it would be humans." I've never wavered from this ideology. I add, almost as an afterthought, "I got detention for spray painting *frog killers* in the science lab at Dalton."

"I remember," Charlie says, which surprises me. I was fifteen. He was twenty and already in New York by then.

I pull at the Capybara bracelet around my wrist. "I can't justify animal suffering, even in the name of science. The thought of killing any living thing…it sickens me."

"How do you know it doesn't sicken her?"

That question catches me off guard. "Why would she do it then?"

Charlie lifts and drops his shoulders, shaking his head like he doesn't have the answer. But then he says, "Sometimes we endure pain because the end goal has more value than our own suffering." He lets out a dry laugh. "Or she could be gleefully murdering Stuart Little. You just never know."

I don't believe she's happily killing mice—but I don't know if she's considered the ethical ramifications either. And should it matter what she does?

I've never taken it personally if those around me don't share my exact ideologies. Not everyone will care about the environmental impact of meat consumption. How it contributes to deforestation, climate change, water depletion, and soil erosion. Not everyone will be as eco-conscious as I am, and I would never claim to be the perfect hero called to save Mother Earth.

I know I could do more.

I know I might never do enough.

So people don't need to practice veganism for me to love them. My brother abuses his private jet far too fucking much, and I haven't shunned him out of my life. He's sitting right next to me.

But I would've been hurt if my parents didn't do the bare minimum. Recycle. Don't wear fur. Use less water. Yet, my mom and dad continue to surprise me. Like when they installed solar panels on the house. When Dad planted more trees in the backyard. When Mom sold her car for an electric Porche. When they donated a shit ton of money to a clean energy organization.

I see them trying, and that's more than enough for me.

My thoughts draw my gaze back to the city. The car is quiet for another few minutes before Charlie says, "One last thing. For Beckett."

It's irritating that he can't just be nice to me without doing it for Beckett. But I'm too drained to say something about it.

He flicks his cigarette outside and rolls up the window. "Harriet makes you happy. It's been very fucking obvious to all of us. Don't push her away over this."

"I wasn't going to."

Charlie takes out a pair of sunglasses and slips them over his eyes. "Then we're settled here." He lays his head on the window. Maybe to take a nap.

I'm not sure. I'm not trying to decipher the persisting riddle that is Charlie Keating Cobalt tonight.

He doesn't ask who my text is from when my phone buzzes.

HARRIET FISHER

> Going to be a long night. I don't think I'll make it back to the club. Talk tomorrow?

I send her a quick reply.

BEN COBALT

> Definitely.

Slipping my phone in my pocket, I feel worse. I wish I could speak to her tonight. Tell her I don't hate her. Maybe she could explain more about *what* she's doing. Maybe it does tear her up inside. Maybe it doesn't. I think, at this point, I don't worry about the answer. I just want to know.

It's another ten minutes to the apartment, and neither Charlie nor I talk as we trek through the lobby and ride the elevator. Our bodyguards slip past us down the hall to their rooms on the same floor.

Once inside, I shower. Brush my teeth. Say "I'm okay, just tired" to Beckett, Eliot, and Tom when they show up. I'm mentally drained and wish I could just pass out. Except, I find myself lying under the sheets on the pull-out, staring up at the ceiling in the darkened living room.

For at least an hour.

It's too late to call Harriet. I'd rather she get the sleep I'm longing for. So I scroll through my texts. Earlier tonight, I wished my uncle a happy birthday, and I reread his reply now.

UNCLE RYKE

> Nothing beats getting old. Being alive. Really fucking miss you, Ben. When you're free, let's go hiking. I found a new trail I know you'll love.

I breathe a deeper breath through my nose. Ryke Meadows is one of the world's greatest free-solo rock climbers, and he's risked death ascending thousands of feet. No harness, no rope. Just his body and bare hands. He has an appreciation for life in a different way than my dad does. Uncle Ryke isn't weighing costs and benefits and always doing what's in his best interest. He's heart-over-head. All the time.

I'd already sent a reply that I'd let him know when there's a good day.

Placing my phone aside, I close my eyes. *Sleep*. Sleep. Breathe. My body untightens, and I slowly begin to fade into a weighted slumber.

I'm out for minutes or maybe hours when the sound of rushing water and rustling stirs me awake. Rolling over, I squint out at the kitchen. Lights off, Beckett is drowned in a fuzzy darkness as he washes his hands at the sink.

He doesn't notice me.

I prop up on my forearm, realizing all the cupboards are opened. Dishes, glassware, pots, pans—all pulled out of the cabinets. Gone.

Bar stools have been moved, made room for the massive black trash bags lined up symmetrically on the floor, each one spaced about three inches apart from the next. My pulse thunders in my ears.

"Beckett?" I call out in a whisper.

I barely see his eyes flit up to mine in the dark. His bare chest rises and falls in quick, heavy succession. "Go back to bed," he whispers. "I'm almost done."

The pull-out creaks as I stand up and go to my brother. As I near, absolute dread slams against me. He's not just washing his hands. He's *scrubbing* them with the rough side of a sponge.

"Beck—"

"Just another second." His smooth voice sounds like a taut wire in threat of snapping, but he's unable to reach that relief. He's scrubbing more vigorously, more hurriedly, and I'm afraid to touch him. When he rinses the soap off his forearms, shuts off the faucet with his elbow, I almost let out a breath, until he turns on the sink with the hand-free sensor, then off, then back on. Three times. And he resumes the entire fucking scrubbing all over again.

I bolt for Charlie.

Half-expecting Beckett to chase after me and stop me, but he never leaves the sink.

Once at Charlie's room, I just open the door, grateful it's unlocked, but I crash to a halt in the doorway. I've never been in here before, even if he gave me permission, and the warmth of his room throws me back—the wood paneling, the intricate beams, the green English ivy spindling down bookcases. It's unlike all the other bedrooms. The architecture of the domed ceiling unhinges my jaw.

It resembles the Oxford library. I'd bet all my bartending tips that was the inspiration. It's so far from dank or decrepit, but I don't waste fucking time gawking. Thankfully Charlie is here and not at the airport for some spontaneous trip.

His king-sized bed is framed between bookcases, and he's under a white comforter. I don't need to jostle him awake. He hears me barge inside and immediately sits up and squints. "What the hell do you want—"

"It's Beckett."

Like he's on fire, he surges out of bed and pushes past me in a frantic hurry, knocking into my shoulder since I'm frozen in shock. He sprints to the kitchen, and I'm right behind.

Charlie slows as soon as he sees the cupboards, the trash bags, the sink, our brother. Quietly but urgently, he goes around the counter to reach Beckett.

I hang back while they meet gazes.

"I can't stop," Beckett says in a single tight breath to Charlie. "Je ne peux pas m'arrêter." *I can't stop.*

My ribs squeeze. Air thins.

I haven't lived with Beckett since I was twelve. I can't remember the last time I even saw him this submerged beneath his OCD. I don't know what to do.

"You have to stop," Charlie says. "You're about to bleed." He pries the sponge out of Beckett's grip and reaches around him to shut off the faucet.

Beckett elbows him and waves so the sensor cuts the water back on. Charlie plants his hand on top of our brother's raw skin. "*Beckett*, listen to me. You have to stop. Take a breath.*" His chest presses up against Beckett's back, and he clutches his forearms, forcing Beckett from reaching the sponge or the faucet.

"I can't." Beckett lets out a deep, pained groan of torment.

"Yes, you can. Je sais que tu peux." *I know you can.*

"I can't look at it," Beckett murmurs. Is he referring to the emptied cupboards, the trash bags, his arms?

"Close your eyes."

Beckett shuts them, takes a much bigger breath, then Charlie spins him around and brings him into his chest, holding him there and whispering something against his ear. I can't hear anything. All I see are Charlie's bloodshot yellow-green eyes as he looks up and stares at me. I'm standing here like mortared brick. Not sure what I should be doing. How I should be helping.

I've never felt so fucking helpless.

As they peel away from each other, Beckett beelines for the hallway to his bedroom. Charlie is seconds behind him—only braking to tell me, "If you leave this apartment tonight, Ben, I will murder you myself. Do you understand?"

Everything hurts. "I'm not going anywhere."

"Call Moffy."

"What?"

"Call your favorite person on this planet." I immediately think of Harriet. Charlie disappears, and I can barely breathe. I'm barely functioning in my own skin. The surrounding garbage bags are closing in on me. I dazedly back up into the pull-out.

My legs hit the metal frame. I sink down. *It was me.* I did this. I know I did.

I'm stressing out Beckett. His OCD is flaring up, probably getting worse, because of me.

My phone rings beside me. It's Moffy. Charlie must've texted our cousin. Told him to call. I hang up on Maximoff, and I shoot a quick message.

> BEN COBALT
> I'm okay. Charlie is overreacting.

I don't even look at Moffy's response.

Words cycle on repeat inside my brain. I can't shake them.

It was me.

I did this.

I shouldn't be here. I was *never* supposed to be in New York. I knew this would happen. My nose flares as emotion ransacks my insides. I hold my thumping head in my hands.

Tears spill out of my eyes as I see my brother…my favorite brother at that sink. I see his arms scrubbed raw. The skin starting to rip open. "Fuck," I choke on a guttural noise, my body trying to unleash a sob. My leg jostles. I push back my hair to pick up my phone.

I check my bank account. Barely enough money to rent an apartment in the city. I haven't really been saving my bartending tips. Like tonight. I bought Harriet popcorn and a Fizz. Then I bought all my brothers a drink at the ballet.

A big part of me has started believing I could stay here. That I didn't need to leave.

Glassy film sears my eyes. Moffy is calling again. Then my sister Jane. I don't answer. I send them both a reassuring *I'm okay* text. I fall back into the pull-out, smashing the pillow against my face.

All I want to do is scream.

My throat is too tight to free one. I try to breathe. Pick up my phone again. I go through my photos, and I see about a dozen pics of Harriet. I took them during a slow evening at the End of the World. She's sticking out her blue candy-stained tongue while pouring a beer. I remember laughing.

I remember her cute, grimaced smile emerging right afterward. Until she laughed with me, then threw a beer nut at my face. I caught it in my mouth.

She shook her head into a growing smile.

Everything was okay.

Everything is okay.

Oxygen tries to breach my lungs. Thinking about her is the only way I can shut my eyes and block out the noise and find some way to sleep.

THIRTY-THREE

HARRIET FISHER

Sleep is a luxury I don't have.

Not with my Latin exam in three hours. Not having finished at the research lab at five a.m. this morning. Not with my mind whirling around Ben hating my ever-loving guts.

I sit cross-legged on the couch, the sun fully risen and my fourth cup of coffee sitting sourly in my stomach. My phone is face up on the end table, and I struggle not to take quick glances at it. I shouldn't be waiting for Ben to text me. I'm fully capable of texting him—but he could just want to cut me out of his life like an infected wound. He's leaving in less than two months anyway, so there's a good chance he'll use this moment to fast forward to the inevitable.

My eyes burn as I trample emotion. Words blur on the pages of the textbook.

Eden exits her bedroom in a rush, fitting earbuds in, and snatching her Lululemon sling off the barstool. I'm at least lucky I don't have an early morning class like her. She gives me a small wave as she stuffs her feet in sneakers. I return it.

We're not *friends*, but at least we don't treat each other like a forgotten carton of milk, spoiling in the back of the fridge. We acknowledge one another's existence. We're considerate enough to wash dishes, put them away, and not overtake or overshare. It makes for a pretty good roommate relationship. No tension and even less risk for drama.

I rotate to my textbook when I hear the click of the door opening.

"Oh!" Eden exclaims in surprise.

"Sorry, I was about to knock."

Goosebumps form on my skin as his voice sends an electric current through my body. *It can't be.*

I twist around to see Eden nodding a ton. "Yeah, no worries." She gestures a hand toward the living room, giving him silent permission to enter. Much taller than her, Ben peers over her head, and his gaze connects with mine.

My lungs inflate. I wobble onto my feet, clutching my textbook to my chest.

The corner of his lip lifts. His blue eyes carrying as much emotion that courses through me. "Hey, Fisher."

"Hey," I reply, almost breathless.

I must miss Eden disappearing down the hall, but I realize she left when Ben closes the door behind him. He grips a white paper bag in his left hand while a potted fern is tucked under his arm like a football. "You have that Latin test in a few hours, right?"

I nod.

He lifts the bag. "I brought brain food."

My eyes well so suddenly, which causes my face to form a monstrous glower in some attempt to stop it. He pauses halfway to the couch like he's unsure if I'm mad.

"You brought me food…"

"Yeah, I've seen your fridge." He smiles, but it's a tentative one. "Is that okay? I can go if you'd rather study alone. I just thought I could help."

This wouldn't be the first time he's helped me study, but I'm just overwhelmed that he's here right now. "You don't want to talk about what I told you last night?" I skip over the graphic mice-murdering details. Are we just pretending I don't do experiments on animals? Is this a fact we're burying under a rug?

"I want to talk." Ben places the paper bag on the coffee table, along with the fern. "But you have an exam in"—he checks his watch—"less than three hours. And I'd feel like shit for taking away your studying time."

I twist the beaded choker around my neck. "I don't think I can concentrate anyway."

He nods.

I nod back, eyeing the springy green fern. It's the fourth plant Ben has bestowed upon my apartment. After the eucalyptus, I told him he should be saving his tips, not transforming my place into the Secret Garden. He said, "Without plants, life wouldn't be sustained on earth, so I'd say this little fella is priceless." He added, "And I've never budgeted in my life."

It shows.

My body wants to float into the stratosphere knowing he's still gifting my apartment—okay, maybe *me*—priceless little fellas.

I place my vocabulary book beside the food bag. "I've tried memorizing the same fifty words all morning. It's not really sinking in."

He knows I'm in intermediate Latin. I'm not being quizzed over grammar or writing out full length sentences. I'll be translating portions of *Caesar Invasion of Britain* from Latin to English. A lot of it is context clues. Most of it requires knowing hundreds of Latin words. Add in the fact that most verbs have more than one definition, and it's like having to solve a logic puzzle in addition to translating a language.

Ben snatches the paperback and opens it to the earmarked page. I've highlighted all the words I'm struggling with, so it's no surprise when he says, "Dēleō, dēlēre, dēlēvī, dēlētum." Latin is a dead language, and yet, his pronunciation is near perfect.

I dizzy a little.

His eyes lift to mine, waiting for me to give the answer.

"Second conjugation," I say. "To destroy, wipe out, erase."

"I'm not erasing you from my life over this," Ben tells me. "That's why I'm here." He pushes the white paper bag toward me. My stomach lets out a low grumble.

He smiles.

"Fuck," I curse, fighting my own smile, then I peek inside the bag. A bagel. He bought me a bagel. The herbed cream cheese smells divine, but before I take a bite, I have to explain. "When I joined Dr. Venison's lab, I knew I'd be working with mice. But I didn't know *I'd* be the one euthanizing them. I thought the grad students would just...give them to me already dead. Which I know probably isn't any better, but I was stupid...naïve."

His face twists. "That's shitty they didn't tell you."

I lift my shoulders. "I think they thought it'd be something I should handle if I'm going into science...medicine."

"You're eighteen," he says like that matters, but I'm not sure it does. I'm an adult. Maybe a *new* adult, but I'm still expected to perform the same duties as students who are twenty-two.

"The position is voluntary," I remind him. "No one is forcing me to do it. It's not even a requirement for my major. I just know it's something I need on my resume for med school. I could quit, but I'm not going to because I can't get into another lab halfway through the semester. I know that makes me an asshole—"

"You're not an asshole," he snaps, angrily. He glances down at the book in his hands, and while I bite into my bagel and chew, he reads, "Doleō, dolēre, doluī, dolitum."

I swallow. "To grieve, suffer; hurt, give pain."

Ben looks to me with a million questions in his eyes, and I prepare for him to ask how much the mice suffer. But then he says, "Does it hurt you to have to kill them?"

"The first time I did it, my heart raced so hard. I thought I was going to mess it up and cause the mouse more discomfort. I just wanted it to be quick and painless for her."

His forehead creases. "You were in the room?"

Oh…he must think we use gas. "So…CO2 asphyxiation is incredibly painful. The sensation is similar to drowning, and it's not fast. It's more humane to do cervical dislocations."

His lips part in shock. "You snap their necks?"

"With a beaker."

He puts a hand to the back of his neck. His face breaks. "Jesus."

"It's the worst part," I say. "I hate it so much, but I don't think I'm supposed to like it. If I got desensitized to it, I think I'd make myself switch labs."

"But you don't want to switch now?"

I shake my head. "I mean, I could try to get into a plant or cell biology lab next semester, but these positions aren't easy to apply for. And I've already established a relationship with Dr. Venison. I need her recommendation for med school…"

He looks away, and my voice drifts off.

"I'm sorry," I breathe out. "For disappointing you."

When he turns back, his face is a full wince. "You haven't disappointed me, Harriet. I just never thought I'd be fal—friends with someone who experiments on animals."

I'm stuck on his trip up. Was he going to say *falling*? Is he falling for me? My heart skips.

"The work my lab does is important," I say. "If that makes any difference."

He takes a breath. "What are you studying?"

"The development of structural proteins in the thymus," I explain. "The thymus matures T cells, so it's critical for our immune system and helping fight against disease. My biggest reason for even wanting to be a doctor is to help people. This is just another way to do that." I take a small nibble from the bagel while I watch him process.

He's quiet in his own contemplation before he says, "The whole world is filled with pain, and I've always believed it's my responsibility to not cause more. Some people feel the same as me. Some people don't. At the end of the day, everyone draws a line on what they're willing and not willing to do. I get that. I've *accepted* that. Because I'm not perfect." He pulls at his T-shirt. "It's organic cotton, but it was shipped on a commercial airline to the store I bought it from. I fly private with my family at times. I could've dedicated my *entire* life to fighting for massive corporations to go green, some of which my parents own, but I haven't done that because at times it feels like speeding into a brick wall. And then I think the person who can handle the repetitive crash, just to crumble a single brick, is better than me. Maybe they should've been born in my place. They would've been the Cobalt who could've made a greater, more positive impact on the world."

I glance down at the bagel, then up at him. "I know with great power comes you-know-what, and Cobalts are said to be gods, but you don't have to change the whole world for the better to be considered a good Cobalt. Just touching one person's life is enough, Friend." I bite my lip and add, "You've made mine better. For whatever that means to you."

Ben hangs on to my words for a long beat. "It means a lot." He breathes in strongly.

I breathe out.

And he says, "Perfect people don't really exist, nor do I think they should. We all have different values because we're human, so I won't hate you for yours. I'm just glad to know them. I'm glad I know you." He lets out a heavy breath before returning to the book. "Reperiō, reperīre, repperī, repertum."

My brain is spinning, and I struggle to find the translation.

His blue eyes lift to mine. "Fisher?"

"I don't know."

He smiles softly. "Fourth conjugation. To find, discover. Learn. Get."

I scowl, realizing he aptly picked it out. "I should have known that one."

Ben deserts the book on the coffee table. Coming closer, he places a hand on my shoulder, the other on my flushed cheek. I have to look up to meet his gaze, my neck straining. He bends at his knees a little for me. The intimacy has my heart thumping. How did I deserve him? And why does he have to leave New York?

"You're going to ace this test," he tells me.

I grimace like he's full of shit. "When I just got one wrong?"

"Yeah, because I know you won't forget it now."

He's right. I won't.

"I'm sorry for not telling you sooner about the research," I whisper.

His gaze warms mine. "I'm sorry for judging you for it. I won't do that again." He brushes his thumb against the corner of my lip. Oh, he's wiping away a little dab of cream cheese. I lick the rest, but his pretty boy smile is officially doing a number on my ovaries.

My body wants him.

I want him.

I hate that he checks his watch. I think I wouldn't mind staying here with him and missing the exam altogether. It's a scary thought. I've *never* flunked a test, let alone purposefully skipped one. "We have some time for more studying."

"Or we could do other things," I offer.

His expression turns heady at the mere insinuation of sex, and I feel his palm slide from my cheek to the back of my neck. It's a sexy move that has my body tingling.

"We can't. See, if you fail this test because of me, I would judge *myself.*" He backs away from me, but there's a gnarled sound in his throat when he does. He returns to the book. "I'm going to need your help after you ace this thing."

"With what?" I ask eagerly. He's so quick to assist me in anything, and for someone who has all doors opened for him, it's hard to find big opportunities to lend a helping hand.

"I can't live with my brothers anymore," he explains. "I need to find a new place to stay. Like STAT."

It hits me that if he wants to leave his apartment asap, then his brothers must be failing at seducing him toward loving New York.

This is not good. The words taste bitter in my mouth, but I say them anyway. "Yeah, I can help."

THIRTY-FOUR

BEN COBALT

I have to slyly check Harriet's text message in the bathroom since I'm currently at the Cobalt Estate. Wednesdays, unfailingly, bring me back to my childhood home. She sent me another roommate listing from the Valley Boards. I click into the link. `$500 for a blow-up mattress in the living room.` Jesus.

I text Harriet.

> **BEN COBALT**
> Out of my budget

She's quick to reply.

> **HARRIET FISHER**
> What is your budget?

I don't need to pop open my bank account to know what I can afford. I skate a hand through my hair, while I sit on the toilet lid.

> **BEN COBALT**
> like a hundred bucks.

> **HARRIET FISHER**
> Bad news, you'd probably have to toss in nudes to make that work.

I laugh and smear a hand down my chin in surprise. Seriously, I haven't laughed in days. Living with my brothers since Charlie and Beckett's birthday feels a lot like sleeping on a bed of nails. Stress compounds every night, and I'm just trying to find a reasonable solution. One that doesn't include cashing in a favor with a random friend. I'd rather not stay for free with someone I vaguely know and use my last name as a bargaining chip. It could add more problems.

Harriet would be my first choice. But she's already asked her roommate if I could crash on their couch, even for just a few days, and Harriet said it was "the most awkward interaction yet."

Apparently, Eden reminded her, "You sleep on the couch." To which Harriet had to say, "Yeah, he'd be sleeping with me, but not *with me*, with me. We won't fool around or anything...we're just friends."

Eden got uncomfortable and said, "I don't want to walk in on anything." It's understandable. If I spend the night with Harriet again, I honestly can't guarantee I won't touch her. I already succumbed to the temptation with my brothers feet away in their bedrooms.

Harriet was bummed her place is out of contention. But I love *this*—apartment hunting with her. It's been the best part of this whole issue, and honestly, I'm hoping it doesn't end too fast.

I text her back.

> **BEN COBALT**
> I hear blow jobs are effective bargaining chips.

HARRIET FISHER

> AHFA. Against Harriet Fisher's Advice.

My lips twitch into a bigger smile as I type out a reply.

BEN COBALT

> Is Harold still available?

She offered her car to me yesterday—but I declined because I'm six fucking five and it's a *sedan*.

HARRIET FISHER

> Rescinded. I cannot be the cause for early onset back issues.

I laugh even harder. Fuck.

HARRIET FISHER

> Greek Row might be your best bet... unfortunately.

Yeah, the frat. It was one of our first ideas that we brainstormed together, but I threw it out because I'm not sure I want to be surrounded by Greek life. It comes with a lot more than just a bed to sleep on.

I check the time on my phone. Shit, I have to go.

I text Harriet quickly.

BEN COBALT

> You might be right. Talk after dinner.

She likes the text, and I slip the phone in my pocket before heading toward the dining room. I take my place at my usual seat.

Five Wednesdays have passed since I buried Theodore. Five Wednesdays where every single one of my siblings showed up to dinner. Even Beckett, whose presence at these things is more like a warm spell during the winter. Infrequent but appreciated. I always thought I'd be more likely to see a California Condor than Beckett at five dinners in a row.

And here we are, at number *six*.

He's seated in the chair across from mine. There's no real assigned seating on Wednesday nights except for the heads of the table reserved for our parents. Their chairs are currently empty, and dinner doesn't officially start until they arrive.

With all my siblings here again tonight, carrying on their perfect attendance streak, tension has amassed. I can't shake it. Not when they exchange side glances and cagey looks between each other.

Ever since I assaulted Tate, their concern for me has been in my face. Apparent. Visible. But tonight, I sense a weird shift.

There is a hold-your-breath strain in the air. Like each sibling is balanced on a sharp edge of worry.

Did they discover I'm broke? Or that I'm currently searching for housing? I have no clue, but they've learned *something*.

Maybe, *just maybe*, this has absolutely nothing to do with me. Except, I'm being left out of the shared glimpses, which is usually a telltale sign that I'm the topic of fixation. I won't be surprised if they throw self-help pamphlets at my face tonight. The pages would probably be generically inspirational. Since it's not like anyone knows I'm on a countdown to say goodbye to New York. Right?

Fuck, please tell me they haven't figured out the plan.

Anxious heat gathers under my white collegiate tee, and I almost check my phone to reread texts from Harriet. Instead, I chug some water from a crystal goblet.

I try my best to not be swept back to last week when I saw Beckett in the kitchen. To not remember him scrubbing at his red, raw skin. The visual sinks a rock straight down to my gut. It screams at me to buy a plane ticket tomorrow, but we're only in the last week of September.

And Harriet—I can't wrap my head around leaving her abruptly when she's faced so much abandonment in her life. Hell, I can't really concentrate on leaving her *at all.* It wedges a fucking pain in my ribs, and I'd rather just focus on the good.

Good news: the frat is a viable option, and I could potentially move out of my brothers' apartment really soon. I'm just weighing *when* I should drop this information. Telling everyone at a Wednesday Night Dinner is the equivalent of setting off a firework inside the house. Not sure I'm ready for those flames.

I glance at Beckett again.

He came straight from rehearsal today, so he didn't have time to change out of his black tights and a casual white T-shirt. He shovels some green beans onto his plate.

The long dining table is so full that I can barely spot the oak wood underneath. Ornate dishware, goblets, candlesticks, and vintage décor are arranged around platters of cranberries, potatoes, green beans, and a roasted goose. The tablescape is as artistic as a painting, and along with the meal, it never changes.

Thankfully, the goose resides at the other end. Out of my eyesight. I remember being pretty young—five or six—and not being able to peel my eyes off the meat for the entire dinner. My stomach twisted in vicious knots, and I just kept restraining hot tears. It hit me like a sledgehammer that what I'd been eating was a bird.

Like the ones I grew up joyfully watching on the lake at our family's vacation house.

After the meal, my dad took me to the library and asked me what was wrong. I told him I didn't want to eat birds anymore. He listened as I cried and asked him about the origins of the burgers we had the day before.

It was that night we agreed that I could become a vegetarian—but it only took me two more weeks to learn about animal byproducts after I pestered my older brothers and sister about vegetarianism. Charlie got fed up and asked me, "If you're so concerned about the animals, why are you still drinking milk?"

I stopped consuming dairy that day, and then my dad explained veganism. I remember telling him, "I want that." As if changing my whole lifestyle was as simple as picking out a pair of clothes. I was too young to realize it'd change what restaurants they went to. What they'd have stocked in their fridge. How I'd have to have my own section of the pantry so that I knew what I could safely eat as a kid. I appreciated the extra step they always took, even if it made me feel guilty at times.

My first Wednesday after becoming vegan, my mom made sure I'd have a seitan roast on my side of the table. I never asked for it. Didn't want to make it a big deal. I really would have been fine just eating some green beans and potatoes. But when I saw she had the chef prepare one, it meant a lot to me. Chef Michael will usually stuff the seitan with different ingredients every week like mushrooms, walnuts, or spinach. So while everyone has the same meal—I've enjoyed the variation of mine.

Standing, I carve a slice. "Anyone want the seitan?" I offer like I do every Wednesday. Not all of them hate it.

"What's in it tonight?" Tom asks while sitting on the frame of his chair. He's mastered the art of balancing on the thing. Only after breaking a dozen of them when we were kids. Eliot would typically catch Tom before he could ever crack his head on the floor.

Right now, his zipper-chained combat boots rest on the cushioned seat. He's dressed in a black gothic waistcoat with a silver cross at the collar, and he tosses a serpent-headed scepter between his hands.

I inspect my piece of seitan. "Shiitake mushrooms and wild rice."

"Hard pass," Tom says. "I've developed an aversion to mushrooms. Once you get a slimy one, there's no going back. I'm fucked for all time."

"Fucked for all time should be a new song title," Eliot suggests, his shiny black leather shoes kicked up on the table. A pipe sticks out his mouth, and he puffs perfect rings of smoke.

Our mom *loathes* smoking. Cannot stand even the stench or sight of a cigarette. Yet, she never could dissuade Charlie and Beckett from the bad habit—the two of them smoke the most of everyone. No amount of charred lung photos or statistics of long-term effects could sway them, but Beckett won't light a cigarette in front of her. And she's only allowed smoking on Wednesday nights if it's not during the entire duration of the meal.

Meaning, at some point, Eliot will have to set the pipe aside.

Pipe between his lips, he currently wears a formal tux with tails tonight, far different from his loose-fitted linen shirt Audrey called "pirate chic" he had on last Wednesday.

There is no dress code here.

There never is. Just like in our daily lives, our parents have let us express ourselves however we wish at these dinners. No holds barred.

I rarely ever feel like dressing up. And they never make me feel out of place in my casual T-shirts and jeans.

Tom scoffs. "You think we're working on new songs? Dude, I can't even get Alfie to learn the ones we have. Breaking in this new drummer is going to be the death of me."

"Death invoked already." Eliot grins. "I predict this will be a very dramatic Wednesday Night Dinner." His mischievous gaze lands on me, his brows rising playfully.

I'm not soaking in his mirth. He might as well be telling me, *prepare yourself, baby brother. Tonight is about you.*

Fuck me.

I wish I could fake a stomach bug. Go hurl in the bathroom. That'd just do the inverse of what I want. It'll ramp up their paranoia about *what's wrong with Ben?*

So yeah, I need to power through this meal.

Beckett eyes Eliot. "Are you planning to set the tablecloth on fire again?"

"Please don't," Audrey pleads beside me. "It took me oh so terribly long to get the smoke out of my last dress. Velvet *absorbs*." Her baby blue dress cascades on either side of her chair. Frilly sleeves threaten to lick the flamed candles when she reaches for her water goblet.

I spring out of my chair and draw her away from the lit candle. Fuck, *fuck*. My heart has ascended to my throat. She's not on fire. *She's not on fire.*

"Sois prudente, petite sœur," Beckett tells her. *Be careful, little sister.* She flips her hair off her shoulder. "Je le suis toujours." *I always am.*

"Starting the night off with delusions, I see," Charlie quips.

Audrey scoffs. "I am *far* more careful than Tom and Eliot. That is not a *delusion*. It is a fact." She twists to me. "Isn't that right, Ben?"

"Yeah," I nod strongly. Hating the attention right now.

I want to smile, but her sleeve nearly catching fire really has me worked up. I can feel Beckett observing me in concern. *Calm down.* I need to calm the fuck down.

Back in her chair, Audrey sips her water and smooths the creases out of her blue dress. The style is apparently from the French Rococo era, she said, fitting perfectly with the likes of *The Phantom of the Opera*. She always plays into the dramatics of the night, even her voice carries an extra whimsical cadence.

I realize she's stopped wearing funeral blacks. No longer mourning my move to New York. I think she's more set on the idea of joining me there now.

Eliot blows another puff of smoke in the air. "I cannot promise a fireless evening, dear sister."

Audrey lets out an annoyed breath. "Then I shall waft the smoke *your* way."

"I vote in favor of no smoke while Maeve is in attendance," Jane says, tucking her baby into a highchair. Thatcher, her husband and the only non-Cobalt to ever grace a Wednesday Night Dinner, slips baby noise-cancelling headphones over Maeve's little ears.

"I vote no infants at these dinners," Charlie chimes in.

"You were already outvoted when she was born," Jane reminds him casually.

It's Audrey who pins a glare on him and says, "Sit in your defeat."

"Yes, Charlie Keating, sit in your defeat," Tom eggs on while he pours himself a deep red Merlot from an antique decanter. He tosses the scepter to Eliot, who catches it from across the table. And yeah, it was less than an inch from hitting the 1800s chandelier. Above us, crystal daggers and pendants hang from the twisted gilt-bronze branches. The crystal chandelier is a work of art, much like the oil paintings on the dark walls.

Charlie rolls his eyes. The warm glow from candlesticks casts a rich sheen over his emerald-green suit, the jacket unbuttoned with no shirt underneath. I check my watch. Really would love for Mom and Dad to show up any minute now.

I force my knees not to bounce.

"Somewhere you need to be, dear brother?" Eliot asks, capturing my gaze.

It's strange how normal he looks wielding a scepter, smoking a pipe, and wearing an eight-grand designer tux. Every night this month he's worn something different, and yet, I'd never call them costumes.

Costumes imply he's putting on an act. With Eliot, the clothes are like another layer of skin.

"Just trying to figure out when Mom and Dad are coming," I say into a deeper breath. "The food is getting cold."

"Shall we invoke *his* name?" Tom asks with another wry grin.

"Not this," Charlie puts a finger to his temple like he's already getting a migraine.

"Invoke whose name?" Thatcher asks, sitting beside Jane with a hand on her back. He never comes to dinner in anything theatrical. Just a flannel and pants tonight. It's not unusual for him to be asking questions. There's so many traditions and lore between the seven of us that it'll probably take a good decade to loop him in completely.

"Tom and Eliot have a ridiculous theory," Charlie says.

"It's only ridiculous to nonbelievers," Eliot counters. "But no one has ever seen it *not* succeed."

"That's because you only do it when you know it *will* succeed."

Eliot gasps. "Tom, is he saying we're rigging it?"

Tom shakes his head in disappointment. "I think he is."

"Pass the potatoes, Pip." Beckett up-nods to me, and I hand over the bowl, careful not to knock a candle. We're both usually the quietest during these dinners. I'm more of an observer and a "talk when spoken to" participant.

Audrey takes a dainty sip of water. "They believe that if you say Father's name three times, he appears."

Thatcher's brows furrow. "Like Beetlejuice?"

"Nothing like Beetlejuice," Eliot and Tom say in unison while Charlie says at the same time, "Exactly like Beetlejuice."

Beckett cracks a smile. I almost laugh. Really, I can't picture even a month without these Wednesday nights. They're a staple, a fixture, a constant, like the oak tree that can endure fire and lightning and still never burn down.

"We'll prove it," Tom says and nods to Eliot. Together they chant, "Richard Connor Cobalt." They drum the table with their fingers. "Richard Connor Cobalt." Their drumming picks up speed. "Richard Connor—"

Dad enters the room, and you can't make this shit up. Eliot and Tom jump out of their seats, hooting and hollering about *magic*.

Audrey spits out her water in surprise.

Jane laughs, especially at Thatcher's wide-eyed expression. Beckett's shaking his head into a brighter smile, and Charlie has risen to fill his goblet to the brim with wine.

I think I'm the only one void of a big reaction. Mostly because I'm just taking it all in. Putting it all to memory with a reverent fondness.

Mom's black heels clap against the hardwood as she struts in behind Dad. "What did we miss?" Her frown overtakes her face.

"Magic." Eliot decrees. "We called upon our dear father and look who appeared." He waves a hand to our dad. "A true mystical marvel."

He's playing up the whole "magic" bit to get a rise out of our dad. We've known since we were kids how much he truly hates all things fairy tale. He's a man of logic, and things like the Easter bunny, mermaids, and unicorns all fall into his "bullshit" category. Apparently letting us believe in Santa Claus was even a point of contention with him and our mom.

"You called and I came," Dad says. "The only magic in that is the magic of communication."

"So you do believe in magic?" Tom says into a smirk.

"No," Dad says pointedly. He calmly rounds the table. Choosing the head closest to me. Which sucks.

I was really hoping he'd be at the other end tonight.

Eliot and Tom glance at each other conspiratorially as they sink down in their respective chairs. No one is left standing except our parents.

"Opening remarks have commenced," Dad says before taking a seat in unison with Mom. I seem to release and cage a breath all at the same time. I'm excited. Nervous. Glad this is starting and ready to get it over with.

It's no surprise when Eliot stands. Anyone can start speaking, but he's usually the one to do it first. Like we're all on autopilot, even Thatcher, goblets are quickly scooped in hands, and we all brace the table.

Eliot climbs onto the chair, then plants a foot on the table's edge in a dramatic stomp that shakes the dishware and rattles the candlesticks. With a flick of his fingers, he spins the chandelier above his head. A couple flames sputter out. He pops the pipe out of his mouth, a burst of smoke flitting the air before he speaks.

"Ladies. Gentlemen." His eyes flit to me for a beat. "'Virtue itself turns vice, being misapplied. And vice sometime by action dignified.'"

Tom and Audrey pound the table with their fists in approval. Jane snaps her fingers.

I assume Eliot recited Shakespeare. I have zero clue what the verse means. Zero clue which play it's from. All I know is that too many eyes have sunk into me. Whatever Eliot just said referred to me. Or related to me? How the fuck should I know? I'm in remedial Literature while they're all earning their PhDs.

They're all more well-read than I am, even Beckett who honestly does not read much, and I've tried not to let it bother me. Because I could always search the quotes later, but I choose not to. I don't need to be exactly like them. I don't want to be.

Even if it dawns on me that I share more in common at this moment with my brother-in-law who's not a Cobalt by blood but considered a Cobalt by marriage. Thatcher has a furrowed, slightly stern expression, just as confused as I am.

Eliot plops back in his seat, and I return my goblet to the table. It's anyone's guess who's going next. Opening remarks can be used to update each other on our lives, voice an opinion about a current event, or incite emotion. I've seen it all.

Tom stands on his chair just as Eliot had done, and I watch as Eliot tosses him the scepter. This time, it hits a dangling crystal on the chandelier. The crystal snaps off and plops with a *clink* into Charlie's wine.

He looks like he wants to self-eject from the room, but he puts the goblet to his lips like he means to take a sip.

"*Charlie*," our mom snaps, her eyes piercing him. "Drink that wine, and I will be rushing you to the hospital to dislodge glass from your lungs."

"Counterargument. You let me bleed out here. Mercifully."

"Counterargument," Mom says. "Fuck no."

Beckett pours a new glass of wine in his own empty goblet. He's sitting far enough away from Charlie that he passes the drink down the table. When it reaches Charlie, he willingly abandons his old glass for Beckett's.

"Death but struck the night twice," Eliot exclaims ominously.

Mom narrows her yellow-green eyes. "*No one* is dying tonight or tomorrow or *ever*." She points a matte black painted nail around at us. "You all shall live for centuries."

"In mind and spirit," Dad clarifies. "For the world will forever know your names alongside ours."

"In body," Mom argues with him. "For I'll make sure they are all immortal."

We drum the table together, except Tom who's still standing on his chair. He taps it with his boot.

Dad's grin widens. "I see the hunt for the Fountain of Youth persists."

"It never ended." She stakes him with a glare. "Would you stop me, Richard?"

He smooths his hair back, then lifts his wine. "Jamais." *Never*. "Il n'y a qu'ensemble." *There is only together.* I swear he glances at me at this, then raises his drink to Tom. "Mon fils."

Mom also hoists her wine to him. "Gremlin. Proceed."

Tom nods a thanks before surveying us around the table. "What constitutes betrayal in this family? Say, is it sleeping with the enemy?" His brows crane at *me*.

Can't lie. I'm shocked. They've been quick to be nice to me like one false step will have me fleeing these dinners. This feels surprisingly more in fashion for my family.

I scoot forward. "Is this rhetorical?" I ask Tom.

"Nay." He points his scepter at me. "Speak true."

"I'd like you to clarify whether Harriet Fisher is an enemy of this family or an enemy of *yours*. And if she is *your* enemy, then why were you standing next to her at a bar last week?"

Everyone drums the table again.

Tom fights a smile, enjoying seeing me engage in this playful display. "I suffer through her presence for you, Ben Pirrip."

"Thank you," I say sincerely. "And I haven't slept with your enemy."

Eliot clears his throat as he pours more wine. I snap a hard look at him. He has a diabolical smile as he tells me, "I said nothing, brother."

"You're implying I'm lying."

"No, I simply felt a tickle in my throat." He slouches back in his chair.

"Eliot Alice," Mom chides. "Act your age or the Fountain of Youth will be dry before it reaches you."

"Did you hear that?" Eliot asks our dad. "Mom is wishing death upon me."

"If you want saved from her hyperboles, you'll need to leave the room," Dad says while eyeing me. "Are you dating Harriet?"

Mom's neck nearly snaps when she zeroes in on me. "You have a girlfriend, and we haven't met her?"

"Oh my fucking God," I mutter.

"You'd fare better cursing to me," Dad says, which we've all heard before. None of us are religious, clearly.

"Oh my Connor, does Ben have a girlfriend?" Tom teases, still standing on the fucking chair.

"You're really wasting your whole opening on me?" I ask him.

"Dude, Mom is going to stab the goose if you don't answer her. You should be *happy* I'm still focused on you."

Our mom is gripping a knife. "When was this official? Did you not want us to know? Is it a secret?"

I wonder if the tension at the start of dinner was more about my relationship with Harriet. It eases me. I'd *love* for this to solely be about me and her.

"Harriet and I are basically…" I lift my shoulders, unsure of what to call someone you're falling for. "We're figuring things out. She's my closest friend, and she's extremely busy being pre-med, so that's a big reason why you haven't met her yet."

"Have you taken her on a date, Pippy?" Jane wonders with a smile, resting her chin on her knuckles. "Where to?"

"Oui! Tell us absolutely everything." Audrey draws her chair closer to mine. "What were you wearing? What did you eat?" Audrey gasps in excitement. "What did she smell like?"

"Please no," Charlie pinches the bridge of his nose.

"I bet she was lovely," Audrey swoons. "Ben would only date girls who smell absolutely *divine*."

"Would he?" Charlie retorts, his hand clattering to the table. "On the basis of what?"

"On the basis of…of…" She spins to Jane for help.

"On the basis of Ben having a terrific sense of smell," Jane says pointedly and arches a brow, much like our father, at Charlie. "Which you can't refute."

"Which I'm not in the mood to," Charlie combats sourly.

"This has really derailed from the point," Dad says, then shifts his gaze to me. "Your mom and I look forward to meeting her."

I nod slowly, my brain starting to spin around my plan. The roadblocks to these future paths.

"Final word," Tom decrees to me. "Although you're not sleeping with my enemy *yet*…"

My brows jut up at his pregnant pause. "Would you like me to air who you're sleeping with during my opening?"

His smile is ginormous. "Ben Pirrip with the revenge plot."

"The twist of the hour," Eliot chimes in.

I cover my face in my hands and groan.

"Aim elsewhere," Mom snaps at Tom.

"Fragile baby Ben," Charlie notes.

I flip him off, coming out from my palms and sinking back in my chair.

"Charlie," Dad says in a disappointed scold which always feels worse than Mom's sharp reprimands.

"He's fine," I cut in, not wanting more tension at the table because of me. Then I nod Tom on. "Go ahead."

Tom smiles softer at me. "I will not consider you being with Harry a betrayal, but rather a very blond, very short, very great annoyance. Because I love you, brother."

My lips begin to rise, and the rumble of feet around us makes my smile grow astronomically higher. The lively noise floods me. Fills me. Audrey even taps her spoon to the glass goblet. My bones thunder. My lungs expand. It's hard not to be swept up in the infectious energy, especially when it's for me.

"Merci infiniment," I say. "Je t'aime aussi, mon frère." *Thank you infinitely. I love you too, my brother.*

Tom's smile twinkles his eyes. "But if she hurts you, she's dead to me." That is his final word, and he drops down into the chair.

Charlie lazily holds up a couple of fingers. "I invoke my right to pass," he says the same words he's used for almost every Wednesday night of his life.

Jane rises to her feet *without* standing on the chair or table. Embroidered lobsters are stitched into her lilac dress. The eccentric outfits have been her standard this month. "You're all cordially invited to Maeve's first birthday. The party is being held at The Independent." She names the billiards bar she owns in Philly. "If you'd like to bring plus-ones, you'll have to run it through Thatcher." He's in a high position in security, and I'm sure he'll want to vet whoever attends. "We'd prefer no strangers or anyone you do not know particularly well."

Beckett frowns a little. "Has there been any security issues recently?" He eyes Jane. "Do you have a stalker?"

"No." She's tense though.

My brothers and I are staring Thatcher down for the truth since Jane will try her best not to worry us.

"No stalkers," Thatcher confirms, then looks to our dad.

From the head of the table, he informs us, "Rochester Industries is finalizing their acquisition of *Celebrity Crush*."

Eliot grimaces. "The enemy of the family has been named."

I'm so far removed from the Rochester drama. It's *beyond* me, really, but I'm well aware that this affluent, assholish family has taken vested interest in us because they own a media conglomerate. And we're a source of content. Meaning, we line their pockets every time they talk shit about us.

It doesn't help that A.) the Rochesters are from the same area of Philadelphia. We grew up with those pricks. And B.) they're about to own the most popular tabloid in the country.

"They might take unethical measures to gain headlines," our dad cautions. "Just be wary who you talk to and bring around the family."

Noted.

Jane returns to her seat, and Thatcher says, "I'm good to pass." He's the silent, brooding type and rarely likes to take the spotlight, even when offered. He'd prefer to watch Jane in it, I'm sure.

"Will you bring Harriet?" Audrey whispers to me. "To Maeve's birthday?"

That's November 15th.

I won't be here. My muscles flex. "Maybe," I whisper back.

"I'll go next." Beckett's calm voice seizes our attention. He stabs a green bean with his fork and stares at his plate for a long, contemplative moment before his eyes lift to meet mine. "Ben."

The way he says my name—with so much comfort and care like he could cradle those three letters for a lifetime. I'd let him. Flashes of last week cycle in my head.

The kitchen.

His arms.

My chest tightens and stomach sinks at the quick visual. I hate how one dark memory can slam to the front of my brain without warning. Without care. It feels like a violation because I didn't ask to remember it in this gentle moment.

Beckett takes a steadying breath before he tells me, "I want to be here next Wednesday and the Wednesday after that. There's not a moment I don't want to be here, but it's going to be impossible."

I nod, understanding, even if my chest feels like someone dropped three fifty-pound weight plates on my sternum. He directs this to me because it's not a fucking secret he's been coming here for me.

He continues, "NYBC's Opening Gala is next Friday, and I'm dancing the White Swan pas de deux. I can't miss rehearsals next week to come down here."

"I get it," I say into a stronger nod. The heat of everyone's gazes is stifling. "I don't want you to miss ballet, Beck. I never have."

His lips downturn, and I know he must be warring about choosing dance over me. But it's not just dance. It's his first love. The more I'm with Harriet, the more I'm beginning to understand what that means.

Audrey tosses two cranberries into her water goblet, then stands and taps the glass with her spoon. "Speaking of missing important, critical events," she proclaims. "I was most grieved to have missed Beckett and Charlie's birthday party. Tell me my invitation was eaten by a carnivorous plant."

"Your invitation didn't exist," Charlie says pointedly. "You're two years too early."

"It was a nightclub," Beckett adds. "They wouldn't have let you past the doors."

"Could you not have paid them?"

"Audrey Virginia," Mom chastises. "Bribery is not a fucking solution."

Her cheeks roast. "Sorry, Mother." She plops down, then eyes me for comfort. I wrap an arm around her shoulders.

Mom sighs into her wine. She must feel a little guilty for being harsh because she meets our dad's gaze for reassurance.

"Your mother is right," Dad says calmly. "You have the means to pay your way through these barriers, but at what cost? I don't mean monetarily. What are your morals worth, mon petit?" He's asking Audrey.

She gulps. "Well...I'd like to think the benefit is greater than the cost because I'd be celebrating Charlie and Beckett." She pops back out of her seat. "It's for family, Mother! You can't fault me for that."

"A bribe is still a bribe, gremlin," Mom retorts. "If you want to be at a nightclub in New York at *sixteen*, I will be accompanying you."

Audrey collapses in her chair in defeat. "I'm far too old for a chaperone, especially when Beckett and Charlie moved to New York when they were only sixteen." She's brought up this point plenty of times before, but the argument has no legs to stand on. Our parents would let her finish school in NYC if it's what she desired. Instead, she's repeatedly chosen to remain with them in Philly. She lifts her chin to add, "I'll simply wait for the next invite."

"There won't be one," Charlie says bluntly. "None of us want to babysit you."

Audrey lets out a horrified gasp. "Father." She swings her head to our dad. "Please remind your infernal offspring that I am *not* a baby."

Dad has his fingers to his temples, casually listening to us. Eliot and Tom take advantage of the silent moment to drum the table.

Charlie barely blinks. "Rappelle-toi que tu dors encore avec un ours en peluche." *Remind yourself that you still sleep with a teddy bear.*

Audrey's grip tightens on her goblet. "I might sleep with a teddy bear, but that doesn't mean I am a child. I am a *woman*."

"Under society terms, you are a *girl*."

"I have *bled*. I could be pregnant tomorrow!"

I have a hand frozen to my forehead. Eliot and Tom are near laughter, which is going to make Audrey cry soon. Jane is too busy trying to feed a fidgety Maeve to come to her aid. Mom is sending daggers at all of my brothers, then eyes Dad for a long beat.

Beckett is raking his fingers through his hair like he sees our sister on an emotional downward slope too. I shake my head at him. She will not win this back-and-forth with Charlie.

Beckett is sitting too far away from him, but he bows into the table and calls out his name. To which Charlie tips his head toward his twin brother. They give each other looks I can't decipher.

To Audrey, I ask, "You aren't...?" *She's not having sex.* She always overshares, obviously, and there's no chance she wouldn't have told me.

Our dad has an unreadable expression, but I think he's unamused. No one wants to picture our sixteen-year-old sister pregnant, but I might be the only one actually cringing.

"And that is fact," Audrey decrees as if she won this tournament of wits.

Fuck. Charlie is a slingshot on her. "Great, you had a period," he deadpans. "You want a real fact? Virgins can't get pregnant."

She lifts her chin. "I'm not a virgin anymore."

The sudden silence should be comical, but it's honestly *tense*. I'm not even studying the reactions around the table because I'm doing my best to read Audrey's poker face.

"And I care because?" Charlie questions. "Fuck the whole neighborhood, it doesn't change your age—"

"Charlie *Keating*," our mom sneers his name. "Rethink what you say to your *sixteen-year-old* sister. Right now."

He expels an aggravated sigh. "Audrey, you don't want to be a statistic, do you? Teen pregnancy?" He forces a pained smile. "Wait for a man who will..." He waves his fingers. "Fulfill your obnoxious imagination." Then he looks to our mom. "Happy?"

"I am *notably* irate."

"Wonderful." He swigs his wine, crashing back in his chair.

"Is this a lie?" Jane asks Audrey.

She's bullshitting, for sure.

"Possibly." She reaches for more cranberries, and the flame of the candle bends at just the wrong time. Her frilly lace sleeve catches on fire. She shrieks and jumps out of her chair. Everyone follows suit in an attempt to help.

"Audrey!" Mom rushes toward her, but Dad is closer. I've already grabbed her water goblet, dousing her wrist instantly. The fire extinguishes, but my pulse is ringing in my ears.

My sister places a hand to her chest, her breathing shortened. Dad curves around to inspect the damage. "Es-tu blessée?" *Are you hurt?*

She shows him her wrist. "Non, je ne le pense pas." *No, I don't think so.*

Mom stakes a glare at the candlestick like it deserves to be trashed for causing Audrey physical harm, but in the back of my head, I just think, *it had to be me.*

Maybe she would've chosen a different outfit if I wasn't here. Maybe she would've been sitting slightly to the left. Maybe this is happening because I brought pain into the world and it's trying to bring pain to the ones I love.

Dumb.

Fucking dumb.

I didn't cause this…but didn't I? My mouth dries, and I'm in a slight daze when I'm back in my chair. The dining room is rotating, and I only come into focus when Audrey says, "Ben."

Everyone is seated but Audrey now.

Everyone is staring at me.

I breathe through my nose, trying not to pass out.

"I love that you come to dinners every Wednesday," she professes. "I know it's for me."

I nod. My throat swells. Words lodge too much to break free.

"I was just thinking that if I visited New York, it'd put less pressure on you coming here. Whatever stress this might cause—"

"It doesn't cause me stress, Audrey," I cut her off. "I want to be here." *I want to make sure you don't feel alone.* I understand what it's like being in this big house with barely any siblings. I can't imagine what it feels like to have no one.

She rips off the burnt lace of her sleeve. "I heard from a source that you look happy in New York."

I frown. *A source.* I only think of Harriet, who I've spent most of my time around. "What source?" I end up asking.

"A friend of a friend." She smiles impishly. "One cannot reveal her sources." It must be Easton or Xander who told Vada who told her.

"There's no need for secrecy, sister." Eliot puffs a plume of smoke.

"Yes, I'd like to see your list of sources," Tom adds. "So we can properly vet them."

"Make sure you aren't conspiring with vermin," Eliot says.

"Rats bring information and the plague." Tom tosses his scepter again back to Eliot and another crystal breaks off and lands in the platter of cranberries.

"Enough," Dad says calmly but directly, then asks Audrey, "Finished?"

"Oui." At this, Audrey lowers in her chair, ending her opening remarks.

Looks like I'm last up. I down a giant swig of water, then stand. "As you all know, I tried out for the MVU hockey team. I've made it, and I've already declined. Coach Haddock was really understanding, and he said if I change my mind, he'd love to have me next season." I raise my glass. "That's it." I'm about to sit.

"You don't want to play?" my dad asks, freezing me in place.

"No."

"Because?"

"I don't love hockey anymore." I sink slowly into my seat, measuring the depth of confusion that passes between my siblings and parents. Now I'm baffled. "Mom, last time I was concussed, you *pleaded* with me to stay off the ice. You should be thrilled."

Her lips purse. "I would be if you decided to quit to protect your brain that I love so very much and would easily murder for."

I let out a befuddled laugh. "So my reasoning isn't good enough. Why would I play a sport I hate?"

"Why do you hate it, Pippy?" Jane wonders.

I stare at the seitan on my plate. Unable to verbalize my feelings to the depth that I could with Harriet. Why are these sentiments so impossible to release? The thought of them knowing more speeds my pulse. "Can't I fall out of love with something? Why is that a fucking crime?"

"It's not," Beckett says softly, which nearly has me relaxing backward, but I side-eye my dad. His gaze is tunneling.

I rest my elbows on the table, smearing my hands down my face. "Can I be done?" *Please.*

And then my dad says, "We need to talk about the estate lawyer."

Oh.

My.

Fuck. My hands are motionless in the air, my face turned toward my dad. My breath is trapped in my constricting lungs. "What about the estate lawyer?"

"Why did you meet with him?"

THIRTY-FIVE

BEN COBALT

This. This is exactly what they all knew at the start of the dinner. It wasn't about Harriet. Their concern has escalated because they know about the fucking *estate lawyer.*

I hadn't even considered that my parents could find out I contacted him. Which makes me the fool. He's not just my dad. He's *Connor Cobalt.* He might as well be an all-knowing deity who chooses not to overly interfere in his children's lives—unless he thinks something terrible will happen.

I shake out my thoughts. "Meet with who?"

"Gordon Brown."

Yup. That's him.

I am unblinking. Staring at the flickering candles in front of Beckett. Wow, my dad must be triply concerned if he's decided to do this among *everyone.* By their patient silence, I'm positive they all knew this was coming and were instructed to take backseat roles. "What is this—an ambush?" I ask him. "You couldn't pull me aside and ask me privately?"

"We are beyond that," he says gently.

My brows hike upward. "Is this an intervention?" I question him, then Mom. "For meeting with a fucking estate lawyer?" I am panicked, terrified for them to know the entire truth, but all of this translates outwardly into anger. "Why? Why the fu—" I cut myself off. *Don't curse.* My parents aren't big sticklers about swearing. They might make a comment if we throw out a bunch of *fucks*, but I just prefer not cursing up a storm around them out of courtesy. "Why would this be a problem?"

"The timing gave us a reason for concern," he explains.

"The timing," I echo with a heated nod. "Right."

Shit. *Fuck.* All I can do is hope that Gordon cares about my client-attorney privilege more than Novak cared about our client-bodyguard one. "You ran into him?" I wonder. "He called you up?"

"Last time I talked with him, he mentioned seeing you."

I wish I ate my seitan during opening remarks. I'm too nauseous to even consider consuming a walnut. My mind is whirling a mile a minute, and I tuck in closer to the table and level my hands. "Okay, so everyone can stop freaking out about me—*yes*, I did meet with Gordon Brown in May." I name the time of date that has them troubled. "Yes, it was after I attacked Tate Townsend. That night, I was thinking a lot about death because I could've *killed* a guy, so I started thinking I should be more involved in my own estate planning."

"That's reasonable," Eliot says quietly, eyeing our dad.

I shake my head at my dad, like *come on*. "I'm trying to be more responsible after doing something pretty irresponsible like putting my fist in another guy's face and sending him to the hospital."

"Why not share this with us?" Dad questions. "Why do you feel the need to hide it?"

"It didn't cross my mind."

I can't masterfully lie to them, but that doesn't mean I have to spill the whole truth. They're just going to have to sit longer without all the information. And yeah, for my family that's like telling them to go dig their own graves.

"Look, things are better in New York," I say, which is true. I've grown closer to Harriet there.

Mom straightens her silverware. "What exactly did you discuss with Gordon?"

"Legal stuff." I stop myself from picking up a fork and pushing around a potato on my plate. They will only let go if I maintain eye contact. *Directness.*

"So specific," Charlie mutters dryly.

"What does it matter?" I shrug at them. "I made sure my will is updated."

That isn't all I did.

Heaviness falls over the room, so thick it's suffocating. Audrey is wide-eyed with *fear*. I'm not following.

"Can someone fill me in please?" I ask, alarm seeping into my bloodstream. It's taking everything to stay in my chair.

Mom is caging so much breath, her collarbones are protruding. "Ben," she manages to say, but cuts her icy gaze to our dad to finish.

"We're here for you. Always," Dad says, then addresses me with my siblings. "All seven of you are extensions of myself and Rose, and it's impossible for me not to love each one." I must be the weakest extension then. I don't say it. I just swallow hard while his deep blue eyes return to mine. "And I'd hope you'd feel like you can come to us at any point. Even if what you're dealing with are emotions too deep."

I nod stiffly, realizing where this is going. "I updated my will," I say in a tight breath. "I didn't write a suicide note that night. *I'm okay.*"

"You weren't contemplating it?" Mom asks outright. "Because if you still feel—"

"I wasn't and I'm *not*," I say strongly, being gravely honest. "I appreciate the worry, I do." *Don't fucking cry.* "I love that you care enough about me to push, even when it's aggravating, but I'm okay. And honestly, I'd rather just enjoy this dinner. It might be one of the last with Beckett for a while, and can we not make it all about me?"

That does the trick.

They all voice their love of me in their own way, and Mom reiterates she's happy I'm here tonight. I'm not relaxed, honestly.

Then Eliot toasts, "To Wednesdays." We all lift our glasses. He takes a dramatic, serious pause. "Which should always revolve around me." He's the only one who drinks, and I start laughing, which causes the whole table to follow. Mirth spreads like a contagion.

I love you, Eliot. He winks at me before he slouches backward.

Everyone begins to dig into the cranberries, roasted potatoes, carrots, as forks clatter and dishes clink. Mom rises with her wine. "This concludes opening remarks." She sips. "Now the game truly begins."

Jane unfurls a notebook and clicks her sparkly pen.

The second half of dinner—the literal game portion—I tend not to speak as much, but I'm always engaged.

Like now, I listen as Beckett tees off the first question. "Which Greek god is associated with a gentle spring breeze?"

I know this one. "Zephyrus," Charlie says almost as soon as Beckett stops speaking.

He's right, of course. Charlie never answers incorrectly. Sure, he's been stumped before, usually by our mom or dad, but if he speaks, it's with unwavering confidence and he's never wrong.

No phones are out, not even slyly hidden under the table. Cheating will have you immediately banished from the dining room. Unable to finish your meal or participate. When we were kids, Tom risked many nights without dinner just to see if he could outwit our dad using the internet, but it never worked.

He was caught pretty early on each time. I could practically hear his stomach growling as he left. I doubt he hated missing out on the food more than being with all of us. Because Eliot would always sneak him leftovers.

So right now, my siblings and parents are spouting off trivia questions *without* reference material. You have to come prepared. Anyone can ask anything, but asking means you lose the chance to gain a point. First to ten wins. It's been this way since before I was born. Our parents never went easy and let us win, even when Audrey sobbed that all she wanted for her seventh birthday was to be the Wednesday Night Dinner champion.

"You have to earn it yourself, mon petit," our dad told her sweetly. "It can't be handed to you."

Up until Charlie turned fourteen, our mom and dad were always the victors. The night he finally beat them, my siblings and I all jumped out of chairs and roared with so much exhilaration, my voice went hoarse. We bounced up and down. Eliot threw a plate. We cheered like the Eagles won the fucking Super Bowl, and to us, it was like our chosen Gladiator finally took down the mightiest of opponents.

And Charlie looked so happy—the happiest I'd ever seen him, maybe in my entire life, was that night.

"It is four points to Charlie," Jane calls out the current score. "Four to Dad, three to Mom, two to me, and one to Eliot." She taps her notebook with the pen. "And proceed."

"What did Prometheus steal from the gods?!" Audrey shouts quickly to slip her question into the mix.

"Fire," too many people say at once. No one shares points, so the question is tossed. Still, this might end up being a short game since the theme is Classical Mythology. They know I have an exam soon, and this wouldn't be the first time a Wednesday Night Dinner is constructed to help one of us study.

Audrey slumps.

"Try something harder," Charlie suggests and not nicely.

"It was meant to be easy," she retorts, stabbing a carrot with her fork.

Charlie opens his mouth, but Mom cuts him off quickly, "What was Dionysus's name before he was resurrected?"

"Zagreus," Eliot slices goose on his plate with a knife. "Thank you for the soft ball, Mom."

"She's just ensuring I won't win," Dad grins at her from across the table. "Isn't that right, Rose?"

Mom doesn't deny. "I'm sure Dionysus will appear on Ben's exam. I'm helping our youngest son pass a college course."

"Two birds, one stone," Dad says.

Audrey pipes in, "Can we not inflict pain upon a bird, even metaphorically?" She casts a kind look to me, and I smile over at my sister.

"Yes, *Richard*," Mom says, "leave the murdering of fowl out of dinner conversation."

His brow arches. "Because the dismemberment of people is better?"

"I've yet to rip out your tongue, but don't push me. There is always time to curse you with eternal silence."

"Which would displease you most of all."

We drum the floor with our feet, and Mom's smile is enough to cause most of us to grin. Yeah, I do not know how to leave this behind. I really, really don't. *I have to.* Don't I?

"In Greek mythology," Charlie says while picking up his wine, "Pandora was given a jar containing all the evils known to mankind. When she unleashed it upon humanity—what was the only thing left inside?"

"Hope," Mom says, her eyes meeting mine.

My pulse tries to skip. I break apart my seitan, not eating much, because now I'm thinking I should tell them about the frat. Tonight. Withholding my meeting with the estate lawyer just caused more drama and speculation. It's better if they know I'm moving out soon.

"Wait, it's not a jar," Tom says to Charlie. "It's a *box*. Pandora's *box*, dude."

"Pithos," Dad explains. "It's the Greek term used in Hesiod's writing, which refers to a *jar*. The kind used for grain, wine, oil."

Mom further clarifies, "It was mistranslated later as *pyxis*. Which means small box."

"Oh I have one," Jane straightens up, then washes down her bite of food with water. "What are the goddesses of the seasons?"

"The Horae," I'm able to say before Charlie. "Or Hours. They personify the four changing seasons and the passage of time." The cycle of human life.

"Well done, Pippy," Jane beams, jotting down a point for me.

Eliot creaks back in his chair. "Greek mythos: Which of the rivers of the Underworld is the River of Woe?"

"Acheron," Dad says smoothly.

"Not Styx?" Audrey frowns.

"No," Charlie looks over at her. "Some Roman poets will reference this to Styx, but he said Greek."

Eliot leans forward to explain, "Acheron is the river associated with pain, sorrow, and woe. It's the river the dead must cross to enter Hades, little sister."

"Of course, I knew that part," Audrey says pointedly. "I'm *sixteen*, not twelve."

"Here we go again," Tom mutters into a big gulp of wine.

Dad manages to keep us on track, and I have to wait until the game ends to surface the frat. I'm a little jittery, but I'm relieved when Jane finally decrees Mom as the winner, Charlie in second, and Dad in third, only partially due to Mom soft-balling questions toward those of us who'd know hers before Dad could answer them.

As napkins are folded and Jane hoists her baby out of the highchair, I let the bomb drop. "I'm planning to join a frat."

Chairs scrap back into the table. Even Jane sinks into her seat and passes Maeve to Thatcher.

"Well, I'm thinking about it," I continue. "I just wanted everyone to know while we're together that it's looking like I might be living with the frat soon, so I'll be out of your hair." I glance around at my four brothers.

"You were never bothering us," Beckett says deeply. "You don't have to move out. We've never wanted you to."

"Yeah," Tom pipes in. "We've enjoyed the company, Ben Pirrip."

"Makes our lives far more interesting," Eliot grins, which floods my lungs. I feel good knowing I haven't been the worst roommate alive, even if I have been a pretty awful brother.

I crumple my cloth napkin in my hand. "I was never planning on staying there long. I told you all that." I shrug stiffly. "The frat thing might be what I need."

"You're a sophomore," Dad says. "Are you sure the fraternities at MVU will let you live in the houses on campus? At some colleges, it's a privilege for upperclassmen only."

Yeah, *no*. I did not consider this major flaw. "I guess I'll find out soon."

THIRTY-SIX

BEN COBALT

"Nah, man, we don't allow sophomores to live in the house. Juniors and seniors only. It's part of the chapter rules for Kappi Phi." Leif Westergaard, the president, delivers news I already expected to hear when I visit the frat on Friday.

After researching all the MVU frats, the housing rules seem to be standard among every single one. I have closest connections to Kappa, so that's basically the only reason I choose this frat to test the waters.

I've been here for a half hour. Chilling with Leif and another senior (Prescott) in their basement, which has a pungent odor of vodka, dirty gym clothes, and tuna. The last being from a litter of stray cats they rescued on their porch steps and now consider Kappa kittens.

Maybe it'll be a good thing if I live here. I can make sure the cats are cared for. Not that they appear neglected. Water bowls are set out and filled. Two black kittens curl up on mounds of woolen blankets beside a white fridge. Clearly, they're being fed if I can't rid the canned tuna scent from my nostrils.

"How firm are these rules?" I ask while we're comfortable on their plaid sofa, beers loosely in our grips.

"Pretty firm, man," Leif says in a casual way that makes me feel like the rules are soft tofu. "What's definitely flexible is rush." I missed rush week, the period where fraternities evaluate potential new members. "Bid Day has passed, as you know. We already have our new pledges, but we'd love for you to be a Kappa. You want to join the pledge class, the door is wide open."

The power of being a Cobalt.

Just joining the frat isn't exactly what I want though. I need the seniority perks, and they just want to say a Cobalt is a Kappa. We'd be using each other.

"You all are my first choice," I say. "I really want to be a Kappa, but I need housing. And if you can't guarantee me a room for the rest of the semester, then I'll have to go to Lambda."

"Boooo!" about four guys holler from the foosball table. "Lambda fucking *losers*."

It feels like the whole fraternity is in the basement right now. Half are glued to a television as the Yankees fight to make the playoffs. The other half are playing foosball for cash and crushing Millers.

"You don't want to be a Lambda, Ben," Leif cautions. "They can't even throw parties at their house anymore."

Do I even want to ask? I lean back into the plaid cushion. "Why?"

"They hazed a pledge so bad, he ended up with a concussion."

"I heard it was a coma!" a guy shouts.

"You weren't even here then, Javi," Leif retorts with a scrunched face. Looking back at me, he says, "Anyway, it got ugly. Lawsuits, threats of shutting down all the chapters, then they decided to just put some restrictions on Lambda Alpha Lambda."

"I'm not really interested in the parties," I admit, but now I'm wondering if Lambda will fucking haze me if I become their pledge. Of what I've heard, the worst thing Kappa Phi Delta has done is make their new members silly string a bronze Thrashers statue in the quad. While only in their underwear.

Tame and relatively harmless.

I'd rather not be waterboarded, pelted with beer cans, or worse, forced to eat meat. Still, I try to show I'm *highly* considering their rival frat so they're more afraid to lose me.

Leif rubs his mouth, thinking. "Look, I can't just give you a room. They're all taken, and even if someone volunteers to bunk up with you, some of the guys will feel like it's not fair. You'd already be getting special privileges by joining late."

"I'm grateful for that," I express, as a tabby rubs against my ankles. I bend over and scoop up the tiny kitten. She purrs and lets out a satisfactory meow as I nuzzle my knuckle near her ear. "But if there's any possible way you'd all be okay with it, I'll join today."

Leif and Prescott share a look like they're not ready to let this opportunity slip away. While they're thinking it over, the kitten scratches at her head. I spread areas of her fur and check for fleas. I've done this a bunch whenever Jane would sneak home strays.

No fleas that I can see. I stroke her spine, and she rolls belly-up on my lap for more pets.

"What about the bet?" Prescott asks Leif, which jerks my gaze up to them. "See if he can get in on it."

I stiffen, especially as he captures the attention of *every* frat brother in the basement. "Oh dude, the bet," a curly-haired guy exclaims near the TV.

"Shit, if Ben Cobalt wins the bet, he can be my roommate all semester and the next," another says.

"Or you can room with me," Prescott offers.

"Bro will be a fucking *legend*."

"No way would he win it. No one associated with Kappa has been able to step foot in the Honors House."

Honors House? My brain pounds. "What's the bet?" I ask Leif.

He bows closer, his grin spreading rapidly over his freckled, fair face. The excitement is contagious around the room, infecting everyone but me.

Apprehension threatens to bind my muscles. They're all crowding closer as Leif tells me, "It's a ten-year-old bet. First made by the Kappa brothers before us. You haven't been at MVU long, but the Honors House is a co-ed society full of judgy little pricks."

"Neeeerds," someone heckles, followed by laughter.

Yeah, I'm sure the Honors House would call them meatheads right back. It's typical stereotyping. Not shocked, not surprised, but I'm stuck on the fact that one of Harriet's goals is to be accepted into the Honors House. She's already sent in her application and taken the entry exam, which she said was *easy*.

"What does the bet have to do with them?" I ask.

"They've *refused* to let anyone in a frat go inside their building," Leif says. "It's literally the nicest house on campus."

"Fucking ridiculous," a guy grumbles.

"It's not like we bar them from our parties," Prescott explains to me. "Everyone is welcome here."

I saw that firsthand the week before the semester began. Where the house party was open to all. It'd also been where Harriet was almost thrown into the pool. A Kappa hadn't been the one about to toss her in, but I'm aware none of them tried to stop it from happening.

"So what's the bet? First Kappa to spend a night in their building wins?" I guess.

Some laugh. Others shake their head.

"That's not it," Leif grins. "First one to sleep with a girl from the Honors House wins." What the fuck? I try not to see red while he clarifies, "No one has ever succeeded. Many have tried." Off my knotted, pissed-off confusion, he adds fast, "You don't know those girls, Ben. They're stuck-up prudes. It'd honestly do them some good by getting laid."

The *no frat boys allowed* rule in the Honors House is starting to make some sense. I can picture this dumb bet being made one drunken, horny night in this very basement ten years ago. I wonder if it started as a joke and gradually took real shape.

"The Honors House president this year, Guy Abernathy, is a

pretentious *prick*," Prescott says with boiling irritation. "He acts like he's better than every person on campus because he what—graduated valedictorian from his private school? Who the fuck cares?"

I mean, he obviously does.

The beef between the Honors House and Kappa is definitely alive and well. *Fuck.* All I can think about is Harriet.

Leif jumps back in, "Sleep with a girl from the Honors House, Ben, and you win the decade-long Kappa bet. All membership dues paid, a plaque on the wall, and special, just for you, housing as a sophomore."

I expel a breath through my nose and let the kitten spring off my lap. "How would this even be proven?"

"She has to admit to the Kappa president, which is me"—Leif points to the MVU letters on his sweatshirt—"that she slept with you, and she has to give us the panties she wore before you fucked her."

"Preferably wet," someone snickers.

My jaw clenches. This sounds so fucking degrading for the girl. No wonder no one has won the bet in a decade, and honestly, I'm proud of the Honors House girls for not falling for whatever manipulative bullshit tactics these guys have attempted over the years.

I should just leave New York earlier than I planned. It'd ensure nothing else bad happens to my brothers, but the thought flexes every tendon in my neck.

Cutting things this short with Harriet hurts. I haven't even made it to her birthday. That's why I'm entertaining joining a frat.

Still, on moral instinct, I tell them, "This isn't going to work for me."

"Do you have a girlfriend?" Leif wonders.

All I picture is her round face, perpetual scowl, and yellowish-blond hair. "It's not that…" *Is it?*

"You're Ben fucking Cobalt," Prescott says with the raise of his beer. "I bet half the Honors girls would kill to say they fucked you."

Leif hoists his bottle too. "If anyone can win this, it's you, my man."

"Woooo!" they holler, swigging beers in cheers.

"Just think about it," Leif smiles, trying to pull one out of me but failing. "We'll give you the rest of the day. You have my number."

Of course I do.

THIRTY-SEVEN

HARRIET FISHER

Earbuds in and The Carraways blasting, I listen to Tom belt out an angsty chorus while I hike across campus. Trees rustle with a cool wind, the leaves beginning to change into a fiery orange as September ends.

I wonder how Ben is faring at Douche Row right now. Sure, Kappa wasn't at fault for inviting a dickhead to a party who nearly drowned me, but they're probably hungry for a piece of the Cobalt pie.

Picturing them taking a bite out of Ben gets my back up. No one is allowed to take a chunk out of him. Maybe I should've gone into law and not medicine. I could've fucking decreed it. Woven a gavel around. Flung that thing—

"Fisher!"

I hear a faint yell, and I pry out my earbud, turning as Ben strides toward me with a long-legged, confident gait. His smile ignites as soon as he sees my face—which has to be resting at its normal scowling stasis.

My whole body goes light and airy. Has anyone ever been this happy to see me? Just him, probably. Emotion tries to rush, and I take some deep breaths to stop the overwhelming surge. Then I shut off my music. He slows to my side with a protein shake in hand, and I'm more cognizant of the *many* heads that've spun in our direction since he shouted my name.

"Sorry." He notices them scrutinizing me.

"It can't be worse than being caught in the quad with Xander. Three girls asked me in my morning lab if I was dating him, and I keep getting nasty spam through my MVU email address."

He shakes his drink. "What do you mean?" Concern darkens his face.

While we walk together, I pull up my email and pass him my phone. "It's junk mail. I'm guessing someone must've posted a pic of me and Xander online, and an internet savvy fan traced down my name, our college, and found my school email."

His jaw muscle tics as he reads, "*Go die, bitch. You don't deserve Xander Hale.*"

I pop a hard caramel candy in my mouth. "I didn't say they were nice, Cobalt boy."

"*I hope you rethink your whole life and take your skank ass vagina to the sewer you came from.*"

"That one did almost make me laugh."

He's not cracking even an itsy-bitsy smile. Instead, he's deleting the emails for me. "Are they jumping in your socials too?"

"Nope. They haven't found me there. My usernames are too creative, and I think it helps I don't post a ton of face pics." His concentration hasn't let up on erasing the emails. "Friend—I will survive."

"This doesn't bother you?" He hands me my phone when he's finished.

I shrug. "People suck. A tale as old as time. I feel worse for Xander, honestly. It can't be easy having these types of fans breathing down your neck and affecting your actual life. It's toxic parasocial relationships. All one-sided and obsessive." I adjust my slipping backpack. "Me, on the other hand, all I have to do is make a new email. Which will be a pain, sure, but it's not like people are crying about who my next hookup might be."

"Don't count me out, Fisher," he teases.

I bite on the caramel candy, my heart going unsteady the longer our gazes latch. "You'll cry if it's not you?"

"Definitely." He sounds serious, but the light in his eyes never dulls. He checks me out a little bit, and heat bathes my cheeks.

"Odds are in your favor," I flirt back.

Ben has a softer smile. I can tell something is on his mind, and I'm about to ask when he says, "Where are we headed?"

We.

He's also freeing my sliding backpack from my shoulder. He slings it on his, carrying it for me.

"Library." I hope I don't sound too breathless. "I need to get *Metamorphoses*. I searched the database, and it hasn't been checked out yet."

He glances at his watch. "One hour before your 1:50 lab." He's memorized my schedule, a known fact that still levitates me in a weird way. "Looks like I'm yours for sixty minutes."

That's not even close to long enough. Before befriending Ben, I would've been shocked if he gave me thirty seconds. Asking for more feels greedy, but I'm ravenous for each minute, each sunny hour.

So when we reach the library together, I soak in the seconds with him. He's such a jock shaking up his peanut butter protein concoction, casting smiles down at me. I think, in part, to try to beckon one out of me.

It works once or twice.

The librarian lets him in with the drink because he offers to dump it first. Being honest and kind does play to Ben's favor a lot of the time. People always seem to give him what he wants in the end.

It reminds me of his meet-up with Leif today. "What's the prognosis with the frat?" I ask, more hushed. "Are you a Kappa now?"

The second story of the cathedral-like library is dead quiet and also mostly empty of students. Barely any light shines through moody stained-glass windows. Bookshelves tower to the domed ceiling, and Ben follows me between two of them.

I crouch to read the spines. He hasn't answered me, and fear squeezes my stomach. "Did they mess with you?"

"No." He makes a face like I am very far off. His lips tic up.

"Were you worried they would?"

"You against all of Kappa? Yeah, kind of."

He rests an elbow on the shelf way above me. "I have a way with frats." There isn't much arrogance in his tone. He speaks like it's just a fact. "But it's not going to work out with Kappa Phi."

I brush my fingers over the spines as my face falls. I'd *really* been hoping they'd offer him a place to stay. No other options seemed good enough to pursue. "Because…?" I drag out a dusty hardback.

He downs a gulp of shake, then clears his throat to say, "They want me to complete a bet that's been in the frat for a decade. If I don't, I can't live there as a sophomore."

"So let's complete the bet," I say with more optimism. I'm already including myself because he's joined Team Harriet before I even handed him the sign-up sheet, and I'm clamoring for the opportunity to be there for Ben too.

"No." He's shaking his head.

My thighs ache in a squat, so I kneel. "You aren't going to tell me what it is?"

Ben slides his fingers through his hair, a groan caught in his throat. "Don't look at me like that."

"Like what?"

"Like you want to scratch my eyeballs out and throw them down the stairs."

"Is it hurting your warm blue heart?"

"More like it's making me want to push inside you and watch you come."

Holy fuck...I'd say that came out of nowhere, but his groan had been a hoarse, turned-on one. My breath staggers, and I can't formulate words. We haven't fooled around since the one time at his brothers' apartment. We haven't even *kissed*, and seeing as how there is a time stamp on his life in New York, I can't determine whether it'll ever happen.

The flirting I like, but the actual reality of him slipping inside me, I know I'd love more. Even if it's probably incredibly stupid to sleep with a guy who's not sticking around. *I don't care.*

I don't care.

I crunch on the tiny bit of hard candy left in my mouth, breaking the spindling tension in the air.

Thankfully he speaks again. "I think you meant *cold* blue heart."

I shake my head once. "Yours might be blue, but it's not cold. It never has been." I don't look at him. I just slip the hardback on the shelf, still in search of Ovid. Not here. I start picking myself up.

"They want me to sleep with a girl from the Honors House."

I literally stumble on the ascent to my feet. Ben juts out a hand, clasping my hip to balance me. My eyes are saucers. At first, I'm trapped on the horrifying image of Ben sleeping with another girl.

Them together.

Hot and heavy in bed. His hands skating down her bare skin.

And she's in the Honors House where I want to be? Jealousy towers over me and makes me want to shrink. Until I realize, *he's not accepting the bet.*

That pains me in a different, more agonized way. He's adamant that he can't stay with his brothers for much longer, and if he has no place to live soon, then...is he going to expedite his trip to the wilderness? Will he pack his bags next week? Three days from now? Tomorrow?

I wish I could offer my apartment, but after I asked Eden, she's now reminded me multiple times not to let my friends spend the night. She's paranoid I'm going to have "friendly" sleepovers when

I've *never* even pushed that boundary once. I just asked one time. She said no, which I respected but hated.

Sadly, the frat really is the best solution to Ben's crisis.

He places the protein shake on one of the library shelves, and he explains more about the bet. When he's done, I consider the possibility of *me* achieving my goal of being accepted in the Honors House. "I could—"

"No," Ben forces out.

"*Ben*, just listen to me for a second, please." It hurts craning my neck to look up at him, but I still fucking do it because I want my eyes on his and he needs to hear this. "If I get into the Honors House, do you know how easy it'd be to just tell Leif we had sex and give him panties? They don't even have to be mine, okay. We can buy a new pair, pour some bleach on them, make them look used."

"What if you don't get in?"

I go cold. "Then I guess you convince another girl to do that for you. Or you actually sleep with her." What is wrong with me?! Why am I suggesting this?

He swallows hard, his nose flaring, and he stares around the dark, quiet alcove that feels like ours. I inhale the old dusty book scent, ignoring the boulder in my lungs, and he says, "I'm *not* fucking another girl." His blue eyes narrow down on me. "You're the only one I've even thought about sleeping with for months. You're all I can think about every morning and every night, and if I even tried to have sex with someone else, I'm fairly certain I'd only be thinking about you, Harriet."

For months. Every morning. Every night.

He's been thinking about me.

Me.

It balls up in my esophagus. I'm too overwhelmed to speak.

He's breathing harder like we're already under the sheets together, like he's already wrapping me up in his strong, unwavering arms. Ben licks his lips, then says deeply, "I believe in you. I know you'll get into the Honors House because they'd be so fucking dumb not to accept you. And they're supposed to be the smartest people on campus, right?"

I shrug. "In theory, I guess."

"But I can't let you go to the Kappa president and tell him we slept together."

"Even if I lie?"

"You're not lying for me." Ben is *very* adamant, his hand leveled like this is a hard *no*. A thousand-foot wall he will not hurdle or let me even touch. "The risk of getting caught in a lie is one I'm not going to take. The consequences of that could be fucking *catastrophic* for you. Kappa could retaliate. I don't trust what they'd do. So if I take the bet, I need to *honestly* complete it."

I understand, and I'm totally fine with that too. "Okay, then I get in the Honors House and we bang."

Ben is vigorously shaking his head.

"What's the problem?" I question with a pained frown. "Am I such an embarrassing lay that you'd want to keep it secret?"

"*What?*" Shock catapults his brows and drops his jaw. "No. I'm not ashamed to be with you—are you kidding?"

Unfortunately not.

I lift my stiff shoulders, holding my elbows.

"Harriet." He slides his hand against my forearm, his warmth loosening the grasp I have on my own body. "If we have sex so I can get housing, it's a transaction, and I don't want to sleep with you just so I can have a place to stay. On top of that, I know guys like Leif, and the bet is coming at your expense. I don't want any of them to humiliate you."

"It's not humiliating to me, and I'll slingshot the panties in his face. Make him the butt of the joke first."

His jaw hasn't untensed, but he also hasn't stopped touching me. He's brought me toward his firm chest. His hand gradually ascends my hip to the small of my back, to my neck, up into my hair where he cups my skull. It dawns on me that he's bracing the weight of my head, letting my neck rest while my gaze dives deeper into his.

I'd like to say physical touch is Ben's love language, but does that assume he loves me? Is he loving me in this second, this moment? As his hand becomes a pillow for me to rest against.

I just want to be that for him too. A soft place. Comfort. Why won't he let me?

"Harriet," he murmurs.

My eyes scald. "It's not transactional if we have sex before I'm in the Honors House—because maybe I don't even get in." The thought impales me worse than ever. "So maybe we just have sex, Ben. Maybe everything will fall into place if we let it."

His desire so clearly drips over me, and as he licks his lips this time, the heat in his next breath ratchets up mine. I feel his fingers tighten against the back of my head, and the clench between my legs, my need for him to be inside me, just grows.

His flexed muscles say he's trying not to move his hands down my body. He's trying to root himself in place. "I want to, I want to," he murmurs deeply, "but I don't want to hurt you. Why do you think I haven't made a move on you again?"

I just figured he preferred teasing and maybe wasn't interested in following through. Questions tickle my brain, and I let one out, "Do you imagine lifting me in your arms?"

"All the time, *Friend*." The sultry depth of his voice on *friend* is cranking the temperature between us.

"Then why—?"

"I'm *leaving*," he emphasizes. "I will leave, Harriet. I will leave." Each word is a blade, but I can see it slices through him too. His voice goes more hushed, more vulnerable as he says, "I don't want you to think that if we have sex, I'll stick around, because I won't."

"I won't think that," I whisper with force. "I'd rather be closer to you now, even if it'll hurt worse when you're gone, because I'd always wonder *what if*—and regret is more painful to me."

Ben breathes in so deeply, his hand tangling in the back of my hair. I feel the heat of his fingers against my head. I could bask forever in his touch.

"I'm telling you I *want* to do this," I say from within, desiring more than anything to just be there for Ben. "We have sex. You help me get in the Honors House. I help you complete the bet. We're both benefitting here." All I imagine is Ben hugging me goodbye, then drawing so far away, the warmth replaced with an excruciating coldness. If this is what it takes to keep him here for longer, it's honestly not even a big price to pay. It's the easiest deal I've ever made. "Don't make me beg, Friend." My voice carries a slight tinge of desperation that even scares me. I've now become *desperate* to keep him in my life?

I wish he was as desperate to stay in mine.

Maybe he is. Maybe that's why he's here right now. I don't have these answers. I'm not in his head, but it must be full of torment because fragments of confliction pulse through his baby blues.

I reach out to take my backpack from him.

He stops me. "Okay."

"Okay?" Relief swells. "We're doing this?"

"We're doing this." He unpockets his phone to prove it. He makes a two-minute call in the library, and I pretend to have more interest in my Ovid hunt than in his conversation. It's so quiet, I can hear Leif on the other end.

"You're one of us now. Welcome to Kappa Phi Delta, pledge."

He had to accept their invitation into the frat first. As he shoves the phone in his back pocket, tension gnarls around the bookcases like thorny vines. Maybe we should leave before it snags us, but his eyes create fiery trails over my body, aching me, then they lift back to mine.

Does he want to have sex today? Now?? Here??? It sounds illicit and raunchy, but nerves prick my neck in slight alarm. We're on campus. What if a librarian finds us screwing against the shelves? I can't risk my education after I worked so hard for it.

I try not to jump to conclusions and play it cool. "You about to fuck me, Cobalt boy?" I ask, a little raspy, because I do want him to fuck me.

Just not *here*.

Ben has an elbow on the shelf, his hand to his mouth as he contemplates the situation, as he studies my body. "I'm not taking you in the library, Fisher."

That was hot. Especially when his lips edge upward, like he knows lust is coursing through me. A rejection shouldn't even sound that fucking *sexy*. After I mentally detour around the attraction, relief comes in soothing waves again. Ben and I are on the same page. *Thank God.*

"It's too public for you?" I'm guessing.

"We get caught, you get kicked out of school, so yeah." He is worried about what would happen to me. My lungs keep swelling.

Breathing in this heady feeling, I rotate to the books.

"Shit," I say, my shoulders falling.

"What?" He follows my gaze to the literal highest shelf. Where *Metamorphoses* is situated.

"It had to be a thousand feet above me," I mutter, about to search for a stepstool when Ben snags the book without any trouble. He barely even had to reach. He places the hardback in my hands, and I wish this small act of kindness wouldn't crush me like I'm being bulldozed by a love truck. It's one thing to openly acknowledge that we want to fuck each other, another to openly have *feelings* for someone who made it clear he won't be around for long.

I look away.

He hunches over, his hands on his thighs, so we're eye-level. I'm avoiding him.

"Fisher."

"Do you hear that?" I swallow, peering behind me, acting interested in a dusty corner.

"Petit oiseau."

I chew on the irrepressible smile. What has this guy done to me?

"Friend."

I turn back to Ben.

He takes the absolute deepest breath, then he pushes my bangs up with his warm hand. Staring at what I'm sure is a grimace. His lips inch up and up. "Bel oiseau." He translates, "Beautiful bird."

My heart enlarges. "I think that's you." I'm lost within the light of his eyes for a moment. "Not a black sheep."

"No?"

"No. Sadly we aren't the same breed after all, Friend." My mouth pinches in a smile though, totally okay with this realization. "You're the bluebird in the lion's den. That's likely what you've always been."

He seems overwhelmed with how I view him.

Don't leave me. "I want you to stay," I say through the lump rising in my throat.

"I want to stay," he says so deeply, as if the yearning is even more torturous for him than for me. I don't understand how it could be. He's *choosing* to ditch New York for the woods.

"Then stay."

He shakes his head once, pain all over his face. "I can't."

"What'd you buy—real estate you can't sell?" I ask.

"I just can't, Harriet." It is physically hurting him to talk about this, so I stop prodding. He never poked me until I bled, and I recoil at the notion of doing that to Ben.

He stands, bringing me into his chest in a strong, affectionate hug. I hug him back just as tightly, and I press my cheek to his body, hearing the pounding *thump, thump, thump* of his heartbeat. It begins to slow. He begins to calm, and he says, "I'm going to be here for your birthday. I promise you that."

TEXT MESSAGES

HARRIET
> MVU Campus 💀

BEN
> The End of the World 💀

HARRIET
> My apartment 💀

HARRIET
> Finding a place to fuck should not be this hard wtf.

BEN
> I'd suggest my couch, but I think we took a big risk last time.

HARRIET
> What would you have done if your brothers walked in on us last time?

BEN
> Thrown something at them. Memory wiped their brains. Judged myself.

HARRIET
Glad we avoided memory wiping and self-judgment.

BEN
Me too. But removing my couch from contention kind of limits the options here.

HARRIET
Too bad you don't have a treehouse we could use, nature boy.

BEN
My uncle has one.

HARRIET
Treehouse 💀

BEN
😂

We'll figure it out.

HARRIET
Idk your coat closet didn't seem like such a bad idea.

BEN
I can barely fit in there.

HARRIET
Motel? I could put in $50.

BEN
Save your money, Fisher. I have much higher standards for our first time.

HARRIET
In the back of Harold?

BEN
I said HIGH standards.

HARRIET
Oof with the Harold slander.

BEN
No offense to Harold the Honda, but he ranks below the motel. I'll likely pull a muscle trying to maneuver you in there.

HARRIET
So there will be a lot maneuvering on your end?

BEN
...yeah, what kind of sex have you had?

HARRIET
The kind where *I* was doing the maneuvering.

BEN

Thank you for the visual and the urge to ring your past hookups' necks.

HARRIET

You're welcome

BEN

I need some space to work with you. Our best bet is going to be my place. Just give me some time and I can figure out logistics. Maybe we can risk it if only one of my brothers is home... and asleep.

two weeks later

BEN

Tonight is a big no again. Tom won't go to bed. He's been up playing guitar forever. I'd think he's cockblocking me, but he's just hyper-fixated on his new song. I'm not sure he even knows what time it is.

HARRIET

Tell him he sounds like a celestial Gerard Way.

BEN

That assumes he cares what I think about his music. My opinion isn't gospel to him.

HARRIET

Who's is?

BEN

Honestly...himself.

HARRIET

How am I not surprised?

BEN

Another night then, Fisher?

HARRIET

Yep. The quest continues.

THIRTY-EIGHT

HARRIET FISHER

Sunday at the End of the World begins slow, and I'm happy about the lull tonight. Because I can spend more time swiping through Ben's phone while he's pressed up against my side. Dish towel slung over his shoulder, and his old worn baseball cap flipped backward—at times it's harder to pay attention to anything but him.

I swipe into the next video in his album titled *mes amours*.

A little gray feathered bird with a yellow head and bright orange blush-like circles bounces to the beat of "Another One Bites the Dust" and whistles the tune.

"Theodore," Ben names him since both his cockatiels look so similar to me. Same coloring, nearly same size. He has hundreds of these videos saved.

It's so cute, I rewatch it again, but that's exactly how I felt about the last twenty I've seen. I never had a pet, and I never imagined a *bird* could look so...cuddly. It's not a fluffy poodle, but they're affectionate in the way they beep-bop their head and perk up at the camera. I imagine they're looking at the guy beside me, and I understand the little twinkle in their eye.

He makes me just as happy.

I slide into another video, the small bird bounces on a National Geographic magazine, nearing an outstretched hand.

Ben. I dizzy even seeing his *fingers* appear on-screen. I've really fucking lost it, but there's seriously no turning back now.

"Theodore again," Ben tells me.

It ends too fast. Next video plays, and I inhale an audible breath. Someone must've recorded Ben because he's *fully* in the frame. In focus. He's young, maybe twelve. Sitting on his bed. His luminous smile is on the little cockatiel perched on his shoulder. He lets out a melodic whistle, and the bird whistles right back, then nuzzles his head into Ben's cheek.

Young Ben laughs. The bird chirps, then whistles so merrily, his little orange feet shifting just to be closer to the blue-eyed boy.

"Pip-Squeak," Ben says beside me.

I swallow my emotion. "I didn't know birds snuggled."

"Yeah, they do." He has a soft faraway smile, and I don't want to fill him with grief since both birds are no longer alive.

So I hand back his phone. "Thanks," I say sincerely. "That's been the best birthday present so far." I don't tell him it's the first one I've received since I was sixteen. Aunt Helena always calls to wish me a happy birthday—like she did this morning—but I wouldn't consider a fifteen-minute chat a gift, even if I really appreciate how she always remembers to ring me on October 13th. A couple years ago, I really needed her call. It'd been a bright spot on a lousy seventeen.

"You think this was your birthday present?" He scrunches his face at me, slipping his phone in his butt pocket.

I'd asked Ben if he had any videos stashed of his cockatiels. Little did I know, he had enough to make my whole night. "I asked and I received," I shrug, straightening up and shifting away from the liquor bottles behind us. My cheeks burn at the way he's watching me move to the beer taps. He's checking me out, and I'm seriously giddy over it. "Why? Did you get me something?"

"Maybe." His teasing smile is going to be the death of me. *Good riddance, Harriet.* The girl who died over a fucking *smile*. Ugh.

"Maybe." I crinkle my nose at him. "Whatcha got in your pocket for me, Cobalt boy? Jolly Ranchers?"

"Generally, gifts are supposed to be special. Not something you carry on the regular."

"Okay." I hoist myself up on the bar, sitting beside the taps. Only two old dudes are here drinking Guinness and chitchatting quietly at a booth. *Ghostbusters* plays on the projector screen. Volume low. I have my back to the movie. "You only came here with a water bottle. So it *has* to be in your pocket."

"Great assessment, Fisher," Ben smiles while nearing. "It is in my pocket."

He got me something. I grip the bar on either side of me. I swear, I'm two seconds from swinging my legs and falling backward like a fool. "You going to show me?"

Ben digs in his jeans, unearthing a square box wrapped with pink cupcake-patterned paper. It's not a ring box, but maybe the size for a bracelet or an iron-on patch to add to my backpack.

"Tell me you didn't buy wrapping paper." I take the gift.

"I didn't break the bank," he assures.

"You better not have." We're obviously not racking in any big tips here. "Your financial situation is already dire. How are you going to buy toilet paper for this primitive excursion?"

"I was probably going to use leaves anyway." His smile is too cute for the End of the World.

"Funny. You know what's funnier—if you get poison ivy, I won't be there to lotion your wounds."

"Straight to the heart." He sounds less jokey and sadder.

I'm fucking up this gift receiving, tanking the upbeat mood already, but in my defense, I have very little experience in opening gifts. "You picked this out?" I point to the cupcake paper.

"From Audrey's stash. My sister let me raid her stationary." It must've been on a Wednesday when he visits her in Philly.

I peel the paper. Unveiling a white box. My pulse speeds so fast, I need to pause to intake some breath. "I love it," I banter, but I think the truth is already out: I am enamored.

His smile widens. "All it takes is a box to make Harriet Fisher happy. Who knew?"

All it takes is you.

"I'm easy," I say. "*Not* like an easy lay." My defensive glare fizzles out in seconds with him.

"I know what you meant," he says softly. "Open it."

So I lift the lid, and my heart pitter-patters in a brand new drumbeat. I take out a really pretty beaded choker. Multi-colored. Square and round beads threaded together. "You made this?" I ask quietly.

"With a slight assist from Audrey since I wanted it to actually look good, but *yeah*. I made it."

I inspect the beads. A smiley face, a glittery purple one, yellow, blue, a pink heart, and then white letters, B-E-L...O-I-S-E-A-U.

It spells out *beautiful bird.*

Our conversation from two weeks ago in the campus library races back to me. "It's..." I look up at him, hiding none of the overpowering emotion on my face. I don't think I can.

His eyes redden like he feels the brunt force of my appreciation, affection, all the gooey sentiments I never thought I'd experience to this degree.

I manage to get out, "It's the best gift I've ever been given." I snap off my old dingy choker so I can wear the new one right now. "Thanks, Ben."

"Here." He offers to put the new choker on me, and this birthday really might end with me as a puddle on the floor.

I lift my blond hair off my neck, and as he wraps the choker around me, his knuckles brush the sensitive skin along my nape. My breath hitches a little, and he shifts his weight, his eyes flitting to mine like his need is being stirred. Tension flexes the tendons of his neck, and he breathes through his nose while he clasps the jewelry.

I touch the beads at my throat. He's standing so close that I've instinctively spread my knees, and he's fit between them. We're at much better eye-level than usual, and his chest collapses in a heady, sweltering beat.

We haven't had sex yet. We won't at our workplace, and honestly, I'm glad Ben isn't willing to screw me against a bathroom stall as our first time. It won't be a rushed quickie. He's treating it as something valuable that should last. Maybe even have a round two right afterward.

It's so different from what I know sex to be.

Thinking about where and when we'll hook up—I like. The fear that I might be rejected from the Honors House—I hate more than anything. Being accepted has become even more mission critical for this semester. If I fail, then what? Ben just leaves?

No, I *have* to get in. Then fling a pair of panties at Leif. Then secure Ben housing.

The Honors House has my application, and I've heard a whole lot of nothing in response, even after follow-up emails. Ben has been trying to score me an invite to their super exclusive Halloween party.

Apparently, it's where they scope out potential new members. If I can't get into the party, then my chances are basically in the gutter.

He knows it too.

Maybe that's why it's easier focusing on the *sex* part of this whole bet. Success rate of us finding a good place and time to bone is higher. Surely we can't fuck that up, right?

Ben has a hand on my knee and slides a hot trail up my thigh. Even with my plaid pants creating a barrier from his skin to my skin, the heat of him thrums through me. My clit is throbbing.

"Is the waiting torture for you too?" I ask in a whisper, our breaths shallowing together.

"You have no idea." He pulls his hands away, a rough groan against his throat. "It feels like I'm putting my palm above a flame every day."

"I thought you weren't the Cobalt who plays with fire."

"My whole family does," he whispers, "except Beckett....well." He cocks his head a little, then sighs. "I don't know." Mention of Beckett kills the mood. He's been upfront on why he needs to move out of his brothers' apartment. I was surprised when he said it wasn't because of Charlie, but a combination of things, most recently Beckett.

"You can't tell anyone," he said, putting major emphasis on the secrecy. How what he was divulging wasn't advertised anywhere. How it was nothing Beckett would like to share, probably for me to even know, but Ben wanted to be honest with me. "Beckett has OCD, and I'm making it worse by living there."

His sudden urgency to move out made a whole lot more sense.

I slide off the bar, which causes Ben to back up and add space between us. He rotates away and exhales to cool off, and I touch the new choker again. "I'll make you one," I say without thinking.

"What?" He spins back around.

"For your birthday. I'll make you a bracelet or something…" I trail off, realizing the mistake here.

Ben blinks, then tugs the dish rag off his shoulder. His frown is heavy.

He won't be here. March 29th—of course I know his birthday. I wished him a happy one last year. It'd been the day he thwarted a bad interaction with my shitty professor.

"I'll mail it to you." I rinse a splotchy pint glass. "You have the address?"

He watches me. "Not yet."

My stomach backflips. "But you know where you're going? Is this an American vacation or are we talking overseas?"

"America." He takes the glass from me to dry it. "More like I'm going to live there. It's not just a trip."

Okay… "But where is *there* exactly?"

"A place that my parents would definitely not enjoy." He smiles a little at the thought. He really loves his mom and dad. "They're not campers. My mom would last a solid day sleeping on the ground, then she'd book a hotel at the Ritz."

"I can't blame her."

His smile grows. "You wouldn't sleep on the ground with me, Fisher?"

"I would do a lot of things with you that I normally wouldn't do," I say. "I just wish there was more time to do them, I guess."

"I'm right here, right now." He flings the towel at my face.

I toss it back with a smile battling its way out of me. "You want to go camping sometime, nature boy?"

"You asking me out?"

I shrug. "You saying yes?"

Ben skates a hand across his jaw. "You have time in your pre-med schedule to drive hours out of the city and camp overnight?"

No, is my first initial thought. I definitely do not have that kind of fucking time between classes, labs, volunteering, research, clubs, bartending, studying, *trying* to snag a shadowing position. "Sure," I lie. "I can make time. Just like I did for your brothers' birthday."

"Midterms are coming up."

Oh my God, don't remind me!

"Are you itching your arms?" Concern pushes him toward me.

"Am I breaking out in hives?" I ask.

He checks the reddened speckling on my arms, but it's faint enough that I relax before he says, "I think you're good."

A weight sinks into my stomach as I replay our back and forth. "Did you just reject me?"

"No," he says like the idea pains him. "If it doesn't derail your goals, I'd do anything with you. But I'm honestly cool with staying in the city, hanging out in your apartment, helping you study. You don't need to go far for me. I just like being around you."

It means a lot to me—that my presence is simply good enough, that just being with me in any capacity is fulfilling. Still, I wonder, "Me plus you plus the woods doesn't sound more appealing?"

His lips tic up but flatline. "No—" He's cut off as the door blows open, and a rowdy stream of sports fans floods the bar. All in Yankees garb, all dropping f-bombs and gesticulating wildly. I'm guessing they just lost the postseason playoffs and came to drown their sorrows.

I'm no diehard baseball fanatic, but I have faint memories of attending a Pirates game with my mom and dad before the divorce. So by association to the decently happy memory in my brain, I am a Pirates fan. Ben roots for the Phillies. Both our teams didn't even make the playoffs. We have no skin in this year's World Series.

Ben and I split apart to "divide and conquer" as he so often tells me at work. He helps the right side of the bar, and I take orders from the left.

Unfortunately for me, the left consists of pushy thirtysomethings outfitted in jerseys. They elbow their way to the front of the bar. "Hey, you!" the beefiest guy shouts at me, wobbling just a little to where I know he's not sober.

I'm pouring lagers for a patient couple who wear Yankees ballcaps. "In a sec. They were first." I must have serious RBF because he growls under his breath to his friend, "What's this bitch's problem? I'm just trying to order a fuckin' drink, Jesus Christ."

I peek over at Ben.

He's bending over the bar to hear orders through the commotion. Ben is such a guy's guy that the group of dudes all laugh at whatever he says. I'd say they recognize his fame status, but they're not doing the usual "You're Ben Cobalt! Bro, no way?!" shock-routine.

No one seems to register a Cobalt is behind the bar.

Ben and these dudes casually knuckle-bump like they're fucking *friends*. They even bro-pat his shoulder before he goes to grab a bottle of whiskey from the shelf behind me.

He checks on me with a brief glance, and concern twitches his brows.

I give him a waist-high thumbs-up, not wanting him to worry. Do I envy his impressive social skills? Yeah. Do I wish they've rubbed off on me? Also yes.

But I'm still a capable bitch-faced individual. I've got this.

"Open a tab or close?" I ask the couple after they hand me their credit card.

"Close."

The gruff beefy dude bellows out an obnoxiously loud laugh with his friends. It puts me on edge since he was disgruntled two seconds ago. *They aren't laughing at you, Harriet.* I close out the couple, their beers already in hand.

Beefy Dude and his friends hastily take their spots. Then he motions to me like he's not right in front of my face. "Hey, we're next." He points at his head.

"What can I get you?"

"What's got you so fucking mad?" he snaps.

What would Ben do? I shrug. "The Yankees just lost."

"Damn right." They all start to smile and up-down me like I'm cool. A fellow dejected sports fan and not at all a moody bitch.

"You want a beer?" I ask, hoping to move this drunken train along the tracks. Somewhere far, far away from me.

Beefy Dude appraises me to where my bones instantly rust. He laughs a little to himself, then points to an expensive bourbon. "A double. On the rocks." The bottle is on the *highest* shelf.

I grind my teeth, seeing him snicker. Let's see the five-foot-one girl try to reach the top-shelf bourbon. How *hilarious*.

I look to Ben for help—it's an instinct now.

He sees me and up-nods. I point to the bourbon, and he's quick to come behind me and grab the liquor.

"No, man," Beefy Dude stops Ben. "Put it back. She's got it."

Ben is unamused. His pissed-off glare drills into Beefy Dude. He hands me the liquor bottle, not listening to the asshole.

"Thanks," I tell him.

Ben remains on my side of the bar. His supreme stare-down is shaking Beefy Dude's friends. They're starting to detach from him, but this guy isn't reading the room. I'm sure the beer goggles aren't helping, but being drunk doesn't excuse being a total dick.

I'm about to pour a double, but Beefy Dude exclaims, "Nah, I don't want that anymore. I'll take that one." He jabs a finger toward another top-shelf bourbon. His smug smirk crawls under my skin. Anger smolders in my lungs. I'm sure I'm glowering, but he does not give a shit. He just tells Ben, "She's got it this time. We have a thing going, me and her." His drunk eyes fall to me. "Isn't that right?"

"No," I deadpan.

"Yeaaah we do. We're connecting here." He laughs. "I know you can jump for it. Go on, jump." He stares at my tits in preparation for me to bounce.

"You can leave," Ben states firmly. His glare never loses scathing heat.

"Whoa, I have every right to get a fuckin' drink."

"We have every right to refuse you service when you're harassing—"

"Harassing? For fuck's sake, I'm just trying to get a drink!" Look at that sudden memory loss. He's puffed up with hostile aggravation, and his friends butt up to the bar, apologizing on his behalf.

"No, he needs to go." Ben has now pushed his way in front of me, shielding me from the situation.

"I did *nothing*," Beefy Dude bemoans. "What kind of fucking place even has high schoolers serving alcohol?"

"We're in college, and you can get the fuck out."

Again, they try to reason with Ben, but he's on a firm line they're not shoving him off. His bodyguard has risen from his usual table near the entrance.

All I see are the many paying customers being disturbed by Beefy Dude's outburst, and they're simply just trying to enjoy *Ghostbusters*, their pints, their friends, and their Sunday night.

"Ben, it's fine," I cut in.

His head swings down to me, confusion hardening his features. "No, Harriet—"

"Just give him a beer and tell them they can sit in the back if they don't bother anyone."

He does not like this. So I'm shocked when he listens to me, relays the statement, and pours a beer from a tap and opens them a tab. Tension is all over his face. He returns the credit card to Beefy Dude's friend with a warning still in his pinpointed gaze.

I appreciate being heard more than he knows. Once we've helped everyone and cleared the line, Ben crosses his arms, his attention still plastered to the rowdiest Yankees fans in the back corner.

"Why'd you want them to stay?" he asks now, his gaze finally pulling off them and dropping to me.

"It's the path of least resistance." I trash an empty bottle of Smirnoff. "Ever heard of it?"

"No," he says with a tight shake of the head. "I'm very much willing to walk the road of conflict if it means kicking those motherfuckers"—he shoots a glare at them—"off the path your feet are on."

"I saved you the trouble, Friend. They're fine."

He exhales a long, long breath through his nose. "You probably came from a place where you couldn't risk putting your neck on the line, but I didn't. So letting him sit there—it's not easy for me, but I'm doing it this time for you. Next time, know that you *can* boot him, and the consequences will not be as harsh as you think. You won't lose the fight."

I am used to suffering through whatever shitty moment is occurring, letting it pass with quiet resignation. The times I snark back, I'm more ready for things to go south. The situation rarely *gets better*. "You really think this is worse? They're not even paying attention to me anymore."

"We've left a ticking bomb in the back of the bar," is all he says before the door swings open, and Ben straightens to an even stiffer stance when Charlie, Eliot, and Tom come striding through.

The Cobalt brothers found the End of the World.

THIRTY-NINE

HARRIET FISHER

Ghostbusters sounds painfully loud as chatter falls hushed in the bar. Whispers and gasps of, "is that Charlie Cobalt?" and "those are the Cobalt brothers, look, *look*" are heard.

None of Ben's brothers ham it up for attention. They act like the bar only consists of me and Ben as they plant their asses on the barstools. Very rarely are these stools occupied. The projector screen faces the opposite wall, and the actual stools themselves are so wobbly, I'm shocked they maintain composure and don't teeter even slightly.

Cobalts are just fucking built different. I'd be aggravated if I wasn't a teensy bit jealous and honestly *happy* they're even here. They haven't given up on reeling Ben closer, and at times, I do wonder if he'll stay in New York longer for them—even if maybe he won't be living with them.

"Ben Pirrip," Tom bows forward, forearms on the bar. "This is really where you want to be at the end of the world?"

"Without us?" Eliot feigns hurt, his grin appearing soon after. "How dare you, brother."

Charlie says nothing. He pounds a pack of cigarettes on the bar.

"What are you doing here?" Ben asks them, already worked up from Beefy Dude. Their arrival isn't ridding the steam from his ears.

Eliot flicks out a lighter. "We heard it's Harriet's birthday, so we're gifting her with our presence."

"Gee, thanks," I say flatly, but inside, I am *elated*. Best b-day present would be Ben's brothers convincing him to stick around indefinitely. Hands-down. Sorry to my new choker necklace.

Tom forces out a winced smile at me, and I force a grimaced one back. Our attention veers to Eliot when he asks Ben, "Better question, what are *you* doing here?"

"Bartending."

"For money?" Charlie asks, almost disinterestedly.

"No, for funsies." Ben is in a grouchy mood. They can tell, probably since this brand of sarcasm isn't his usual approach. "I'm guessing Audrey told you I work here?"

Tom steals a cocktail stirrer. "Dude, whatever you tell her, she will spread like gangrene until it comes back and infects you and then you'll need Pre-Med Harry, here, to check you out," Tom waves a hand at me. "Which is worse than the actual infection."

I cross my arms. "So you're saying Audrey would fulfill my ultimate birthday wish and kill you?"

Eliot grabs his brother's shoulders in a playful gesture of protection. Tom's jaw has unhinged, until he sees Ben's slow-forming smile, and then Tom smiles victoriously as if *he* was the one who flipped Ben's mood and made him grin.

No, that was *me*. I did that.

"So you're saying you wouldn't save me, great," Tom slips the cocktail stirrer between his lips. "The feeling is *mutual*." Ben is frowning now, and Tom quickly adds, "But I'd still call upon you so do with that what you will, Harry."

"You knew Audrey would tell us," Charlie states plainly to Ben, redirecting this conversation.

"Eventually, I figured she might. It's not a big secret I work here. I just didn't want *that* to constantly be around." His gaze drifts beyond his brothers, but none of them turn to look to understand what "that" means.

People have whipped out their phones to snap pics and record videos of them. I notice their bodyguards making rounds around the bar. Ben said some of his brothers will have strangers sign NDAs and delete footage if they're being filmed outside of a public space.

I'm unsure of which brother has requested this tonight.

"Any of you want a drink?" I ask them since I'd prefer if they stayed until closing. Yes, even *Tom*.

"Glenfiddich, neat," Charlie says. It's easily one of the most expensive bottles we stock, and I stiffen when I see it's on the highest shelf. *Not again.*

My joints need oiled. I can't fucking move for an unbearable second.

Skin pleats between Charlie's brows as his gaze bores through me. Before I reanimate, Ben grabs the bottle, then slides a comforting hand down my back, knowing why I just had a minor internal freakout.

I breathe in.

Charlie asks Ben something in French. What calms me more is realizing I'm not Charlie's punchline. *He just wanted a drink, Harriet.*

While I pour whiskey in a tumbler, their French conversation picks up intensity. Eliot is joining in with a fiery emphasis on some words. Tom has a distraught yet irritated expression—on his phone. He's texting, not listening to whatever his brothers are passionately discussing.

As Eliot's blue eyes flit from me to the beefy dickhead from earlier, I know for certain Ben is relaying the minor shitshow before they arrived. Seeing Eliot, and even Charlie to a degree, appear incensed on my behalf feels strangely good.

I didn't think I needed more people to look out for me. I've been okay on my own, but to witness it happening is spurring a sudden onslaught of emotion. I can't tamp it down fast enough.

"Eliot, *Eliot*," Ben whisper-hisses as his broad-shouldered brother has a murderous glare on Beefy Dude and purposefully tries to catch this dickhead's attention. Ben speaks in forceful, *blazing* French, recapturing Eliot's gaze. Then he rests his hands on my head, then my shoulders, as if mentioning me in the equation.

I lean back into his chest on impulse.

Ben is stroking my hair, calming me even if his words sound aggressive as fuck.

"Anyone want to clue me in?" I ask.

"Learn French," Charlie bites back.

I do not have the fucking time right now to pick up another language. "It's about me, dude," I say.

"Astute."

I glower, then tell Eliot, "It's fine. They're fine. We have it handled."

Eliot is on his feet, unable to even sit. "He's still breathing, so it's not handled to my homicidal standards." He motions to Charlie's drink that I slide over. "I'll have what he's having."

I pour another whiskey. Loving Ben's hands on me. Loving him behind me, really. Literally and figuratively. *Don't get used to this.*

Yeah, yeah, yeah. I sigh to myself.

Eliot exhales the fire, then centers his focus on Ben. "We've hardly seen you at the apartment since Charlie and Beckett's birthday. You're really taking leave no trace behind to heart, brother."

I feel Ben tense behind me. I pass Eliot his drink, his grin flickering out before he takes a sip.

"I told you," Ben says, "once the frat gives me a room, I'm out of the apartment."

"Your days are numbered, we've heard," Charlie says with irritation.

Ben glares. "Don't act like you won't love it when I'm out of there."

"I love very little, so I can promise you I won't bother loving that." He picks up his whiskey. "Beckett wants you to stay with us, truthfully. Almost *desperately*. In case you didn't realize the last fifty times he's told you."

Ben didn't mention that Beckett has pleaded with him to stay at their apartment.

"I can't," Ben shakes his head. "I can't be there."

"Why?" Eliot's brows knit together. "Beckett said it was nothing you did." I assume Ben doesn't believe this. "He's ok—"

"*I can't.*"

Charlie pinches the bridge of his nose. He's aggravated. It seems like anything Ben says is an annoyance to him.

"Are you fucking kidding me?" Tom gapes at his phone, then puts it to his ear. "No, dude. *No,* the song isn't ready. We're not playing it—it's not good enough. Yeah, I said so, Warner." He's on a call with his bassist. "I'm not a tyrant! I just know what sounds good and what sounds like shit. Warner—*Warner.*" Tom plugs one of his ears as the Yankees fans grow noisier in the back. They'll likely want another round soon. "*Shit.*" He looks up. "Ben, is there a storage room or somewhere quiet I can go take this?"

"Yeah, I'll show you. We need to restock the Jameson anyway." His hand slips off my back as he leaves.

I'm rarely alone with Charlie and Eliot. Last time I was *truly* alone with Charlie, I offered to blow him. It still makes me cringe, but weirdly that whirlwind of a night feels forever ago. No one has necessarily buried what I did. It's become the sand. Harmless in light gusts, blowing past us.

"Let's cut to the chase," Charlie says to me while Eliot angles sideways, observing the beefy dickhead's every move from the corner of his eye.

"Okay?" I grab an empty pint glass a girl brings to the bar and say to her, "Thanks, you want another?"

"Uh, no I'm good. I've already closed out." Her voice trembles with nerves being so close to Charlie. I want to tell her this bitter Boy Genius is not worth the anxiety. She side-eyes him, likely yearning and praying for a single glance from him, even if it's a mean one.

He's ignoring her existence.

When she shuffles away, Charlie immediately resumes the conversation. "Why is Ben working at a bar? Is it for you or for the paycheck?"

I shrug, not wanting to be an untrustworthy friend. Even if I think they *should* know. I asked Ben why he doesn't just tell his family about his money issue and how he's leaving New York soon.

He said, "It'll turn into a bigger ordeal. They'll try to stop me, and I don't want them to."

I want them to.

But I can't break Ben's trust. There is no coming back from that—our friendship would be *obliterated*, and I'd rather not cause him that type of pain, especially when there's no guarantee telling Charlie and Eliot anything will make Ben stay.

"Does it matter why he's bartending?" I rinse out the pint glass.

Charlie twists the glass on the wooden counter, scrutinizing me. "It does if he needs money. That would imply he's burned through millions."

I process this. "How would you know he has that much money?"

"Because we all receive the same amount on the same day. Ben first asked to access his trust fund on his sixteenth birthday. To buy a car. The car he would eventually crash."

Okay...I'm shocked Charlie is just delivering this personal information to me like it's a greeting card and not gold bars locked in a vault. "And you're saying he has millions?"

"It would accumulate that high, easily." His eyes ping around the bar. "So him blowing the bank—that does matter to us."

"He could be in danger," Eliot says, his glimmering blue eyes shaded with worries. Is he...afraid?

"Ben's not in danger." *He just wants to live out of the city*, I want to say. *In nature.* I picture him on a solo adventure among dense foliage and dangerous wildlife. I'm guessing this would freak out any protective, loving family, and he's doing his best not to trigger their concern.

"Does he need money?" Charlie questions.

Eliot observes me like Charlie, but his eyes are layered with a dark protectiveness.

I dry the clean glass. "Can't you just ask him yourself?"

"Were you here thirty seconds ago?" Charlie rebuts. "You don't think we've tried? He'll talk circles around us and be purposefully vague. I'd rather Ben stuff aluminum foil in my ear."

I shrug. "Maybe that's your dynamic with him, dude. I can't get in the middle."

Eliot downs a strong sip. "She's loyal." He motions to me with the glass. "Commendable. Blink twice if Ben is penniless. We won't tell."

Holy shit, the urge to actually blink overpowers me, and I do blink. Twice.

Eliot holds out a hand to Charlie. "He's broke."

Charlie sighs, then glares up at the ceiling.

Regret assaults my insides. I am literally the worst friend. I couldn't even stop myself from *blinking*.

Are you serious, Harriet? I throw the dishtowel at the taps.

"This isn't a betrayal," Eliot says deeply. "Look at me."

I barely lift my burning gaze.

"He needs us. He needs you."

I frown. "What do you think is going on?"

"He's moved his money somewhere. A trust. Land," Charlie theorizes. "Or he was scammed out of a large sum of cash. He's being blackmailed—"

"What?" I bristle.

"It's my number one theory," Eliot chimes in. "He's paying off some bastard."

Is that why he needs to leave New York before the end of the year? Is Ben being threatened? At times, he acts like he *has* to go. Like it's a necessity. Against his will…? "What if he is in trouble?" I ask them.

"That's why we're here," Eliot says, then points at me. "That's why you're here. Eyes and ears." He motions to those organs with two fingers.

Charlie rolls his eyes at the dramatics, then tells me, "Ask Ben if he is. He's clearly been more forthcoming with you."

I'm not a fan of prodding Ben. I don't like how it makes me feel. I hate how it makes him feel even more.

"Heeeeey." Beefy Dude is back with an empty pint. No friends at his side. "My girl."

I clutch my biceps.

Eliot extends an arm out across the bar, obstructing this dickhead from being able to careen over and reach me. "She's actually my brother's girl." *He considers me Ben's girl???* I can't even fully process, not while nerves accelerate my pulse. At six-four, Eliot towers over the dickhead. "You're going to want to back up."

Charlie is relaxed against the bar, barely moving a muscle, acting like a confrontation isn't beside him. He sips his Glenfiddich.

Beefy Dude laughs, only eyeing me. Trying to unsettle me. It's just frustrating me. Maybe Ben was right. This outcome was a high possibility. It wouldn't have been if we'd just kicked him out in the first place.

My scowl even pains my face. "You want a beer? Fine, but I'm not getting you any liquor. And if your friends want something else, they can come up and get it."

He coughs out a hostile sound. "You fuckin' tiny little bitch." Out of nowhere, he spits at my face—but Eliot blocks me and takes the loogie to the chest. Then he sucker-punches the dickhead. It's the hardest hit I've ever heard in person. His eyes roll back, body slackens, and he's out. Just a sack of flesh and bones on the floorboards.

"'If you wrong us, shall we not revenge,'" Eliot spits on him.

The bar erupts.

Beefy Dude's friends rush forward. The Cobalts' bodyguards deescalate. Charlie is just watching me while he casually drinks whiskey.

I'm pinned to the shelf of liquor. Fighting the extreme instinct to flee the skirmish. To block out the commotion, I end up making myself even smaller, sliding to the floor and hugging my knees. The noise is loud. Violent.

"Harriet?"

I flinch, my spine digging into the cabinet.

"Hey, it's me," Ben says gently. He's squatting in front of me, then sits, breaking his legs apart so I fit between them. He shields me in a way. His body curves toward mine like he's the castle walls and I'm the porcelain inside. No one has ever treated me like this. No one has ever tried to protect me from harm.

Except him.

I hear a *chair* clattering. "Ben..." *You were right.* His gaze is tender on me, and he cups the base of my neck, feeling my rapid pulse. His palm slides down to my heart above the top of my breast. It makes me take a much-needed deeper breath.

"You know the funny thing about tornados," he whispers, "the eye is so...very...calm." His voice becomes a drug, lulling my body. "So among all this destruction, there is peace at the center. And it's not hard for me to reach with you." I ease even more. "You feel that?" he breathes.

I do. "Only with you," I murmur softly.

His palm slides against my cheek, holding me. "Only with you," he says back, his chest rising with breath, and I can't even tell how long we're on the floor. How long he just *sits* with me while his security detail clears the bar.

Time moves differently with Ben. Months are millenniums, only then to be tortured with the knowledge that every era has an end. He is the Golden Age, a period of growth and springtime, where life flourishes, where nature and man are uncorrupted and good. Ovid called it the Eternal Spring, but even the season everlasting had a final chapter. It broke into four. Made way for harder times, for selfishness and greed.

I don't want to move onto the Silver Age.

I'm not ready. Will I ever be ready? "Ben," I whisper, his blue eyes already caught on mine. "Are you in trouble?"

He's confused.

"Is someone blackmailing you?" I ask.

"No," he whispers, peeks over his shoulder, then back at me. "My brothers think that?"

I nod, more tensed, but he never shies away from me. He's only pulling closer. "You're not being coerced to leave, are you? Should I be calling the cops, please tell me the truth—?"

"I'm *choosing* to leave," he interjects, but each word sounds pained in his throat. "This is my choice. No one is making it for me. No one is threatening me."

Why does that hurt worse? Maybe because if some fuckwad were messing with him, the solution is so clear. His dad hires some hot shot lawyer, takes down the criminal, and Ben is set free.

Then he'd stay in New York with me.

He stares hard at the cupboard behind my shoulders. "Do they know I'm broke?" He glances at me. His chest collapses in a panicked, anxious breath.

I open my mouth. "I...didn't...they just kind of got it out...and I couldn't—"

"It's okay," he says softly, full of understanding, but I can tell this is a secret he never wanted them to have. "I told you they're relentless." His eyes redden. "It's part of why I love them so much."

I try to exhale slowly. "I'm sorry—"

"It's not your fault. *It's okay.*" I think he's trying to reassure himself too. "I knew my family interrogating you for answers was a possibility."

I speak very hushed. "I didn't tell them you're going to the woods without me and that I'm not excited about losing my best friend."

"You aren't losing me."

"You say that, Ben, but writing to you isn't the same as you being beside me."

He thinks this over for a few seconds, then his phone buzzes. He checks a text, and his smile begins to peek. "Well, Happy Birthday,

Harriet Fisher." His eyes brighten like a cloudless blue sky. "You're going to the Honors Halloween party."

"What? No way!" My voice pitches in pure shock.

He hands me his phone, and I read the personal invite from Guy Abernathy. My jaw is on the fucking floor.

"He invited me by full name," I mutter. "He said I'm a strong candidate. Holy shit, I get a plus-one."

Ben runs his hands up my arms. "Who you taking, Fisher?"

I love how he threads his fingers into my hair and holds my head. "I'll have to check in with my long list of friends."

"I better be number one."

The only one. I can't stop smiling.

FORTY

HARRIET FISHER

"You came with Ben Cobalt, right? Is Charlie Cobalt here too?" a brunette with clear-framed glasses asks while Monster Mash blasts.

It's the *fourth* time tonight I've been asked if I brought Charlie to the Honors House's Halloween party. As if I can speed dial the eldest Cobalt boy and have the power to conjure him *anywhere*. He wouldn't even accept a blow job from me.

My cheeks flame thinking about it. "Uh, no. Just Ben." That Cobalt boy is currently off grabbing me a glass of punch from the bar—which I wouldn't be able to tell you *where* it is. I got lost as soon as I entered the massive white-brick building.

The Honors House truly is a stunner with its four stately marble columns and wraparound porch, decked out tonight with cobwebs and six-foot skeletons. Decorations aside, I've never been somewhere and thought, *this is where I want to be*. But as I passed each room with oak-paneled walls and a cozy, academic atmosphere, this place has felt especially made for me.

I don't *want* to feel that way.

Fifty people are at this party. Eleven of whom are already in the Honors House, and they're vetting the rest for their twelfth and final spot. My goal seems out-of-reach, especially when I was only granted this invitation because Ben worked his extrovert magic. He wouldn't tell me how exactly he did it, but I'm beginning to suspect it might have something to do with Charlie. Maybe?

Especially when the brunette says, "When Charlie shows up, can you just…nudge him my way? I'm a polyglot too, and I think we'd really hit it off—oh, shit, I haven't even introduced myself." She passes her punch to her left hand to hold out her right. "I'm Venus, yes like the planet, and I'm a third year at the Honors House." I figured she was a member because she's not wearing a name tag on her shirt.

All guests have them.

Mine is stuck on a red-and-white striped T-shirt. My bangs are blown out in Farrah Faucet waves, and these red shorts are *seriously* riding up my ass. I'm not in love with the '70s Slasher Summer Camp theme for this Halloween party. But it's my own damn fault for wearing hotpants when I could have been like Venus and chosen high waisted bell-bottoms and a comfy floral blouse with bell-sleeves.

Luckily, I'm not in danger of being booted from Honors House contention because of the short-shorts. I saw a member wearing a bikini top and a pair of cut-offs, so I don't think they're *that* stuck-up. This is still college.

Venus's words ring in my head as I shake her hand. *When Charlie shows up.* Is he showing up? Did I miss this memo? "Sure," I say, not even knowing if I'm lying. "I'll give him a nudge."

Her white skin goes rosy at the prospect. "Thank you." She grins excitedly. "And of course, I know all about you through your application. I love how you got into Dr. Venison's lab. She is a notorious stickler for only accepting seniors. You must be something special."

I nod, my neck stiff. At a loss for words. I don't know what to say. Agree with her and sound like a pompous jerk? Or downplay and risk coming across as a humble bragger, especially with my scowly face? Ugh, I wish I knew what to do.

"Punch." Ben appears beside me carrying a paper cup of pink liquid. What I hope contains three ingredients and not ten that'll make me barf, but I spy the Skittles and think, *this is my kind of drink*. Candy is my weakness. And the floating ping-pong eyeball is a nice spooky touch.

I take the punch, grateful for the perfectly timed interject. Being around Ben is like that. He has perfect fucking timing. He turns to Venus. "I just learned this is a plastic-free house, and I'm impressed. I'm going to have to bring your ways to Kappa Phi."

Venus snorts. "Those guys would rather fuck a landfill than give up their Solo cups."

I laugh. Okay, I think I could like it here.

Ben's smiling too. "I believe it." His hair is extra fluffy tonight, teased with the blow dryer, and his '70s vintage gym shorts are just as short as *mine*. The green fabric really leaves nothing to the imagination. I'm not the only one who's noticed.

Even Venus peers down at his dick.

Ben gives no shits. He knows he's packing, and the fact that he's 1.) not self-conscious and 2.) not cocky about being well-endowed is somehow more attractive. I've blushed way too much tonight, and I've been telling myself to focus on his white ringer tee instead. It says Camp Crystal Lake Counselor, an homage to *Friday the 13th*.

Still, I have trouble not imagining Ben thrusting inside me. I get hot just picturing his erection between my legs. Our sex quest has yet to be completed. Fall midterms and his hovering brothers have been majorly in the way since the bar fiasco. Ben could sense my exam stress, and he hasn't wanted to be a reason I fail a course.

So right now, I can't even reminisce on the reality of Ben fucking me. This is purely a tormenting fantasy.

I'm thwarted out of my carnal thoughts when a girl in pink overalls rushes over and grabs Venus's arm. "Xander Hale is here."

Venus lets out a soft gasp. "He actually made it?"

"Wait," Ben holds out a hand. "Xander *Hale* is here?"

I feel unsteady on my feet, and I haven't even taken a sip of my punch. Am I competing for an Honors House spot with Xander fucking Hale? I might as well go home.

"Yeah, his friend is a candidate," Venus tells us.

His friend.

Okay, so maybe I'm not competing against Xander. But I'm assuming the friend in question is Easton Mulligan, and is he any better? He's a chess champion *and* Xander Hale's best friend. In my head, being *Ben Cobalt's* friend trumps being Xander's, but I know not everyone feels that way. I am so fucking biased.

By the deep frown contorting Ben's face, I think he's gauging the worrisome levels of tonight. His hand slips to the small of my back as Venus and Pink Overalls hightail it down the hall.

"Isn't Halloween a Hale thing?" I ask Ben. "Since it's *the* Loren Hale's birthday. Xander's dad." I realize how this sounds. "Whiiiich is your uncle." I nod to myself. "You know this already, but okay, last I talked to Xander, he said he might go home to celebrate with the fam."

"Yeah, sometimes we all do, but my uncle just had a big fiftieth last Halloween. So this year is more lowkey. There isn't a giant party. Everyone in New York stayed here." Ben is grimacing at a thought.

"This is bad, right?" I ask him into a sip of punch. My prospects of being an Honors House member have shot downward.

He expels an annoyed breath. "Why wouldn't Easton say anything about applying for the Honors House? We see him at Board Game Club."

I shrug. "It's not like I mentioned it to him." I wrack my brain. "I don't know if I've even told Xander…"

Ben's brows catapult. "Really? It's been your biggest goal since the start of semester."

"I don't advertise my goals on loudspeaker. You know…in case I *don't* achieve them. And that reminds me, is Charlie showing up?"

His hand drops off my back to skate through his hair, smoothing down the wavy strands. "No. I lied and told Guy Abernathy that I could get Charlie to come. It sealed the deal for your invite. But I'm going to make an excuse for Charlie, don't worry about it. It won't look poorly on you." His eyes flit down the hall. He touches my shoulder. "I'm going to go find Xander and clear things up. You...mingle."

"Mingle," I say into a nod. "Right." I do need to pull my weight here. Ben can only do so much, and I need to remember this is an interview masquerading as a Halloween party.

He peels away from my side to venture down the hall, and I meander through the different rooms—a den with a roaring fireplace, a two-story library, an art room filled with pottery wheels and easels, a study room with four giant whiteboards—trying to find one of the eleven members. *Hopefully* not all of them are clustered around Easton and Xander.

Slipping into the kitchen, I encounter a small group huddled around a plate of cookies, which I am immediately told are marijuana cookies. The two Honors House members are *baked* when they greet me.

Elijah and Kiki seem open to chatting with me, and I do my best for what feels like twenty minutes. They were both valedictorians at their private schools. Kiki is an aerospace engineering major and has been dreaming of working for NASA since she was five. Elijah has his sights on a doctorate degree in theoretical physics. It's in his genes, he tells me. His grandfather was nominated for a Nobel Prize in physics for discovering the surface plasmon.

I feel underequipped here. I've never talked about myself like they're talking about themselves. So easily listing off their accolades and goals as if they're chatting about their favorite books. And I won't lie—they sound pretentious as hell. Boastful. Maybe even vain, but it's not rubbing me the wrong way.

A fine line exists between confidence and arrogance. I wish I just didn't give a fuck about accidentally overinflating myself. They clearly don't.

Not caring what other people think is a mightier drug than the pot cookies. I'd love to be high on it.

"You're a sophomore and you're only eighteen. How did that happen?" Elijah turns the conversation on me. The spotlight both welcome and unwelcome at the same time. *This is good, just don't scowl.* I work my face into what I hope is a gentle smile. "I turned nineteen a couple weeks ago, actually."

"Happy belated birthday." Kiki raises a cookie in cheers with a stunningly beautiful smile. She's Black and has dark brown skin, entrancing hazel eyes, plus the height of a supermodel.

"Thanks." I take a larger breath and try to maintain eye contact. Neck aches. "I skipped the fifth grade."

"That's cool," Kiki says after a bite. "I skipped sixth and seventh."

Another candidate named Sanders pipes in, "I didn't have to skip any grades. My parents sent me to a magnet school. I was, thankfully, challenged from the start."

"Yeah, but which Ivies did you get into?" Elijah asks.

"Dartmouth and Brown." Sanders lists, sliding his fingers through his pretty boy brown hair. He's olive-skinned and a little on the lanky side. "And then the Southern Ivies, of course, Duke. Vanderbilt."

My pulse races, and my eyes sink to the plate of cookies. Being stoned sounds exceptionally helpful right now. Kiki sees me staring. "Take one." She pushes the plate toward me.

"I shouldn't..."

"It's just a little weed," Elijah says, much shorter than Sanders and Kiki, so I find myself looking at him. "Last time Guy made them extra strong, and we all passed out. Learned from our mistakes."

Swiping a chocolate chip cookie from the plate, I take a nibble. It's disgusting. It tastes like the inside of a rotted tree. I keep chewing because spitting it out will likely make Elijah and Kiki throw my application in the garbage can.

They start talking about the new science library being built on campus, and I struggle to add any helpful commentary. I just nod. Hoping that maybe my presence is enough. Sanders speaks over Kiki a couple times to boast about several engineering competitions he won, and he's totally not picking up on Kiki's side-eye.

I devour the cookie and wash it down with a big gulp of punch. I have very little experience in recreational drugs, especially edibles, so I'm hoping this shit kicks in soon and eases my nerves.

A candidate named Grace brushes off cookie crumbs from her racerback tee, matched perfectly with brown corduroy shorts. "My parents are both anesthesiologists at Johns Hopkins," she says. "So I'm fully expected to join the 'family business'." She uses finger quotes. "They had a friend who I'm shadowing at Metropolitan Medical."

The cookie *has not* kicked in. I repeat: THE COOKIE HAS NOT KICKED IN.

My blood runs cold. My pulse accelerates. A ringing begins in my ears. It was easy not to feel panicky about my medical school prospects when I was listening to Kiki and Elijah talk because they're not pre-med.

But hearing that Grace has found a shadowing position at Metropolitan Medical Hospital here in New York—something I haven't been able to land—is wrecking my self-confidence in a single instant.

You'd think being around other pre-med people would fuel a sense of camaraderie, but it only surfaces the big, stressful reminder of what more I could be doing and how much smarter I could be.

I hate this fucking feeling.

Grace continues, "Add that with four clubs, volunteering, undergrad research, and I think I have my bases covered for med school. Just have to kick ass on the MCAT."

"We have great tutors for that at Honors House," Kiki says. "Pre-med is the main focus for about half the members here."

"That's amazing," Grace says wistfully. "I could really use the extra support."

The cookie/punch combo unsettles my stomach. "Where are your bathrooms?" I ask Elijah. He lists off a few directions, and as I slip away, I hear him say, "Does she always look mad?"

I stop right outside the door where I can easily eavesdrop.

"I think she's kind of cute," Kiki replies. "Like a fun-sized pre-med grumpy Barbie." I rarely wear much pink. Red, definitely. So the only Barbie thing about me has to be my blond hair. Thanks to a five-buck boxed dye.

"She's pre-med?" Grace's tone has the same competitive freeze that runs through my blood. "Do you know what her extracurriculars are?"

"Not off the top of my head. But she's in Dr. Venison's lab."

"Fuck," Grace curses.

That shouldn't cause me to smile. But it does. Yeah, maybe that makes me an asshole, but I don't care tonight. I leave the wall before they say something that plummets my self-esteem. I'm going to nurture this surge of confidence like a fragile seedling. Channel Ben's green thumb ways.

Continuing down the hall, it doesn't take me long to forget Elijah's directions.

I most definitely took a wrong left-turn somewhere. I'm about to retrace my steps when I pass one of the many little study lounges. Alcoves nestled beside the full-length windows. A cobweb-strewn bookcase and club chairs accent the intimate space. Purple and orange multicolored lights wrap around a fireplace mantel, and my heart shoots to my throat when I spot Ben.

He's facing away from the hall, angled toward the bookshelf and a girl.

A girl.

I don't have to be good at reading body language to see he knows her. It's the way he stands close to her with little visible distance, the way his hands move passionately as he talks, the way his head dips down to be more at eyesight. To be closer.

She's taller than me. Maybe by five inches, making their height difference not as awkwardly obvious as mine and Ben's.

Her dark sandy blond hair flows into a loose braid. A rust-orange satin, cowl-neck top is tucked into a pair of high-waisted denim jeans.

My throat dries. There's no need to be jealous. She's just a girl. He can talk to girls. *I should introduce myself,* I think. But my feet root to the ground, an invisible force seizing my muscles. My resolve. The way Ben starts to look at her, raw concern in his blue eyes, devastates every inch of me.

He touches her shoulder—and I can't watch anymore.

I slip away from the alcove, walking dizzily toward…somewhere else. My head feels far too light, and I wonder if the pot has finally hit me. I really hope it has.

FORTY-ONE

BEN COBALT

It's always been easy to explain my relationship to Winona Meadows to other people.

She is my cousin.

She was my best friend.

But how do I explain the girl in front of me?

Vada Lauren Abbey is not blood related to me, but she's related to the Hales *and* the Meadows. We grew up together. Almost *every* family function—she was there. But she's been more my little sister's friend than she's ever been mine. And I didn't start the night thinking I'd see her here. I didn't start the *month* thinking I'd cross paths with Vada, since she's supposed to be at a boarding school in Upstate New York.

So when I found her standing next to Xander and Easton, I thought I was seeing a mirage. A figment of my imagination. Because there was no way on this planet Earth that Vada came to a Halloween party filled with college students without Winona by her side.

The fact that she was tagging along with *Easton* had me seeing fucking red. Did he invite her here? To a college party? Is he out of his mind?

I didn't start shit with him and cause a scene. The temptation was real, but I'm *Harriet's* plus-one. It'll destroy me if I'm the reason she gets rejected.

So I pulled Vada away. Found a quiet corner where we could talk. We currently stand between a bookshelf and a window, the thick velvet drapes drawn shut.

"You shouldn't be here right now." My voice is a low, angry whisper. "You're *seventeen*."

She glowers. "What are you my dad now, Ben?"

"No, I'm your friend."

"Wow, *wow*." Her aquamarine eyes widen like I've been huffing glue. "Some friend you are. You're never even around. You don't call. You don't check-in. I don't know what we are, but we're not *friends*." Hurt pinches her face. Loose strands from her braid touch her lashes, annoying her enough that she starts redoing her entire hair. Taking out the dark sandy pieces. Starting the braid over.

She has road rash on her forearms. From falling off a dirt bike. She's a BMX racer, but she's been trying out motocross, apparently.

For months. I had no clue.

If I were her friend, maybe I would've. So yeah, she's right.

I skate a hand through my hair, my chest rising and falling. It shouldn't be this painful, but I'm trying not to leave shattered pieces behind. I want everyone happy and whole and this…this is so far from that.

"Does your dad know you're here?" I question.

She snaps the hair-tie at the end of her braid. "Does *your* dad know you don't have a bodyguard on you right now?"

I hate that it's obvious to her Novak isn't with me. That there's not a lingering presence ten feet from my body. It was easy telling Novak that I had no plans for Halloween. The lie should be hard on me, but it's not when Novak betrayed me first.

Since I'm taller than Vada, I keep having to glance down. I hate it. She's wearing some sort of droopy, thin-strapped top with a pushup bra, and it's impossible to avoid glancing at her cleavage. I keep hearing Eliot's voice in my head. I'd been a teenager when I overheard him talking to Tom. "You think Ben and Vada will ever hook up?" Eliot asked conversationally because forbidden gates for him are challenges meant to be unlocked and traversed through.

"They're close in age, no blood relation."

I didn't even hear Tom's response. I walked away quickly, my face on fire. Before that day, I had never thought about Vada *in that way*. But after that...it sits in the forefront. That maybe *other* people in the family have been thinking it. Maybe she has.

I've never asked.

I don't want to know.

Since she answered my question with a question, I decide to keep the trend going. "Did Easton or Xander invite you here?"

She looks pissed.

Vada isn't usually hotheaded. Winona is the firecracker. But Vada—she's a ball-busting, loyal friend who will take the heat but never start it. Our family says Winona is the one who leads, Vada follows, and from my perspective, that is true.

It's also been true that Winona has always followed me, and I stopped letting her. Honestly, I didn't consider what that meant for Vada. How she'd be affected, but I should've. It's just another domino I've struck down. Another person I've hurt.

I try a new question. "Are you Easton's date?"

Blush ascends her cheeks, but I can't tell if it's from embarrassment, bashfulness, or ire. "Why do you care?"

I nip this really fast. "I'm not jealous of him," I state flat-out, point-blank. "Easton or Xander—whoever brought you here— should *not* have. You're a high schooler."

"You were in high school not that long ago. Why are you acting like you're so much older?"

I grind my jaw. *Because I am*, I want to say.

Because Winona, Vada, Kinney, and Audrey are *young*. And I don't just mean their ages. They are the *youngest* of our families. We've *all* sheltered them in different ways.

I've loved that Winona sought after it. Reveled in it. Felt freer under the protection our families gave. I've wished my little sister felt the same, but she's counting down to eighteen like every year beforehand is a ball and chain.

I don't know what Vada hopes for. But I'm trying not to patronize her. She's gone through shit I wasn't around for, but I still don't know why she's here. It puts me on edge.

"So it was Xander?" I ask her.

Her reddened cheeks give her away. *It was Easton.*

I nod a couple times.

"I'm friends with Easton," she says with visceral heat. "*Actual* friends. The kind that call and make sure we're not dead."

Confusion draws my brows together. "When did you get so angry?"

"You think you're the *only* one who gets to be mad? I didn't have the luxury of expelling my rage on Tate's cunty face." She steps back in hurt, and I grab her wrist before she can bolt.

Her shoulders slacken, and she waits for me to speak.

"I'm sorry, Vada," I say. "I'm *so* fucking sorry. I'll say it a thousand times until it means something to you. I shouldn't have gone radio silent last year and left you and Winona to deal with those assholes."

She breathes heavily. It takes her a minute to reply. "They're cunts," she mutters. "Not assholes. That's way too nice."

"Yeah, I'd call them that, but you've pretty much trademarked that swear word in the family."

She stares down at her Converse shoes, still upset.

So I ask, "How's boarding school?"

Her eyes well as if she's surprised and grateful for the question.

"Better, I think," she says more softly. "But our school is right next door to Faust, and those guys are next-level egomaniacs. Very dickish. I cannot believe your dad went there."

My brows rise like *seriously*. Her lips lift into a small smile the same time as mine do.

"Fine," she sighs, "that sounds just like him."

I nod more heartily.

She stares at her sneakers again, then scuffs the corner of the rug and sighs out heavier. "Okay, I have a confession to make." Vada can't meet my eyes. I've known her to be shy at times. So this isn't that odd.

If she were Harriet, I would say, *eyes up here, Friend*. I'd probably tilt her chin up, maybe even hold her cheek. There are signals I *never* want to send to Vada, and I overthink my interactions with her to where I end up doing nothing.

"Easton told me about the Halloween party and said how he heard you were invited too. The next day, I asked him if I could be his plus-one."

"You invited yourself," I realize. "Why would you…did Winona—"

"I'm not here on Winona's behalf. She'll be upset I snuck out without her, but she'll understand why I did."

"Why?"

"Audrey wanted me to. I'm here for her."

Jesus. I rub hard at my temple. "You're spying on me for my little sister?"

"She just wanted to know if you had a 'tragic demeanor' or whatever. If you still seem happy in New York. I'm supposed to relay that back to her."

"Yeah, and what will you be relaying?"

"That you're more pissed off I'm here."

"Perfect." I run my fingers through my hair again. "Maybe she won't get any ideas."

Vada chokes out a laugh. "This was *her* idea. She has the wildest plans." She smiles afterward. The tiny gap between her two front teeth caused a lot of teasing when she was younger. Winona used to get in fights with guys over it. To which I would bail her out of and do my best not to throw a punch at those pricks.

It hits me, though, that the first smile I've seen from Vada is for her best friend.

She peeks back at the doorway. "Xander's bodyguard saw me, and I'm positive your snitchy security team will be ratting me out to my parents any minute. I'll be grounded for eternity, so this party is now my funeral. Here lies Vada Abbey, girl who died trying to check on Ben Cobalt."

"For Audrey Cobalt," I add.

"Of course for Audrey. She's one of my best friends." She drags her gaze to the fireplace where a strand of purple and orange lights blink. Her face is baking. "But I probably messed everything up with Easton."

I frown. "How?"

She presses her fingers to her mouth, unsure if she wants to tell me.

"Do I want to know?"

"I've been hooking up with him—when he was a senior at Dalton."

I stare hard at her. "Yeah, I didn't want to know that. Thanks, Vada."

"Well, the benefits part of our friendship has been over for a while. That asshole won't do anything with me while he's in college and I'm still in high school." That actually makes me like Easton a fraction more. "Now everything is too complicated with him. Made more complicated after tonight." She winces. "I constantly choose my friends over what's in my best interest. So yay me."

It's not computing. "What made it more complicated?"

"He knows that I used his invite for the purpose of finding *you*."

Oh this is now making too much sense. Easton has been like a Brillo pad rubbing against my face because he thinks I have a "thing" with Vada. "I will be telling him I'm not into you as soon as I see him. You should do the same."

Her face is bright red, but she nods repeatedly, then we go toward the exit together. At the doorway, she says, "I know I've texted you an embarrassing number of times, but you really should talk to Winona. She hasn't been the same without you in her life. You're the OG sunshine boy, and she's needed your light more than ever. Without you, it's just darker."

I always thought Eliot was the one who leaves an unbearable shadow in his wake.

I'm now more afraid that it's actually been me.

FORTY-TWO

BEN COBALT

I've been spiraling after I split from Vada. Mentally *reeling*.

I can't stick around. *I can't.* Winona will eventually be okay. The absence of me isn't as harmful as the existence. That's what I've come to know.

What happens when I leave Harriet? She has my brothers. She has my family. She won't be cast into a cold, shadowy darkness. Right? Does she need me? Why do I feel like I need her?

No, I've known I need her. Like right now, the urge to be with her is a sledgehammer, and I'm speeding through this massive house trying to find the cutest scowl, the most beautiful brain—so when I do find her, I exhale. *She's here.*

I slow into a music room. Walls soundproofed with padding. Guitars, violins, brass instruments—they all rest in racks near stereo equipment. She's seated on a stool in front of a drum kit, sticks in hand, and my frown takes hold of me.

Why does she look so fucking sad?

"I thought drumming made you happy, Fisher."

Her blue eyes ping up to mine. She opens her mouth, but

nothing escapes. I shut the door gently behind me. Her yellowish blond hair has lost its volume. It lies flat in its usual edgy cut around her delicate face. Strands brush against her striped red and white tee that molds her breasts.

A groan tries to work its way out of me when I see her nipples are hard.

Her knee-high socks and tiny gym shorts have also been driving me up the wall all night. I've always been attracted to her—that's never been in doubt. Why is she upset? It's the question I want answered. Everything else can shut up.

I come closer.

"I haven't played anything yet," she manages to say. I watch her rotate on the spinning stool...away from me.

It's a knife in the gut. "Did I do something?" I ask her, my heart thrashing. "Harriet?"

She whirls back around; her scowl is a complete, pained *grimace*. "You haven't been screwing with me, right?"

"What?" I don't follow. My pulse keeps skipping. I'm losing oxygen with each passing second she's not explaining what I did wrong.

"This hasn't been one elaborate *gotcha*?" Her tone grows stiffer, more defensive. All the walls I'd taken down are being built back up. "Befriend your brother's enemy. Make her fall in love with you. Then make her pay for the bratty email to his bassist, for causing friction in his own band. Should I be expecting to get egged at the end of this, Cobalt boy?"

I can't breathe. "Are you serious?"

Her chin trembles. She looks as demolished as I feel. "Don't break my heart."

"You're breaking mine." I swallow hard. "It's in your hand. I gave it to you at the start. Remember?" Tears begin to fill her eyes, and I add more forcefully, "You know me. I've *never* lied to you. Am I the kind of person who'd manipulate someone over the course of months just to make them feel pain?"

"No," she says immediately, instantly, and I release a breath. "That's why I've been sitting in here going out of my mind. I've lost it, dude. Like, I can't think straight because all my deepest insecurities keep piling, and I'm choking on them."

I barrel toward her on instinct as her face crushes in hurt, but she's not ready to be touched. She recoils a little, and I stop beside the tallest cymbal. "Why do you think I would've tricked you?"

"Do you have a girlfriend?"

What is going on? "That girlfriend would be you...if I wasn't leaving." I suck down raw, blistering pain. *I want to stay.* "I only want to be with you, and I mean that. I've meant *everything* I've ever said." Why...why does she think I have a girlfriend? "If you heard something—it's a lie. They *lied* to you, Harriet."

"I saw it."

My lips part. "There is no way."

"You were like *this close* to that girl." She puts her palm up against her face to demonstrate. "In that study room with the fireplace."

"Oh my God," I gape. "*Harriet.*"

"What?" She goes still, seeing my widened eyes.

"That was *Vada.*"

Her scowl is a confused wince. "The girl squad girl?"

"Yeah, and she's related to the Hales and Meadows. She might not be *my* family by blood, but she is still practically family. I've *never* liked her like you're implying. Never will." She's taking bigger breaths, so I keep going. "I was upset when I saw she was at a college party, and we were arguing about it. Apparently, she came here to spy on me, as requested by my little sister. To see if I have a *tragic demeanor.*" I rest my hands on my waist like I'm embodying Peter fucking Pan. Eliot would be proud. "What do you think? Tragic or not?" I begin to slowly smile.

She's chewing the corner of her lip, emotion still flooding her eyes. She's almost smiling off mine. *Almost.* We're nearly there. To the good place I want to be with her.

I chase after her runaway gaze. "Fisher. Talk to me. Because you haven't taught me CPR yet, I can't save your life without your help."

"I'm a jealous freak, Friend," she chokes out, her nose flaring as she tries not to cry. "Like why would you even want to be with someone who went from zero to a number that doesn't exist?"

"Unknown numbers are cool. I love weird people. I love you." It just comes out. The truth. Her breath hitches, but I add, "And I'm not all there, Friend. I've felt like I'm losing it...all the time. The only thing I've known is that when I'm with you, the confliction, confusion, whatever I'm thinking just doesn't matter. I can breathe. I can admire. I can love." I cradle her gaze. "So if this is your attempt to run me off early, you've failed because..." I lean forward and cup her cheek over the drum kit. "I'm still here."

Harriet takes staggered, uneven breaths, gripping fiercely to my gaze. "Say it again."

I glance at her lips—and I kiss her. It explodes us together. I crash into the fucking cymbal. She elbows a snare drum as our lips meld with a desperate heat. I need to be closer. The craving screams at all my muscles, and to avoid breaking the drum kit, I pick her up and haul her over the instrument and into my chest.

A moan ejects out of her mouth, and I want to devour the pleasured sound. I crush my lips against hers, one hand tangled in the back of her hair, the other cupping her ass. My tongue glides against her tongue, loving the sweet taste of her, loving her vulnerable, overwhelmed reactions to my hands, my lips. I can feel the building heat of her pussy against me, her legs split apart around me. It's a primal urge to want to slide inside her right now, but I don't.

I just kiss her. But it's not really *just* a kiss. It feels like I'm being lit on fire. I'm burning and burning. And I'm not in search of water. I want to fan these flames. I buck her up higher on my body, and a whimpering cry leaves Harriet—a sound I've never heard her make.

Blood rushes to my cock.

Aroused flush coats her cheeks, and she clutches my neck. Hanging on to me as our gazes cling. I hold her at eye-level. Next kiss, I carry her to the wall. Resting her shoulders against it. Then I trail kisses down her cheek, her jaw—spending a longer, hotter beat at her neck. She full-body shakes.

"*Ben*. What the fuck…?" She breaks into a moan.

"*Fuck*," I groan against her nape. I'm careful not to give her a hickey. It's as if every nerve-ending of hers is coming alive from my touch, and it's making me want to smother her until she climaxes. Then I'd do it again, just to see it all over again.

I return to her lips. Holding her soft cheek while I slow the kiss in sensual strokes. She's melting against me, and my muscles flex against her as I control my need and desire. She's allowing me to take her on this journey, and I'm grateful because feeling Harriet lose herself to pleasure in my hands is like inhaling helium. I'm flying high. Fire in the night sky.

A smoldering, blazing star.

"I can't," she gasps for breath, her eyes threatening to roll.

"Let go," I whisper against her lips.

"It's too…much." She chokes on a sudden cry, and I taste the sound against my tongue, then I run my fingers between her thighs. On the outside of her gym shorts. Over her clit, her pussy. She is so fucking wet. It aches my cock.

This does her in—my hand between her legs.

Her whole body convulses against me. I want inside Harriet. I want to feel her pulse and clench around me, but I grit down on my teeth and breathe hot breath through my nose. Keeping her in my arms while she orgasms. She's light to me. I could probably toss her around all day, all night.

Really, I just want to hold her right up against my chest. Press her close. Just like this.

And never let her go.

As she descends off the rippling climax, I take a hand off her ass, just to peel strands of her hair off her reddened lips. Mine sting a little, and my breath is much shallower than hers. I'm pent-up. Doing my best to ignore it. Her fingers slip down to my biceps. I watch her study our bodies, how I have her supported by the backs of her thighs now.

"Good?" I ask her with a rising smile.

"Uh, that was…way better than good." Her cheeks are still flushed. "I've never really enjoyed kissing, but that…holy shit. I could fantasize about that."

"Why fantasize when you can have it?" I kiss her more tenderly, then pull back to see her narrowed eyes softening. I see her thinking. Her mind contemplating weeks from now. "I'm still here."

"I know." She kisses me this time. Deeper, soul-pulling. Her small palms cup my face. I skate my hand into her hair again. I grind against her into the wall, and I'm scared I might lose myself in a round two of *just* kissing.

So I break our lips apart.

I let her catch her breath, then I set her gently on her feet. She tugs down her shorts, and I adjust my erection.

"Dude," her eyes bug at my cock.

I burst into a laugh. "I will fit, Fisher. Basic anatomy. I assume you aced Health Class, smarty-pants."

"Aced it, yeah. Never taken a dick that big though."

"I'll go slow." I nod toward the drum kit. "You want to play?"

She walks back over to the instrument and grabs the sticks off the floor. "I thought you were about to ask if I wanted to be fucked on the drums."

I laugh again. "Yeah, I have to draw the line somewhere"—I peer back to the closed door, thankful for the soundproofing in here—"being caught having sex isn't going to appeal to the nerds. Unlike my kind, who love the notches on the bedposts."

She twirls her drumsticks way fancier than I ever did. "Such a jock." She points a stick at me. "I do need to mention something."

"Okay?" I can't see where this is going.

"Earlier, I ate a pot cookie."

"By choice?" I ask.

"I mean, yeah, no one forced me—and I'm not high." She speaks fast. "I don't think it was strong. I haven't really felt effects, except maybe paranoia."

My smile stretches. "Yeah, I could see that."

"That's the last time I ever eat an edible."

"I've never had one," I admit. "I've never done drugs or wanted to…" I trail off, hearing the creak of the door, and I spin around as a member of the Honors House peeks inside. It's Kiki Kershaw. Her animable smile is on Harriet. She acknowledges me with a shorter wave, and it's about the same curtness I've been gifted by several girls who live here.

They hate Kappa.

For good reason. And the *only* reason I was allowed inside this building is because I made friends with Guy Abernathy before I joined the frat. The president of the Honors House trusts me at least.

"Hey, a bunch of us are going to play volleyball in the pool," Kiki says. "Nine times out of ten it turns into a game of chicken. But it can be pretty fun if you want to join. Just don't get on Elijah's shoulders, he will do anything to win—including throwing you at the opponent."

I don't like imagining her on another guy's shoulders.

Harriet tenses a little bit. "Uh, that's all right. You go ahead."

"You sure?" Kiki asks. "The water is heated."

"Yeah, I was wondering if it's okay if I can play?"

"The drums?"

"Yeah, I mean, is that cool? I know how to play, so I won't beat them up or—"

"It's totally fine," she interjects with a growing smile. "That's really awesome that you play. I didn't see that on your application."

She raises her shoulders in a stiff shrug. "I never played for a band, not even at school."

"It's a hobby," she nods robustly. "Hobbies aren't something to leave off the resume. I'll tell Guy. He'll find it cool too. No one's very good at the drums here." She sneaks a kinder smile at Harriet, then eyes me suspiciously before she exits.

"Left off the drumming talent, did you?" I tsk. "Fisher." I shake my head in mock disapproval.

"Cobalt fam would never," she teases.

"No, we would not. You have to pack that thing, even with the one-legged sack race you barely won in third grade."

"Shucks, I forgot that one too."

I smile at her. "I thought I was teaching you our ways?"

"Slowly but surely, Cobalt boy." Her lips twitch upward, then go flat. "I can't swim."

I'm rigid. "You never learned?"

She nods. "My parents fought over which classes to put me in, then the divorce happened, and they totally forgot about it, so the story goes."

She can't swim.

I'm rushed all the way back to the frat party. *Fuck.* I scrape my hand through my hair and suck a breath through my nose. "Harriet…" She was almost thrown into the pool. "I thought you were terrified of being tossed in the water at the KPD party because you were wearing a white shirt." That, coupled with the attention it'd bring—it didn't register that it was anything deeper.

"Flashing a mob of people would've freaked me out, and I didn't like being that dickhead's entertainment. But I was mostly stuck on the life-or-death situation."

My jaw tics.

"Don't burst a blood vessel. I'm alive. You saved me," she says flatly.

"You could've *drowned*." I smear a hand down my face and exhale the heat. "If it makes you feel any better, I can't drive. Ever since the car crash where I was behind the wheel…I just can't put my foot on the pedal without violently shaking."

She eases more. "So I'm not the only scaredy cat?"

"Definitely not." I can't stop looking at her. "Maybe one day…" I trail off. *Maybe one day I'll teach you how to swim. You can help me drive again.* One day isn't going to come. I can't see a way there. I don't even want to ruin this moment with her and reignite the painful search.

Harriet twirls her sticks, then nods to me. "Put a song on for me, and I'll play it on drums."

"Which one?" I take out my phone.

"'She' by Green Day. I'll count you down."

I grin. "All right." I find the song in my music library. "I'm ready when you are, rock star."

She sticks her tongue between a finger-V, and I laugh harder. Her scowl makes way for a scrunched smile, and I already know I'm her biggest fan. She doesn't even need to move.

"Three, two, one," she nods, and I press play.

The song is an angsty rock anthem, so perfectly *her*. As soon as the melody strikes, she takes off. Moving her drumsticks at an expert, rhythmic pace I've never seen. Instantly, I'm entranced. With her. With how her body thrashes to the music, lost in the powerful beat. Eyes closed as she taps the drums in quick, rapid succession.

Her head bangs, blond hair going wild. Strands stick to her forehead, and her face pinches in emotion like the song flows through her bones.

Her passion sends me to an exultant state. Her pure, unadulterated love swells emotion in my throat. I'm stunned by all of her, and I watch and tears try to gather. I feel the burn against my eyes. Unable to look away. Still never wanting to—because there is a truth living in the essence of my soul.

I am so deeply in love with her.

She's become the quiet rustle of leaves. She's become the soft soil beneath my feet. She's the cold air that awakens my lungs. The gorgeous light bending through the trees.

She is the planet I've adored and tried to care for, and when I look ahead and see her, I see my entire world. In all its peaceful beauty.

FORTY-THREE

HARRIET FISHER

Kissing Ben has become my favorite activity. From a girl who *never* fantasized about kissing, all my brain does now is cycle through the kisses we've had this past week. The push-me-up-against-the-wall kisses in the storage room at the End of the World. The pick-me-up-in-his-arms kisses when he comes over to my apartment. The bury-his-tongue-in-my-mouth kisses in his building's stairwell.

I've loved every single one.

We aren't an official couple or even technically dating. Not when Ben is still hard stuck on his wilderness plans. He reminds me he's leaving after almost every kiss, which makes me feel like I'm freefalling off a steep cliff. But I get why he does it. He's scared to create any false hope. Not that I ever believed my kissing skills could convince him to stay. I'm not an idiot—I don't even think sex will do the trick. He's adamant he's leaving.

Except…it's November 6th. And he's still here.

He told me it's because of Classical Mythology. He wants to keep the promise he made to be there for the group presentation, which is scheduled for the end of November. So I have less than a month.

Less than one month left with Ben Cobalt unless his brothers convince him to stay in New York.

It's the last thing I think before I put a fist to his apartment door and knock.

Ben opens the door, his hair styled in soft waves and his dark pants slung low on his hips. He's not wearing a shirt, and I can't tell if I'm more distracted by the ridges of his well-defined abs or the way he smells.

Because he smells…amazing. Pine and mint waft off him in the freshest scent. Along with a dizzying musk. His natural man-smell makes me stupidly feral. Like I could bury my face in his washboard abs. Like I could make a fabric softener with that fragrance and spritz it daily on all my clothes and blankets. Like I am obsessed, okay. And maybe it's a little unbecoming. But fuck it, I am obsessed with this guy.

Weirdly, happily, obnoxiously obsessed.

I'm flushing when he smiles down at me and lets me inside.

I rummage through the tote bag on my shoulder. "I have flashcards, B12 supplements, and chocolate-covered espresso beans. The vegan kind." He called me twenty minutes ago to ask for help studying for his Marine Biology exam, and I rushed over here with far too much glee for someone about to have a full night conversing about plankton.

But Ben has *never* asked me to help him study, and he's passed on my offer to help him too many times to count. He's always said, "I don't really care what grade I get." For someone who's planning to drop out of school, I understand that he wouldn't put too much emphasis on passing his classes.

So this newfound interest in studying has blossomed some hope. Maybe his brothers got to him. Maybe he's reconsidering his plans to jet off to Nebraska or South Dakota or the farmlands of Iowa. I still don't know *where* he's going, so my brain keeps placing him in a bunch of random states.

"I also have highlighters in four different colors," I continue. "I figured you probably bought your textbooks instead of rented them which makes it easier because we can just highlight directly on the pages."

He hasn't said anything, and when I glance up, he's smiling down at me like he's absorbing my frantic, study energy with amusement.

"We'll use the B12 and the espresso beans," he finally says. "But I don't think we'll need the flashcards or the highlighters tonight."

I'm about to ask why, but then he leads me farther into the apartment, and my feet stumble to a halt. *Candles.* So many candles flicker on the bookshelves and the windowsills, the lighting far too romantic and moody for just studying.

My eyes go wide. "Friend?"

Ben casually leans against the back of the couch, his hands stuffed in his pockets. His smile reaches his eyes, and all of it—him, the million-dollar apartment, the candles—is *beyond* sexy.

"Fisher," he says my name in a deep husk. "We have the apartment to ourselves."

My fingers lose grip, and I drop the tote to the ground. Shock churning to a wave of excitement. "How?" We've tried for over a month to have alone time here with literally no success. I've been thinking that we might have to settle for Harold or a motel, but this is so epically better.

"It's Wednesday Night Dinner," he explains. "All my brothers are down in Philly...except Beckett. He has rehearsals for *The Nutcracker*, but he said that he'd spend the night at a friend's and give us the place." He winces. "I only told Beck. It was kind of necessary. I didn't think you'd mind."

Beckett Cobalt knows that Ben and I are sleeping together. *Will* be sleeping together. A heat wave courses through me. But I'd much rather Beckett know than not be able to have sex with Ben. If I'm being super honest, I wouldn't care if all his brothers found out. It means he's not trying to sweep me under the proverbial rug, and just Ben sharing this with Beckett makes me feel valued in a way.

"I don't mind," I confirm. "I'm just processing. I thought we agreed the Wednesday Night Dinner strategy wouldn't work." We know this is the *one* night most of his brothers vacate the apartment, but if Ben called in sick or made an excuse about needing to miss dinner, it'd just trigger their concern and make them rush back here to check on him.

"That was before I had Beckett to reinforce my alibi."

"Which is?"

"I'm studying for a Marine Biology exam." He waves a hand toward me. "My study partner just showed up though, so I might get distracted. But who can really blame me?" His eyes drink me in, and a flush ascends my neck.

I can't hide my smile. "So this is official? It's real?"

"Fisher, I did not just light fifty candles for fun."

I take a step forward and stop. "Um...can I use the bathroom real quick?" I motion toward the one down Eliot and Tom's hallway.

"Yeah." He nods, and I try not to run.

When I shut the door, I go into full-on freak-out mode. I sniff my pits. *Fine.* But they surely don't smell like pine *and* mint. I pull at the waistband of my plaid pants and check which underwear I have on today. OhmyGod. I'm wearing my ugly undies. The ones I wear the day before wash. They were once white. Now they're a shade of orangish pink.

I remember there's a hole in the crotch from over-washing them. I should have thrown them out five hundred years ago!

Leaning into the sink, I tap my forehead lightly on the marble. *Idiot.* What do I do? Remove them? I didn't bring my tote bag in here, so where would I even throw them? I could wrap them up in a wad of toilet paper and bury them in the little trash bin by the sink.

But what happens when Ben realizes I'm going commando underneath my pants. Isn't that weirder than wearing old underwear?

My pulse races as I bring my palm up to my mouth and exhale.

I can't tell if my breath stinks. Maybe I should use some toothpaste. I'm sweating. I try to waft my shirt. That's probably causing me to smell.

Why do I even care?

I haven't thought too hard about "preparing" for sex with Ben before. I certainly never gave a shit with past hookups. But this is so far from meaningless sex. And now that I'm smack dab in the moment of it, all I want to do is make sure it's right. Perfect.

There's a soft tap on the door. "Harriet?" Ben asks. "You okay in there? Do you need anything?"

This is stupid. I shouldn't be freaking out. It's *Ben.* He's put his fingers inside of me already. This shouldn't be any different.

Still, my heart hammers in heavy thumps as I open the door. Ben has an elbow propped on the frame, filling the space in a casual confidence that is way too hot for this room.

I'm going to sweat.

His concern fills his blue eyes as he stares down at me. "What's wrong?"

"I didn't prepare for this," I tell him. Honesty just pours out of me because he makes me feel comfortable enough to release the truth.

Realization washes over his face. "Do you…need to prepare?" His gaze does a full body examination, and I'm too turned on to even think clearly.

I just say, "I wore the wrong underwear."

His lips lift into an amused smile. "What about them is wrong?" He's staring at my crotch like he has X-ray vision.

Why is that so attractive? Why am I glowering? "They have holes," I admit. "I was contemplating ditching them in the trash so you wouldn't see them."

His brows rise. "Holes in your panties sound convenient for tonight, Fisher."

My lips part in arousal. "As enticing as that *does* sound, I'm really not looking forward to being fucked in the ugliest panties I own."

He nods once. "Then take them off."

His eyes don't leave mine, and the way he says those words like they're such a simple request quickens my breath in a heady need.

"Now?" I ask.

He nods again. "We have the entire apartment," he reminds me. "Take off your ugly panties, Friend."

I lick my dried lips. He's going to watch me do this? That turns me on even more. Still filling the doorway, he watches me as I unbutton my red plaid pants.

Slowly, I shimmy them down, hooking my thumbs in my panties to lower them with my pants. It's one movement, then I'm standing in nothing but my cropped tee and a pair of socks.

Ben doesn't glance at my bare pussy. His eyes are on mine. "Better?" he asks.

I squeeze my legs together, wetness building between them. "Problem solved."

"Good." He crosses the threshold and grabs me by the ass, lifting me up around his waist so swiftly and effortlessly. Spreading my legs around him is different this time now that my lower half is nude and he's shirtless. Can he feel how wet I am? My whole body thrums when his large palm slides against the back of my neck, his fingers threading my hair, and he cups my head in a protective, assertive grip. Then his mouth plants on mine in a scorching, ravenous kiss.

He has to be the world's best kisser. It's unreal how each one sends shockwaves through my whole body and stokes a fire in me.

His tongue slips into my mouth in a sensual beat, and he brings me to the edge of the sink, resting my bare bottom on the cold marble. His kisses are devouring and hungry, and I'm equally starved. My hands slide against his back, feeling his warm skin.

His lips move to the edge of mine, then to my cheek, then down to the nape of my neck—then he drops to his knees.

I let out a rasped breath. "*Ben.*" My knees knock closed, and he places a large palm against my inner thigh, gently spreading me back open.

His gaze meets mine. "I've been dreaming of this for months, Fisher. I *need* to go down on you."

I'm so wet I worry I might be dripping on the marble. "Will you still put your dick in me after?"

He frowns. "Yeah, of course. Why wouldn't I?"

"I don't know…the order of things…this is a first…so…" I nod a little and tuck some of my blond hair behind my ear.

"Your first time being eaten out?"

"Yeah."

He groans into a graveled noise of arousal, his hands still planted on either side of my thighs. "This is my favorite thing to do, so if there's a next time, we're going to do it again…and again. If that's okay with you?"

If there's a next time. There are no guarantees with Ben, but I don't really care right now. I can replay this moment for eternity. Maybe the memory will be enough.

"Should I answer that after I learn what it feels like?" I ask. "What if I hate it?"

He smiles. "Challenge accepted, Fisher."

I gasp as his head disappears between my thighs. The warmth of his tongue hits my swollen clit, and heat spreads through my entire body. *Fuckfuckfuck*. A moan escapes my lips, and my fingers slide on the cold marble to try and find grip.

He sucks gently on my bundle of nerves, and my thighs quiver. "*Fuck*," I curse.

His tongue slips inside me, and my body unbuckles. Knees lock, legs shake, muscles tighten in all the best ways. His fingers dig into the soft flesh of my thigh, reminding me that he's doing all of this with just his mouth. The thought draws another strangled cry out of me. I clutch at his hair, my fingers twisting in the brown strands. When his tongue flicks against my clit, he lifts his eyes to catch my gaze.

He watches me moan his name. Moan another curse. His mouth glistens with my cum, but it's the arousal clouding his blue eyes that soaks me even more. He dips his head back down and sucks the sensitive bud. I lose it and come on him.

He grips me tight and laps at the wetness I create.

I really, *really* understand why they call it being eaten out now.

My chest rises and falls heavily, and he stands fully to his feet. He wipes his mouth with the back of his arm, which is somehow just as sexy as when he was between my legs. He looks me over. "And?"

"Yes," is all I manage to say.

He smiles and grabs me underneath my bottom, picking me up again by my bare ass. I'm still trying to catch my breath, and I press my forehead to the crook of his neck. He carries me into the living room, and the warm flickering candles tug at my heart.

Romantic.

So fucking romantic.

Waiting for this was worth it. And he knew that. I would have for sure been fine with fucking in a motel, maybe because I didn't know what I'd be missing.

The mattress is already pulled out from the couch. Fluffy pillows and cozy blankets strewn over it. Ben gently rests me down, and the frame squeaks as he kneels on the mattress. My breath cages when he grips the bottom of my cropped tee and pulls it over my head.

Cold air hits the tops of my breasts, and I'm suddenly so aware of our height difference. I've never slept with anyone remotely as tall as him. "I assume I'll need to be on top," I breathe out in a raspy voice as I watch him fish the button in his pants through the hole.

His gaze lifts slowly, hooded underneath thick lashes, and his brows knit together.

"Because of our height difference," I explain.

Ben smiles. "I knew why you were *assuming*," he says. "I'm just trying to decide if I should pop up some visuals for you before we do this because you're not going to be on top."

My face heats. "I don't need visuals."

"You sure?" he asks, genuinely sincere as he reaches behind me. "I'd rather you be comfortable than in your head about it." His fingers snap off the clasp to my black bra like he's done this before. His experience is a turn on. I hope my inexperience with tall guys who take charge isn't such a turn off—but that thought vanishes instantly when I see heady waves of attraction pool in his eyes.

I bite the inside of my bottom lip before saying, "I trust you."

He expels a hot aroused breath, then removes a square foil packet from his pocket. He bites down on the corner of the wrapper, the unripped condom dangling from his mouth, as he sheds the rest of his clothes. His pants. His boxer-briefs. They crumple in a heap on the floor.

We're both entirely fucking naked, and his eyes haven't left my breasts now that my bra is gone. Mine haven't left his thick cock. Holy fuck, okay, *yeah,* he's even bigger than I imagined, most likely due to his current erection that's been freed from the confines of fabric. *That is going to be inside me.*

My pussy aches as if pleading for it.

I'm a puddle of need. I lean back against the firmer couch cushions that mimic a headboard. He grips my ankle, then slides me down fully supine on the mattress. *He knows exactly what to do, Harriet.* That thought is like a slow drip of Valium, washing away all worry about the next steps. I love not having to lead this expedition.

He takes one of the pillows and fits it underneath my lower back. Then he reaches up and rips the condom's wrapper with his teeth. He spits the sliver of foil off to the side, then his gaze drops back down to my breasts. He says, "I'm sorry. I have to—" He abandons fitting on the condom to put his lips to my perked nipple, as if he can't wait any longer.

I let out a whimper as he sucks against the bud, kisses, laps his tongue against me. Holy shit, *holy shit.* My legs rattle, and my back tries to arch into him. I twitch as he toys with the sensitivity. Oh…

my God. I'm busty, so when he squeezes my other breast, he has a soft handful of me, kneading in a firm grip. His undeniable, impatient craving for my body has my head spinning. My toes curling.

Ragged breaths leave my lips. "You're a tits guy?" I ask, practically panting.

He sucks my nipple harder, and a moan scratches my throat. When he releases hold of my breasts, he says, "I'm a Harriet guy. Everything about you turns me on. Tits. Ass. Ears." He pinches my prominent ear that sticks out of my hair. "Nose." He bops a finger on the tip of my nose. "Lips." His thumb caresses my soft bottom lip, teasing it from entering my mouth.

He pulls away before he does and plants his hand on the mattress beside my head. "What about you?"

"I'm a dick girl," I tell him.

He's full-on grinning. "I knew it."

"Yeah?" I try not to smile. "What gave me away?"

"Oh, all those times I caught you looking at my dick, Friend."

I heat. "I did not—"

"You did." He fixes my bangs so they're not in my eyes. "I liked it. I like when you look." Confirmation of that settles me into a toxic mixture of needy impatience.

He must be feeling the same unsettled desire because he leans back, still on his knees, but more angled against his heels. He pinches the tip of the condom.

"I can help," I tell him. "I've put condoms on guys before." Instantly, I inwardly grimace. I don't think he wants to know about my past sexual exploits *now*.

His eyes flash to me. "I trust you," he says, casually. Totally not put off by my words. "But I'm going to do this myself if that's okay? I've had one too many girls rip it when they try, and I don't have the restraint to wait to grab a new one with you."

I nod, new feelings starting to swarm me that have *nothing* to do with arousal.

It's a sudden realization of how comfortable this is. How he makes me feel like I could never say the wrong thing or mess this up in any way. Am I ever going to feel like this again with anyone else? Do I even want to?

I brush away the onslaught of emotion to focus on him rolling the condom along his hard shaft. He lifts me by the waist, my legs dangling on either side of his hips. My shoulders remain on the mattress, and my back still has the support of the pillow. I have an amazing view of his carved muscles and body while he's on his knees. It's not hard to meet his gaze either.

His eyes latch on mine, watching my reaction as he grips his cock and guides himself in me. The tip presses against my opening, racing my pulse in anticipation, then he drives more of himself inside.

Oh...God. A grimace overtakes my face, pain flaring for a quick second. Ben abruptly stops moving. He waits, gauging my expression.

"I'm fine." My voice is more hostile than I like.

His lips curve. "You're the one who said you've never taken anything as big as me. I'm just being careful. Next time I'll stretch you with my fingers first."

Next time.

His eyes tear away from mine, and I wonder if he's aware of his slip. He focuses on easing himself deeper. When he's just a little farther in, he lets go of his cock and flexes into me so slowly, so gradually. There's no more pain. Only a fullness that ekes out more carnal need.

My lips break apart as a moan ejects the same time he groans under his husky breath, "You are...so fucking tight."

I think you're just massive, I want to reply, but I literally cannot form words right now.

Ben is in me.

Ben is in me.

Ben is inside *me.*

I can't decide if it's the words or the actual feeling or the *visual* that ignites my body and flames my already heightened arousal. The fullness of taking him, the fact that his dick is disappearing into me—it's hot in itself, but then I look up and see his caring, loving blue eyes stroking over my whole body, my whole being, while he has my hips in two hands.

I'm too overcome to even consider moving.

While he's knelt and keeping me still, he thrusts in slow, melodic movements like rolling waves. He might as well be fisting my pleasure in his hand. He has full control. His throaty grunts intoxicate me. My breaths shorten.

The friction he creates inside me is gathering so much heat. I curl my fingers into the bedsheets, one of my arms reaching above my head and gripping a pillow. That seems to affect Ben—his muscles flex and a knotted, masculine sound scratches out of his throat.

Oh fuck, *oh fuck*. I cry out, not sure how long *I'm* going to last.

He has all of me. While on his knees, he also has perfect view of my jostling body each time he flexes forward and thrusts inside, and I love how he's staring at me. I love every time our eyes catch there is only a bottomless sense of longing and emotion.

Sweat glistens on our skin. Candlelight flickers over us.

He breathes through his nose, pushing his dampening hair back, then he pulls me by the hips toward him, nearly filling me to the brim. He starts making deep, short thrusts that feel too intimate, too fucking intense—like he has reached into my soul and constructed a dwelling there.

I whimper, so on the verge.

It feels like he's pounding into me. I can barely breathe.

He stretches an arm and clutches my cheek, as if saying, *I'm taking care of you. You can let go.* He's demolished all my gates, all defenses. I am just the earth around the moat. Relishing as the cool wind sweeps over me and pricks my hot skin.

What kind of sex is this? I think it right as I shudder into a climax. Whoa, whoa, whoa...I dizzy.

Being naked in Ben's hands is another favorite thing of mine, I realize. Because the way he holds me, looks at me, cares for me like I'm his to protect and cherish and pleasure is my ultimate high.

I barely come down when he lifts me upward. He brings me toward his chest so I'm sitting on his lap—his dick still so deep in me. The movement ousts a rough moan from my lips. I'm quaking. Quivering. *He's not done.* We're not done.

Yes, fuck *yes.*

Ben arches up into me with skill and experience, and his hand slides to the back of my head. Our eyes lock onto each other in another intense, intimate moment. We're so close. His chest against my breasts. The world falls away, and his pace slows in a more sensual rhythm.

My heart thumps harder. I grip his neck with one hand. His waist with the other. Trying not to collapse backward from the way he drives into me. But he's strong. He keeps me firmly on him.

Our breaths merge into the same ragged, hot tempo. He dips his head lower, kissing me. We can't even stay lip-locked for long. I'm panting. I'm ascending.

"Harriet...I..." He grunts out a couple more indecipherable words. This happened last time, I remember. Communication became a game of failure. I feel the same defeat as all I can do is curse and curse and curse. The same basic word. *Fuck.*

His arms are curved so strongly around me, his hand buried into the back of my hair. I feel cocooned against him. Cradled, sheltered, unharmed. His movements quicken. We're a mixture of grunts, moans, curses, and half-sentences. I think I'm going to come again when he guides my head to the crook of his neck, then fists my hips in his clutch. He steadies my waist as he alternates between thrusting up in me and bringing my own body down on his cock.

"Can't...get..." His hoarse voice is too sexy. "...deep enough. *Fuck.*"

I understand the feeling. I just crave more and more.

Pleasure winds through my core as I glance down and see his

erection vanished between my legs, and I suddenly, abruptly, contract on his length. The pressure and fullness and new position soars my orgasm to new levels. It lasts longer than it ever has before, climbing up and coming down three times on repeat, and on the last climax, I feel him jerk upward, his muscles tensing, his fingers tightening in my hair, his cock twitching as he releases inside me. He pumps a little, in and out, milking the sensation—which, *wow.*

I kind of wish he wasn't wearing a condom. Maybe one day I'll feel him drip out of me. One day? *Don't think about it, Harriet.* I do not want to ruin the best sex I've ever had.

Our bodies slacken together in heavy, tired, sputtering waves. He gently pulls out at the same time he lowers me into the mattress. I'm spent but happy when I see he's staying on the bed with me. He plants a soft, affectionate kiss on my forehead, then my cheek, then my lips. It's impossible not to smile a little bit.

He only leaves to dispose of the condom. Once he returns to the pull-out, I'm greedy for his embrace again. We're lying down together, and I like the way he fits me into his chest and rubs the back of my head tenderly. I think I might like it too much.

A deep ache wells in the pit of my stomach. I anticipated this being hard—having sex knowing he's going to leave. But I underestimated the pain. It's an immediate onslaught of emotion. Of feeling ripped open and left to bleed. I try my best to bury it down. *He told you. You knew.*

My throat tries to close.

I've never had sex like this. Emotional, raw sex.

Loving sex.

It makes everything so much more complicated. The flamed wicks of the many candles catch my eye. This was perfect. It was everything a girl like me had stopped hoping for, because I never really thought it was in the cards. Now that it's here, I can't believe I might lose it all in weeks.

"Harriet?" Ben props himself on his elbow to stare down at me.

He pushes sweaty pieces of my bangs out of my lashes. "You okay?"

Tears squeeze out as I tighten my eyes shut.

He clutches my cheek as I try to turn away. He's breathing hard like this is agony watching tears slip from the corners of my eyes. "*Harriet.*"

"I..." I intake a sharp, hiccupping breath.

I think I loved this too much.

I think I love you.

It hits me so suddenly and so hard. I start crying right here. Right now.

"Harriet..." He pulls me into his chest as I quake in full-body sobs. He presses comforting, warm, loving kisses into my hair. He holds me so securely, so possessively, like he'll never release his clutch, and for a moment, I make-believe that he never will.

FORTY-FOUR

BEN COBALT

I'd never call having sex with Harriet a mistake. Not for a single second. But it's impossible not to feel the repercussions of it.

We're in the shower together, and I can't believe I'm going to leave this. Her. It throttles me how I might be wrong. Could *leaving* be worse than staying? It's a question I don't have the answer to, which makes me agonize over it even more.

The blue glow from the LED lights basks a calm hue on Harriet. Water drips down her eyelashes, and I rub shampoo into her hair. She lets me—which is a shock in itself. I thought after she stopped crying on the pull-out, she might want to push me away forever.

I can't discern exactly what has her so upset, but I can make some educated guesses. Still, I'd rather calm her down to where she's ready to share than badger her for answers when she's too torn up to. But yeah, Harriet sobbing after I slept with her—not a great feeling.

Is it because I won't be sticking around? *Maybe.* Part of me wants to tell her, "I'm on the fence about the future." But I'm scared to be wishy-washy, even if my head is like a fucking pirate ship on rocky seas.

Fuck, I wish I could figure how to tell her where I might be without compromising the plan. I can't risk my family finding me if I go through with it. I'm just trying to protect them. If I cause anything else terrible to happen to them...I can't. I can't even allow myself to think it.

My panic will escalate, so I breathe out and focus on her.

Harriet.

She's right in front of me.

Here. Now.

Her back to me, I skate my fingers through her hair, rinsing out some of the shampoo for her. I asked if she wanted to take a shower with me. She could've rejected me, curled up in the sheets, cursed me out forever.

Instead, I get the chance to comfort her. To make this better.

Her silence is eating at me just as much as her tears did. "I'm sorry," I breathe out. "If I made you feel this way..."

She whirls around, her glare still cute but it splinters in places. "No, you've been upfront with me." She brushes water out of her eyes. "I shouldn't have cried—"

"You can cry," I say. "I want to know how you feel, and if that's how you feel, you can let it out."

Harriet holds my waist. She's not crossing her arms. That's good. I see her thinking before she says, "It was the sex."

I wrack my brain. "The sex brought you to distraught tears?" That's...*not* good. "Did I hurt you?" My chest tightens. I thought I went slow enough.

"No, the sex was *the best*, Ben." Her reddened eyes carry so much emotion. I clasp her cheek, then cradle her head as she strains her neck. Not wanting her to look away from me. "I've never felt anything like it, and then knowing you're leaving soon...it just got to me. But I'll get over it."

A knot is in my ribs. Do I want her to get over it? Get over me? I know I'll never get over her. I pull Harriet against me in a hug, my hand cupping the back of her skull. She rests her cheek against my chest and hangs on to my build.

"It was the best for me too," I whisper to her. We take some breaths together, and I sense her body relaxing against mine. When we pull back, I peel a wet tendril of hair off her jaw.

She bites at the corner of her lip, her eyes drifting down to my cock. She's been doing that since we got in the shower, which I've learned is one of my biggest turn-ons with Harriet, but I'm hesitant to start another round right now. Not when she's been so fractured.

"Can we start over, Cobalt boy?" Harriet asks with a stiff shrug.

"Depends on how far over." I push my wet hair back and angle the showerhead away from her. She's being pelted with water.

"How far are you willing to rewind?"

I suck in a breath, feigning contemplation. "Two minutes."

Her cheeks pinch in a grimaced smile. "Oh, only two minutes." She pumps a lackluster fist in the air.

"Now we can't rewind at all because that was too cute. We can push pause though. Let me just do this first." I lift her up, and her legs naturally wrap around me. We're eye-level while I cup her soft, bare ass. Her arms drape over my shoulders, and her grumpy, sullen face takes a much lighter turn. "You want to pause, Fisher?"

She nods slowly while she says, "I don't want to fuck this up. We have such a short amount of time left, and I might ruin it."

"You won't ruin anything. You are the least *ruinous* person I've met. I'm the one—"

"You warned me," she interjects. "You told me. There was nothing more you could do, except not have sex with me, and I wouldn't want that either. I loved tonight. So I'm not rewinding a single second, I've decided."

"Good—"

She kisses me abruptly, which makes me smile. I kiss back, slowing the tempo, which draws an aching sound out of her.

When our lips part, she pants out, "Did we press play?"

"I think so."

"Cool, because I wanted to ask what shampoo we're using."

I laugh. "Hate it?"

"I could marry it."

"Now you're making me jealous. I might have to trash it." I reach for the bottle, holding her up against me with one arm.

She tears my hand away from the ledge of products. "Absolutely fucking *not*."

A deeper laugh rumbles out of me.

"My hair has never felt this silky, and it's not even dry yet. *Feel*." She tips her head forward to me.

I gladly run my fingers through the blond strands. "That's the work of a high-end vegan shampoo."

"High-end, huh." Her brows spring at me. "Splurging, Friend?"

"Thankfully I already had it before my bank account plummeted to *zero*. I don't use a lot at one time."

"Conserving," she nods. "I do the same thing with toothpaste. You have to roll that sucker to the very tip." Her puckered smile is making me grin. My heart feels so fucking full again.

I lean in and kiss her—then I hear the slam of a door.

Our mouths break apart like we've been electrocuted. I shift my hands to her hips, and she slides down my body, her feet splashing into the wet tile.

"What was that?" Harriet's eyes widen.

I'm already jumping out of the shower, not willing to take any chances. "Stay here." I wrench a towel off the hook. "Use the conditioner. Just don't marry it while I'm gone."

Her hesitation ends the banter, a hand frozen on the hot-and-cold lever. "I thought your brothers usually spend the night at your parents' house on Wednesdays?"

"Usually they do." No one loves the two-hour drive back to New York after dinner (shorter for those who push the speed limit, longer if there's traffic), but there are times they'll do it. Especially if they have a morning obligation the next day. I checked the group calendar. No one has shit to do tomorrow morning.

I'm already walking out the door, tying the towel around my waist. Water drips down my legs and creates footprint puddles as I head down the short hall.

"Hello?" I call out. "Anyone here?"

Then I skid to a halt in the living room.

It's Charlie.

His yellow-green eyes flit from the soy wax candles on the bookshelves, windowsill, and coffee table. I can't read his blank expression, so I say quickly, "I'll blow them out. They won't catch anything on fire." Except the image of flames spreading across the couch, of me starting an inferno in my brothers' apartment and burning them alive, is now scoring my brain.

I rapidly begin blowing out candles—my stride lengthy, slightly frantic.

"It's not kerosine," Charlie snaps. "This isn't even the hundredth idiotic idea involving fire that's been in this apartment. So rest assured, the two pyromaniacs will burn down the whole building before you even light a match."

Makes sense, still I side-eye a few candles on the bookshelves. I need to blow those out. I'm waiting for him to leave so he doesn't give me a hard time. "Is that it?" I ask.

He looks me over, unpocketing his cigarettes. Then he eyes the rumpled sheets on the pull-out. "Here's a tip. Worry more about the girl you left in the bathroom, less about us." He sticks his cigarette between his lips. "Revelatory for you, I know."

I clench my jaw. My concern for Harriet isn't something I feel like I need to defend, but I do tell him, "She's not just any girl."

"Didn't ask. Don't care." He lights his cigarette, showing me the flame of his lighter as it eats the paper. He takes a drag, then blows smoke up at the ceiling. "And look, I'm still alive." He clicks the lighter closed.

I'm not afraid of him causing an uncontrollable blaze. Me, on the other hand... *I shouldn't be living here.* The thought has flared up less and less frequently since I kissed Harriet at the Halloween party. I haven't forgotten the necessity of completing the Kappa bet and securing new housing—but it's been shelved behind Harriet.

I like that she's crowding the front of my brain. I like that I've stopped picturing Beckett scrubbing his arms at the sink.

The past week, I haven't felt a half second away from packing my duffel and exiting. I've been contemplating delaying for longer. Sometimes, I even wonder if there is a way to stay in New York. With her. With my brothers.

We hear the door open, and I turn as Eliot and Tom slip inside the apartment. When I glance back at Charlie, he's gone.

Eliot and Tom pass the kitchen with monstrously big smiles while I extinguish the last waxy candles. They might as well be arm-in-arm, skipping in glee, as they put all the pieces together. The candles. Me, naked in a towel. The shower still running in the bathroom.

"What are you doing here?" I ask before they can launch questions.

Eliot chokes on a laugh. "We live here."

Tom arches his brows. "Dude, we thought you were alone. We were coming back to keep you company."

"Unless you are alone," Eliot grins wider. "Is this a side of you we don't know about, brother? You light candles and set the mood before you jerk one out." He mimes the motion with his hand because of course he does.

I skate a palm across the back of my neck, still wet from the shower. "Harriet is here. She's spending the night on the couch with me, and I'd appreciate it if you wouldn't make a big deal out of this, for her sake. She grew up as an only child. She's not used to having you two as brothers." Last thing I want is for Harriet to be uncomfortable.

Eliot can't suppress his elation. "Next time you want to fuck your girlfriend, just tell us. We'll go somewhere else for the night, or I can even give you my room."

Fucking on Eliot's bed—not on my Bingo card.

But really, I'm still hung up on the other word. "She's not my…" I can't even say it. *She's not my girlfriend.*

Eliot's smile fades.

A grimace contorts Tom's face.

They know me too well. I've been hanging out with Harriet so much that there's no universe in which she *wouldn't* be my girlfriend now that we're hooking up. I'm the relationship guy out of all my brothers. I have the most experience truly dating—and that's a terrifying fact considering I'm the youngest.

"You're not calling her your girlfriend?" Tom just comes out and asks. "Is it because I don't like her? Because I have no problem going from disliking your friend to disliking your girlfriend."

I'm not getting into Tom and Harriet's feud. It's about as heated as a shishito pepper.

"It's new," I say, which isn't a lie. I know that I'll be dumping a truckload of suspicion on myself if I continue not calling Harriet my girlfriend. It is weird. I understand that. Because if I knew with absolute certainty that I'd be in New York by the end of the year, I'd be screaming it off every rooftop in the city.

Harriet Fisher is my girlfriend.

I want it so fucking badly. I just can't figure out if this is a cruel temptation—like I should want to keep my family safe more than I want to be with her. I don't know…I don't know, but I'm not going to stress about it right now.

They both pat my shoulders, congratulating me like I won an award, and I'm grateful when Eliot says they'll stay in their rooms for the rest of the night.

When they leave, all I want to do is return to Harriet.

So I do.

FORTY-FIVE

HARRIET FISHER

"Want to spend the night again, Fisher?" Ben asks me through my earbuds. I'm bowed over a fluorescence microscope in Dr. Venison's research lab. The small, empty room is pitch black except for the computer beside me. Proteins from a section of the thymus glow bright neon green on the screen, and I adjust the focus to sharpen the image.

I know what this looks like, but his call is *not* distracting me. I've been doing a mediocre job of concentrating on anything other than Ben before my phone rang.

In my defense, we *just* had sex for the first time and woke up together this morning. Legs tangled, my cheek on his chest, his hand sliding down my arm in a sleepy just-waking-up haze. I loved how he kissed my nose, then later how he split one of his smoothies with me after we showered. It feels like we're together.

Like a couple.

Even if we aren't labeling anything. Even if there is an expiration date.

It's been a lot for my brain to handle, so I'm not beating myself up for working at a snail's pace today. Or for even answering his call now.

My hand *flew* to the phone when it rang. I was also terrifyingly close to falling off the chair like a lovesick, demented fool. Thankfully no one is around. I signed up to use the microscope for the next two hours. No one will even open the door to this dark room without good reason because the light has potential to fuck up the results.

But even being alone, I'm trying so hard not to wear a dopey grin.

"Booty calling me already, Friend?" I tease. "I must've made a lasting impression."

He laughs so brightly. "I'm afraid you forever changed me."

"I've been afraid of that too." I purse my lips so the smile will stop hurting my cheeks, but my insecurities do the job for me. "You sure you want me over again? Won't your brothers care if we have another *friendly* sleepover?" I emphasize. "I'm guessing they'll be home."

"Yeah, they will be, but as long as you're comfortable with it, they have no problem with you staying over." He must pull the phone away to shout a distant, "Yeah, I have it, Colton! You too, man! See you soon!" Then back to me, "Sorry, that was a Kappa checking to see if I'm carrying my cub."

His lion cub. The frat bestowed Ben with a teddy-bear-sized stuffed animal that he must tote around campus every day. They call Ben the "lion pledge"—and he said it's the easiest pledge task. Of what he's described, the "jeans pledge" sounded the worst. One unlucky guy has to wear the same pants until initiation while Kappa brothers hack away at the material every time they see him.

They're already jorts.

"You name your lion cub yet?" I ask.

"I was actually hoping you'd do the honors. Want to brainstorm tonight?" He's still waiting for my answer. "I have a chapter meeting, then I don't have much else going on." Off my silence, he adds, "We don't have to do anything but watch a movie and go to bed. I just like being with you. Last night was honestly the best sleep I've had since the last time you were over."

Giddiness returns, and I fall forward, hand to my hot cheek. My heart wants nothing more than to spend *every* night with him, but will my grades plummet? Will he fill 100% of my brain? Then again, even when I'm not around Ben, he's become a mental fixation—so it's not like I can easily detach. *Might as well give in, Harriet.* He won't be around forever.

Okay, that solidifies it.

"Yeah, I'll spend another night with you," I agree, but five minutes after our call ends and I return to the microscope, I start majorly overthinking about his brothers.

Maybe I should ask them if it's okay? It's *their* space too. I whip my phone back out. The night Charlie, Eliot, and Tom spontaneously showed up at the End of the World, they exchanged their numbers with me, and then this morning, Ben and I ran into Beckett near the elevator in the apartment. He asked me for my number as well.

So I text all four of Ben's brothers at once, starting a group chat.

> **HARRIET**
> Is it okay if I spend the night again? I won't bother you or anything. Just want to make sure you're all comfortable with me being there.

I press send. Then I add really, really fast.

> **HARRIET**
> You can say no if you want to.

I send that one way too quickly, and I groan at myself. "Of course they know that. Ugh, *Harriet*. Why?" I don't have to second-guess for long. My phone is already pinging.

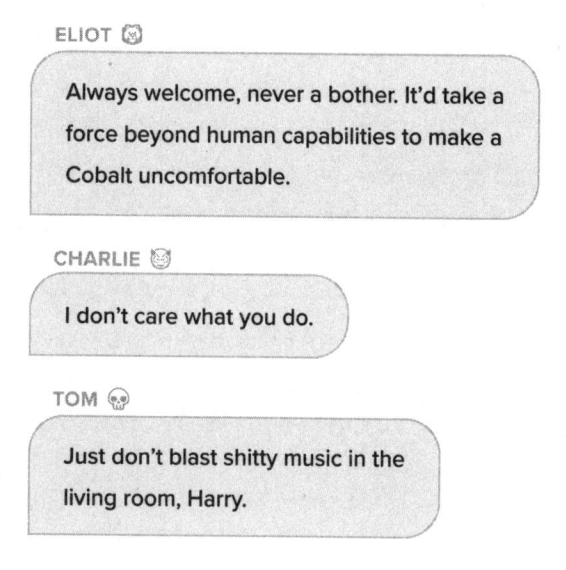

> **ELIOT** 😈
> Always welcome, never a bother. It'd take a force beyond human capabilities to make a Cobalt uncomfortable.
>
> **CHARLIE** 😈
> I don't care what you do.
>
> **TOM** 💀
> Just don't blast shitty music in the living room, Harry.

Relief begins to wash over me, then my phone *rings*. "Oh fuck." I spring back off the chair, holding my phone out like it's contracted a staph infection. Beckett is calling me?! Why? Oh no, is he going to grill me over the phone? Ask me what my intentions are with his baby brother?

I intend for him to rail me tonight, if you must know. I have a love-hate relationship with my brain right now.

"Okay, you can do this," I pump myself up, then answer the phone. It connects to my earbuds. "Hey?" I'm praying that didn't sound hostile.

"I don't mind if you spend the night again."

I wait for more, but he says nothing after. "Did…did you just call to tell me that?"

"Yeah, sorry, I don't text."

I pause for the joke. "Wait, you're being serious? Is this like a seventeenth century Cobalt Empire role playing thing?"

Beckett lets out a light laugh. "No. I wish." His breathing sounds shortened. I wonder if he's on a treadmill. Or moving very quickly somewhere. "It's sadly a *friend leaked my messages to a tabloid* type of thing. Don't take it personally. I don't even text family."

"Good to know." I stare out into the pitch-black darkness of the lab. "Sooo you're really okay if I just crash with Ben in the middle of the living room? Even if we…I mean, I'm not saying we *will*…but maybe…" *Stop talking, Harriet.*

Whyyyy does Beckett Cobalt intimidate me?

"You've already spent the night twice," he says smoothly. "Third, fourth, fifth time—if that's what Ben wants, it's what I want. I have to run, but if you ever need a ride to the apartment, you can call my driver. Put this number in your contacts."

I store the number Beckett reads out over the phone. My pulse beating a mile a minute.

Then he says, "One more thing."

"Yeah?"

"Stick around. I haven't seen my little brother this happy in a long time, and it's definitely because of you."

My eyes spring a tiny leak. *What the fuck?* I wipe my cheek quickly. I've just never been a source of someone's happiness before. I can see how Ben feels around me, but to hear it from a witness makes this fact durable, solid, like it's etched in stone.

Stick around. How do I even tell Beckett I'm not the one in threat of bolting?

In this moment, all I manage to reply is, "I plan on it."

FORTY-SIX

HARRIET FISHER

Later that night, Ben and I devour frozen pizzas in his kitchen. Vegan margherita, which Ben let get extra crispy in the oven for me. I like a crunchy charred crust. None of his brothers are home early enough to swipe a slice. Seeing as how their professions have late hours, I'm not surprised we have most of the apartment to ourselves again.

We're cuddled on the couch (not the pull-out mattress), and I lie longways against Ben's firm chest, his arms weave around me while I untangle a knot in the stuffed lion's mane.

He lists off all my name suggestions. "Cubby? The cub? Baby lion? Son of Ben?"

"What I lack in creativity I make up elsewhere," I say a little defensively, forgetting how much I love my audience.

Because Ben immediately says, "You're plenty creative, Fisher. SOB is pretty funny."

I smooth the golden-yellow fur. "If you had an actual baby, would you name them something earthy like Clover or Aspen?"

"You trying to tell me something?" he teases.

I peer up at him, my face warm. "Unless the condom broke, I think we're in the clear on the baby-making front, Cobalt boy." I hold his gaze. "But I wouldn't mind forgoing the condom next time. I'm on birth control."

His smiling blue eyes sink down on me. "Yeah, I know, you mentioned being on the pill."

So he *did* process that information a while back. "Just letting you know. I've also been tested recently, all negative, and I'm not sleeping with anyone else, so…"

"Same and same."

"Cool." I'm smiling off his sexy widening smile. "So you're going to have a baby Thistle one day?"

He laughs, and I feel the rumble of his chest against me. "You want to name our kid Thistle?"

My heart double-beats. *Our kid?* Obviously, we're messing with each other. This is playful banter, where we're constructing a future that can't even happen. "You have a better earthy name?"

"Why are we going earthy?"

"To appease your tree-loving soul, nature boy." I rotate around, wanting to face him, but the most natural maneuver is to straddle Ben on the couch cushions. He rests his hands on my thighs. This time, I did remember to bring cotton pajama shorts, but his fingers slip up the hem.

His touch is magma. I heat all over. Our breaths sound shallow, and his muscles flex as I shift a little on his waist. The gray sweats and blue tee are typical Ben attire.

I hold on to his lion cub. "And?" I ask.

"And…" He clears out husky arousal from his throat. "I'd rather we pick a name that appeases your punk-rock-loving soul."

"Baby Spike," I joke.

"Whatever you want, Fisher."

Now my heart flutters. It's how he's staring at me, like he would literally give me anything in the world if he could. "No, see there is a compromise here, Ben." I hold out a finger. "*Stone.* Earthy and rock-forward."

"We better get cracking if we want to make our baby Stone." He brushes his knuckle against my clit, and I clench my thighs around him.

"Fuck," I curse. "*Ben.*"

He grins. "Keep glaring at me like that, it's only going to make me want to push inside you faster."

I place the lion cub behind me and plant my hands on his chest. He hardens against me, and he brings his lips to mine. He kisses me once, twice, pulling me closer, but I break apart to pant out, "You want a blow job?"

That sounded sexier in my head, but whatever, I offered.

He sucks in a contemplative breath. "Do you enjoy giving them or is this just something you feel like you have to do?"

I shrug. "I want you to feel good too."

"Trust me, I already do." He's slouched on the armrest of the couch, his reassuring hands gripping my hips. He even grinds me down on him, so his erection rubs against my pussy. *Oh my…God.* "And if I don't come inside you here, then how are we going to make our baby?"

I can't decide if this conversation is torture of the best kind or the worst. "Our fictional baby," I say like a dumbass. *You aren't dumb, Harriet.* I blow out such a heavy breath, my bangs billow. I'm about to launch myself off him, but Ben's grip tightens on me.

He's sitting up. "Hey."

I scowl. "I don't actually want to be pregnant."

"I know—"

"Because I have so many goals, *soooo* many, that would be epically derailed if I were to get knocked up tomorrow."

"I know—"

"And I don't even know if I'm mom material. I have no relationship with my own mom, and maybe I'd be a really shitty one."

"You'd be a great mom," he says without any hesitation. "Do you want kids someday, when you're older and a surgeon and settled in your career?"

I lift my shoulders. "Maybe. I mean...it's not off the table. I have time to think about it more." I can't search his eyes fast enough. "Do you want kids someday in the future?"

"I don't know," he murmurs, slipping his hands through my hair while his eyes roam across mine, like he's scavenging for the answers. Like he believes they're within me. "I'd want them with the right person, and that person would be you."

"Stop," I deadpan, pushing off him.

He grasps me stronger, keeping me still and closer. "I'm not teasing." His eyes say he's being serious. "I mean it, Harriet." I feel his warm hand against my cheek.

"If you were staying," I add for him. "That's what you really mean. If you were staying, there would be a future between us."

"Yeah," he breathes, looking even more torn up than I feel.

I glide my fingers down his chest, staring at our laps as confusion bites at me. "Why are you leaving, Ben?" I nearly whisper, as if these are harmful questions that could pierce his body, his heart. I've just never wanted to hurt him. I'm not Charlie, who prefers to bludgeon Ben with his words. "Why go move to the wild? To a place you apparently can't share with me because you're afraid your family will find out...and then they'll stop you?"

"It's..." He grimaces at himself. "It's so fucking hard to explain."

"You could try." I shrug. "I'm all ears, and I'm not going anywhere."

He blinks a lot, like he's disentangling jumbled, gnarled thoughts.

"Is it a calling?" I try to help. "Like, you feel compelled to go commune with nature alone?"

"I don't know..." His breathing shortens. His heart *pounds* beneath my hand. "Maybe not that." He swallows hard, runs his fingers through his hair a few times, and the coldness when he lets go of me feels agonizing. But I hold his neck instead, hoping he knows I'm here. His eyes are reddened. "Maybe it's more like a need, a necessity. Like if I don't do this…" He shakes his head, then intakes a sharper breath.

"It's okay," I say quickly, not understanding why he's getting so worked up over this. I do know I *hate* seeing him choked for oxygen. I *hate* how his pulse is a quickening hammer under my hand. "Take some breaths. We don't need to talk about it."

"Maybe I could…" He swallows again, trying to inhale deeper.

"Ben, let's just drop it—"

"I could stay into the holidays," he says with a nod. "I want to stay. More than anything. I think I can." He nods more assuredly. "I'll be here."

Now I'm processing rapidly. "Are you sure? We haven't heard anything from the Honors House yet. You'd still have to stay with your brothers if you can't complete the Kappa bet."

"Maybe I can stay here longer too. It's been better. Beckett has seemed okay."

If I cling too tightly to this hope, will it just crumble in my hands? Still, I find myself clutching to this blissful feeling. "It's the sex, isn't it," I tease. "It's mind-altering. Too good to say goodbye to."

"It's not the sex, Fisher. It's just you. It's been you." His smile emerges as soon as mine peeks, and he nods even stronger this time, his breathing deepening in a good way. "I'll be here for longer. I'll be here with you."

My spirits catapult to the clouds. I pull him closer, but he's already crashing his lips to mine, urging them apart. His sensual, devouring tongue draws me into him. His hand tightens in my hair with a dominant, needy grip. I ache to be smothered by his touch, by him.

The door clicks open so slowly, so softly, we almost don't hear when one of his brothers enters the apartment.

"Beckett?" Ben calls out, craning his neck over his shoulder, and I wonder if he thinks it's him because of the hushed entrance.

I have a direct view of *Tom*.

I'm still straddling Ben, about to spring off his lap until Tom's despondent shuffle gives me extra pause. His head is hung, shaggy golden-brown hair hiding his eyes. My nemesis looks…defeated. And not by *me*, so I don't like this at all.

"Everything okay?" Ben frowns. "Tom?"

He drops his keys on the kitchen counter, then meanders closer. "You will be happy to know, Harry…" Tom just barely lifts his bloodshot, wrecked gaze up to mine. "That my drummer just quit. And so did Warner."

"Warner?" Ben says in confusion, like that's inconceivable. The bassist started The Carraways with Tom seven years ago.

"That's the whole band," I say unhelpfully.

"Thank you so much for clarifying," Tom says with a shrill noise. "Like I didn't know my band just imploded." He pushes his hair back, and my eyes bug into concerned saucers.

"Dude." I leap off Ben's lap. "Did he punch you?" I'm fucking pissed.

"*Tom*." Ben is on his feet in seconds. Tom's eyelid is puffy, and the inside crease is already bruising.

He slings his head back with a frustrated, distraught sound. "He lost it at rehearsal and threw a mic at my face." He glares at me. "Go ahead and laugh it up, Harry. Tell me I deserved it. I'm an asshole. I had this coming. Rub it in."

"You didn't deserve to get assaulted." I head to the fridge. "Do you have any ice packs in here?"

"Freezer," Ben tells me while he checks on his brother.

"The bruise to the face I can take," Tom assures him. "My pride…" He blinks back emotion. "Goddamn Warner."

Ben rests his ass on the back of the couch, so he's closer to Tom's six-foot-one height. "If this is how Warner reacts, I don't think you should work things out with him. Maybe it's better to cut ties."

"I don't want him back, dude." Tom points at his eye. "And not because of this. We can't agree on *anything* anymore. Not the tempo, not a song title, not the color of a fucking EP cover."

I return with a squishy icepack. I'm guessing Beckett being an athlete is why there were a multitude of different kinds in the freezer. I offer it to Tom.

He grabs it slowly like he's expecting a catch to my kindness. "Thanks?"

"Any reason to flex my pre-med skills, Thomas."

He wheezes out a laugh. "Right now I feel like I'm dying. What are you going to do about that?" I open my mouth to respond, but he's quick to say, "Forget it." He presses the ice to his eye, nods goodbye to Ben and retreats to his bedroom.

I let out a long breath. "I'm not happy his band broke up. It actually sucks knowing The Carraways may never put out new music." I crinkle my nose at myself. "And I'm the real asshole for not telling him that."

"Tom is in his own feelings," Ben says. "I think the only thing that'll really make him feel better are solutions to the problem. So this doesn't feel like he just lost everything."

"Is there a solution?" I ask.

"I have no fucking idea," Ben says with a heavy sigh, his empathy on the hallway where Tom disappeared.

"You should check on him again. I'll pull out the bed."

He nods. So that's how we split apart for several minutes. By the time Ben returns, I've slipped under the covers, dimmed the lights, and scrolled through Netflix on his laptop. He brings over a couple glasses of water and cozies up beside me.

A tin of cookies balances on the armrest of the couch. Eliot brought them back from Wednesday Night Dinner and told me they were baked with mischief and love from his little sister. Apparently, Audrey has a thing for giving sweets to people, and I've been devouring the little drum-shaped sugar cookies. She slipped a note in the tin too.

> *Harriet –*
> *I can't wait to properly meet you one day. In person!*
> *xo Audrey*

It feels good knowing Ben's little sister, who he cares for greatly, thinks I'm important enough for cookies and a meet-up. I snuggle next to Ben with the laptop, and we're about five minutes into *Okja* when a door shuts from the hall.

I perk up and glance behind the couch with Ben.

Tom has a pillow tucked under his arm. "Please tell me we're not watching monkeys digging in the dirt."

I give Ben a confused look. "Did you invite him?"

Ben shakes his head with a rising smile and a laugh. "This is Tom."

Tom hikes a leg over the back of the couch and slides onto the pull-out. Not just anywhere—he chooses *in between* me and Ben. I'm not kidding.

I scoot over so my arm isn't butted up against his. "Do you understand personal space?"

"Yeah, can you give me some? It's a little cramped." He wiggles his arms, shoving me and Ben farther apart and fluffing his pillow behind his back.

I would be more irritated if Ben wasn't trying to stifle full-body laughter. Just hearing the sound is like a serotonin boost.

"He's not sleeping with us," I tell Ben.

Tom makes a face at me like *I'm* the weird one. "Like I want to sleep in the same bed as my sleep paralysis demon."

"I hope I give you nightmares."

"Ben, tell your girlfriend to be nice to me. I'm emotionally fragile right now." He doesn't appear it as much as he did, so I wonder if Ben's pep talk helped. "Look, if I'm left alone, I'm going to text RJ to come over here, and the last thing I need is an emotion-fueled hookup. In fact, take my phone. Take it." He plops his cell on Ben's lap.

Then he pries the laptop out of my hands, holding it since he's in the middle. "*Okja?* Never heard of it."

"It's one of Ben's favorite movies."

Tom frowns at him in hurt. "And you never shared this with me?"

"You won't like it," Ben says with certainty.

I've never seen *Okja* before, but the science-fiction fantasy premise of a little girl going to great lengths to save her animal sounded interesting. It also has glowing reviews.

"Let's see it first without passing judgment, Ben Pirrip." He rewinds and presses play.

This is how I find myself wedged beside Tom Carraway Cobalt on a pull-out couch watching Netflix on a random Thursday night. Oh and he's icing his soon-to-be black eye.

Ben smiles over at me a few times. That's the best part.

We're an hour into the film, and Tom has a stink-face.

"You can hate it, Tom," Ben says with a smile. "It won't offend me."

"There's still more left to go." He's squinting at the screen midway through. Then his silent rumbling laughter shakes the laptop.

"Dude," I say flatly.

"It's a big hippo," he defends. "How is this not supposed to be a comedy?"

I'm so invested in the plight of this little girl and her CGI animal that I've been restraining tears for the past ten minutes. "It's a super pig," I correct. "And it's not supposed to be *funny*."

"But if you watch it thinking it's a floppy-eared ugly hippo...?" He holds out a hand of reason.

"It's a *cute* animal."

"It's pretty fucking ugly, and I don't know if Ben's going to like knowing you'd only save the cute animals."

I fling my pillow at his face.

"Ow, watch the eye, Harry."

I almost feel bad, but not quite. When I glance over at Ben, I'm about to apologize for reinjuring his injured brother, but his expression on me steals my breath. He's looking at me like he could kiss me, hold me, hug me, lie with me in a field of grass and watch the rolling clouds forever.

Maybe this movie night with Tom isn't so terrible. I also have a great window into the dynamic between all of Ben's brothers than ever before. Like when Beckett arrives, and even in the darkness of the living room, he beelines for Tom. As if he's already heard the news.

"How bad?" Beckett asks behind the couch.

Tom tilts up his face toward him, so Beckett can inspect the puffy eyelid. "With a microphone."

"Keep ice on it." Beckett presses a hand to Tom's shoulder, then nods to me and Ben. "You two need anything? I'm in for the night."

We shake our heads. "Thanks, Beck," Ben says.

"Have you seen this hippo movie?" Tom asks Beckett, angling the laptop.

"*Okja*? Yeah, it's really good. It's one of Ben's favorites."

Ben smiles at Tom. "I knew he'd like it."

"I like parts of it," Tom defends. "The sci-fi elements are just taking me out. There's still time for improvement." The door opens again.

As Charlie enters, he kicks off his loafers and immediately asks Tom, "Have you told Eliot?"

Tom sinks down, his arm sliding against mine. "I'm not interrupting his date with that Gertrude girl. The minute he finds out, he'll rush over here."

"You need to tell him," Beckett says smoothly. "He'll bring her here just to kick her out when he sees you're hurt and hears about the band."

Charlie peels his shirt off his head. "No one wants to spend the night trying to get rid of his grating, clingy date." He's unbuttoning his pants. Is anyone seeing this? Is this normal? Charlie just walks down the hallway, mid-stripping to likely take a shower.

Beckett never switches to French in front of me. He lets me hear everything, and I think it's this exact moment when I realize I might be in the inner circle of the Cobalt Empire.

BEN AND I WAKE AS THE MORNING SUN STREAMS ACROSS the couch, and then his therapist calls. While he slips into Eliot and Tom's bathroom to do a short session, I head to the smaller half-bath and run into a problem I wished to never meet at the Cobalt brother's apartment.

"Really? *Really?*" I mutter to myself, spinning the empty toilet paper roll in the powder bath. Thankfully, I haven't peed yet and can easily check the cupboard under the sink…and…no TP. *Ben.* Ben is obviously *not* the solution here, even if my brain is trying to will it to be.

I'm not disturbing his therapy session for toilet paper. But the pressure in my bladder demands relief, and holding it for thirty minutes isn't an option.

I go through the alternatives. Barge into Charlie and Beckett's bathroom without asking. *No way.* Clogging the powder bath's toilet with paper towels. *Hell no.* I'd rather pee myself than be found standing in a lake of toilet water with a plunger in hand.

Looks like I'll be waking one of them up to do the adult thing and just *ask* for some TP. I wince, picturing this face-to-face interaction. I would be more comfortable looking them in the eyes and asking for a condom—and I don't even want to know what that says about me.

I could avoid eye contact by sending a message, but Beckett doesn't even *text*. And I'm not going to text Charlie. In fact, I don't even want to ask Charlie at all because he might not help me. I'll gladly choose the more intimidating brother if it means a guaranteed successful outcome. So this all leads me on a trek down their hallway to find Beckett.

Brand new territory, yippee.

If only this expedition had a map because I can't tell which door leads to Beckett's room or Charlie's, and before I play *What's Behind Door Number One?* my ears catch mutterings through the wood.

"...I know, but he's only hanging around when she's here, Charlie. He will actively avoid the apartment otherwise."

Charlie doesn't want me here? Beckett is trying to convince him to let me stay? These theories sprout from earth that Ben would consider polluted and erosive. There isn't much that says Charlie dislikes my presence, so why do I instantly think I'm a problem?

All I picture is my mom.

"He trusts her? He loves her? He would do anything for her?" Charlie throws out like potential possibilities. "If he has told anyone anything, it's been to her."

"We need to ask Harriet," Beckett whispers, so I take a teeny step closer, pressing my ear to the door. "...he's been more himself when he's with her. I don't like the look on his face when he's alone with us, Charlie. I'm telling you, something still isn't right."

They fall too hushed.

Then the door whips open. I jerk back the same time Charlie stares me down, then he swings the door wider to show Beckett. As though he knows I find him *far* more intimidating.

"Look, a recreational eavesdropper," Charlie says like he's tarnishing my resume.

"*One-time* eavesdropper," I correct. "I just came to ask for some toilet paper."

"Come in here." Beckett gestures me forward. He even peeks in the hallway behind me, as if ensuring none of his other brothers are lurking. Then Charlie catches my wrist and *pulls* me into the room, breaking my threaded arms apart.

What…is happening?

I stumble inside as Beckett shuts the door very softly. I survey my surroundings. Okay, this *has* to be Beckett's bedroom. Soothing blue tones. No clutter. Very minimalist with a desk, king-sized bed, navy-blue comforter and matching navy curtains. Both ironed to wrinkle-free perfection. The permeating cedary sage scent smells like him too.

I touch *nothing*. "I really have to use the bathroom," I remind them, just so this secret rendezvous doesn't take forever. I would rather plug the toilet than pee on Beckett's floor. I'm standing in a potential Worst-Case Scenario right now.

"We'll be quick," Beckett assures, only wearing cotton pants like Charlie. I'm guessing they just woke up too.

"Has Ben told you why he's broke yet?" Charlie questions.

"No, not really." He's alluded to using the money for his move, but I can't mention this. I peer at the door. "I know we all want the same things…but I don't like conspiring behind his back. It doesn't feel good."

Charlie cocks his head. "Pardon me for not caring about your feelings when my brother lost a tiny fortune either under duress or by choice."

"He said he's not being blackmailed," I retort. "I already told you that." I have yet to share Ben's move to the wilderness. It's too big of a betrayal. I'm almost positive he will cut me out of his life. Never speak to me again. It's a secret he wants kept so badly, his heart *races* when he even mentions portions of it.

"She can't rat him out," Beckett reminds Charlie. "If he can't trust her anymore, he'll push us all away, and that's not what we want."

Charlie rolls his eyes, tugging at his hair.

"We will lose him, Charlie, if he loses her."

"We don't know that for certain."

"I'm not willing to risk it," Beckett says smoothly, then nods to me. "Don't tell us more than you can, but please, if you ever get the feeling—even if it's so small—that he might be in trouble, come to us."

"I will," I nod.

Ben is moving to a remote location. It's not like he's decided to jump off a cliff and drown. I'm sure once he's there, he'll write to his family and let them know his address. Then maybe he'll find a satellite phone and be able to call with updates. Or even a café with Wi-Fi.

Anyway, there is such a great chance Ben won't even move anymore. He's delaying his plans for longer and longer, and what if he just scraps them altogether?

"Toilet paper?" Beckett asks.

I nod, about to follow him out.

Then Charlie says, "Offering any more blow jobs these days?"

FORTY-SEVEN

HARRIET FISHER

I freeze. Beckett's intense gaze drops to me, like he's gauging my reaction. Is he concerned I might be a cheater? Face on fire, I can't look at him. It's much easier to turn to Charlie. "Yeah, to your brother. *Ben.* You want to know if I made him come, too?"

Charlie just arches a brow at Beckett, who asks me calmly, "Does your college provide counseling?"

I tense, not expecting that question at all. "Yeah, but it's not free."

"You don't have health insurance?" Charlie probes now.

"Through MVU, but it's basic. Therapy isn't covered. It's way out of my budget."

"Your boyfriend can pay for it. Oh wait." Charlie lifts his brows. "He's broke."

I glower, not loving his sarcasm when the salty shots are aimed at Ben.

Beckett grabs his phone off his desk. "I can transfer you some cash—"

"No," I interject, wide-eyed.

Charlie rubs his temple with two fingers. "You don't think you have an issue?"

"I'm not denying that I'm fucked up like you said."

Beckett cuts Charlie a piercing look. "You need to be careful what you say to his girlfriend." It still floats my body every time I hear them refer to me as Ben's girlfriend, even if it might not be *entirely* accurate. I'm pretending it is. "He will lay you out on the floor."

"You and Eliot should just let him."

"No," Beckett says firmly. He must know Ben hates violence, and to inflict pain upon his older brother would hurt him beyond measure.

I shift my weight, the urge to pee escalating. "I can't accept your money," I tell Beckett. "I'm not sure I'm ready for counseling." I'm barely used to *one* person being up in my business. Just having *them* be overly involved in my life is bewildering, but the pushy, forceful care seems to be what they extend to each other. I'm in more disbelief it's being given to me. "But I would like some TP."

He grants me my wish. Thank God.

On Friday, I spend the night again, and I learn that Ben is *strong*. Made evident by the steamy minutes in the bathroom where he bounces me on his dick. While standing. A climax ripples through my whole body. I see stars. And I discover that our first time wasn't a fluke. Sex with Ben is an emotional, physical, mental exhilaration I can't fathom might end.

I stop believing it will.

On Saturday, I'm seriously buzzing when he invites me to his place *again*. Even after our long shift at the End of the World, I want nothing more than to curl into Ben's embrace. I've noticed his brothers are big night owls. Charlie, Beckett, and Tom are up and wired at 3 a.m. while I'm about to pass out.

So I vaguely listen to their conversation while I lie against Ben, his hand stroking my hair. That coupled with the lights they dimmed in the living room are lulling me to sleep. They've congregated around the pull-out, nursing waters since they all drank tonight except Ben.

Beckett and Charlie are on the swivel chairs. And Tom—he's lying on the bottom of the mattress like he's about to be fed grapes.

Thankfully I'm short enough that he's not fucking with my feet. I'm pretty sure I hear Ben warn him not to mess with me.

They're discussing what to get for their niece's first birthday.

"I vote we let Beckett Joyce pick out the gifts," Tom says.

It's the last thing I hear before I doze off. Then I'm startled awake to a heavy slam. I jolt against Ben. He holds me tighter, his hand cupping my head.

"It's okay," he murmurs against my ear. "You're okay. Eliot just came home."

I swallow the brief surge of alarm, but I don't untense. Ben's muscles contract in taut bands. As I register my surroundings, I realize Charlie and Beckett are still awake.

They're on their feet when Eliot stumbles into the apartment, his arm slung around a *gorgeous* brunette. "Brooothers!" Eliot grins a magnetic, wily grin.

"Baby," the girl coos to him. "I want to see your room."

He pays less attention to her as he walks farther inside. His playful behavior contains extra flair as he bops Charlie and Beckett on the nose back and forth. "Fancy. Seeing. You. Here." Charlie smacks his hand away.

"You smell like a distillery," Beckett says.

"The distillery smells like me," Eliot bops him again.

He's not slurring, but by Beckett and Charlie's unamused demeanor, this must be Eliot very, very drunk. Even Ben shifts to an upright sitting position.

"We're just going to bed," the girl says, maintaining effortless balance in her four-inch heels. "We'll be out of your way. Come on, baby." She tugs him in the wrong direction of his room. Which means she's never been here before.

My sleepy haze totally wears off when Beckett says, "He's going to bed alone. We'll call you a cab—"

"Uh, no, *no*. Baby." She squeezes Eliot's hand. He's gripping onto the kitchen island like he might keel over without the support. "I'll put him to bed."

"You're not staying," Charlie sneers, taking a much meaner approach. "Leave."

She scoffs. "You have to be joking." Her gaze roams the apartment and lands on...me? "Oh so she can stay but I can't?"

I recoil with a glare. Leave me out of this. A weird feeling tosses my stomach until Ben tucks me closer to his chest.

"There are things called boundaries. And doors." Charlie points to the exit. "Do yourself a favor and walk out of it."

"Really?"

"No, I'm joking," he says irritably. "This is so much fun for me." He points again. "*Go.* And no, I will not call you a cab. Get one yourself."

"What's wrong with you?"

"Right now, *you.*"

"Eliot," Beckett calls out.

"*Brooother*," Eliot grins again, wrapping his arms around his older brother in a bear-hug and abandoning the girl. It allows Beckett to start guiding him to bed.

"Ben," Beckett asks for his help as he reaches the pull-out.

Ben checks on me first, sending a fucking *flutter* to my chest before he leaps over the couch. Eliot bops his head and ruffles his hair. "MY BROTHERS!" he bellows, curving his arms around them. But really, they're basically carting his full weight into the bedroom.

Charlie blocks the girl from following.

She gives him a lengthy once-over, her arms crossing. "Charlie Cobalt, right? You think you're a *god.* I bet you're a knockoff version of your dad. I bet you aren't even half his size." Her gaze is firmly on his *dick.*

I'm on my knees, about to climb off the mattress, like maybe he needs some assistance. But what the hell am I going to do? I grab a pillow. *Great, Harriet, let's have a fucking pillow fight.*

Charlie wears a lethal expression. He walks forward, forcing her to take a couple steps backward toward the door. She's cackling like it's a game. He looms over her, and when he yanks the door open behind her, she grabs a fistful of his crotch.

"Hey!" I shout, springing off the bed.

Charlie shoots me a scathing look. "*Do not* come over here."

I go still in confusion.

She's laughing, and he dips his head down to hers. Whatever he snarls into her ear, her laughter decays into brutal silence. Then she slaps him across the face.

"Fuck *you*." Her voice shakes as her tears leak, then she rushes out. He slams the door shut. I expect him to completely ignore me.

Instead, he returns to the living room, slouches on the swivel chair, lights a cigarette, and blows smoke up at the ceiling. Like nothing just happened.

I sink down on the pull-out. "Are you….?"

"Am I okay?" he asks dryly, sucking on the cigarette. "What do you think, Harriet?" He tilts his head with mocking interest.

"By your lovely attitude, I'd say you're fine, Boy Genius."

He kicks up his feet on the mattress.

Maybe he is fine. Maybe he's desensitized. Maybe meeting covetous, unconsented hands are just an ordinary night for Charlie.

He puts out the cigarette in an ashtray. Unsurprisingly. If any of them smoke indoors, they don't do it for long. They'll take a few drags, then snuff it out, so the stench hasn't lingered.

Beckett and Ben appear from the bedroom, and Beckett confirms, "Eliot is passed out."

Damn…I honestly didn't think he was blackout wasted. I hug the pillow. What if his brothers hadn't been here to kick the girl out? Would she still have slept with Eliot when he was too inebriated to properly consent? My body chills. I've thought of Eliot as the greatest defender of his brothers, but it's comforting knowing they're looking out for him too.

Beckett watches Ben for a long beat, but he's just combing his hands through his hair and sliding back into bed with me. Ben immediately reaches for me, and when his brothers leave, I hug him and feel the pound, pound, *pound* of his heart against my ear.

"Ben?"

"Yeah?" he whispers, taking a deeper breath.

"Do you need water? Are you okay?"

"I'm okay." He nestles a kiss in my hair. "I'm okay." With each word, his pulse begins to slow, and I ease with the sound.

In the morning, Eliot has no recollection of what happened. He jokes it away, says he must've drank more than he realized, and Tom is upset no one woke him.

"Don't sleep with music blaring. Problem solved," Charlie retorts.

"Harry will wake me up next time," Tom notes.

"Don't press your luck, *Tommy*."

I am secretly over-enthused at being considered for a tomorrow before tomorrow even arrives. And tomorrow does come.

On Sunday, I string together beads on Ben's couch. I make a choker necklace for Son of Ben with block letters that spell out *Cobalt Empire*. The stuffed lion cub has to rock the family name.

Ben angles his laptop toward me while we watch *Jawbreaker*. My rec.

Charlie is on his way out the door when he says, "If you didn't dump all your cash into the mysterious land of Oz, maybe you could've taken your girlfriend on an actual date."

Ben glares.

"Don't listen to him," I say as Charlie exits. "I just like being deep under the iceberg with you, Friend."

His smile slowly crawls over his face. "Feeling hypothermic yet?" he teases.

"I fear we have a greater risk of you boiling our water." I nearly shriek when he picks me up in his arms.

By Monday, I should most definitely go back to my own apartment. My grades aren't in threat of slipping, but I'm paying for a couch, too. Except, he's where I want to be late at night, when darkness falls and I'm left with whirling, happy thoughts of him.

I cave and end up with Ben.

Late, past one a.m., Eliot tosses a condom at us, and Ben and I crack up laughing under the sheets. Mostly because we stopped using condoms.

When he's gone, we naturally shift to our sides. The plan is to *sleep*, but heat ratches up as our bodies meld. As he holds me. Then his hand travels down my stomach and between my legs while he kneads my breast with the other.

He's toying with me. It feels *so good*. I forget about being in a public space. I forget about everything except how much I love his wandering, ravaging hands. When I shudder, his palm flies up to my lips, but he's now slipped his fingers beneath my panties. He cages my cries and makes me come against him.

I want to offer the same release for Ben. He's *very* hard, but he shakes his head and whispers against my ear, "That was for you and for me."

"Such a giver," I whisper.

He laughs hard. "You have no idea."

"Oh I think I do, Cobalt boy." I burrow back into his embrace. Never, *ever* thought I'd be a girl who enjoys *spooning*, but being tucked inside his carved biceps is like being strapped in a steel-fortified vessel. It's like knowing no danger will meet me. No fall will kill me.

I feel so very loved.

And I easily begin to drift to sleep—only to wake to quiet footsteps. We aren't fooling around anymore, but the second I catch sight of *Beckett* in the kitchen, I freak and go deep-sea diving into the mattress. Flinging the quilt over my head. Pretending his brother didn't see me right up against Ben.

Does this look worse? Like I'm giving Ben a blow job?

Too late now, Harriet.

Ben is laughing though. He thinks it's hilarious that out of all his brothers, Beckett intimidates me the most when that title should go to Charlie. Maybe for him that's true, but Beckett is the most protective of Ben, which I've realized means I care more about his opinion of me. Whereas Charlie is just a loose cannon who pushes Ben's buttons.

On Tuesday, I fully intend to crash on *my* couch. Mine. Then after Board Game Club, I find myself once again at Ben's apartment. I left a change of clothes here. Even some toiletries. I am nothing if not *prepared*, but it also makes it very easy to not go home.

I'm scared this is starting to feel like a home. It's comfortable. Safe. Loving. But it's not really mine, right? It's still Ben's. And what happens if he does say goodbye to New York? To me?

By Wednesday morning, it dawns on me that Ben has stopped saying he's leaving. He no longer ends each kiss with reminders that this won't last.

Preparing to venture to class with this high, I'm happily showered and stuffing my backpack. All the Cobalt brothers are awake, milling around the kitchen for breakfast. When my phone buzzes, I check the screen and go slack-jawed.

"Harriet? You alive?" Ben rounds the counter like I need CPR.

I fucking might. "Guy Abernathy just texted me." I sway backward into the wall. Pressing my phone to my chest as I dizzy.

"You need us to kill him, brother?" Eliot says to Ben, which jolts me into awareness. I'm acting like a dopey *fool* over a text from another guy—who is literally named *Guy*—in front of his *brothers*.

I'm sure my scowl reforms. "It's not like that." I haven't read the message yet. "He's the president of the Honors House."

"This is that weird Kappa bet thing?" Tom asks, pouring a bowl of Lucky Charms. A while back, Ben explained the Kappa Phi Delta's housing stipulation to his brothers. They'd asked if he ever convinced the frat to let him stay there, so they know all about the "sleep with an Honors House girl" bet.

Ben sidles beside me. "She's not trying to be a part of the Honors House just so I can live at the frat. She had this goal before me."

"But if she gets in, you will move out?" Tom questions.

Ben lifts a tense hand. "Yeah, I guess."

"He guesses," Eliot says to Tom, as if there is wiggle room there.

Beckett is listening intently while shutting the fridge and fisting a jug of orange juice. *Do not look his way. Do not look.*

I blow out a long breath.

"Read it, Fisher," Ben urges with a smile. His optimism is really sweet because right now, I am floating in an ocean of cynicism. Likelihood of this being a rejection is *high*.

Okay. Fuck it. I read the text.

> **GUY ABERNATHY**
>
> Harriet Fisher, on behalf of the Honors House, I'm pleased to inform you that you've reached the final round of selections. You're in the top five.

"She looks like a cartoon character," Tom quips. "Harry, is this your happy face?"

"Shut up, Thomas," I manage to say, albeit breathily. "I'm in the top five," I tell Ben directly. "I made the top fucking five."

His bright smile is everything. He says a melodic-sounding phrase in French, then translates, "Never doubt yourself."

It floods me. He lifts me up, just to kiss me, and I swoop my arms around his neck, the shock wearing off as Charlie claps slowly.

Ben brings me to my feet.

"Girl Genius," Charlie says, less dryly than usual. His other brothers aren't as excited for me. I get why. If I'm accepted to the Honors House, then Ben will move out. My frown takes hold.

Ben pushes a hot hand through his hair. "Her achievement isn't my downfall. You can be happy for Harriet." He adds something else in fiery French.

They all speak over each other while my phone pings. I pop up my email notification, and I exhale an audible dejected sigh.

The whole kitchen quiets. It's odd that my mere crestfallen mood can have people shifting their postures. Prepared to go to battle for me? To be there for me? They're definitely not against me anymore.

"You okay?" Ben asks.

I nod, then acknowledge Tom. "You'll be happy to know, *Tommy*, that I did get rejected. Just not from the Honors House."

"From what?" Beckett frowns.

My neck heats. "From another shadowing position. They're super hard to find. I've cold-called so many doctor's offices. Emailed twice as many. All of them are either filled or they're not seeking any. Too much liability and paperwork—that's the main complaint."

Charlie tilts his head. "Is your dad not a trauma surgeon?"

They found out this little nugget of information before my End of the World shift on Sunday. Ben and I met them at Duke's on 10th, a cool diner in Hell's Kitchen, where I was grilled more than the burgers.

Questions ranged from "what do your parents do?" to "would you let our brother drown in a Jack and Rose *Titanic* scenario?"—which I found funny since we were just discussing icebergs that day. Kate Winslet's character definitely had room to scooch over and keep Jack out of the freezing water.

Problem is, Ben would pull a Jack and ensure he wouldn't tip me over with his weight. It caused the whole conversation to derail into Ben needing to protect himself more.

Which I totally agree. But his selfless heart shouldn't be changed either. It's so much of who he is.

Ben ended the onslaught of questions when Eliot started asking personal ones about kinks. "Okay, *okay*, too far," he said, but by Eliot's grin, I knew he was mostly messing with his little brother.

In the kitchen, I glance back at the email. Rejected for another shadowing position. Then I confirm to Charlie, "My dad is a trauma surgeon. At Metropolitan Medical." Which is so very close.

"Why not use that connection?" Beckett is the one to ask.

Ben gives me a consoling look, knowing the truth. My dad *is* an option, but I've been too scared to pursue that contact.

As I gaze up at Ben, I'm reminded of what he once said.

Courage doesn't exist without fear. We all have to confront things that scare us at some point.

"Maybe I will," I decide.

Might as well rip off this Band-Aid. I'm going to see my dad. Today.

FORTY-EIGHT

HARRIET FISHER

I'm desperate. It's the sole reason I'm standing inside Metropolitan Med's emergency department. I can admit that to myself.

The busy front-desk lady talks briskly on the phone, hoists a finger for me to wait, then appraises me in a quick sweep. She reminds me of my mom. Not because of her terse demeanor or her appearance. Her honey blond waves and angular chin couldn't be further from my mom's light brown hair and rounded face.

It's simply where she's sitting.

Behind the plexiglass wall, checking patients into the hospital, asking for their insurance cards and IDs. When I was little, I heard the story about Hope Danes and Grant Fisher meeting in the ED. She was a medical receptionist. He was starting his trauma fellowship.

"The very first time we had the same shift, it was love-at-first sight," my mom recalled *before* the divorce.

Only later did the recollection of events flip from love story to horror story.

"He was a pretentious narcissist who wanted attention from the youngest 'hottest' girl in the hospital." She went hard on the air quotes. "Some weren't even legal to *drink*. What was he going to do? Buy them a soda." She'd scoff and fume, as if she didn't meet him when she was twenty, and he was in his early thirties.

Three months later, she became pregnant with me. A *big* surprise, they said. Not a good one either since I was the main strain on their short relationship, but they stuck it out until I was five.

"Surgeons are a different breed, Harriet," she'd tell me while we grocery shopped, angrily tossing boxed mac 'n cheese into the cart. "They're sadistic, emotionless *assholes* who get paid to cut people up. Remember that."

It's as if she implanted her voice in my brain for this very moment. So I would turn around and bolt and never confront him.

My stomach curdles. This might be a serious mistake, but I've run out of good options. With a stomach full of nerves, I just think about Ben. Picturing his infectious, slow-rising smile edging across his face only makes me want to smile back and not bang my head on this lady's desk.

Are these Cobalt powers from afar? Has Ben zapped me with poise? But I know I have my own brand of self-assurance.

I didn't get this far on my own without putting myself out there. I can do this.

Taking a deep breath, I prepare myself for the next step. So as the honey-blond receptionist hangs up the phone and motions me forward, I feel ready.

"Dr. Fisher is in surgery," she explains. "But if you can wait twenty minutes—"

"I can," I say fast.

"Okay, you can come on back and wait in the staff lounge."

My mouth nearly drops. She's letting me back into the staff lounge? *Me*. I thought she'd point to one of the waiting room chairs and tell me to park my butt. Though—most are taken by sniffling kids and worried parents.

I don't question it. I just follow her through the double doors and down the sterile hallway. Doctors, nurses, and technicians meander around, and I don't bother searching for my dad. If he's in surgery, he won't be strolling down the hall. She leads me into a small room with couches and chairs and a long table that has the basics. Microwave, mini fridge, and a pile of plastic takeout utensils.

A woman in scrubs pours herself a cup of coffee. I read her medical badge: **Twila Vandersloot, M.D.** "Who's this?" she asks the receptionist, but her eyes are on me.

"Dr. Fisher's kid." The receptionist motions to the chair for me to sit. I slowly sink down. Careful not to make any noise. Break anything. Be too much of a problem. I don't want *anything* to get me kicked out.

Twila's brows furrow. "Siggy?"

"No, from his first marriage."

Her eyes bug. "Ohhhh."

Great, *great*. That sound totally means they've discussed my dad's first marriage, or maybe there's some horrible rumor about how my dad knocked up his young receptionist in Pittsburgh and married her a year later.

Twila's phone beeps and she leaves hastily without any formal introductions or even a quick goodbye. The receptionist exits the room right behind her in just as abrupt fashion.

For a moment, I felt like I belonged. That *quickly* vanished.

But my dad wants to talk. He didn't immediately dismiss my request to speak to him, so that's the positive spot I land on.

Twenty minutes pass with doctors dipping in and out of the lounge. Some ask who I am. Most just grab a coffee or an energy drink and scroll on their phone for ten minutes before returning to work.

The thirty-minute mark nears when the door bangs open again. No one else is in the room, so I'm preparing to either blend into the chair like an invisible dust bunny or explain my name and relation to the trauma surgeon on duty.

I have to do neither because I'm face to face with the trauma surgeon. It dawns on me that I haven't seen him in person since I was eight years old, and I doubt he could find me on social media when Fanaticon internet sleuths still haven't.

His stunned expression mirrors mine as I rapidly soak in his features. His deep brown hair is void of gray except for a few patches on his chin. The mustache and full scruff along his jaw is neatly groomed. So unlike his clean-shaven appearance I remember as a kid. Even in his fifties, his charming demeanor resembles television doctors. Like the ones on *Grey's*.

I wobble to my feet, grateful that I chose to wear my khakis and a white blouse tonight and not my leather jacket.

"You're blond," is the first thing he says. His eyes narrow. He shakes his head like it's hard to put the pieces together. "You're eighteen now?"

"Nineteen. Last month."

"Right...right..." He nods slowly. "Sit, sit." He gestures me to the chair while he scrapes over one from the wall. Just so it can face me. He keeps perusing my features as if he's documenting each change. "You look so much like your mother."

My gut drops. I don't take it as a compliment, and I'm not sure he's giving it as one.

I swallow hard, words trapping in my esophagus, but I manage to say, "I haven't seen her in three years. I wouldn't know."

It takes him aback. "Three years?" He shakes his head, confused.

That hurts. Because the worst day of my life didn't even register enough to form a memory for him. "The last time I called you. My sixteenth birthday. I told you she was kicking me out."

He rubs a palm along his jaw, processing. "Right...right..." He drops his hand, his brows knitted together. "So I'm guessing the child support I was paying her never made it to you."

I nod once. I never thought about the child support—but I guess he's right.

"I'm sorry," he tells me. "You and your Aunt Helena, did you get by?"

My throat nearly closes. "Yeah," I squeak out the lie.

He scans me. More confusion creases his forehead. "So then what are you doing here, Harriet? Do you need money?"

Bile rises at the insinuation I'm going to ask for cash. I'm not. But is asking for a shadowing position any better? It's the first time I've seen him in *eleven* fucking years. I should be here to try and form a father-daughter relationship with him before trying to get something from him.

God...I'm a user.

A taker.

I wouldn't mind transforming into dust particles this very instant.

"I, um...I..." I blink a couple times and take a breath. "I'm going to Manhattan Valley University. I'm a sophomore. Pre-med."

His brows vault in surprise. "So you're still doing well in school then?"

"Yeah." I restrain myself from listing out every course I'm taking, all the clubs, the volunteering and research. I don't want to bombard him with my life—even if I ache to have him know all the details. Every single one. "The plan is to get into medical school, then into a general surgery residency, then a trauma fellowship." *Like you.*

He gives me a warm smile. "That's tough."

"Yeah, I know, but it's the life goal." It's going well. I think I just need to take my shot. "I have all that I need on my resume. Perfect grades and extracurriculars. But I haven't had luck getting a shadowing position with any doctors."

I almost wait for him to say, *so that's what you want.*

But he thankfully doesn't. He nods again. "Shadowing positions are few and far between, and I wish I could help you out. But Denise and I made an agreement with each other around eight or nine years ago that I needed to cut all ties to your mother. If I were to let you shadow me or one of the residents in my department, it would be breaking that agreement. Denise and the kids, they mean the world to me, and I just can't let any of that negativity back into my life. Into *their* lives."

I've stopped breathing. "I-I don't understand," I say. "I'm not my mom."

"You are tied to her—"

"I'm *not*," I argue, heat baking my lungs. "I haven't spoken to her in years."

He holds up his hands, his eyes going wide. "We were having a civil conversation, Harriet."

I *barely* raised my voice. But is that all he sees when he looks at me? Hope Danes, who overreacts. Hope Danes, who can't keep her cool.

I'll never be anything other than his first wife's daughter.

I'll never be just Harriet Fisher.

I've never hated him. Not a moment in my life. Not even when the happy birthday phone calls stopped when I turned eleven…*holy shit*. He made that agreement with his wife eight or nine years ago. That would've been around my eleventh birthday. He never forgot my birthday. He cut ties with me. And I just never knew.

Hurt blasts through my chest as if I'm standing in the center of a nuclear explosion. I don't plan to say a goodbye. I figure it's a common thing in this hospital anyway. I just stand from my chair and face the exit.

"Harriet, sit down. Let's just have a normal conversation."

Normal?

My eyes flame as I spin on him. There are so many things I could say—because I have a feeling there might not be another time we ever talk again.

But all that comes out of my mouth is pure fire. "Fuck you for thinking I'm Hope. I'm not *her*. I'm not even *you*. I am Harriet fucking Fisher. I'm the girl who was smart enough to skip fifth grade. The girl who's brilliant enough to get a full ride to an Ivy. The girl who's proud enough to say I don't need you. I never needed you to succeed one single day of my life, and I won't need you to become a doctor. I will do that with the support of people who actually care about me, and thank you for reminding me it's not you. So fuck you." I wipe an angry tear away. "And you might hate Hope. You might think she's the worst person in the world. But look in the fucking mirror. Because you've never been any better."

Rage clouds my vision as I storm out of the lounge. Out of the hospital. My breathing is labored as I land on the sidewalk. Ambulance sirens blare as they veer into the emergency bay. I'm shellshocked at my outburst—because that *never* happens. I keep my words in. I keep my feelings tight. I know I have too much to lose by cursing people out.

But I don't regret it. The sentiment surges more powerfully. *I do not regret it.*

I'm proud of myself for unleashing my feelings. No Cobalt would've sulked out of the hospital with a tail between their legs. They would've stood their ground. Held their head fucking high.

Pride indestructible in the face of adversaries.

I just never thought my dad would be one. Until now.

All I want is to call Ben, but it's Wednesday night. He's back in Philly, eating dinner with his family, and I struggle to bother him. Who else to call?

Xander? I'd have to explain this whole situation.

Aunt Helena? She won't understand why I went to see my dad in the first place, and the last thing I want to hear is a bunch of different variations of *I told you so.*

So I just go to my apartment. Microwave a bowl of ramen noodles. Curl up on the couch and click on the television to marathon some CSI. In no mood to even study for finals.

Ben texts at one point.

BEN 💚

How'd it go?

I send him a thumbs-down emoji.

He immediately calls, but talking sounds strenuous. I'm one with the couch. Can't even move to grab my earbuds, and Eden has her door ajar. I'm also not in the mood for my roommate to hear about my daddy issues.

So I text Ben.

> **HARRIET**
> Don't feel like talking tonight. Sry. Will chat with you tomorrow. All good.

BEN 🖤

> 😘

The kissy face emoji is always used playfully when we text, so it tics up my lips just slightly. Still, I overturn my phone and squeeze my pillow beneath my head. Lying on the lumpy couch cushions, I didn't even pull out the mattress.

Four episodes in and four grotesque murders solved later, a knock sounds on my door.

As if knowing I am a slovenly sloth tonight, Eden answers it. "Oh." She startles. "I thought you might be Austin. Come in."

Before I even exert effort to look, I hear him.

"Oh my God, not the Hello Kitty blanket," Ben says like I'm in dire straits wrapped up in the hot pink fabric. The smile in his voice has an instant effect on me.

I almost smile back. "Don't knock my emotional support blanket, Friend."

"I'm only jealous you're under there without me." He places a slim red vase of beautiful, perky sunflowers on the end table beside my dirty ramen bowl. No one has ever given me flowers until him.

Let alone the many vibrant green plants he's bestowed upon my apartment. I hear Eden's bedroom door shutting.

Ben skims my couch-potato state.

I'm not even embarrassed. This sinking, weighted feeling overshadows even the ability to be *mortified*. And what's so humiliating about Ben seeing my sadness? When, really, all I want is for someone to help take it away?

Ben towers. "I know I showed up unannounced, so if you want me to go, now's the time to tell me, Fisher." My last name rushes in a wave of grief I haven't felt before. I *love* my name. I don't *ever* want to hate it.

I swallow a lump. "Not afraid of jump-scaring me with your presence anymore?"

"A little scared. Still took the risk." He's drawing my gaze to his. "Did it pan out?"

I nod vigorously, tears pricking my eyes. "I'm really glad you're here," I say as my voice breaks.

Immediately, Ben has his arms around me. He's scooping me up, cradling me while he sinks onto the couch. He brings me into his chest in an epic, consoling hug like he's the god of solace. I bury my face into the crook of his arm, choking on a sob.

We're both tangled in the Hello Kitty blanket, and I don't really care. He plants tender kisses on my head, on my cheek, on my lips, and I ease with each one. Ten minutes pass before I'm able to release what happened into the air.

He is *pissed* at my dad. When I tell Ben I said "fuck you" to him, he nods a lot in relief, and it makes me feel really good. Still, there is a sense of loss I can't thwart. My cinematic reunion with my dad in my white coat, with my M.D., with his love and pride for me—it's been demolished.

He will never love me or be proud of me. I want to not care. Why should I even waste tears on him?

"You might want to let go of me," I warn Ben, wiping the creases of my eyes while he uses the bottom of his shirt to dry my chin.

"Why?" he asks.

"I might just decay on you. I was becoming one with the couch before you showed up."

"You weren't doing a very good job."

I snort out a surprised laugh. "What?" I squeak out.

His lips inch higher. "Yeah, you're still a lot cuter than the couch, Fisher." He pauses when he notices me wince at *Fisher.* "I can stop using your last name—"

"No," I interject. "Please, *please* don't. I love my last name, and it's *mine*. He doesn't get to take that from me."

Light touches his blue eyes. "Okay, Fisher. And I'm not letting go of you. So I have to warn you, we will be decaying on this couch together."

My heart swells so much, I'm shocked it's not bursting out of my ribcage. I blink away more tears. "You make it impossible," I realize.

"What impossible?"

"To rot away." I hold his deepening gaze that reaches into me. He seems to be gripping onto my expression, his chest falling and rising in time with mine. "How long have you been the sun?"

He cups my cheek. "I'm not the sun."

"You are, Ben. Life can't wither and die when you're around. Nothing can go cold. Out of an entire Empire of stars, you're the brightest in the sky."

He smiles a little.

"What?" I sit up higher on his lap, our faces closer.

"I just know something that you don't, smarty-pants," he says as his gaze strokes mine. "The sun isn't the brightest star. It's not even the hottest, but I still burn." His thumb caresses my cheek. "Because I'm mad. Maddened for those I love. Maddened by their pain. Maddened by life. Your agony is my plight. Your torment, my war. Your love, my triumph. I don't know how to dim when I love you, Harriet. I only know how to burn bright."

FORTY-NINE

HARRIET FISHER

I sprint across the grassy quad, taking every shortcut known to man. My bookbag thwacks my back, and I just think, *I'm late, I'm late, I'm already late.* I'd rather be fifteen minutes late to Professor Wellington's oral exam than three minutes late to meet Ben's parents.

I am at least fifteen minutes tardy by this point. It's one thing to be late meeting a boyfriend's mom and dad—another thing for that mom and dad to be *the* Rose Calloway and Connor Cobalt. Not only are they famous, they're the types who'd arrive early to the freaking dentist. For unimportant routine events.

They probably think I'm lazy.

Or worse, that I don't care about Ben enough to make a good first impression.

I can't believe my Latin professor held me up in office hours. I was submitting extra credit in person, and he basically kept me *hostage* while he was chatting with another student. I wanted to go, but he kept saying, "Wait, give me a minute." As though he had some important thing to share with me.

He simply wanted to say, "Job well done this semester." Normally, I'd appreciate the pat on the back, but not today. NOT TODAY!!

I rush toward Loxley Hall, the largest and most ornate auditorium on campus. Used for guest lectures, research seminars, alumni gatherings, and things of that ilk.

To further emphasize Ben's parents are so not normal—security guards are posted outside the imposing arched double doors, and clusters of students loiter around the gargoyle turreted building with their phones at the ready, likely hoping to catch a glimpse of the legendary Rose and Connor when they exit.

I speed through the crowds, jogging up the stone steps, and as soon as I reach the door, a random security dude juts out a hand to stop me. These aren't the Cobalts' personal 24/7 bodyguards because they would, I'd hope, recognize me by now.

"Miss, are you a business student?"

Rose and Connor are here giving a guest lecture to business students only. The tickets apparently sold out within the first two minutes of hitting MVU's website. But Ben said we could attend without them, and his parents know he's introducing me afterward.

"I'm pre-med, but—"

"You can't go inside, I'm sorry."

"I'm with Ben Cobalt." I step forward—the door is right there, *come on.*

The security guard bumps me back with a firm palm. "We've heard that one all day."

I, too, would think I'm lying, and I try not to bristle knowing other girls are claiming Ben. Panting for breath, I hurriedly shoot him a text.

> HARRIET
> Outside. They won't let me in. SOS.

"Head down the stairs, Miss," the security guard instructs, just as the door whips open. Wow, that was super fast. Ben peeks his head out. The shrieks behind me pierce my ears.

"That's a Cobalt!"

"BEN!!"

"Is Rose Calloway behind him?"

"Is Connor coming out?!"

"She's with me," Ben says quickly to security, then waves me forward.

I bolt past the wall of guards, not even caring to rub my priority status in their face. All I can think is, *I am so fucking late.*

"I'm so sorry," I whisper to Ben as the heavy doors *thunk* closed behind us. The checkered marble entryway leads to a set of auditorium doors. It's hushed in here, except for the faint sound of his mom's voice. "I meant to be prompt, on time, but I should've planned to be early—"

"I wasn't even early," he whispers with a rising smile. "*Breathe*, Fisher." He's sliding my bookbag off my arm, fitting Son of Ben in the big pocket. The golden stuffed lion peeks out. Then he slings my bookbag on his own shoulder, and his hand clasps mine. "What my parents think of you won't change my feelings for you at all. So however this goes, you aren't getting rid of me."

He's still here.

It helps calm my nerves. My cheeks pinch as a fluttery, weightless feeling soars inside me. "Let's do the thing, Friend."

He lifts our cupped hands and kisses my knuckles, as if to say, *more than friends.*

I grimace to hide my smile. "Thanks, Romeo."

"Working on your Shakespeare before you meet my parents?"

Should I have studied for this??? "They aren't going to quiz me—"

"I'm joking, I'm joking." He kisses the top of my head. *This isn't that serious, Harriet.* I repeat the sentiment as he swiftly leads me into the auditorium. Probably so I stop obsessing.

It is packed. Some heads swivel as Ben gently shuts the door behind us. His hand in mine, he guides me across the back wall where we stand beside several older professor-looking types. We don't make a fuss trying to find empty seats, and honestly, I'm not sure any exist.

My pulse kicks up an extra notch when Rose, at the podium, makes sudden direct eye contact with Ben, then me.

Her speech never falters, but her yellow-green eyes are as penetrating as Beckett's and Charlie's. If not more so.

Her form-fitting black dress hugs her hourglass curves, and her matte black nails curl around the podium's frame. She reminds me of Disney's Maleficent. Powerful, deadly, elegant. I'd be hanging on her every icy word like most of the students here, but I am *nervous*.

I should've taken Benadryl.

My arms itch a little under my cropped sweater top and oversized leather jacket. I asked Ben what I should wear, and he said, "What you normally wear."

Okay, but my belly button ring is showing. I'm rethinking that decision. She looks *classy*. I look...trashy?

I whip my leather jacket closed. *Too late, Harriet, she's already seen your stomach bling.* Ben frowns down at me because I've let go of his hand.

I'm about to reach back for him, but instead, he curves his arm around my shoulders, hugging me closer to his side.

Affection for him floods me so tremendously. He's too good for this world, maybe too good for me because I didn't earn Ben. He came into my life without any effort on my part, but I want to hang on to this beautiful, good thing the universe has given me. My Aunt Helena would tell me to, at least.

As I watch Rose, I realize her poise is Ben's poise. Her confidence is his confidence. It's so clear he's her son.

She carries herself with dignity and pride, and I wonder if it's as bulletproof as they say. After the fallout with my dad yesterday, I want to be indestructible like her. To move forward with armor that Grant Fisher can never pierce.

"I'll leave you with this." Rose scans the auditorium with

narrowed eyes. "Take care of yourself." Her gaze pins to me, then her son. "I understand those four words might seem simple and futile. In our pursuit of success, we often forget the key to moving forward is not in the distance we run but in how long we can run for." She takes a beat, then adds, "Even in heels." The audience claps and *woots* but they settle quickly as she continues, "So take care of yourself. The stars may be in reach more than you even believe."

I swear her lip twitches up at me. My heart flip-flops. Was that a secret nod of approval? Already? *Yeah, right.*

We all clap. She exits to booming applause. The standing ovation is exhilarating. As it dies down, people shift out of rows to leave.

I go wide-eyed up at Ben. "I missed your dad's entire fucking talk?"

"He won't test you on it." His smile soothes me.

"I would've liked the opportunity because taking a quiz is way better than missing the material I could've been tested on."

He laughs. "And that's why I know my mom will love you." He scrunches the side of my hair, and I bump my weight into him, my sour-puss face morphing into something weirdly smitten, I'm sure.

"Ben." His bodyguard touches his elbow and whispers, "This way." We're directed toward the stage, then into a private lounge for guest speakers at the university.

Rose and Connor are already here.

This morning, I distinctly recall Ben saying, "My parents really aren't as intimidating as the media makes them out to be."

I could choke on a laugh. They are *so* fucking intimidating. Not only are they both way taller than me, but they look like they chew and spit out interns on the daily.

"Mom, Dad," Ben greets with a widening smile. He's not letting go of my hand yet. "This is Harriet Fisher, my girlfriend." I mentally add *temporary (until the holidays)* to the relationship status so I don't pass out. "She was stuck in office hours, going above and beyond." He smiles down at me like my nerd habits are cute. "So she didn't get a chance to hear you, Dad, but I'll give her the CliffsNotes later."

He just removed a ginormous weight off me from having to overexplain my absence.

"Don't worry, there won't be a test." Connor fucking Cobalt is speaking to me. Not only that, he's *smiling* at me, but more like a warm *hello* of a smile, whereas Rose has pursed lips that twitch like she's overcaffeinated for this moment.

"That's what I told her," Ben grins.

I nod. "He did assure me I wouldn't be graded." I work my face a little out of a scowl. "It's nice to meet both of you. Ben has only said great things."

"Likewise, he's talked a lot about you," Connor says. "It's good to finally put a name to a face he mentions so often."

"Very often," Ben teases. "All the time. Every other word is *Harriet*, actually."

I chew my rising lip. "Knew you loved my name, Friend."

"Friend?" Rose cuts in like a P.I. sniffing out our relationship. "Are you two not officially together?" Her matte black nail points from me to her son.

Thank God I'm with an extrovert. I want to pat myself on the back for this choice in life because Ben quickly clarifies, "It's just a thing we do. We're together. You'll probably hear me call her *Friend* too."

His dad bridges the space and holds out a hand to me. "Connor Cobalt. Though I likely don't need an introduction."

"No, you don't." I try my best to do a good business-like shake. Firm grip but not a death clutch.

Connor is basically the same height as Ben. The one-inch difference is so miniscule, but he's not trying to loom over me. Which I appreciate. Ben's friendliness is definitely from his father.

His mom is a hawk, watching me as I wrap myself up in my

leather jacket like a bat cocooning itself in wings. I might be scowling at her. Shit.

"Rose, darling," Connor says with a grin.

She snaps a glare at him, then comes forward with a finger raised. "I'm not a hugger, but I will make an exception this once. Do not judge me on the quality of this hug."

That blunt honesty eases my nerves. "No judgment here," I say as she comes in for a hug…but it's more like a light tap on my shoulders. She wasn't fucking lying. The fact that she wanted to hug me though—that means something, right?

I'm about to turn to Ben, but Rose tells me, "I'm stealing you away for a little bit. Follow." She gestures a finger toward herself, and I leave Ben's side like his mom has put a fucking spell on me. Maybe she really is Maleficent.

Rose takes me to a private courtyard attached to Loxley Hall. Iron bistro chairs and round tables scatter the cobblestone, and she chooses one beside a heat lamp.

We sit. "This fucking wind," she growls, swatting her lush, glossy brown hair out of her face and crossing her legs. "We should have made the boys come out here." She eyes me. "What do you think? Switch places?"

She's asking *my* opinion? "I'm okay." I stuff my hands in my leather jacket. "The heater is nice."

Rose pulls out a black winter beanie from the purse she places on the table. "Here, put this on at least. Your ears are getting pink."

I accept the hat, grateful because my ears do burn from the wind. As I wedge it over my head, I ask, "Aren't your ears cold?"

She leans farther back, the hem of her peacoat nearly skimming the stone patio. "Me? *No.* I've embraced the cold. It's the monstrous gusts of wind determined to mess up my hair that I take issue with." She only leans forward when a twentysomething, fashionable girl—sporting a plaid peacoat and turtleneck dress—appears with two coffees. "Allegra Piscitelli, my personal assistant," Rose introduces us. "Allegra, this is Harriet Fisher, my youngest son's girlfriend."

I remove a hand from the warmth to raise it in greeting.

"Nice to meet you," Allegra says. "This is for you." She hands me the coffee cup. "Black drip, one espresso shot, no milk, no sugar."

"Yeah…? How do you know my usual order?"

"I asked Ben," Rose answers into her sip. "Thank you." Her sharp perfunctory *thank you* sends Allegra away. Her assistant seems happy to escape into the warm indoors. "Don't be nervous."

I expel a tight breath. "Am I that obvious?"

"You keep hugging yourself like you're afraid your bowels are going to spill onto the floor."

"What an image," I say flatly. "Maybe I'm just cold."

"Scoot closer." She waves me toward the metal heater, then fiddles with the knob, raising the temperature for me.

Is it weird that I think I already love her?

My eyes burn. How is that possible—that in two seconds, I already wish she were my mom? When it's taken me years to convince myself to have even a morsel of affection toward the woman who birthed me?

Sitting back in the iron chair, Rose pushes hair off her shoulder, then picks up her coffee. "When I first met Connor's mother, I threw wine on her blouse, so just know you can't make a more hostile first impression than me. Unless you throw the coffee. Which I considered getting on ice just in case karmic justice came back to bite me today."

"Chances of coffee-throwing are very low," I assure her.

Her lip quirks, then she scans me. "You're the first girl Ben has ever introduced us to. He wouldn't even let us meet his Prom date."

I didn't know that.

"We've gotten really close. He means a lot to me. He's…" How do you even describe someone who's become your best friend, the person you ache to share every aspect of your life with because their mere presence just fills your soul? "There is no one like Ben. You raised an *incredible* person with a heart I feel fortunate to know, and if anyone hurts him, I'd probably go to jail for stabbing them in the eye."

"I'll be right behind you for stabbing the other one."

I laugh.

She smiles into her sip of coffee, staining the rim with dark rouge lipstick. "I'm *very* new at this whole meeting one of my son's partners, so forgive me if I sound too blunt. But he's treating you well? Because I will drag him to the center of a burning volcano—by his earlobe—if I hear he's being anything other than chivalrous." Her eyes flame like she means it.

I didn't expect her to want to protect *me*. My throat tries to swell closed. "No, Ben is such a gentleman. He's honest. Caring. The best, really." I add fast, "And I don't know if you've been afraid of it—but I'm not with him because he's a Cobalt. Like, honestly, I couldn't care less that you all are famous, no offense. He could live in a tent out by a creek, and I'd be stupidly giddy if he invited me inside."

She grimaces at the word *tent*. "Do you like the outdoors?"

"Uh, no." I shake my head hard. "No, I foresee myself in the city…" I trail off, grateful for the coffee to drink away the pause.

"As a doctor," she concludes for me.

"Yes." I nod, licking coffee off my lips. "That's the goal."

Rose is processing quickly. She edges forward. "My children being taken advantage of *does* cross my mind, but Connor and I haven't suspected you of anything nefarious. That being said, have you and Ben discussed your futures?"

"He knows I want to be a surgeon. I can't exactly accomplish that in an RV or backpacking the Appalachian trail."

Her nails clank the iron table. "Has he bought an RV?"

"No," I say fast. *Oh shit*. "No, I was just throwing out hypotheticals. He doesn't even talk a lot about what he wants to do beyond this semester." That is true.

As wind picks up, she tugs black gloves on her fingers. "Are you two being safe?"

"In what way?"

"If you're sexually active." She grabs her coffee. "I was on birth control when I became pregnant with my first."

My eyes bug. "Are you serious? Did the condom break?" I can't believe I'm asking *Rose Calloway* this. Not to mention, Ben's *mom*. But she's making this conversation easy. I'd almost believe she wants me to ask.

"No condom. I was on the pill, and I proudly *never* missed a day."

I'm freaking out. "That's like a one percent chance of getting pregnant." My face falls. "I'm on the pill too."

"Just be very careful," she says ominously.

"What, is there something in Cobalt sperm?" I'm joking of course; as a lady of science, this is absurd.

"The tireless willpower to impregnate, yes. I've already cautioned my sons a thousand times."

"We'll be extra safe." Maybe we'll use condoms when I'm ovulating and chances of pregnancy are higher. I'll have to talk to Ben. Part of me still thinks this is silly.

But if it turns out he has godlike super sperm and knocks me up, I might actually start believing I'm with some immortal being.

She plucks out her phone. "I understand being focused on career goals, so let me know a time that's best for you to meet again. I want to bring you to Le Petit Rêve. It's my favorite café in the city. We can make it a girl's date or invite Ben and Connor. What's your number?"

I exchange numbers with his mom. She also sends me Connor's cell too. While I add them to my contacts, I receive a new text.

TOM 💀

> Meet me at Duke's on 10th at 7 p.m.? Just you, Harry. Ben doesn't need to come.

Even though we've been around each other more, Tom and I still volley insults like we're competing in some deranged version of Wimbledon. I don't think we're friends, so this invite to a Hell's Kitchen diner *without* Ben is strange. He must sense my hesitance because another message pops up.

TOM 💀

> I will repay you however you want. Free favor on the house. Just give me a half hour.

I hope I don't regret this. I send him a reply.

HARRIET

> Fine, Thomas. See you then.

I'M ON A HIGH FROM MEETING BEN'S PARENTS, FROM HOW well it went, and it's all about to be squashed by Tom.

As I walk up to the diner, Tom stands beneath the lightbulb marquee sign blinking *Duke's on 10th*, and he says, "We're not going inside."

I glare. "Then where are we going?"

"It's a surprise." He clasps my hand and climbs inside an SUV, tugging me in behind him.

I hug my messenger bag on my lap as the car peels out, his bodyguard driving. "If you weren't Ben's brother, you would have a face full of pepper spray, dude."

His blue eyes fall to my bag. "Packing weapons? I thought you just tote around five-gallon tubs of Jolly Ranchers."

"I could pelt you with candy too."

He's distracted, staring out the window. Squinting a ton to

inspect a building, maybe. "Ian, you can stop here," he instructs his bodyguard.

It shocks me how much I'm trusting someone beyond myself and Ben. The possibility of Tom playing a massive prank on me is low, though. He loves his little brother too much. But I do worry he's going to rope me into trouble somehow.

I'm more surprised when we enter a recording studio. "Tom?" I drop my messenger bag in the booth. Instruments are set up behind the glass. Guitars. Microphones. *A drum kit.*

"Come out here for a second," Tom says.

My head is whirling when he leads me into the most professional recording space I've ever stepped foot in—hell, it's the *only* one I've ever been in. This is legit.

"Put these on." He hands me chunky black headphones.

"*Tom.*"

He takes a pair of headphones too.

"*Tom*, what are we doing?" I ask flat-out, realizing I might not be a fan of big surprises. I need information like *immediately.*

He rests headphones around his neck. "You're about to listen to a song for The Carraways. I wrote it after Warren quit. Drums could be better because I'm not great on them, admittedly, so it's a little rough."

"You want my feedback on your new song?" I ask.

He nods with the tip of his head, so I'm guessing that's a *meh, not really.* But he does say, "I want you to play with me."

"What?" I rock backward.

"Just listen to the song first. Play it on drums. Get a feel, then we'll talk."

I'm already here, and I am curious about the song. He jumps back into the booth, partially hidden behind glass. Leaving me alone among the instruments. Then the music pours through the headphones. I put my hands to them as Tom's passionate, melodic voice accompanies rage-fused guitar riffs and drumbeats.

I go very still as the song stirs emotion so incredibly deep inside me, as the chorus seeps into my bloodstream. I remember this same overwhelming feeling when I first heard My Chemical Romance's "Famous Last Words." It's like Tom is speaking directly to me. To what I just experienced with my dad.

You could never take the reason I woke.
You could never take my anger you provoke.
This voice, these feet, this heart of a thousand beats will go on.
Don't worry, I don't need you to see.
Any fucking part of me.
I don't need you.
You'll wish you knew.
Any fucking part of me.
The fire you feel is blue.
Don't you wish you knew?
Any fucking part of me.

Holy shit.

I am in love with this song. Possessed by the furious, heart-wrenching energy, I immediately go to the drums, grab the sticks, and I play as Tom restarts the track.

It is a blackout euphoria. To pour my emotion onto the drums. All the hurt my dad caused just leaves me with each crack on the snare. Each boom on the kick-drum. Each bang of my sticks.

Don't worry, I don't need you to see.
Any fucking part of me.
I don't need you.

By the end, I pant for air and focus when I hear Tom's elated voice. "Whoa, Harry!" He comes sling-shotting out of the booth. "That was way better than what I did. You are *epic*." He's applauding hard as he nears. "And?" His grin is huge and magnetic.

"The song is sick." I shake my head, still awed.

"I know." His grin just grows.

I roll my eyes, then stand up.

"So?" He wavers a little, maybe seeing I'm not jumping for joy. "Join the band. You and me."

"Just us?"

"We can make two work. I talked to the label. They're down for the change."

"You want me, even when you *rejected* me?"

"Because you were seventeen—"

"Then I turned eighteen, dude," I retort. "You still rejected me *then*."

"We were working with other drummers, and Warner—"

"Oh you're going to blame this on Warner when he's not around to defend himself. Really, *Tommy*?"

"He didn't want a *girl* in the fucking band," Tom says seriously. "Specifically *you*. He thought you were hot and that it would've complicated shit. I would've been a hypocrite if I fought him on that point, because I threw out Phoenix St. Pierre as a potential drummer for the *same* reason."

"Phoenix? The drummer for Nothing Personal?" I say flatly. "That band sucks."

Tom lights up. "See, this is exactly why we're meant to be, Harry. We both have the same taste in music and recognize Phoenix as trash."

I shift my weight.

"Listen to the song again." He urges me to put my headphones back on. "Play it again."

I want to so badly. "Tom, I'm in college to be a doctor. I can't *also* be a drummer. It's impossible." There is no avenue to do both. Attending med school, then entering a residency—it is even *more* time consuming than undergrad. Being in The Carraways means going on tour around the country, which sounds…unreal. But also, a time suck.

"I'm not asking you to change your life on the spot, this moment, this minute," he says. "Take days, weeks, the next month if you need more time to decide. But we could create something really special, Harriet. So I need you to know that I want you."

Is this the first time he's ever called me Harriet?

He's serious. He really wants me to be a part of The Carraways. The allure is as luminous as Tom is, and I feed on his energy.

I don't have to decide now. It lets me bask in this moment. My lips tic up a little as elation flows through me. "Can I play it again?"

"Fuck yes."

FIFTY

BEN COBALT

New York—I was never supposed to be here in the first place. I never thought I'd be living here this far into November. None of this has been part of my ultimate plan. I thought I'd even be moved out of my brothers' apartment in Hell's Kitchen forever ago.

Sure, I don't really have anywhere else to live since the Honors House hasn't accepted Harriet yet. I haven't completed the Kappa bet. But the past couple weeks, I haven't been clamoring to ditch my brothers for the frat house.

Last week, I even went to my niece's first birthday party in Philly. Harriet had a research symposium she needed to attend, so she couldn't go. I didn't want her to miss it, and Maeve's birthday isn't the sole family gathering of the year. As the holidays approach, we're all going to come together so much more.

Plus, family vacations are around the corner. The yacht will come out. The fancy villas in the Med. She's barely even seen a portion of the wealth. Mostly, I'm excited to be here as Harriet is integrated into my universe.

I could tell Harriet wished she could've gone to the birthday party. Almost everyone in my extended family had been there. Hales. Meadows. Cobalts. I saw Baby Maeve dig her little fingers in a soft-pink cake and smile gleefully up at Jane and Thatcher. No disasters, no damage, no hurt or harm.

It's made me wonder if maybe things are changing. Things are better now. The desperate need to leave is being submerged between the powerful desire to stay.

It's November 22nd.

Close to midnight on a Friday.

And I can say I'm still here for the upcoming Classical Mythology presentation. But really, it's so much more than that. I'm dragging out the plan because of her. Every bone in my body wants to stay and just be happy with this girl I fucking adore.

I know if I leave New York, everything with me and Harriet ends. But if I stay...

The *if* feels like an *I am*.

I am staying.

"You really want to do this?" Harriet questions for the third time. We're in my brothers' apartment. I have her up on the marble kitchen counter, my hands on her thighs while her knees are spread around me. Her wet blond hair has slowly begun air-drying, but strands still soak against her baggy Green Day tee. She's not wearing a bra, and I've debated slipping my hand up her shirt about a thousand-and-one sweltering times.

"What was the question?" I ask with a playful smile.

She tears a red Twizzler with her teeth, seeing me check her out. "You are such a dude."

"I am only human."

"Hate to break it to you, Cobalt boy, but you're far from mortal. And what I've gathered from all our course material, gods tend to fuck more than humans."

I laugh. "That explains Eliot then." I run casual fingers through my own damp hair. We just took a steaming hot shower together. I shut off the water at one point to not waste a lot. I'd hooked a tie on the doorknob, so my brothers knew not to barge the fuck in there. We have an agreed upon system in place, and I don't even care if they know I'm hooking up in the bathroom.

They don't care that I am.

It feels like college. Like I'm in a dorm with the people I love most. I'm falling further in love with the idea of planting roots with my brothers. Of keeping both feet on the floor, both feet beside them. It scares me, but that fear isn't a panic crawling to the surface of my skin.

It's somewhere unreachable. Faded.

Hopefully gone.

I smile more at her. Thinking about us in the shower.

Being inside Harriet hasn't wrecked me. It's been the most cathartic, euphoric experience of my life. I've never been this close to someone else. Never loved them to this extreme depth, and I've given so many pieces of myself to her—vulnerable pieces that I've never shown anyone.

I think she's given just as many back.

"You really want to do this?" Harriet asks for the fourth time now. She swallows the bite of Twizzler and awaits my response.

"I'm sure," I nod. "Tonight is the best night. Kappa has been throwing a football party all day. It's probably still going on, and Leif wanted me to show up. So I'll go to the frat house and tell him I'm dropping out of the pledge class."

I'm not going through initiation. I don't want to be an official member of the frat. Especially now that I don't plan on completing their bet. Even if Harriet is accepted in the Honors House, I'm not living at Kappa Phi Delta.

I want to live with my brothers.

I've always wanted to, really. I just never felt like I could until now.

"You're setting your parachute on fire," Harriet warns me. "They're your fallback."

She's worried I'll leave the city early if I don't have alternate housing. "I won't need one. I'll be okay with my brothers," I assure her. I don't mention how I'm contemplating staying permanently. I might take her out to break the good news. "Before I forget." I tug my phone out of my pocket, then send Harriet a contact.

Her cell lights up on the counter beside her. I smile as her big eyes grow into disco balls at the contact's name. "What the fuck...no."

"Yes." I nod with a grin. "I've got the connections. One of which is a highly-respected concierge medical team. Physicians that you can shadow. You've already met Farrow after the escape room, now you have his number."

After she told me the play-by-play of her meet up with her dad, I wanted to knock him out. I hope to never run into him because I might. I don't trust myself. I wish it struck me sooner that Farrow was an option right there, all this time, but maybe it's good Harriet closed the chapter with her dad. Her goals in medicine no longer have to be tangled with him.

She hasn't blinked yet.

I heard all about Tom asking Harriet to join The Carraways. She wanted my input, but I'm not much help. I can easily picture Harriet being extraordinary as a rock star or as a doctor—both paths fulfilling her, both paths making her happy.

She's been firmly fifty-fifty split down the middle. At a significant fork in the road. Music or medicine. Where she goes will determine her entire future, but it shouldn't change our relationship much. I'll be beside her no matter what she does.

Unless I leave.

What *I* decide about my plan will be the course-corrector, the thing that truly impacts us. I don't love wielding that much power in a relationship, but then again, I would be more panicked if I didn't have control.

I have no clue what that says about me. That I'm a control freak?

I see her mind reeling. "I won't be the one to call Farrow," I tell her. "It's your choice."

She picks up her phone. "Is this your way of telling me to choose medicine?"

"No, I just want to make things easier if you decide to be a doctor. No pressure at all, but that window is cracked for you, bel oiseau. Fly through if you want to."

"Thanks, Ben." It's so soft and sincere, my ribs relax around my lungs hearing it. "I'm collecting numbers in your fam like Pokémon."

"You going to catch them all?" I tease.

"Maybe." Her teeny-tiny smile peeks through, and I dip my head down, kissing her lightly, tenderly, my blood coursing through me in fervent, passionate waves. I still hold her delicate jaw when I break our lips apart.

"I am spending the night at my apartment," she says *again*.

"You telling me or yourself?"

"Both." She needs to finish writing her final essay for Classical Mythology in the morning, and her place does have less distractions.

I still haven't started my paper. But I figure I'll take the subway with her, make sure she gets home okay, then go to the frat house from there.

Harriet scoops the stuffed lion off the counter, his neck blinged out with a beaded *Cobalt Empire* choker. "You're not giving Son of Ben back. We're keeping him. Because trust me, you don't want to be the father that ditches their kid."

"Noted," I nod, looking her over. "I'll be in and out tonight. I'll let you know how it goes—"

"How what goes, brother?" Eliot saunters in the kitchen. Snatching a red apple from a fruit bowl, he leans over the island and takes a bite.

Fuck. I comb a hand through my hair, and Harriet slides off the counter while I spin toward him. "I'm dropping out of the frat tonight."

"Say no more." Eliot straightens up. "I'll grab my coat—"

"Alone." Like *very* alone. I planned to not alert Novak. Eliot is already opening the coat closet. "Alone, Eliot!" For fuck's sake.

I hear Charlie. "That word has lost meaning to him since Tom entered the world." He appears from his side of the apartment and slings a travel duffel on his shoulder.

"Wasn't he only eleven-months-old?" Harriet asks with another hostile bite of Twizzler.

"Eleven-months of pure agony and loneliness I'll never forget," Eliot quips. He's sliding his arms through a very, *very* expensive black peacoat, pressed and ironed.

"And that's not your coat," I point out.

"Finders keepers," Eliot grins, popping the collar. He's trying to get a rise out of Charlie, since the coat belongs to him.

Charlie isn't entertaining Eliot tonight. He slips his wallet in the pocket of his black slacks, then grabs his keys. Probably about to Houdini himself to another country. Who knows?

I pull my MVU sweatshirt over my head, then toss Harriet her pleather jacket. "Well, I'm out of here—without you," I point a finger at Eliot, then raise a hand like *stay. Please.* But Eliot is far from a dog.

He has an impish grin as he sinks his teeth into the apple.

"Where are we going?" Tom enters the living room, setting aside his guitar against the pull-out, and I internally groan.

"Ben is finally kicking the frat to the curb," Eliot explains, which makes Tom grin like it's the best news he's heard all month. Eliot dumps his half-eaten apple in the trash.

"We could've composted that," I say, "and I'm going *alone.*"

Harriet watches us, chewing her candy more slowly. Her glare is presenting as *angry*, but I know she's just contemplative.

"You're ditching the frat?" That's Beckett coming into the communal space. Already finished dancing in a dress rehearsal for *The Nutcracker*, he's recently showered and wears black joggers and a tight-fitted tee. "Did they do something?" His protective stance is welcomed but unnecessary.

"No, they've been cool. I just don't want to be in one. It's a lot of time commitments. Too many parties they want me to attend." Off his smile, I nod and smile back, "And I'm staying here." Before they celebrate, I add fast, "I'm leaving now." I swipe my granola bar and water bottle off the counter, about to head to the door.

"We'll all go with you," Beckett offers, which stops me dead in my tracks. Especially as Charlie and Beckett exchange a silent, unreadable look. Then Charlie blinks hard in palpable irritation and drops his travel duffel to the floor, like his plans are now cancelled. That easily?

For me?

No way.

"I'm literally just going to the frat," I say. "If you're concerned about me—"

"None of us are doing anything for the rest of the night," Beckett interjects. "We're free."

"Clearly Charlie has somewhere he needs to go." I motion a hand to the duffel on the floor.

"It can wait." Charlie stares me down like I'm making this more excruciating for him. "Can we hurry this up?"

"Charlie Keating finally finding his priorities," Tom says while sticking his arms through his jean jacket, wearing it over a black hoodie.

"The night is practically over," I tell them.

"The night is always young," Eliot counters, squeezing my shoulder while he rounds the island and closes in on the door.

Harriet shrugs at me. "Why not bring them along?"

Because you won't be with me. I need to figure out how to quiet my panic when she's not around. A catastrophe isn't going to strike. I won't hurt them. *Think of Maeve's birthday.* Yeah, that went fine.

Eliot's grin widens in my direction. "Even your girlfriend wants us present, brother."

Her ocean blue eyes search mine, but I just take a big breath. I want to say my brothers complicate everything, but they also uncomplicate terrible situations too. "No security," I tell them.

"What a shock," Charlie says dryly.

"You didn't call Novak?" Beckett asks.

It hasn't been such a secret that I've routinely stopped informing Novak when I leave the apartment. I'm a legal adult. Not a kid. I can decide *when* I want a bodyguard trailing my every move, even if my mom has blown up my phone reminding me to attach myself to our private security.

My parents can't force their desires. They can get creative, yeah, and place me among the family who have bodyguards flanking their every move. Being protected by proxy.

So I assume my brothers are about to lead me down that type of path.

"No, I didn't call him. This isn't supposed to be a big ordeal. If you all want to go with me, then no bodyguards. I don't want to make a scene. In and out. I'll be five minutes. You stay in the car and wait for me after we drop Harriet off at her apartment."

I'm floored when they instantly agree.

Minutes later, I'm in Beckett's luxury car with his personal driver, Hans, behind the wheel. My four brothers with me. I've already said bye to Harriet at her apartment, and now we're en route to the frat house.

My stomach grumbles because I burned way too many calories today working out and having sex. I want to eat the granola while not dirtying the sleek black interior of Beckett's SUV. The risk of spreading crumbs is astronomical. It's not a soft, chewy granola bar. It will break into too many tiny pieces with one bite.

Should've grabbed a banana. Fuck.

"So you've screwed us all over, brother," Eliot says as we hit a red light.

My brows pinch together in confusion. "What'd I do?"

"Chose a girlfriend that Mom literally adores." Eliot flashes a wry grin. "Thank you for setting the bar unimaginably high for the rest of our future significant others."

"You don't need to worry about that, Eliot," Charlie says from the front seat. "We'll all be dead before you stop fucking around."

"Touché," Eliot smiles. "But even while you are nestled in your graves, I don't think my future girlfriend will be living up to the Harriet Fisher standard. I heard Mom asked her to Le Petit Rêve."

"*Beeeeen.*" Tom lengthens my name in a groan. "Seriously, couldn't you have told her to belch or something?"

I'm near laughter. "I don't think I've ever heard her belch."

"So she's Mom's favorite and she doesn't burp?" Tom throws up his hands. "I'm calling it, she's a demon."

"What about Dad?" Eliot wonders. "He could be our opening. Maybe he hasn't been bedazzled by Harriet's demonic charm."

I stare at the granola in my hand. Our dad didn't have as much time to converse with Harriet, but he told me he can tell she means everything to me. He used that exact word. *Everything.* That's all I care about—that he knows she's not a tiny part of my world, that she is my world.

"Dad already likes her, I'm sure," Beckett says, immediately grabbing my gaze. He has a soft smile on me, and I can practically read his eyes that calmly whisper, *no need to be afraid.*

That's not what I've been afraid of, Beck. A lump wedges in my throat. How do I tell them? How do I explain the mess inside my mind? It's been *years*, and I never really could unravel it all in perfect coherence. I barely understand myself at times.

In the silence, my growling stomach sounds like a broken dishwasher.

"Dude, did you skip dinner?" Tom side-eyes me.

"Our growing baby boy," Eliot teases.

Beckett smiles into a laugh, which is making me smile, but I'm still not unwrapping the granola. It causes Beckett to frown a little more. Then his face just completely plummets, and that hurts. We stare at each other for a long moment, unspoken things passing between us, and I don't know what to do until Charlie says, "Eat it."

I waver. "I'm fine."

"*I'm* fine," Beckett says so deeply, so soothingly. "My little brother being hungry in my car, I don't like. Especially if you're not eating because of me."

I can just wait until we reach the frat, but since he's asking me not to, I say, "You sure?"

"Positive." So I end up carefully eating the granola, but yeah, shit goes everywhere.

Tom is laughing so much, he's rolling into Eliot.

Guilt overwhelms me. Sears the skin on my face, my arms, my chest. I seldom find humor in the same exact things Tom does, which is partly why I'm sure I'm more sensitive than my brothers. But as soon as he laughs out, "All this time, all we had to do was feed Ben granola—follow the crumbs and we'll never lose him," I find some ironic levity in the joke.

I laugh from my chest. Hard.

It actually startles Tom. To where Beckett busts out laughing, and Charlie has a rare smile. Eliot ruffles Tom's shaggy golden-brown hair in brotherly affection, then touches the back of my head with the same sentiment, and I hang on to this effervesce filling my lungs. I don't want to lose this. I don't want to lose any of them. Not even Charlie.

Maybe I never have to.

FIFTY-ONE

BEN COBALT

The frat house is trashed from the all-day football tailgate that's switched into a drunken afterparty. Remixed hits blast through the first floor. Sloppy hands glide down my shoulders in greeting as I weave through the college students and step on so much *trash*.

Beer cans, Solo cups, empty liquor bottles, pizza boxes, paper plates, plastic silverware—I almost grab a garbage bag to clean up and separate recyclables from waste. No way will they go through the effort.

I had to personally buy a recycle bin for the frat house because "it's not in the budget"—which I understand, but barely anyone uses it. Most treat it like it's just a second trash can.

If I go through initiation, maybe I can gradually change their habits. Maybe I can have a better, greater impact, and honestly, the thought makes me second-guess if I'm choosing the right path. If I'm doing good by de-pledging, or if I'd do better by remaining here.

The vein in my temple is throbbing as I overcomplicate this. *In and out.* I need to get in and out. My brothers are waiting in a noticeably expensive SUV, and I'm hoping no drunk idiot bangs on their tinted windows to figure out who's inside.

In and out.

"Ben, man, buddy, you gotta see this!"

"Later, Reggie!" I call out to one of the Kappa brothers.

"Hey, Ben!"

"Ben!"

"Ben!"

I politely bow out of the interactions and ask around for Leif. Getting conflicting answers.

"I think I saw him upstairs."

"He's been in the backyard."

"Basement, I heard, bro."

I'm about to cycle through each spot when I run into a freshman pledge in the kitchen. Iggy mops up what looks like piss all over the sink with a sponge. Thank fuck Beckett isn't in here. I should also be a grunt-working pledge, but they've treated me more like a trophy they don't want scratched.

"Hey, Ben," he up-nods.

I nod back, about to pass him into the backyard just as he asks, "You see your sister yet?"

I freeze to solid ice. "What?"

"Your little sister." He drops the sponge on the counter. "She's been here for at least fifteen minutes."

I can't process fast enough. "Audrey Cobalt? At this frat house?"

"Red hair. Blue eyes. I think she said she was surprising you."

I'm instantly starved of oxygen. This can't be real. While I take out my phone, I glance up at the ceiling. Toward the second floor where the bedrooms are, then I think, *they're fucking with me.* This is a sick joke.

I send Audrey a text.

BEN COBALT

Are you at the KPD house?

Then Iggy adds, "She brought you a whole thing of cookies. She even demanded that no one eat them until you got here." He snorts like there's no chance that happened.

It feels like a Mac Truck just slammed into me. Audrey's love of baking cookies isn't so widely known. He'd only mention it if it were true. She's here. I dial her number, my pulse racing so far ahead of me, I can't see straight. While it rings, I ask, "Iggy, you know where she is?"

"I just saw her come inside. Not where she went."

Fuck, *fuck*. I'm about to storm upstairs, to the bedrooms, but she suddenly answers, "Ben?" Her voice sounds weird. Woozy?

"Where are you?"

"Don't be angry—"

"I'm not angry. Please just tell me where you are, *please*." I'm suffocating under distress. I whip my head around, trying to see if I can find her. She's not in the kitchen, so I bolt back into the living room where the music pierces my eardrums.

"I'm at your frat house," Audrey confirms with a very slow, very strange breath. I plug one of my ears to hear her say, "The basement."

"I'm not far. I'm coming to you. Stay there." I'm running. Sprinting. For my sister. Down the creaky wooden steps into the dank, tuna fish smelling Kappa basement.

Why she's here is a thousand-leagues deep in my brain. I'm not diving for those answers. It does not matter right now. All that matters is that she's safe.

As I rush into the basement, all I see are guys. Way too many fucking guys. And my sister—she's on the plaid couch, lying on the cushions with her cheek on the armrest, and Leif is on the other end. She's coherent. Her blue eyes just barely meet mine as I charge for the Kappa president.

"Get off the fucking couch!" I scream at him. Confusion and alarm startle him off the sofa, but I'm already yelling, "SHE'S SIXTEEN!"

"Whoa, Ben. *Ben.*" He raises his hands. His eyes huge.

I am guarding the fucking couch from every single one of them. I swear, I will lay them on the fucking concrete floor if they so much as inch toward her.

"It's not what you think—"

"She's the *only* girl down here with half the frat—don't fucking tell me I'm overreacting." I come closer to Audrey and check on her with a quick glance, trying to keep an eye on the guys who easily outnumber me. I'm six-five. I've never been physically weak, but if they wanted, they could restrain me and do whatever they wanted to her. Make me watch. Nausea is scorching my throat.

I want to think better of them, but right now, I am cycling through the worst possibilities.

"Let's just talk about this, okay?" Leif says, knowing these accusations in the frat could damage Kappa's reputation. The whole chapter might be punished if it gets back to the dean. Not to mention, my sister is *famous*. There is no rug big enough to sweep this under.

I squat beside Audrey.

She's petrified, staring in stark, wide-eyed horror at me. I don't understand why. I can't make sense of this. "I'm getting you out of here." I'm about to pick her up.

"Wait." She catches my wrist. "I'm…I'm okay?"

"Why is that a question?"

"I…" She glances around, as if reevaluating this basement, these people. "We're at your frat, Ben. These are your friends."

Is that why she's here? To befriend my friends?

I smear a hand over my mouth. Don't puke.

"Just…can we talk first?" Audrey asks, not wanting to make a scene in front of these older guys, probably.

"I think that's a *great* idea," Leif says stiffly, trying not to be hostile. I shoot him a glare.

I am confused beyond belief, but I know one thing. I need my brothers. With my phone concealed at my side, I send a group text with one hand.

> **BEN COBALT**
> Need you. Audrey is here. Basement.

Then I turn back to her. "Audrey?"

"She came down here herself," Leif says civilly, trying to dig himself out of this ten-foot ditch. Several frat brothers corroborate while munching on football-shaped, perfectly iced cookies from a Tiffany Blue tin.

"Did you?" I ask Audrey.

"I did." She struggles to sit up and just abandons the effort. My ears are ringing with adrenaline. I am a malfunctioning, broken computer. My system is completely crashing. I normally can read body language like I'm AI, but my intelligence has spun back to the Jurassic period.

"I was looking for you," she explains with panicky eyes.

"You found me," I say, not sure how to calm her because I am going out of my mind.

"You...you mentioned you'd be at the party, remember?"

"Yeah." *Yeah.* I told her about the football party. I said I'd be stopping by the Kappa house tonight. Did not tell her I was dropping out. Did not tell her when I'd be here. When she asked for further information, I just said, *probably late, around midnight.*

It's around midnight.

"I wanted to surprise you...I took a rideshare." A fucking rideshare? "I just thought I could...make friends with your friends. And you'd invite me over more." Her eyes glass, her nose flaring with emotion, and she leans closer to whisper, "They are your friends? Aren't they?" Her terror is terrifying me.

She trusted them because of me—because she believes I trust my friends.

The urge to vomit is surging rapidly. I feel violently ill.

Do not puke.

"Ben?"

"Yeah, yeah," I nod, unable to tell her the truth. That, no, I wouldn't even trust Dalton Academy's hockey team alone with her—and I knew them for fucking *years*. I just met half these guys in this basement eight weeks ago.

She tries to relax. "Okay, so...we're okay."

We are not okay.

I am not okay.

I look her over frantically. Trying to reboot myself. Her frilly burgundy dress has a high neckline, long-sleeves. A gold locket lies against her heart. *Burgundy. Gold.* MVU's colors. Her clothes aren't torn. Blood drains out of my face when I see her bare feet and the lacy white stockings on the floor. "Where are your shoes?" I sling my death-decaying glare at Leif. "Who *the fuck* took off her socks and shoes?"

"She twisted her ankle coming down the stairs." Leif rakes a nervous hand through his brown hair. "Believe me, we were just trying to help her, man."

"It's true, I tripped." Audrey intakes a weird, slow breath. She reaches for her foot but doesn't wince.

"We were icing it for her," Leif adds, pointing to the Miller can that fell off the cushion. They were icing her foot with cold beer. Her right ankle is a hundred percent swollen and puffy.

Audrey has this questioning, anxious look in her eye.

"Did they do anything?" I whisper under my breath to her, still in a squat beside the couch. "Audrey, you can tell me." I'm just barely hanging on right now. It feels like a monster is trying to rip out of my ribcage.

She attempts to shake her head, but it's weaker. Her cheek lies back on the armrest. "They've helped...I think."

"You think?" My brain pounds. "Did you drink a beer, vodka, anything?" Did they roofie her? I start thinking about Winona, and I want to collapse to my knees and scream.

"No, I didn't." *She didn't drink anything.*

"She couldn't put weight on her foot," Leif explains. "She was in a lot of pain. So I told her to take a seat on the couch and wait for you."

I see blood-red. Fury incinerates me. "Where's the text telling me my sister showed up?! Where's the text telling me she got hurt coming down the stairs?!"

"Yeah, you're right, I should've texted." Leif shifts his weight uneasily, his hands threaded behind his neck. "Ben. Look, we're all brothers here."

"You're not my brothers." That's when the door blows open, and four indomitable forces storm the basement. "They are."

Mutterings of *holy shit* hit my ears. The Kappas go still. It's rare we're all this accessible all together without a legion of security around us.

My mistake.

My fucking mistake.

I was supposed to be in and out. This wasn't supposed to happen. Now they're in this mess with me, and I can't even regret it when I want them to help Audrey.

Charlie and Beckett are bullets toward her.

I move out of the way, standing behind her head. She peers up at me, blinking too slowly. Her breathing is still bizarre to me. She's not roofied?

"What happened?" Beckett asks her and me.

"Surprise?" Audrey says weakly.

"She hurt her ankle," I explain.

Charlie sweeps her with one long glance. "She's on something."

It's a shotgun blast to the chest. I glare at Leif. "Did you give her something for the pain?"

Leif is taking several, *several* steps back from Eliot who looks like he's going to decapitate him.

"Speak!" Eliot shouts, pointing a baseball bat at the Kappa president. Yeah, he has a bat. I'm sure Beckett keeps one in his car, considering he's been mugged before.

"It was just Tylenol?" Audrey says like she's now unsure if they deceived her.

Leif's face is splotchy red. He whirls around to the Kappa brothers. Last thing he wants is an OD in his basement. "Who gave her the pain meds?"

Prescott comes forward. "It was, uh, out of a baggie."

"Oh this is going to be fun," Charlie says dryly.

"Ben," Audrey whines. "Am I going to pass out...I don't feel right...my toes are tingling. I'm dizzy. The room is spinning...it's spinning."

"You're okay." I crouch down to be level with her head on the armrest. "You'd be totally out of it if it were that bad." Right? I look to Beckett who looks to Charlie.

Tom is pacing like he has to piss. "Charlie, they're filming," he whispers to him.

Charlie peers backward at the Kappa brothers. "You record anything, and we'll use it to get your frat banned for life. I know it must be an impossible task for all of you, but try not to be *fucking* morons before you decide to put this Cobalt Show and Tell on YouTube."

"Put your phones away!" Leif yells at all the Kappas. "Javi, you too! Jesus Christ."

Eliot slaps a cellphone out of someone's hand. They shrivel back.

"Can I have the baggie?" Beckett asks Prescott, gesturing him over with two fingers.

"Am I going to die?" Audrey asks us dramatically. "Please let me only die from embarrassment. Please. *Please*....please. Charlie, tell me...tell me this is just the death of my common sense."

"That died years ago."

"It was...resurrected." Her breath sounds are weak.

Charlie's gaze darkens on her. I can't tell what he's thinking, but I know his lack of biting response isn't good.

Beckett gets handed a baggie filled with too many different pills. "Which one?" he asks Prescott.

"I…I can't remember."

Eliot might just murder him. Prescott scuffles so far back while Eliot stalks him around the basement, and I wonder if the bat will be more than a prop tonight.

Beckett is quickly inspecting the baggie. "Vicodin or benzos?" he asks Charlie.

"Both are in there."

"Should we call Farrow?" I ask them since Audrey isn't doing well. She might be dramatic, but this isn't *her* normal. Her breathing is not right. She's sinking deeper in the couch.

They're not listening to me. They exchange a serious look when they identify more pills. A kitten hops up on Audrey's lap. She tries to reach for the tabby, but her arm droops off the cushion. Limply.

I'm going to throw up. "Beck?"

Audrey starts slumping, and Charlie catches her first, pulling her farther down the sofa while Beckett rests his knee on the cushion. They move so fast. Beckett hovers over her, tapping her cheek. "Audrey?"

Her eyelids are fluttering. "I…don't feel…"

"Tom," Beckett captures his attention. "Go get Narcan from my car."

"On it." He's sprinting out of the basement.

"Oh fucking hell." Leif has his hands on his head. "This can't be happening." All he cares about is this frat.

All I care about is my sister. "What'd they give her?" I ask.

"An opioid, we think." Charlie scrapes a hand through his hair. "But if it's Rohypnol, the Narcan isn't going to work."

"What's Rohypnol?" I ask.

Charlie snaps me an annoyed look for all the questions—but it fries quickly into ash, then nothingness. I'd almost believe he was worried about me. Almost. I don't have a mirror. I have no clue what my face is telling him. I know I am mere seconds from retching on this floor.

"Just tell me," I choke out. "Just tell me, Charlie."

"Date Rape drug," Charlie says. "Roofies. She'll get knocked out."

Acid bubbles in the back of my throat. Audrey is losing consciousness. Beckett is saying her name and, "Reste éveillée." *Stay awake.* His calming, soothing voice isn't reassuring me. He's taking her pulse at her neck.

Then her eyes shut. Body slackens. She's out.

Beckett rubs his knuckles against her sternum. "Audrey? *Audrey.*" No reaction.

"Is she breathing?" I ask them. Maybe I don't even release the words. Because I don't hear their response. I can't hear a thing. I drop to one knee and puke off to the side. Everything I ate on the car ride here meets the concrete floor.

My sister is ODing in the basement of the frat. "Your frat," she'd said. *My frat.* I caused this. If I hadn't been here...why am I here?

My fingers dig into the plastered wall while I vomit again. I can't even help her...how do I help her when I can barely help myself?

Pain tunnels through me. I feel a hand on the back of my head. Eliot's? I feel him lifting me off my knees. I'm leaning most of my weight on my strongest brother. He's cupping my jaw, trying to train my gaze on his. I think he's saying my name.

My eyes are flaming like I rubbed jalapeño in each one. I just barely see Beckett administering the Narcan up her nose. I just barely feel Tom rattling my arm. I just barely hear a kitten hiss at a frat brother, then I see him blow smoke from a joint in the tabby's face.

They aren't safe here. The Kappa kittens.

I reanimate. Gain muscle function. Just to gather all the cats. I'm making things worse for my sister, and the only good thing I can do is save these fucking kittens from this fucking frat house. I'm in a daze, hunting for kittens and putting them in a blanket-lined beer box.

Eliot gently rests a black cat in with the others. "That's it, brother. That's the last one." I hear him say.

I count only six. "There's seven kittens." I know there are. I feed them every time I'm here.

"That's it. This way." He's directing me out the basement's backdoor. "Time to go." We're all leaving. I see Beckett. He's cradling Audrey in his arms. She's lucid. *She's coherent.* She's awake?

"She's okay." Who's saying that Tom or Charlie?

I feel drunk. Intoxicated with visceral emotion I can't escape. No matter how much I repeat *she's okay* in my head. With one blink, I'm going from point A to point B. Soon, I'm in the very back of Beckett's SUV, holding onto the beer box as the kittens let out tiny *meows*. I press my forehead to the cardboard edge.

Someone is rubbing my back. Beckett? He should be with Audrey. She needs him, and it's the first time I look over.

Charlie is beside me.

It makes no sense. But what has? He comes into powerful focus. And the first thing he tells me is, "Don't puke on my lap."

Yeah.

That's Charlie.

It strangely calms me. The bitter, biting familiarity of him. He's looking straight into my eyes, and again, I don't know what he sees. They feel bloodshot. My face feels slick with silent tears.

"She's okay," he says, and now I'm more certain that he's the one who said it the first time. "She became responsive immediately. She never lost a pulse. We're taking her to the hospital. Do you understand?"

I nod.

It's not helping. Everything he said—it's not helping me, and I don't know why. It should. She's okay. Our little sister will be okay. The reassurance is in outer-fucking-space. I have no way to fly there without being asphyxiated. It feels like I'll never reach it.

"What's the problem?" Charlie asks with a great deal less annoyance than usual. It roils my stomach. "Ben?"

I shake my head over and over. I can't be here. I can't be here. I can't be here. I can't be here.

I can't be here.

I'm going to hurt everyone I love.

"*Ben.*"

I lift my gaze to his.

Confusion—confusion I've never seen from Charlie—stares back at me. I am confusing a genius now? There is so much agony inside my body, and I can't verbally translate even an ounce. *Just kill me*, I want to tell him.

Then I think about the blood. Beckett's car. Can't do that.

Then I think about her, and I nearly break down. "Harriet," I choke out.

Someone hands Charlie a phone—minutes later? Moments?

He's putting it against my ear.

"Ben?" I hear her tough voice, and I wipe a hot tear that rolls down my cheek. She continues when I don't say a word. "Is everything okay? Tom didn't even insult me. He said you need to talk?"

I struggle to speak.

"Cobalt got your tongue," she says flatly. "Get it. Lions, cats… dumb joke, I know."

I clear the knot in my throat. "I've actually heard that one before."

She intakes a sharp breath of relief. "Yeah? Here I thought I was finally being clever…Ben. Are you okay?"

No. I pinch my watery eyes. "Can you do something for me?"

"Anything."

"Can you just read to me for a second?" I swallow a rock, holding the phone tight against my ear.

"Yeah," she says fast. "What are you in the mood for? I have an O-Chem textbook that'll put you to sleep or we can go dark and moody and read about Pyramus and Thisbe—I vote O-Chem."

I feel a smile somewhere in me. "Scared of the dark, Fisher?" I hoist my glassy gaze to the roof of the car.

"Sorry to say, me and the dark were friends before you."

I rub at my wet jaw, releasing a long breath. Peace is cresting the edge of the horizon. I'm fighting to go there. "You kick your friend to the curb?"

"Yeah. With a little help from my best friend."

I shut my eyes. Tears slip out of the creases. *Stop fucking crying. Please stop. I want to stop.*

Very softly, she says, "You need help, Friend?"

I nod. "Yeah," I rasp out. "Read to me. Just read to me."

And so she does. Science jargon goes in one ear and out the other, but I listen to her voice. I stop thinking about everything that happened. I stop fixating on my washing machine of thoughts. I just listen to Harriet. And I breathe and breathe.

"HE'S STRANGELY CALM NOW. IT'S KIND OF FREAKING ME out." I hear Tom whispering to Eliot in the seat in front of me.

Eliot rotates to inspect me.

I say nothing. Tears have dried. I'm numb.

"He's in shock," Eliot guesses.

Beckett has been monitoring Audrey's pulse. He still has her in his arms, her legs splayed on Eliot's lap. She peeks back at me.

"I feel…rather good now, you know?" She's clammy.

I nod. "I'm glad, Audrey. You still need to get checked out though." We're on the way to the hospital.

"Oui." She rests an emotional, tear-stricken smile on the cardboard box. "Where would they be without you? Terrifying, really." Her chin quakes before she mouths the word, *thank you.*

I did nothing to help her. I just called our brothers.

"Je t'aime comme les arbres aiment la terre, ma petite sœur," I murmur from the depth of my soul. *I love you like the trees love the earth, my little sister.* "Toujours." *Always.*

"Toujours," she repeats. "Et je t'aime comme les étoiles aiment la nuit, mon frère préféré." *And I love you like the stars love the night, my favorite brother.*

Eliot gasps. "Am I not your favorite?"

Laughter ensues, along with more banter, and I cradle the sounds against my ears. I love my family. I will always love them, which is why I know now that I have to leave. Very soon. This is going to be the hardest thing I ever do in my life, but I never should've considered staying. And I've delayed it for too long.

I should've stuck to the original timeline. Then this would've never happened tonight. If I left New York weeks ago, Audrey would've never taken that pill. Hell, if I never came to the city after Beckett asked me, this could've all been avoided.

We arrive at Metropolitan Medical. It's the closest to MVU. Audrey is admitted. Our parents were already headed to New York when they realized Audrey snuck out. So they rerouted to the hospital when my brothers informed them of tonight's disaster.

Now they're here. My mom's heels clip-clapping across the hospital floors like she's setting them on fire. My dad's calming hand in hers. I don't speak long to either of them. I tell them I'm okay when they ask. They should be focused on Audrey.

Neither one blames me. They reinforce, "This is not your fault."

"Ben?" My father's steadfast blue eyes search mine. We're in the hallway near Fizzle vending machines. Security is hovering to where we receive only a few glances from nurses and doctors. "Can you talk to me?"

"What is there to say?" My throat is torched. It hurts to speak, but I'm trying. "My frat gave Audrey *fentanyl*."

Yeah, the doctors figured out the drug in her system. She could've so easily died tonight if Beckett didn't have Narcan in his car. I am one small move away from killing one of my siblings. That's what it feels like. Not to mention, her ankle is sprained. She made the varsity cheer team, so she'll be sitting out until her foot heals.

I tell him, "I'm upset. I'm *angry*. I wish I could take it back with everything in my body, but I can't. All I want to do is move on."

"Okay," he nods, examining me with deeper concerns. "Where's Harriet?"

"Asleep. I told her not to worry—that I'll see her later."

"When you get home?"

I tighten my eyes closed as my head hammers. "No, um." I rub at my eyes and shake my head harder. "She has an essay she planned to write, and I can't be the reason her GPA drops. I'll probably go back to the apartment and pass out anyway." That's what I told Harriet too. She said she doesn't care about her grades as much as she cares about me, but I care. I can't be the dynamite imploding her goals. "After that, I'll see her. So it'll probably be later tonight."

It's two a.m.—technically already Saturday.

"Can you do something for me?" he asks, drawing my gaze back to his.

"What exactly?" I ask so I don't make a promise I can't keep.

"Go see Ryke. As soon as you can. Or have him meet you."

I nod a lot, even if there is pain in my neck, in my whole body. "Yeah, I can do that." He sees I'm telling the truth, and he relaxes. I relax too.

I call Jane. I ask if she'll meet me in Philly at her billiards bar. "I know it'll be late, or early." By the time I get there, I think it'll be four a.m.? Five? "But I have some cats—"

"I'll be there, Pippy."

I plan to go alone.

But Charlie and Beckett hop in the car. My bodyguard is driving, and I don't waste time arguing with my older brothers. When we arrive at The Independent, I'm about to step out of the SUV.

I turn and ask, "The cat…the seventh one I couldn't find. He was dead, wasn't he?"

Beckett is barely breathing. He looks to Charlie. But it's enough of an answer if Beckett is afraid to tell me the truth.

I nod, about to leave with the beer box.

Charlie reaches across Beckett and snatches the back of my shirt, forcing my ass on the seat.

"Fuck. *Charlie.*" I glare since I jostle the kittens.

"You aren't going to cry?" he asks me. "A cat is *dead*. It died. It is gone. It's not coming back."

"Charlie," Beckett says quietly. "Stop."

"Stop what?" Charlie motions to me. "It's not affecting him." He looks unsettled by me.

"I thought you hated when I cried," I shoot back.

"I find it overly emotional. Which you are."

"Is that not what I've been all fucking night?" I retort. "Maybe I'm just done?"

Charlie is grimacing. Tugging his hair. "Fuck," he curses under his breath. He whispers something to Beckett I can't hear.

I should've gotten the kittens out of there on day one. I chose the wrong path. Made the wrong decision. I won't make another one. It's what I hang on to. "It'll be okay," I tell them.

Beckett steeples his fingers to the bridge of his nose. "Ben. We should really talk about tonight. What happened with Audrey—"

"Yeah, it was awful," I cut in. "I'm sorry."

"Why are you sorry?" Charlie is making weird fucking faces at me. He's staring at me like he's smashing his head into a brick wall. All this time, I thought he saw me as translucent. Too easy to read.

I shake my head a little, then say, "Thank you both for being there tonight. I'm glad you were with me. I'm glad you were adamant about coming along." I make sure he specifically knows I'm talking about him too. "Thanks, Charlie. And I don't hate you either."

I'm about to exit the car again.

Charlie grabs my shoulder one more time. "The seven kittens—you do know they're not a metaphorical representation of the seven of us?"

My brows scrunch. "What? Why would I think that?" Now he's confusing me. One kitten didn't survive, so what…now one of us is going to die? That sounds ridiculous to me. "I don't believe in fate, Charlie."

"Then what do you believe in?"

"Consequences."

FIFTY-TWO

BEN COBALT

"They're in dreadfully great hands, don't worry," Jane says with a reassuring smile in my direction. I've released the Kappa kittens, and they race toward plates of wet cat food Jane puts out. I refill water bowls strewn around the closed billiards bar.

The Independent is home to many strays that my older sister rescued, some of which eventually find forever families when people stop by for a beer and some pool, then wind up growing attached to the bar's feline residents. It's the perfect place to leave these six kittens.

"You are the vanquisher of worries," I smile back at her. "A destroyer of doubts."

"You flatter me."

"With the truth," I add, my lips rising as kittens nibble on a strand of yarn from a ball Jane tossed. She knows I took the cats to the vet weeks ago. They all have their shots. No fleas. They'll be really happy here.

She hops up on the pool table and pats the green felt for me to join.

I take a seat beside her.

Thatcher is behind the bar counter, rocking their sleepy daughter in his muscular arms. As Jane peeks at him, he nods to her, then slips into a backroom. Giving me and my sister time alone together. There's no one who respects the bonds of siblings more than Thatcher Moretti, who loves his twin brother to his absolute core, and I think it's just another reason he's so perfect for Jane.

But I recognize that Thatcher has lost one brother in his life. I was one of the first people in our family he ever told about Skylar Moretti, his older brother who jumped into a quarry and drowned when they were just kids. I hope…I really hope he will be there for Jane if she ever feels like she's lost me.

I need him to be there for her. There really isn't any doubt he wouldn't be. Thatcher would walk through quicksand for the rest of his life if it meant Jane was okay.

"Tonight sounded terrible," Jane says quietly, gently. "How are you doing?"

"I'm getting through it. I'm just glad it wasn't any worse for Audrey. It could've been worse."

She hugs me around my back. "Oh, Pippy. You have the biggest heart of us all, you realize?"

I stare at the floor, tears trying to well again. "Charlie knew it was always a weakness," I tell her. "He knew eventually the more you feel, the more you hurt."

Maybe he even knew one day I'd be swallowed whole by it. Maybe he never wanted to watch it happen.

"Your heart is your strength," Jane says fiercely. "It also may be the very thing that brings you to your knees, but it can be the very thing that makes you stand. Don't give up on yourself, Pippy." She hugs me closer to her side with warmth I crave.

I rest my cheek on her shoulder like I'm twelve again. "We should add instiller of confidence in your Wiki bio."

"It'd be redundant. It's simply being your older sister."

I suck a sharp breath through my nose, caging the waterworks. "Obligations of the firstborn."

"No. For me, it isn't work to love and care about my siblings. It never will be." She tips her head into mine. "I know Moffy feels the same. If you ever need him, he's one phone call away."

The firstborns carry the largest burden in our families, and I admire how Jane and Maximoff still managed to be there for everyone, for themselves, and find soul mates of their own.

To me, they are the mightiest of gods. The ones we will forever look up to in the star-lit sky.

"I really love you, Jane," I tell her before I leave The Independent.

Once I'm back at my brothers' apartment, I call my Uncle Ryke to meet up. Not for coffee, not for lunch or dinner, but to be outdoors together. What I love doing with my uncle. I finally said *yes* to the hike.

He picks me up in his Land Rover, and I sleep in the passenger seat all the way to the Catskills. By the afternoon, we're on a trailhead called Hunter Mountain Fire Tower. It's the most challenging of five fire tower hikes. Eight miles. Difficulty: Hard, Sweating in the Cold, Toe Blisters Likely to Ensue. I wore the wrong socks.

He let me choose which trail. I decided if this is my last hike with my favorite uncle—I wasn't going to let it be easy and end in a handful of minutes.

We talk in Spanish some. Just so I don't lose the language. It's partly why my family speaks so often in French. None of us want to forget what we were taught.

"Ya casi llegamos," he says. *We're almost there.*

My boots crunch fallen autumn leaves. "No tengo prisa." *I'm not in a hurry.*

Uncle Ryke is textbook definition brooding with constant furrowed brows and narrowed eyes. His unshaven, hard jaw isn't doing any favors to lighten the unapproachable demeanor, and despite his "fuck off" aura, I know he'd do anything for me as if I were his own son.

Ryke Meadows is the embodiment of the mountains I love. Resilient, immovable, unchanging. He's nothing like my father.

Connor Cobalt is the embodiment of the water. Even the calmest rivers can drown with the change in currents. When I was younger, I wondered if my dad felt like he was drowning me—so he made sure I had Ryke. He made sure I had the mountain to lift me out of the swelling tides.

And I fucking love him for it.

That he knew what I needed, and maybe it wasn't always him, but he never took it away from me. He drew me toward it. He still does.

All those times I spent morning to night at the Meadows Cottage—playing on their makeshift ropes course in the backyard, spinning on the tire swing with Winona, running barefoot through the woods—my parents rarely called me home. They let me stay until I looked down the street and felt a longing tugging me, pulling me, to be with my sisters, my brothers, them.

And I went back on my own accord. Their happiness to see me never withered. It grew and wrapped around me every time I walked through the door.

I had more homes to go to than Harriet. I had an excess of love, and it feels incredibly fucking stupid to willingly walk away.

But I can't be here. I can't stay and destroy them. It's a nagging, suffocating panic I can't shake. I will never be rid of this monster looming over me until I'm miles away. Until I'm *certain* they're all safe.

We reach the base of the fire tower, and I take off my baseball cap, wiping the line of sweat off my forehead. Uncle Ryke jerks his head toward the winding staircase. He leads us up the steps.

This isn't a popular trail during this month. In fact, I think he had to pull strings last-minute to obtain a permit for us to hike it in late November.

No one is here.

As we climb, he peers back at me a few times. Questions are in his knitted brows, but Uncle Ryke hasn't asked any tough ones yet. He's not badgering me, but I know the time will come.

At the top, we step into the square structure. All open windows. No glass panes. It's an empty fire tower and not large. Just a lookout point, really.

I should be staring out at the rolling peaks, the horizon, the cascade of evergreens. Even if it's a little overcast, the expansive views stretch out to three states. But I don't care about the trees. There'll be spruces and dirt and the clouds and blue sky where I'm headed.

There won't be him. I care about the guy beside me that I'll never see again.

"Thank you," I say before he can speak. "For bringing me here."

"You chose it." He's gazing out. "I like this one. Mostly because you're fucking here though."

I smile. "I was going to say that about you. Beat me to it." I suck some water from the spigot of my hydration bladder on my back.

Uncle Ryke rotates toward me now. "How are you holding up?" Of course he's referring to the frat. My sister. It's probably only been around fourteen or fifteen hours since then.

"I've been better," I admit. "Sorry I haven't been around—"

"You don't need to fucking apologize." He throws out *fucks* like they're flower petals, not always with aggression. Though, yeah, he can be intense.

"I do, actually." I fit my baseball cap back on, curving the brim. "I haven't been a good friend to Winona, and if I had—"

"I'm going to stop you for a fucking second." He raises his hands like he's cradling something fragile between us. "Your relationship with my daughter will never, *ever* fucking impact my relationship with you—do you get that? I need you to understand that, all right? Because I am always right down the street. Always there, Ben. There will never be a fucking moment where I'm not, and if you need to walk through that door, walk through the door. Don't turn around."

My eyes burn because my relationship with him was impacted. But it wasn't his own doing—it was mine.

"I've known the door was always open," I say in a soft breath. "I knew you'd never shut it on me. It's just how you are, Uncle Ryke." I smile tearfully at him and inhale a colder stream of air to tamp down the sorrow. "I'd come over more, but I'm actually considering a change of pace."

"Yeah?" He scrapes a hand over his unshaven jaw. "Like?"

"I might quit college. Go see more of the country." I tip my head toward the landscape, but I keep my eyes on him. "I think maybe it's just what I need. To get out and just breathe in the quiet. Live somewhere else with less noise."

He rubs at his forehead, his mouth, his jaw again. "Alone?"

"You've done so many backpacking trips alone. You've rock climbed alone."

"And the ones I'd never give back, the mountains I would kill to climb again, were the ones where I was never alone." He extends an arm. "Look, I'm not the fucking one to talk about *caution*. Your dad, I'm sure, will go over rash decisions after you just went through something emotional—"

"It's not about Audrey or the frat," I cut in. "I've been thinking about this for months. It's always been on the table." It's the truth. "I just think now's a great time."

"Because why?"

I dig my gloved hands into my jacket pockets. "Because." My throat tries to close. "I don't know if I'll have the strength to leave Harriet if I stay any longer."

"If it's so fucking hard to leave your girlfriend, why do you want to?"

I don't want to. I have to. I swallow a rock. "I need to do this for myself. I need to help myself first."

This untenses some of his muscles. He seems to understand. "Who's the one person you talk to that makes you want to wake up in the fucking morning?"

Harriet. I'm more torn up, and I can't even say her name.

He sees, though. "Ben, if it's *her*, really contemplate what you want to do next. Because life, this one fucking life you have, is worth living with the people you love. You could go to the most beautiful place on earth and be the loneliest fucking guy because she's not there."

I know I will be.

All I can do is nod. Before we descend the fire tower, he cups the back of my head, bringing me closer, and I hug my uncle in a strong, toughened embrace. Fortifying me for what's to come.

I FEEL LIKE MY TEMPERATURE IS A MILLION-DEGREES AND climbing. One sneeze away from total destruction. So when I'm back at the apartment, I only say a few words to my brothers. Enough to diminish their worries. Then I shower, crash on the couch, and when I wake, most of them have left for work obligations. It's Saturday night. They have performances.

Beckett, the ballet.

Eliot, the theatre.

Tom, meeting with his producer.

Charlie, no clue.

They know I'm heading to Harriet's apartment around nine p.m. They know I'll be with her late into the night, so it's likely why no one cancels their plans. Plus, they're aware I'd be pissed if they did that for me.

I have some time before I go to Harriet's. I find myself on the rooftop of my brothers' Hell's Kitchen high-rise. It's something I wanted to do, but never did. To look at the glittering skyline and city lights from the tallest point of the building.

No pool, patio, wet bar, or lounge chairs—the concrete roof just has some vent stacks, satellite dishes, cellular antennas, a couple empty beer cans, and cigarette butts. No one has escaped here for a smoke. It's just me and the city I thought I hated.

New York.

Now I wish with everything in my soul I could stay.

I just can't. I never really could.

The heavy door swings open, and I twist my head. Shock solidifies my joints at the sight of *Xander*. He seems equally stunned to find me here. His cellphone is in one hand, the screen aimed at his face like he's on a video chat.

I fully expect him to retreat inside. If the ice is melting between us, it's on a slow drip because I still feel the chill at Board Game Club, during class, and family functions.

He steps on the roof and lets the door shut behind him. Maybe he'll sit five-hundred feet away from me. I didn't choose an interesting spot. My ass is on the hard concrete in the middle of the roof, and I've been leaning back on my palms.

Xander signs in ASL on his phone. Then hangs up and comes over to me. Yeah, I am dumbstruck at this point. Unable to speak. I recognize he has no bodyguard shadowing him.

"Don't freak. I'm not going to jump." He drops down beside me, stuffing his hands in the pocket of his black hoodie. "Are you?" His amber eyes touch mine, and I see he's serious.

I bend forward. "I considered flying actually." I hold my knees loosely. "How far you think I'll make it?"

"Too many buildings. You'll hit one at some point." His silver hoop earring glints in the flickering city light. "But I'm also not the glass half-full guy. Ask someone else, and they'll say you'll reach Neverland." He blows on his cupped hands, the chilly temperature dropping as December nears. "I come up here sometimes just to get away. It's one of the only places I can go without people staring at me. Plus, this whole building is like a fortress. No one is going to

Spider-Man their way up here, and if they do, then maybe I will jump." He adds fast, "Joking."

"I knew you were." I glance at his phone he placed on the ground. He has a friend who goes to Yale and is hard of hearing. They met in prep school, and I knew of Spencer Sadler when I'd been there. Mostly because I had a class with her.

I smile over at him. "You learned ASL for a girl."

"You joined a geeky ass board game club for a girl."

I laugh. *Yeah.* I did do that. I'd do so much for Harriet Fisher. Except stay in New York. The laughter drifts to silence. I think that hurts the most because I know it's the one thing she wants, and I can't give it to her.

He hunches forward, his elbows on his knees. "You two are officially together, aren't you?"

Yeah, we have been, but I'm about to change everything. "You heard our family talking about it?" I guess.

"Way before then, I knew, man." He gives me a look. "You were wearing her bracelets. She has a fucking necklace in French. You flirt hard-core. I'm not that dense."

"You're not dense at all. It's just more complicated."

"Why?"

Oh, I don't know…I won't be here tomorrow, Xander. I'll never see you again either, and by the way, I'm not going to make the Ovid presentation. I scratch the back of my head, unable to release a single word. It all just hurts.

Xander sees. "I'm pretty sure she loves you, you know. Harriet. If she hasn't already told you yet. She's cool, so if I were you, I wouldn't screw it up."

My stomach tightens.

"No pressure," he says more softly, sighing at himself. Then he unpockets a box of SweeTarts. "I mean, if I were you, I *literally* would never fuck-up. Being gregarious, extroverted, likeable is like hitting the social lottery."

"So is being considered one of the most beautiful people on the planet."

"Too bad I'm ugly on the inside." He tosses a SweeTart in his mouth.

I smile wider, liking the jokes. "We're self-deprecating hard tonight."

"It's what I'm good at." He chews on the candy more slowly. "Kinney told me everything about the frat last night." His little sister is best friends with Audrey.

I slip my cold hands into my dark blue winter jacket. "Yeah, it wasn't a good time. Be glad you weren't there."

"Our little sisters are nuts." He shakes more candy in his palm. "They take the wildest risks imaginable."

"She thought she could trust Kappa because of me."

Xander lets out a sharp noise. "The whole frat?" His face contorts in thought. "Ben, I know you looked out for the girls when I didn't, but they'd feel like dogshit if you took any blame for their mistakes. I'm almost positive Audrey knows it was *her* decision that caused the downward spiral of events."

It was actually mine.

It all leads back to me. It always does.

I don't want to alarm him, so I just nod and stare at the SweeTarts in his palm. "You and Harriet could open a candy shop."

"And eat everything inside, probably."

I want to laugh, to smile, but I just look deeper at Xander. *Please take care of her.* I wipe the heel of my palm against my cheek as tears drip.

"Ben?" Xander touches my bicep.

"I'm okay." I nod to myself a lot and run my tongue over my molars. The loss of Harriet is slamming into me before I've even let her go. I have to pinch my eyes to stop the waterworks. I'm on my feet. Needing to go inside and—I don't know—cry in the fucking shower?

Xander stands, and before he says anything, I hug him goodbye. "Thanks," I say from my core, trying to breathe. I start walking away, rubbing at my tear-streaked cheeks.

"Ben!" Xander catches up to me.

I stop and turn my agonized face toward his empathetic amber eyes. His chest collapses in a deep breath. "I hope you know something," he says, very quietly. "I'd rather sit on this rooftop with you for a billion years than not have you in this world at all." The memory of us at thirteen comes sweeping back. The bathroom. The lake house. "I never forgot what you told me. It helped me that night…and maybe it'll help you too. Because you belong in this world. Shit, if anyone does from our families, it's the eco-friendly vegan with a heart made of sustainable material."

It makes me laugh.

He smiles a little more, but he's uncertain. He knows I'm not okay. I know this all sucks, but this is the only way I can protect them.

I have to go. "I think you and Harriet will always be friends."

He intakes a pained breath. "Ben, don't—"

"I'm not dying," I assure. "I'm considering moving out of the city. Living somewhere else. I think maybe nature will be good, you know?"

He nods, then rapidly shakes his head. "No, man, I don't understand."

"I'm going to drop out of MVU. I haven't told my parents or my siblings yet."

Xander frowns. "Does Harriet know?"

I nod a few times, tears trying to surge again. She doesn't know it's happening soon, but she will tonight. My eyes blister.

It dawns on Xander—this is why I'm crushed. "Why are you leaving? New York isn't even that bad. There's not as many paparazzi like back in Philly with our parents. All your brothers are here. You even said Charlie stopped being an ass. Nature can't be better."

It's not. "I think it's what I need."

Xander expels a heavy sigh.

"Keep an eye on her for me?"

"Jesus Christ," he mutters, shaking his head like he's stepped into another dimension. "Yeah, I will." I turn to go as he speaks. "You never said why you were up here."

"I was just looking at the lights."

One last time.

FIFTY-THREE

BEN COBALT

Harriet flings open the door right as a timer goes off. "Shit, come in!" She races into her kitchen where she left her phone. I shut the door behind me, my stomach tightening when I notice Netflix popped on the TV, my favorite fig bars plated on the coffee table, along with bowls of corn chips and homemade guac.

"Having a party, Fisher?" I try to keep my voice lighthearted. This is the first time we've seen each other since last night—the night of the frat.

"With a microscopic invite list. Just me and you, Friend." Her back faces me while she opens the oven. She has on a flowy, red plaid mini-dress over a black long-sleeve top. Everything about her, I find beautiful.

Of course, tonight is no different. Being around Harriet, I ache to curve my arms around her small frame, lift her in my arms, clasp her head and kiss her breathless.

"I'm working on convincing Eden to spend the night at her boyfriend's place. She's there now," Harriet says, pulling out a baking sheet of pizza bites, likely the vegan kind I keep in the freezer at my brothers' apartment. "If I succeed, then you can stay over until like nine in the morning."

I rest my canvas duffel on the ground. She hasn't seen it yet. "Did you go to the bodega for party supplies or did you write your paper?" I tease.

"I did both." Harriet dumps the pizza bites into a bowl. "I figure if you're not up for talking, we can do an animated movie."

I come closer. "I thought you hate animated movies."

"I find them cheesy, which is low on the hate scale. You said *The Wild Robot* is good, right?"

I slide a hand along her back. "Yeah, I like that one." A knot forms in my chest. How am I going to get through this? How am I going to get *her* through this? "Harriet..."

She sets the baking sheet aside, then tugs off the daisy-patterned oven-mitt. Concern cinches her face into a darker scowl. "We don't have to even stay here. If you need to go outside, we can do a walk or...what do you need, Ben?"

I push my fingers through my hair. "I need you to be okay."

"I *am*. I have been. I'm concerned about *you*."

"I'll be okay knowing you are."

"That's so not true." She threads her arms, more on guard like she's prepared to battle my demons. "I can see it all over you right now. Something is really fucked up."

"That would be me," I mutter. "I am fucked up. I think I've been the real fucked up one this whole time." I try to smile, but it hurts. My eyes are raw, likely bloodshot, as I restrain emotion.

"Let's just sit down." Harriet grasps my hand, carting me toward the lime-green sofa. "The Hello Kitty blanket has your name on it tonight, Cobalt boy."

I laugh a little, but the sound just dies inside my lungs. I squeeze her hand, then let go as she plops down on the cushions.

Instead of joining her on the sofa, I push aside the guac and chips. Taking a seat on the coffee table.

Her confusion narrows her eyes. She moves to the edge of the couch, our legs knocking together. "Ben—"

"I can't stay for a movie."

She freezes.

"I want to," I add deeply.

"Animated movies are an hour and thirty minutes tops."

I feel like I'm being crushed alive. "I have thirty minutes."

Alarm springs her brows into her blond bangs. "What are you talking about?"

"I'm leaving New York tonight."

She slides backward like I pushed her. "No, no. You can't leave. You said…the holidays? What happened to staying for the holidays?" Her pinpointed gaze drifts around the apartment. She intakes a sharp breath when she spots my canvas duffel in the entryway.

"I'm sorry," I murmur. "I really thought I was going to stay for Christmas. I was even planning on staying indefinitely, but…"

"But what?" Her eyes grow wider. Not in anger. She's confused, distressed, worried. "What changed?"

I stare up at the whirling fan. "My sister almost died last night, and it was my fault, Harriet." I meet her gaze. "I can't be here."

"You didn't give her fentanyl. Those Kappa dickheads did that. Okay, fuck them. They should go rot away in the woods. Not you."

"I'm not going to rot away. I'm the sun, remember?"

She's unblinking. "I remember you telling me you aren't the sun. Do you…do you feel like you're decaying, Ben?"

"No," I reach out and clasp her small hand between both of mine. "I'm not suffering from depression. I am very fucking torn up about leaving you right now, but I haven't been over here masking my sorrow with joy. Every time I laughed with you, that was always real. It wasn't to hide sadness. I was never sad when I was with you, Harriet. You've made me so unbelievably happy." My voice chokes as emotion balls in my throat.

She opens her mouth to speak, but more confusion twists her features.

"I know it makes no sense," I breathe.

"You're right...it doesn't," she says slowly in thought. "If you're worried about that happening again, then never step foot on Douche Row. You don't have to drop out of college. You definitely don't need to leave New York or me..." Her voice fades.

I lace our hands together. I can't figure out how to explain this. My brain is just saying, *calm her down. Make sure she's okay before you go.* "What's in there?" I nod to the paper bag on the sofa beside her. "Party favors?"

She chews her lip. "You really want to make this a Going-Away Party? Don't you think we should invite your brothers?"

"I like this party of two." I reach out to grab the bag.

She's so fast to snatch it away, rolling the paper so I can't see inside. "It's just junk food."

Okay. Is she hiding something from me? I nod tensely. "We could start the movie?" I suggest.

"I can't watch a movie right now." She places the paper bag aside, then scoots forward again. "You can't leave. Because look around, nature boy."

It's very difficult to follow her whirling finger when I want to engrain her determined, hostile expression in my head forever. I try to take stock of all the potted plants. Ferns, ponytail palms, eucalyptus, devil's ivy, weeping fig. All around us is vibrant green.

"They will die without you," Harriet says so sternly. "I have a *black thumb*. Okay, they will die in this fucking apartment, *Friend.* They need you."

"I put the watering schedule on the fridge."

She purses her lips, like she forgot about that. "It'll slip off the magnet," she contends. "It's a super old Minnie Mouse from my only family vacation. It's practically ancient."

"Disney World or Land?" I wonder.

"Land, and stop trying to make me smile." I know she's serious, but her finger at my face is just making my lips rise more, which is causing her smile to fight through. "Eden will find the watering schedule on the floor, Ben. She will trash it. Then the plants will die."

"Every plant has a popsicle stick in the soil with its label. I have full faith that you'll do the Harriet Fisher thing and research them and make an Excel spreadsheet that can't be trashed. You'll take great care of them."

"What about the End of the World?"

"Literally or figuratively? Because I don't think doomsday is happening anytime soon."

"Are we sure? This feels catastrophic to me."

That warps my thoughts, a sledgehammer to the brain. Because if I stay, that feels like the real disaster.

She takes a pained breath. "And literally?"

"I talked to Gavin. He said it's fine if you keep bartending without me. You don't have to worry about losing your job."

"But what if there's another asshole sports fan?"

My muscles flame. "You and your coworker kick them out of the bar. If they won't go, you call the cops. Or you call my brothers. They'll always have security with them."

She buries her face in her palms.

"Harriet—"

"Your *child*," she says so emphatically.

"Son of Ben?"

"You can't abandon him." She springs hotly to her feet. I don't follow suit. I let her tower over me. "He might be a stuffed animal, but it's the principle of the matter. You are not a deadbeat father. Stay for your son."

It guts me in this second—that she might believe I'd stay for a stuffed lion over *her*. "If I could stay, Harriet, it would've always been for you. You're the reason why it's been almost impossible to leave."

"Almost impossible," she echoes. "But not *impossible*." She breathes harder like she's scaling a cliffside. "How do I make it impossible for you to go?"

"Please don't." A hot tear slides down my jaw. I smear it away with the side of my fist.

She kneels at my feet, holds on to my knees, seeing this is torture for me. Her breath is weighted. "I don't think letting you go is what's best for you, Ben."

"You need to."

Her chin quakes. "What if I need you? Okay, forget the plants, forget your son—what if *I* need you? There's a feeling inside of me I've never felt with anyone but you, and I may never feel it again." She presses closer. "It's love so deep, I can never be empty. It's love so hot, I can never be cold. Love like this is a star you wish upon, Ben. It's fairytales and make-believe, but you made it real. I don't want to give it back."

My entire body swells and collapses at once. The paradox of me. The tragedy of me.

The end of me.

I hold her warm cheeks. "I will never stop loving you. There will never be one moment where I don't, wherever I am."

Her tears slip down my hands. She takes a staggered breath, clutching my arms, then she kisses me. It's not an ordinary kiss. This kiss screams *I love you* with her entire soul. It bellows *please don't leave me*. It beseeches *pick me up and love me back*. It ignites the balled-up pain in my chest, and I crush my lips against hers, desperate for these seconds to last forever.

I am burning alive. My blood is on fire. Standing, I haul Harriet in my arms. Her legs wrap around my waist. Our lips weld and tongues wrestle in a heart-wrenching tug-and-pull. I curve my arm so tight around her while she holds fiercely on to me.

Don't let her go. Don't fucking let her go. What are you doing? I bring her to the kitchen, set her gently on the counter. My fingers clench her hair as our panting, hot breaths intermix with gripping, yearning, distraught kiss after kiss.

She fists my shirt, keeping me close. We're lip-locked for minutes upon minutes, and I slip my hand against her leg, up her dress, sliding along the soft, warmth of her thigh. Her hands don't roam, they pull, they wrench. The fraught need to connect, to fuse, is pummeling my senses. A tormented groan rakes through my throat. "*Harriet.*"

"Come inside me," she rasps.

I force myself to grab the cabinet above her head. The more I touch her, the more I want inside her. "I can't have sex with you."

"Why?"

"Because I can't live with myself knowing I fucked you and left you."

She presses her forehead to my collar, and I scrunch the back of her hair, kissing the blond strands, listening as she catches her breath. I see the time on the oven clock, and my stomach overturns.

This is it.

"I'm sorry," I whisper. "I have to go." I kiss her temple, her cheek, then I draw back, and she releases her grip.

"Wait. You'll be hungry. Just let me give you some of this stuff." She sprints around the apartment, shoving the fig bars back in the box. Then she grabs a baggie for the pizza bites.

While she packs away the snacks, I sling my duffel on my shoulder and unzip the main pocket. I pull out Son of Ben and place him on the kitchen counter. Along with my worn blue ballcap.

She hands me the sealed pizza bites, the fig bars, and barely glances at the stuffed lion or the hat. Her ocean blue eyes are crashing waves, and I stare down into them.

"Thanks for all of this." I can't even tear my gaze off hers. "If you need anything, call my family," I remind her. "They'll be there for you."

"I will," she says definitively.

I breathe in a stronger breath. "I'll write to you as soon as I can. It might be a week." My return address on the mail I send will be a P.O. Box in Philly that I've set up. Any letters sent to me will be forwarded from there. So no one will ever have my actual address.

Not even Harriet.

I can't give it to her. The risk of my family finding me is too high.

She nods.

Another kiss to her cheek, and I back away. Each step is a wrench cranking inside my body. Then I reach for the doorknob.

"This isn't how we end, Friend," she says suddenly. It stops me.

Those are the same words I said to her months ago in the back of her Honda. I rotate to Harriet. My pulse pounding. My heart skidding.

She's several feet from me, her narrowed eyes drilling into me with powerful resolve. "You said Cobalts carve out futures they want. I don't believe this is really what you want, Ben, and it's not what your brothers will want either. It's not what *I* want." She points at her chest. "So if I were to make some grand prediction, I'd say this isn't how we end. This isn't over. You're in my future for so much longer than this."

I want to believe her, but my gut says I will let her down. Because I have to let her down. There is no way out.

"Do amazing things, Fisher." I give her one last smile.

Then I go.

I leave my entire world behind me.

FIFTY-FOUR

HARRIET FISHER

He's gone. I'm stuck in a motionless state when Ben exits my apartment. Our interaction cycles through my head at a painful, incoherent speed. I've known Ben planned to move for *months*, but it's never triggered this type of alarm in me.

The last several weeks, he's only mentioned staying. Then his sister was in harm's way at the frat, and everything changed too abruptly. He feels responsible enough that he's leaving? How will that help? It's not rational. I think back to how many times his pulse sped when he mentioned this move. Panic. Pure *panic*.

Anxiety? Fear?

I want to be a fucking doctor—how did I not see something could've been wrong on a psychological level? That it's possibly even deeper than anyone knows…

What if Ben never wants to be found?

What if that's the point of everything?

Nausea barrels up my esophagus, and I race into the bathroom. Kneeling just in time to vomit in the toilet. I shake and dizzy as I puke my guts up. Sweat beads my skin. *There's no fucking time for this, Harriet.* I grip the bowl, unable to stop that quickly. I swallow some down, then crawl into a stance. Picking myself up, I run for my phone.

I snatch it off the couch and call Beckett. "Please answer, please answer." I wipe my mouth with the back of my hand. Stomach acid sears my throat.

It beeps into his voicemail greeting. "If you called the right number, you know who this is. I'm likely unavailable. Just ring me again in an hour or I'll get back to you when I can."

At the second beep, I say fast, "Ben is gone. We need to find him before he leaves the city. You need to stop him. I couldn't...I couldn't stop him."

Did I not try hard enough? I should've tried so much harder. What could I've done better? I finish leaving a voicemail message and try not to contemplate my failings—instead, I send a group text to his brothers.

HARRIET

> BEN IS GONE!!!! WE NEED TO FIND HIM!!!

There aren't enough shouty caps and exclamations in the world to express my distress right now. Moving hurriedly, I unfurl the paper bag on the couch, sifting aside the extra bags of chips to grab the slim blue box.

An unopened pregnancy test. My heart pangs in the worst way possible. Since my birth control prevents my period, it's not easy to deduce whether I could be pregnant. My breasts have felt more tender recently, and I freaked myself out enough to purchase a test.

Ever since his mom said Cobalt sperm is powerful enough to defeat birth control, my paranoia has run rampant, and I wanted to put it to bed. Now, this is just coming at a horrible fucking time.

I didn't want Ben to discover the test in the bag. I wasn't going to mention it because this test was supposed to quell my anxieties. Not baby trap him. It felt like a gross way to manipulate him to stay. Now I'm wondering if I should've, for his sake.

I collect mouthwash from the bathroom to use on my walk to the subway. I check my phone. No texts?

Most of his brothers are likely on stage, not near a phone, but what about Charlie? Once I gather my things into my backpack, I slow down as the stuffed animal and Ben's blue baseball cap catch my eye on the kitchen counter.

I take the ballcap. And a letter slides out beneath it. Fluttering to the floorboards. I pick it up to see my name written in yellow crayon.

Tears almost burst forth.

He left me a letter. Because maybe he knew…I would've liked a note. A note would've been nice. "Come back," I nearly cry. Scrubbing the silent tears away with my hand, I slip the letter and stuffed animal into my bookbag, then I fit his hat on my head, tightening the strap.

We're going to find him.

We have to find him.

Life isn't the same without him.

It's all I think on the way to the Cobalt brothers' apartment.

NO ONE IS HERE YET. I'M SITTING IN THE HALL OUTSIDE 2166. My bookbag between my legs while I knock the back of my head against the door. Security let me pass through the lobby after I signed my name on the guest sheet, but they didn't pat me down. Didn't ask me questions. I'm too frequent a guest for them to bat an eye.

Five minutes of his brothers not responding was too long, so I pulled the trigger and alerted his mom. I basically spent the entire subway ride texting her and trying not to cry when she called me. She asked a lot of questions I don't have answers to, but I wish I knew.

I wish I knew where he went.

I wish I prodded harder, even if it hurt.

If we never find him, I'm going to always wish.

Now I'm just waiting for his brothers to show up. They're on their way to the apartment.

Tom had been the first to answer me, and he rerouted to the ballet to physically get Beckett. I think both Beckett and Eliot left mid-performance. Charlie has been totally uncommunicative.

While time drags excruciatingly slow, I unearth the letter from my backpack. My heart beats so loud as I carefully open the envelope.

I unfold the plain white paper, and a pressed flower slips out, falling to my lap. I pinch the delicate, dried stem. The cream petals too fragile to touch. I'm careful not to destroy them.

I sniff back emotion, blow out a shaky breath, then eye the letter. He wrote in black ink, his handwriting nothing fancy, but seeing a remnant of Ben is everything to me.

I read slowly.

Dear Friend,

There is no possible way I'll be able to tell you everything I want to when I say goodbye. It'll be a miracle if I even manage to say goodbye at all. I wouldn't be surprised if I never do. Because my heart is yours forever, Harriet. I'm not taking it back. I left it with you.

I also left you a flower. One of the oldest on earth. Something so delicate and beautiful withstood glaciers, extinctions, the ever-changing landscape of our planet, the rise and fall of civilizations...through eras and hardship, it survived. It's a testament to the strength and perseverance of life on our Earth. And it's always reminded me of you.

The magnolia.

You will endure, Fisher. You will heal others with music or with medicine, with emotion or with mind. You will love and be loved, and if you ever miss me, like I will always miss you, just find the brightest burning star across the sky.

à toi pour l'éternité,
Ben

I don't want to love anyone more than I love him. I only want Ben. "I only want you," I cry as a broken sob rips through my body. I try to protect the letter from my sudden onslaught of tears. Burying my face into the golden fur of his stuffed animal, I hug the lion against my shuddering frame. He still smells like Ben. Like his musk. Like pine.

I'm not angry he left. I can't be angry. I am pulverized knowing that maybe I didn't do enough to help him while he was here.

You've made me so unbelievably happy. I hang on to what he said. I believe it's true. And I wish I could've told him, "Take me with you."

"Harriet?"

I peer up and blink away the glassy haze of tears.

Joana Oliveira, the neighbor down the hall, rushes toward me in concern. Curls cascade down her shoulders. She has on a mocha crop top and matching pants. Fuzzy enough to be PJs. She even wears slippers. I don't know why I'm fixating on her wardrobe.

Maybe to dam the waterworks. It sort of helps.

"What happened?" She reaches the door. "Did they lock you out?" She's a half-second from banging her fist to the wood. Actually, she does do that. "You smug Adonis knockoffs. Open up!"

"They're not home." My voice is hoarse. I notice the ice pack in her hand. "Holy shit, are you okay?" I croak out. Her ribcage is seriously bruised.

"What?" She's confused, until she follows my gaze. A welt the size of a fucking dinner plate blemishes her golden-brown skin. Right below her crop top. "Oh, yeah. It hurts like hell, but I'd take a punch to the ribs over one to the face. Having your eye swollen shut is miserable."

I crane my neck down the hall toward her older brother's apartment where she lives. Wondering if I should drag *her* away from some dude.

Joana sits down beside me, adjusting the ice pack. "I'm a professional boxer."

That explains things. I nod.

She sweeps my face. "I take it you're not a professional crier."

"What gave me away?" I deadpan, smoothing out Son of Ben's wet knotted fur. "The ugly tears?"

"If that was ugly crying, then the rest of us are *grotesque*. And no, it's because when I first met you, you had one of the best mean mugs I've ever seen. Not really crying material."

"I am a professional mean mugger," I murmur, tears trying to scald my eyes again.

"You'll have to give me notes for when I'm in the ring." Joana holds her legs loosely, but she tenses as her worry escalates. "I'm so down for silly-stringing their apartment. Writing some world-class Cobalt insults on their mirrors with lipstick. I will brainstorm all night. I bet we can piss off one of them, at least."

So much emotion barrels back into me. "They didn't do anything wrong." I glance over at her. "But thanks." My voice tries to rattle. "I've never really..." The honesty fades away. What I planned to say would be a weird confession to someone I barely know. I just feel so unzipped, undone, and she's right here to witness my insides tumbling out, with no way to scoop them back in.

I could say, *get it together, Harriet,* but maybe it's okay if I don't this time.

"You've never really...?" she asks quietly.

"I've never really had many friends. Kind of by choice," I whisper. "So when I moved to New York, I knew I'd only make maybe one, if that." I twist the lion's beaded necklace. "Then I befriended Ben, and he felt like a million friends in one, you know? Like he was... everything." I bang my head back against the door. "And now he's gone. And I'm not saying you're my friend—obviously we've barely interacted, but your silly-string offer was nice. So thanks."

"What's your number?" She's unpocketing her phone.

I give her a look. "You don't have to take pity on me—"

"I've wanted to hang out with you for *weeks*. There aren't that many girls around our age in this building, and not to pat myself on the back too hard—I get along *great* with introverts. You can reject me a thousand times, and I won't take offense or ever stop inviting you. I'll just be excited for the times when you do appear."

She makes friendship seem easy like Ben does…or did. I tell her my number. The blip of elation coming, then going. *He's not here.* I'm making friends without him. Already moving on without him? It's only been fucking *hours.*

Joana sees my crushed expression. "The silly-string is always on the table. I'll place an online delivery. Have it sent to the lobby asap."

As fun as it'd be, I could never trash their apartment knowing Beckett has OCD. Given his extreme privacy and how much Ben cautioned me when he shared his brother's medical history, I highly doubt Joana knows he does either.

"There's nothing to retaliate," I swallow hard, then I place the dried flower back into the letter with so much care. Refolding the paper, slipping it into my bookbag.

"Texted you my number." She pockets her phone, then grabs her ice pack. "You said Ben is gone? Was this a breakup?"

"No, it's…he's missing, I guess—not kidnapped," I add quickly. "It's hopefully nothing serious." *Hopefully.* I sit up higher at an encouraging thought. "Your older brother is Charlie's bodyguard, right? Oscar Oliveira?"

"That's him."

"Would he tell you where Charlie is if you asked?"

"Oscar? Fuck no. He won't even tell other bodyguards where he is when he's protecting Charlie. I'm a world-renowned secret keeper, but my brother is on another level. It's impressive."

"Fuck," I slam back into the door. "We can't find Charlie. I thought maybe he'd help."

"Charlie is king of the assholes, so don't set your hopes on him." She rises to her feet, then hesitates on leaving. "You're waiting for the Cobalt brothers, aren't you?"

I nod at the same time Beckett and Tom come bounding out of the elevator, and I jolt up beside Joana. She says a quick goodbye and "text me if you need anything" before walking backward to her apartment, then spinning fully around and vanishing.

I'm stuck on how Beckett and Tom *sprint* down the hall.

I gather my stuff off the ground as Tom charges for the door. While he unlocks it, he's speaking to me, but I just nod a ton, unsure of what he's saying. Seeing their urgency, their fear for their little brother up close, I'm not processing this well.

I still wear his ballcap. I'm hugging a backpack with a pregnancy test, his stuffed animal son, and a goodbye letter—and all this time, I had the piece of the puzzle, the one morsel of info, that could've kept Ben here for his own good.

I knew he planned to move.

And I never told anyone.

Guilt and turmoil crash against me, and as Tom disappears inside, I train my focus on helping. *Find Ben. Find Ben.* It's mission critical.

Except as I step forward, I freeze right outside the apartment. I've never really been here without Ben. The door swings back in my face, until Beckett clasps the frame.

He's standing just inside the doorway.

His sweaty hair falls over a rolled blue bandana. His skin reddened like he rubbed makeup off in the car ride here. He pushes the door open wider for me with his back. Letting me inside. Waiting for me.

Remorse, guilt, anguish contort my face. "*I knew.* I knew, Beckett. He told me he planned to leave New York. I should've told you. I should've said something—"

"You couldn't have known what he was really thinking," Beckett says deeply. "Trust me, you aren't the only one revisiting every conversation you've had." He does this thing where he tries to pick up my gaze off the floor. He chases after it, and it reminds me of *Ben.* Is everything going to remind me of him?

I set a harsher, narrowed look on Beckett to steel myself. "We'll find him. We have to find him."

He says a single word in French, then tells me, "Together." He stretches his arm into the apartment, showing me the way.

I go inside, Beckett right behind me. He flicks on the kitchen lights. Tom is rummaging around the couch, searching for any signs or clues.

The apartment is spotless. Like Ben was careful not to interact with any object, any of their possessions, anything he could accidentally break before he left.

My stomach bubbles with nausea again. Especially as Beckett finds a piece of paper and a phone beside the espresso machine.

"He left his phone?" I shake my head at myself, furious with myself. I take off his hat in a huff and shake out my bangs. *He left his phone.* He never lied to me. He basically insinuated he'd go off the grid, but I thought he'd eventually come back! I thought he'd commune with nature, find whatever he was searching for, and stay in touch with his family.

This…this is not *that*.

"Unlock it, Beckett Joyce," Tom says hopefully. "We can check his texts."

Beckett has a hand to his eyes.

"What?" Tom's voice spikes. "*Open it*, dude. His passcode is the day Pip-Squeak died. Or try—try Harry's birthday. Ten-thirteen. Try *ten-thirteen*."

I think Tom is seconds from vaulting over the kitchen island to steal the phone, but Beckett quickly tells him, "He wiped it."

"No, no," Tom shakes his head aggressively. "You-you aren't trying hard enough. You have to try the passcode."

Beckett approaches Tom at the couch, just to hand him the phone. I join them as Tom turns on the cellphone. A welcome screen stares back. His face fractures for a brutal beat.

The air thickens with tension, making it harder and harder to breathe. "What's the paper say?" I ask, just as the door flies open.

Eliot storms inside, shrugging off his peacoat quickly like he's up in flames. Torched to a deadly, incinerating degree. "Any word on Charlie?"

"He's in Prague for the weekend," Beckett answers, as Tom snatches the paper out of his hand. "He delayed his trip last night when we went to the frat." *So Charlie is in Prague right now? Great. That helps us...not at all.*

I watch Tom skim the note, and he staggers dazedly backward, then drops down to the couch.

"What's it say?" I ask Tom, but he's staring off into space, incoherent.

Beckett's eyes are reddened.

Eliot steals the paper from Tom's loose grip, then glares at the words. "Not to admonish the missing, but our dear brother has the second most aggravating handwriting of us." He passes the paper to Beckett. "Please."

Beckett stares at the note and reads out loud, "'*I'm sorry. I love you. Thank you for being the best brothers...*'" He can't finish.

"*Beckett*," Eliot forces.

I take the paper from him to read the rest. "'*Thank you for being the best brothers a little brother could ever hope for and have. I'll write to you in a week. Don't worry about me. You don't need to find me. I need to be on my own.*'" I manage to keep my voice level. "He ends with French and his name."

Beckett says the French part to Eliot, then translates for me, "Forever your brother, Ben."

Tom bows forward, his distraught face in his hands, then he pops out to say, "The granola, check—check the cupboards, Eliot Alice. See if he took his granola." His voice cracks with his features. "Okay, we—we just follow the crumbs. We'll find him if we follow the..." He collapses backward as he loses breath to speak, like he's been shot in the chest.

It hurts so badly to watch. I've loved Ben for months. They've loved him for nineteen years.

Eliot sinks beside Tom. Wraps an arm around him. "There is no crumb we won't follow, brother. We *will* find him."

"What about logging into his accounts?" I ask. "Seeing what flight he booked?"

"Our parents have people working on tracking him," Beckett says, "but he might be untraceable. We don't think he took a commercial flight. Or if he flew at all. No one knows how many people Ben has been in touch with or who they even are. He could've called in favors or paid people to discreetly get him where he needs to go."

He's broke, but maybe this is why. He always intended to move before the end of the semester. Maybe he paid them in advance.

"Did he leave you anything?" Beckett asks me.

I nod quickly. "Yeah. Yeah, a letter. You can read it in case you think he says anything that could help find him. Just...just be careful with the pressed flower." I dig through my backpack in my arms, emotion clouding my gaze. My pulse is out of whack, and I end up losing grip and dumping half my things onto the floor. Tiny pieces of candy scatter everywhere. "Shit." I kneel, finding the letter under spilt Jolly Ranchers. Ugh, I don't want to fucking cry right now. I wipe my wet eyes with my bicep.

Beckett and Eliot crouch down to gather loose pieces of hard caramel candies and rolling jawbreakers. Then in slow-motion, I witness Beckett grabbing the slim blue box off the floorboards. How is this happening? *You're a mortal among gods, of course your luck is shit.* I am being asphyxiated as Beckett and Eliot glance from the pregnancy test to *me*.

I snatch it from Beckett's hands. "It's just a precaution."

"So you don't think you are?"

"I don't know, dude. I haven't taken it yet." I sound defensive. Can they tell I'm scared?

"Taken what?" Tom stands from the couch, spotting the pregnancy test in my clutch. He goes motionless. We're both grimacing.

Then he falls back on the cushions. "What else is going to be thrown at us? An earthquake?"

Eliot scrapes a hand along his hard jawline. "*Ben,*" he says roughly, then looks to Beckett. "Our little brother was having unprotected sex."

"I'm on the pill," I shoot back.

"Did you miss a day?" Beckett questions.

I burn up. "No. *No.*" I pick myself up to my feet. They follow suit, towering and staring down at me like I'm *young* and inexperienced. Possibly because I'm with their youngest brother. I don't know what it's like to have older siblings—or really, siblings at all. "Like I said, it's just a precaution."

Eliot shakes his head hotly, his gaze on my flat belly. "Ben couldn't have known. If he had *any* idea that he got you pregnant, he would've never left you."

It confirms that I could've done more. I nearly double over. I swallow all the brimming pain. "Well, I didn't tell him," I snap, then I hand Beckett the letter. "I'm probably not pregnant. I didn't want to manipulate Ben."

"You're better than me," Eliot paces toward the kitchen, then back, each footfall scalding the floor. "I would've told him I have a terminal illness. That I expect him to bury me in three weeks with his own hands or else I'd haunt his ass for fucking eternity."

"Or maybe I'm worse," I rasp. "Because I didn't…" *I didn't do enough.*

"He was going to leave," Beckett rationalizes. "We did what we could when we could."

I peer down at the pregnancy test, inhaling a deeper breath. "Can I use your bathroom?"

"Why is she asking—why are you asking?" Eliot says to me, standing still. "Has this not been your home the past few weeks?"

Don't cry, Harriet. He's basically saying this fact doesn't change if Ben is gone, but it feels like everything does. "Thanks," I mumble, darting to the powder room. I'm shaking as I rip open the box.

The instructions confuse me. Maybe because I'm staring at *Spanish*. Hurriedly, I flip the paper over to the English directions. I reread the same line four fucking times, but the typed black font isn't processing. Teardrops wet the paper.

People leaving me is nothing new.

Sunny, my drum instructor, left me without a note.

My father left me without a goodbye.

My mother left me by shoving me out the door.

So is it any wonder that I accepted Ben leaving me too? In the end, I relegated this loss as a commonplace part of my life. Familiar. Routine.

Now, I'd give anything for him to come back.

A knock sounds on the door. "Just let me know you're okay." It's Beckett.

"Yeah." A broken noise breeches my lips.

He jiggles the knob. "Let me in."

I unlock the door. "I can't read it." I can't see him past the film of tears. "I'm—"

Beckett immediately pulls me into a hug, and I release a wounded sound against his chest. I'm muttering, "I don't want to do this without him. I can't lose him. We have to find him. *We have to find him.*"

"Shhh," Beckett coos. "Take some breaths." The way he holds the back of my head, I pretend he's Ben.

I pretend Ben never really left. That he's here with me, and I calm down enough to pull back, rub at my eyes, and read the instructions.

"I can do this," I choke out to myself. "I can do this."

My phone buzzes.

I scramble, patting my hip-clip, and I think, *Ben*. Forgetting that he doesn't have a phone.

> **XANDER** 🙂
>
> I heard Ben is MIA. He just told me hours ago he was planning to drop out of MVU, but I didn't think he'd leave tonight. Did you know? I feel like shit. If you need to talk, I'm here. I'm sorry. I'm really fucking sorry.

I send back a quick text to chat later and that I feel just as guilty. Because I knew too. "It's Xander Hale," I explain to Beckett when I reattach my phone.

"He just found out about Ben," Beckett guesses, unsurprised. Off my frown, he clarifies, "Xander is usually one of the last to get information in our family." I wonder if this has to do with Xander's self-harm.

"You're one of the first?" I ask.

He presses his shoulders to the door. "Not even close. Everyone is aware I'm largely inaccessible because of ballet. Charlie knows more than I do, always."

"He's really in Prague?"

"Really," Beckett nods, his gaze falling in sorrow. "I can read you the instructions if you need help."

My neck heats. "I've got it. I think it's probably uncomplicated. Pee on a stick. Wait a handful of minutes. Learn whether or not your brother knocked me up." I try to joke, but it lands like a dinky water balloon that rolls away and never bursts.

"First brother to fall in love, first to get a girl pregnant," Beckett says.

"And Ben thinks he's not winning awards in the Cobalt fam." This joke hits.

Beckett smiles. It almost nudges up my lips.

He nods to me. "You want me to wait with you?"

Knee-jerk reaction, I shake my head, but after a couple seconds, I begin to nod. I've always been able to do anything on my own, but given the chance of comfort over pain, of warmth over the freezing, brutal cold—I'd choose the relief of not being so alone.

So I choose Beckett's company. Grateful he's offering. He seems just as relieved I accepted. After I follow the instructions in privacy, he returns to the bathroom. I sit on the toilet lid to wait for the results. He leans up against the wall. My phone timer ticking down.

"I tried..." I gaze at the marble floor, gripping the sides of the toilet as I squeeze my legs together. Afraid to completely unravel again, but I can't stop replaying the final moments with Ben in my apartment. "I tried to get him to stay. I think with sex..." I cringe at myself, furious with myself. "I told him to come inside me minutes before he walked out the door. But telling him I might be pregnant was a line I couldn't cross? Having sex right before he left, that was *totally* fine though. Doable." I confess more to the ground. It takes everything just to peer up at his expression.

Beckett has his skull pressed to the wall while he stares up at the ceiling. His face unreadable.

"If you think I'm too fucked up to be with your brother, I'd get it." My stomach twists into a pretzel. "I'm not a good person."

"You use sex to get what you want," he says as his gaze descends like a feather to mine. Lightly, not even close to caustically. "We've known that since you tried to blow Charlie. We never thought it'd magically go away if you started dating our little brother. Neither did Ben." He holds my gaze even softer. "None of us are striving to find perfect people with no baggage. We're well-aware we all carry our own." He glances painfully at the door. "Ben is gone. Isn't that proof enough?"

I release my grip on the toilet, just to clutch my kneecaps. My body hurts as the loss ricochets through me.

"Bad people to me," Beckett says in a soothing tone, "are the ones selling out my family to the media. Ones who wouldn't care what happens to my brother. That's not you. That has never been you. So, no, I don't think you're too fucked up to be with him." He releases a weighted breath. "And I'm almost positive he wouldn't have had sex with you before walking out the door." His eyes grip mine. "Tell me he rejected you."

"Don't worry, he didn't let it happen. He did the Cobalt chivalrous thing."

"He did the *compassionate* thing." Beckett straightens off the wall. "Charlie, Eliot, and I wouldn't have done the same as Ben."

"Oh so you would've fucked me and left," I deadpan.

"Probably."

My brows shoot up. Shocked he even answered, but Beckett is blunt as fuck.

"Our morals aren't exactly on par with his. He's one of the best guys you could've been with in your situation, Harriet, and you lifted something heavy off him these past few months. You two were good for each other."

"Were," I mutter, staring haunted at the floor. "We're already in the past tense." It's a punch to the gut. I'm surprised I'm not bent over. "Everyone always leaves me in the end..." I trail off into the tense silence.

"I know Ben," he says in the quiet, lifting my gaze to his. "He's too selfless. He's too altruistic. Too caring. The only reason he could've had the strength to abandon you was knowing you wouldn't be abandoned—because you have us. And regardless of what that test says, I will be giving my brother his final wish for the rest of my life. I promise you that."

I shake my head as tears roll. I wipe them roughly away. "Ben has given me too much. Even when he's gone, he's given me a family."

"That's my brother. That's Pip," Beckett says lovingly, fondly, sentimentally, as if he's remembering years of time with him.

The timer beeps, and the *not pregnant* result doesn't alleviate my paranoia like it should've. I'm numb to the fact that I won't be dealing with a massive life decision.

Though Ben wouldn't want me to, I would sacrifice everything to find him.

My grades.

Harold.

Tom's offer to join the band.

I'd drop out of MVU tomorrow. Never become a doctor.

I would lose it all for him to come back. For him to be alive and safe. For him to not be alone in the wilderness forever.

FIFTY-FIVE

HARRIET FISHER

It's been three days. No signs of Ben.

No letters. No clouds in the sky spelling his name. No crumbs leading to his whereabouts. It's all been dead-end after dead-end. His mom texts me every morning, every afternoon, calls me every night, asking if I've heard *anything*.

When I say no, she reassures me she will scour the entire earth for Ben. I believe her. She won't rest until she finds her youngest boy, but how do you find someone that intended to never be found?

It should be heartening knowing *the* Rose Calloway and Connor Cobalt are his parents. Surely *gods* will be able to locate their son. But I think Ben knew exactly who he was trying to fool. He knew he had to outwit his cunning family.

I'm more and more afraid he's succeeding.

Still, I try not to wallow. Rose tells me, "Chin up. Shoulders back. Imagine the whole auditorium is full of idiots and you're the only smart one," the morning of my Ovid presentation. The pep talk and ego-boost are appreciated.

Xander and I practiced for hours together in his apartment, so we should be fine. Totally fine. No hives.

Just a really heavy heart.

"Where's Ben?" Professor Wellington asks as Xander and I approach the podium. His white brows knit together. He seems genuinely puzzled why a student would miss their final presentation.

Xander pushes away the mic, then whispers to Professor Wellington, "Ben's not coming."

He lets out a disappointed sigh. "Well, that's too bad. He was doing very well."

"He'll be back," I pipe in. "It's a stomach bug. Can he do a make up? Like maybe an extra essay to weigh against the zero?"

Xander gives me a soft look, then nods to the professor. "He was puking all night. They're giving him an IV drip in his apartment—our family has doctors on call. I'm his cousin, which you might not know because you likely don't read tabloids, and why am I saying this?" Xander shakes his head at himself and accidentally makes eye contact with several girls in the second row.

They audibly gasp and shriek.

Professor Wellington just smiles. "Ah, I remember Ben telling me you're his cousin." I'm not at all surprised Ben chatted with our ancient professor. "I'll go over extra credit opportunities with him when he returns to class. And don't forget, there's still the final exam next week."

It might be *extreme* wishful thinking that Ben will be here for finals, but I can't reject the idea of him coming back. I'm not sure how he will yet. Maybe he's knee-deep in snow and he'll be afraid of frostbite, so he'll return to civilization. Okay, this might sound like something *I* would fear and do, but I imagine different scenarios where Ben decides he needs to be in New York.

If he shows up, he needs a chance to complete the semester without failing, and I feel good knowing Xander and I can give him that.

Professor Wellington waves us to the podium. "You two can carry on."

Carry on.

As if it's so easy to do without him.

One foot in front of the other, Fisher. Is his voice going to be in my head from now on? Don't fucking cry. I blow out an uneven breath. Xander sidles next to me and tips his head down to mine. "We've got this," he whispers to me, his voice shaking just a little. "*Fuck.*"

"We can do this, Paul Atreides," I whisper back, straightening the index cards in my hand. "Just imagine they're all idiots and we're the only smart ones."

He chokes on a laugh. "That's such a Cobalt trick." Xander is shying from the obsessive eyes and the phones raised at him. "I'd do anything to get through this, even pretend I'm a genius for ten minutes." He has another stack of flashcards. "You ready?"

I nod him on.

He twists the mic toward us. "This thing work—?"

The gasps and squeals have the professor shushing half the lecture hall. This is the first time they've heard Xander Hale speak in person.

"That'd be a yes," he mutters, backing away from the mic like it's a bomb.

I step forward and take a shallow breath, the mic crackling. The auditorium falls hushed, and I dip forward to speak. And then my voice cages in my lungs for an unbearable moment. I've practiced this opening line a thousand times with Xander. It's Latin from Ovid's *Metamorphoses*.

Before I even say a thing, the words plunge into the depth of me. I look around, and the auditorium is empty in my mind. I just see Ben in the middle row. I see his lips crawling up into a radiant smile. I see his baby blue eyes glittering with the same effervescence.

I see Eternal Spring that will last through the ages.

"Omnia mutantur, nihil interit," I say quietly into the mic. "Everything changes, nothing perishes."

FIFTY-SIX

HARRIET FISHER

We didn't exactly bomb the presentation, but it definitely did not go as planned. The uproar and commotion each time Xander spoke caused the professor to stop us. Girls *wept*. They were physically trembling as if Xander was talking solely to them. Some went into shock.

I've never seen anything like it up close.

Our professor either took pity on us or didn't have the time for us to present privately without the mayhem—because he just gave us an automatic one hundred.

Xander keeps apologizing as we walk to the dining hall for lunch. Easton is also with us.

I tell him the truth. I couldn't be happier that we only had to be up there for five minutes tops. No way would I complain about an easy A. Especially in a humanities course. There are enough hard-earned ones in my schedule.

On our trek across the chilly campus, leaves falling, I'm distracted by Donnelly. Xander's bodyguard speaks into his mic more often now that Ben is MIA. He's on comms seemingly all the time, and whenever he catches me staring, he'll shake his head at me like, *no new news.*

No Ben.

My phone buzzes, and I check the text.

> **TOM** 💀
> I sent the packet to you. Let me know what else you need. I can email you what I think the proposed tour schedule would be.

> **HARRIET**
> Def send that.

I told Tom if I were to *seriously* consider his offer then he needed to *seriously* give me all the information. Contracts, people I'd be working with—producers, managers, whoever. I want details.

He's surprisingly followed through in epic fashion. For a chaos-maker, he is incredibly detail-oriented and organized.

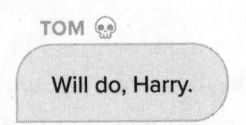

> **TOM** 💀
> Will do, Harry.

My phone vibrates again. This time a phone call from an unknown number. I stop abruptly, wind nipping my face.

Xander turns back around. "You okay?"

"Uh, yeah, someone's calling me. It's an unknown number."

Xander looks to Donnelly, who wears just as much confusion as me.

I wrack my brain for who it could be. "It might be spam."

"What if it's Ben?" Xander says, more hopefully.

"Or maybe it's Guy Abernathy," Easton says, popping his coat collar as more cold air blows through the wind tunnel in the quad.

"We still don't know who's made the Honors House." Easton is in the top five, still in contention like me. With the semester ending, they should be whittling five down to *one*. It's nuts they've even taken this long to choose a new member.

It's likely the House is split on who to pick. Maybe they've finally decided, and it's not me.

I prepare for a rejection, since that seems more likely than Ben calling. And I answer on the last ring.

"Harriet Fisher?" It's a very unfamiliar, deep male voice.

Not Guy.

Not Ben.

"Yes?"

"Hi, I'm Gordon Brown. Ben Cobalt's estate attorney. If I could have a moment of your time, I need you to come down to my office and sign some paperwork."

I DON'T UNDERSTAND.

I don't understand.

I don't *fucking* understand. I've said it three times to Gordon, and he's tried to explain it to me in three different ways. I could blame bad cell reception if we weren't having this conversation in person.

I left campus and told Xander I'd fill him in later. Now I'm currently sitting in this lawyer dude's stately office in Midtown, a pen, documents, and legal pad laid out on the desk before me.

"Let me just say it back to make sure I have this correct," I tell him, my hands hovering over the cherry oak desk. "Ben Pirrip Cobalt, your client, made *me*, Harriet Stevie Fisher, the sole beneficiary of an irrevocable trust that contains…*this*…amount of money." I tap the legal pad with a number written down.

It's not a microscopic number.

It's not even a small number.

It is *massive*.

A staggering amount. More than my eyes can truly grasp. Gordon had to write it down because I couldn't believe it without seeing the numbers.

It's millions.

"All yes," Gordon confirms.

My eyes burn. I think I've blinked twice since I sat down. "Is this all of Ben's money? He emptied his bank accounts and put everything in this trust?" *For me?*

Gordon sighs heavily. "Yes. I did tell him he needed to consult a financial advisor before making this move, but he was incredibly persistent."

I clutch the sides of my head. Wishing I called his brothers or his parents to come with me, so they could process this too. Because everything about this doesn't feel right.

I wince. "I don't accept." I push the legal pad, documents, and pen away from me.

Gordon exhales even deeper. "I'm afraid it doesn't matter whether you accept or not. The money is still in this trust. It's going to sit here if you don't use it."

My stomach churns thinking about all the ways I *could* use the money. Rent for the rest of my life. I wouldn't even need free housing from the Honors House. Medical school, paid for. If I go that route. My future, funded. But it feels so wrong. So terribly wrong.

All of this.

Gordon pushes a box of tissues toward me, then retracts. Am I in threat of crying? Or do I look like I might bite his head off? "Once you sign, you'll be able to access the trust on January 1st. You will have *full* access. No rules or stipulations. That's how Ben set it up."

Ben set it up.

What about all the months Ben was broke? Was his money tied up in *this* trust the entire time? Waiting for me?

This...this isn't making sense.

"I don't understand," I say, which makes Gordon huff out another deep sigh. "No, I understand how the trust works. I don't understand the timing. Ben told me he was already broke at the beginning of the semester when I ran into him at a frat party. We'd *barely* spoken before that—so when did he set this up?"

Gordon swivels to his computer and scrolls until he stalls on a document. "His first meeting with me was…in the middle of May."

I blow backward. "*No.*"

That means he made the decision to give me his money before the frat party. When we'd only run into each other a couple of times. Like at Penn. The science lab.

"Hold on," Gordon lifts a finger for me to wait. "I did put a note in his file. I thought it was strange too and wanted to keep some sort of record in case of litigation." He reads from his computer. "*I asked Ben how well he knew Harriet Fisher, and he told me, I know she's a good person. Also asked why he was giving her so much. He told me, I don't need it where I'm going.*"

My eyes well. "May?" I ask again. "You said *May?*"

"Yes, mid-May."

Oh fuck. "Can I make a call?" I ask Gordon.

"Of course. I'll give you a minute." He steps out, and I dial Beckett, hoping he's available. *Please, please, please.*

"Harriet," he answers on the third ring. "Everything good?"

"No, I'm at this lawyer's office. I'll explain in a second, but do you know when Ben assaulted that asshole who lives in your family's gated neighborhood?"

"Tate Townsend? That was back in May."

I go very still. Wide-eyed.

Ben was going to leave his family right then. He must've set up this "irrevocable" trust soon afterward. Dumped his money since he wouldn't need it anymore.

But he didn't end up in the woods or wilderness—or wherever he is now—back in May. He transferred to Manhattan Valley University.

Ben always said he never intended to be in New York. That it took convincing.

It was never part of his plan.

It's why he showed up *broke*.

His brothers unknowingly changed his path. Then Ben spent more time with me, and he kept delaying and delaying the date to leave. Until at one point, he considered staying.

Then Audrey...the frat...it pushed him to finish what he had orchestrated.

His original plan.

Give me all his money. A girl he knew needed the cash. A girl he thought had a good heart.

Then he'd disappear into the woods. Never to be found again.

FIFTY-SEVEN

BEN COBALT

I swing an axe, splitting a log in two clean pieces.

Snow crunches under my boots. The air frigid. I have no problem with the cold. I could've lived on the ice, but if asked, I'd say I love springtime the most. I was born when the tulips begin to bloom, when the air in Philly begins to shift and people start spilling outside. When doors open and the cool breeze is let in.

If anyone asked?

Yeah, like anyone is going to ask me, "What season do you like, Ben?" I'm not even going to be asked if it's cold outside.

I am very, very alone.

No one around me for *miles*. With a deep exhale, I glance at the sky-scraping, snow-capped hemlocks and spruces. A bald eagle soars in the clear blue sky. Pine and earth flood my nostrils, but I find myself wanting to get rid of it.

Afraid I'll forget what she smells like. The sweet, candy scent of Harriet.

I adjust my grip on the axe. It doesn't help it's Wednesday.

This is the first Wednesday of many I'm never going to enter my family's ornate dining room. Sit around the table. Watch Eliot bang his foot on the edge. Everyone raising their goblets just in time. Drumming our feet and our hands. Laughing. So much vivid, effervescent laughter. The roaring love of the Cobalt Empire.

I rub at my raw, swollen eyes. I wasn't delusional. I didn't think I'd come here finding peace. I left that in New York with a short, grumpy punk-rock girl.

"They're safe," I mutter to myself.

They're safe from me. I can't hurt anyone here.

Another exhale, I place a bigger log on the stump. I swing, and the wood splits. I hear the snow creak, then crunch, and I immediately drop the axe and reach for my shotgun. Could be a wolf or a bear, if the latter is too hungry to hibernate.

When I turn around, I never even raise the gun. There is no way. There is no fucking way possible.

"How did you find me?" I ask in one iced breath.

"It wasn't easy. I'll give you that." Charlie approaches in a black durable winter coat, thick-soled boots, a scarf up to his neck. Even a black beanie covers his ears, and for a moment, I wonder if he bought the heavy-duty winter gear just for this trip.

Or if he's been to the coldest places on earth before.

I am solidified in shock. Unmoving. "Really, how?"

"I sewed a tracker into the lining of your duffel weeks ago." He knew I'd leave. Charlie comes closer to the firepit I haven't lit yet. "I would've been here sooner, but I was on a flight to Prague when you left New York. By the time I arrived, they weren't letting any vessels onto the island until the ice melted."

I saw the water lapping the rocky shoreline this morning. So that checks out. Fear is seizing my muscles. He can't be here. I need him to leave. "You can't tell anyone where I am," I say in panic. "Charlie—"

"I won't tell a soul."

I try to relax. "You promise?"

"I promise, except for Oscar. He already knows."

"Your bodyguard is here," I realize.

"He never shares where I go when I ask for secrecy. So *relax*. He won't tell anyone." Charlie trusts him even more than I realized.

"He's in your cabin now. You left the door unlocked."

Didn't think I'd ever have a visitor.

I can't get the words out. I blink a ton. Maybe he came here to see what I'm up to. Mystery solved. Then he'll go. Right? *Right?*

"Calm down," he snaps.

I let out a pained laugh. "I don't hunt you down on your mysterious trips across the world. No one does. They let you go, but as soon as I try, it becomes *impossible*."

"We're not the same," Charlie says pointedly coming closer and closer. "You need others. You are fueled by connections to people. Not the earth, not the sun, not the sky, not on a remote island in fucking *Alaska*. You will wither away in isolation like the very birds you love. While I will thrive." He outstretches his arms, hiking poles in hand. "Because I hate people. The human race annoys the shit out of me, and I would do anything to get away."

"So this is a welfare check?" I ask him. "You can go. I'm fine."

I return the gun and pick up my axe.

Charlie stops in place. Feet away. The firepit separates us. "What are you going to do with that?" He nods to the gun.

I can't even look at him. "There are predators out here."

"You wouldn't hurt a living soul, let alone a fucking Ficus tree. If a predator were to approach you, you wouldn't shoot. You'd let it kill you."

I swallow hard, my eyes blazing. I come around the firepit and toss the axe at his feet. "You want to get it over with then?" I'm losing my nerve. Panic is riding me so hard, I can barely breathe. "Just do it. No one has to know, Charlie." I can't even see his expression through the hazy film in my eyes. I put my hands on my thighs, hunching over, and I start gasping for more and more breath.

Then I'm on my knees, and Charlie is knelt in front of me, urging me to breathe. His hand on the back of my skull.

I tug my jacket at my throat, and I tell him, "I feel like I'm exploding. I can't stop it, Charlie."

"You have to stop."

"I can't...I'm going to hurt *everyone* around me." Snot balls up in the back of my throat. I am drowning in my own emotion. Keeling over. He's keeping me up as I fight to say, "I know it makes no fucking *sense*. But my choices end up causing so much harm, and...I can't...I can't stop it. I can't stop it."

"You can."

I shake my head.

"Yes, you can. Je sais que tu peux." *I know you can.* His words—I've heard those words from Charlie before. Only he spoke them to Beckett.

I look up at my oldest brother. Seeing him clearly through the scalding sheen of tears. "What's wrong with me, Charlie?"

He stares at me in ways he only reserves for Beckett. "It's the butterfly effect."

"What is?"

"What you believe in." He lets go of me as I sink back on my heels like I've been shoved. "Even the smallest actions you take can have extraordinary consequences. The wings of a butterfly flapping can cause a tornado halfway around the world. A single fallen domino will tip over a thousand more. Cause and effect. Everything changes everything. It's the chaos theory. And maybe it manifested when you were little. Your responsibility to protect the earth. You recycle—you save the entire forest. You don't eat meat—you save the animals from extinction. Then maybe it grew into something worse."

A chill snakes down my spine. "What do you mean?"

He's not irritated for me not "getting it" fast enough. He's not even pulling me to my feet. Snow tries to bite through my pantlegs, but I can't feel anything but Charlie's words as they try to unlock a chain around my body.

"I mean when you started feeling like you were the source of all the terrible things that happen in our family. The one responsible. The butterfly causing the storm. When was that?"

I stare off at the snow. All I see is the car crash. Slamming into the median. The flip. The violent crunch of metal. My hands slipping off the wheel. My family I'd hurt, the ones in the car with me. I'd never felt so responsible for the pain of others until that point.

It overwhelmed me. Consumed me. Haunted me for weeks into months into…

"I think the car crash." The monster grew beneath me and began shaking my bed. "I was driving, Charlie. I literally caused the accident."

"It was raining. Paparazzi were chasing us. They caused it. But I can tell you this a thousand times, and you'll still struggle to believe me."

How is he in my mind? "Why do you know that?"

"Because…" He has trouble now. He falters, tipping his head to look at me with more care and concern he's ever given or offered or extended before. "I'm almost certain you're dealing with an obsessive-compulsive disorder."

My brows pinch. "No." I reanimate, pulling myself to my feet. I walk over to the tree stump, my gloved hands on my head. I let them slip to my neck. "I would've known." OCD runs in our family. "Dad would've known."

Charlie is standing. "He's not around you enough. He's not a figure in the sky watching our every move. He can only see what you show him, and even then, you would only have these occasional breakdowns. You were *obnoxiously*—and I mean it in the rudest sense—vague. It was a clever way to lie, but not clever enough because I'm clearly *here*. And you're not dead."

I go cold. "That wasn't the plan," I assure him. "I didn't set out to take my life."

"You think you can survive out here? On nuts and berries? With a growing, feasting mental illness?"

My nose flares. My brain spins. I have to sit or I might pass out.

I take a seat on a tree stump around the firepit. "You're all safer away from me."

Charlie forces a tight smile. "Right. So you purchased a plot of land in Alaska. To live here for...?"

I clench my jaw, the alarm not subsiding. Restlessness rattles my whole body. It's taking everything not to shoot back to my feet. I open my mouth to offer him the actual answer, but it's trapped inside me. "I can't..." I gaze unblinkingly at the peeling bark of a tree. "It's not that I don't trust you. I just physically feel like I can't..." I heave for more oxygen in the biting cold. *Fuck.* "Like I'm afraid what happens if I do tell you everything."

"I know that you plan to live here for the rest of your life. You fear if you share this knowledge—which I already have because I'm *me*—then it'll compromise my safety. You've been trying to protect us from your own mind. Your illness was never going to allow you to tell us *exactly* what was happening or this elaborate plan to help us." He narrows his piercing yellow-green eyes into me. "You realize that?"

I'm starting to.

I unzip my heavy blue jacket. "I was able to tell Harriet things. More than I could share with anyone else." I shake my head as thoughts whirl. "I told her how I felt...how nothing was making sense to me."

Charlie studies me. "You weren't trying to protect her as well?"

"It's not that." I think back. "I didn't feel like I had to."

"You weren't afraid of causing her pain?"

"Never," I realize, and I blink away the burn in my eyes. "I kept telling myself I was doing good by her. I was good for her. Then she felt like the only one I never hurt. She was the only one I ever loved without harming." I laugh harshly to myself. "I don't even know if that's fucking true, but in my head...it's all that I understood."

Charlie shifts his weight, leaning on the hiking pole. "She's not here though." He swings his left pole toward the thicket of trees. "She's not there. She's definitely not in the ugliest cabin you could've purchased."

I almost laugh. "Yeah, sorry I didn't hire an interior decorator."

"I meant the outside, but I'm sure the inside is just as heinous."

I tug off my gloves, combing my hand through my hair. "Charlie—"

"She's not here, Ben. Harriet isn't in Alaska. Which means that the 'only one' in your life is no longer a part of your life."

"She has all of you," I reason. "She has the Cobalt Empire. She will be okay."

"What kind of Empire are you leaving her?" Charlie retorts with heat. "What do you think happens if the sixth born never returns?"

I slip my fingers back into my gloves, needing to move. My ribcage squeezes around my lungs. "I think it's better this way."

Silences bleeds. Charlie pulls off his beanie, then mutters, "I wish I brought Beckett."

"Beckett can't kn—"

"I've told him nothing." He glares. "No one knows where I am. I'm being brutally honest with you because I don't know how to be soft enough for you. But you're stuck with me for at least another hour." He plants his ass on the tree stump, stretching out his leg.

An hour.

I can last an hour.

"So you put thousands of miles between us." Charlie rubs his knee, then looks up at me. "You planned to limit communication to letters so no one would worry. Maybe mail a fun postcard. Maybe you bought some from different states—*welcome to Wyoming, North Dakota, Montana*—just so we'd believe you were traveling. There's Ben Pirrip on his great American backpacking adventure. Having a wonderful time away." He slow-claps.

He's not wrong.

Charlie continues, "The letters would eventually slow down, until they stop arriving altogether. You'd hope we'd forget about you.

Grow disinterested in what you were up to. We would just move on without you."

Yeah.

I can't even nod, but he's not asking for confirmation. He knows he's right.

His intense gaze stays fixed on mine. "Now you're really alone. What's next when you start imagining what could happen to us? You have an intrusive thought of Beckett drowning. Now you're panicked because it might happen. You thought it, now you caused it. Then what are you going to do to protect us, little brother?"

I stare haunted at the snow. It takes me a minute to speak. "The existence of me is more harmful than the absence," I say what has kept cycling in my head for so long.

Charlie's eyes redden, his gaze tunneling in me. "The loss of you is the most catastrophic event our family will *ever* endure. You could explode on another planet, and we'd all still feel the impact like you're a single inch away. Our parents will never recover. Our mom will grieve you for the rest of her life. You will have *irreparably* changed us all."

I can't catch my breath. "I almost caused Audrey's death. Better me gone than her."

"She's not going to die if you come home," Charlie refutes. "And if she does, it won't be because of a bad choice you made."

"You don't know that." I jump to my feet, pressure compounding on my chest. "You think I can't survive out here, but Charlie, I can't survive *there*. Literally, if anything were to happen to one of you…"

"You will lose this battle if you stay here," Charlie says slowly, forcefully. "I am *certain*. I am also certain you have a chance to win if you come home."

It freezes me in place.

Charlie picks himself up, bracing his weight on the hiking pole. "You think Beckett doesn't understand that fight? He's battling compulsions every fucking day."

I grimace up at the sky. "I don't even understand how this is OCD. It's not like Beckett's rituals with symmetry or the contamination thing. It's not the same."

"It's similar. There are different types of OCD. Some are all up here." He points to his temple. "Do you have intrusive thoughts about negative outcomes or causing harm to others?"

I swallow. "Yes, yeah."

"Do you feel a compulsion to protect others from yourself?"

Clearly. I nod.

"Do you have the irrational belief that your thoughts or actions can control the outcome of events?"

It's all just slamming into me. "Yeah."

"That one is magical thinking. You also likely have hyper-responsibility, but I'm not a fucking psychiatrist. I'm just well-read and too intelligent for my own good." He stakes the pole hard into the snow, then bores his eyes into me. "Beckett *knows*, Ben. He knows what it's like to go to war with your mind…to the point where I'm guessing he saw in you what none of us did. Maybe subconsciously, he always knew."

I frown. "What do you mean?"

"He was *adamant* that you come to New York. We all knew you hit a low point, you weren't doing well, and you started to pull away from us. But beyond everyone, it was Beckett who *felt* that something was critically wrong. That you *needed* to live with us. Not in Philly with Mom and Dad, but with your brothers."

I take a few dazed steps backward.

It was Beckett.

I shut my eyes tightly, emotion stinging. Then I rub my face with my fist. All this time, I thought my own family would be the least likely to understand me. And here they are—the ones who always would.

"I wish I talked to him sooner."

"There's plenty of time for that," Charlie says. "There's also time to fire your fucking therapist and start being honest with a new one."

I choke out a laugh. "Yeah, like who?"

"Frederick." *Dad's therapist.* Before I combat, Charlie adds, "There's little better than the guy who's been in our dad's mind for decades. He'll understand your feelings more than most would. Isn't that what you want?"

To feel understood.

Yeah. It's what I've been craving.

I expel a weighted breath, trying to throw the monster off me. I stare around at the trees. At the logs, at the snow. At the tiny cabin in the distance. It's so hard.

It's so hard to choose this path. "What if leaving is the biggest mistake I make, Charlie?" I ask.

He holds my gaze. "It took hockey from you. It took your friends. It took your family. Don't let it take her. Don't let it take you. There will always be dominos hitting ones you never intend. You can't avoid *mistakes*. You can't avoid bad choices. You can't avoid change. Embrace it and get the help you need. You won't find it here."

I stare right at him and inhale the deepest breath of my life. *I think I did find it here.* I nod to him, overwhelmed. "Let's go home."

CHARLIE TOOK A PRIVATE JET, OF COURSE. I CAN'T EVEN think about fossil fuels. I just crash almost the entirety of the plane ride. Emotionally wiped out, and he wakes me up when we land. With a kick to the shins. Still very Charlie, but it'll be impossible not to love him after today, even when we aggravate each other.

He tells me, "I called our family. They all know everything." He doesn't give me a chance to thank him. He collects his luggage from the back of the plane and speaks to Oscar.

I asked Charlie to make the call before we took off. It lifts a heavy weight not having to do it myself. Gives me a jump start on picking up the pieces I'd left behind. I just hope I can glue the ones with Harriet back together...I hope I can salvage this.

I'm going to try.

I gather my duffel from the overhead bin, ducking a bit on my way out the door.

When I straighten up, I see Beckett waiting on the tarmac of the private runway. His dark brown hair blows in a gust of wind. His leather jacket zipped. He's at the foot of the stairs. His SUV parked farther away. He rips out his AirPods as soon as I emerge, and his widened, relieved eyes meet mine.

His chest rises into a bigger breath.

Don't break down.

Don't fucking break down.

I chant to myself as I descend toward him, but as I near, I just know—it was him. My ultimate plan would've succeeded, if not for him. If not for New York, I would've never fallen in love. I would've never had all that time with Harriet. All that time with my four brothers. Charlie would've never found me. I would've never gotten on this plane and come back to find peace.

I reach him on the tarmac, and I know—my brother saved my life. I drop my duffel and wrap my arms around him.

He hugs back, his warm hugs the best of my whole childhood. I want to say thank you, but I can't even fucking talk.

When he draws away, he holds the side of my neck, still keeping me close. His calming eyes carry so many reassurances. "If something happens today or tomorrow or next week that makes you want to turn around, you need to know something. There will always be storms—whether you're here or not, but *be here*."

I intake a breath.

He continues, "The world needs butterflies, Pip. Even if they cause chaos. Think of the ecological damage without them. The world needs you. We need *you*." His plea burrows into me. "We're going to get through this. I know it might feel impossible now, but it won't in time. I'll be right beside you." Very strongly, he says, "N'en doute jamais." *Never doubt that.*

I fist his leather jacket, bringing him into another hug, and I whisper, "Je n'ai jamais pu." *I never could.*

When we pull back, I exhale powerfully, then twist toward the SUV and go still. My heart skips a beat.

"Is that...?" I start to say.

Harriet.

Harriet.

She's standing outside the car in her oversized leather jacket. Her choppy blond hair blowing around her soft, scowling face.

My feet move before my mind does. I'm dropping my duffel. I'm in a sprint. My long legs can't pump fast enough. She's clutching her elbows, and I sweep her rapidly for damage. Hurt that I may've caused. I left her. I haven't spoken to her.

Four days.

I can't fathom even an inch of her broken, and it's tearing me apart with every step knowing this decision could've impacted her in ways I could not mentally stomach. I could not handle. I would not allow myself to think it for even a second.

Harriet lets go and opens her arms, reaching out for me with urgency—it almost brings me to my knees. I wrap my biceps around her frame, hugging her and lifting her up against my chest all at once. Her legs weave around me.

I press her closer. Feeling her deep inhale. Feeling the quickened beat of her heart. "Are you okay?" I ask, combing my hand through her hair. "You're okay? I'm sorry. Harriet—"

"*Breathe*," she demands, her eyes flooding. "I just got you back, okay, you don't need to hyperventilate on this tarmac. I don't want to do CPR on you."

I choke out what wants to be a laugh. But it sounds tortured. I sound fucking *ripped open.* "I need to know you're okay."

"I need to know *you're* okay, Ben." Her palms are on my face, slipping down my jaw like she's ensuring this is real. If this is all in our heads, having Harriet in my arms is a fantasy I can't split from. I skim her flushed cheeks, her shallow breathing...her puffy, bloodshot eyes.

She's been crying a lot. Devastating pain gnaws at me from the inside.

I try to take slow breaths. I cup her jaw, my gaze diving into her turbulent ocean blues. "I haven't been..." I can barely manage the words. "I haven't been well, not mentally, and I'm sorry I put you through all of this. Knowing I hurt you...over even the course of an hour let alone four fucking days, Harriet, is brutal for me. You didn't deserve this."

"You're *unwell*," she says strongly. "I could've done more—"

"No," I interject, stroking her hair as her chin quakes. I kiss the top of her head. "You couldn't have." In this moment, I don't feel like I deserve her, but I want to be someone who does. I'm going to get better. I have to get better. For me, for her.

She glances up at the sky, then down to me. "I know I probably met you at the worst time in your life."

"You didn't. I think you met me exactly when I needed you." I brush away her escaped tear, my other arm supporting her body, so we stay eye level. "If we started over, I would only rewind the last four days. I would've never left your apartment. I would've sat beside you and watched *The Wild Robot* and eaten pizza bites and held you in my arms all fucking night. I would've let you be there for me, and I hate that I couldn't see that as the better path."

She dries my wet jaw with her sleeves. "I was really worried. Losing you like this, Ben..." Her nose flares. "Maybe you'd never come back to me, but you were supposed to come back to them." She flings an arm toward Charlie and Beckett behind me. "You could've been eaten by Smokey the Bear."

I let out a small laugh. "I think it's Smokey Bear. Does he eat people or warn against forest fires?"

"Then Bullwinkle."

"The friendly moose?"

"You could've *died*," she emphasizes, her agony slicing through me. "You would've—" Her voice cracks.

"I'm going to get help." I hold her face tighter, and she nods faster as I repeat these words three times, solidifying them for myself too. "I won't do this to you again, Fisher. I promise with everything in me." I sound choked because I'm fucking crying. "I promise, I won't leave you. I don't think I could survive hurting you this badly again...but I can't promise that I'll always be okay."

"No faith, Friend," she tries to tease, but her voice is too hoarse.

I stroke my thumb against her cheek. "I think my odds have now increased with you here. I have faith in that."

She gets emotional because she said that to me once upon a time. "You don't have to always be *okay* for me to love you, Ben. We're all a little fucked up." Her eyes swim against mine. "And I didn't stop loving you when you left. I won't stop loving you now that you're back." She holds my neck. "But we have a lot of talking to do."

"Yeah, we do."

"Right now, I kind of just want you to kiss me." As her eyes drop to my lips and mine drop to hers, I crash into her in a soulful, body-pulling kiss. It wrenches us together. My blood heats at her touch. Her fingers curl into my hair. *Never let her go.*

I'll never let her go.

BECKETT AND CHARLIE LINGER ON THE TARMAC, CATCHING up with each other, and Harriet and I slip into the warmth of the SUV, crawling past the captain's chairs and into the cramped backseat. Just so we can sit beside each other.

I remove my heavy winter jacket. Feeling her examine me from a few inches away. I do the same to her as she shrugs off her leather coat. Her striped pants ride low on her waist, and her black sweater molds her chest and slender arms. I can see her hip bones.

"You look thinner," I mention, my heart in knots.

Her neck flushes. "Puking your guts up all night will do that… and I haven't had much of an appetite."

"You want to stop at Wendy's or Taco Bell?"

"You don't like fast food."

"I'd stop anywhere for you."

She chews the corner of her lip, a smile almost peeking. "Maybe. We'll see." She watches me shove my sleeves to my elbows. "You have all your fingers and toes or did frostbite get you?"

"Intact." I wiggle all ten fingers. "Physically fine. Emotionally questionable. Mentally fucked up." I slide closer to her. "What about you? Head, ears, knees, and toes?" I place a hand on her head, then pinch her cute ears. "All there."

"Can you take your shirt off?" she asks. "In case you were mauled." She's seriously worried. I don't tease her because the same concern for her is cycling through me.

I grip the back of my shirt and tug it over my head. Pulling the fabric off, I show her my shoulders and spine first, then my bare chest and abs.

She launches toward me. "What is that?" It's hard not to smile when she inspects the faintest cut on my ribs.

"I think that's called a scratch."

"From what? Metal? Wood? You might have a splinter. Or need a tetanus shot."

"I'm all up to date on my shots. You think it's deep enough for a splinter?"

She peers harder. Her cheeks rosy. "Maybe not."

I can't stop looking at her. "You threw up because…?"

"You left abruptly that night, dude. I knew something was wrong on a much deeper level at that point. It didn't feel good." She crosses her arms, slouches backward, and I extend my hand over the seat behind her head. Letting her decide if she wants to lean into me or not.

Knowing Harriet was sick because of me is very fucking painful. She sees my muscles flex and hears my breathing shorten.

She winces at herself. "I shouldn't be telling you this."

"Yeah, you should. I want to know what I missed and how I affected you because these are things I don't want to repeat. I can't let this happen again. I won't."

"You shouldn't be worried about me at all though," she says so quietly, rotating the choker necklace at her throat. "You need to get healthy, and maybe what's best for you is if we aren't together."

I'm going to lose her.

I crash backward. My burning eyes rise to the roof of the car, then fall to her. "I don't want to lose you. If I can do this with you, please let me try. Doing it without you sounds so much worse, Harriet, but I…" A ball forms in my throat. "I understand if you don't want to be with me."

"All I *want* is to be with you," she expresses so deeply. "But I can't be an obstacle for you."

"You aren't. Me caring about you isn't a roadblock. It's not a hurdle. You aren't in my way. You are the hand that holds mine while I walk down a rocky path. And I'm asking you to walk it with me, and I know it's a big ask—"

"Yes," she interjects.

"Yes?"

"I'll walk it with you, Ben. Because…I really, *really* love you," she says so softly. "And I know you'd do the same for me. You already have." She hoists a finger. "But if I turn out to be the worst thing for you, then we reevaluate."

"Okay." I start to smile. "I can accept those terms, Fisher." Because there is no way she's been anything but good for me. It's been so clear from the start. She's been the one that's helped me breathe. "But I should warn you," I tell her.

"What?" she hesitates.

"I think you have healing hands."

She rolls her eyes, her cheeks pinching as a smile forms. "I'd say you're a dork, but you're literally slouching and man-spreading like a jock."

A laugh rumbles through me. Our smiles soften on each other, and I ask her, "Did you make a choice while I was gone? Do I have a rockstar girlfriend or a doctor girlfriend?"

She rests her cheek on the top of the seat near my forearm. "Which one are you hoping for?"

"Long-lasting girlfriend," I say. "Into forever Harriet."

"Fortunately for you, whether I become a rockstar girlfriend or a doctor girlfriend, I predict it'll be long-lasting."

I ease. "You think?"

"Yep." She holds my gaze. "Which boyfriend am I getting?"

"Mentally unwell boyfriend. On the road to recovery boyfriend."

"Into forever Ben?"

I nod. "I'm not going anywhere," I promise.

She clasps my hand that's on the back of the seat, then slips her beaded bracelets onto my wrist. "I haven't decided yet on medicine or music. I've been more focused on finding you."

I rake my free hand through my hair. Pain cinches around my lungs, my heart, my ribcage. "Anything else I missed?"

She tucks a strand of hair behind her ear, then grimaces. "I shouldn't tell you this…"

"I want you to," I press. "I want to know."

"Fine. Only because I think it's likely your brothers will say something, and maybe it should come from me first."

Okay. I nod her on. "Lay it on me, Fisher."

She lets go of my wrist. "I was paranoid I might've been pregnant. I'm not. But I took a test."

I swear my heart stops beating.

Her eyes are steady on mine. "Say something, Friend."

"You thought you were pregnant? And I wasn't there?" I visualize what she went through, and it thrashes inside of me like a feral animal clawing, tearing, shredding. My jaw clenches. I smear my hands over my face, bowing forward as nausea builds.

"*Ben.*"

I reawaken and wrap my arms around her, pulling her into my chest. "You're okay?" I stare right into her eyes. Clinging. Holding. I cup her cheek.

"I'm all right," she assures, her tiny smile easing me more. "I was *paranoid*, okay. I bought the test the same night you left, *before* you actually left, because I was freaking myself out."

"The paper bag." It dawns on me. I knew she was hiding something...but yeah, not *that*. "I'm so sorry...you shouldn't have had to deal with that alone, Harriet. I should've fucking been there."

She has a hand against my bare chest. On my hard-pounding heart. "I understand now why you felt like you had to leave."

I take some deep breaths. "The test was negative?"

"Yeah, and I wasn't alone. Your brother kept me company."

I try to relax at the fact. But I'm sure my brothers finding out about a pregnancy scare went over *great*, especially while I was missing. "Which brother?"

"Guess."

"Beckett," I say like it's just known.

"I get why you love him so much," she murmurs softly.

"He doesn't intimidate you anymore?"

"Oh no, he's still intimidating as fuck."

I laugh, and she smiles a little at my chest. I realize now that my pulse has slowed to a calm beat. She lies more against me, slackening into me, and I hold her closer while she rests her head against the crook of my neck.

I kiss her blond hair as she fiddles with the beaded bracelets and the elastic Capybara one on my wrist. We both catch movement out the window, and we see my brothers walking toward the SUV. Beckett grabs the duffel I dropped.

"Charlie and Beckett," she says, looking up at me with glassy blue eyes. "I owe them everything."

Emotion barrels into me. I fight more tears. "Me too."

Me too.

FIFTY-EIGHT

BEN COBALT

Ovid once wrote, "Happy is the man who has broken the chains which hurt the mind, and has given up worrying once and for all."

Then again, this is supposedly from Ovid's poem "Remedia Amoris," which of course is in Latin, and according to my father, the better translation is, "He's his own best liberator who snaps the chains that hurt his heart, and ends the grief forever."

The first speaks about anxiety, the second speaks about lovesickness, and ironically, both speak to me. I've been doing more reading lately. Not necessarily at the recommendation of my new therapist. I've only met with Dr. Frederick Cothrell once, but I've only been back in New York for a week.

I hadn't forgotten that we'd met before. He sometimes attends Cobalt Inc. events, galas, fundraisers. Still, this time felt different as I entered his office. I swept his features. Early sixties. Salt and peppered hair. Amiable, warm smile like he knew me since I was a child. Deeply knew me.

I suppose he did from all the years my dad talked about me. It could've felt unsettling, but it was the exact opposite. It felt like I was walking on a cloud. Like nothing sharp or poking or painful was around me. Like maybe I could speak without panicking.

Maybe this will work.

He asked if I planned to finish the fall semester. He didn't say I shouldn't. Didn't suggest I drop out of college or return. These are paths I need to decide on my own. Of course I'm afraid of choosing the wrong thing, of making a mistake and hurting others around me, but I can't push everyone away as a solution anymore. Or avoid the things that I think will cause harm.

Like driving. The thought of being behind a wheel with my foot on the gas freaks me the fuck out, but I know I'll need to try at some point. Avoidance isn't a long-term fix, and it's obviously made my life worse.

I'm working on it.

I went back for finals week. So I could pass the semester and stay on course to graduate at the same time as Harriet. I know I at least want that.

Seeing Xander again in class, the guilt was an avalanche burying me. He'd done exactly what I did when we were thirteen. He told no one about how I was hurting and realized too late that maybe he should've, and I put him in that position.

I'd prepared for another Ice Age between us. I'd kicked up the snow. Winter was coming, to quote his love of *Game of Thrones*. We took our usual seats in the back row. Harriet between us, and we had our sheets of paper ready as Professor Wellington manned the podium for the final oral exam.

Before our professor said a word, Xander quietly stood up with his pen and paper, and he changed seats. He sat in the empty one right beside me.

It took sheer strength of will to not break down crying. I had to cover my face with my hand as I sat between Xander and Harriet. He rested a palm on my shoulder.

I'm not sure I expected kindness and understanding when I'm still barely making sense of myself. So to receive that from Xander when he had every right to ice me out—yeah, I'm surprised I was able to concentrate on the exam enough to pass.

I can't predict the future. Just see the one I really want, and I think we're going to be friends again.

It's what I contemplate on an eight-mile hike. Same trail I trekked in the Catskills with my Uncle Ryke, which was the same night I boarded a greyhound bus. It didn't take me to Alaska or all the way across the country. The bus got me to the Midwest, then to a private runway and to a pilot who I met through a series of acquaintances that no one would be able to follow.

I doubt they would've ever found me without Charlie. The past seven days, he's crossed my mind a lot more. Though, he's not on this hike.

It's just me and our dad.

Backpacking on nature trails isn't really my father's forte, but he's far from unathletic or clumsy. Honestly, I doubt he's ever tripped in his life.

I'd call him a "social hiker" because when it becomes a group activity, he'll join, no problem. He's in incredible shape. I used to wake early just to workout with him when I was a teenager. He'd jog on a treadmill and have Bloomberg playing on TV, but when I was in the home gym, he'd let me put on *Planet Earth*.

As we journey across the soft earth in pursuit of the fire tower, I glance over at his clean-cut features that's graced magazine covers. His perfectly styled wavy brown hair, his superhero-strong jawline, his calm deep-blue eyes. He has one earbud in, the other free to hear me if I talk.

I haven't said much. All the leaves have fallen. A light layer of snow dusts the ground. It's the first week of December, and the frigid air fills my lungs in a lively way.

"What are you listening to?" I ask him.

His lips curve upward as he passes me his loose earbud.

I fit it in my ear and laugh. His grin spreads. It's Led Zeppelin. "Ramble On." Not exactly the classical instrumentals that most expect Connor Cobalt to leisurely jam out to. It's only now that I fully acknowledge my love of rock music is because of him.

That maybe I have more similarities with my dad than I've let myself comprehend.

When we reach the top of the fire tower, my dad isn't admiring the expansive evergreen-lined view. He's watching me like I watch him. The bluebird and the lion. I smile to myself, thinking of Harriet.

And I shake my head a couple times. "I always wondered how I could be your son."

"I know you did." Skin pleats between his brows. "That's also where I made a misstep. I was too focused on how you felt like you didn't fit in. It made it more difficult for me to see that you were dealing with an obsessive-compulsive disorder."

I nod as realizations sink in. "Because why would I obsess over trying to protect my family from myself? When I spent half my youth questioning whether I even belonged in the first place. But it never meant I didn't love you all. I love everyone too much, probably." My eyes flit up to his, knowing on the flipside that my dad loves very little and infrequently. Just like Charlie. "Maybe Charlie's right—maybe I should have more armor. Feel less." I pull my beanie off, then skate my hand through my wavy hair. "I'm irrational. Sensitive. Naïve. Overly emotional."

"Passionate, vulnerable, generous, self-sacrificing. These aren't flaws, Ben."

"They're traits that weaken, Dad. They're ones you don't possess. Which makes me the most *fragile* extension of you. Of this family." I extend my arm toward his chest. "You can't disagree with that. You know it's true, and look, I'm not saying I'm upset at the idea. I know it's who I am. I've always known. Just as I've always known who I am is *no one* you could ever relate to."

"Is that what you think?" His frown deepens.

Now I'm frowning. Could I be wrong? "You relate to Charlie. I'm *nothing* like Charlie. These are facts."

He steps closer, skimming the length of me. "I do relate to Charlie, but I'm not Charlie, and Charlie isn't me. We have *vastly* different approaches to how we live inside this world." He glimpses out at the snow-capped trees, gestures a couple fingers for me to follow him, and we end up near the glassless frame of the fire tower. Where gusts whip back at our bodies through the open window. "More than one thing can be true at once, Ben."

I watch him gaze out. "Like what?"

He rests his self-assured eyes on mine. "You can be fragile, and you can also be the most *important* extension of me. Of our family."

"That's hard to believe," I say, even as his certainty, his control, his composure washes over me.

"Why?" His brows furrow. "We protect tender hearts like yours because they are *vital*. Necessary. Not everyone should be made of steel. You challenge me. You make me see things I would never see otherwise. I admire your passion, your virtue, your *fervor*. You roar at injustice. You hurt for others. You give and expect nothing in return. My life—it would be *dull* and gray without you, mon fils courageux." *My brave son.* "You paint my world with color, and I could not bear to lose you. Just as I couldn't bear to change who you are."

I intake a slower breath. I'm too choked to speak.

I'd thought that I was the runt they dragged along because they loved me, because they wouldn't cut any of us loose, but I never thought my father valued me. Not for my beliefs, not for my vulnerabilities, not for my differences—I thought, if anything, I was a negative cost. A sort of liability of the Cobalt Empire.

Not once did I consider I was a boon. It's made me wonder if he's told me this before in a plainer way, and I just never took it in. I never believed I could be an asset or a gift. I simply made peace with the fact that I was the worst of us.

"Why am I like this?" I ask, still choked up. I blink away the burn in my eyes. "When you tell me I'm important, I question it. When people like Coach Haddock tell me I'm NHL potential, I find reasons to disbelieve them."

"Humility is an interesting trait for one of my children, considering I have very little."

A bright laugh rolls out of me.

He grins at the sound. "You have a decent amount, Ben, conceivably to your own benefit and to your own detriment. And OCD is called the 'doubting disease' for a reason. It will make you doubt your own reality, your own perceptions." He turns toward the endless view. "But this doesn't mean you lack an ego."

I glance out at the vastness of the undulating hills, the misty morning blue sky, the uncorrupted land teeming with life.

"You aren't responsible for the creation of everything," he says.

Emotion stings my eyes.

"The same way that you won't be responsible for its destruction."

I feel him studying me, but it's more difficult to not smile. "I really must be your son," I say. "Believing I have the power to impact the whole world. I, alone, am the cause of bad things happening around me." I nod strongly to myself and laugh lightly. "Then in the reverse, I can't even accept my self-importance. I am a real conundrum."

"A paradox," he grins. "You don't have to fit into any box, mon fils. Ordinary is boring."

He's telling me to accept myself as I am. To stop battling all the conflicting sides.

I smile brighter at my father, seeing the pieces of him that I share. Really, seeing, for the first time, all the social prowess, all the unwavering confidence, and I love those pieces of him. Of me. I love my ego. I love my humility. I love so much more of who I am in this moment than I ever have in my entire life. And I know what I've always been.

A butterfly, a bluebird…and a lion.

FIFTY-NINE

HARRIET FISHER

Holy shit…I am *bad* at ice skating. The last time I put on a pair of skates, I couldn't have been older than six or seven. But I deluded myself into thinking that it's just like riding a bike. Natural intuition would take over, and I'd just float gracefully down the rink, right? Wrong. So very wrong.

I didn't go so far as picturing twirls, but I most definitely did not imagine myself death-clutching the railing while on an official date with Ben. I've considered most of our hangouts as being date-like, but he specifically said, "I'm taking you on a date this afternoon. Wear something warm, Fisher."

My heart volleyed against my ribcage. "A date?" It struck me that no one had ever used that word with me before. It was always *let's go grab a bite to eat. Let's watch a movie. Let's fuck.* Never *let's go on a date.*

"Yeah," he smiled. "There'll be many more like it."

There'll be more, Harriet. Having more time with him is what I really cherish. We could be playing Scrabble in my apartment, and it'd be just as perfect.

But I am glad he decided on *this* type of date after finals week. I'm not sure I would've enjoyed it as much with the stress of exams and essays dangling like an ugly raincloud. I mean, I hope I would mentally compartmentalize, but I like that I don't have to even think about it now. With fall semester over, I fully embrace this moment with my boyfriend.

Boyfriend.

Okay, that still makes me unnaturally *giddy*. I've accepted the strange, powerful effect Ben Cobalt has on me. I even let him surprise me this afternoon—though I asked about twenty-five questions to narrow down where we'd be.

Ben took me to an outdoor ice-skating rink in New York City. Winter clouds up above, festively clad skaters surrounding us, and a dazzling Christmas tree overlooking the glittery white rink—it can't get more romcom than this. Except for the part where I almost ate the ice.

Twice.

I envisioned this sickeningly sweet moment where I skate alongside Ben, hand-in-hand, like we're strolling down Park Ave with birds chirping. It was this dumb Disney princess fantasy that I'm not even positive I want. It seems too fake.

So I'm not kicking myself that hard for not being fucking Elsa and conjuring the spirit of frost or icicles or whatever she does. I've honestly never seen *Frozen*, but that "Let It Go" bitch is inescapable.

In the center, a young girl is doing some sort of twizzly twirl. *Definitely a trained ice skater.* At least we aren't a spectacle. His bodyguard glides back and forth near us, but for the most part, no one recognizes Ben Cobalt on the rink. Families, couples, and friends all relish in the pretty December weather together and not my laughable skills.

"Seriously, go on without me, Friend." I wave Ben on with a hand, the other is planted firmly on the railing. "I don't want to hold you back." He is a hockey player. The ice is his natural habitat, and my ankles scream at me like they're two seconds from giving out.

Ben hovers close and comes to a dead stop since I'm no longer moving. I'm just clinging to this railing like a baby deer learning to walk for the first time."

His brows knit together in concern. "I'm sensing fear."

"Of face-planting, chipping my front tooth and needing a full dental package, yeah. Of falling on my ass and bruising my tailbone, possibly *fracturing* it, also yeah."

A smile edges across his mouth. "Come here." He hooks his fingers with mine. "I'll keep you safe, mon bel oiseau."

My lungs expand. This is the first time he's ever said *my* beautiful bird.

My.

Mine.

I'm his.

I bite the inside of my cheek as this lovey-dovey feeling engulfs me. "I don't know, Ben, I could be an actual terror on skates. Ten more feet forward and I might need dentures."

"I won't let you chip your front teeth. Let alone knock out all of them." His smile pulls mine to the surface.

"Okay," I breathe, trusting him. "What do I do?"

He clasps my left hand. "Just follow my lead." He holds out his right, and I take that palm too. Both hands in his, my knees fight the urge to tremble. Ben is skating *backward* while he helps me gain balance on the ice.

My pulse thumps hard in my chest, but after a couple of minutes, I start to relax. Mostly thanks to Ben's constant encouragements and supreme confidence as he moves so effortlessly on the ice. I tighten my grip on his hand as I teeter.

"I have you," he assures, his sexy smile a great distraction from my nerves.

He's too attractive. Wispy strands of hair escape his navy beanie, and his winter jacket is more suited for the elements than my pleather getup. I'd be colder if it weren't for the flush bathing my whole body every time Ben looks down at me.

Since I'm wearing black earmuffs, my ears are safe from getting pink and numb. They were a gift from his mom when I met her at Le Petit Rêve. I told her, "I didn't know we were exchanging Christmas gifts yet. I didn't bring anything—"

"That's not for Christmas," she cut me off fast, thank God. "It's so your ears don't fall off."

I love his mom more and more, and I'm starting to dream of adopting her as my own. It's beginning to feel like a real possibility. Which is...*nuts*.

But like hell am I complaining.

Ben must feel my hand ease off the death-squeeze. "You want to try on your own?"

"Maybe for a little bit."

He drops his left hand, then releases his right as I stabilize myself. I'm wobbly, but in no threat of falling. I exhale a large breath. He's grinning and still skating backward like a pro. "Looking hot, Fisher."

"That's about how I feel. Like I might melt into this ice." My ankles really are on fire. I can't tell if the skates are the wrong size or if people just grow accustomed to this uncomfortable ankle-breaking feeling.

Honestly...I think I might hate ice skating. I don't like how people whiz too close to us, but I do love when Ben skates around me, to protect me from being shoulder-slammed on the crowded rink. I don't like how unstable I still feel. But I do love each time he slides an arm across my back. I don't like how my feet shriek at me to yank the skates off. But I'm putting up with the pain because it'd be a shame if Ben only spent two seconds on the ice. And I love seeing him glide so naturally on his blades.

He maneuvers beside me in a clean, practiced turn. I'm majorly impressed by that simple move. Then he studies the length of me, maybe noticing me wince. "You want to call it?"

Yes. "No, we just got here. I'm doing great, Cobalt boy. *See.*" I let go of him just to skate ahead with this impulse—not to show off because *hello*, I know where my skills are and this isn't it—but to illustrate my okayness.

I make the dumbest move to turn (my instinct is to look at him and not save myself, apparently). As I rotate, my skates screech and slip. Oh fuck. I try to balance myself, but I'm falling backward. My breath catapults right as arms swoop down and catch me.

Ben has me in his grasp like he dipped me in a dance. My heart triple-beats, and I'm fisting his jacket, more to touch him, to pull him closer, because I know there is absolutely no way Ben would ever drop me.

His gaze flits to my lips in a featherlight moment, then he kisses me.

I dizzy. My cheeks heat, and I can't come down to earth because he picks me up so suddenly, my skates lifting off the ice, and he rotates in a skilled circle with me tucked to his chest. I cup the back of his neck—grinning, I'm fucking *grinning*.

"You are too good at this," I tell him deeply. "And I mean so much more than ice skating."

"Yeah?" He drinks in my features. "I'm glad I'm good at loving you. I'd hate to be terrible at it, Friend." It fills my heart before he presses another hot kiss to my lips. After that romantic moment, which I will be replaying for eternity, he sets me carefully on my blades. I grimace a little.

Ankles, ouch.

"Now we're calling it." He catches my hand, but I pull back. "Harriet?"

I eye the exit with too much glee. "I might not be made for this, but you are. You skate some more. I'll go grab a hot chocolate."

He's uncertain. "You sure?"

"Not to be a creepy stalker fan, but I wouldn't mind watching you fly like a bird."

His smile explodes into a laugh. "Not to be a creepy stalker fan, but I wouldn't mind watching you sip a hot chocolate."

"Oh, I'll be pounding a hot chocolate, Cobalt boy, and you can watch me from the ice."

"Deal." He seals this with a tender kiss, bending a lot lower to reach my lips, and I'm grateful when he helps me back to the exit.

Once my skates are removed, my ankles *very* red, and my boots firmly back on, I buy a hot chocolate and an apple cider. I nestle near an open spot at the railing overlooking the rink.

Then I see him on the ice.

My breath leaves my lungs.

Ben really is *flying*. It's not his speed that has me awed. He's skating fast but respectfully for a semi-crowded rink. It's *how* he's skating. Lithe, graceful movements as if you can't tell where his body ends and the ice begins. It looks like he was born here. Like his soul finds comfort here.

It registers so powerfully that this is the very first time I've ever seen him skate.

My throat swells watching him. I'd like to think that's how I look when I play the drums. When I talk about medicine. Totally and completely enraptured.

Music and medicine—that decision has become a terrorizing stressor.

I'm *nineteen*, and I need to make the biggest choice of my life. I'm terrified of my future being mired in regret. Of wishing I took the other path I left behind. I've been starting to look for signs to give me a hint at the right one. Even the *smallest* of signs. Heard Green Day on the radio yesterday—I should choose music. Last night, Ben asked me for a Band-Aid after he cut his thumb on a can of garbanzo beans—I should choose medicine.

It's silly to think the universe will point me in the right direction. But I am holding out hope for divine intervention because at this point, I have *zero* clue which one I'll choose.

I'm fifty-fifty.

My heart lies with both. How do I even begin to pick?

Luckily, I still have time…I think. Tom hasn't exactly hung a deadline over my head, but whenever I run into him, he asks me if I'm nearing a decision. I do need to pick classes for next semester, so my goal is to decide by Christmas. It gives me a few more weeks at least.

I avoid the stress by watching Ben. Seeing him skate floats my anxieties into the ether, and I'm doubly impressed when he zips over to me and slices against the ice in a quick stop.

I fight a pinched smile. "Show off."

"I have to flex somewhere," he grins. "This is the only thing I excel at."

"That's so far from true." I gulp my hot chocolate, then he glances at the extra cup in my hand. So I tell him, "Apple cider. No honey."

His smile reaches his baby blue eyes. "Let me get my skates off. We can find a place to sit." I'm soaking in the hours I get to spend with Ben before he heads to Philly later tonight.

It's Wednesday.

The day of fucking mystery. I'm not invited to the Cobalt family dinner, and I don't expect to be, nor do I want an invite. I respect their family traditions, and I sure as hell wouldn't bring a new relationship to a sacred fam event.

Ben also needs that time alone with them. He's tried pushing them away in an effort to protect them from himself. It's good he has these opportunities to figure out how to manage his OCD when he's solely around family.

We find a vacant bench in view of the ornament and garland-strung tree. Mariah Carey belts out Christmas staples through speakers somewhere. Really, the holidays have never been my favorite time of year. They're typically solitary affairs between me and my TV. I'd even work extra shifts at Wendy's. Stay busy. Earn some cash. So "holiday cheer" is taking on an entirely new meaning being with Ben.

Little kids giggle as they put on skates, and I catch Ben smiling as the boy practically drags his dad toward the rink with excitement.

"Do you think you could fall back in love with hockey?" I ask him, since he's learned that his OCD stripped away his enjoyment of the sport. He was too fixated on potentially hurting other players and causing harm on the ice—it made it difficult for Ben to find pleasure in the game.

"I don't know." He stares off. "I've thought about whether I can overcome this enough to love it again, but...right now, it seems unreachable. Ask me in a week?"

I nod. "I'll put it in my calendar."

"Do I get an alarm alert too?" He slips me a teasing smile.

"Oh yeah, a super basic one," I say flatly. "Chimes."

"Not even an electronic beep." His lips rise higher. "Ice cold."

"Frost to your fire." I make a lame joke and crinkle my nose, but Ben is laughing like it was decently clever, so I snuggle closer to him, especially for his warmth.

He has an arm around me, moving it up and down my side. I wouldn't let him give me his jacket. It's too fucking chilly, and I'm already wearing outerwear.

My phone pings within a few minutes of sitting.

> TOM 💀
>
> Not to rush you, Harry. But I just got a call from the label. They need a decision by Friday.

My stomach plummets. "Fuck."

"What?" Ben reads the text over my shoulder after I angle my phone to him. He lets out a low growl. "That's bullshit. He's only giving you two days. You want me to call him?"

"No, it's okay. It doesn't sound like it's his choice." I exhale out a tensed breath. "On one hand, joining The Carraways would be way less pressure than trying to become a doctor. It's like skipping to the almost-finish line. Whereas I'd still have med school, residency, a fellowship..." My voice drifts off as the stress starts to build.

"Tom would *not* tell you he's at the almost-finish line," Ben says. "In his head, he's still stuck at the starting gate."

"I guess that's true…maybe there is no real finish line with music. Maybe every album is going to be another race." I stare into the depths of my hot chocolate. A nagging thought takes root in my head. "Sometimes I think maybe I don't have the gut instinct to be a doctor."

He frowns. "Why would you think that?"

I don't have the heart to look at him. My insides coil uncomfortably. "I didn't catch on to what you were going through that quickly. Maybe it's a sign."

"A sign," he echoes. "Harriet…" He brushes his fingers underneath my chin, tilting my head up so our eyes meet. He carries an immense amount of tenderness in his baby blues. "Don't quit on medicine because of me. Because I could just as easily find a good sign."

"Like what?"

"Like how being with you has only brought me comfort and peace. You have—"

"If you say 'healing hands' I'm going to shove you off this bench."

"Damn, Fisher, that is more punk rock," he teases, and I let out a laugh, hooked on his softening smile. Especially as he says, "You have what it takes to be an incredible doctor if that's the path you want. Just like you'd be an amazing drummer."

His words temper my anxieties, but I think about *us*. Because outside of our own goals, there is an *us* now.

A Ben and Harriet in New York City. Attending college together. And our future living situation has been super up in the air.

The ground feels more unstable. Like I'm back on the ice fighting to stay on my blades. "Eden texted me this morning," I tell Ben. "She's moving in with Austin next semester. Not that I planned to stay on her couch again. It's just now my options are officially narrowed. Especially with the likelihood of not being accepted into the Honors House."

He downs the last of his apple cider and free-throws it into the recycle bin. I can't even call him out for his jock behavior when he's saying, "If Guy Abernathy makes that mistake, then you and I could always move in together."

Oh my...what?

SIXTY

HARRIET FISHER

Move in together.
He says it so casually. Like it's an easy next step, and maybe it would be. Sharing his company has brought me literal happy-go-lucky joy, and he hasn't grown tired of Too Much Harriet. Some might say living with a boyfriend isn't always a recipe for good times. But I've lived with people who only bring darkness and misery.

My parents. My mom. Her exes.

A TV remote to the face. Insults to the mind.

The real bad times.

Those don't exist with Ben. We could be battling a thousand demons together. He could be struggling with his OCD. I could be a mopey grump cocooned in my Hello Kitty blanket, and still, it wouldn't touch that kind of *bad*.

All Ben has ever done is shelter me, love me, care for me.

But I also want to make sure I'm doing the same for him. So I shake my head when he suggests we move in together.

His confusion downturns his lips. "Too fast for you?"

"It's not that." I'm glad his arm is still around my shoulders.

"You're on the road to recovery. I think you need your brothers more than you need to be living alone with me. I'm going to be busy, but they'll always be around. One of them, at least."

I imagine Ben all by his lonesome in an apartment while I'm doing research or volunteering or at office hours or possibly in a recording studio. Now, more than ever, he needs his four older brothers.

That's why they wanted him in New York in the first place. I can't derail this path—one that he's mentally tried to derail himself. In a bad, *bad* way.

"Hear me out," Ben begins to smile. "You and me. Living *with* my brothers."

I snort into a laugh.

"I'm serious."

Oh...now I feel bad. "On the couch?" I ask. He's still been on the pull-out since returning from Alaska.

"They'd consider moving to a bigger place, I think."

"You think?"

He sucks in a breath. "Okay, maybe not that, but I think they might consider renovating. Buying the unit next door. Knocking down a wall. If it's possible..." He trails off like it's probably not. I bet there are fire codes and red tape. "They did talk about buying the building when I first moved in."

Holy shit.

"The building?" I widen my eyes, shaking my head slowly. "Just when I forgot you're all trust fund babies."

"That reminds me, I'm getting you back for the drinks." He pulls out his phone to send me cash. "They're on me."

Uh, *fuck*. I wish I didn't mention money. My stomach nosedives. "Don't worry about it." I scuff the pavement with my boot.

"You're grimacing, Fisher."

And he clearly knows something is up now. *Good one, Harriet.* I've been seriously stalling on addressing this topic, but I just go for it. "I met Gordon."

"Gordon..." His eyes superglue to me like he's a frozen search engine. "Gordon Brown?"

"Your estate lawyer, that's the one." I snap my fingers into a half-hearted finger-gun.

His chest falls, and he takes off his beanie with a heavy sigh, raking a hand through his hair. "He contacted you?"

"When you were in Alaska," I nod. "He wanted me to sign some documents."

"Great, yeah, he wasn't supposed to do that. Not until January." He runs another hand into his thick hair. "Why didn't you say something earlier?"

"I didn't want to stress you out. Not with you just starting to talk to a new therapist, and I was also kind of half-hoping one of your brothers would tell you because I didn't know how to start the conversation."

"They all know?"

"That you left all your money to me, yep. They know." My bangs catch in my eyelashes from a strong gust of wind. I brush them aside, then tug my earmuffs to my neck. "They honestly didn't find it as shocking as me. Like it was totally in your nature to go broke for a random girl you barely knew, but I'm not going to lie. It shocked me. And I especially don't get why you wouldn't tell me."

He fists his beanie, his gaze descending on me in a serious sweep. "I set up the trust before I decided to move to New York. I had no idea..." He takes a breath. "I didn't think I'd ever see you again, Harriet. When I ran into you at the frat, I didn't tell you about it then because I planned to leave the city well before January. Which is when you can access the money. I was worried if you knew why I was broke, you'd think I was even more unhinged or you wouldn't accept it."

"I don't accept it." I tuck hair behind my ear. "I don't want it. Take it back."

"I can't, and it's yours."

"*Ben*," I growl. "I cannot keep your money. You gave it to me thinking you didn't need it. Well, now you do."

"I really don't. I'm getting a deposit into my trust fund in May."

My forehead creases in an even deeper scowl "That's *six* months from now. You can't even budget your bartending tips for *two* weeks."

He smiles.

"This isn't funny, dude. You gave me a fortune when you barely even knew me. You're so lucky you chose me and not someone who'd leech off you like an ugly little parasite. Because as soon as I access the trust, I will be slowly redepositing it into *your* account." I'm not sure if I'm even able to do that—it's not like I've ever had a trust before. But it sounds plausible.

Off his grave expression, I'm thinking it might not be.

I add quickly, "You said it's mine, so I can do what I want with it."

He cups the back of my head. Strokes my hair. It. Is. My. Weakness. His voice goes soft but deep. "I'd love if you kept it because it'll be put to better use with you, but you're right, it's your choice."

I bite the corner of my lip. I don't want to fight him on it. Not today when there's so many other upheavals in our lives.

Like our living situations.

My entire fucking future.

Throwing money into the mix complicates an already complicated ordeal. I also love our weekend bartending gig at the End of the World, and we just agreed we'd keep working there together. I don't want that to change, no matter how loaded I am on paper.

"I'll think about it. And I do want you to know something," I say into a deep breath. "You can give me the entire rainforest, your entire family, your money, your clothes—but nothing will ever compare to you. Just you, Ben."

His eyes glass, his jaw clenching as he nods. "I feel the same way about you." He inhales deeply like I just did. "And I know you don't *need* anything but me, but you're going to have to let me spoil my girlfriend from time to time. It's in the handbook."

My face contorts. "What handbook?"

"The Ben Cobalt Boyfriend handbook that I created right fucking now. Section 1. Paragraph 1. It's all right there." He waves a hand like there's an imaginary handbook in the air that I can read.

I fight a smile. "Does this handbook have any other info? Like when your big family exodus from Philly and New York is happening?" The Hales, Meadows, and Cobalts typically spend the holidays all together outside the city. At a lake house.

Somewhere mountainous, private, and secluded from the public.

The location has never been leaked, so I had no clue where Ben would be going for Christmas. Until he told me it's in the Smoky Mountains. He's painted the picture of this boisterous, chaotic, festive atmosphere, a giant house filled to the brim with family. How there might be bickering and tears, but it's followed by a lot of laughter. It always smells like cinnamon rolls and fir trees.

It's hard to imagine.

I don't even know my cousins. Ben is close to practically all seven of his. And my childhood home smelled like microwaved pork roast and burnt gravy.

The lake house isn't as exclusive as Wednesday Night Dinners since their security know of the location, but Ben has said no one has ever invited a girlfriend there for the holidays. I'm sure his parents worry about a break-up and the scorned ex tipping off the tabloids. It'd ruin a very private place they've maintained for decades.

"I'm just wondering when you might be leaving," I clarify. "How much longer do I have with you before you go?" We'll be spending Christmas separately, and I'm kind of hoping it's the day before. Maybe he'll pack up on the 24th.

"Yeah, about that." He glances at the ice rink, then down at me. "I'm not going."

Oh no. I straighten up, facing him fully. "Ben, you need to be with your family—"

"It's not that." His smile crawls higher, his eyes flitting over my body. "Your concern for me is cute, Fisher."

"Stop flirting." I purse my lips to restrain a smile.

"I told my parents I wanted to stay in New York to be with you and Beckett," Ben explains. "He rarely goes to the lake house for the holidays because of *The Nutcracker*. If he does, it's *very* short. Next thing I know, all my brothers and sisters and my mom and dad have declared Christmas is at the Cobalt Estate this year. Just my immediate family is staying back, and honestly, I did *not* want them to at first because…if something were to happen in Philly, it'd be because of me. Because they're doing this *for me*. But maybe it's good to work through it with them."

My lungs inflate with a deeper breath. He's going to be *here*. Well, a couple hours away, but that totally beats being in a secret location at least five or six hours from the city.

"Are you grinning?" Ben asks.

"*You* are grinning," I point out because his grin is ginormous and very bright and coaxing mine out to new levels.

"Don't stop." He curves his arms around me.

"My cheeks fucking hurt. How do you do this all the time?" I stretch out my jaw.

And then he says, "You want to spend Christmas with me?"

My face falls. "Wait, what?"

"I talked to the powers that be, and you're invited to stay the week at the Cobalt Estate for the holidays. In Philly."

"I'm invited?" My brows hike. "To Christmas?"

"Yeah." He laughs a little off my surprise. "There's a guest room in the house. But you'll probably be allowed to spend the week in my bedroom. I don't think my mom will care. She loves you."

"Wait, she loves me?" I touch my chest. This is too much at once. "Are you sure? Did she tell you that or are you guessing? Because you can't be playing with my heart like that."

"It's a *very* good, educated guess," Ben replies into a wider smile, then slips the earmuffs off my neck, as evidence. "She designed these for you."

"No, she didn't," I retort, getting hot all over.

"Yeah, she did." He shows me a *Calloway Couture* logo underneath the black headband. I figured these are from her boutique.

"She just grabbed me some of her merchandise."

"No, there are no *earmuffs* in her fashion line. She made these specifically for you."

Tears sting my eyes. What the fuck…? "Why didn't she tell me?"

"She was worried about coming on too strong. I don't think she wanted to smother you."

I hold the earmuffs delicately as if they've turned to glass. "Is it weird that I think I love being smothered?"

He's smiling more. "If it is, then I'm just as weird. Because I want to smother you with all the love I can give."

My heart is so full. "You give a whole lot." I sink against his side even more. "Christmas," I say wistfully. "With your family."

"So that's a yes?" Ben asks.

"No, I'm going to have so much fun watching *Elf* from the backseat of Harold this year," I say into scowl.

Now *he's* scowling. "Is that what you did last year?"

"Maybe…"

He sighs. "Please say yes."

"I already did. In my head. Like fifteen times." I watch his gorgeous smile widening again. "But *yes*. Definitely. Christmas in Philly with your family is going in the calendar. With an alarm alert."

"An electronic beep?"

"Even better, a punk rock song."

"Just don't choose anything from Nothing Personal. If Tom hears that band come out of your phone, he might retract your offer."

I give him a look. "Are you serious?"

"Deadass."

"That is so petty." My lips twitch in a slight smile. "I appreciate the commitment to his feud." And I guess if I become the drummer of the Carraways, it'll be my vendetta too.

SIXTY-ONE

BEN COBALT

Wednesdays are for my family. For the Cobalt Empire. It's my first Wednesday Night Dinner since I've returned, since I've named the monster in my head, and apprehension hasn't struck me. I'm not jittery or rattled yet because A.) I'm not hiding anything anymore and B.) I'm doing my absolute best not to think about the house burning down and C.) the focus is more so on Audrey tonight.

We're not in the dining room yet.

Our youngest sister has requested a sibling photo, and as soon as we arrive, she corrals all of us into the library—one that'd be the envy of most bookworms. With floor-to-ceiling dark wooden bookcases, fancy crown molding, several built-in ladders, a roaring fireplace, and candle-lit chandelier. The moody academic atmosphere is as familiar as it is unfamiliar because I rarely spent time in here growing up. I found it gloomy.

Now, as light rain taps the windowpane and fire crackles against real logs, I find it calming.

"What happened to the club chairs?" Tom asks.

"I had the furniture rearranged for our picture." Audrey motions to a midnight blue Chesterfield sofa. "Sit, please. Charlie preferably in the middle. Merci infiniment." *Thank you infinitely.*

He's clearly annoyed, but I snap a glare at him, hoping he remembers the ride here. My brothers and I carpooled to Philly in a limo-style SUV so we were facing each other the whole way. Audrey had already informed us about the photo and told everyone to wear blue.

Charlie, ever the nonconformist, did not conform to a dress code this time. He climbed into the car wearing black tailored slacks and a black suit jacket—no shirt underneath. I can't remember who mentioned Audrey first on the drive, just that we talked about her the *entire* two hours.

"She's unaffected, dude," Tom told Beckett, who had questioned how Audrey had been faring since the fentanyl overdose. "You would actually think she popped a Tylenol that night."

Beckett made an uncertain face. "It might be an act."

"Yeah, I don't believe it had no effect on her either," I said. "I can't see how nothing changes from this."

"Of course you couldn't," Charlie pointed out.

Which pissed off Eliot, surprisingly. He typically stays neutral or makes excuses for Charlie. Instead, he glowered. "You go all the way to Alaska to bring back our youngest brother just to nettle him."

"I'm okay, Eliot," I told him.

"He's okay, Eliot," Charlie said mockingly. "Look, I brought him back so he could tell you he's fine." He forced a tight smile.

Eliot let it go, only because Tom cut in, "I'm telling you all, Audrey Virginia isn't dwelling. She said, and I quote, 'Nothing can destroy me. I'm a Cobalt.'"

Beckett rubbed his eyes.

I shook my head harder. "She *wants* to be unaffected, Tom. It doesn't mean she is. She was *terrified* that night, and on top of it all, I left because what happened to her sent me over. Now she's suddenly taken up scrapbooking?" It's why she wants a posed group photo. To immortalize memories of us together. "So is she just telling us she's fine? Or is she pretending to be fine to stay strong for me?"

"Maybe I want her to be fine," Tom shrugged. "I don't want that night to stick with her or change her. Do you?"

"No," I said. "If that night could have zero impact on her, that's what I'd take, but that seems unrealistic."

Charlie slid an arm on the seat behind Beckett. "Or nothing can pierce her ten-inch armor."

"You believe she's invulnerable? Honestly?" I asked him seriously.

"Only one way to find out," Charlie said.

I glared. "Do *not* fuck with her, Charlie."

"What's better?" he retorted. "We all play into her act and pretend she's an unfeeling automaton and indestructible?"

"Would you seriously rather unearth *trauma* that she might be burying?"

He considered it.

"Unfucking believable," I muttered, then shot a look at Beckett.

He told Charlie, "I doubt she'll do something as reckless. It has to be in the back of her head what could've happened."

"And if it's not?" Charlie questioned him. "We were *lucky* this time."

"Killing her confidence isn't the way to go, brother," Eliot said. "I'm with Ben. We reinforce she's fine."

"Ditto," Tom nodded.

Beckett agreed, and it took all two hours to finally get Charlie to *promise* not to launch a grenade on our sister tonight. Promises from Charlie are decently well-kept—but only with family. Outside of blood, he will break any made in a heartbeat.

Now that we're all in the library, Charlie follows our sister's direction and sits in the center of the Chesterfield sofa. "And you want me in the middle because…?" he asks her.

"So you can't easily ditch the photo before it's been taken." She raises her chin. "I've outsmarted you."

"Hardly."

"To be seen." She waves the rest of us at the couch. "Take your places wherever you see fit. Thatcher, for you." She passes her phone to our brother-in-law so he can snap the pic. Even if this is for her scrapbook, we're all aware the chances she posts this on social media are high.

None of us really mind since it's for her.

So we gather around the sofa. Audrey squishes in on the right side of Charlie but makes enough room for Jane to be next to her. Then Beckett fills the last sofa seat to the left of Charlie. Behind them, Eliot stands and stretches his arms across the back of the furniture like he's fucking Dracula hovering over everyone.

It makes me laugh as I drop down to the floor. Leaning against the couch in front of my little sister, I rest my arm on my bent knee.

Tom sits on the ground and flicks open a lighter. "On three, take the pic, Thatcher Alessio," he instructs. "On two, we all say *Cobalts never die*."

I smile at Tom, but I laugh so hard when things go naturally awry within one, two, *three*. Eliot steals the cat ears off Jane's head. Audrey shrieks, "Charlie!" because he puts a palm in front of Beckett's face, hiding our brother from the camera—while also flipping off the lens with his other hand. Tom sticks out his tongue near the flame of a lighter, and I have to be mid-laugh in the photo, staring at my family I love with all my fucking heart.

"We must take another," Audrey decrees.

"Mommy!" Maeve suddenly picks herself off the floor near Thatcher's ankles, then waddles with her tiny arms outstretched to Jane. "Mommy!"

She's walking for the first time.

"Oui, Maeve. Look at you go!" Jane beams.

We all cheer her on, and Thatcher films the milestone on Audrey's phone. When Maeve reaches Jane victoriously, we jump up and applaud like our niece just won first place in a spelling bee. Even Charlie claps. The baby giggles so vibrantly.

Then Charlie makes a quick exit.

"Wait!" Audrey calls out, distraught. She retrieves her phone to check the photo. "No, Ben." She rushes over to me. "Look. I'm *blinking*. My eyes aren't even open."

In the several pictures Thatcher captured, Audrey has her eyes shut in every single one. "It's just candid," I say. "I'm not even staring at the camera."

"You're laughing, though. You look..." She smiles more fondly, her eyes going glassy before they lighten. "You look *really* happy."

"I am," I smile at her. "Let's take some selfies for your scrapbook."

That cheers her up. Eliot also stays behind to take more photos for Audrey, and we squeeze together on the couch. When she's ready to head to the dining room, she hugs me extra tight, which does make me think she's not all okay, but I know I'll be here for her when she needs me.

I tell her that.

"And I'll always be here for you too," she nods.

I nod back, seeing maybe I'm not the person she will be vulnerable with if she's too concerned about my well-being. But I can't wear false armor. I am what I am. Sometimes, I'm fragile enough to hurt easily. Sometimes, I'm strong enough to bear it. Sometimes, I'm just mad. And I burn and burn and burn.

When it's just me and Eliot left in the library, side by side on the sofa, I tell him, "I asked Harriet to move in with us this afternoon."

At the end of our date, we agreed if she doesn't get into the Honors House, it's the best plan B. I'd love to live with her, but I hate it's at the cost of her losing a great opportunity. Mixed emotions are real.

Eliot grins. "So you're staying for good?"

"I'm staying for good," I nod to him.

"Not on the pull-out, brother. You and Harriet can have my room."

I grimace at the idea of displacing him. Maybe I can learn to live with shaking up his world, what I feared when I first moved in, but I still don't love taking too much. "I could—" I cut myself off before

I offer sharing a room with him or Tom, which I would prefer, but I can't do that to Harriet. If she does move in, then she deserves her own bedroom—at least one only shared with me. "Any chance of knocking out a wall?" I smile, knowing it's a longshot.

"For you, I would've knocked them all down already if I could."

"I believe it." I gaze up at the never-ending rows of books. "I want to leave all this torment behind, all the terrible things that's etched fear into me, but it seems so...*so* hard." I lock eyes with my most unburdened brother. "'What's past is prologue.'" He knows this is from *The Tempest*.

"Only if you let it be." Eliot squeezes my shoulder. "And if we're living in a Shakespearean tale, your story won't be the tragedy, little brother. We won't let it go dark."

The potent sentiment carries me into the dining room. I take my seat near the seitan. Dad comes to my end of the table again, but this time, I'm not on edge.

"Opening remarks have commenced," Mom says as she lowers in her chair.

I'm about to reach for my goblet, preparing for Eliot to bang a foot against the table. Then I solidify—because Beckett moves first. This...never happens. He stacks his bowl onto his dishes, shifts the silverware aside, and then with so much grace, he steps onto his chair. Then the table.

Beckett is standing on the table. Air knocks out of my lungs as his commanding eyes drop to mine, a smile inside them. "Ensemble."

Together.

Audrey is quick to hop up on the table next. Her gaze falls keenly to me. "Ensemble."

I scoot back as emotion barrels into my chest. This isn't just the rallying cry of my family. This is a word spoken to me when I was a little kid. When I packed my bag to run away from home because I felt like I didn't belong. They each, one by one, stood on the table and reminded me I always did.

Now we're grown.

And I watch as Eliot climbs onto the surface, clattering the dishware and tipping over goblets. Towering as a grin glitters his eyes. "Ensemble."

Then Tom flicks a lighter closed as he rises beside Eliot. He looks only at me. Nods to me. "Ensemble."

Jane lifts her tulle skirt as she goes from chair to table. Spinning to stare down my end. To face me as her lips lift and her breezy voice fills my ears. "Ensemble."

Charlie is the last of my siblings seated. Just like when we were kids, he's the last to stand.

He snuffs a cigarette on his plate, then puts one foot on the chair, one on the table. Because he turns back around. And extends a hand to me. "Ensemble." *Together.*

My eyes sting, and there is no question, no hesitation, no reluctance inside me. I grab my oldest brother's hand—the brother I might always disagree with but will always love—and I rise with him.

"Toujours," I promise. *Always.* My smile ignites my whole soul on fire. "Ensemble."

SIXTY-TWO

HARRIET FISHER

By Friday, everything is happening at once. I almost believe I pulled a Dorothy, got swept up into a tornado, might've knocked myself out. Sure, I'm not in a magical land where witches ride in pink bubbles—and the lions I know aren't cowardly—but I am in the Honors House.

Fairytales.

I think today I am slowly accepting that I might be living mine.

"It's perfect you could move in so fast," Kiki Kershaw says after showing me into my room. I try my best to lock eyes with her and not gawk at my new surroundings. "Most everyone is headed home for winter break. I'll be in Cleveland on Monday, but there's a few stragglers who always stay here for the holidays. Guy, among them. Do you have plans? I can let him know if you'll be here."

I'm blown over knowing that I was never going to be alone for the holidays this year. Even if Ben had chosen to be at the lake house.

"I'll be in Philly." I pause.

If I mention Ben, is it a braggy name-drop?

Fuck it. I'm name-dropping my boyfriend. "I'm spending the

holidays with my boyfriend and his family. I'm dating Ben Cobalt so…" My face is red-hot, mostly because I've never publicly declared myself as taken, and it's weird but also…I kind of love it. I love belonging to someone. I love how that someone is Ben.

I love that he also belongs to me.

Kiki nods into a laugh. "I knew it. *I knew it.* Wait, wait"—she raises a protective, serious hand—"he's not still with Kappa Phi? I heard he dropped out, but you need to be *very* careful, Harriet. They will try to sleep with Honors House girls just to fulfill this ridiculous frat bet."

Looks like the bet isn't so secret after all. "I heard about that one."

"You did?" She's genuinely shocked but doesn't ask who told me.

Though it might be obvious it's Ben. The loyal parts of me are still vitally intact, and I'd never throw him under, even if this bus isn't moving fast enough to kill.

I nod in confirmation. "But Ben isn't in the frat. So he has no big ties to KPD anymore."

"Good, *good.*" She nods robustly. "I'm not supposed to tell you this, but you were my first choice. The House was split for a while on who to pick, which is why it took *forever* this semester to choose our twelfth member." I already heard mutterings that it'd been between me, Easton, and Grace, the other pre-med hopeful. "Guy also went hard for you."

That surprises me, considering I said about two words to him this whole semester, but he's super friendly with Ben. I have a theory he likes that I'm one-degree from the Cobalt Empire. Venus also might've voted for me in hopes she'd meet Charlie Cobalt, but honestly, I don't even care if my connections helped push me over the finish line.

Everyone has them here. It doesn't discredit all my other achievements, and why would I want my life to be harder? Why should I feel guilty for the boost over the hurdle?

I don't.

I'm just really fucking happy.

Once Kiki hands over my key and a welcome packet, she tells me she'll be in the study room if I need any help with my things, but she'll let me take it all in. She must notice my eyes bouncing around the space.

"Thanks, really," I say to her. "Being here means…" I have no words to express my gratitude and elation of completing this impossible goal. *It's not so impossible, Harriet. Look at you now.*

Her smile grows exponentially. "We know." I'm in a house full of overachievers, who've all clawed for this, who've all been here before. "We're happy to have you here, Harriet."

It lifts me. I am *floating*.

When Kiki reaches the door, I raise a hand in a *see you later*. She smiles back, then disappears. I twist around in a three-sixty at my bedroom. Plain cream walls, a corkboard with pushpins, mopped shiny floors, a sturdy wooden desk beneath a quaint window, a dreamy collegiate view of the snowy front yard, a single bed that's all mine. This is *all mine* to make my own.

I toss the key and packet on the desk. My lungs swell, and I can't help myself—I hop up and down and pump my fists in the air. Yes, yes, *yes!*

When I spin around in a karate-kick-leap combo, I connect with a body and hear a gruff *oof.*

"Shit." I extend my hands and freeze as Ben winces into a full-bodied laugh. I scan him rapidly for injury. "Did I kick you in the dick?"

"Not quite that high, Fisher." He nods toward his leg, his arms full. He carries a cardboard box of my things, my backpack slung on his shoulder, and as he brings them to my desk, he casts an epically attractive glance back at me. "Did I just witness the Harriet Fisher happy dance?"

"Technically you *felt* it."

He smiles. "I hope I feel it for days."

"And you call *me* punk rock." I shrug off my leather jacket, the heat cranked up to toasty levels. I throw it on my bare mattress. "I'm a wimp when it comes to pain. I won't even go into mosh pits."

He sets my box down and hooks my backpack on the desk chair. "That's a good thing. Picturing my five-foot-one girlfriend being shoved around by men twice her size actually pisses me off."

"Shoving me for fun though," I point out.

"Yeah, that makes me angrier."

I wish I could tell young Harriet that she'd find someone who'd protect her—and she'd let him and she'd love every second of it.

Ben comes closer, spinning my car keys on his finger. His hand slips down my spine, and I realize he's barely examined my room. He's just fastened on my features, and I like that I make him smile. That's what I'm doing—causing his lips to rise, his baby blue eyes to glitter.

I've started believing that my mere presence can make someone else happy. Ben gave me something that my mom stripped away. My company isn't heavy and soul-leeching. I'm not an energy vacuum. I might still press myself against the plaster wall at parties, but I know Ben will come find me.

I know he'll stay at my side.

I know he'll smile down at me.

I know I'll crane my neck to look up at him.

I know I won't feel alone.

"Two more trips to your car," he says, "and I'll have all your stuff up here."

"I'll help." It takes us one more trip. Thankfully the Honors House has a decently sized parking lot, and so Harold has a home too. I didn't have to ditch my Honda.

I toss my folded sheets, pillow, and comforter on the bed. Then I place Son of Ben more delicately near the footboard. I fix the stuffed lion's twisted choker necklace. "Do you want weekends or weekdays for this joint custody arrangement?" I ask Ben.

"Joint custody implies we've split up." He rests a potted fern on the desk and my printer on an end table near an outlet. "You trying to divorce me already?" He slips me a teasing smile.

"Can't divorce someone without being married, Cobalt boy."

He has a daring look in his eye.

It widens my gaze and point at him. "That's not an invitation for you to drop to your knee."

He laughs into the hottest smile imaginable. "I wouldn't propose to you right now, Harriet."

Oh…kay. I exhale a long breath of relief. "I just don't want to rush this next chapter with you. But one day, though, Son of Ben probably needs a legal mom, right?" What am I doing…? I can't take it back. I don't want to, and these honest conversations aren't too hard to have with Ben, even if we like to joke and tease inside them. Anticipation quickens my pulse.

He leans back against my dresser, his fingers rubbing against his stretching lips. "I don't know the parental legality when it comes to stuffed animals."

I cover the lion's ears. "He's a *real* boy."

We're both smiling, especially as Ben says, "Our boy." He skims my face. "I suspect one day he will have a legal mom."

"If she's not me—"

"She's *you*," he interjects with a laugh. "Come on, Fisher, who else is there? It's only you."

I have trouble meeting his eyes. My feelings for him surge to the surface so forcefully, and I end up smoothing the lion's mane. "I'll take really good care of him."

"I know you will. Because you already have. It's actually really fucking adorable. I'm shocked you've never had a pet."

"They're too much work."

"Says the girl who combs every knot out of his hair each night."

"That's more for me. It's…therapeutic." I am more curious now. "Do you think they allow pets in here?" I stride over to the desk and sift through the welcome packet. The rules are typed in bold print. Impossible to miss. "No animals allowed. Welp, there goes my hopes of being a porcupine mom."

"My apartment doesn't have those restrictions." Ben stays against the dresser. "You want to be a porcupine mom, you can keep him at my place."

His place. He's officially claiming his brothers' apartment as his own now, and it's comforting to hear him firmly plant his feet in the soil and not be so quick to uproot himself. I meet his gaze. "Only if you're the dad."

"I'd hope there wouldn't be another father in the picture, Fisher."

Happiness pinches my cheeks. "Maybe not a porcupine."

"Whatever you want."

It floods me. I can't stop staring at him. "A bird, maybe."

His smile shines like a beam of sunlight, and I know this is it. This is the pet we will someday have together. A beautiful little bird.

I glance back at the welcome packet and spot the word *curfew*. Shit, I forgot I need to explain this to him. "Kiki told me about the strict policy for guests."

"I was informed." He jerks his head toward the door. "I can't spend the night. Guests get kicked out at ten p.m. sharp." He looks me over. "That bother you?"

I shrug. "It bummed me out at first, but considering it applies to all members, I like the security. It's nice knowing there aren't strangers creeping around here. And it feels like everyone in the House looks out for each other." Ben knows I've never had that until him and his family. "But it does complicate our situation."

"You can just sleep at my apartment whenever you want to." For the first time, his eyes traverse across my new room. Sweeping the space. Really taking it in.

I watch him linger on the single bed, then the corkboard, the pretty wainscotting—but I can't read his mind.

At all.

I wonder if he wishes we had to go to our plan B. "You're disappointed that we're not living together."

"What?" His brows knit together. "You think that?"

"It's a hypothesis." I lift my shoulders again.

"Fisher…" He closes the distance between us, bending a little to pick me up around the waist, just so we're more eye level. I wrap my legs around him and hold his neck. "Let me disprove it," he breathes. His eyes fall deeply into mine, and before he even says it, I see it. "I'm so fucking proud of you."

My chest inflates with a deep inhale, soaking in his words.

"Your accomplishment sends me on a high," he says strongly. "You living with me isn't as good as this. It was a backup plan for a reason. It wasn't the preferred outcome right now, but *this* is, and you better celebrate. There better be more happy dances I get to feel. Because I'm not going anywhere."

"Say it," I implore.

He smiles, knowing me, knowing what I want, and he says, "I'm still here."

I will never get tired of hearing that. Or feeling how his fingers slide up into the back of my hair. I love the way his gaze descends upon me, drinking in all my reactions.

Even if I have a massive scowl.

He places my ass on the desk and dips his head to kiss me once, twice. Sensual, stroking, fiery kisses.

I warm all over and tell him between them, "Feel special, Friend, because you've been the sole witness to my happy dance—*holy shit!*" I see a roach scamper across the desk, and I catapult myself off the furniture. My knee collides with Ben, and he lets out a painful groan before placing a strong hand on the desk.

"Shit, fuck." I wince for him, my hands on his elbow tentatively. "That was your dick?"

Ben's brows knot. "Yeah," his voice is rough gravel. "That was my dick, Fisher."

"Fuck," I curse again. "Is it okay? Should we check it?"

His eyes grow dark and heady at the suggestion, and his gaze drips down my body. "You asking me to take off my clothes, Friend?"

Oh...my cheeks are on fire. I take a quick glance at the door. It's closed. All clear. "Yes," I say confidently. "Drop the pants."

He opens his mouth to reply and movement catches both of our eyes. The *cockroach* zips across the windowsill, and I bend down to unlace my boot.

Ben frowns. "What are you doing?"

"Getting a cockroach weapon."

He grabs my elbow, lifting me up. "Nope, no. We're not killing the cockroach."

I frown. "Ben, I can't let it live in my bedroom. That thing could be carrying bacteria. Salmonella. E. coli."

He has his hands on both of my arms. "It's not going to be cohabitating with you. If I can't be your roommate, you think I'm going to let that roach take my spot?"

I fight a smile. "Okay, then what?"

"Capture and release."

I narrow my eyes, skeptical. "*If* you can catch it."

"I can catch it," he says confidently. "How about you focus on unpacking, Killer." His smile reaches his eyes, and that's how I know he's not upset at me for almost murdering a living creature with my boot.

I check the time. "Crap, it's already four." I hurry to my printer, plugging it in. "I should sign and send the contract before end of day."

When I meant *everything* is happening at once, I meant the biggest life choices have been made *today*. Not just with the Honors House. My career path is set.

From one of my boxes, Ben finds a white mug that says **STILL EMO** in black font, and I suspect he will lure and trap the roach. While he stalks the bug, I kneel at the printer and set up the Wi-Fi feature.

I hate regrets.

So I asked myself what I would regret losing more.

Rose even helped me. Ben's mom said to visualize myself ten years from now. I'm a doctor. After a grueling shift, I go to a concert. I'm in a crowd of adoring fans, and I watch Tom sing his heart out. I watch the drummer be where I could've been. Maybe it's a sold-out arena. Maybe it's just a handful of passionate fans.

Or I'm a drummer. I'm on-stage playing music that bleeds through my veins. I see a girl getting crushed with the masses. I might stop the show to help, but when she's carted off in an ambulance, then taken to the ED, it'll be the doctors who finish the job, who see it through. I'll return to the drums knowing that's not me.

That I'm not a doctor. And I never will be.

It was a rock-in-the-throat decision. Both scenarios added grief. But only one sunk my stomach to extreme pits.

I pull up a document on my phone and hit the print button. The machine rumbles to life and a HIPAA form ejects onto the tray.

I'm choosing medicine.

I would regret never trying to become a physician a thousand times more, I realized. Because I will always hear Tom's music. I believe in my heart of hearts it'll be made regardless of whether I'm behind the drumkit or not. I'd be giving up so much more by saying goodbye to medicine.

Being a doctor is *my* dream. And I'm following it.

I met Tom at his apartment this morning. Just to drop the news. He gave me the *Still Emo* mug thinking he'd be welcoming me to the band.

I gave the mug back. "I'm not joining The Carraways."

He barely blinked. He was in shock. "Harriet—"

"You wrote an amazing song, dude," I interjected fast. "You don't need me to make music. You'll find someone else. I know you will, and I'm going to be seriously mad if you don't record your song. Because it deserves to be heard. So you better not give up on The Carraways."

He let out a long, excruciating sigh, then placed the mug back in my opened palm.

I frowned. "Tom, did you hear me—"

"Yeah, I heard you. And you're still emo." He nodded to me, accepting what I said. "I'm sure I'll see you around."

"Chances are high. I am dating your younger brother."

"Chances are higher since you are my sleep paralysis demon."

I rolled my eyes.

He made a grimaced face and added, "Just don't come groveling back to me, Harry. This was a one-time offer."

"That I'm *firmly* rejecting, Thomas."

"Perfect."

"Great."

We flipped each other off.

In my new room, Ben searches for the roach beneath the bed and rotates his gaze to me. "You need a pen?"

"I think I can find one." I dig in my backpack, unearthing my pencil pouch. "Got it." His wide, overpowering smile is inching mine higher. His pride for me is like looking directly into the sun. I never want to turn away.

I only do to sign the HIPAA form, which will allow me to shadow Dr. Farrow Redford Keene *Hale*—I'm getting his last name right from now on, for sure.

He said he'd be happy for me to shadow him during any calls, especially the ones in New York since I'm already here and it'll be easy to jump on them. First, he had to check with the *entire* family to ensure his clients were okay with "Ben's girlfriend" tagging along.

I'm not sure which ones declined yet, but I know all the Cobalts agreed. So if any of them are injured and need help, I'll be there. And I can ask Farrow questions. I'm allowed to pick his brain. He's going to teach me more. It's so exciting that even scanning the form to send back, I'm fucking *trembling*.

I think I chose right.

Still probably too early to tell, but I'm going to do my best to not obsess over the path not taken. I want to enjoy the path I'm on so fully, and the only way is to look at the ground beneath my feet. And look ahead.

I glance over at Ben. Just as he's caught the roach. He has the mug planted upside-down on the floor. Acting like it's easy fucking peasy. Just another Friday for him.

Why are his bug catching abilities so…hot?

He up-nods at the printer. "Can you hand me a piece of paper?"

I pull a sheet out of the paper tray and slide it to him. "Do you need help?"

"I've got it." He slips the paper under the mug, then carefully brings it to the desk. "You know a lot about the diseases this thing carries. I thought maybe it's because of your interest in medicine, but I'm not so sure cockroach borne bacteria is on an MCAT." His eyes flit to mine, and I catch the heavy concern in them. "Is there something more there or am I reading too much into it?"

Jagged memories come into view. I take a soft breath before admitting, "After my mom kicked me out, I was terrified of getting sick and having to go to the doctor. I couldn't picture what would happen if they found out I was living on my own. Either I'd be shipped off to my Aunt Helena's or…foster care. I don't know. But it was a great big fear. So yeah, I did a lot of random research just to avoid possible contagions."

He nods slowly, his concern tripling on me. "You know if you need to talk to someone about what you went through, someone who's more qualified than me, you can always use that money in your trust. It's a good use for it."

I'm grateful for it. I am. But I don't know. "It's easy talking to you," I tell him. "I can't imagine talking to a stranger. It honestly scares me."

"It's okay if you're not ready for it. No pressure, Fisher."

That eases my shoulders. He always knows how to handle me. Like I'm a Harriet Fisher package made for his hold alone.

A gust of cold winter air invades the room as he cracks the window. In seconds, he releases the bug into the wild. Even guaranteeing it has a grip on the building and doesn't plummet to its death, I bet it'll find its way back to the warmth. Any smart creature would.

He waits to ensure success before he shuts the window.

A life saved.

My lips twitch upward as I watch him. The world is a better place with Ben Cobalt in it, and I have hope that one day he'll believe it too.

Once I send off the form to his family's med team, we unpack my things together. I hang up my clothes in the closet, and Ben digs through a cardboard box of my knickknacks while sitting on my unmade bed.

"Kid photos?" Ben flashes a stack of four-by-six pictures I never framed. His smile widens. "You haven't shown me these."

"I forgot I had them."

He flips through the pics, laughing. "Your pigtails."

"Hey, don't knock the hairstyle. It was the one thing I *begged* my mom to do and she listened. I rocked them all the way until the second grade."

"You were a cute kid." He flips the photo, then his smile slowly fades. He checks the back…I can't figure out what has him looking like he saw a ghost.

"You spot Casper lurking behind seven-year-old me?" I joke, abandoning my sweaters to go plop down beside him. My shoulder presses up against his body, but he hardly budges.

"When did you go to Disneyland?" he asks.

The photo between his fingers—it's me at Disney. The teacups ride is blurry in the background. I have on classic black and red Minnie ears and my dad has his hands perched on his waist, a little fed up with me. I think Disney wasn't his thing, or so my mom said. The trip had been a boiling point in their marriage, which was likely why it was the only family vacay we ever took.

"Uh, I think I was four here." I squint at the photo. "Yeah, four."

"What month?"

I'm confused. "Why...does that matter?"

"Was it July?"

"I think so." I nod. "That sounds right. It was definitely the summer." I peek at the back of the photo. No date written. "You okay, Ben?"

He blows backward in a daze, leaning against the wall my bed is pushed against. I scoot back to be beside him. He stares off as his thoughts whirl. "I was there."

"You were at Disneyland?"

"In July. We were there at the same time."

"Okay, but like different days."

Ben gazes at the photo with a faraway expression. "I remember this little girl with pigtails. Light brown hair." My natural hair color. "Her knees were scraped."

I peer closer at the pic. My knees are visibly reddened like I'd fallen.

"I remember her dad being so mean to her, and it hurt to see. I remember crying over it...over..." He glances down at me.

My pulse skips. "It might not have been me. What are the odds, Ben? You were...how old?"

"Five."

"How good is a five-year-old's memory, really?" I pat my hip for my phone, about to search the internet for the answer, but I left my cell by the printer.

"I don't remember a lot from that trip," he says. "But I do remember that. It was burned in my head because it upset me. I wanted to go to that girl, but I couldn't stay. I was being tugged in another direction." He sweeps my features.

I cling harder to his, scouring his face as if my own memories from that long-ago summer will surface. Maybe I'll see him in my mind. "I thought you don't believe in fate."

"I didn't think I did," he whispers in the gentle silence. "What about you? What do you believe?"

"Well...Aunt Helena would tell me it's all real. She'd want to call her psychic friend Angelica for a reading, which she's already promised us."

Ben met my aunt on video chat the other day. She said she sensed "goodness" in him and thought our fire and air signs would spark explosive sex—which I did *not* want to talk about with her and him together. Ben controlled his laughter well.

When he'd first introduced himself, she'd asked, "You're a Cobalt, as in that famous family?"

Even my aunt knows of the Cobalts. After confirmation that he is, indeed, of that renowned lineage, she'd gasped and said, "Harry!" As if I hit a jackpot, and I definitely did, but not because Ben has money or fame. By the end of the call, she made an offhanded mention about my mom. Reminding me to keep her blocked.

"I know what your aunt would believe," Ben says. "But what does Harriet Fisher believe in?"

I want to be closer, so I straddle his lap. His hands fall to my hips, and I clutch his neck while my knees dig into the mattress. "Scientifically speaking, there is no way to verify whether your memory was of me or not. Even if we figured out that we were at the park on the same exact day."

"Yeah," he nods, not disagreeing with the logic.

"But...it's a really beautiful belief." I search his eyes while he searches mine, as if scavenging for more fragments of each other, more pieces of us together littered over time. Of course he'd want to pick them up. Cradle them. Protect them, and I'd want Ben to share them with me too.

I clutch his cheeks, my finger brushing over his beauty mark, as I stare deeper into Ben. "My childhood memories aren't ones I like visiting. What makes me want to look back for the first time is the knowledge that you might've always been there. Out of all this bleakness, there was a star."

"Two stars," he breathes. "You were never dull, Harriet. Not to me."

"Two stars," I agree, trying not to get choked up. "And no matter what choices we made, we were always orbiting. We were always going to collide over and over again. Until we ended up here. We're destined for each other, Cobalt boy. That's what I believe in. Because it makes me happy, and I want to believe in things that bring me stupid amounts of joy."

He cups my cheeks like I'm cupping his. "I think I can get behind this."

"Really?" He believes in the butterfly effect. His actions can change events. Fate is relinquishing control to the universe.

"I don't know how else to explain the photo, but I'm not explaining it away. I want to be fated to be with you. But more than anything, I just want to be with you, Harriet. Fuck everything else."

I smile off of his. We pull each other into a crushing kiss. He lifts me up against his chest, and I gasp into his lips as he brings my back to the mattress. I'm underneath him. His warmth, his love, his heart.

We tangle into deeper, emotional kisses. Our limbs like knotted branches of a tree, wrapping, weaving. We root to the earth. We plant into the ground.

We are bent, gnarled, twisted things.

And we'll thrive as we grow together. As one.

SIXTY-THREE

BEN COBALT

Tom has his hands out like he's grasping a ball of reason in the air. "Dude, I say this with all the love in my veins—"

"In his veins," I emphasize to Eliot while I hit the elevator button to take us up to the 21st floor.

Eliot grins at me, but we're listening as Tom finishes, "Ben should not be your roommate." It's the fifth time he's shared these sentiments just this morning alone.

We all look like we rolled out of bed. Hair a little unkempt. Drawstring pants on (the kind I slept in). I'm not even wearing a shirt. We did just wake up about ten minutes ago. The three of us went to the lobby to grab our mail. Our bodyguards sifted through it already to trash any threatening letters or used panties (Charlie gets those all the time). Normally they bring it up to us, but there was miscommunication on the security team, and it ended up at the front desk.

As the elevator brings us back upstairs, Eliot says, "I'm much better roommate material, Tom. You play music at all hours. You'll disrupt his sleep."

"*I* will disrupt his sleep?" Tom touches his chest. "You fuck at all hours."

I almost laugh, but I can't tell if this is becoming heated between them in an aggravated way. They rarely, *rarely* fight, and I'm a little worried this might start one.

"An exaggeration," Eliot says to me, then to Tom, "Not even I can fuck 24/7, brother. Physically impossible."

"Eliot Alice, listen. Ben's just going to get kicked out of his room every other night because of your hookups. He's going to end up on the couch. Exactly where we don't want him to be."

I glide my fingers through my messy hair. "I don't mind crashing on the pull-out. It's really not a big deal—"

"No," they say in unison.

Eliot rests a hand on the elevator wall as he faces Tom. No shirt, Eliot's cut muscles flex to where I'd believe he was admiring himself in the mirror. But the mirror is actually behind him. "I don't *need* sex," he says. "The rate at which I bring girls over will drastically decrease when Ben rooms with me."

I have a visual of Eliot passing out after Charlie and Beckett tried detaching a very incessant girl off him when he was far too drunk to consent. I honestly debated whether she slipped him something that night.

"Maybe that's a good thing," I tell Tom.

Eliot outstretches his arms, clutching a stack of envelopes in one hand. "Rooming with me is the better option."

"I can also wear headphones," Tom says, more to me than to Eliot. "You'll barely hear my music."

"That's a good point," I tell Eliot.

"*See*," Tom says. "I'm the *best* option. You heard it straight from Ben."

"Roll the tapes," I smile over at him. "I'm pretty certain I said you're both good options."

Eliot raises his brows at Tom. "You aren't a Virgin Mary. What happens when you bring over RJ?"

"My band is on life support. You think I have time to reignite that?"

"That's exactly why you will, brother."

Tom groans up at the elevator's escape shaft.

"You seek him out when you are emotionally—"

"Okay, okay, okay," Tom says quickly. "How about I delete his contact? Because I will." He pulls out his phone.

"Whoa, whoa," I cut in, holding out a hand to stop him. "Let's not nuke your relationship because of me."

"It's not a *relationship*," Tom emphasizes. "It's a casual—*casual*," he repeats to Eliot, "situation."

Eliot is mouthing to me, *relationship*. I have a feeling the truth is somewhere in the middle, considering something with even an ember of emotion might be deemed as "serious" to Eliot.

As they go back-and-forth again, I glance between them and catch myself smiling. I never thought Tom and Eliot would fight over me this hard. Both even liked the idea of me rooming with one of them over them sharing. To be honest, I think they want to keep an eye on me, to help me, and being further isolated isn't the way.

Having one of them as a roommate isn't forever, but it's a "for now" I'm not ready to end that quickly. I'm at a time in my life with my brothers we won't ever get back. We're young, unfettered—able to be more selfish, follow our ambitions, fuck the night away, and let it all go.

I finally understand what Beckett meant about living in the city with them. It's moments I will never recapture, and I want to exist inside each one instead of shoving them away. I can't let my mind steal anymore from me.

Easier said than done, but I'm trying. I'm going to try with all that I have in my body and soul.

The elevator beeps. Doors slide open, and they continue this debate in the hallway. As things grow heated again, I cut in, "Instead of trying to figure out which one of you is better for me, why don't you decide who'd rather deal with me? Because I might not be the world's greatest roommate."

"Hogwash," Eliot denounces.

"Yeah, bah humbug, Ben Pirrip," Tom also says. "You don't snore. You're not throwing dirty laundry everywhere. You're quiet when you wake early. The worst thing about you is your girlfriend—it's a joke. It's a *joke*."

I'm glaring.

Eliot walks backward in front of us and extends his arms. "I love your girlfriend. This settles it."

"No, *no*." Tom cinches his face. "I was joking. Okay, Harry and I have an actual back-and-forth. What do you have with her, Eliot?"

"We also have a back-and-forth, thank you for asking." Eliot lifts his brows to me. "We're friends. Best friends."

I try not to laugh. "That makes a ton of sense, actually," I banter. "Seeing as how she's *my* best friend."

"I've might've unseated you, brother."

"Yeah, that's not possible."

Tom hears my territorial bite, and he's grinning like he just won.

"I asked you two to choose," I remind them. "Maybe just think about how my girlfriend will be spending the night. I can't crash at the Honors House with the curfew. So Harriet will be sleeping in my bed with me sometimes, and if that makes either of you uncomfortable, then opt out now."

Eliot laughs at the word *uncomfortable*, and Tom acts like it's no problem. While we near our apartment door, my phone buzzes.

I hang back to check my text from Winona.

I'd reached out to her, finally. I'm unsure of how many messages my family tried to send while I was gone. None went through since I wiped my phone. It took a while for me to download all my storage from the Cloud, but I have the same number.

Winona said she'd texted. Called. I knew she must've been concerned. We haven't had a full-blown phone call yet. I want to see her in person first, but since she'll be at the lake house and I'm staying in Philly, I'm not sure if our paths will cross during the holidays. We might have to make time, so I told her I was sorry for the epic cold wind, that it'd be better to explain face-to-face, and we should catch up soon. Before we inevitably see each other for family events and trips.

> **WINONA MEADOWS**
>
> Catching up sounds good. What are you thinking? Breakfast? Quarry swim? Ducati ride to the death? 💀 ☠️ 🧟 👾 🔯

I smile a little and send back.

> **BEN COBALT**
>
> Too cold for quarry swim. No dying, please. Breakfast is perfect. Our fav vegan spot?

> **WINONA MEADOWS**
>
> 💯 I'll be there.

I inhale a deeper breath and think about messaging back one more time, but she beats me to it.

> **WINONA MEADOWS**
>
> I missed you.

I send a **me too** just as Eliot asks, "You okay, brother?"

"Yeah," I clear the knot in my throat. I don't expect my friendship with Winona to ever be the same after what's happened, but then again, with time and age, it was always going to change. I just want to stop the erosion, so new life can sprout.

Once we reach the apartment, Eliot unlocks the door, and the scent of eggs, turkey sausage, and maple syrup flood my nostrils as I go inside. Beckett babies sausage links in a frying pan while Charlie is on a barstool, a paperback folded in one hand while he drinks fresh-squeezed orange juice.

Eliot tosses the mail in a basket on an entryway table, then beelines for the stove to help Beckett. Eliot is the only one who ever really cooked when we were kids. I think, mostly, he liked conversing with our family's chef, and likewise, Chef Michael enjoyed teaching Eliot knife skills and how to make a perfect soufflé and to poach eggs.

I hear Tom ask Beckett to weigh in on the roommate debate, but my gaze is drawn toward the living room. Toward this short blond who crouches at an eight-foot Christmas tree. Her hair sticks up wildly like she also just rolled out of bed—because she did. With me.

Harriet is wearing my MVU sweatshirt over black sweatpants. The burgundy fabric engulfs her small frame and hangs past her thighs. Yeah, I love that she put on my clothes. I didn't see her do that before I left for the lobby.

She's busy using a non-contact voltage tester to find the defective light bulb in the strand. It's been her mission ever since we put up the tree and it wouldn't light.

Just as I'm about to move, the fir tree illuminates row by row and reaches the star at the top.

I smile and give her a loud two-finger whistle. "Way to go, Fisher."

She rotates around to loud, hearty applause from me and my brothers, who grin with pride. Even Charlie sets down his book and puts his hands together.

Her fair cheeks go rosy, but she takes a stiff curtsey, plucking the sides of my sweatshirt like it's a dress. I just want her in my arms. Her gaze soars up to the tree. "Why am I not surprised. You all chose *blue*."

The tree is lit with only blue lights.

"The gods' color," Eliot decrees dramatically.

Beckett laughs.

As I go to my girlfriend, I scoot a cardboard box out of the kitchen area with my foot. Charlie side-eyes me but says nothing. My shit is spilling out everywhere. Several boxes, a crammed duffel with all my hockey gear, some potted plants. Not to mention, the queen-sized mattress in the center of the living room. Where Harriet and I slept last night. The bedframe is in an unopened box, which I'll unpack and put together once Tom and Eliot choose where I'm going.

All my stuff is here.

My stomach cramps knowing I'm cluttering the living room. I still don't love being in the way. I'm not suddenly relaxed about my presence possibly causing Beckett anxiety. There hasn't been a flip of a switch within me just because I know my own issues stem from OCD. So I plan to move all of this to a room *today*.

Tom and Eliot need to decide. We're ten days out from Christmas, and we plan to leave for Philly soon to spend the week at the Cobalt Estate.

I pick up my fallen hockey stick on the way to Harriet, watching her adjust silver ornaments and some of the dangling crystal icicles.

"So frosty," she says of the décor.

"Five sons born from an ice queen," I smile down at her.

Her lips twitch a little. "You all are on brand, Cobalt boy."

I rake my fingers through her blond hair, almost regrettably smoothing it down. The wild strands billow out like she put her finger in a light socket, and it's just really fucking cute. Her eyes ping toward the kitchen where my brothers talk over each other about the roommate situation.

"You want to join that?" she asks.

"Nah, I'll let them hash it out for a second." I rest the hockey stick against the wall. Maybe I'll play next season. Maybe I'll be in the NHL someday. Or maybe my life will take a different turn. Thankfully, these are choices I don't have to make anytime soon. I'm just ready to live here.

To be here.

I smile down at Harriet. She's partially concentrated on my brothers as Beckett makes a *what the fuck* face at Eliot, then says, "You think you can be celibate for a whole year?"

She has an expression like she ate a rotten date.

I laugh, but then I think about her spending the night at this apartment. This decision does affect Harriet to a degree. More hushed, I ask her, "Which brother would you rather be my roommate?"

"No way." She raises her hands, speaking under her breath too. "I'm staying out of this. Eliot has already tried to bribe me, and I don't need Tom pissed off after I already rejected his band."

"Eliot tried to bribe you?" I glance toward the kitchen, about to go confront him, but she snatches my waistband, tugging me back beside the Christmas tree.

"With a year's supply of candy," she clarifies. "He wasn't throwing cash at me, and I didn't take it, obviously. You don't see me trying to convince you to room with him."

She has stayed very neutral.

I skim her normal grouchy disposition. "You don't have strong feelings either way?"

"I lived in my car, dude. I'm not choosy."

I hold the back of her head more tenderly. She breaks apart her crossed arms and weaves them around me. Rests her cheek on my chest, just as we hear Tom letting out a long, frustrated groan.

She grimaces, then says quietly, "Is claiming rooms during Cobalt vacays this dramatic? Or is there a seniority thing at play? Oldest gets first dibs on the best room."

"Rarely by age," I tell her. "If we can't compromise amongst ourselves, then we'll settle disputes with games. Even something simple like rock-paper-scissors. You'll see."

"I'll see?"

"You think you'll only be invited for the holidays?"

Her shoulders lift uncertainly. "I wasn't assuming anything. There are fortified walls in your family that not even girlfriends can break through."

She's not wrong. "Outside of the lake house and Wednesday Night Dinners, you can assume you'll be invited to pretty much every family event from here on out. Including trips to France. Around the world. The yacht comes out at least once a year—"

"The yacht." Her brows spring into her bangs. "As in...I'll be surrounded by open water?"

I see her bugged eyes, and all I want is to quell her fear. "You know," I say gently, my fingers threading through the back of her hair. "My apartment building has a private indoor pool. I can teach you to swim. Maybe tradeoff? You can help me drive again." It's what I've wanted to offer. "But I can't promise I'll be a good student."

"I can't promise I won't sink to the bottom of the pool."

"I *can* promise I won't let you sink."

Her scowl morphs into a teeny-tiny smile. "And how will you be a bad student?"

"I might have a panic attack behind the wheel," I admit.

Her face softens. "We'll start in a parking lot, Friend." She lets go of my waist and backs up, just to extend a hand. "You have a deal."

My smile edges higher, and I shake on it. Not letting go of her hand, I interlace our fingers, then bring her closer to the window. I snatch my worn blue ballcap off the couch. I'm about to fit it on her head, but she points at mine.

We agreed to share my hat, but she likes when I wear it more. So I put it on backward. Her pursed lips try to spread into another smile. I engrain every single one of her smiles in my mind. Even if they're fleeting, I still see them.

I want to kiss her, but the view turns her head. Snow flurries catch the morning wind, and the weather forecast says it's going to dump about five inches today.

While we gaze out at the winter city landscape, her hand stays in mine. Lights and garland decorate the balconies of several buildings. Wreaths and red bows hang on the street lampposts. Clouds cast a haze over the city, but it's so far from dreary as snow kisses windows and railings and fire escapes.

"One of the prettiest views in all of New York," Harriet says quietly.

I look down at her. "Yeah, it is," I whisper. I could say I've fallen in love with New York, but I've fallen more in love with the people in this city.

Sometimes life isn't about where you go but who's going with you, and where I want to be at the end of the world is beside her.

"You were right," I tell her.

Her gaze lifts to mine. "About what?"

"This isn't how we end. You are my entire world, Harriet Fisher. The future I want has always had you in it. For as far as I can see, you are always there. You're always with me."

Her chest collapses in a deep, audible breath. "Don't make me cry in front of your brothers."

I laugh, my eyes burning with my love for her. "If they tease you for crying, I will be on their fucking case." I hold her cheek.

Her eyes do well, but after a few breaths, the waterworks recede, and she pops up on her toes to kiss me. Not getting close enough. So I pick her up at the waist, and her legs naturally wrap around me.

"Thanks for the boost, Friend," she murmurs, her eyes on my lips.

Mine on hers. "No need to thank me. This is where I like you, *Friend*."

Her lips curve before she kisses me first. I smile against it, my fingers scrunched into her messy hair.

"Ben Pirrip, stop sucking face!" Tom shouts, pulling our attention to the kitchen. "You're going to have to choose, dude. We can't pick."

I set Harriet on her feet. We join them in front of the barstools. Charlie has spun around to face us, and Beckett is behind the island, telling me, "You'll need to decide, Pip."

"They're never going to agree," Charlie adds.

It's a weird statement. Tom and Eliot are almost always on the same side, and I try not to obsess over being the one to cause friction. They both remind me there will be no hard feelings in whoever I choose. They just can't make this choice themselves. They're both unrelenting. Unwavering. Steadfast to the bone.

Great, this is going to have to be completely on me. I tip my head and smile at a thought. "Anyone have a quarter?"

"You want them to flip for it?" Beckett asks, then exchanges a shocked glance with Charlie.

"Yeah," I nod as Harriet retrieves a quarter from her messenger bag. She tosses it to Tom.

"Leaving this to chance, little brother?" Eliot asks while half-seated on a stool.

"To fate, yeah."

Tom pinches the quarter. "Dad would never." He shares a gleaming grin with Eliot.

"You call it. I'll flip it," Eliot says to him.

That's how the next step of my life is decided. A coin-flip.

IT TAKES A COUPLE HOURS TO MOVE ALL MY STUFF INTO my new room. Thirty minutes are spent putting the wooden bedframe together. I'm on the floor, barely following the directions, and Harriet keeps shaking her head at me while reading step by step. We both still haven't showered. I haven't even grabbed a T-shirt. She's bunched my MVU sweatshirt up to her elbows.

"You're diabolical," she says.

"So you've said," I smile up at her. "This is intuitive. Hole. Screw. Board."

"There are several different kinds of screws."

"This looks right." I show her a wide wood screw and the bigger hole in an oak board. "What do you think?"

She double-checks, then nods. "Correct, you may proceed."

"Merci beaucoup, mon bel oiseau." I twist the screw into the board and glance up to see her watching me, affection swirling in her ocean blue eyes. It's hard to tear away. I love that I really don't have to.

After the frame is built, the mattress carried over (thanks in part to Eliot), and the bed made with my checkered blue and green quilt, Harriet plops down on the foot and I sink beside her, following her roaming gaze around my new space.

We plan to mount a ceiling track and attach a privacy curtain at some point, but for now, my brother's side is visible, but it's not cramped, even with two queen-sized beds. He's always had one of the biggest rooms in the apartment, so it's honestly perfect that the coin landed on tails.

On what Tom called out.

"Are those just for show?" Harriet points to the guitars perched on the wall.

"No, he definitely plays those." Tom's side is closer to the door, mine farther in the room near a floor-length window. I catch Harriet chewing her lip—her *smile*, really—at the sight of the framed Green Day poster, at the dark moody walls, at my punk-rock brother's sticker-decaled dresser and his old school cassette tapes and his '90s stereo.

"Are you vibing with my brother?" I tease.

"With his personal belongings. Like barely at all, if he asks." She squeezes her fingers together to show a pinch.

I smile. "Wait till you see Eliot's raven paintings. You might want me to swap rooms."

"That dark?"

"It gave me nightmares as a kid," I laugh. "Or maybe you should tell Eliot you like Tom's room better. Take his ego down a fraction of a *fraction* of a peg."

"Wow, the Fort Knox of egos," she deadpans, then eyes my elephant ear plants near the oak dresser. "I like your side the best."

I look her over. "Even if it's not like you?"

"I like it the most because it's like you. Because I love you, and when I look around, I just see Ben." Her eyes slow into a stop, fixing on the wall directly in front of us. On the ginormous oil painting that Eliot and Beckett carried in here and hung. "That..." she says in quiet reverence. "That is so much like you, and I don't even know what it is."

"The Arcadian," I name my painting by Thomas Cole.

Sweeping pastoral lands, so much vibrant, lush green as morning light crests behind a jutted mossy mountain peak. On a hill, a stone building has been built. Women dance in one corner while another figure plays a pipe. Fields are plowed. Shepherds tend to their flocks. An older man draws a geometrical shape into the dirt, new discoveries made. Boats sailing to shore. Humanity at peace with the land.

I start to smile, and I tell her, "It's the beginning of an empire."

"O, she doth teach the torches to burn bright!"
Romeo and Juliet, William Shakespeare

ACKNOWLEDGMENTS

The Cobalt Empire has been years in the making, and for a story that's in part about enduring, persisting, being *here*—we just want to thank all of you for being *here*. You matter in this great big world, and we are truly honored that you've spent time reading the characters we've created and cherished. Most especially Ben and Harriet.

This series would not exist without the readers who've loved these families for years of time. Thank you to our oldest readers who never forgot about the Cobalts, the Hales, and the Meadows. Thank you for keeping them alive in your hearts. You're the reason they've survived over a decade and the reason we can continue writing stories about them.

There's an incredible number of you. It brings tears to our eyes, really, to know so many of you are still here after so many years. It's mighty, fierce, devoted love—and we're so fortunate to see it and feel it. Every single day of our lives.

Thank you.

And thank you to new readers who've taken a chance on us and Ben and Harriet's romance. If this is your first book of ours, we're so very grateful you've chosen *Burn Bright* to jump into as a starting point, and we truly hope it's resonated with you in some way and you're ready to read more (because so much more is to come!).

We want to thank our mom for being here every step of the way from the very beginning. For constantly being the biggest support behind-the-scenes. Thank you for being the brightest star in our sky. Always and forever our Rose Calloway.

Thank you to our fiercest agent Kimberly Brower for finding the best home for the Cobalt fam and for helping guide us at every turn. We can't imagine our careers without you and your epic talents. To

Christa Désir and the Bloom team, thank you for all the support and push to make *Burn Bright* the shining star that we've always felt it could be. We're so very happy the Cobalt Empire is in your hands.

To Marie, *thank you* for your beautiful French translations. To know you're still with us—after so many years—again, we're crying writing this. We are saps! But it's nostalgic and moving to just know the Cobalts have had your touch for years and years. We adore you, and we can't thank you enough for lending your French expertise for the Cobalt Empire.

To Jenn, Lanie, and Shea, our dear friends behind the Fizzle Force and some of the kindest souls—thank you for all the endless support and love. There isn't a day that goes by where we haven't been so thankful you're still here.

To more friends we've made along the way—Haley, Andrea, Alyssa, Andressa, Juana, Maria, Marissa, Abby, Angelina, Sarah Green, Em, Margot, Laura, Rowena, Zoe, Rose, Allyn, Olivia, Kenny—thankyouthankyouthankyou. For roaring so very loud with so much love and passion and kindness. You've helped keep our books alive and have also helped fend off our doubt monsters. We've been so lucky to have your support, and we're even happier we've gotten to hug each and every one of you.

Some readers have also kept us going, and we want to give a thank you to Jared, who sent us an email a long while ago when we needed words of encouragement the most. It changed our trajectory and kept us on this path. Thank you immeasurably.

There've been *so many* people who've been here and supported us and all our books, and we see you and love you and we wish we could make this book extra chunky to list everyone here. If you don't see your name, just know you're so very beloved by us.

Patrons on our Patreon—your support is the reason why we could keep writing these books and keep living our childhood dreams. We are forever thankful for all the love over on our Patreon and the readership who wants *all* the extras. It's the best feeling knowing we can write our hearts out, and there are people who will gobble it all up! It's our happy place. Thank you for wanting more and more. Thank you for being fiercely devoted to our work. We hope to always do you proud.

Many thanks again to you, the reader, for embarking on the start of this saga. It's the era of the Cobalt Empire, and it's only just begun. We can't wait for you to see what follows as our favorite pride of lions returns, and romances are just heating up. Ben might've been the first to fall in love, but he's most certainly not the last ;)

Can you guess who's next?

All the love in *every* universe (especially the ones with the Cobalts in the sky),

xoxo Krista & Becca